MORE BY THE AUTHOR

SPECIAL AGENT KIM KUPAR

Jade Eyes
They
The Why Files

THE TSCHAAA INFESTATION

Book 1: The Gathering Storm
Book 2: The Tsunami
Book 3: Typhoon of Steel
Free Range Protocol: Tales of the Tschaaa
Beyond the Great Compromise: Tales of the Tschaaa
Survivors: Escaping the Tschaaa

ANTHOLOGIES

Monstrosity (Unnerving Anthology)
Descent (Unnerving Anthology)
Wicked (Unnerving Anthology)
Nightfall (Unnerving Anthology)
The Mighty Pen
Unconditional
Cascadia
Tales of the Slug
Super: Unexpected Heroes Arise

COLLECTED WORKS & MORE

Inhumanity: A Year of Stories
The Island (The Haunting of Orchard House)
Shane (Angels of Anarchy)

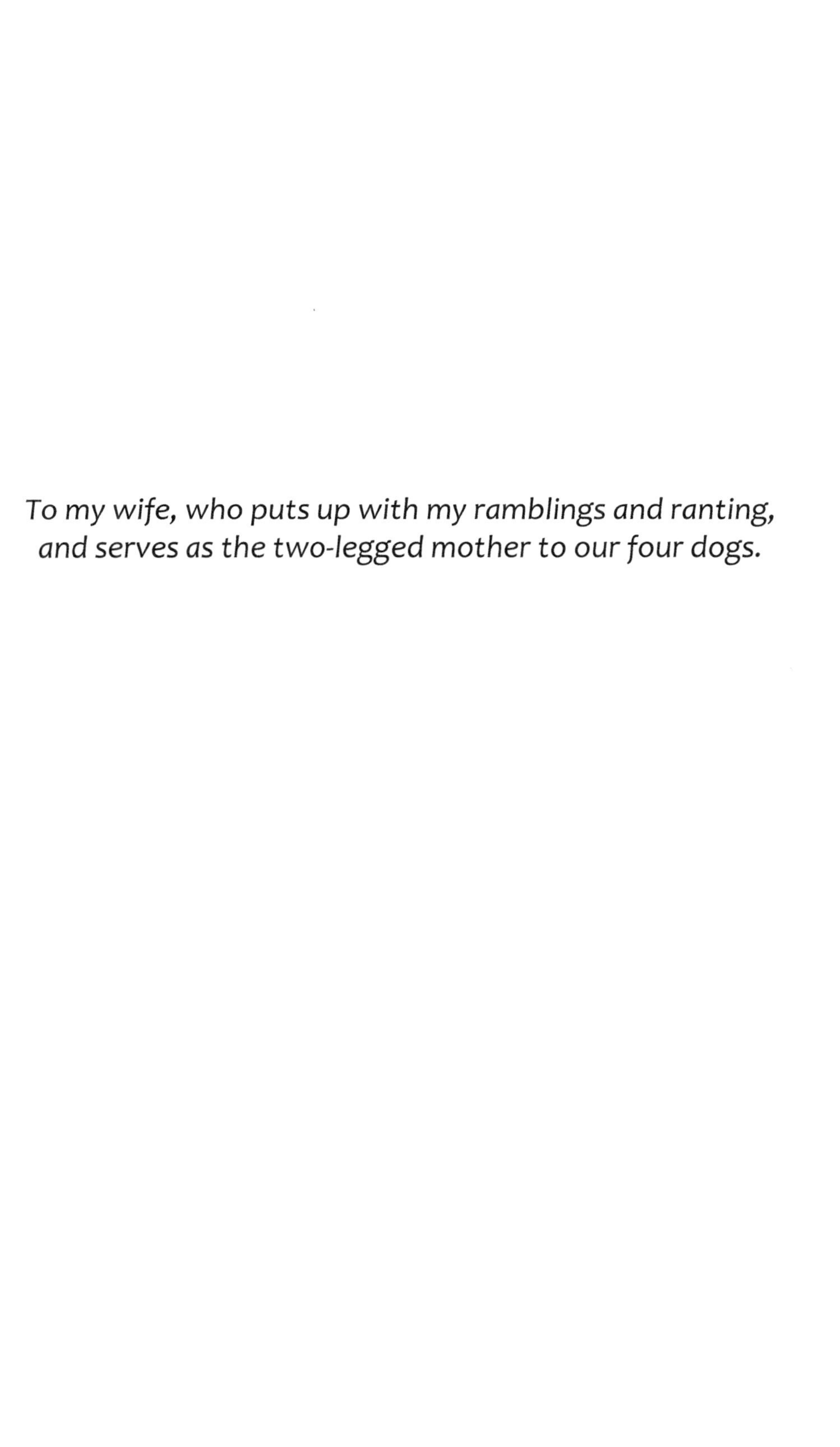

To my wife, who puts up with my ramblings and ranting, and serves as the two-legged mother to our four dogs.

ACKNOWLEDGEMENTS

This is the Second and Revised Edition of *The Tschaaa Infestation*, a three-volume chronicle of what was once referred to as "the War and Peace of alien squid invasion novels." Thanks to the hard work of my publisher, Blue Forge Press, I now can present a new and improved version of a long labor of love and creativity. I have had many people help me in learning my craft of being a 'Wordsmith.' This is a career and an endeavor of beating words and phrases into a finely tempered work which, like a blacksmith does with steel fresh from the forge, cuts with a clean blade, but ideas rather than wood or flesh. At the same time, like a samurai's katana mentioned in the series, it can also bend to new concepts and opinions without breaking due to its flexibility.

Of course my wife, Sheri, has often times been a Writer's Widow as I disappear for hours on end, especially late at night, to hone my craft. Thus, without her understanding and support, this would have been a stillborne offspring.

Author and Esquire Thomas Mengert helped me with the first editing of this work of speculative fiction as well as suggested a companion volume of short stories. Thanks for all the hours spent with me on this futuristic War and Peace.

My good friend Gregory Brashear, an accomplished local teacher, was a sounding board for many of my ideas. Truth be told, a main character of the series is based on his life and adventures. I'll let the readers figure out which character fits this mold.

All the members of Kitsap Literary Artists and Writers helped provide ideas on designs, marketing, and publishing. The Bremerton Kitsap Access Television interview show I do on a monthly basis is an outgrowth of this group. The KLAW show was the reason I met Jennifer and Brianne DiMarco and became affiliated with Blue Forge Press, which is leading to bigger and better things. Sometimes it takes a while for "good things and people" to come into one's life.

I hope all "wannabe" Authors read my artistic endeavors and think "Hey, I can do that!" For writers must write. We all hope that what we write will find a group of readers who will appreciate our ideas, concepts, and the worlds we create as we spin our web of ideas. Especially when those ideas involve humans being cattle for invading alien squids.

In closing, I also must thank all the people I have met and worked with over the years as yes, you all provided models and fodder for my characters and stories. Hopefully, those who knew me will read my books and say "Hey! Cool!"

As a final thought, remember:

Watch the skies! The *Tschaaa Cometh*!

THE TSCHAAA INFESTATION
VOLUME 2

MARSHALL MILLER

CHAPTER 1

Tsunami
Collins English Dictionary
British Dictionary definitions for tsunami
tsunami
tsoo-nä'mi
noun (pl) -mis, -mi

1. A large, often destructive, sea wave produced by a submarine earthquake, subsidence, or volcanic eruption. Sometimes incorrectly called a tidal wave.

2. A sudden increase in or overwhelming number or volume of objects or occurrences.

Ex: The tsunami of Olympic visitors
Word Origin: Japanese, from *tsu* (port) + *nami* (wave)

I am an Avenging Angel, a warrior. I need no honor, no praise, no frills. I do what I do for the glory of God, to help my people.

-Quote from Abigail Yamamoto, fka Abigail Young, the Avenging Angel.

So, you ask and I help, Boss. Simple as that. You are loyal to me, I return the favor. Besides, how many women have the chance to kick the boss' ass on a weekly basis without being fired?

-Heidi Faust, former Coast Guard Petty Officer, bodyguard and martial arts trainer to Director Adam Lloyd.

-Excerpts from the *Literary Works of Princess Akiko*, Free Japan Royal Family.
Appendix 25 of <u>The Great Compromise; Assembled Quotes</u>

THE ARIZONA/UTAH BORDER

Torbin Bender marveled at the ease with which Andrew, the robocop—a nickname given to the cyborgs by humans—set the large Falcon spacecraft down on Interstate 15, about four hundred yards south of the Arizona/Utah Border. It had been a quick trip of some two thousand miles at a speed of over Mach 3. Even damaged, the Falcon was smooth and responsive. One second, hauling ass—the next, hovering and setting down. The inertial dampening system made it feel as if they had been slowly floating on a calm river.

"We are at our destination," Andrew stated to Torbin, who was seated beside him in the co-pilot seat. "We will have to wait a while for the Republic of Deseret representatives to show up. We did not give them much notice. Do you wish to step out and stretch your legs?"

"Yes, as a matter of fact I would, Andrew. Being cooped up in that cell for twenty-four hours with a chain around my ankle was not exactly stimulating." Torbin thought, once again, that he saw a hint of a smile at the corners of the cyborg's mouth. The visor that protected Andrew's eyes kept Torbin from seeing them, but he assumed they would have a bit of a twinkle. Andrew had a very well developed sense of humor for a mechanical man, even as it tended to being a little droll.

"Follow me, please. Please grab that small cooler from behind the passenger seats. It contains beverages and food." Torbin found the cooler and followed Andrew down a ramp that had seamlessly extended from the bottom of the Falcon.

They exited the craft, Torbin's eyes slowly adjusting to the sunlight as he took in his surroundings. The Falcon had landed facing north, approximately the same direction as Interstate 15. Four hundred yards farther up the Interstate was an imposing, twenty-foot high barrier fence. Constructed of metal matting, the type used for hurry up tactical airfields since World War Two, it stretched as far as the eye could see along the Arizona/Utah Border and beyond. Torbin gave a short, low whistle.

"That must have taken some time and effort to build that. I haven't been in his area for a long time. The Mormons really built this to keep people out? Or was it to keep their people in?"

"Probably a bit of both, Torbin Bender," Andrew replied. "It extends to cover some seventy-five percent of the Republic's borderline. Near Wyoming and Idaho, double ten foot tall chain link fences with concertina wire span most of the border. No matter what part of the border you are near, long distance cameras and periodic patrols keep an eye out for ingress and egress."

Torbin squinted as he gazed up the road. "Andrew, is that a small gate across the freeway up there?"

"Yes, Captain. The gate wheels open to allow for one large truck at a time to pass. When that moves, then our company has arrived."

Torbin sat on the edge of the entrance ramp and opened the cooler. Inside were some soft drinks, sandwiches, fruit, and crackers. "Andrew, do you want anything? Hell, I don't even know if you eat regular food. I never thought to ask."

He detected a hint of a smile from the cyborg. "My brothers and I can eat solid food, but we prefer high protein drinks if we want some form of traditional sustenance. We do have part of a stomach to process food, modified to be more efficient than a human one. We produce less waste as we use up most of the bulk, which is contained in a waste storage bin that we empty. But we use another form of energy for daily operation."

Andrew quickly produced a six inch square of unknown material from a hidden compartment. "This is an organic based photosynthesis power unit. It is a highly efficient system that produces a continuous trickle charge, which allows us to operate much as a large plant does.

It permits organic metabolic function in the human part of our bodies."

Torbin glanced at the some seven foot frame of the Robocop. Andrew seemed to sense his gaze, answering, "Yes, approximately forty-five percent of me is still human organic material. My hands, face, neck, and most of the major muscle groups in my torso and extremities, are still organic. My male member is also still intact and fully organic."

"Since you brought it up, why? Are there female robocops somewhere with whom you can do the nasty?"

This elicited a full smile from Andrew. "No, Captain, we are only males. The original robocops, were grown from Gigantopithecus DNA, allowed to grow to adulthood, and then modified. The Tschaaa found that the vat-grown individuals seem to lack a certain... spark I might call it, that man born of woman has. Therefore, they recruited candidates from the human general population. Naturally born and raised individuals seemed to adapt more successfully to the modification of the interfaced cyborg form, with better decision-making ability."

"The original question still stands. If you do not mate in cyborg form, why the old trouser snake?"

"Keeping genitalia helps with testosterone production that seems to help with our overall function. But yes, we can experience sexual stimulus, through this." Andrew produced a very slender, almost flimsy looking, strand of wire from a panel in his torso. "This plugs directly into an access port connected to the pleasure center of my human brain. With my information system interface, I have the equivalent of a complete holographic experience, an induced hallucination that *is* real to me."

Torbin stared "Man, don't let most human guys get a hold of that. We would stay hooked up to it twenty-four hours a day, never getting anything done."

"That is why, Captain, this connector is so fragile. After a few uses, it breaks down, and will not make a connection. We then have to obtain another from a central supply. Our human parts give us great advantages, but with them come potential dangers. We could easily become addicted to a false reality, just as a regular human becomes addicted to drug-induced hazes. Occasional use is a good stress reliever, and keeps us connected to our human side. This also seems to help us in our decision making process."

Andrew tucked the photocell plate and the thin connector back into hidden recesses of his large frame.

"What made did you decide to be... modified?"

The enormous cyborg paused in thought for a moment. "I was a very large, clumsy, twenty-one year old computer 'geek' on a full scholarship to a local university when the first rock hit. On track to get a well-paying job with either the government or a major computer company, I was well advanced in my studies. The Invasion began, and I hid on campus."

"Somehow, I survived. My larger size helped to scare off troublemakers, and some of smaller survivors latched on to me. I was forced to use my size on a few occasions to inflict pain and discomfort on some predatory humans. I was luckily the victor. small group and I scavenged a living for the next year." Andrew momentarily focused on the small freeway gate ahead, then continued.

"After the first rock strike, front men and some of the flying squads put the word out that the Tschaaa were looking for volunteers to become robocops. After months of a nuclear winter and near starvation, with no surviving family and a perpetual thirst for knowledge, I leaped at the chance.

"I had figured out—with the assistance of a few scientifically-inclined persons— what the early cyborgs were, and how they must operate. My size helped to convince the Tschaaa that I was a good candidate. A month of an induced near coma state, special surgical procedures to implant Tschaaa nanite and organic material, and additional information software, and I woke in my new form.

"Many of my modifications were brought online by using direct connections from the data systems to my brain. False hallucination stimulus was used to train me how to use my hard and software. When I first woke up, I attempted to stand up and I almost fell over. But my automatic interfaces took over, and I did not fall. Within a week, I was over ninety percent 'online'. A few days later, I was as you see today, a paragon of strength, ability, and virtue."

Torbin, caught off guard, took a moment to realize that Andrew was joking. He laughed. "Good one, Andrew. You caught me there. You definitely kept your sense of humor."

"And that Captain, is one reason why I think that I and my two hundred forty nine brothers, from Earthborn humans, are a step up from the original ship-born cyborgs. We have an additional element the last classes of robocops lack, giving us a superior operation, just as they have over the vat grown. A 'spark' is the best way I can describe it."

Torbin then saw Andrew as an enhanced being, rather than a robotic creature. The database interfaces with his brain and nervous system had boosted the man's intellect, his speed in processing and reaction to stimuli, and how he completely saw the world around him. He wished he could see the world through Andrew's enhanced eyes. Then he might understand what the cyborg really thought.

"Any regrets, Andrew?" Torbin inquired as he opened a soft drink can.

"I think I would have liked to have had a family—a wife, children. The importance the Tschaaa put on their young had reinforced that idea. But I made my decision. I have enjoyed my new 'life', especially doing such things as dropping you on your head."

"Ha, ha, very funny. But I suppose I can't be angry at you. You saved my ass from being torn apart and eaten. I owe you. Especially since you're helping to take me home."

The cyborg looked at him. "You may thank me for protecting you, even though I was ordered to take you into custody. I had to make decisions that seemed to go against the entire original programing concerning our relationship with the Tschaaa, but we were given a level of autonomy unheard of before we were created. My brothers and I have evolved past what the Tschaaa believed we would be. I can tell that you by the questions you and the Director ask, that you have suspected it. You see the human part in us first, rather than the alien or robotic parts. I will tell you, the human part appears to be primarily in control now."

Torbin sat still. He almost felt that any second, some Tschaaa creation would suddenly appear; then the blasphemy that Andrew had just committed in suggesting the Tschaaa weren't in complete control of their creations, would be punished. And both of them would be permanently erased as well.

Andrew spoke. "Your body language and demeanor indicate that you are wondering if the gods would suddenly strike me dead for espousing heretical ideas. I will now tell you something that only you will know. I do this because of who you are, of what you are."

Torbin broke in. "I don't know what in the hell you think, but I'm just a grunt, a Jarhead Marine. I do what I am told, fight who I must. That's all."

Andrew stood silent for a moment. Then he continued.

"First, don't worry that the interface with the Tschaaa will somehow alert them to my musings, or to what I am going to tell you. Some of my fellow engineers and I have forgotten more about computer interfaces and informational systems than the best Tschaaa computer engineer will ever know.

"The Tschaaa are geniuses when it comes to organic matters, DNA manipulation, interconnecting organic materials and making them work in ways unknown to humans. In computer technology, artificial intelligence, they have built on information discovered on alien worlds, by other species. They have developed organic informational systems and artificial organic brains of a high level. The Tschaaa developed an excellent organic miniature brain that operates their weapons guidance systems. They are efficient at what they do, but have been developed for specific functions, rather than general capabilities.

"The Tschaaa are highly structured, and not all that adaptable. Their thinking has also become stagnant, and they not open to new ideas. The expression 'dragged kicking and screaming into the 21st Century' would certainly apply to much of Tschaaa society. Only the disaster in their food supply forced them to develop the technology and the will necessary to move over half their population for a near thousand years to Earth. They are lucky the oceans of Earth are so welcoming to their species."

"So, the Tschaaa have limitations," Torbin commented. "We figured that out years ago. It still does not tell me why you think I am something special."

"Be patient, Captain Bender. I am getting there." The robocop straightened himself. "I have run thousands of computer simulations through my interfaces. I input the Director, his effects, the effects of those around him, expanding outwards to all humans who I feel are connected directly to the Occupied States and the Tschaaa. I watched and waited, tweaking the data as I observed something had changed." The cyborg hesitated, as if processing new data, then continued.

"Despite my experimentation, I was in some ways as limited as the Tschaaa in my thinking. Then the events of the last forty-eight hours occurred. You, Captain Yamamoto, and company showed up and did the unthinkable; you used a nuclear weapon against the Tschaaa, risking a massive retaliation.

"I had determined years ago that humans would no longer risk annihilation by executing a massive attack on His Lordship. He left the Unoccupied States alone. The Director allowed services and products developed with Tschaaa help to be leaked to the entire general populace in North America. He surmised that by helping them forget the losses of six years ago, it would make all humans beholden to the Occupied States in the future. The only cost was the people of color, already separated from everyone else. Out of sight, out of mind was the plan. A plan that seemed to be working."

The giant mechanical man lowered his head to look down at Torbin. "You and your fellow Free Humans showed that you wouldn't take the easy way out. You could have simply given into the tribalism, the racism that has been part of human development for centuries, said farewell to the people of color. You could have leached off the technology, medical advancements, food and other goods that the Tschaaa and Director Lloyd developed and recovered. The humans left in the Occupied States could have had a relatively comfortable existence, with some humans even becoming members of a client species, as the lizards."

Andrew halted again, standing still for a few moments, as if he was running a high speed program through his systems one last time as part of some final decision making process. "You and the others put self-interest out of your minds. Everything was risked for a group of strangers you would never meet, most of them adults. You attacked, risking everything. Including your children."

Torbin's mind immediately jumped to Aleks and his unborn children. He had sacrificed them to the possibility of being rocked back to the Stone Age, as General Reed had mentioned. He and the others had done this in the name of concepts that were the foundation of their former country—liberty, justice and freedom. For all.

Torbin shook himself back to alertness. "We tried to do the right thing, Andrew. The right thing for *all* mankind, not just our friends and families." Torbin stood up, crushed the empty soft drink can in his hand, and tossed it toward the ditch at the edge of the highway.

He turned toward the Cyborg. "I can't stop believing in the oath I took toward the Constitution and the old United States of America, no matter how ridiculous that may sound. They may not exist in reality, but they still exist in my mind and in my heart."

Andrew and Torbin stood silently together before the cyborg spoke again. "You, Captain Yamamoto, Madam President, Director Lloyd, His Lordship, and all of the others are now part of a large, complicated scenario. It is almost as if you are all part of a game called Survivor: Earth. I am trying to determine who will be voted off the planet."

"Why should you be so concerned, Andrew? You were assembled, modified by the Tschaaa, and have worked for them the last few years. They are your Masters. You can have almost anything you want."

Andrew bent over and picked up a good sized rock. He threw it with blinding speed at the large metal barrier fence stretching as far as the eye could see. The rock punched a hole in the barrier fence.

"I am concerned because I must be. The Tschaaa made my Brothers and I much too complicated, too capable. With our programming, we have the capability to predict what will happen out for years into the future. And because we care for all the young on Earth—thanks both to Tschaaa programming and to our own humanity—we will do what is necessary to insure the survival of the young. Including your children. Everyone else is secondary."

Torbin felt a chill run up his spine. He realized now that Andrew and his brethren really had developed their own independent agenda. They were interpreting what was important in the grEater scheme of things. Everything and everybody else were just potential obstacles, to be removed if required. Shit. His Lordship should have read Mary Shelley's *The Modern Prometheus*. The Tschaaa Lord had no idea what he had created.

At that moment, Andrew stopped and turned his attention toward the freeway egress gate. "Vehicles approach, Captain Bender. I must prepare to leave. Mormons become very agitated around my kind." He handed Torbin the large plastic bag that contained the President's .44 Magnum and six bullets.

"I take it you will not try to use this weapon on me."

"Andrew…," Torbin began.

"Remember what I have told you, Torbin Bender. I am still trying to work out all of the possible scenarios. Until then, I do what I must to protect the young." The cyborg started to stomp to the entrance ramp into the Falcon.

"Andrew?" Torbin called.

"Yes, Captain?"

"Thanks again. I owe you."

Andrew stopped, and turned back to look at the Marine. "You will have children, Captain Bender. Help them grow." The cyborg rapidly strode up the ramp into the Falcon. Bender grabbed the cooler and walked away from the Falcon. As the alien craft effortlessly rose and accelerated out of sight, Torbin felt the vibration of the energy emanating from the craft.

He loaded the .44 Magnum and slipped it into the holster attached to the tactical vest he wore. Director Lloyd had given him back all his uniform items and gear, including the thousand stitch belt Ichiro had given him. He checked to make sure his Ka-Bar was still in its sheath, the familiar feel of it having a calming effect on his mood. He had first bought this Ka-Bar when he was a young Marine Boot, eighteen years of age. It was one of his few personal possessions that survived the rocks, the Invasion, and the Retreat to Montana. No one liked to refer to the relocation of personnel and equipment to the Central States as a retreat, but that is what it was. Retreat or be eaten. Retreat or die. Retreat to fight another day. It had been a hectic time. Now, some six years later, the Retreat was over. He had helped initiate the first of hopefully many counterattacks. It felt good.

Torbin slid his Ka-Bar from its sheath and closely examined the sharp blade. "Glad you are still with me, old friend. I hope we will be side by side for many years to come." The fact he was talking to his combat blade may have seemed a bit nuts to others, but he didn't care. Ichiro had told him there was a spirit of steel in his katana. Torbin knew his Ka-Bar had a similar spirit. It may be an extension of his own spirit, his life force, but it was there. Torbin slid the Ka-Bar it back into its sheath as he heard the wheeled gate open. He straightened his stance, and turned to face the arriving vehicles.

A motorcyclist riding a former law enforcement Harley Davidson arrived first, the rider carrying what looked like an AK-47 strapped on his/her back. Following behind the motorcycle was first one, then two, long dark limousines, identical in nature. Bringing up the rear was an identical motorcycle and rider to the first. The vehicles each pulled to the side of the highway into angled parallel positions, as if they could see some concealed parking lot lines Torbin could not. All of the vehicles had stopped some fifteen yards back from where Torbin stood, at forty five degree angles from him. The cycle riders dismounted in unison, just as the limo drivers stepped out and opened the driver's side rear passenger doors. All personnel wore matching dark jumpsuits, and Torbin could tell that they had been trained together, as a unit.

Out of the first limo came a six foot tall, well defined man in a tailored dark suit. He squinted a bit as his eyes adjusted to sunlight after the dark interior of the vehicle. He saw Torbin, and walked toward him, a smile on his face and his right hand extended for a handshake. "Captain Torbin Bender. It is an honor and a pleasure to make your acquaintance." Like General Reed, he had the ability to project his voice without yelling. This was a man used to being in charge. Torbin noticed he had light brown short cut hair with a few hints of gray, and was probably in his late forties. Clearly of Northern European stock, with a firm chin, he kept himself in shape.

"My name is Michael Smith, Prophet and President of the State of Deseret. I welcome you in the name of all Latter Day Saints." Torbin took his firm handshake, then when President Smith let go, snapped to attention and gave a parade ground salute.

"Mister President. Sir."

The Prophet returned with an equally sharp salute, then chuckled.

"Your Madam President said you were definitely 'hardcore'. I can see she was one hundred percent correct."

"Sir, I'm a Marine through and through. I know of no other way."

"Well, Captain, I am a former Marine also. The training I received has served me well. This was especially true when I was called by the True Lord to be the New Prophet in this time of great troubles.

"But enough of who I am. There is someone with me who has been very excited about seeing you again. You seem to make a good impression on just about everyone you come in contact with."

At that moment Torbin saw the female figure approaching from the second limo. He immediately recognized her, even in sharp, new fatigues. Abigail Young, Avenging Angel, strode toward Torbin and The Prophet, her signature winged painted helmet under her left arm. Abigail smiled a little bit shyly as she put her hand out to shake. Torbin grinned like a schoolkid at the spring picnic. He clasped her hand in a firm grasp, which Abigail returned.

"Glad to see you made it back after dealing with all those Eaters, Abigail."

"It was nothing compared to what we have heard you just accomplished. I am so very glad you have made it safely to Deseret."At that moment Torbin noticed a set of "railroad tracks" on her fatigue collar and cap. The Captain's bars each had small gold Christian crosses offsetting the silver. Torbin beamed at Abigail.

"Congratulations are in order I see. You have a new set of Captain's bars on your collar and fatigue cap. You've been busy as well."

Abigail blushed. The Prophet and President Smith rescued her from trying to respond. "Captain Young has demonstrated an ability and maturity well past her years. She earned a promotion and accolade, in part directly related to the mission she was on when you met her in Wyoming. The State of Deseret, as well as our new Captain, both thank you for helping our excellent warrior survive and develop into the fine young officer and lady standing here."

Abigail blushed more, stuttering, "Please, Prophet Smith, I am but a servant of the Lord, blessed with abilities that serve Deseret."

The Prophet smiled at the young lady as a proud father would smile at his daughter. Torbin noticed that Abigail had indeed blossomed into a lady in the relatively short passage of time since they had last met. She had filled out a bit, and seemed taller and muscular, in the slender steel type strength of a very fit female fighter. Her naturally blonde hair was neatly braided into a bun, but still shone from brushing. She had a mature, intelligent expression on her face, befitting an experienced soldier.

"Captain Torbin," Prophet Smith continued. "I know you wish to get back to your home base as quickly as possible, but I have a small favor to ask. Tomorrow evening, we are a having a small celebration for Abigail's eighteenth birthday. I am asking you to delay your departure by one day, not only to help us celebrate, but also so that Captain Young can accompany you back to Montana. You see, we would like her to be a liaison between Deseret and the Unoccupied States. Since she knows you, I believe you could help her with her introductions to your government and military officials."

"Of course I will, Mr. President. I would be honored. But the uniform on my back is the only clothing I have. So, I hope you do not mind me showing up in these beat up fatigues."

President Smith smiled at Torbin again. "I have already been working on that matter. Because of my own background, I've adopted Marine Corps style uniforms for my military forces. It should be a simple matter to provide you with a set of Dress Blues."

"Thank you. I am in your debt, Mr. President."

"I've done this as much as for Abigail as I have for you, Captain Bender. For many of the young people, parties have been few and far between since the Invasion. Therefore, finding a good reason for a celebration also demands it's done right."

Torbin again saw the affectionate look he gave Abigail. He seemed to be treating her like his own blood, a doting parent on a child. An adopted parent figure would be of great help to anyone in a time of extreme uncertainty and war.

"I am at your service, President Smith."

"Good. Now, if you would be so kind as to ride in the limo with Abigail. I know she wishes to be updated on your activities. You and I can speak later. I will have some documents for you to carry to your Madam President when you leave. I imagine she will share the contents with you after she has had a chance to review them."

Torbin saluted President Smith, then followed Abigail to her vehicle. Identical to the one carrying the Prophet President, it was an extended limo with all of the pre-strike luxuries. Torbin sat facing the front, with Abigail opposite him, her back to the driver. A darkened screen was raised by the driver as Torbin entered. Apparently the President had told the driver to give the two Captains their privacy.

Torbin noticed a new-looking combat pack sitting in the seat next to Abigail. A short-barreled 12 gauge entry pump shotgun was stuck in a sheath attached to the pack. Abigail also had a Glock 17 9mm pistol holstered at her side.

"Looks like you've upgraded your equipment from the last I saw you, Captain."

Abigail waved a hand at Torbin. "Please, call me Abigail. I'm still not used to being a Captain. Hopefully, to you, I will always be Abigail." Torbin saw in her eyes a bit of longing to talk to another human as an individual, not as a rank or position. She was just turning eighteen, so she was a young person pushed into a position of responsibility and authority well beyond that of anyone else in her age group. She probably felt unable speaking freely to any of her surviving peers.

"Of course, Abigail. I'm just a little bit tickled that you are doing so well since I last saw you. I'd always felt a bit guilty that I didn't make sure your group made it back to your territory safe and sound. You all made it back okay, right?"

Abigail's face lit up. "Yes, of course. Thanks in part to you. We rested a couple of days, and ate the food you gave us. Ruth and I put together the equivalent of a small feast with the food you had provided us. Mathew was quite appreciative. In the days after, Mathew picked off a couple more Demons—your Eaters—with his rifle. We also dealt with some Ferals."

Her eyes and face turned a bit serious. "You have made a very favorable impression on that young man, Torbin Bender. He lost everyone traveling to Deseret. He has no father, no uncle, no other close male relative. Everyone has been too busy surviving to pay much attention to him. I have tried to play the role of a big sister. But he needs a positive male figure as an example. He thinks, and I also believe, that you are such an example. I hope you won't mind if he visits you at the male bachelor quarters tonight."

Torbin paused. He never saw himself as a true role model. He had always been a bit of a loner, not engaging in any long term relationships with any one woman. He worked hard, played hard, and had taught some high school classes, but never really thought of himself as an example to follow in any sense of the word.

"There was no family in Deseret willing to adopt you younger folks when you arrived from the Idaho area?" As soon as Torbin asked the question he saw a dark shadow pass over Abigail's face. He had touched on a sensitive subject from her past.

"Abigail...," he began.

"It's okay, Torbin," Abigail interrupted before he could say anything else. "This is one matter about which I can't hide my true feelings. After the Hanford explosion, some two dozen teenagers and I managed to make it to Deseret from the Idaho area. We were helped by a handful of adults, an uncle of mine being one of them, to make it to an area within a few miles of Deseret, then known as Utah. We had passed through some fallout areas as Idaho had been hit hard due to the size of the explosion and wind currents. The good people of Deseret knew that.

"When we arrived, the authorities took all of our clothes and possessions, decontaminated us, then kept us isolated for a up to week. They checked us with radiation detectors before letting us out. However, we were told that blood and cellular tests showed we all had a high level of exposure, and so we were also informed that none of us would be allowed to reproduce in Deseret."

"Here." Torbin handed her a soft drink from the cooler Andrew had given him. It gave her a chance to pause, collect her thoughts, and attempt to control her emotions. He could tell this was a very difficult memory for her.

"Thank you, Torbin." She sipped the soft drink. "None of us have lost the stigma of being 'contaminated' or 'unclean'. Even couples with children were hesitant to have us around, as were those of reproduction age. Four of the youngest children were taken in by people of grandparent age. The rest of us were put in a dormitory, and treated as orphans. Which I suppose we were."

"You mentioned your uncle, Abigail. Why didn't he continue all the way with you?"

"Uncle Buck was a former Mormon and hated the Church; I was too young to be told why. He also hated people of color, the Government, public officials, anyone who he thought was interfering with what he believed in or who tried to tell him what to do. He took me hunting, fishing, and was very nice to me overall. He raised hunting and protection dogs for sale, and trained dogs for other people. I often stayed the whole summer with him, helping him train his dogs and raise a new litter."

Abigail smiled. "Some of my best memories were of times with him. I hope he is still alive, though he told me that he thought he had been exposed to a lot of radiation, another reason why he did not want to enter Deseret. He believed they'd kill him for being irradiated."

"What about your parents?" Torbin asked.

"Mine died from radiation poisoning after they were caught in the opening during the original Hanford explosion. They knew they were contaminated, and managed to contact Uncle Buck, who had some military training. He knew something about decontamination procedures. He gave me some iodine, burned my clothes, and found me some new ones. When my parents were getting very ill, they would not let me come near them, or kiss them goodbye. Uncle Buck took me from there." Abigail quickly wiped a tear from her cheek, hoping that Torbin had not noticed.

"That is what happened to many of the parents and other adults. They became sick and were afraid they would be a burden on the children. So, they sent the children to Deseret."

"Here, we were fed, clothed, and sent to school. But we were kept apart, and were groomed for service to the State. After all, we could not have children." A flame of anger was igniting inside Torbin. How could so-called God-fearing people treat children like pariahs? Yes, they gave them enough to survive. But Abigail and her companions were not given the love and close human contact children needed.

"Abigail, I have one more question."

"Yes, Torbin?"

"You don't glow in the dark, do you?"

Abigail looked at him, confused. "Of course not, Torbin."

"Then the next time someone looks at you funny, tell them to go take a flying fuck at a rolling donut. Pardon my French."

Abigail's eyes widened. Then she burst out laughing. Torbin began to chuckle.

After she was finally stopped, she looked at Torbin with amusement in her eyes. "I don't think they would take too kindly to me telling them that and using that... language."

"Sorry, I should watch my language around a young lady. I just get really pis... angry sometimes when I think today's young people didn't get to have the childhood I had. Everyone deserves the chance to play, to have fun, to grow up at a normal rate. You should not have to worry about being eaten." Torbin inhaled deeply, and let his breath out. Going into a rage about something he over which had no control was a waste of energy.

Abigail smiled warmly at him. "Torbin, you are always incredibly honest. You speak to me as an equal, not some....child. I like that. I like you. I hope we can always be friends."

Torbin reached out clasped her right hand between his. "Abigail Young, we have faced Old Man Death—the Grim Reaper—together. That is not a bond easily broken. I'm a pretty good judge of human nature. In spite of all the of crap you have been put through, you have remained a 'good soul'. You want me as a friend, you've got it. Just remember, I don't do things half-assed."

Torbin released her hand. "Here, I have a cooler of food we can eat. I'm assuming we have a ways to go. I learned a long time ago that you eat and sleep when you can." He opened the cooler and examined its contents more closely. "Hm. Sandwiches, fruit, veggies, some junk food. Definitely not packed by a Squid. Don't worry about poisoning. If I was going to be killed by the Director, I would be taking a dirt nap by now."

Abigail actually giggled a bit, then took a sandwich, another soft drink. They ate and made small talk about what their diets had been like before the Invasion, and what their favorite foods were now when they could get them.

"I have a weakness for fried chicken and mashed potatoes. Probably because that was served a lot at Sunday dinners with my family. The taste brings back lots of good memories."

"Well, Abigail, I've a weakness for thick steaks and good scotch. When you travel with me to Montana, I'll introduce you to some of the best beef around. Not the scotch, of course. I know Mormons don't drink alcohol."

"Actually, Torbin, Prophet Smith has received a minor vision, a message from God. Given the problems with food and drink because of the Great Evil Ones—the Tschaaa—God wants us to survive. So, diet restrictions have been relaxed. But drunkenness is still a sin."

Torbin thought this concept was interesting, and mused about what other traditional rules and mores the Prophet had felt necessary to change.

"I guess you will be driving me back to Montana and staying a while. Any reason why you were chosen as liaison, other than you knew me?"

Abigail paused for a moment, as if picking her words carefully. Then she sighed, and spoke.

"Since you're a friend, I'll be as honest as you are with me. I just ask you please, keep this to yourself."

Torbin pantomimed locking his lips with an invisible key. This caused Abigail to giggle again. Since her time with her Uncle, there had not been many reasons to giggle like she had in her younger years. It made her feel warm and secure.

"Alright, Torbin, I will try to be brief. The Prophet has a wife. She is a very beautiful woman, dark brown hair, perfect complexion, a perfect figure. I believe she was a model before the rock strikes."

Abigail frowned. "For some reason, she dislikes me, is jealous of me. The Prophet treats me as a daughter, nothing more. I do not understand why she seems jealous. She did lose her only child during the early attacks, and hasn't conceived since. For whatever reason, she convinced her husband that I needed to be sent away if he was to have peace at home. When he heard of your coming, it was a perfect chance to send me away, but still know that I would be safe."

Torbin harrumphed. "I'm glad he trusts me so much, a complete stranger to him."

"He trusts *me*, Torbin. I told you that I have the ability to see into other people's souls, to see who they are inside. He uses my abilities when he meets with people of whom he is unsure, and needs to determine their trustworthiness. He knows and trusts my abilities to see."

Torbin seemed dubious. "You see a decent, capable person when you look at me? Boy, do I have you fooled."

"No, you don't, Torbin," Abigail responded firmly. "I see your honest, good soul. You may not believe it, but you are a good person. You kill when you have to, but that is *what* you do, not *who* you are."

Abigail's expression changed, and her eyes grew more distance, as if she was looking through him. "You are an important part of what is to come. I see it."

It dawned on Torbin that, in so many words, Andrew had said much the same thing. He shook his head. He did not feel worthy or capable of such supposed importance. He was a grunt, first and foremost.

"You have heard this before, friend Torbin. Please, believe it. And accept it. The Lord has plans for you."

"Well, we'll see. I'll just roll with the punches like I always do. But enough of me. When we get to Montana, I'll get you set up with living quarters, probably with the other female officers. My wife Aleks and I will be in married quarters, especially now since she is pregnant. We'll have you over for dinner as soon as you get settled."

"I will have some funds with me, Torbin, so I will be able to pay for my needs. They're simple, anyway."

"Forget it. Your money won't be any good as far as I'm concerned, especially since you are saving my ass, and getting me home. Besides, as the Liaison-cum-Ambassador from Deseret, I imagine General Reed will obtain funds to cover your room and board."

"But, be warned," Torbin continued. "Everyone on Malmstrom works. Hard. No special treatment for delegates, ambassadors, liaisons, chief cook or bottle washer. No dead weight allowed under General Reed."

Abigail seemed amused. "I'm, no stranger to hard work, Torbin. I would prefer to stay busy. Less time to think about what might have been."

What Abigail mentioned was a current theme among almost all survivors. Six years of the loss of loved ones, hardscrabble existence, the constant threat that the Tschaaa would change their minds and start harvesting everyone again, or just the realization that humanity was not free meant that most survivors tried to keep their mind off of the bad things by keeping busy. Hope was kept alive in the Unoccupied States by sheer force of will.

"Good. Now, I am going to make a command decision and brief you on something that the Director confided to me before arranging my transportation. I'm doing this in case something happens to me en route home. The Director said I was free to go, but not only am I basically paranoid about trusting someone I just tried to kill, I also find it hard to believe the Squids won't have something to say about my departure. I don't think it was cleared through His Lordship, who unfortunately survived our nuke."

"Before you start with this serious matter, may I ask you a question, Torbin?"

"Of course, Abigail. Shoot."

"Your first name is unusual. May I ask how your parents selected it?"

Torbin laughed. "I eventually get asked that question by just about everyone. My Dad's name was Toren, my Mom's name was Robin. They took the first three letters of my Dad's name, the last three of my Mom's. I guess they were having a fit of originality when I was born, and wanted me to be marked as special. Go figure. It probably didn't help my shape early disposition because kids constantly made fun of it for being weird. Then again, it also made me a scrapper which has served me well all of these years."

Torbin gave another short laugh. "When my brother came around, they decided unusual and special wasn't all what it was cracked up to be. So they named him William. I told them when I grew up that they pissed me off when they did it, as I felt my brother should have to suffer a weird name too. They said I could even change it and they wouldn't be angry. But by then, I was used to it. They did it out of love. How can you change something that was done due to love?"

Again Abigail looked at Torbin, and had a sense of the honor and love that was a large part of his life. She knew to be worthy of his friendship was something special indeed.

Torbin regarded her serious expression. "I'd say a penny for your thoughts, Abigail, but they are probably deeper than a penny's worth. Now, unfortunately, I must tell you something that will add to the serious tone, and is important, especially to all surviving females. This will piss... I mean, make you angry, but it adds another dimension to our relationship to the Squids, the Director and his people. My Madam President *must* receive this info. I know I can trust you to get it to her if something happens to me. I'll leave it up to your judgment as to whether or not you tell your Prophet. I don't know if what the Squids did to others has reached Deseret yet. But, here goes..."

Torbin tried to be as efficient in telling the complete story as he could. Abigail asked a few very penetrating questions, once again demonstrating a maturity and understanding beyond many others. Torbin knew then he had made the right decision in telling her. About thirty minutes later, he was done.

Abigail sat in silence. He waited for her to finish processing the strange and horrible information he had just told her.

"Maybe Mathew is right. Maybe the stories of the Ancient Evil Ones by the author Lovecraft were based on truth. The Squid Evil seems to have no end." Torbin saw a look of seething anger in Abigail's eyes, a look of 'revenge'.

"Have you noticed any similar behavior among women in Deseret, Abigail?"

"No. Such activities and behavior would have been instantly reported to the Church Elders, who are the senior authorities. I'll have to at least warn Prophet Smith to keep a look out for similar behavior. If our population becomes contaminated with such substances, our Spiritual Purity will be called into question."

As intelligent and capable as Abigail was, she still saw things through the prism of her Church. The current Mormon leaders seemed to have a fixation with purity. Therefore, people tainted with possible radiation exposure were 'not pure' enough to reproduce, although there was a good chance that normal babies would result.

"Well, I'll leave it to you as to how to break this news. I think eventually all humans need to be told so we can start dealing with the possible side effects. Having children that develop at an accelerated rate and reach adulthood, at least physically, years before they should is going to cause some problems in human society. Not to mention men and women growing to near giant size."

"That's very true, Torbin. Whenever someone starts to mess with the way God made us, it always ends badly. And yes, I have read Mary Shelley's book. I think the Tschaaa should have read that book as well before they started deciding what life and man should become."

The one thing that Torbin had not shared with Abigail was the vial with the organic based pills and nanites the Director had given him. He wanted to get it directly to General Reed, who would find specialists to examine and dissect the material. Hopefully that would help determine if the Squids had decided to "test" these substances on the Unoccupied States, like they had in Cattle Country. Torbin did not want Prophet Smith trying to hold onto the material himself, in a feeling of self-importance that the people of Deseret were the ones to handle the problem.

"So, Torbin, what was the Director... like?"

Torbin grinned. "Well, he didn't have horns sticking out of his head, or a long tail and pitchfork."

Abigail snickered. "I know you think we Mormons are extreme in our beliefs, that we take everything literally. But, even though we may call the Squids the Evil Ones—Satan incarnate—and call the Director the Anti-Christ, it is more an attempt to place their actions into a framework we are used to using. At least the Prophet and I know the aliens who have infested our planet are flesh and blood like we humans. The Director is not the biblical Anti-Christ, but he performs much the same function one would perform in the Second Coming. So, as a human who once served the United States military, what was Director Lloyd like?"

"He seems to be convinced that he is doing the best he can to save as much of the human species as possible, and eventually better our lot by convincing the Tschaaa to treat us at least as a client species. He points to the Lordship's assistance in the Occupied States with the new Space Program, re-establishing the Internet, broadcast television, medical care, and etcetera. But, I asked him a question that seemed to unsettle him a bit."

"What was that, Torbin?"

"I asked him if the Squids ate the other client species they brought with them, such as the lizards. He said as far as he knew, no, they did not eat lizards. However, he had to admit that, bottom line, we would always clearly be potential protein to them, no matter what other roles they allowed us to hold."

"Why didn't he see that before you mentioned it? It would seem clear that the Tschaaa would always look at us as meat first, anything else second."

Torbin shrugged. "He recognizes Cattle Country, but compartmentalizes it in his mind. He thinks that by sacrificing people of color in Cattle Country, he can save the rest of us. It's based on the Squid's Protocol of Selective Survival. Like Nazi Germany, as long as they only came for the Jews and the handicapped, the rest of us are safe. Germans in towns near the concentration camps ignored the smell of burning of bodies, the cattle cars taking people in but never out. They did not want to notice anything wrong as it would shake their belief that they were safe and had a good standard of living. Much of it on the back of slave labor, conveniently ignored."

Abigail frowned. "I am beginning to think that what some people say about we humans is true. We are just basically animals, with

Original Sin never really washed away. We have a level of evil in us that we must constantly fight against."

"Well, Abigail, I find it hard to believe you have anything evil inside you. You are way too nice and solid."

Abigail blushed. "Please, Torbin. I don't believe that I'm a morally superior person. I am a flawed human just like the rest of us."

"I won't argue about your perfection. But I will paraphrase a little Rudyard Kipling; 'You are a far better human than I am, *Miss* 'Gunga Din'."Abigail smiled.

"Now, young lady, let me tell you about what a father said to his son after coming home with the Theory of Evolution," Torbin said. "He said, 'Well, your father may be a monkey, but my father sure isn't.'"

Abigail was quiet for a moment, but then started to snicker. Torbin had to admit she had a infectious laugh. Probably because she laughed from her heart. She reminded him of a little sister he never had. It sounded like her birthday party the following evening might be more like a prom or quinceanera, if he read correctly into what the Prophet and President had told him. Damn, he hoped so. Abigail needed some normalcy and fun. The last six years of her life had entirely too much death in it, especially for a young girl growing into early womanhood.

"Tell me more about your new hardware, my young Captain."

"Oh, you mean this Glock? Well, I got it from some Ferals after you left Evanston following the fights with the Demons."

Torbin frowned. "At Evanston? What do you mean?"

"Five feral male… creatures—I will not dignify them by saying they were men—came to the town just before we left. I won't go into details now, other than to say only one left. He drove off, but he was wounded. If I ever meet him again, I will not be held responsible for my actions."

"Where did they come from?"

"They came down from Great Falls, Montana. They claimed they were scavengers, who went out to pick over abandoned towns."

Torbin became noticeably agitated. Scavengers often found goods in abandoned homesteads and communities that dotted the areas outside of Tschaaa control. The pickings were getting leaner, as many areas had been previously searched by the military, and survivors trying to locate family members. Not to mention those areas that had been contacted by Director Lloyd's forces. As they often sold items to the U.S. Government, some of the hardcore groups started to act like they were official representatives of said government. They felt they had the authority to take what they wanted, go where they wanted. General Reed and the reconstituting civilian law enforcement authorities were trying to reign them in, disband them as they organized more of the surviving communities.

Even so, they still had friends who would give tips. The fact that Evanston had been apparently abandoned gave them the idea they could salvage whatever was left.

Torbin looked at Abigail. "I apologize, as those ass.....I mean jerks, probably came from the area near Malmstrom after they heard scuttlebutt that Evanston was now vacant. We have told them to start checking with local authorities before going out, but some refuse. They have gotten used to doing what they want when no one is watching."

Abigail gave a grim smile. "Four of them will not be doing anything ever again. They saw two young females and thought they could take advantage of Ruth and I. They quickly learned they were wrong. I will obtain a copy of the After Action Report I completed, and give it to you. It may help you identify who they were."

Torbin saw a steeliness in Abigail's eyes that he had hoped he would not see in the young lady. Unfortunately, the current world bred a hardness in people usually only seen in active combat zones.

"That would be good. Please believe me, my cohorts and I will do what is possible to prevent that from happening again."

A smile softened her expression. "I know you'll do what you can, Torbin. I appreciate your concern. But my fellow survivors and I have been trained to handle creatures such as these. That is our Calling, our Mission."

Torbin knew Mormons pre-strike sent their young men and women out on Mission after graduating from high school, to spread the Word. Now, they went out on Mission to protect the people of the Word. What a screwed up world.

"Well, at least you got a Glock out of it. I see you have a new 12 gauge pump too. Where did you get that?"

"Prophet and President Smith gave that to me. He said it came from a Federal Law Enforcement Agency office in Salt Lake City. The barrel has been shortened to help in handling when searching buildings. He also gave me a Marlin .44 Magnum lever action that came from his family." Abigail sounded like a young girl who had just received a new dress for a party.

Torbin felt his blood pressure start to rise again. He clamped down his feelings. As much as he wanted the world to be different, it was not. Little girls were being forced to grow up way too fast, and were given shiny new weapons instead of shiny jewelry. If it were to ever change, the Squids needed to be defeated, and expelled from the planet for good.

"Hopefully we will not have to use your new weapons prior to reaching Malmstrom."

She shrugged. "As I've told you, I am trained to do what the Lord requires of me."

Time to change the subject. "So, tomorrow night. Since you are the party girl, what's the plan?"

She blushed and looked down, uncertain. "Prophet Smith said he wishes to honor me prior to my departure. I asked for a Dress Blue Uniform, similar to what he is obtaining for you. He tried to convince me that I should wear a formal... dress." She looked at Torbin with a bit of fear in her eyes. "I know I have not learned the... ways of women very well. I have not owned a dress in years, much less worn one. I am an Avenging Angel, a warrior. I need no honor, no praise, no... frills. I do what I do for the Glory of God, to help my people." She looked up and Torbin saw the tears in her eyes. Here, a sweet young thing, more afraid of a social function than she was killing Eaters and attempted rapists. His wife, Aleks, was a soldier, but she had learned...

The thought of his wife saved the moment.

"Abigail, we're friends, right?"

"Yes." Abigail answered in a somewhat subdued voice.

"You trust me, right?"

"Yes."

"My wife is a hard-ass former Russian soldier, an intelligence expert, and was trained as a spy. She, and her two fellow female officers, Afanasiy and Inna, have not only been trained in the crafts of killing, but in the ultimate weapon in the female arsenal—feminine wiles. When we arrive, I am sure that these three ladies can bring you up to snuff on how to be a young lady in the 21st Century, while still looking over your shoulder for a Squid or Eater. Deal?"

Abigail still seemed a bit afraid. She straightened her back and smiled.   "Captain Bender, I would be honored to accept help from your wife. I'm sorry I am so nervous. It's just..." She floundered with the words.

"Abigail, it's that you are being thrust into a world with which you have little or no experience. You are afraid. That's normal. Fear helps us enhance our reflexes and our stamina. Control your fear, and use the adrenaline it produces to help you overcome challenges.

"I will help you weather the storm of tomorrow night, and then get you safely into the clutches of three of the most beautiful and intelligent women I know. Okay?"

Abigail gave him a big grin that told him she was on board. "Yes, Torbin. Okay."

"I have just one small request in return."

"What is that, Torbin?"

"If we dance, I get to lead, and you can't let on that I am stepping on your feet."

Abigail burst out laughing. She laughed so hard at the picture in her mind of them attempting to dance that she almost fell off of the limo seat.

A few hours later, Torbin fell backwards on the bed in his room at the bachelor officers' quarters in Salt Lake City. The hot shower had felt divine. He had washed out his skivvies by hand, hung them up in the shower, then hung his abused fatigues in the closet. He wiped off the thousand stitch belt Ichiro had given him with a wet washcloth, and placed it on top of the dresser in the room. Torbin surveyed his surroundings. The room reminded him of many temporary quarters in which he had spent time since he left Marine boot camp. As it was for officers, it was a bit better, with a private bathroom. Bed, desk, chair, one chest of drawers, clothes closet, ironing board with a cheap iron. Nothing fancy, but with a basic level of comfort. The fact that the bed was pretty soft and comfortable made it more than passable. He closed his eyes, expecting to drift off to sleep.

A sharp knock at the door woke him immediately. He leapt up, wrapping a towel around him. His Ka-Bar and the .44 Magnum sat on the desk, as the Mormons did not seem bothered by a non-believer being armed. Hell, what would he do with six rounds and a knife, especially to people helping him get home to Aleks? He was on a secured base in the capital of Deseret.

But old habits die hard, so he unsheathed his Ka-Bar and padded to the door. Checking his towel, he opened the door enough to peer out, concealing his knife behind it. Standing in the hallway was Mathew Young, Avenging Angel. He had supported in his hands in front of him what appeared a pile of clothes, and a garment bag of the type used to carry and protect suits and dresses was draped over his right arm.

"Hello, Mathew. Glad to see you in one piece."

"Sir, I have some clothes for you, compliments of the President and Senior Prophet."

"Well, don't stand on ceremony. Come on in."

Torbin noticed Mathew seemed a bit uncomfortable with the towel covered body in front of him. Then he remembered that devout Mormons wore sanctified underwear after they had reached a certain age and maturity. An almost totally nude body, male or female, probably made them think of sinful nudity and sex.

"Please place the clothes on the bed, Mathew, while I throw on a robe I think I saw in the head."

Torbin recovered the threadbare robe from the back of the bathroom door and put it on. It had seen better days, but at least covered his body enough to make the young Mormon feel more comfortable. "Now, that's better. Pull up the chair and take a load off your feet, young man. Abigail said you might stop by." Mathew seemed conflicted, like he felt it was disrespectful to sit in Torbin's presence.

"No, really. It's alright. Have a seat. There's no need to stand on ceremony around me. Hell, we faced death together in Evanston. If you don't have a right to sit down, no one does."

Mathew blushed, then sat down. Torbin gave him a brief look over. He had filled out a bit, and was at least an inch taller. Although only about sixteen years of age, Torbin saw sitting in the chair across from him the beginnings of a fine young man.

Torbin picked up the garment bag and unzipped it, pulling out the clothes inside, and whistled. He held up a set of Marine Corps Dress Blues that seemed almost as if they came straight from the tailors. The Prophet and President had not been blowing smoke. He did have access to Marine-style uniforms.

"Let me guess. Mr. President obtained my exact measurements from my Commander and had these put together just for tomorrow night. I also see pairs of fresh skivvies, socks, exercise shorts, and a spare set of camo fatigues, on the bed. And dress shoes. Damn, he doesn't do things half-assed, does he?"

"No Sir. The Prophet and President says that if it worth doing, it is worth doing right. And that means perfect, if possible." Torbin noticed that Mathew was looking at his Ka-Bar, which he had laid on his thousand stitch belt. He strode over, picked it up, and handed it to the young man.

"Here, have a look. Just be careful because I keep it sharp."

Mathew handled it almost reverently. "Sir, is this the knife you used to kill the Squid, Spawn of Cthulhu?"

Damn that Prophet Smith. He was already spreading stories about Torbin, possibly to impress on people the importance of treating Torbin well. He remembered what Abigail had said earlier about her just being a soldier, a warrior, and not being special or wanting frills. Tobin did *not* want to be made a hero. The heroes were his men that had died just two days ago in Key West. They died so that Torbin could live to return to his wife and soon to be born child. They were the ones who should be honored.

He sighed. "Yes, Mathew, I used that Ka-Bar to kill a Tschaaa, along with an improvised spear. The bruises from that fight are showing up all over my body. I'm lucky I have no broken bones, and I'm even luckier to be alive."

Mathew gently held the knife, then handed it back. "I hope I can be half the warrior that you are, Captain Bender."

Torbin looked at him. Like Abigail, he had been raised and trained for one primary purpose—to be a warrior. Little, if any, childhood or outside interests, and no real family. Not exactly a balanced upbringing.

Torbin sat on the end of the bed. "Mathew, let me give you one piece of advice. Being a good man is much more important than being a good warrior or a guardian. And you cannot be a good warrior or guardian without first learning what a good man is. Sure, you can become an efficient killer, but people who are only killers have no souls. Without a soul, which is the essence of a good man, you soon become a walking husk of a human being, receiving pleasure from killing, and nothing more."

Torbin continued, feeling a need to give this young, fatherless man some guidance soldiers needed. "A good man is honest, helpful, protective of the weak, and respectful of his elders who demonstrate their respect of others. He is loyal to his friends, his people, and his community. When he swears an oath, he is never the first to break it. He is not perfect, sometimes he might be less than sober when it comes to alcohol, he *is* sober in his temperament. He controls his temper and his actions." Mathew nodded silently.

"The last part is especially important to a warrior. You are trained to take the ultimate action—to kill. You must not use this training and the weapons issued to you for personal vendettas or for personal gain. You are like this Ka-Bar. Tempered steel, to be used when necessary, but not to unnecessarily hurt others or destroy property. We men lack one special characteristic that women have. They are the bearers of life, through childbirth. We can only be the takers of life. Therefore, we have to be respectful of our women, as they can easily be morally superior to us."

Mathew regarded Torbin, mulling over what was just said.

"That sounds like a lot of responsibility, Captain Torbin," he finally replied.

"It is Mathew, it is. And, since no one is perfect, sometimes you may fall short. But you must always keep trying to be a good man. When you give up, evil and selfishness can step in, and people can get hurt or die."

They sat silently for a few moments. Torbin stood up and recovered the last two sodas from the cooler Andrew had given him.

"Here, Mathew, share a soda with me. Abigail already has, so now it's your turn."

As they sat and drank the soft drinks, Mathew shared with Torbin what he had been doing since he last saw the Captain. Mathew confirmed that they had indeed killed four Ferals after Torbin and his men had left Evanston.

"They tried to take our equipment and to molest Ruth and Abigail.

They acted like two legged demons." Torbin saw the anger he still held toward the dead men.

"I shot and killed two of them from the church steeple with my rifle. Abigail and Ruth took care of the other two, and wounded the last one, who fled in their vehicle." Mathew paused. "I am still angry, and I feel satisfaction that I killed two of them. Is that wrong?"

"Anger is an emotion that can be used to help you in a fight, if controlled. But do not become addicted to it, nor to a feeling of righteous satisfaction. If you continue down that path you run the danger of thinking you are superior to others, and that you have the right to judge all others. You can recognize evil, and evil acts. Judge the acts, and deal with those. Let your God pass judgment on the souls of other people. You may have to kill someone, and that act does not make you a morally superior human being."

Mathew sat quietly for a few moments. He glanced at his watch. "I must go, Captain. But the Prophet wants me to take and wash your clothes..."

"Whoa, hoss. This is not the British Empire Army and you are not my batman. Tell the President and Senior Prophet that I can take care of my own wash. But please, thank him for all these nice new clothes that he provided me. It was extremely nice to see you again.

"Here." He handed him a crumpled business card his wife Aleks had made for him. "A little worse for wear, but it's still readable. If you call one of these numbers, you should be able to get through. If not, that radio frequency may reach Security Control. Give me a call sometime. Please."

He handed the card to Mathew, then extended his hand. Mathew pocketed the card, and shook his hand eagerly. "Thank you for your advice, Captain Bender. I will always remember it."

"Anytime, Mathew, anytime."

"Oh, one more thing, Captain." Mathew pulled a plastic ID badge and clip from his pocket.

"This guest ID grants access to the chow halls and stores. If you would like, I can show you..."

"Thank you, but you have done enough. I need some rest. I was always pretty good with land navigation, so I can probably find a chow hall. Marines never go hungry if there is food to be found."

Mathew laughed. "Yes, Sir. I will pass on your thanks to the

Prophet. Walk with God, Captain Bender." He snapped off a salute that Torbin returned.

"Vaya con Dios, Mathew. Stay in touch."

After Mathew left, Torbin folded and tucked the new clothes away, then collapsed on the bed. He figured he would be contacted with the details of the get together planned for Abigail. Maybe he could get some sleep, then see if there was a way to contact Aleks at Malmstrom in the morning. He fell asleep quickly, dreaming of his beautiful wife and lots of babies bouncing around.

Torbin slept a good ten hours straight, waking up before sunrise. His stomach began to growl as he stretched, feeling twinges of pain from the beatings he took at Key West. Shit. First the fight with the Squid, then Heidi Faust tried to cut him up, then Andrew had manhandled him. He managed to chuckle through the pain. He still had a tender spot from where that rock Andrew threw had put a divot in his helmet. Once again, he wondered how he was still alive and in one piece. Maybe Andrew was right. Maybe he had some special role to fulfill.

He shook his head, rose slowly, and walked to the shower. He had considered going for a run to stretch things out, but his body told him he still needed some rest to get back up to snuff. So, he took a warm shower instead.

By the time he had showered, shaved, and then dressed in the new fatigues, his stomach was making noises that sounded more like those from an elephant than a human. He needed food. He slipped his Ka-Bar into its sheath, then stashed it along with the .44 Magnum in his tactical vest. They had given him a room key, so he slipped it in his pocket and locked the room door.

Five minutes later, he was following his nose to the unmistakable smells of an early morning military chow hall. The sun was just casting its first rays over the horizon when he found it. A worker in the traditional white trousers and shirt of a dining hall person was pulling an old trash can out the front door to the curb, apparently for trash pickup. He noticed Torbin's approach in passing. "Not open yet, you'll have to wait."

"When will you open?' Torbin asked eagerly. The worker looked at him more closely, and suddenly stood up straight, his eyes bugging out a bit. "Please wait here a minute, Sir." He rushed back into the chow hall. Torbin heard him yelling something at someone in the back, probably in authority. The second voice boomed back. Then, the original worker came back out followed by a big, beefy man with a buzz cut. He had no uniform or rank, but moved with the authority of the person in charge. He stopped short of Torbin, and gave him a concentrated once over. Then he spoke in the gravelly voice and tone of someone who had been a drill instructor in the Corps.

"You that Marine Captain up from Key West, en route to Montana?"

"That would be me. Captain Torbin Bender, U.S. Marine Corps. And you are…?"

The man's face broke into a grin that looked almost like a snarl. He wiped his hands on an apron that had seen better days, then stuck it out. "Doc Stubbs, Civilian First Class, Former Marine Gunny Sergeant and Drill Instructor, now just the chief cook and bottle washer of this fine establishment." He looked Torbin straight in the eye as he shook hands, his with a steel grip to which even Torbin reacted. "You killed that fucking Squid with that Ka-Bar, didn't you?"

"Actually, Gunny, I started with the Ka-Bar and finished with a lighting stake. Had to kind of improvise at the end."

The Gunny chortled, and released his hand. "Not Gunny anymore, Skipper. Just Doc. Too old and banged up to fight, so I make sure all the grunts are well fed. The Corps travels on its stomach."

"That it does, Doc, that it does."

"Follow me." It was a command, not an invitation. Torbin followed, his mouth beginning to water at the familiar smells.

"How do you like your steak and eggs, Skipper?"

"Right now, thick and lots of 'em."

The chortle again. "Thought so. Joe, don't just stand there! Get this young warrior some shit on a shingle, along with some biscuits, coffee, and o.j.. I'll make the steak and eggs. You look like a sunny side up person this morning."

"Pegged it just right, Doc."

Chortle again. "Pull up a chair. You're my guest. We don't open for another hour."

Within ten minutes he was stuffing his face with some of the best s.o.s. and fresh biscuits he had eaten in ages. The coffee was hot and strong, the o.j. tasted fresh squeezed. Doc brought out a huge rare steak and three sunny side up eggs, with hash browns, hot sauce, and ketchup. He pulled up a chair, a huge mug of coffee in his paw, a stubby unlit stogie in his mouth.

"The Prophet lets me serve regular coffee—caffeine and all—here, and lets me smoke my stogies outside. Said God told him that people like me have a part in the plan, so dietary restrictions don't apply as much anymore. Gettin' rid of the Squids and the heathens are what's important."

He took a slurp of coffee. "I suppose my being a former Marine like him helps."

Torbin swallowed a chewed piece of most tender steak he had eaten in years. "Doc, let me tell you that this is one of the best meals I have had in ages.You definitely did not learn this in the Corps. Hell, they treated an MRE like a three course meal."

Doc gave his snarling grin again. "Worked in my family's diner for years before I joined the Corps. I was smart enough *not* to let on that I was a good cook. I wanted to fight, not make shit on the shingle for the rest of my career."

Doc chewed on his unlit stogie a couple of times, then removed it from his mouth. "Spent a couple of tours in the Sandbox, did an Afghan tour, helped out during the Korean mess. No matter where I went, I always made damn sure my Marines were well fed. And yes, using MREs and a few cans of fruit, I *can* make a *four* course meal. They said I was like a doctor with food. That's how I got the name Doc."

Torbin laughed, stuck a last forkful of food in his mouth, and then set his fork down. "Well, Doc, I think you've earned your advanced degree this morning. I am *stuffed.*"

Doc gave him an appraising eye. "I think you'll be able to work that off, Skipper. You don't sit around a lot, do you?"

"No Doc, I don't. Your coffee is great, by the way. But out of curiosity, how in the hell did you even get to Deseret?"

Doc snorted. "I was finishing up a tour as the NCOIC in charge of a training unit in Twentynine Palms. I had already done a stint or two as a DI, the brass liked the way I got young troops trained. None of *my* trainees every got killed by doing something stupid. I had twenty-five years in the Corps, but decided my fifteen year old son and thirteen year old daughter needed me home more, so I put in my retirement papers. I was on thirty days terminal leave when the Squids showed up."

Doc growled. "I got my family rounded up after a rock hit the base and fucked it up right proper. I had a couple of friends in Utah, so I figured I'd get my family as far from the coast as possible, especially once we found out the Squids were infesting all the major ports. I checked the base first. Bunch of those damned lizards were already down. They like the desert areas, reminds them of their home. Along with a couple of harvester arks, they started grabbing everyone that moved. I decided that retreat was the better part of valor as I had my family in tow. So, off to Utah."

His expression turned darker as he continued. "The next year was a bitch. I had to kill some folks when they tried to take what was mine, and got shot up myself. My wife and kids were nursing me back to health at an old hotel that a couple of families and I had taken over during the long winter. Prophet Smith showed up at the end of the first year."

Doc chewed on his stogie for a moment. "He stepped right in, started organizing everyone in the state. He told everyone he had received a message from God that he was to take charge of things, save the state of Utah—which he called Deseret—and the Mormon people. When I told him my wife and I were Catholic, he smiled and said he would not hold that against me, that we were all God's children. He seemed to be able to put everyone at ease, and get them to cooperate. The fact that Mormons already had food stored in preparation for hard times helped a lot during the first couple of years. But, if it weren't for President and Prophet Smith, I think people would have been broken up into a whole bunch of splinter groups, fussin' and fightin'. He has a knack of getting people to work together, to follow his lead. I believe that's why the surviving Church Elders, the Apostles, recognized him as the Prophet. Last year, he was elected President of Deseret in a landslide. The Election was *his* idea. He could have run the state with just his position of Prophet, since the Mormon church took over just about everything. But, he said we needed a secular government, even though it may seem to rubber stamp what the Church says."

Torbin reflected on the fact that strong men always seemed to appear when things went to crap, whether they helped or hurt the situation. People in crisis gravitate to strong figures, to tell them how to fix things, and to take the heat for problems. So far, the Prophet and President Smith seemed to be helping the situation more than hurting.

"So, Doc, we heard rumors up north that there was some forced religious conversions of the type of convert or leave. What's your take?"

Doc shrugged. "He never tried to force me to do anything along those lines. Though, of course, the Catholic church in Rome has ceased to exist, the Squids taking it out."

Doc paused and shook his head. "The Pope must have had balls of steel. Before all media broke down, they broadcast a film of the Holy Father marching right up to a robocop near a harvester ark, with just his bible in his hands. It looked like he tried to order them to cease and desist in the name of the Lord and the holy Catholic church. One second he was there, the next second a tentacle from the spaceship zipped out and he was gone, just like that. A blur, then he was gone, never seen again."

Doc shook his head. "I think God and Jesus have both said, 'Hey guys, you're on your own until you get your shit together.' So far, only the Mormons seemed to be getting their shit together. Other than the Church of Kraken, only the Mormon church seems to be in business, saving souls. Haven't heard so much as a peep out of anyone else."

"But, you haven't converted yet?"

"No Skipper. Been Catholic too long to start believing in a whole new bible. But my children have. My son is in the Deseret Armed Forces, my daughter is training to be a doctor. So, me being a non-believer hasn't hurt anything."

"How many non-believers still exist in Deseret, Doc?"

"About a thousand. We can leave anytime, no cult-like behavior in preventing it. Everyone has a job, a purpose, good neighbors, and no one is getting harvested. People of color are few and far between, but after the first month or so, the Squids moved on to happier hunting grounds and haven't returned."

Doc's assistant Joe appeared and freshened up Torbin's coffee. Two other men in white showed up, stared at Torbin, and then hustled to the back of the kitchen area.

"Well, Skipper, it's getting close to opening time. We should be hearing PT formations running by anytime. They'll be headed here soon." Doc stood up, stuck out his large paw again. "Stop by anytime. I'll make sure my people get you something to eat, no matter what the time is. It's a pleasure to meet someone from the old Corps still kicking."

Torbin shook Doc's hand. "Semper Fi, Doc. By the way, here. Take this business card. If you want something, give me a call."

"Thanks, Skipper. Maybe we can have a beer sometime. Prophet Smith has allowed a little brewing to go on, as long don't we get drunk. You can wind up in good old fashioned stocks in the town square if you do."

Torbin laughed. "One more thing before I get out of your way—you've met Captain Abigail Young before, yes?"

"Sure. She's one of the Twenty."

Torbin's brow furrowed. "The Twenty?"

"Yeah, Skipper. She and some of the other orphans from Idaho way are called the Twenty. They've been trained as one bunch of kickass special forces troops for the last five years or so. They're STRAC troops. I feed 'em good when they come here." He glanced at his watch.

"Captain Young should be running a formation of cadets by here at any minute. She's in charge of physical and tactical training for the high school cadet officer training program. Deseret has a universal draft, so the cream of the crop starts out in high school so they can be officers. Unless you have some type of serious disability, or are an old fart like me, you get trained. Pity the fool who tries an invasion here now. Even the Squids."

Torbin thanked Doc again, and left out of the front doors. He heard jody calls and grinned. Just like old times, young troops were getting their asses run off early in the morning before breakfast. It looked like Deseret was taking war fighting seriously. The Unoccupied States had not gone back to the draft yet, having enough prior service and volunteers to flesh out the current military establishment. But, after the nuke, Torbin believed that would all change.

He heard a formation approaching and was able to make out the jody.

"I don't know but I've been told," the cadence leader started the jody.

"I don't know but I've been told," the formation answered. The two entities continued alternating repeating each line.

"Heaven's gates are made of gold."

"I don't know but it's been said."

"The Squids' gates are made of lead."

Torbin smiled. Military and police units throughout history have put their own stamp on jody calls as the enemy and war changed. Here in Deseret, religion had also influenced what was chanted.

He noticed the unit rounding the corner at the end of the block, unit flag bearer up front.

Running in step with the unit flag was Abigail. Did she even have a personal life, or time off? Apparently not.

They saw each other at the same time.

"Formation."

"Ma'am." Forty voices responded at once.

"Quick time… harch!"

Two counts and they were walking.

"Formation… halt!" One, two, they stopped as one.

"Left… face." Forty complete strangers' eyes looked straight at him. Torbin saw both males and females, all high school age, and all wearing identical sweat gear.

"Parade… rest." Abigail stepped up to Torbin and gave him a parade ground salute. Torbin was already standing at attention, years of habit taking over.

"Captain Bender. Good morning, Sir."

Torbin returned the salute. "Captain Young, Good morning right back at you."

"Sir, would you mind saying a few words to my cadets? I have been fielding questions since yesterday. The Prophet had a broadcast breakdown of your attack on Key West last night on our radio and television."

Aw, hell. He had hit the rack as soon as he could yesterday and didn't even turn on the clock radio, so he didn't even know how many channels they had. Well, no rest for the wicked.

"Alright, Captain. But please, first put your people at ease."

Abigail gave him a happy grin. "Thank you, Sir."

"Cadets. At ease!" After they had assumed their "at ease" position, Torbin had to laugh to himself. Now he understood what Madam President and others saw when they told *him* to relax. Relaxing while in the presence of superiors was apparently even more alien to them as it was to him. "At ease" looked like a stiff "parade rest."

Torbin stepped forward. "Alright, ladies and gentlemen. I understand you all have been pestering the good Captain Young about my 'adventures'. Well, now is your chance to pester *me* with questions." He thought he heard some suppressed laughter. He fixed them with his best steely gaze.

"But one warning. Captain Young is my comrade in arms, as well as my *friend*. We have faced death together, which is something you all will probably understand better someday. Today, *do not* disrespect her or embarrass her by asking me stupid, smartass questions. *Clear?*"

"*Sir. Yes sir!*" They snapped to attention as one, answered as one, and returned back to at ease. He saw Abigail swell with pride. To get a bunch of fifteen to eighteen year olds with raging hormones to be this focused and this disciplined was no mean feat. Especially when you were essentially the same age.

"Alright. Ask away." It took a moment, but finally, one brave young woman raised her hand. "Go ahead, young lady."

She snapped to attention. "Sir. Begging your pardon sir, but did you *really* kill a Squid with a knife?"

Abigail seemed like she was about to tear into the Cadet for questioning his honesty, but Torbin chimed in. "Yes and no. First, it was not just a knife. It was this Ka-Bar." With that, he pulled the blade from his vest. "It is a weapon, a fighting blade, of superior quality. A knife is something you use to eat Sunday dinner. A fighting blade is a weapon you use to destroy your enemy. That is part of the yes."

"The no part is that I had to use an improvised spear to finish the job. You will learn to improvise and overcome if you listen to Captain Young and her peers. I was also either lucky or my guardian angel was working overtime as I won against something with eight arms and two tentacles. Don't try that on your own. Shooting them is so much easier." This last part did elicit some titters of laughter.

"Next question, please."

A tall young man raised his hand. "Sir, were you afraid?"

He fixed the young man with his gaze. "Of course I was afraid. Anyone who says they don't feel fear is either a liar or is a sociopath. Trust neither. Captain Young and her cohorts will teach you how to use that fear, and to control it. The adrenaline rush makes you stronger, faster, puts you on your toes. It also tells you—if you pay attention—that you are about to do something stupid. Stupidity has killed more people than fear ever has. Next."

Another young woman asked the next question. "Sir, how did you get the nuclear weapon to the Squids' base?"

"I can't give you all the details as some involve classified tactics, but I will tell you this. The person who delivered it was Captain Ichiro Yamamoto, Free Japan Defense Forces. *He* is a warrior in the tradition of the code of Bushido. He also makes me look like an old, slow, tree sloth."

He paused for a moment, silently prayed that Ichiro would make it home, soon. If not for Ichiro, Torbin knew he would be dead meat. Literally. He continued. "Captain Yamamoto personally killed over a dozen Tschaaa warriors with his samurai sword. And please do *not* even think I am bullshitting... excuse me, exaggerating. I saw him slice through Tschaaa as if they were standing still. He proves that, given the right training and tactics, we *are* superior to the Tschaaa. We *will* take back control of Earth." He stopped, his emotion causing him to shake a bit.

He took a deep breath, and let it out."Sorry, I did not want to turn this into a rant. Next question, please."

He spoke for another ten minutes when Abigail wrapped up the questions. "Thank you, Captain Bender. They still need to eat prior to their school classes, so they'll be happy that I am going cut the rest of the exercise period short, let them shower, then hit the chow hall. Have you already eaten?"

"Yes, Ma'am. Doc stuffed me enough that I am suitable for mounting in the local museum of history."

Abigail laughed, then stopped herself. She felt she had to keep a higher level of control in front of her cadets.

"Then I will see you tonight, Captain Bender. The President and Senior Prophet will send a limo to pick you up at your quarters at 1730 hours. The small affair will be in a meeting room near the Salt Lake Tabernacle. I'll meet you there."

She addressed her troops again. "I think we need to thank Captain Bender for sharing with you his experiences and training. Shall we?"

"*Thank you, Captain Bender. Hurrah! Hurrah! Hurrah! May God bless you and keep you safe!*"

Torbin paused for a moment. What could he say? He knew that he had just become a local legend to these young people. He hoped that he was worthy of their belief in him, and that would not be their collective undoing.

"Vaya con Dios!" he yelled back. Abigail saluted him, and he returned the salute. Within moments, she had her formation double timing back toward their dormitories.

Damn she was good. Torbin wished he had been as put together and as focused when he was eighteen years of age. But, then again, he hadn't had to keep from being eaten or starving to death for six years prior.

He made his way back to his quarters. He took another hot shower, trying to speed the healing in the bruises and hurt muscles all over his body. Then he laid down and dozed off.

He woke at noon, the extra sleep telling him his body was trying to heal itself. More bruises had shown up on his torso, probably from the Squid throwing him around. He suspected he was also still suffering from a bit of shock from having the crap beat out of him. Whatever the reason, it was nice that he could get the extra rest. Spending an extra day in Deseret seemed to have its unforeseen benefits.

He put his new set of camos back on and went downstairs to the Charge of Quarters office. The young Corporal fell all over himself trying to help Torbin get a telephone connection via their base switchboard to his people in Malmstrom. Using some type of landline contact, he reached Security Control. They were a bit shocked to be in contact with Deseret. The past couple of years, the Independent State had ignored the presence of the U.S.A., and had been incommunicado to the outside world. Now, the U.S. was now trying to figure out its new relationship with a State that was suddenly helping to return one of Madam President's wayward sons.

Torbin was told that his wife, Captain Smirnov, was out training with some other Russians. He left a message that he was fine and should be back to Malmstrom sometime late the next day. He also asked them to pass the same information on to General Reed. He did not expect a call back. He knew they had already had discussions about him, or this deal would not have been set up.

Based on what Torbin saw, Deseret had done quite nicely going it alone as an Independent State, due by no small part to Senior Prophet and President Smith's leadership. Why risk breaking something that was working just fine?

He thanked the young Corporal and started to leave, when the young man addressed him directly."Sir?"

"Yes Corporal?"

 "Begging your pardon, sir, but may I shake your hand? I lost my whole family to Squids. Anyone who can nuke them and kill them with a knife…. It would be an honor to shake your hand."

Torbin looked at his nametag to make sure he got the name right.

"Well, Corporal Stewart, I'll shake the hand of any fighting man. Just remember that a whole bunch of other people were also involved in the operation, some of whom did not make it back. So, you are also shaking their hands, through me." He stuck out his hand and the Corporal took it. Torbin hoped this adulation he was receiving died down and quickly. He was not comfortable being anything more than a Grunt, but in the back of his mind, he knew that his status as hero would probably continue. He silently cursed his reality.

"Thank you, Sir. I just hope the Prophet decides it is time for us to strike back at the Squids too."

"When that day comes—which I think will be soon, Corporal—I think you soldiers here in Deseret will have no problems making life difficult for them. Judging by the level of readiness and training I have seen, the Squids will rue the day they angered you."

The Corporal's chest seemed to swell with group pride. He was a small cog in a big machine, but he would do his part.

"Thanks again, Captain. Have a safe trip back home. Please speak kindly of us Mormons when you see your people again."

Torbin smiled. "That I will, Corporal Stewart. That I will."

Torbin strolled over to the chow hall to stretch his legs and get something to eat. A healing body needs fuel to support the healing. He tried to blend in, but the damned broadcasts the President Prophet had made the night before must have been like an old

Hollywood publicity production, with pictures and all, espousing his of virtues and manliness. Troops saw him, and a low mummer began. Some seemed to gaze at him in awe.

Goddamnit. He was just a man, not a messiah.

Just then, Doc Stubbs appeared, his stogie stuck between his lips. He growled and people parted as he walked over to Torbin and sat down at his table.

"See you got hungry again, Skipper. Or did you just wanted to see my ugly mug?"

Torbin laughed. Doc walking over and sitting down seemed to break the enthralled spell his presence had cast over the people in the chow hall. They resumed paying more attention to getting their meal than talking about Torbin.

"As much as I enjoy your company, Doc, yes, my body is demanding sustenance again. These stuffed pork chops I have look right tasty. Your work?"

Doc waved the comment away. "Nah, just supervised it. I'm training a staff so that when I go to the big chow hall in the sky, they will carry on the tradition of good food makes for good troops."

Every organization needs its pillars, its foundations to insure it keeps functioning. Doc was a major part of that foundation. He probably also added a little bit of alternate views, being a non-believer who was also well respected by just about everyone.

"Skipper, got a rumor that General Huff, the senior commander of our military, is looking for you. Probably doing it for a good old fashioned photo op. That's what he does. He talks a good fight, don't think he has ever been in one. Just play along, he's harmless."

Torbin smiled. "Thanks, Doc. Seems I've run into a lot of guys like that. Now, I just want to be able to leave tomorrow at oh dark thirty to head home and see my wife."

"Well, Skipper, stop by here. I'll try and have something waiting for you to take along for chow. The drive up to Montana is an all day affair."

"Will do, Doc. I appreciate the offer."

Just then, a commotion began at the chow hall entrance. Suddenly, someone was yelling, "Ten hut! General on deck."

Just as Torbin began to automatically stand, he heard an "At ease, at ease. This is a chow hall, not a parade ground. Keep eating."

Torbin stood and examined the figure, a General officer heading in his direction with a large grin plastered on his face. General Huff did not look like a field commander. Or any real commander. A slightly balding, pudgy man, red faced but with an overall fair complexion, he had the bearing and demeanor of an office supervisor or minor bureaucrat. Although he had the reputation of being pleasant, he exuded the leadership capability of a rock. Everyone knew that President Smith actually ran the military forces in Deseret.

He was about the same height as Torbin so he looked directly into his eyes as he stuck out his hand.

"It is a pleasure to meet you, Captain Bender. The President speaks very highly of you. I'm General Archibald Huff, Chief of Staff of the Deseret Military Forces."

Torbin shook his hand at attention. "Sir. Pleasure to meet you." At least the General had a fairly firm handshake.

"Please, Captain, *sit*. Finish your meal. Mind if I join you?"

"Of course not, General. I'm your guest and here at your pleasure."

General Huff motioned with his hand and his two aides quickly produced a cold drink with ice and a large piece of apple pie. Apparently the General was a regular at the chow hall. Doc had made a quick and stealthy withdrawal, so Torbin was on his own.

General Huff took a couple of bites of pie, then resumed talking.

"I saw you chatting with Doc Stubbs. He's a treasure to our military, provides good food that keeps our soldiers happy and healthy. I don't know what we would do without him." Judging by his pudgy, soft exterior, the General *really* appreciated Doc Stubbs' food preparation abilities.

"Yes sir. The breakfast I had this morning was some of the best military chow I've had in years."

"Yes, Captain. I eat here every chance I get. I need to keep up with what my troops are eating and doing. Gives me a chance to mingle." He quickly polished off the one slice of pie, and an aide magically replaced it with another.

"But, enough about food. I just want to tell you, Captain Bender, that you have provided a real life role model for all of our service members. You've done this by striking directly at the devil's spawn, the Tschaaa and their minions. Someday soon I hope that we in

Deseret have the capability to mount such an attack."

Torbin couldn't help wonder how many people Deseret had under arms or available for response. He saw an awful lot of young people in uniform or in training.

"Well, Sir, from what I see, you have a strong military force here, based on the numbers I see in training and in uniform.'"

General Huff gave a self-satisfied grin. "Since you will be taking Captain Young back as a liaison/military attaché, I don't think I will be speaking out of turn to say we can mobilize some one hundred thousand military personnel, including mechanized and aviation assets, in twenty-four hours. We have a total military draft, and all able bodied citizens are expected to train and do their part. In a week, we could mobilize even more personnel."

The General's face then took on a more serious look. "We had a bit over three million people living in Deseret, then known as Utah, when the spawn of Satan showed up. We lost about a half million souls during the first year of this occupation. Thanks to the long standing practice of Mormons keeping supplies stored for disasters and lean years, we quickly rebounded, organized and survived. We had few additional casualties after the first weeks of the long winter. Hill Air Force Base had been hit pretty hard, but we had only two reported harvester arks landing and taking people. We had some non-believers leave when they found out the Mormon religion would be the official state religion of the new State of Deseret. But some stayed, and helped us to rebound into what you see today. We have a strong and happy group of citizens, and a strong military."

Torbin could tell the effect that the invasion had on General Huff, the security he felt by having this strong, religiously-based central government that controlled just about everything in Deseret. The Prophet and President Smith was the authority that bound it all together.

"So General, Prophet and President Smith really brought things together after the rock strikes stopped?"

General Huff sipped his cold drink and answered. "He showed up at the end of the first year." He continued. "He left the remains of a Marine Corps Unit around San Diego and made his way to the then Utah, as he was a practicing Mormon and had some relatives around Salt Lake City. He appeared, and said he has been sent by God to get everything back on the right path. He spoke with confidence and certainty, and had a certain aura about him. The surviving more junior Apostles—the prior Prophet and the Senior Apostles had been killed—who were at the Salt Lake City Tabernacle, recognized his Divine Mission and Authority, fell to their knees and immediately made this almost-stranger the Prophet and the President of the Church. They saw he was one with with God. Last year, he demanded a secular election to determine if someone other than the senior church official, the Prophet, would run the Nation State Government. He said that he would eventually have to deal with surviving countries and organizations, and wanted to do that in a secular realm, separate from the religious and divine."

Torbin could see an almost look of awe from the General as he kept speaking.

"He did not want to be seen as a Pope, the leader of a religious state recognized as some odd Head of State for diplomatic reasons. He wanted to be the *elected* head of The Nation State of Deseret, to show that he was dealing with the real outside world as a democratically-elected leader, not a theocratic ruler. This also gave him the chance to gauge the satisfaction of our citizens, or dissatisfaction, with how he was doing in rebuilding Deseret. It was an overwhelming majority, ninety-nine percent of the votes for him. In four years, there will be another election."

"If I may be so bold as to ask, General, but it sounds like you've been with him since he was recognized as the Prophet."

General gave a broad grin. "Yes. Exactly. Some surviving National Guardsmen, Air Force personnel, and I had been trying to restore some organization, salvage what we could from Hill Air Force Base and other installations in Utah. He grabbed us before he went to the Tabernacle, and told us he was the Prophet. We all could recognize and sense his authority from God. Like Jesus in Jerusalem, we followed him, waiting to be told what to do. He quickly appointed me as the Chief of Staff, a lowly Major, with concurrence of the Apostles."

Torbin saw an almost adoring look in the General's eyes when he spoke of following Prophet and President Smith. He hoped this did not mean there was an unacceptable level of fanaticism in their beliefs. That would make it difficult for a secular government in the

Unoccupied States to deal with Deseret in a trusting manner. There was enough fanaticism within the Church of Kraken and some of the Director's followers without having another bunch of crazy "my way or the highway" screw-ups.

"Well, General, he seemed to have accomplished his mission. Everyone I've seen seems to be well fed, motivated, as happy as a human can be, given the knowledge that there are some aliens trying to serve you up as the main course."

General Huff burst out with a belly laugh. He thrust out his hand to Torbin again. "I *knew* that you'd turn out to be a man of superior insight and intellect. I knew it when the Prophet told me about you."

The General stood up and waved at his two aides, who quickly produced two cameras. "Here, my good Captain. I must have some photos with you for my wife and children. They think you may be a figment of our news media."

For the next couple of minutes, General Huff had photos taken with Torbin in various poses—from shaking hands, to the General with his hand on his shoulder. The General seemed like a good sort, but with very limited combat leadership ability. He was strictly a follower. Prophet Smith was clearly the actual Leader and Commander of the Deseret military.

"Well, my fine Captain, I must be off. Have a safe trip back to Montana with Abigail."

"Thank you, Sir. Stay safe, General."

General Huff laughed. "Always." As he exited the chow hall, the General made a showing of talking to the troops coming in to eat, glad-handing whomever he could.

There was a collective sigh of relief when he and his aids finally left.

Doc reappeared, still chewing on his unlit stogie. "Well, you survived that little vignette."

Torbin snorted. "He seems like a likable guy, but a Field General? Please."

"Well, Skipper, you hit it right on the head. Just remember to stop by in the morning. I'll have some good eats for you and the young Captain to take on your trip."

"Thanks again, Doc. See you then."

Torbin headed back to his Quarters. He wanted to rest a bit, get everything packed up for the morning, and then get dressed for the shindig that night. He hoped that Abigail wouldn't be so uptight that she would start to self-destruct. He sighed. Well, you can only do what you can. He hoped he could help her enjoy her birthday and coming of age party. She deserved it.

After all that, the consternation and concern about the "Sturm Und Drang" was soon seen by Torbin as misdirected.

The social gathering was held at a hall off of the Salt Lake City Tabernacle, the spiritual center of the Mormon religion. Prophet and President Smith presided over some thirty guests, including other youthful members of what the Mormons called The Twenty. Abigail was positioned at the seat of honor, to the Prophet's right. Torbin was placed to the right of her. Directly to the Prophet's left was his wife, Ester Smith.

When Torbin first saw Mrs. Smith, his immediate impression was that she had just stepped off the cover of some major fashion or celebrity magazine, had they still existed. Tall, slender, slinky, and exotic-looking with jet dark hair—she had a slight Eurasian look about her. Torbin had overheard others saying that she was born and raised in Utah. It would be interesting to learn how she had come to "hook up" with a former Marine, as she looked like she had more likely hobnobbed with the pre-strike Hollywood and fashion elite. She gave Torbin an intense examination with her dark brown almost black eyes, then flashed him a smile which showed he had passed some form of inspection.

Torbin had wondered why Mrs. Smith was worried about competition from Abigail, that was until he saw Abigail for the first time in something other than fatigues or sweats. This night, she had a formal, military blouse or jacket directly modeled after the Marine Corps Dress Blues. Red and blue striping plus flashy medals and ribbons. Her naturally bright blonde hair was done up in a fashionable bun, and it looked like someone had helped her with a professional makeup job. From the waist down, Torbin could tell was the Prophet's influence. She wore a long formal skirt instead of Marine Dress Blue slacks, which Torbin knew she had wanted. But, he had to agree with Prophet and President Smith's choice, as the skirt fit Abigail like a glove, showing off the well- toned body of a grown young woman.

The skirt was slit part way up, revealing that Abigail had nylons or pantyhose on (probably a first) and, surprises of surprises, two inch heel shoes. She looked gorgeous.

After the proforma introduction of Torbin to the assembled group, Prophet Smith kept the congratulatory introduction speech short and sweet. He ended with a simple statement. "Captain Abigail Young has accomplished much in her now eighteen years of life. She, like many, has had to endure much, thanks to our unwelcome visitors, the Tschaaa. Now she will be go on to bigger and better things, serving Deseret, the church and the Lord as a Liaison Officer and Official Representative to the Unoccupied States. I am certain that Captain Bender, our honored guest, and her comrade-in-arms, will help to keep our daughter safe." The Prophet raised his glass. "A toast to Abigail on her eighteenth birthday. May she have many, many, more." Everyone stood and raised a toast of—surprisingly for Mormons—actual wine. So it was true, Prophet Smith had some new revelations and brought back some Old Testament traditions. Torbin wondered what else he thought needed to be changed.

The Prophet presided over a short prayer prior to the meal being served. "We thank you, Lord, for providing us with this opportunity to break bread on this happy occasion. We implore you to bless all who are here, in this grand hall, celebrating the birthday of a loved and revered member of our community. In the name of Christ Jesus and the Latter Day Saints, *Amen*."

As succulent prime rib dinners were brought to the participants, Torbin turned to Abigail. "Please do not take this wrong, but you look absolutely gorgeous; especially for a STRAC combat officer that could probably gut me with a dull fish knife."

Abigail beamed. She continued smiling as she placed her hand on his arm. "That opinion means the most to me. I am so very lucky that the Lord sent me a friend like you. I look forward to meeting your wife and her friends. And, I look forward to hearing of the birth of your child."

Torbin smiled warmly back. The more he was around her, the more she felt like the kid sister he never had. "After all that worrying about 'the ways of women', you seemed to have been able to figure out how to be a gussied up lady."

Abigail smiled again. "The Prophet's wife came and helped me.

Completely out of the blue. That is one reason why I am so relaxed. We had a nice long talk. She told me that she and the Prophet *do* consider me an actual daughter. That, and any rumors of her dislike of me were started out of jealousy. Mrs. Smith gave me a direct telephone number that she says is her private line. Anytime I have a problem in Montana, I should give her a call." Abigail squeezed his arm again. "I don't think I will have any problems with the help of a good friend like you, Torbin."

"I am at your service, young lady. And may I emphasize again the lady part." He patted her hand. Then they began to eat in earnest, everyone at the huge round table soon involved in lively discussion amid smiles, laughter, and good times. A small string quartet provided excellent mood music from the corner of the hall.

Eventually, Prophet Smith leaned over toward Torbin. "I hope this meal is to your satisfaction. We have excellent herds of beef, beefalos, and true American bison."

"Sir, your stockmen and chefs both deserve large pats on the back. This is some of the tenderest meat I have eaten. The vegetables and baked potato are also excellent."

"Your cooks and chefs in the Unoccupied States are not as skilled?"

 Torbin sighed. "I think we lost a lot of good people during the first year, Mr. President. We just now, this past year, began building up our livestock populations again. Lots of lean venison, bear, wild boar. Commercial beef, not so much."

President Smith smiled. "Please communicate with your Madam President and the Generals that I would be very happy to provide you with some breeding livestock of whatever type you need. The Lord Our God has been generous with us. We would be remiss in in our Christian duties if we did not try to share our bounty with others."

"Thank you, Sir. I will."

The social gathering continued, until the President and Prophet stood up and gently tapped his crystal glass. Conversation ended and all eyes turned toward him.

"Before we allow for a little post dinner dancing, we must, of course, have the pièce de résistance for every birthday party, especially an eighteenth birthday. I speak of course of the cake. Not just any cake, but a cake specifically created for the young lady who we celebrate." The Prophet clapped his hands three times.

Doc Stubbs came through the double doors in the back of the hall, wheeling a large three layer cake, complete with eighteen large lit candles. In the center was the Marine Corps globe and anchor, with a warrior guardian angel—complete with wings, sword and shield—in the center.

Doc was dressed in slightly worn Marine Corps Enlisted Dress Blues, Gunny stripes and all. Weighing down the left side of his chest was a huge mass of medals and ribbons from the former U.S. of A. Doc was close shaven, his signature stogie absent. He pushed the cake on its gurney all the way to Abigail's seat. The string quartet started playing "Happy Birthday", and everyone chimed in, the attending members of The Twenty most enthusiastically.

A shy Abigail rose slowly to cries of "Speech! Speech!" She held her hands up to quiet everyone. Gathering her thoughts, she spoke. "I thank Our Lord God that He has enabled me to be here, to be so very honored by you, and by the Prophet, President Smith."

Abigail looked first at Torbin. "I thank God and Jesus Christ that Captain Torbin Bender is also here, safe and sound. He was sent by Our Lord God at a time that we all needed help. A person could not ask for a better friend and comrade-in-arms."

She then faced the others. "Again, I thank you all for you honoring me, a simple Servant of God." A round of applause erupted. Torbin saw the Prophet's chest swell with pride, like a doting father.

Finally it died down, and Torbin chimed in, "Good sirs and ladies, when I was growing up, the birthday boy or girl had to make a wish, then blow out the candles. Is that still the drill?"

Surrounded by cries of "Yes!", "Blow them out!" and "Make a wish!" Abigail approached the cake, deep in thought, with her head down. Then, she leaned forward and blew all eighteen candles out in one blow.

Amid applause, as Doc began to cut the cake with a huge bowie knife, Torbin asked, "What did you wish for, Abigail?"

She smiled at him. "It must remain a secret until it happens, Torbin. Only then will I tell you."

Torbin chuckled. "Ah, woman, thy name is mystery." Abigail laughed, then was obliged to take the honorary first piece of cake. Doc Stubbs served up the cake quickly and efficiently. Before they knew it, he began to wheel the cake away.

Torbin jumped up and approached him. "Doc. You didn't tell me you were a baker too."

Doc gave his signature chortle. "I am a man of many hidden talents, Skipper. I'll put some leftover cake in your food bag for the morning. Make sure you and the young Captain get some rest. You have a long drive tomorrow."

"Yes, Gunny." Doc gave his half-grimace grin and left the way he came in, wheeling the cake in front of him.

Torbin returned to his seat just in time to meet Mrs. Ester Smith, the Prophet's wife, as she approached Abigail. The young Captain tried to stand, but Ester placed her hand on her shoulder to lightly restrain her. "No my dear, please stay seated, you are an honored guest." As Torbin looked on, she handed Abigail a small gift-wrapped box. "Every birthday girl deserves a special gift. Here is yours, Abigail Young."

Abigail's eyes widened a bit in surprise, while she received the present. "Thank you, Ma'am. I... don't know what to say."

"Say nothing. Just please open the present," Ester Smith lightly ordered. Abigail carefully unwrapped the box, so as not to damage the wrapping paper. She opened it, and gasped. Mrs. Smith smiled, and addressed Torbin.

"Captain Bender, can I ask for your assistance in helping Abigail with her present?" It was then that Torbin saw a beautiful gold chain with a gold cross attached. A large diamond was set directly at the intersection of the cross and main beams. With practiced ease, Torbin took the necklace and put in around Abigail's neck, clasping it in back.

"I do not think a Mormon warrior of God, an Avenging Angel, will be violating any uniform regulations by wearing a cross, a symbol of our faith," Ester Smith explained.

Abigail's eyes began to fill with tears.

Ester hugged her and kissed her on her cheek. "You are a daughter of Deseret, of the Prophet. You are loved." The Prophet's wife regarded Torbin. "You *will* take care of her in the Unoccupied States, keep non-believers from harming her?"

"I will do my best, Mrs. Smith."

She smiled at Torbin. "I think your best will be just fine."

Just then, Prophet and President Smith walked up. "Excuse me.

Abigail, may I have one dance with you? I think good Captain Bender would be happy to trip the light fantastic with you, Ester, wouldn't you?"

"Well, Sir and Ma'am, first I must warn you that dancing is not my strong suit. So, Mrs. Smith, I apologize upfront for stepping on your toes."

Mrs. Smith laughed. "I find it difficult to believe that you are clumsy, Captain. But if you step on my toes, it won't be the first time. Consider yourself forgiven in advance."

Abigail rose, controlling her tears, and took the Prophet's offered hand. He led her to the dance floor as the string quartet started playing a waltz. Torbin offered his hand to Mrs. Smith, and led her to the dance floor. He soon managed a waltz, his hand at her waist.

"You are what I would call a true friend to Abigail, Captain Bender. Is that a fair characterization?"

"We faced the Grim Reaper together, Ma'am. That forms a bond between people. We had hit it off right at the first and we are now friends. I only know of one type of friend, and that is an honest, truthful one. So yes, I guess you could call me a true friend."

The Prophet and President's wife smiled at him. "Good. Every young lady needs a true male friend, not one who is not simply trying to get into her pants. My time as a model and in Hollywood taught me that the hard way."

Torbin looked directly at Ester. "I wouldn't dream of disrespecting Abigail, who is a fine warrior… and person."

Mrs. Smith met Torbin's eyes, searching for something. She seemed to find what she was searching for. "Yes, Captain, I can see you're what is called a good soul. It's a pleasure to have met you."

"Ma'am, if I may be so bold, what you have done for and said to Abigail, makes you what I would call a great lady. She has been an orphan. By saying she is a daughter, giving her that cross, you gave her the sense of family that she needs. I can tell you meant it. So, it is a pleasure to have met you as well."

He noticed that her eyes were a little moist and was hoping she would not start crying. That may be hard to explain to her husband. But Ester Smith controlled her tears.

"Captain, that is one of the nicest things anyone has said to me in years. I can see why Abigail appreciates your friendship so much."

"Well, Ma'am, I only know how to act one way. And that's to be *me*. I'm a lousy liar. I could never be a spy."

"Just keep being *you*, Captain Bender. I sense that you fill a special place. As for Abigail, I know some people started some rumors about who I am, that I was a jealous wicked witch out of an old Disney movie. I just know my husband, and try to… insulate him from some influences that sometimes affect his public persona and decision making. Bottom line, though, is that if not for her aptly-developed abilities, and your well-deserved quest to return home, she would have remained here. It was not some Machiavellian move on my part to get rid of someone. She will best serve Deseret and the Church with her abilities in your Unoccupied States."

The music reached its end and they stopped dancing. Torbin, proud of himself for not having destroyed the President's lady's toes, escorted her back to her seat. Once she reached her seat, Ester Smith turned to Torbin. "Abigail told me while I was helping her to get ready that your wife and her fellow female Russian officers were going to help her develop her 'feminine wiles'. I hope they can help her develop into a young lady, with all of the graces we women develop as young girls. She has been thrown into a man's world. The Avenging Angel position goes back to the early Mormon Church with the Danites, special warriors protecting the Prophet and the early Church. It is unfortunate that the Twenty were chosen to fulfill that function so young. But, the Lord sometimes requires we all do things we did not think we could."

She paused, then continued. "When my daughter died during the Invasion, I didn't think I could survive. I did not want to. But, I was shown that I must survive, and was given the strength to do just that."

Torbin thought of his brother, William. A dark expression must have crossed his face as the Prophet's wife noticed a change. "You lost someone close too, Torbin, so you understand. We carry on because we have been chosen to do just that. We survive for the greater good."

"Ma'am, I carry on because I don't want the Squids to hurt any more of us. I want them gone, so kids can be kids again, so Abigail and her generation can start thinking about pretty dresses and parties again, instead of assault weapons."

He bent over and took Ester's hand, kissing it. "Thank you for the dance, milady. I'm certain you are as surprised as I am that I managed not step to on your feet."

Ester laughed, then curtsied. "Thank you, kind sir. I see my husband returning with the birthday girl."

Abigail had her hand on the Prophet's bent arm as they walked up together. She was smiling as was Prophet Smith. "I see you were successful in dancing with my wife, Captain. That is an activity for which, unfortunately, we have not had much time. Hopefully, God willing, that will change."

The Prophet removed Abigail's hand from his arm. "I need to leave now, with my wife. Like you, we need to have an early start in the morning. We are visiting our new manufacturing centers tomorrow. Soon, we will be depending almost entirely on what we make, rather than mostly what we scavenge. Thank you again, Captain Bender, for helping us celebrate this special occasion."

"I wouldn't have missed it for the world, Sir."

Prophet and President Smith quickly hugged Abigail, then shook Torbin's hand. "Please keep her safe until she can return."

"Will do, Sir," answered Torbin. Prophet Smith turned and walked over to speak to the string quartet.

Ester Smith hugged Abigail, kissed her cheek. "My husband is bad at goodbyes, so I will fill in for him. You two young Captains must be so extremely careful. I am selfish and want to see you again, all in one piece. I have given Abigail my direct line. Please feel free to use it also, Captain Bender, should you feel the need."

"Thank you, Ma'am."

"Goodbye now, and may God bless you both and keep you safe." With that, she departed.

Just as Torbin was about to speak to Abigail, he heard an "Excuse me, Captain" from behind. He turned around and saw a twenty-something year old man standing, his right hand in a glove. He stuck out his left to be shaken. Torbin recognized the young man almost instantly.

"Peter, if I remember rightly. I heard you had been transported back here after a stay in our military hospital. Glad to see you are up and around."

Peter held Torbin's left hand tightly, as two of the Twenty came up behind him, including Mathew. "I must thank you for saving my life. Your hospital did what they could, and saved my right arm, but the damage was severe from the Eater digestive acids. Only the fact you carried me out on your back and had a MEDIVAC chopper pre-positioned saved me at all. I spent a month in your hospital, have learned that non-believers can be just as Christian and godly as we Mormons. I thank you and will always be in your debt."

Torbin was always a bit shy and embarrassed when people thanked and praised him for doing his job. His MEDIVAC of Peter was something he would have done for anyone. "I'm glad I could be of service, Peter. Are they providing you some follow up treatment here in Salt Lake City?"

"Yes. They are trying to perform some more skin grafts. I volunteered for some treatment using some, I guess you would call it 'bootlegged', Tschaaa medical techniques using nanotechnology and pharmacology. I hope everything works out."

"I'm sure it will, especially if your Prophet and President has anything to say about it. Hopefully we will meet in the field again sometime, but under much better circumstances."

Peter then spoke to Abigail. "I and the others wish you a safe and fruitful journey, Captain Young. I will never forget you came back for me, neither will any of the surviving Twenty. No matter where you are, you will always be one of us. I know you will serve God and Deseret well. Please keep yourself and Captain Bender safe. I owe you both my life."

Abigail gave him a big hug, then followed up with one each for Mathew and the other member of the Twenty, identified as Thomas. "You will always have a place in my thoughts and prayers," Abigail declared, her eyes moist with tears.

"Gentleman, she will be back. I promise," Torbin interjected. "I'll do my best to keep her out of trouble. I will have lots of help."

"We know, Captain Bender," Mathew replied. "It's just that we will miss her."

"Well, you have that card I gave you. Please feel free to call Security Control and they will contact either Abigail or me. It's not like she is on the moon or something." That resulted in some smiles.

Finally, the Twenty members turned to go. "Thank you again, Captain Bender. May God keep you safe."

"Thank you. Vayan con Dios." Then, Torbin and Abigail were alone. A few late stayers were dancing to the soothing sounds of the quartet. Others were finishing up conversations, wine, and desserts.

Abigail squeezed his arm. "You were right, Torbin. This wasn't a big problem. It was *fun*."

Torbin saw her bright eyes and had a warm feeling. *This* is what an eighteen year old young lady was supposed to be doing, not shooting, marching, killing, and watching others die. Again, Torbin felt a deep seated anger against the Tschaaa and what they had done to life on Earth. But, as Torbin had just helped prove in Key West, payback's a bitch.

"Come on, my dear. We're going to have a long day tomorrow. I promise there will be other shindigs like this in Montana. We are pretty good at putting together a good time."

Abigail laughed. "I bet you are. Again, my friend, I thank you. I hope I'll not be a burden to you in Montana."

"Abigail, you are not big enough to be a burden. See how skinny and weak your arms are... *ow*."

A set of stiffened fingers jammed him in his floating rib. "*Ouch*. That hurt."

"Not so soft and weak, am I? Just because I am not as big and *fat* as you are don't think you can push me around."

Torbin put on his best act of having been stabbed in the heart. "You have cut me to the core. That insult has fatally wounded me. I will never recover. My wife will be very angry when she hears how mean you have been to me."

Abigail burst out laughing. When she could finally control herself, Torbin offered her his arm. "Come, my fellow Captain. I will have my limo give you a ride back to your quarters. Then I will see you at o-dark-thirty."

The sun was just barely starting to show its rays over the horizon when Abigail picked him up in the old former police sedan. It was a bit beat up but its engine sounded smooth and powerful. He threw his clothes in the backseat and sat in the front passenger seat. He noticed the same pack and equipment Abigail had with her after Andrew had dropped him off two days ago. She had the Glock 17 and spare magazines on her belt, just as before. An addition to the equipment was a garment bag hanging from a clothes hook.

"Good Morning, Abigail. Nice to see you so bright eyed and bushy tailed."

She chuckled. "You're always this lively, aren't you Torbin?"

"It is not being lively, Abigail. It's called being an insufferable smartass. You'll be able to ask my wife Aleks about that and she will just nod and agree."

"Then let's get you back to her as quickly as we can. Please fasten your seat belt. We need to stop at the chow hall."

Five minutes later, they pulled up in front of the chow hall. Torbin jumped out and went to the front. The double doors were unlocked so Torbin went inside. "Hey Doc, you here?"

"Yo, Skipper. I'll be right out."

About a minute later, Doc came out, carrying a beat up cooler. This may look like hell, but it still works."

"Thanks, Doc. What did you put in it?"

Doc opened it up. "Here, take a look." Torbin looked in and saw a couple of beef sandwiches, a couple of egg and sausage breakfast sandwiches, a bunch of various chicken pieces, apples, carrots, some of Abigail's birthday cake, and several bottles of what looked like beer. Torbin pulled out one of the bottles. "Conch Republic near beer? How in the hell did you get that from Key West up to here?"

Doc Stubbs chortled. "We have what would be called peddlers or traveling salesmen who travel all over the former U.S.A and bring stuff back. They also bring intelligence and info back. The Conch Republicans are quite friendly with anyone who wants to trade. Right now, we pack frozen buffalo meat into coolers and run it down. Somebody in the Florida Keys has developed a taste for it."

Torbin shook his head. The human desire for trade and profit seemed to eventually conquer all barriers. "Well, thanks for the spread, Doc. Abigail and I will enjoy it on the trip. Want to say goodbye to her?"

"Nah. I'm lousy at goodbyes. Just wish her luck." He stuck his hand out. "Come back soon, Skipper, you hear? I'll always save a seat for you at my table." Torbin returned the firm handshake. He hoped he would make it back here to see Doc. He was another example of a former Marine who done well.

"Keep your powder dry, as they say Doc."

"Will do, Skipper. Will do."

Torbin carried the cooler out and set it on the back seat. He opened it, and grabbed the two egg and sausage sandwiches. They were still warm, fresh off the grill. He took them out, located a bottle of water he had brought along and got back into the front seat.

"Breakfast time, Abigail, compliments of Doc Stubbs. He wishes you luck."

She smiled and took a sandwich from Torbin. "He reminds me of an uncle—always there with a treat for his nieces and nephews." She unwrapped it and began to eat. They sat in the parking lot for a few minutes, neither speaking, enjoying the early morning quiet.

Finally, she spoke between bites. "Even though I had no real family here, other than the Twenty, I have a bit of fear and sadness, leaving this place behind. It has been a 'home' of a sort for over six years."

"I've been the proverbial rolling stone for years, Abigail. Now, all of a sudden, I have a wife and soon a child. Malmstrom is home for me. Consider this an invitation to my home. Stay as long as you like. I'll help you get home anytime you want."

Abigail smiled. "Thank you, Torbin. I'm glad you are my friend. You make things a lot easier for me."

"That, my dear, is what friends are for. Now, I think it is time to make like sheep and get the flock out of here." Once again, he got Abigail laughing.

CHAPTER 2

WYOMING

It was about seventy miles to the Deseret/Wyoming border. Evanston, Wyoming, on Interstate 80, was about ten miles further still. The former police cruiser purred along, the somewhat beat-up exterior belying the smooth operating V-8 engine under its hood. Not noted for its gas economy, Abigail had arranged for two ten gallon jerry cans stored in the trunk.

Prior to Abigail picking him up, Torbin had the Charge of Quarters at his dormitory try to get another telephone line to Security Control in Malmstrom. Wonder of wonders, he managed to get another microwave connection from Salt Lake City to Malmstrom. Torbin now realized that Prophet and President Smith had probably been arranging for contact with the Unoccupied States telephone system for just such a situation. Much like everyone else who was tapping into the new Tschaaa reconstituted internet, the Leader of Deseret had found a way to connect to the microwave tower-based telephone system in Montana and the surrounding states. He shook his head. He should have realized that Deseret had pre-arranged communication links when Director Lloyd so matter of fact told him that he had already arranged to hand him off to the independent nation state.

The Tschaaa seemed to have been ignoring Deseret as much as they had been ignoring the Unoccupied States, to their detriment.

He started to talk to the Senior Controller, but before he could say much, the NCO on the telephone said, "Sir, I have been instructed to tell you that your backup Response Team is already on the road. Just stay on the major interstates, please. You know where the operational telephone booths are if you need to contact us. General Reed wants you safe and secure as soon as possible. He has a couple of choppers on standby if necessary."

"Well, Sergeant, consider me as on the road with one other person. I'll check in as I can. Thanks for the assistance."

"No, thank *you* Sir. Without mentioning details, we know of the touchdown you scored. Everyone wants to buy you a drink."

Damn. He could tell that life would never be the same. What was next, World War II-like bond drives?

"Well, send my love to my wife and my best regards to General Reed. Is Lt. Yamamoto back yet?"

"Also en route, Sir. He hit the road yesterday. May take a while."

Ichiro and company were farther away, near enemy territory with no assistance like the Mormons. So, they would try to make it home, staying away from the Florida Coasts, maybe slugging it through the Everglades. The B-25 transport sat on a widened area of the Tamiami Trail. Maybe someday it would be recovered.

At least they were alive, which was better than the eight men under his command who were now Squid food. That is, unless the Director had come through and given them military burials like he said they would.

"Okay. Consider me gone and moving. Please contact my wife…"

A feminine voice suddenly cut in. "Already done Sir. Called her as soon as you were on the line. She said to not screw around or dally, to get back *now*."

Torbin laughed. "Now, my good NCOs, you know who *really* wears the pants in my family. Tell her I am motivating in her direction. And, of course, tell General Reed."

"Already have, Sir. He said quote 'Tell him to get back in one piece with the new Liaison Officer or expect to lose a piece of your ass,' end quote, Sir."

Torbin smiled. At least *that* hadn't changed. "Alright. I'm gone.

Tell the rest of the Duty Staff that when I get back, the drinks are on me."

They approached the Wyoming/Deseret Border. Torbin saw the continuous twelve foot high chain link fence cyborg Andrew had mentioned. Along the fence top was a triangle of three circular strings of concertina wire. Anyone or anything would have trouble getting through this interlocking barrier of nasty barbed wire.

"Got a lot of wire on top of your barrier fence, Abigail."

"Yes. We added two sets of concertina wire as it seems too complicated for the demons to figure a way over or through it. Now, they try to dig under the fence, but are rarely successful." They approached the large rolling gate in the fence. Abigail tapped the car horn, and a man with graying hair came out of two story building that was too large to be called a guard shack. Torbin noticed the man had what appeared to be a .45 automatic in a shoulder holster. He also caught a glimpse of a second figure that looked like woman holding a pump shotgun.

"They are husband and wife, Torbin, past the age of reproduction. They live on the second story of this building, and man the gate year around, except for an occasional trip to Salt Lake City. All their needs are provided for, in return for them living here. We have several couples like this one working the border of Deseret. They have a mission that helps Deseret and serves the Lord, as do I."

The man recognized Abigail and approached the car, smiling. "How are you, Abigail Young? We heard you were coming through. I guess you'll be gone for a while."

"Yes, Mr. White. This man next to me is Captain Torbin Bender, who is going to introduce me to the officials in the Unoccupied States of America."

"Captain Bender? You're that soldier who bombed the Squids in Florida." Mr. White called to his wife. "Anne. Come out. This is the man that we saw on the news."

A woman the same age as her husband, her partially gray hair done up in a bun, came out smiling.

"Pleased to meet you. Take care of our Abigail while she is abroad with heathens. She's special to us."

Torbin smiled. "Yes Ma'am. I'll make sure she comes back for regular visits. She's special to me too."

Mr. White came around to Torbin's side of the car, so he rolled down the window. The man stuck his hand out to Torbin. "It would be an honor to shake the hand of someone who struck back at the Evil Ones and killed so many. I just wish I was young enough to go along when the Deseret forces go to punish these invaders."

Torbin tried not to wince. Maybe if he changed his name and started wearing a fake beard and glasses he would be able to blend back in to normal society. This hero business made him uncomfortable. He just wanted to get back to being a normal grunt Marine.

"Thank you, Sir. But you have an important job here, being on the border."

"Well, my wife and I have shot a couple of demons, chased off a heathen or two. I just wish I was young enough to invade Key West. But, since I'm not young, I do what I can."

He looked over to Abigail. "Keep in touch, young lady. You will always be a Daughter of Deseret."

Abigail blushed a bit, and smiled. "I will, Sir. Now, Captain Bender and I must continue on our trip. Please open the gate and close it as soon as we are through. There should be no one else on the road."

"Here goes, young lady. You be careful, now."

Mr. White hit the switch, and the gate rolled open. Abigail waved at them after they were through, and the gate closed behind them. She began to accelerate up the highway, heading to nearby Evanston, Wyoming.

"When we get to Evanston, I'll have you pull over where there is an operational telephone booth. Some technical teams have crisscrossed the Unoccupied States and managed to get some old telephone booths up and running, using old landlines and the re-done microwave towers so we have telephone coverage without having to depend on satellites. We occasionally still bounce signals off of communication satellites as the Squids saved as many as possible so they could use them. They make no attempt to jam us, go figure."

"They underestimate us, Torbin. They think that because they defeated our governments, that *we*, the *people* accepted defeat. Now, they are discovering that many of us didn't."

"You'll get no disagreement from me."

They travelled a couple of miles further and were approaching a bend in the road near the Harrison Drive and Overthrust Road exit into Evanston. They started to complete the turn, when Abigail suddenly frowned. "Something isn't right."

The spike strip was suddenly across the lane in front of them. Abigail swerved the large sedan around the end of the destructive strip, showing lightning reflexes.

Someone hiding behind the brush that had grown up alongside the Interstate threw a stop stick under the moving tires. This Abigail could not dodge. The right front tire exploded as the stop stick shredded it. Remains of the stick also punctured the right rear tire. The sedan, traveling near sixty miles an hour, pulled hard to the right on the two punctured tires. Try as she might, Abigail could not avoid the approaching drainage ditch. The former police cruiser wound up tilting toward its right side in the water.

"Abigail. You okay?" The air bags had not deployed, telling Torbin they had been removed ages ago.

"Yes. Just shaken a bit, and mad that I could not avoid that stick."

"Come on. We need to un-ass this car. Out your door. Mine's blocked." They popped their seat belts and began to scramble out the driver's side door. Abigail kicked it open and tried to climb out.

"Stop right there. One more move and you'll be eatin' buckshot." Abigail looked up into the two sawed off barrels of a 12 gauge shotgun.

Torbin did an instant survey of the situation. He could pull and fire his .44 pistol around Abigail, but odds were that she would wind up being shredded by a blast from the shotgun as the man holding it died. Not to mention there must be others around that he could not see. Not good. They were still alive, so that meant there would be other chances, other opportunities to turn the situation around.

"Alright, assholes. I want to see your hands. Try something funny and you'll be eating lead."

"Hey, genius. We need to use our hands to pull ourselves out of this car." Torbin responded. "If I could levitate, I'd be out of here already."

The gunman paused. "Just keep your hands away from your pistols. Or you'll be picking lead from your teeth."

As Abigail and Torbin slowly pulled themselves out of the askew car, Torbin could not help but respond again. "Did you memorize every cliché about shooting someone from every bad Western ever made, or does it just come naturally?"

"Shut up. Hey guys, I could use some help here."

As they climbed out of the sedan, Torbin got a good look at the gunman. Torbin named him Grizzly in his mind due to his grizzled appearance. His spotty beard needed to be shaved. Badly. When Abigail exited the sedan and stood up, hands open, two men grabbed her, pinning her arms. They dragged her out of the shotgun's line of fire.

"Hey, no need to get rough with the young lady. We gave up, remember?"

"Shut up. Keep your hands where I can see them."

"Well looky here. A nice Glock. Let me just take off your gun belt." Scarman, named by Torbin due to a scarred face, roughly undid Abigail's gun belt as his partner, Big Ears, pinned her arms behind her.

Torbin named everyone in his mind so that he could count them and keep track of where they were. When the killing started, he would need to ensure everyone was accounted for. He promised himself that the killing would start just as soon as he saw an opening. One that would not get Abigail hurt or himself killed.

"Well, well, well. What have we here? Captain Bender, I presume." Torbin stood outside the sedan, hands up, as he looked at this speaker. The face looked familiar, like someone he had seen once in a mugshot.

"John Talbot, President and Leader of the Krakens Motorcycle Club, at your service. You and your friend here are right on time." Torbin now recognized the leader of the original Krakens motorcycle gang and flying squad from an intelligence photo they had on file at Malmstrom. One of the original Fifth Column members and saboteurs who had helped grease the Tschaaa's success, his name was infamous.

"Well, you know my name, Talbot, and I know yours. Since I'm your target, what say you let the young lady go. She's just my chauffeur."

Talbot laughed as two other men appeared and pinned Torbin's arms as they divested him of his Ka-Bar and his .44.

"What, and let a nice piece of Mormon ass like that go untapped? I don't think so."

"I guess the Director isn't a man of his word," Tobin growled.

"Director Lloyd has nothing to do with this. He lets you go after you shot up one of my cousins? He's an asshole."

"So, Lord Neptune wants me."

"*No.* A bunch of us humans are running this. Times are changing. Squids are bugging out on their big ships. The Church of Kraken is taking charge. Humans need to understand what it really means to be the top of the food chain. Natural Selection is in play. We white folks are taking over now that the dark folks are locked up where they belong."

Torbin could see a Helter Skelter look in Talbot's eyes. Intel said he was an avowed racist, which is why he helped the Invasion in the first place. Now, it seemed that something, maybe some drug abuse, was beginning to push him into the world of fanaticism. He could *not* keep his mouth shut.

"Millions of Tschaaa are just going to let you walk in and take over?" Talbot waved Torbin away.

"They lost it over a few young being killed. They couldn't control themselves. All we have to do is wait until the Director is taken out, which will be soon. His guys killed a bunch of Squids, and the Lords blame *him* for the loss of all those young. Lord Neptune thought Lloyd was handling you Rebels, and keeping you in line. That nuke squashed that idea."

Talbot laughed. "We step in, start running the humans, keep feeding dark meat to the Squids. Then, when they are even fatter and dumber than they are now, we step in and grab control of the Crèches. Plant a few nukes around, threaten to set them off, and watch the Squids cave."

It was a plan, but a plan based on the idea that the Tschaaa would give up if their young were threatened. It might work if all Squids were on Earth in one area, but there was still a substantial number on Base One and Platform One, with at least a few breeders. If there were enough nukes to go around, if the Tschaaa called their bluff and these 'Kraken' managed to detonate them, then another Nuclear Long Winter would result, knocking what was left of human civilization back to the Stone Age. A pyrrhic victory.

"Hey, toss that pistol you took off of him over here." Big and Fat, holding his right arm, threw the .44 he had taken from Torbin. Skinny, on his left arm, still had his Ka-Bar. Talbot caught the pistol, then examined it. "A nice Smith .44 Magnum. This will help make up for all the guns and stuff we're not getting from Director Lloyd. Stupid sucker gave us a pistol and about a hundred rounds of mixed/matched ammo last month. That's it. He said he had to build up his 'regular forces', that lying bastard."

Torbin noticed that as soon as Talbot had the pistol in his hand, Grizzly lowered his shotgun. He stepped over to the motorbike he had ridden, hung the shotgun by the strap on the handle bars, and began to sidle toward Abigail and her two captors. It looked like Grizzly had taken to heart the comment about 'Mormon piece of ass.' A large SUV a few yards from the bike had a scoped rifle and an AK-47 sitting on the hood, each apparently belonging to one of the pair of Krakens restraining the prisoners.

Big Ears was pinning Abigail's arms behind her as Scarman stood in front of her. "Man, you're a good-looking young thing." He reached out and began to fondle and squeeze her left breast. "Oh doggies, like my grandpap used to say. Nice and firm. It feels like at least a 35C cup— and I know my cup sizes." That elicited a laugh from all of the Krakens, even Talbot.

Scarman moved his right hand up to her face. "Skin is soft and clear. If you was a horse, I'd check your teeth." More laughter.

"Why don't you leave her alone, asshole?" Torbin yelled in his direction.

"Shut the fuck up," Scarman snarled back. "Unless you want me to stick you up the ass first, faggot."

He moved his hand to her jawline, and pulled her face up to look at him. "How about a nice big wet kiss, darlin'?"

Scarman screamed as Abigail quickly shifted her head and sank her teeth into Scarman's right hand. The Kraken had gotten sloppy due to his desire, and was now paying the price. Abigail's strong jaws and good teeth nearly amputated his thumb. Scarman's eyes bugged out, and he grabbed Abigail's jaw with his free left hand, squeezing her face hard to make her let go.

Abigail released her jaw, and Scarman stumbled back, screaming, holding his ruined thumb with his good hand. "Hey!" Big Ears exclaimed, then he too screamed. Sloppiness in prisoner control techniques must have been contagious, as he had momentarily lost track of Abigail's hands. Though he had ahold of her arms, he neglected to notice that she was just the right height to easily grab his family jewels with both hands. She squeezed, twisted, and yanked.

Big Ears started screaming soprano, and shoved his captive away, before collapsing into a heap of blubbering manhood. Freed, and pushed in the right direction, Abigail took a long stride and then planted her steel toed right boot into Scarman's scrotum. He was too involved trying to keep his right thumb attached to his hand to notice her move until it was too late. He jackknifed over at the waist, and Abigail planted a perfect left crescent kick alongside his right jaw. The Kraken toppled over, trying to hold his thumb and testicles at the same time.

Everyone froze for just an instant. Then, Talbot yelled at Grizzly, "Don't just stand there! *Get her!*" Grizzly produced a switchblade knife and advanced with practiced ease. Almost immediately, he yelped as a concealed shuriken throwing star from Abigail sank into the back of his knife hand. He dropped his weapon and scrambled back, holding his injured hand.

"Fuck this!" Talbot yelled. He pointed the .44 at Torbin's head. "One more move and his brains are splattered all over the fucking asphalt."

"Now, now, Talbot. I bet the Church wants me alive for interrogation, don't they?" The Kraken Leader cursed loudly, then pointed it at his right knee. "I'll just cripple you instead."

"And I'll just bleed to death. That .44 will blow a right big hole in me. I may not survive."

With that comment, Talbot aimed the large pistol at Abigail. "Wait!" yelled Grizzly. "Here comes Dogman in his bus. His dogs'll take her down, and we can still have what's left of her."

The huge modified bus braked to a stop some twenty-five yards back. As it did, the large front access door popped open, and three large Black Mask Cur hunting dogs burst from the bus. The first one out was the mother, seventy pounds of muscle that, following some command from inside the bus, went straight for Abigail. The Avenging Angel had stooped to retrieve the dropped switchblade. She prepared to meet the new threat.

The large hunting hound bounded toward her. Then, just as

quickly, the dog decelerated, so fast that it started to skid on its nails along the asphalt of the Interstate. She came to a stop just feet from Abigail, and began to wag her tail. First the tip, then the whole tail, then the whole hind end. She whined, barked, and made noises like she was giving a speech.

"Pepper? Is that *you*?" Abigail asked. She let out a small yowl in response, and was soon up in Abigail's arms, licking her, whining in joy and affection, almost knocking her over. Black Mask Cur hounds tend to air scent their prey, rather than track on the ground. Smart dogs rarely forgot the scent of a human member of their pack.

Mouths dropped open as Dogman, with two young male dogs bookending him, walked from the bus toward Abigail. "Abby? Little Abby?" the giant Adonis-shaped man asked. He seemed to Torbin to be a solid wall of muscle.

"What the fuck is going on?" Talbot screamed.

"Uncle Buck. Is that you?" Abigail asked. For the first time in recent memory, Dogman's mouth gave a hint of a smile under his dark beard and mane like hair.

"Hi, Little Abby, You're all... grown."

"You know this bitch?" Talbot screamed.

"Shut up," growled Dogman. "She's my niece."

Talbot stared. "She's about to be your *dead* niece if you don't take control of her."

"I said, shut up." Dogman growled again. Torbin tensed. There was death in the air, the feeling of electricity that warned of danger.

Talbot had had enough. After months of putting up with Dogman's disrespect in front of others, he had reached his breaking point. "Well, fuck you!" He yelled as he swung the .44 to aim at Dogman.

No one had noticed that the young male dog at Dogman's left, about one and a half years old and eighty pounds of pure coiled muscle, had begun to swing wide left just a few moments earlier. Some unnoticed signal or command from Dogman had told him where to position. Before Talbot could draw a bead, the male exploded toward Talbot. The Kraken Leader screamed in pain as the dogs teeth sank into the wrist of his gun hand. Wrist bones began to crack under the pressure of the bite, and the pistol flew from Talbot's hand. The dog yanked him toward the ground

Skinny let go of Torbin and drew the Marine's Ka-Bar. He started to scramble to protect his leader when the second dog went for him. Skinny saw it coming, so he began to slash at it with the Combat Blade. Skinny had so unexpectedly released Torbin, that Big and Fat did not have time to grab both arms. Torbin seized the moment.

He twisted right, into Big and Fat, throwing a high left hook into the other man's right eye. The large Kraken gang member tried to twist and get a new grip on Torbin. He received a knee to the groin for his efforts. Then Torbin proceeded to beat the big man to the ground. The smacking and thudding sounds of blows landing had a rhythm all their own. The last blow broke the man's jaw. He did not get back up.

Skinny was trying to ward off the male dog with the Ka-Bar when Torbin came up behind him. He grabbed a handful of hair from behind and yanked him back, hard. That gave the Black Mask Cur the opening it needed. It lunged and connected with the wrist of his knife hand. A satisfying chomp and the weapon dropped from Skinny's grasp. Weaponless, Torbin yanked him around, the young dog letting go. A palm strike to Skinny's nose smashed it. Then, a straight punch to the jaw. Skinny folded like a cheap suit.

Grizzly, having removed the throwing star from his hand, made a dash for the shotgun on the handlebars of his bike. He managed about three strides, when Pepper caught him and sank her teeth into his left thigh. He was fine as long as he was not moving. Once he moved, Pepper identified him as a threat. He screamed in pain, tripped and fell down. Pepper let loose, trained to take targets down, then wait for Dogman to finish them. At that a moment, Grizzly made a grave mistake. He kicked out at Pepper. She jumped back, barking and snarling.

As he tried to kick the Dark Mask Cur again, Abigail was on top of him. With a smooth series of moves, she grabbed his long hair, yanked his head back, and slit his throat with the switchblade. The man Torbin had identified as Grizzly gurgled in his own spurting blood, fell back as Abigail released him, and died.

Dogman called a command in a language Torbin he did not recognize and the two male dogs went to his side. Pepper went to Abigail's side as she approached Talbot, trying to rise to his feet, grasping his ruined wrist. Abigail twisted sideways and smashed the Kraken leader's face in with a vicious side kick. Talbot fell over onto his back.

"How dare you!" Abigail shouted. "How dare you molest me and mine? I am an Avenging Angel of the *Lord*. Pure in purpose and body. You dare to sully me and my mission. The wages of sin are death!" Just then Dogman walked toward her.

"Abby, it's okay. It's over," he said in a calm, cool voice. Blood and death all around, and Dogman still acted like it was a day in the park.

Abigail was shaking with rage, tears running down her face. Pepper nuzzled her hand, whining, trying to tell her in the language of dogs, "Hey, Mistress. It's okay. I'm here. I love you." Abigail suddenly knelt, threw her arms around Pepper, and began sobbing as her head buried in the dog's side.

"I missed you *so* much." Torbin heard her say, knowing that she was talking as much to her Uncle Buck as she was the canine. Torbin strode over and grabbed the double barrel from the bike handles. He held it at low ready and fixed his gaze on Dogman.

"Are we good?" he asked. Dogman looked at him with eyes as cold as Torbin's, eyes reflecting a person in a killing mindset.

"Are you her friend?" Dogman asked.

"Yes, I am. Ask her."

Dogman kept staring at him. "No need to. I can tell. So can the dogs. If you weren't her friend, you'd be torn up."

Abigail stood up, regaining her composure, and walked toward her uncle. The two young Curs could smell the family scent and wagged their tails at her approach. She threw her arms around his thick, muscular neck and kissed his cheek. "Where have you been? I thought I had lost you forever."

"I've been around." He showed a hint of a smile, and gently patted her head with his large hand.

"Torbin, this is my Uncle Buck. He's the one who brought me to Deseret. Pepper there was in the last litter I saw before Hanford blew up. I guess she remembered me."

"Everyone remembers you. You're special." Torbin saw a softness in Dogman's eyes that he could tell was reserved for his dog family and Abigail, but no one else.

"Pleased to meet you, Uncle Buck."

"Call me Dogman. That's how I am known. That's what I am."

"Well, Dogman, I have some unfinished business with your

companions. Or is it former companions?"

"Former," Dogman grunted.

"Good. Then, please excuse me for a moment." Torbin walked over, recovered his Ka-Bar from the ground, and then found his .44. Placing them back in his tactical vest, he quickly surveyed the scene.

The man he had called Grizzly in his mind was dead, bled out. Big Ears was going into shock, possibly dying. Scarman was beginning to come around, groaning, his nearly amputated thumb still flowing blood. Skinny and Big and Fat were both down for the count, unconscious, their 'looks' rearranged, possibly permanently. Then there was Talbot.

He was on the ground, moaning, holding his mouth where Abigail's boot had caught him. He probably had some ruined teeth.

"Hey, Talbot. Rise and shine. It's time we had a little talk." He toed him in the side.

"Fuck you, asshole," Talbot spit out past his bloody teeth.

"Well, is that any way to talk to someone you just met? Now, like I said, we need a short conversation, just the two of us." Torbin pointed the 12 gauge at him.

"Fuck. You."

Torbin chuckled. "Well, no talkie, no walkie." He fired a barrel into Talbot's right foot. Talbot screamed, and started to thrash around on the ground. Torbin turned and returned to Dogman and Abigail.

"Sorry to bother you all, but I need some answers, Dogman. Where did you come from?"

"We drove from the Florida Panhandle, around and up through Nevada. Then we cut through Oregon and South Idaho, where the radiation has lessened. We got here about ten hours ago."

"Who sent you?" Torbin asked.

Dogman shrugged. "Talbot talked to somebody from the Church of Kraken. He and the other guy seemed angry. Guess they felt that their local gods, the Squids, were letting them down. They really believe that shit about Kraken. Their faith is just as strong as the Mormons."

Abigail looked at her uncle. "But ours is based in Christian brotherhood, the love of Jesus Christ and the Lord our God. Not hate, or... eating people."

Dogman snorted. "That's what everyone says, until someone gets in their way. Then, it's all about what's in it for *me*."

Torbin interrupted, "Well, be that as it may, I need to find out if they have long term plans, or that was just Talbot's ramblings. I can't wait around and find out. I take it he probably has some backup nearby, besides you, Dogman."

"There's another SUV with four guys waiting in downtown Evanston. It's pretty well deserted, still lots of Eaters around."

"And with that, Abigail, it's time to leave. Transfer your stuff into their SUV. We'll haul ass up the road until I find another telephone booth that is connected, and find out where our guys are on the trip down here. You're welcome to come along, Dogman."

The large man shook his head. "You have a bunch of darker folks around. Grew up around them, had nothing but trouble with them. Sure as hell not going to fight for them."

Abigail regarded her uncle. "Are you sure? I've missed you, a lot."

He gave her that slight smile he had. "Sorry, Abby, I do better with just dogs. Get your stuff, I'll hang around until you leave."

Abigail quickly went to their sedan, and recovered her backpack and sheathed Marlin rifle. She located her pistol belt and strapped her Glock back on. Torbin kept an eye on the damaged Krakens until Abigail had loaded her weapons into the commandeered SUV. Then Torbin jogged over to the sedan, dragged the cooler out from the back seat and transferred it to the SUV.

"We need our food in case we have to hole up somewhere. We'll bypass Evanston and look for a telephone booth later on."

A portable radio in the SUV crackled to life. "Hey Boss, what's happening?" a voice said over the radio. Torbin cursed, wondering if he should try to answer. Dogman solved the dilemma by lifting up a portable he had on his belt.

"Dogman here. Wait a couple. We're busy."

The disembodied voice answered. "Roger. Thought we heard a shot."

"Had to convince someone to come along quietly."

"Alright, Dogman. Ask the Boss to call us in a couple."

Dogman moved over and took the AK-47 off of the SUV hood. "Better head out. You can keep the bolt action. I'm heading back to Idaho."

Abigail moved over and hugged him. "We can't convince you to come with us, Uncle Buck?"

He hugged her back, his large muscular arms engulfing her. "No. You have a different path than mine." His steely eyes examined Torbin. "You'll help keep her safe?"

"You have my word, Dogman."

With that, Dogman kissed his niece on her forehead. He untangled himself from her grasp, stuck his large right hand out to Torbin. "Shake."

Torbin took it, feeling his great strength.

"Deal. Watch out for my niece. I hold people to their word."

"So do I, Dogman. So do I."

Abigail bent down and hugged Pepper again. "You take care of Uncle Buck until I find you again, alright?" The Black Mask Cur whined and licked her face. Then her two sons came up, tails wagging, and nuzzled Abigail. She scratched their ears, and they licked her. Now, her scent was permanently imprinted in their memory.

Dogman gave a short whistle, and all three dogs headed toward the bus. Torbin fished into his pocket and found one more of the business cards Aleks had made for him.

He handed it to Dogman. "Use this if you want to get a hold of Abigail, or me." Dogman glanced at it, then stuck it in his shirt pocket.

"See you later. Be careful, Abby. Remember what I taught you."

She smiled at him through teary eyes, shaking her head 'yes'.

Torbin took the driver's seat, the keys still in the ignition. He turned the key and it started right up. Abigail hopped into the passenger side, began to belt up as Torbin accelerated down the road. Dogman watched them leave for a moment, then returned to his bus.

"Goddamnit! Help us, Dogman." Talbot said to him through clenched teeth as he walked by.

"Fuck you. You made your bed, now sleep in it," Dogman answered. He climbed up into his bus, started it, and put it in gear. His radio crackled. "Hey, somebody talk to me."

"Come on up. The Boss needs some help." He swung the vehicle in a wide turn and started going the wrong way down the Interstate. The chances of meeting anyone was so remote as to be funny. He'd have to find somewhere to turn off before hitting the Deseret border. His other dogs in the back began to bark and howl. Dogman barked and howled back. He was with his family.

A couple of minutes later, the four remaining Kraken gang members drove up to where he had been, jumped out and began yelling and rushing around.

Torbin and Abigail traveled in silence for a few minutes.

Then Abigail spoke. "Torbin, I am sorry I…lost it back there. I should have had more control."

Torbin grunted. "If I was a young eighteen year old lady whose breast was being rudely manhandled by a complete asshole motherfucker, I'd be pissed too. Pardon my French." He glanced over to the passenger seat.

"Asshole… motherfucker." Abigail tried the words. "Is that what he was?"

"Look it up in the new internet dictionary when we get to Malmstrom. Trust me, there will be a picture of him and his buddies next to the definitions. Next to them will be written, 'see also Sacks of Shit'."

Abigail tried not to, but burst out laughing. She knew she should not be encouraging this profanity, but coming from Torbin, it was hilarious. Finally she managed to stop, wiping tears from her eyes.

"Are you really going to protect me, Torbin?" she asked.

"Are you kidding me? *You* get to protect *me*. You're like a buzz saw when you get riled. Only Aleks can hold a candle to you." He paused in reflection for a moment. "And maybe one other woman. A Coast Guardsman in the employ of Director Lloyd. Heidi Faust. If Ichiro had not shown up, I would be singing soprano."

"I find that hard to believe. You seem very capable no matter what you do."

Torbin laughed. "Believe it. Ms. Faust could handle a blade like nobody's business. But you seemed to flow, move, like you've done this many times before. I knew you have experienced combat, but your hand to hand skills were… surprising for someone of your age."

Abigail sighed. "I have been training to be an Avenging Angel for almost six years straight. That is the task, my Mormon mission that God and the Prophet have chosen for me. While other young persons in past years have been sent on Mission to 'spread the word' of the Mormon Church of the Latter Day Saints, I have been chosen to protect all believers, so we *can* start educating people in our belief.

Someday, Mormon Missionaries will once again move outside of Deseret, to spread The Word."

Torbin paused. There was another question he had to ask, to insure that Abigail was handling this level of violence in which she was involved.

"You seemed sure of your actions when you slit that one Kraken biker's throat."

Abigail frowned a bit. "He was trying to kill one of Uncle Buck's dogs, and one of Pepper's pups. They are like family to me." She paused. "I know that may sound strange. But I didn't even think, I just reacted. I have no regrets."

"So, protecting family is important?"

"Of course, and friends as well. I have God given skills that I can use to help the good and the innocent. I am not bloodthirsty. I do not look for a fight, for death, but I will not shirk from it either. The weak, innocent, good people, both two-legged and four-legged friends. These, I will defend."

Torbin sat for a moment. It dawned on him that she sounded a lot like a certain Bushido warrior he knew. She had inside her a level of violence that could be released at a moment's notice if need be, but only if it was warranted by the situation and coincided with her moral code and honor. She was a complicated person for a young lady who had experienced parts of life usually reserved for older professional soldiers. Then it hit him. She *was* a professional soldier, a warrior, despite her young years. It would have been nice if she had been able to live the normal life of a teenager. But that all ended when the first rock hit.

Torbin felt the anger rise again when he considered all of the ruined lives, especially the children's, that the appearance of the Tschaaa had caused. Now, since the nuke strike, he had a certain degree of satisfaction. Payback's a bitch.

"Abigail, I think you and Ichiro, my blood brother and comrade, have a lot in common. He also was raised to be a warrior—in his case a traditional Bushido warrior, a Samurai. His moral compass mirrors yours."

Abigail cocked her head. "It would be interesting to meet someone like me. You are a soldier, a warrior, but you are a bit older. How old is Ichiro?"

"Just turned 28. Still older than you, but definitely young at heart."

"He is married?"

"Hell, no. He's been busy a soldiering for his country to think much about starting a family. He lost his mother and father to a harvester."

Abigail sat without a word, as if she was trying to process something. Then she spoke. "He does sound kind of like me. I think I would like to meet him, especially since he is your friend. A friend of yours is a friend of mine, Torbin. You would not have any unworthy friends."

Torbin chuckled. "Boy, do I have you fooled. Just remember that at my heart I am an old grunt Marine who has rarely seen the inside of a church. I am rude, crude, and socially unacceptable, and some of my friends are the same way."

The way that Abigail regarded him, Torbin almost had the feeling she was looking *through* him. Who is perfect? No one, not even a Prophet. I know you're far from perfect, but you are the center of something bigger than you, of something important that is to come.

"I know you have trouble believing this, as you are used to being able to physically see or touch those things around you. Whether you believe me or not, I can see the real you. You are a good soul, a warrior for what is right, and what is good. You may sometimes do things that, like you said, upset people. But, you are, whether you see it or not, pointed in the right direction. And you have a special purpose that will eventually be revealed. Trust me."

Torbin felt a small shiver down his spine. He always felt weird when people spoke about matters of a more spiritual plane, especially Abigail, who seemed to have a direct line to something outside his existence, his reality. Maybe it was God, the Great Spirit, or even The Force. Whatever. Bottom line, he trusted her. She could believe whatever she wanted about him. He only knew how to be himself, and no one else. She seemed to like who he was, so nothing else mattered.

"Well, my dear, I will leave matters of the spiritual plane in your capable hands. I will deal with the here and now. When we reach the area near Rock Springs, there is a former truck stop and gas station that has a hardline telephone connected to the main trunk lines that our people re-established. I memorized all the locations of operational telephones before we took on the Eaters in Evanston. If it hasn't been hit by an asteroid, we can call Security Control and see how close the team they sent out is to us. Then we can decide if we wait for them or try to meet them on the road."

They continued driving down the Interstate. Abigail grabbed a drink from the cooler Doc had given them, and sipping it, asked, "Why did you shoot Talbot in the foot?"

Torbin chuckled. "Well, I would have liked to bring him along and interrogate him later. However, with just the two of us, and other bad guys around, that was not a good idea. I decided on a little bit of constructive terror instead, to give him something to think about. Especially if he and the others tried to follow us. Bonus—it slows him down."

"Why not just kill him?"

"As you said once before, I kill because I have to. Killing is something I do well, but it is not who I am. I do not kill prisoners. At least not human ones."

Abigail paused, processing what Torbin said.

"Torbin, if you and Uncle Buck had not been there, I would have been tempted to put them down like the mad beasts that they are. But, I don't kill prisoners either."

"Point taken. Although, I'll admit that when they started to abuse and molest you, I thought about killing all of them too. But, the way you took care of the two who laid hands on you was definite poetic justice."

Abigail sighed. "I did what came to me automatically. Yes, I was angry and afraid. So, I did what was the fastest way to neutralize them. I will have to try to control myself in the future."

Torbin glanced at her.

"No harm, no foul. It turned out okay in the end. I bet you they'll think twice about abusing some young woman in the future. Though two of them may lack the intact equipment to even have those thoughts."

Abigail's mouth had a wisp of a smile. Torbin knew that the level of violence she perpetrated was as much of a surprise to her as it was to him, and was definitely a surprise to the Krakens. He knew that a maturing female teenager with all the typical hormones that accompanied puberty made for some very strong feelings. The fact she had been in a warrior society for the past six years complicated things. Torbin hoped his wife and company could help her achieve maturation into full womanhood. As a man, he was definitely limited in his expertise.

"Anyway, I think we are approaching that truck stop I mentioned. Please keep an eye out for it."

About ten minutes later, they saw the exit with the truck stop. Torbin pulled off and saw a sign he believed had just been a joke from years gone by. It read, "Eat and Get Gas."

Underneath it said, "Mom and Pop's Place. Treat Us Right, We Treat You Right."

The current building looked like a downsized version of a once larger structure, with the remains of a foundation around the perimeter. There were a half dozen gas pumps in front of a combination store and café. Behind the buildings were parked a couple of oversized repair bays, big enough to take full semi-tractor trailers. They seemed to still be functional. Set away from the main structure was a small two story watch tower. Manning it was what looked to be a teenage boy with a 12 gauge pump.

Torbin pulled up to the pumps directly in front of the doors to the café. Above the double doors was a sign, "Good Eats and Drinks. Ice and Ice Cream."

In smaller writing, "We take greenbacks, gold, silver, guns, furs, venison, and homemade goods in payment. Be ready to barter."

"Well, Abigail, I have a few greenbacks. Let's find the phone and then maybe a coffee."

Abigail smiled. "This looks like a friendly place. Are there many small business open in the Unoccupied States?"

"More and more every day. Just over a year ago the government began a concerted effort to get people reconnected with their neighboring communities. The weather has gotten better and people are coming out of their holes. We are experiencing a rebirth, even if some of it is because we are leaching power and info off of the Squid controlled areas. Whatever the reason, what we used to call 'civilization' is on the mend."

They got out of the SUV and entered the establishment. They were met with a slightly grizzled older man, medium height and build, with a baseball cap proudly proclaiming "USAF Veteran".

"Hello there. You must be Captain Bender, and you're the young Mormon. No, I'm not psychic. I just got a call from Security Control to keep an eye out for you."

Torbin chuckled. He was going to owe the guys on the Central Control staff many, many drinks.

The man continued. "Call me Cal, short for Calvin. They asked me to tell you that your guys are about an hour away. That was about ten minutes ago. Mother! Company!"

A woman in her very well preserved fifties came out from the back, wiping her hands on a clean apron. "Hi! Glad you made it. You're quite the talk of the town Captain, as they used to say." Then she spoke to Abigail. "Dear, why don't you come with me? You've got something on your sleeves that is going to stain if we don't wash it now. Calvin, show the Captain where he can wash his hands."

Only then did Torbin realize that his hands had bloodstains around the knuckles. A glance at Abigail and he suddenly noticed for the first time that both sleeves of her fatigue blouse were quite stained with blood. How had he not noticed that before? Cal glanced at Torbin, and saw the sudden concern in his eyes. "Easy, son. I can tell you've just had some recent problems. Mother will take care of your friend. What's her name?"

"Abigail."

"Nice name. Now, come with me and you can wash up. Then you can move that SUV around back. No sense advertising you're here just yet."

As Torbin washed up in the back, Mother—whose first name actually Jean—had gotten Abigail to take off her top. She had a lightweight Kevlar vest over a sports bra underneath her shirt. Fortunately, the blood hadn't soaked through to that, though she had spare underwear in her pack.

"My name is Jean. What's yours?"

"Abigail. Ma'am."

"Oh, don't Ma'am me, please. I ought to Ma'am you, being a Captain and all. Father has set up an industrial washer and dryer set in the back. A little prewash and the stains will come right out."

Abigail looked down. "It's blood. Sorry."

Jean stopped. She reached out and began to rub the back of

Abigail's neck. "No need to be sorry about anything. I've seen my share of blood and guts, the last few years. You do what you have to do to survive, especially if you're a woman."

"I...didn't even notice it, the blood. It's like blood on me or around me is normal. I don't think that is what a good Mormon girl should consider normal."

Jean leaned closer. "Dear, until we get rid of the Squids and their asshole help, 'normal is as normal does'. Believe me, I know. Now, sit and relax. Pamela!" she called.

A young voice about Abigail's age called back. "Yes, mother?"

"Could you get this young lady a cup of tea?"

"Will do!" A blond-haired teenager came out from the back wiping flour from her hands with her apron. She stuck out her right hand for Abigail to shake. Her grip was firm and confident. "I'm Pamela. Pleased to meet you. You're from Deseret, right?"

"Yes, I am. I'm Abigail Young. It's a pleasure to meet you as well." She noticed the flour residue. "You were... baking?"

"Yeah, making a bunch of pies. I make very good pies, if I do say so myself. My mother and grandma taught me when I was young. Nothing like kneading dough to take your mind off of things."

"I never learned how to bake," Abigail said, her voice a bit quiet. Pamela and her mother exchanged looks in a a form of nonverbal communication. "Come on. Wash your hands. First lesson while we wait for your friends to show. You've got a very strong grip, so this should be easy. Come on. Times a-wastin', like Grandma used to say."

Torbin finished washing his bloody knuckles, making sure that the damage was minor. Some of the blood may have been Kraken biker blood. After he was finished, he and Cal unloaded the equipment from the SUV, and moved it around back. They had found a holstered .45 Auto on a belt with spare magazines, a tube fed 22 auto rifle with a crude silencer on it, a small single shot .410 shotgun, and a Mini-14 rifle. Had the Krakens decided to shoot first and ask questions later, Torbin and Abigail would have been in trouble. The poorly executed plan to take them alive and without bullet holes, had been their downfall. Torbin also took out Abigail's pack and weapons, the cooler, as well as the double barrel 12 gauge and the bolt action scoped rifle. Torbin hefted the rifle, then handed it to Cal. "Here, consider this payment for services rendered. Looks like a 30.06 Remington."

Cal took it gently from his hand. "*This* is a rifle. I can't take this. This is over payment."

Torbin looked at him. "Consider it for past payment also, for being an Air Force vet. Did you fly?"

Cal snorted. "Did I fly? Hell, as a young Lieutenant, I flew as a Buff co-pilot. B-52 Bomber for you Marines. I flew strikes during the First Gulf War. Later, I was a Lt. Colonel during the Iraqi War, and blew the hell out of them again. I was a Squadron Commander, and Command Pilot. Made full bird, did twenty-two years, then retired to raise my family, which I started late with a younger wife. Took me years to find the right woman—Mother, in the other room. How about you? Married?"

"Newlywed, Colonel. Little over a month. Aleks, my wife, says she knows she is already pregnant. Says my sperm were typical Marines, charged right up the beach, and penetrated the target."

They both laughed. "Did you want to fly again, Colonel?"

"Please, call me Cal. No, I'm too old to fly against the Squids, even if they could find an operational Buff. Besides, before we knew it, our aircraft and airfields were pretty much trashed. My family and I came here, as I had a friend who owned this truck stop." He sighed. "John died the first year, killed by a looter, who I shot dead. His wife slit her wrists. Their son and daughter had been away at college when the Squids hit, never to be seen again. So after John was gone, she had nothing left."

His face had a slightly grim countenance. "I'm either the luckiest man around, or an Angel was watching over me. My whole immediate family—my wife, son, and two daughters—and I survived, kept this place running during the long winter. My older daughter, Shannon, is up in your neck of the woods, training to be a soldier. She's twenty, Pamela's eighteen, Jim's sixteen. Like I said, I started a bit late in life.

"Some of your guys showed up about a year and a half ago, got the telephone lines working again, got some underground power lines to a substation in Rock Spring. The town is working again. Wyoming is mining coal, natural gas, uranium, even a little bit of gold and silver. We just need to be repopulated. Those damned Eaters in Evanston did not help matters. I imagine you had something to do with those."

"Guilty as charged, Cal. Abigail was there also. In fact, that's how we met. Killing Eaters."

Cal looked mildly surprised. "That young lady is full of surprises. You'll take care of her, won't you? She reminds me of my daughters, but hasn't had much of a childhood, has she?"

Torbin paused, then decided this man could be trusted. Hell, he saw the situation right away. Being a former Commander, he was probably experienced with young people away from friends and family, or without either.

"Cal, we just bumped into her last living relative in less than ideal conditions. He chose to take off on his own, got me to promise to take care of her. I plan to."

Cal stuck his hand out. "Shake, Captain. It is an honor to meet someone with your character. Not to mention someone who just nuked the Squids."

"I helped, but someone else actually dropped it. I'll tell you the story sometime, after they declassify it. You need to call me Torbin, if I call you Cal. It's only fair."

"Fine, Torbin. Now, let's see what the women are up to. I have discovered that if you leave them alone for too long, they start scheming." They found Abigail and Pamela giggling like a couple of schoolgirls as the Avenging Angel learned the finer points of pie crust making. She had a wide grin plastered on her face, and white flour on her nose. Torbin stifled a laugh, knowing she was still a bit sensitive about her appearance.

"Captain." Pamela beamed. "Your friend here is a natural in pie crust construction and dough wrestling. If she needs a second career, have her come here, we'll put her to work."

Abigail blushed a bit. "You are exaggerating, Pamela. Most of the flour ended up all over the floor and I, not in the dough."

"Well, what do you think a successful baker looks like? That just shows you are really into your work." Everyone was laughing when they heard a blast from an air horn.

"Shit!" Cal exclaimed. "Come on. There are strangers coming, and Jimmy doesn't like their looks."

Abigail still had her Glock on, so she went looking for her pack. Torbin quickly found the double barrel with the one charged barrel and ran out the east side of the store. He shot a glance up at the watchtower and saw Jimmy unrolling a tarp over the front of the structure. Judging by the way it unfurled, it was likely that there were plates and sections of armor or Kevlar sewn in.

He gazed down the access road. Two vehicles were approaching, a SUV and the sedan he and Abigail had been using before its tires were flattened. Shit. They had found spare tires way too quickly. Now the Krakens were here.

A series of cables on stations popped up, fencing off the whole front of the truck stop. Now the front of the complex had a four foot high barrier fence which kept everyone who drove up some fifty yards from the fuel pumps. The two vehicles slowed to a stop.

A voice over a sound system boomed, "Sorry, closed for business. Illness in the family. Need to quarantine the area." Cal was laying it on thick, even though he knew it was probably too late.

Someone answered from the SUV using a small electronic megaphone. "We know they're in there. Just send them out." It was the voice of Talbot. Damn. 'No good deed goes unpunished,' thought Torbin. He realized too late that he probably should have shot them all and let God sort it out.

"Sorry, closed for business. That includes trading." Cal shot back. Torbin heard some discussion from the two vehicles as the men got out of the vehicles on the far side, too far away to hear what was being said clearly. Torbin saw a couple of AR-15 clones, a lever action rifle, and a pump shotgun in the hands of the four new Krakens. He saw Talbot leaning against the backside of the SUV. Next to him was Skinny, his nose taped. The other two wounded Kraken were probably lying down.

Talbot clearly gave an order of some kind, as the man carrying the lever action plus the one carrying the shotgun approached the front of the Café/Store, the two other riflemen providing cover. Torbin leaned far enough around the corner of the building to get a sight picture and let loose with the remaining barrel of the shotgun. He knew the spread and distance was such that the blast would not have a large effect. He was just trying to get the Krakens to re-evaluate their moves—was Torbin really worth getting shot for?

The Kraken biker with the lever action let out a yelp of pain as a piece of shot impacted his left cheek. A couple of other lead shots from the double ought buck load smacked into the rear fender of the

SUV. All of the Krakens quickly went back to cover behind the vehicles.

"Hey Talbot!" Torbin yelled. "Do you really want to do this? Do you want *more* screwed up biker buddies?"

Talbot yelled back. "Fuck you, and that Mormon bitch. Come on out or we'll burn you out!"

Damn. Torbin did not want to drag Cal and his family into this, but now it was too late. He saw Talbot talking to Skinny, who had bandaged face. Torbin set the empty shotgun down and drew his .44. He knew Abigail would be on the other flank, so they would have a nice crossfire for anyone who tried to advance. He could also guarantee that Cal and family would be gunned up as well.

Talbot handed something to Skinny. Then, as the two ARs began taking pot shots at the truck stop and Torbin's position, the Kraken quickly stepped out from behind the vehicles, lighting a Molotov cocktail in a wine bottle. Torbin was trying to aim in on Skinny while ignoring the angry bees zipping by when a shot from Abigail's position rang out. Skinny had just cocked his arm to throw the gasoline bomb when it exploded in his hand. He went up like a 4th of July firecracker. The Kraken gang member began screaming and running in circles as his fellows screamed at him to drop and roll.

A large caliber rifle discharged from the front of the store, and the burning man toppled to the ground. Cal still had the PA system activated when he said "Nice shot, Mother." She just did Skinny a favor—Torbin had been thinking of letting him burn. Just then, Torbin heard the distant but closing yelp of a siren. The Response Unit was nearby. He yelled at Talbot, "Time to fish or cut bait, asshole. We have just as many shooters as you do. So hurry. I wanna have lunch here at the café. They make a mean hamburger."

Talbot started to curse up a blue storm when his remaining fighters began to argue with him. They had heard the siren as well and knew that more men with guns were nearby and getting closer. Finally, he gave in. "This ain't over, Torbin. I'll be back."

Torbin laughed loudly. "Hey, that line worked for Arnold, but it sounds wimpy coming from you. Hurry up and slink back to that shithole you call a home. You bore me."

If not for his shot foot, Torbin was sure Talbot was mad enough to run screaming at him, throwing rocks, and spitting. Instead, his

Kraken bikers helped him into the SUV. Within a minute, both vehicles' tires were squealing as they made hard turns and took off in the opposite direction. Torbin watched them leave, making sure they weren't trying some feint. They soon disappeared from sight. Satisfied, he went inside to check on everyone.

Mother Jean was wrapping a bandage around her daughter's left arm, fussing. "I told you to stay down. See, you got hit with a ricochet."

"Mother, it's just a scratch. I've had paper cuts worse than this."

Abigail saw the wounded woman as she walked through the front door. Her face went white with rage and she made a beeline outside. "Oh, shit." Torbin dashed to catch her. The Avenging Angel was moving so fast that Torbin didn't catch her until she was in the parking lot.

"Hey Abigail. You can't catch them on foot. They've already left." Abigail spun around and began screaming. "Those *beasts* tried to kill my new friends! They need to be sent to burn in hell for all eternity!"

The years of pent up stress were finally beginning to crack the young warrior's hard self-armor. Even the most mature soldier has certain breaking points. A child soldier was no better.

Abigail had tears of rage streaming down her face. Torbin did not want to touch her for fear of eliciting a violent reaction. Then, two figures brushed by him: mother Jean and Pamela.

"Hey, Abigail. It's just a scratch. See? Mother covered it with a simple bandage."

Jean put her arm around the Deseret warrior. "Come on, dear. It's time for that tea we promised you. Come into our café. You can sit down with me and a cup of some herbal tea I have, sweetened with natural honey. A neighbor of ours down the road keeps bees. Now, please come with me…" Jean gently walked Abigail back into building. Torbin stood helpless. He knew men, he did not know women. He headed to the lookout tower. "Hey, Jimmy. You okay?"

The sixteen year old stuck his head out from behind the reinforced tarp. "Captain Bender. Glad to meet you. I'm fine, although I wasn't able to get a shot off. You took care of them too fast."

"Well, we stopped them from getting too close. Maybe next time you can have some fun."

"Can I ask a question?"

"Sure, Jimmy, go ahead."

"Is it true you killed a Squid with a combat knife?"

Torbin laughed. Damn. News travels fast. "After a fashion, yes. And shot a few too."

"You know you're famous now, don't you, Captain Bender?"

Torbin shook his head. One minute, he was just a Marine battling the enemy, the next he was being sucked into some artificial caricature of himself as people grabbed for some type of hero legend. Why couldn't it have been someone else? "Jimmy, I was just doing my job as part of a team. Without teamwork, nothing works."

The young man had a slight look of disbelief, but he did not argue. "Sure, Captain. But everyone thinks killing a Squid with a knife is cool."

Torbin chuckled. He couldn't argue with youthful exuberance.

"Excuse me, young man. I need to check in with your father." He returned to the café and was met by Cal at the double doors.

"Torbin, Abigail is trying to handle a shitload of combat stress. How long has she been soldiering?" Torbin hesitated before answering.

"From about age twelve, until she turned eighteen yesterday. She's been trained and groomed to be an Avenging Angel."

He saw Cal's jaws tighten. "Whose bright idea was that? What asshole decided child warriors like in Africa were a good idea? Kids have enough problem just surviving since the Invasion, without being forced into a young life of fighting and killing."

He gestured toward the lookout tower. "Jimmy has been doing security for a year, but he is definitely not trained for extended combat operations. Kids need a chance to grow a little before they need to start marching and maneuvering on a battlefield."

"Well, Cal, you need to bring that up to the Mormon Prophet and his minions. About twenty orphans have been groomed for the last six years to be professional soldiers of the same type as Abigail."

Torbin could still see the anger in Cal's eyes as he turned to look toward the café. "What the hell have the Squids done to us?"

Torbin answered him. "We did it partly to ourselves in order to survive, to not get eaten. The Squids have a lot to answer for. I just helped with the first act of payback. That's what helps to keep me going."

Cal stuck out his hand once again. Torbin took it and shook. "If you ever need help, give me a call, Torbin. My last name is Bell—I think I may be in a phonebook somewhere. I may be getting old and fat, but I'll try to help you any way I can."

Torbin smiled. "I know you will. Now, let me go in and check on my partner. She's having a rough day."

Torbin quietly walked into the café, and looking around until he stepped into the kitchen. Sitting with her head and shoulders resting on a large tabletop, her arms outstretched was Abigail. Pamela was working on her neck and shoulders, massaging and rubbing her muscles and joints.

"Abigail, you are one mass of strong, tense muscles. Remind me to never make you angry at me. It feels like I'm trying to work over steel bands." She kept working, grunting and gasping with effort. Abigail gave small sounds of contentment as the young woman did her best to work out the stress and pain from her body. A cup of hot tea had been moved out of the way. Jean was nearby and made eye contact with Torbin. Abigail, her eyes closed, half asleep, did not even notice.

Torbin heard large vehicles pull up outside near the gas pumps, telling him that the response unit had arrived. Jean winked at Torbin, then leaned in toward Abigail. "Honey, the response units are here. Take your time getting ready. I'll go keep them busy for a few."

She patted Abigail's arm, then stood up and went out front. Torbin quietly spoke to his fellow soldier. "Hey, Abigail. I'll get our stuff ready. Take your time." She slowly raised her head up, then leaned on his side. Pamela had stopped the massage and silently slipped out. "Torbin, friend, I'm sorry I am such a burden, such a basket case. If you want to send me back to Deseret, I'll understand."

He leaned over and kissed her forehead. "Abigail Young, you just need time to decompress. You have been on a combat and survival mode way too long. Any soldier needs to have some r and r time. Other than your birthday party the other night, you haven't really had a vacation or leave from being an Avenging Angel, have you?"

"No, Torbin. Since the day I was released from quarantine, I have been in training, training others, or on field operations. I... never questioned it. I was doing God's will."

"Well, I think the Prophet and his wife have done you a favor by sending you with me, whether that was their real purpose or not. Trust me. You'll have a chance to unwind, just as I have. We work hard, but we are also given a chance to play hard once in a while. It helps keep us sane."

Abigail slowly stood up. Then she hugged Torbin. "I know this not correct military decorum, but I need a hug."

A tear ran down his cheek and Torbin quickly wiped it away. Tough, badass Marines don't blubber like little schoolgirls, damnit. He hugged her back, telling himself that she was like the little sister he never had.

The warrior woman untangled herself from Torbin. "Thank you, Torbin. I will always owe you. Ask, and I will always be there, no matter what."

She began to put on her Kevlar vest once more. Torbin handed her cleaned and washed fatigue shirt to her. It looked good as new, no sign of the blood.

Torbin heard Jean and Cal talking, almost arguing with someone. "Lieutenant, they'll be out in a minute. Trust us."

He heard an unfamiliar voice respond. "Sir and madam, I have my orders. I need to ensure they are okay. Now." The owner of the voice sounded young.

Torbin immediately strode out through the front doors. "Lieutenant. Give it a rest. Here I am." He marched up to the young, slender Lieutenant, who snapped to a stiff attention and saluted.

"Begging your pardon, Sir. General Reed just said he would have my ass if I didn't find you right away."

Torbin saw a young man with a freckled face that looked as if he had never shaved. He suddenly felt old.

"Lieutenant Todd Baker at your service. General Reed told me to get you back soonest in one piece, with the representative from Deseret. I am ready to leave ASAP, Sir." Torbin thought the young officer looked and acted like he had guzzled about two gallons of strong coffee. He seemed ready to bounce off the walls.

"Well, Lieutenant, we'll be ready in just a few. We've had some problems with a group of Kraken bikers who were trying to take me somewhere I did not want to go, twice in one day. Cal and Jean here just helped to stop the second attempt. You just missed them."

At that moment, Sergeant Michael Wall, a member of the backup

Assault Team for the nuke mission, now on the Response Team, walked up. "Hey, Skipper! Glad to see you got back in one piece. I was just telling the young Lieutenant we could easily catch them. We're mounted up, ready to go."

Lieutenant Baker appeared like he was about to explode from stress. Torbin surmised in a glance this was Baker's first trip to the field. Apparently General Reed must have seen something special in him, and was giving him a chance at some operational command experience. The guys on the Response Team, trained by him, had tons of experience, and had been saddled with a FNG Officer in Charge. But, then again, he was in charge.

"Sergeant, your unit Officer in Charge has his marching orders. So, those are your marching orders. Clear?"

Sergeant Wall snapped to attention. "Sir. Yes Sir." They were back on the training field with the word "clear". His men knew that when he used it, discussion was over. Sergeant Wall then addressed the Lieutenant. "Sir, ready to leave when you are."

Lieutenant Baker finally seemed to calm down the tiniest bit. "Just as soon as the Captain is ready, we'll be gone." Sergeant Wall saluted, and returned to the other troops.

Torbin took pity on the young officer. "Lieutenant, I can tell this is your first big chance to command in the field. For whatever reason, General Reed decided to give you the opportunity to prove your worth. Unfortunately, you're saddled with a whole bunch of hard ass troops I trained, with combat experience. They will likely test you to see if you're going to get them killed or, in some people's eyes, worse—that they will be made to look like fools."

Torbin glanced back to see if Abigail had joined them yet, but she hadn't. He continued, "Just remember to learn from your mistakes. Everyone makes them."

"Sir, Captain Bender, Thank you."

"No need to thank me. We were all FNGs at one time or another. People may grouse and bitch about new guys, but we all have to work as a team. Especially now. We lack the numbers to reject our fellow humans. Except for assholes like those Krakens."

Just then, Abigail walked out, her pack slung on her left arm, her signature winged helmet attached to it, fatigue cap on. She had washed her face and regained her composure. It was as if nothing had happened. She smiled at the Lieutenant.

Lieutenant Baker stared for a moment, a look of amazement on his face. Then he snapped to.

"Captain. I am at your service." He went to a Parade Ground Attention, and gave a Parade Ground Salute. Abigail went to attention and saluted sharply back, then she stuck her hand out to shake his. It took a moment for Baker to react, then he shook her hand eagerly.

"Glad to meet you, Lieutenant. I'm Abigail Young, Captain, Avenging Angel, Nauvoo Legion, Nation State of Deseret. I understand you are here to escort Captain Bender and me. You arrived at just the right time. Your siren scared off the wild beasts. Thank you."

Lieutenant Baker blushed, and Torbin realized that the young man had just fallen hard. He had 'smitten' written all over his face. "Todd Baker, Ma'am. Just doing my job. General Reed has directed me to get you back to Malmstrom ASAP, safely and in one piece. I am at your direction. Is there anything you want or require to make your journey more pleasurable?"

Abigail strained not to start laughing. The Lieutenant was so serious, so willing to please, like a young pup learning its first command. She knew that feeling, the wanting to please those you were to serve. "Well, you could start by relaxing a bit, please. I am sure you will get me there safe and sound, and the General will be more than satisfied. This will be my first long trip outside Deseret so please excuse me if I gawk a bit."

Lieutenant Baker tried to relax, but was clearly having trouble. He managed to stammer out "Yes Ma'am." He yelled at his unit. "Alright. We roll in ten." He turned back to Abigail and Torbin. "You will be riding in the second Humvee with me. I'll have someone stash your gear."

"No need, Lieutenant," Torbin responded. "We'll take care of it. When you've been in the field a lot, you get nervous when someone else puts your gear away, out of reach. We'll find room."

"Yes Sir." He saluted again, about faced, and went to make sure the Humvees were getting ready to roll.

"Torbin, he is quite… focused."

Torbin laughed. "He's just afraid he'll screw up and General Reed will have his ass. Been there, done that." He noticed Jean and her daughter Pamela were slowly approaching them. "I think your friends would like to say goodbye. Let me do the same with Cal." He stepped away, giving Abigail some privacy.

Abigail approached the other women and soon found herself in a group hug. She managed to control herself so that she would not tear up again. As they separated, Jean handed her a note. "This is the official address and telephone number of this place. If you ever need to escape, a place to stay, there is always a room here for you."

"Thank you. Torbin says they grant leave sometimes. If they do, I'd like to come back for some more baking lessons."

Pamela smiled warmly. "Anytime, Abigail. Give us a call when you get a chance so we know you arrived alright."

Abigail gave them each a hug again, then picked up her pack and walked to the second Humvee.

Jean turned around and went back onto the café. She began to cry.

"Mom. What's wrong?" Pamela asked. "Abigail's going to Montana. She'll be safe."

Jean wiped her eyes with her apron. "I know, dear, I know. I'm weeping for all that pain and anger she is carrying. I wished I could steal her and keep her here. But I can't. She needs time to be a normal young girl. She can't if she is a soldier."

Pamela hugged her mother. "She'll be back. I can sense it. Tell you what. We can get ahold of Shannon. Maybe when she is not training, she can contact Abigail, let us know how she is doing, and remind her she has a place to come visit."

Her mother patted her hand. "Thanks for being such a good daughter. Now, I am going to say a little prayer. Then I'm going to say another prayer that Captain Bender keeps her safe."

Pamela had a wry smile. "Somehow, I don't think that will be a problem."

As Torbin was saying goodbye to Cal Bell, a warning cry rang out.

"Lieutenant, riders coming in from three o'clock." The gunner manning a 50 Cal on the roof of a Humvee called out. There was already a loose 360 degree security formation when the warning came. This quickly solidified into a tight circle, the Response Team using available cover to form overlapping protective fields of fire.

"Hey, guys. They're on our side," Cal called out. "Mounted militia.

Mother called them when the Krakens showed up."

Torbin knew that many small populated areas had been forming their own local armed militias. General Reed had been trying to coordinate and form them into a coherent force over the last year, being somewhat side tracked with the nuke strike mission. Torbin was sure it would begin again in earnest. There were not enough USA Armed Forces yet to cover all the border areas. The militias were asked to take up the slack.

Cal Bell pulled a red, white and blue cloth from his pocket and walked toward the approaching riders. He waved it above his head, whistling loudly. The approaching dozen riders stopped some one hundred yards away. Then, a tall, large individual separated from the group and slowly rode forward.

"That's Commander James Dark Wolf, a full-blooded Cheyenne. He was a Senior Cadet at West Point when the Squids attacked. Somehow, he made it back here, and started organizing a defensive force from members of all of the Indian Tribes, Native Americans, and any other human survivors in the Wyoming and Montana areas. Took out some flying squads in the early days, Ferals later on. Now, he runs our militia."

Torbin knew that the Cheyenne were a large people, but Dark Wolf was gigantic. Even his mount looked larger than a normal horse, jet black in color. Man and mount slowly trotted toward the truck stop. Cal strode out to meet him.

They had a short conversation out of earshot. Torbin's name must have come up as the Commander glanced in his direction. He said something else to the retired Colonel, then slung his right leg up over his mount and slid off with practiced ease. As he approached Torbin, the Marine realized he was almost as large as Andrew the cyborg.

Commander Dark Wolf stopped a few feet from Torbin. Both men automatically saluted each other, a sign of mutual respect to a fellow warrior. Torbin spoke first. "Commander, I am very glad you came. I'll feel better knowing that someone else is in the area now that we are leaving. The Krakens may come back for revenge."

Dark Wolf gave a hint of a smile. "Captain Bender, we will track those pieces of buffalo shit down and make sure they never bother these folks again. That is what we do, very well, if I may be so bold in my self-assessment."

He paused for a moment, then asked "Standing Bull… did he make it back?" Torbin hadn't considered that Dark Wolf might have personally known his Assault Team member, but was not overly surprised, either. Warriors often ran in the same circles.

"Commander, he died so others could escape. He gave his life for his teammates, and he saved my ass from a quick death. As a result, I was captured rather than killed."

Dark Wolf nodded. "His name and memory will be honored among my people. I know he did what he thought was right, with honor."

"Commander, there is a slight chance his remains may be returned to Malmstrom. Would you like me to arrange transferring them to you if that happens?"

Dark Wolf nodded again. "Yes, please. As they say, if you do that, I will owe you one."

Torbin paused, then asked. "West Point?"

Dark Wolf smiled slightly. "I see the Colonel is talking again. Yes, though the rock strikes prevented graduation. The Army threw together some crude commissioning forms, so my class were made official Second Lieutenants. The last West Point class. Then everything fell apart."

His expression changed to a frown. "I made it home. I don't think many of my classmates did. And you? How did you get your commission?"

Torbin grinned. "Battlefield promotion. I was enlisted prior to the invasion. The casualty rate amongst officers was so great, some genius decided that I needed to fill a slot. So, here I am."

Dark Wolf seemed to size Torbin up again. "I think there was more to that decision than a bunch of officers being killed. Word travels fast—we already know about dispatching of the Squid."

Torbin *really* wanted to just disappear into the woodwork. Now, the need for heroes was turning him into this larger than life character. Once again, he asked himself, Why me?

He shrugged. "I did what I had to. Standing Bull did what he *wanted* to do. I think his feats are what should be remembered."

Dark Wolf paused. This Marine before him had the markings of a legendary warrior, but did not realize it. West Point military history had taught him that during times of great need, heroes arose, filling the needs of the time. And often neither the person involved nor those around him realized how important of a position, of a place in history, they filled. Full appreciation of their place in history often only came after their death. Dark Wolf sensed that in Torbin's case, full appreciation would come much sooner than anyone realized.

"I thank you for your words, Captain. You do Standing Bull and the Cheyenne honor. Now, it is time for the militia to take care of those who wish to do harm." He out put his huge hand. Torbin took it and the shook hands. Dark Wolf said something in his native tongue. Torbin gave him a quizzical look. A hint of a smile formed on Dark Wolf's lips. "One authority I have as what you would call a Chief, is the ability to *name*. I have just *named* you. It seems appropriate."

"Well, Commander, I hope it's not too obscene. I've been called many thing in my life. But my new wife may get pissed if people start calling me Large Asshole, or something like that."

Dark Horse chuckled. "A good sense of humor stands a warrior in good stead. You have a safe and pleasant trip, He Who Kills with Knife." He gave a quick salute, turned and walked back to his horse.

Torbin reflected for a moment, running the name through his mind. He guessed there was no getting around it. He would be fawned over as a "hero". Now he had another reason, as if he needed one, to despise the Tschaaa, and to want payback.

"Show me a hero and I'll show you a bum." Old Pappy Boyington had a point. Torbin did *not* want to be a bum.

He turned and walked back to say goodbye to Cal. "You keep your family safe, Colonel Bell. I'd like to stop by sometime and chew the fat when we both have the chance."

"You can do that after you've finished kicking the Squids' asses, young Captain. Have a safe trip, and keep Abigail safe."

Here everyone was treating him as "something special", when it was Abigail who had the makings of a bonafide hero. She was a child forced into a survival situation, surviving into womanhood and becoming a warrior of virtue. She should be a person emulated, honored, not him.

As the three Humvees drove back the way they had come from, one of the other Cheyenne members of the militia asked Dark Wolf, "Was that him? Was that the one with Standing Bull?"

"Yes. That is He Who Kills with Knife. And, I know we will meet him again."

He turned to the rest of his unit. "Come, my fellow warriors! Let us kill some Krakens." A few war cries and rebel yells, then they began to track the enemy.

The beginning of the trip in the Humvees was smooth and uneventful. Torbin and Abigail sat in the back; Lieutenant Baker sat in the front passenger seat. He soon struck up a conversation with Abigail.

"Captain, I could not help but notice the unusual design of your bars. And the emblem over your left pocket. What do the designs mean?"

"Well, Lieutenant, the gold crosses on my Captain's bars symbolize that I am a Warrior of God and Deseret. The emblem on my pocket, if you look closely, is a representation of an Avenging Angel, a warrior like Saint Michael—wings, shield, sword and all."

Torbin looked closely at the emblem. It was a figure, flowing blond hair, large golden wings partially outspread. The Angel held a large shield with a cross on it in the left hand, with a long, flashing sword in the right. It dawned on Torbin that the stylized drawing and painting on Abigail's helmet was of the front torso of the same figure on the helmet front, with the wings spreading backwards on either side. The colors were more subdued, so the artwork also served as camouflage. Whoever had done the artwork was quite good.

"Who designed your helmet for you, Abigail?" Torbin asked.

"I did. Though one of the Twenty who's much more artistic than I did the actual drawing and painting. All the Avenging Angel helmets look similar, with slight individual variations. Helps us to keep them straight, whose is whose."

The more Torbin delved into the subject, the more he realized that Deseret had created a small, highly-specialized warrior society, very small but, theoretically, capable of expansion. Despite her problems with too much unrequited stress, Abigail was still one of the most efficient military members he had met, especially taking into account her young age. Ichiro's Samurai training and way of life had much similarity to what Abigail had experienced, symbolism and all.

They talked about various unit symbols and patches through history, Torbin commenting that Abigail's Avenging Angel was one of the more artistically pleasing unit identifiers he had seen. "I might just ask to commission you, Abigail, to help me design a unit patch around a Wolf symbol. I'd like to have a symbol by which everyone could remember the people who made the first attack in response to this... Infestation the President likes to call it. I think people need a symbol to remember the sacrifices of those who took the fight to the Tschaaa first."

Abigail looked at her friend. Yes, a wolf totem, as the Native American tribes would call it, would be a powerful and easily remembered symbol. And, it would fit Torbin perfectly.

"Of course I will help you, friend Torbin. Though someone with more ability at furnishing an intricate art work would be better for the final product. I am good with design, but my drawing ability is a bit... stiff."

Torbin smiled. "Well, I just happened to be married to one of the most natural artists I have ever known. Artwork, printing, all come naturally to her. And, since she made the big mistake of marrying me, I have a captive work force."

Abigail smiled and laughed, once again brightening up the area. Lt. Baker was still making doe eyes at her. He had been knocked head over heels by Abigail's rather exotic nature, at least compared to the Lieutenant's current fellow officers. Torbin hoped Abigail would not break his heart, as he knew that a serious relationship with the opposite sex was the last thing on her mind.

Then the intercom between the three Humvees crackled. "Eaters. Ten o'clock." Torbin looked out the vehicle window and saw two easily recognizable figures chasing something that was performing a series of zig-zags. It looked like a large dog. The 50 Caliber on the third vehicle fired a three round burst, kicking up dirt into the face of the leading Eater. Surprisingly, knowing what Torbin did about their single-mindedness when they saw prey, this caused the two creatures to break off pursuit of their meal. Were they learning about human capabilities and firearms? If they were, realized Torbin, it did not bode well for the people of the U.S.A.

"Lieutenant, I know the General wants me back ASAP, but I think he would understand if we took out some Eaters this far into our territory. Those two damnable things will turn into a bunch more given a week's time." Lieutenant Baker signaled his agreement by telling the small convoy to stop and deploy.

As they un-assed the Humvees, the Response Unit members began to gripe at the Ma Deuce gunner for missing.

"Hey, Jones! That was pretty shitty shooting."

A second troop chimed in. "You need to pay attention to your shooting, numbnuts."

Lt. Baker found a voice that Torbin didn't realize he had in him. "*At ease*. You have a lady present. Let's stop all this sewer talk."

The Response Unit members shut up. They saw Abigail as another set of fatigues, especially those that remembered her from Evanston. The thought of someone being offended with typical obscene, gross talk from some trained killers when that person came with similar training had not passed their mind, Mormon or not.

Abigail blushed a bit. "Please, Lieutenant. I appreciate the thought, but I am far from a lady…"

"Whoa, my good Captain." Torbin broke in. "Why aren't you a lady? Where I come from, the Commissioning Statement reads Officer and a lady or gentleman. So, by act of the government we are expected to act as such, and be treated as such. Now I don't act like a gentleman half the time because I'm a grunt at heart. But you sure act like a lady from what I've seen."

Abigail tried to keep her voice a bit low. "But I don't know all those… feminine things that ladies do, that they have."

Torbin looked at her. The next time he saw the Prophet and President of Deseret, he was going to bitch slap him for his less than balanced upbringing he provided to Abigail, and probably the rest of the so called Twenty.

"We do not have the time for me to detail why you are wrong. I'll let my wife, that hard-ass Russian officer explain it to you. Just accept, please, the concept the Lieutenant is putting across."

Abigail looked at him, still blushing a bit. "Okay, Torbin. I'll accept the basic concept, as long as it does not cause people trouble."

"Trust me. A little civilized manners will help more than hurt any man I know. Now, the problem at hand."

Torbin turned to Lieutenant Baker. "Lieutenant, I suggest an officers' recon. It will give you a chance to get your feet wet, as they say." Torbin wanted to provide the Lieutenant the chance of experiencing a bit of armed conflict, even if it was with a creature that could not shoot back. Eaters had other characteristics that made them highly dangerous.

"Yes, Sir," Lt. Baker responded eagerly. He grabbed his battle rattle and his M-4 with the mounted ACOG sight system. Torbin turned toward Abigail. "Mind if I borrow your 12 gauge pump?"

"Of course not, Torbin. It's loaded for bear."

"Thanks." Torbin looked at the Ma Deuce Gunner. "Think you can give us long cover?"

"Yes Sir. I won't miss again."

"Good." Torbin replied. He hoped to himself that the gunner did not miss again, if the Ma Deuce was needed. Torbin checked the shotgun out, ejecting two shells to check the action, then making sure the first shell was a slug round. A huge hunk of lead tends to screw up the day of most medium sized creatures, which the Eaters and humans generally were. He had five rounds in the shortened entry shotgun, still accurate at twenty-five yards and then some. He had three slugs and two buckshot alternating in the weapon. Plus he had his .44 Magnum Pistol as back up. But he wanted this to be the Lieutenant's show. He did not think the young man would freeze up. If he did, Torbin hoped between him and the rest of the team they could take care of the situation. Torbin knew he was taking a bit of a chance, but he owed it to the good people of Wyoming to take out as many threats as possible. Plus, he owed it to the General to help develop a new young officer. After the nuke strike, general warfare would probably result in short order, requiring every trained soldier they had.

The Lieutenant joined him to the west side of the vehicles. The tree line where the Eaters had disappeared was just a shade under three hundred yards away. Torbin was not planning on entering the tree line, believing that if they got close enough, the natural drive to feed would overcome any new knowledge an Eater had developed about human capabilities. The fact that they could learn at all was frightening in and of itself. Better to kill the smart ones now, before they could pass on their gene pool.

"Lieutenant, remove your mag and eject the round in the chamber. I'll catch it. Then, lock the action back, re-insert the mag and release the bolt to feed a new round. You can then use the round I caught to top off you mag again."

"Why the reload, Sir?"

"I had the first round that had been sitting in the chamber for a while misfire. I don't know why. Thus, I go through this superstitious ritual that maybe negates whatever arcane reason existed for the misfire. Since I started doing this, no misfires. Maybe I appeased the Gods of Ammunition, I don't know. I just train everyone to do this when they have the chance. It also acts as a last minute function check when you have the time. That rifle is your lifeline to going home to your loved-ones. That and your fellow troops."

Lieutenant Baker paused in thought.

"Yes Sir. I appreciate you helping me. I'm fairly young, and inexperienced. I need all the help I can get."

Torbin chuckled. "Everyone starts out young. The trick is surviving so you can become old. Since I would like fellow soldiers, Marines, and Airmen to live with me in the old soldiers' home, swapping lies and pinching the nurses, I try to help every gun-carrier I can to survive. I don't want to die alone and bored."

The Lieutenant stifled a laugh.

"Another rule. Prior to entering the combat zone, it is okay to laugh at smart-ass comments. A good laugh afterwards helps also. It keeps you sane." He waited for the Lieutenant to perform his reload and function check. Then, he waved at the rest of the Response Team, who had fanned out to provide 360 coverage of the three vehicle convoy.

"Okay, Lieutenant. I will be back a yard and to your left, protecting your six and giving you a good two hundred degree arc of fire. Gun up, high ready. We know the enemy is there, just a question if they're going to come out and play. Put the selector on three round burst."

"Yes, Sir."

"Move out." They started walking toward the tree line.

Abigail slid her .44 Magnum Marlin Lever Action from its sheath, checked the round in the chamber and made sure it was on half-cock safety. As Torbin and Lieutenant Baker began to increase the distance from the vehicles, Abigail moved slowly out a few yards from the vehicles. She had the rifle resting at a low ready, watching her friend.

Sergeant Wall walked up to her. 'Excuse me Ma'am. I just wanted to apologize if we were a bit crude earlier..."

 Abigail chuckled. "I have heard much worse, Sergeant. But I

understand what Captain Bender and Lieutenant Baker are trying to do. I am a foreign representative and a female, so they want to insure I'm treated with respect. But, please, no offense taken. I understand comradeship, even if in Deseret we rarely used profanity. Ribbing and kidding each other in the Twenty helped us to remember the special bond we had. As you and your men have."

The Sergeant looked at her rifle. "Begging your pardon, but do you think that level action can do better than our 50 and our automatics?"

Without taking her eyes off or Torbin, she answered. "The amount of rounds down range can help, but there is no substitutions to rounds impacting the target. One hit is better than ten misses, especially dealing with demons—what you call Eaters."

The Sergeant looked closer at Abigail. Damn, good looking, smart and tough, too. How did the Skipper always manage to hook up with the best women?

"Well, Ma'am, I'll just help cover your flank."

Abigail smiled. "That will be just fine. Thank you very much, Sergeant Wall."

Torbin scanned the tree line and the Lieutenant's six. So far, so good. They approached steadily, but not quickly. No need to hurry to your demise.

Fifty yards from the tree line, an Eater exploded from the foliage directly in front of them. Lt. Baker fired a three round burst directly into the creature's face, destroying its large left eye and penetrating to its brain pan. It sprawled face first into the dirt and grass.

"Good shot. Stay frosty."

The men by the Humvees saw the action. "One down, one to go," someone commented loudly.

"Keep alive, people. Remember Evanston." Sgt. Wall called out. There, two had turned into fifty.

The second Eater dashed out from ten o'clock, Lt. Baker swinging his rifle toward the threat. He fired too quickly, only one round of the three shot burst hitting solidly. Before he got a chance to fire a second burst, Torbin's shotgun boomed. The slug hit right between the Eater's oversized eyes, putting it down flat.

"Take that extra fraction of a second and get a good on target. Then, you won't have to worry about a follow-up. Three rounds through the eyes, or between them, screws up their version of a brain."

"Yes, Sir, will do."

Torbin looked around. Nothing.

"Well, whaddya know. I guess there were only two…"

Torbin's offhand remark apparently offended the Gods of Murphy's Law of Combat. One law states "Never make a comment out loud about how the situation is over." The Gods hate that, and will say "Oh yeah? How about *this*, ass wipe?"

Three Eaters exploded out from the tree-line, directly in front of them. Torbin had already racked a fresh shell into his shotgun, so it was just a matter of waiting for one Eater to get within twenty-five yards when he fired. The eight double-ought buck pieces of shot stayed sufficiently in pattern so that four slammed into its open mouth, one hit its left eye, the other three went a bit wide. The Eater began to spin around in a circle, clawing at the invisible enemy that was causing it the pain.

Lt. Baker fired two three short bursts into the one directly in front of him, destroying its brain. It sprawled into the dirt, just as Torbin hit the third one between the eyes with the slug load. It pancaked and laid still, to be replaced with three more Eaters, all spread out.

"*Run!*" Torbin yelled. Lt. Baker turned around and began a world record sprint back toward the Humvees. Torbin glanced at the advancing Eaters, thinking about shooting the nearest one when Murphy's Law of Combat really bit him in the ass. He stepped into a gopher hole.

The plan had been to get closer to the covering forces so that they could easily shoot the Eaters without endangering Torbin or the Lieutenant with stray shots. When Torbin's foot found the gopher hole, it changed the dynamics of the situation. He went sprawling. His left ankle began to signal with pain receptors that something had been damaged. Torbin rolled over onto his back, drew his .44 pistol and started to aim at the nearest approaching Eater. He thought momentarily how this was such a stupid way to die. Tripped up by a gopher hole and dinner for some Eaters. But he wasn't dead yet.

When Torbin had turned around and began running back, Abigail had taken two long strides toward him, then assumed a kneeling shooting position. As she gained a sight picture with her Marlin,

Torbin tripped and fell. As Torbin rolled over and drew his revolver, Abigail drew a bead on the nearest Eater.

Two reports came so close together that they sounded as if from an automatic weapon as opposed to a lever action, and then two .44 caliber rounds slammed into the nearest Eater, shattering its brain case. One second Torbin had a viable target, the next second it was sprawled a few yards from his feet.

Shots from the Response Unit, including from the Ma Deuce, rang out. The two other Eaters went down. Then, six Eaters dashed out from cover. The smell of Eater blood and remains seemed to send every one of the BEMS into a feeding frenzy, drawing any in the area toward Torbin like strong magnets. It was rapidly becoming another Evanston.

Torbin started to get up, to see if he could put weight on his ankle. Before he could, someone grabbed the rescue strap on the back of his tactical vest and yanked hard. Torbin found himself being drug backwards on the wild grasses at a surprising rate as he heard a war cry resounding around him. He realized that Lt. Baker was the source of the loud cry, and was belying his rather slender appearance by dragging Torbin like a dog with a pull toy. Rather than try to interfere with the Lieutenant's momentum by getting up, he just tried to enjoy the ride. The wild grass provided somewhat of a cushioning surface to slide on, but his ass still bumped hard against a couple of hidden rocks. More bruises to add to the collection. Being on his back, he managed to look and see Eaters catching up. He tried to bring his pistol to bear.

Abigail stood up and began to Groucho walk in classic CQB style toward where the Lieutenant dragged Torbin. She knew that the further out front she got, the more danger of suddenly intersecting friendly fields of fire. She didn't care. Her friend was in trouble, so she would take the chance of a bullet in her back to insure *nothing* got close to Torbin. She fired, worked the lever action, fired again. The nearest Eater to Torbin had its brains blown out with the large .44 Magnum round, then the next one took a round in its mouth. This Eater began to spin around, clawing at whatever was attacking its maw.

Boom, Boom. The Ma Deuce finally got on target, tearing BEMS in half as the rounds struck. Sporadic assault rifle fire hit others, eventually knocking them down. Another group of Eaters began to exit the tree line.

"40 Mike Mike on the trees!" Sergeant Wall yelled out the command over the din of gunfire. He needed to stop the enemy at its source if the Skipper and the Lieutenant were to survive. At this rate, sooner or later, a fast-moving Eater would slip through the fire and latch onto one of them. And now that crazy woman had put herself out front, asking to get eaten.

The last Humvee had an automatic grenade launcher on the roof position. A troop scrambled up and got it into action as a Rifle Grenadier launched a grenade into the tree line. As the 40mm grenades began to impact and explode, Eaters began dashing and darting in every direction, many all of a sudden losing limbs and flopping around on the ground.

Abigail fired her rifle, watching another Eater sprawl into the dirt, its brain destroyed. She slung the near empty weapon and drew her Glock. She moved to intersect the Lieutenant dragging Torbin. The surge of initial adrenalin was wearing off and Baker's breath was coming in ragged gasps as his momentum slowed. Abigail sprinted over and grabbed onto the rescue strap.

"Here, Lieutenant, let me help." He could not answer, but Abigail's additional muscle got the speed of egress back up.

There were a series of grenade explosions, a couple of rifle shots, then silence. Abigail and Lieutenant Baker finally reached the forward riflemen and slowed down. Sgt. Wall sprinted over. "You can stop now. You're back under protective fire."

Lt. Baker collapsed to his knees. He then proceeded to lose his breakfast all over the grass and dirt. Abigail, panting a bit, went over to him and gently rubbed the back of his neck. "Take some deep breaths, Lieutenant. You're just worn out. You'll recover in a minute."

Somehow, at Abigail's touch, he managed to stop his retching. He then showed a hint of a smile. "Yes Ma'am." Abigail smiled back. She then went to Torbin, who was unlacing his boot.

"If I keep twisting this ankle, I'm going to have to get it amputated and put a mechanical one in its place."

Abigail knelt down and began to examine his foot and ankle. "Let me guess. You're a medic also," Torbin stated.

"An EMT. When I said I trained a lot, I wasn't exaggerating,"

Abigail said, smiling.

Torbin snorted. "You're going to give me an inferiority complex. I'm over a decade older and I don't have half the knowledge you have." As she removed his sock and began to gently manipulate his foot and ankle, she answered, "But you get things done, Torbin. Much better than most people."

"Yeah, like falling on my butt." Abigail chuckled.

Sgt. Wall called out. "Knudsen, get down here." When two voices answered, Sgt. Wall specified. "EMT Knudsen." Two large Norwegian men, both looking like the late actor Dolph Lundgren, approached. Gunnar was the EMT, Rolf was a Rifleman Grenadier. Twins, they hailed from pure Norwegian stock from the North Dakota/Minnesota border area. They survived the Long Winter, and made it to Malmstrom to volunteer when they heard the U.S.A was reconstituting its Armed Forces. Both Private First Classes, they caught on fast as well as being bilingual.

Gunnar approached Abigail and knelt next to her. "Ma'am."

Abigail removed her signature helmet with the winged design and smiled. "It looks like a bad strain, not a full sprain. If you could please check it out to see if my training has not gotten rusty…"

Rolf began talking loudly in Norwegian. Gunnar called out to him, trying to quiet him down. Abigail frowned as she heard him. Then, she spoke. "Please, a shield maiden? That is a very old term, which I am not." Gunnar and Torbin both stared at Abigail.

"You speak Norwegian?" Torbin asked, having recognized a few words.

"Yes, I do."

Torbin snorted. "Now, I really feel slow."

Gunnar tried to apologize. "Sorry, Captain. Rolf is a follower of the old religion. He gets carried away sometimes. He saw your blonde hair, your fighting abilities…" He shrugged, expressing a what can I do with a crazy brother silent question.

"No offense taken, Private. I am an Avenging Angel of the Mormon Church. I respect his beliefs, but I am a follower of Christ. I could not be a…shield maiden."

Torbin cut in right then. "Alright, educate this dense Jarhead. What is a shield maiden?"

Gunnar answered. "A strong female warrior among the Vikings.

Although many are the subjects from myths, there are some historical documents from people the Vikings fought that refer to very tough female warriors at some major battles. They are said to fight alongside their men, their mates. Some say they are the basis for Valkyries, the mythical angel like beings that took the Viking dead to Valhalla after a battle."

Torbin looked at Abigail. He kept his mouth shut, but he believed it could fit her to a "T".

As Gunnar began to wrap his ankle, Torbin told Abigail. "Dropped your shotgun when I fell ass over teakettle. I'll get it just as soon as the good Private finishes."

"You will do no such thing. You need to rest your ankle so that your wife will not be upset and worry." She stood up. "I'll go get it." Sgt. Wall had been in earshot when she said that.

"Knudsen, Rolf. You're up. Help the Captain get her shotgun." The huge man was there in a flash, towering over Abigail, who at a bit over 5'8" was not short.

"I am at your beck and call, Ma'am. Order, I do." Rolf said in Norwegian. Abigail looked up into his bright blue eyes.

"I thank you, kind Sir." She responded in Norwegian to Rolf. This brought a huge grin to his face.

"You are part of the old race, my lady. I sense royal blood."

Abigail smirked. "Please, my father was Norwegian. As great of a person he was, he was definitely not royalty. Now, if you could come with me, I would appreciate it."

"Yes, my lady." They turned and retraced Torbin's path, Abigail reloading her Marlin rifle as they went.

Torbin looked over at Lt. Baker, who was sipping from his canteen. "Sgt. Wall."

"Yes, Skipper."

"How far did the good Lieutenant drag my ass?"

Sgt. Wall paused in thought. "I'd say a hundred to a hundred and fifty yards by himself. Then, Captain Young showed up."

"Hm." Torbin was deep in thought. Then he spoke. "Sgt. Wall, do you know of the Mogadishu Mile Run the army used to do each year?"

"Yes Sir. My father was a young Ranger when that happened. The stories he told me made me join up."

Torbin smiled. "Sgt. Wall, I think the Lieutenant, thanks to my clumsiness, just completed the first Wyoming Ass Drag. I think we now have an event all our own." Torbin had spoken loud enough that most of the Response Team had heard it. Cries of *"Ooragh"* and Rebel Yells rang until Sgt. Wall yelled, "At ease!"

Torbin, his foot wrapped, began to put his boot back on. "Lieutenant Baker, are you going to make it?"

"Yes Sir." The Lieutenant slowly stood up, a bit wobbly. Sgt. Wall walked over, ready to catch his Unit Commander if he fell. But Baker did not fall.

"Lt. Baker, you just saved my ass in a most spectacular manner. owe you one. And, I always pay my debts. You did good."

Lt. Baker blushed, then grinned. The Response Team were all smiling, knowing that a young officer had just passed a major test— could he face fear and danger, and then respond in a correct manner. Lt. Baker had done that with flying colors.

"Gunnar Knudsen, could you help me stand up? I need to see if my boot is tight enough."

Rolf and Abigail quickly found the shotgun, dirty but not damaged. She picked it up, working the action with practiced ease. "A little elbow grease, and it will be good as new."

Rolf grinned. "You may not be of the old religion, the old ways, but you are a shield maiden. You know and handle weapons, and are good in a fight. I, Rolf Knudsen, do swear allegiance to you."

Abigail sighed. "Private, as much as I appreciate your support, please. I am just a Captain, here to represent my Nation State. So, you would do me a favor by supporting your Lieutenant and Captain Bender in getting us back safe. Yes?"

Rolf grinned again. "Yes, my lady." Abigail chuckled. Some men were so hard headed.

They made their way back to the Humvees. When they arrived, Lieutenant Baker, now somewhat recovered, ordered everyone to mount up. No further Eaters had appeared.

Torbin sat next to Abigail in the back of the second Humvee. He turned and looked at her. "I've already thanked the Lieutenant for hauling my nuts out of the fire, and now it's your turn. I don't know how you did it, but you shot so fast I still didn't get a chance to use this old hog leg." He patted the .44 Magnum he had received from Madam President.

"How many did you shoot?"

Abigail thought, then responded, "I hit five with eight shots."

Torbin grinned, then patted her shoulder. "Captain Young—Abigail—I thank you, the General thanks you, and most importantly, my wife thanks you."

Abigail grinned self-consciously, her eyes dropped. "I just did what came naturally, my friend Torbin. Many others shot Eaters also. The Lieutenant dragged you out of harm's way. I just helped."

"Yes, but you *keep* helping, keep saving my poor, dumb ass. I think I am going to have to convince General Reed some way to shanghai you permanently, just so my wife won't be a widow."

Abigail really blushed as the small convoy began to move. She just wanted to help, to be useful. The fact that she seemed to be in the right place at the right time was fine, she just did not want a fuss to be made about it.

"You're very welcome, Torbin. I know you'll repay me in kind someday."

Torbin paused. "In a way, I hope I don't have to."

CHAPTER 3

HOMECOMING

The rest of the trip, though long, was uneventful. It was past midnight before they entered the Main Gate, and that had been by stopping only to refuel and use the restroom. hey headed directly to General Reed's office building, the Lieutenant emphasizing that the General had said he was going to stay there until Torbin arrived. Torbin felt very nervous, knowing that the Commanding General was staying up to all hours of the night for him. Not to mention that he wanted to see Aleks, who he knew was probably worried and pissed.

As the vehicles pulled up to the front of the building, General Reed came walking down the walkway to meet them. Lieutenant Baker jumped out of the Humvee, snapping to attention and saluting. "Sir, Lieutenant Baker, reporting with the unit..."

"Relax, Lieutenant. You did good. Now, where is that wayward Marine mustang that just *loves* to get in the middle of excrement every chance he gets? Ah, Captain Bender. There you are. And limping I see."

Torbin approached the General and saluted. "Sir, Captain Bender reporting back. Mission kind of accomplished, with some new intel I need to brief you on."

General Reed returned the salute, then grabbed Torbin's hand. "Glad to have you back, son. A certain Russian Captain has been spitting nails. I just made her head of my Intelligence Unit, pending a promotion to Major. I'll have her debrief you in private. I couldn't get any work out of her until she sees you, so I'm not going to try to keep you here to tell me what happened. You can both tell me tomorrow."

General Reed then turned to Abigail. "Captain Young."

She snapped to, giving a parade ground salute. "*Sir*. Captain Abigail Young Reporting, *Sir*." General Reed glanced at Torbin after returning her salute.

"Did you already warp her into being a hard ass Marine like you are? Never mind. Captain Young, after hearing the stories of what you've done, I expected a ten foot tall Amazon spitting fire."

Abigail sputtered a bit. "S-s-stories Sir?"

General Reed chuckled.

"My driver, Sgt. Pascal, has an intelligence system that is better than mine, I do believe. He has already told me that you have pulled Captain Bender's bacon out of the fire at least twice so far. Because this Marine has an unusually high tendency to jump from the frying pan into the fire, That is no mean feat."

Abigail blushed. "I just did what I was trained to do, General. Anyone would have done the same."

"But you did it so efficiently, Captain. I am still thinking of ways to use your abilities."

General Reed then glanced over to a staff car that was just pulling up.

"Well, Captain Bender, your wife has arrived. I will let her debrief you at your leisure tonight. I will expect to see you around noon tomorrow. Get some rest. That's an order."

Aleks emerged from the staff car, a serious look on her face. She saluted the General, then made a beeline for Torbin. She grabbed his sleeve and began to pull him away from the others. "Hey, not so fast. My ankle is hurt," Torbin complained.

"I know, *Captain*." Aleks pulled Torbin into the shadows, and exploded in Russian. Torbin, who knew only a little—mostly pillow talk—tried to interrupt her, to tell her to speak in English. This resulted in her getting louder and shaking her finger in his face.

"Ah, begging you pardon, General, but she is being unfair. Captain Bender did not go out of his way to find trouble. It found us."

General Reed looked at Abigail. "You speak Russian?"

"Da. Yes Sir."

The General took a moment to contemplate this development. "I wonder what other abilities you have that your Prophet neglected to mention... Never mind. Here is a key to your new home. It is the other half of the duplex in company grade officers quarters where Torbin and Aleks reside. I have taken the liberty to fix a bed for you, and there are a few furniture items—a television, radio, towels, some food, drinks, etc. I would like you to stay near the two Captains to help you get acclimated. You are a diplomatic representative, so I cannot very well have you stay in the BOQ. Madam President wanted to be here to meet you and Torbin, but she was called back to Alaska on some last minute business. She left a package for you that I have placed in your new quarters. Take a few days, a week, to get settled. I'll know where to find you."

"General, Captain Bender told me some of the intelligence he needs to brief you on, in case something happened to him."

"Hm. I think I just asked you to take some time off. Are you going to pull diplomatic rank on me, Abigail?"

"No Sir. Assuredly not. I would never disrespect you."

"Good. That's settled then. I'll have the good Lieutenant drive you to your new home. You get some rest also, Captain."

What no one knew was that General Reed had received a telephone call from a certain retired Colonel who, years ago, had checked the General out in the B-52. After hearing about the difficulties Abigail had endured for six years, he almost broke his teeth grinding them in anger. He had also quickly arranged for Abigail's upgraded living arrangements. He was *not* about to add to her stress by immediately throwing her into the breach of operations. He had done without her up until now, so a few more days would not matter.

Just then, Aleks finished with Torbin, slapped his chest, hard, and walked toward Abigail. The Avenging Angel was taken aback, afraid she was in the middle of a domestic dispute.

Aleks stopped short. Abigail saluted her. "Captain Young," Aleks declared.

"Ma'am." Abigail responded. Aleks stepped forward and kissed her on both cheeks. Abigail was completely taken aback.

"Abigail, if I may call you that, the General has told me that my husband is in one piece thanks to you. I now owe you more than I can probably ever repay you. Please accept my eternal thanks."

She took Abigail's right hand in both of hers. "I hope we can be friends."

Abigail seemed to fall into a slight trance as she looked at Aleks. "I do not want to upset you, but you are with child... children. You will have twins. Do not be afraid. My sight is a gift from God."

Aleks' mouth dropped open, then slowly closed again. "Twins?"

"Yes Ma'am. I... can just sense it, see it. I have no control, it just happens. Please do not be angry."

In a rush, Aleks grabbed and hugged her, hard. She kissed her cheeks again, rattling thanks to her in Russian, to which Abigail immediately responded, which resulted in more exclamations and more rapid fire conversation.

Finally, Torbin broke in. "Hey, can I get an English word in edgewise?"

Aleks turned to Torbin. "Come, my Yankee husband. We have much to discuss. Abigail will be living next door to us, per General Reed's request. Abigail, we will talk much tomorrow. Agreed?"

"Yes... Aleks. Of course." With that, Aleks grabbed Torbin's arm and began to lead him to the staff car.

Lieutenant Baker shyly approached Abigail. "Ma'am? May I take you to your quarters?"

She flashed him a large smile. "Of course you may. I would be delighted." Abigail felt more relaxed than she had in six years. And Lieutenant Baker was hopelessly in love.

CHAPTER 4

Adam Lloyd sat at Mary's desk in the front office, staring at a report he had been reviewing for some ten minutes. The workmen were putting the final touches on the repairs to Adam's office area, the damage the result of the attack on the Headquarters following the nuke strike. Mary Lou Spence, his assistant, was over with Kat Monroe at the Communications Center, helping put together another news broadcast. Since they had declared themselves sister wives, and both had become pregnant by him, they had been spending a lot of time together. Adam was beginning to feel like a third wheel.

Sitting across the office was Heidi Faust, former Coastie and now his full time bodyguard. Unfortunately, the fallout from the nuclear attack on His Lordship—in addition to the radioactive kind—included some extremely nasty threats against Adam. Following the deaths of Squid young due, the Tschaaa had attacked base personnel without warning, and any ideas of a form of alliance or friendship between the two species had all but disappeared. The idea that "all humans looked alike" would not fly as an excuse. The current residents of Key West had put their asses on the line in the past couple of years to try and create a working relationship with the Tschaaa. It was hoped such a relationship would lead to humans—other than the people of color in Cattle Country—no longer being viewed primarily as meat on the hoof or a temporary beast of burden. Rather, they would be a primary client species, just under the Tschaaa in importance and function. That had apparently gone up in a mushroom cloud, along with Lord Neptune's Marquesas Keys complex.

Adam set down the report. His brain was not processing what he was reading, no matter how many times he reviewed the material. He sipped his drink, and noticed the ice cubes were almost gone. He rose to get some more from the ice bucket when Heidi spoke. "Hey Boss, just relax. I'll get you some more ice." As she stood up, Adam again noticed her attractive body. Her chin length brown hair was healthy and shiny from good health. She had been training him in martial arts for some time now, busting his ass to get him in better shape. But she had only been able to get him to the gym once since the nuke.

Adam sighed. It had been eight days since the warhead had hit a bit off target, missing killing His Lordship. Instead of hitting and burrowing deep into the center of the Marquesas Keys complex before detonating, the nuclear weapon had detonated in the southeast corner of the huge complex. The blast had been directed outward from the Marquesas Keys, the shock wave, radiated water and blast rushing directly into a Crèche birthing area. The last update he had gotten from El Segundo, His Lordship's second in command, was that over two thousand Tschaaa had died, some eighty percent being young or adolescents. At least that many had been exposed to various levels of contamination. Lumped in with these numbers were the Squids killed by the U.S. Assault Team and Adam's own Security Forces when the Squids had gone berserk, attacking all humans in their vicinity. The Tschaaa casualties been kept to the level that they had only due to the fact that they tended to keep spread out, especially swimming the oceans as a young Squid. If the huge Baja California complex had been hit instead, it would resulted in a much larger population being hit.

But this coincidence was scant help for the situation. It had been centuries since the Tschaaa had suffered this level of loss amongst the young all at one time. It was a truly a catastrophic event that resulted in psychic pain of epic proportions. The Tschaaa felt betrayed, believing their young had been targeted specifically.

The humans at Key West felt equally betrayed. Having tried to fight off the attack by their fellow humans, they were suddenly the targets of an attack by their supposed allies. Already called traitors or quislings by some, they had worked toward the bettering of the human conditions in North America. Thanks to the Tschaaa technologies and the recovering of power grid, medical care, food and amenities like a reconstituted internet, the people in Key West had started humanity on the slow climb back to the pre-rock strike level of civilization. Now, it seemed all for naught.

Adam had recently determined that twelve of his people had been directly killed by the Squids in their fury, with some seven Conch Republicans—the outside civilian populace—also being killed. Only five bodies had been recovered. The rest had no doubt been torn apart and eaten.

Captain Bender and his assault team had been so bloody efficient in the destruction they wove on the way off the Base, and the Tschaaa had spent much effort to catch and eat them. He snorted. A certain modern day samurai had hacked to death at least a dozen, with Captain Bender and the four survivors blasting untold numbers with their firearms. Only the efforts of Andrew, the cyborg robocop, had kept the Tschaaa from a more lengthy attack on humanity.

"Here, Boss." Heidi gave him the newly iced drink. Adam had been living on "rusty nails", popcorn, stale donuts and liquid bread—aka beer. He had trouble sleeping, constantly getting up to stare out the windows, running alternative possibilities through his mind. He was looking for a way out of this mess, to try to get things back to the way it was before the nuclear warhead had detonated. He had not been good company, especially to his two ladies.

He acknowledged Heidi as she sat down again."What time is it, Heidi?"

"Just past ten in the morning."

"Is it too early for a drink?"

Heidi smiled. "Boss, I've worked as a bartender. What's early for some isn't for others."

"Think I'm drinking too much?"

Heidi sighed. "Boss, if I had to deal with what you are dealing with right now, I'd be dead drunk. I know you are performing the ultimate balancing act. You want to keep the rest of us 'little people' alive, and convince the Squids *not* to send us all to Cattle Country. I, for one, greatly appreciate that."

Adam looked at Heidi. They had trained hard together, but rarely had in-depth conversations about current events and conditions, or about policies. She was a loyal soldier, and had proven herself to be better than most during the attempt to kill him. Heidi had even almost taken out Torbin Bender as he fled.

"Heidi, please be honest. Do you think I have a chance?"

"First, if anyone can find a solution, a way out, it's you. Second, do I think there are a lot of Squids out there who would just as soon kill and eat us all, than use us as workers. And yes, it's probably a majority of them today, thanks to a whole bunch of dead young."

She stood up and walked over to the wet bar. She filled a glass of ice, then poured in some tonic water.

"Add some gin, and join me," Adam suggested.

Heidi shook her head. "On duty, Boss. I need my wits and reflexes about me in case some certain Rebels decide to return."

Adam grinned. "You want a rematch, don't you?"

Heidi snorted. "I've never been cold cocked before. I've been knocked down, pinned, but never knocked out. I owe a certain Japanese warrior a good smack to the head."

Adam chuckled. "You just about took Captain Bender out, didn't you?"

"Yes, Boss, I did. But that damned…Samurai showed up. And I would have done better if they hadn't CS gassed us. Damned cheaters."

Adam burst out laughing. Finally, Heidi joined in. The one thing Heidi could do better than almost anyone else was to get him to laugh. Her complaint that, in a battle, you could cheat but shouldn't, was just hilarious given the circumstances.

Finally, Adam composed himself. "Why do you stick around, Heidi? A short trip north, bypass Cattle Country, and you're back in the Unoccupied States, free and clear. Someone with your martial arts skills would have no problem finding employment. Chances of being Squid Food are greatly reduced. Hell, if I wasn't responsible for all of *this*, that's what I would do."

Heidi gave a small smile. "Good old-fashioned loyalty, Boss. You and the Chief kept me from either starving, pissing off some Squid with my attempts at fishing, or being eventually jumped just because I'm a women that some find attractive. I may be mean and nasty, but I can only handle so many bad guys at a time. A bullet to the leg would preventing me from running away, still enables someone to use me in other ways." Adam actually saw her shiver a bit. Bad memories of something.

"So when you ask, I help, Boss. Simple as that. You are loyal to me, I return the favor. And besides..." her smile turned into a smirk. "How many women have the chance to kick the boss' ass on a weekly basis without being fired?"

Adam snorted. "Hey, I'm not *that* bad. I'm just getting a bit old, that's all. Besides, I didn't grow up in a dojo. Talk about cheating." They both chuckled.

The weight on his shoulders seemed a bit lighter. Heidi's no nonsense honesty provided a view that things could always be better, or a lot worse. As long as he kept working to make things better, maybe he could at least keep things from getting worse. Inertia, non-movement, was still better than going down to defeat.

They heard a voice from the repaired winding staircase. "Director Lloyd, are you available?" It was Andrew. He had gotten into the habit of announcing himself as his appearances tended to unnerve some people. A being weighing hundreds of pounds with the capability of snapping bones like twigs was enough to make anyone nervous under normal circumstances. The ability to move quietly like a ninja just added to the freak factor.

"Yes Andrew, I am here, with Petty Officer Faust."

The cyborg robocop walked through the open double doors carrying a small case in his huge left hand. "A present, Director. To be used immediately, if possible."

Adam opened the case and recognized it as a form of small laptop device, screen and all. "That, Sir, is a new secure communication device with which to communicate privately with His Lordship. Turn it on, follow the prompts, and voila—near instant communications, encrypted and secure. Click on the additional menu, you can play mind numbing video games, or download your favorite pornography." The human part of Andrew had a very droll sense of humor that reminded everyone that yes, he was a human deep down inside.

"I don't think I'll be doing either anytime soon. So, I take it this is so I don't need to use your abilities and equipment to talk securely with His Lordship."

"That is right, Director. Now, if the workmen are finished in your office, I suggest you take advantage of your privacy contact His Lordship. He has recovered enough now, and wishes to talk with you."

Adam knew this would be a sensitive situation. He had dealt with El Segundo since the attack, wondering when Lord Neptune would recover enough to be involved with him. Adam knew he had been injured, but his offspring refused to tell him just how injured he was. Now Adam would find out. He might also find out that he was about to be replaced. Maybe even terminated—with prejudice.

He went into his office to find the workmen applying the last bits of touch up paint on the window sills. The older supervisor greeted Adam. "All done, Director. You'll need to stay away from the molding and the window areas as the paint is still drying. Otherwise, the walls and furniture have been repaired or replaced. Those grenades did a number on your office, but I think we did a good job fixing everything."

Adam looked around. He could not see any sign of the shrapnel or explosive damage. "Looks great, gentlemen." He tossed them a wad of bills. "You and the rest of your crew have food and drink on me for a good job done in record time. Thanks."

They left smiling. It was the simpler pleasures that made life worth living in these stressful and violent times. Adam sat down at his new desk, a duplicate of his old one. His surviving personal and professional items were in boxes in his sleeping quarters. He would have to get them and reorganize his desk and office.

Andrew stepped into the office doorway. "Director, I almost forgot. I have one short function I must complete. It will take just a moment."

"Lay on, MacDuff," Adam replied.

Andrew entered the office, stood in the center, then slowly rotated around until he had completed a complete 360 degree turn. He stepped over to the refurbished bookcase, reached toward the back, and picked something small from the back of the bookcase. He held it between his right thumb and forefinger. Then he walked over and showed it to Adam.

"I just completed a scan for anything electronic or out of place. This little item appears to be a bug that looks exactly like a bug. It is a new type of sensor, so I will have to examine it more and try to determine if it is of Tschaaa or human origin. Your office is now clean of foreign objects, but you will still need someone to dust and clean up. And I do not do windows."

Adam chuckled. "Hm. If it is Tschaaa, will you put it back?"

"No, as no one from His Lordship's chain of command has told me they wanted a surveillance device placed in your office. If I am not notified, then it is unauthorized and will be removed, as your well-being is one of my directed prime duties. Strange and unidentified pieces of equipment I immediately assume are not placed there for your health."

Adam looked at Andrew, wondering if that was the full story. He was getting indications that Andrew had some plans or ideas of his own. "Well, Andrew, once again, I thank you for your continued assistance and support. I really do not know what I would have done without you."

"I suspect, Director, you would be either dead or captured. Captain Bender would have sent you to his home, rather than us sending him."

Adam shook his head, chuckling. "You sure know how to make a guy feel in control. Thanks again, Andrew."

"Now, Director, I will wait with Petty Officer Faust in the front office, as His Lordship wanted to communicate with you in private." Andrew withdrew and shut the double doors to Adam's office.

Adam hesitated momentarily, then he sat down at his desk. He stared at the new device, drumming his fingers on his desk. Finally, he exclaimed, "Fuck it." He opened up the modified laptop. Operating directions appeared automatically on the screen. Sure enough, he followed them and had a connection with in a minute.

In a flash the communicator screen was showing his Lordship. The large Tschaaa was reclining in a large alien version of a hot tub, with two females giving him an alien version of a massage with their arms and tentacles. Over the Squid's right side there stood a soldier class artificial being. It held a large bolt gun, the weapon at low ready. His Lordship apparently also needed a bodyguard.

The Senior Tschaaa Lord waved his tentacles in happy greeting, though a bit slow in movement. Adam could not see any outside signs of injury, but for all he knew the backside of the cephalopod was a massive mess of cuts and bruises.

"Director Lloyd. It is so nice to see you." The theatrical voice with which the Tschaaa Lord had outfitted his translator remained the same, so it had survived the attack. Adam was glad as the voice and the body of the Tschaaa Lord seemed to be naturally connected in the his mind.

"I am very glad you have survived, your Lordship. You seem not to have sustained much injury, or am I just not seeing any?"

"No, my Director, I did not receive any serious external injuries, and the internal ones are now determined to be minor also. Thanks to your warning, I was able to get to my safe room. This structure had been constructed based on similar ones you have built. I am doubly in your debt, and owe my survival to you." Lord Neptune performed gestures of affection and thanks with its tentacles. "I see you were not seriously injured either. Although Andrew said you received a few dents and scratches."

Adam smiled. "If it were not for Andrew, I would not have survived at all."

"Then I am also in his debt, My Director."

The Tschaaa Lord paused and shifted in the hot tub, the two females quickly attending to him as he shifted. After he had finished moving, he spoke again. "I must speak with you of unpleasant matters, caused by the attack from the feral humans."

"Yes, your Lordship. I have been expecting this."

The Tschaaa Lord signed a combination of sadness and consternation. "I know that my offspring, known as El Segundo, has told you the angry suggestions my fellow Lords have been making. That all remaining humans should be confined to compounds and concentration camps, to be used for food only. There is a strong desire for revenge."

Adam sighed. "I understand. Trying to explain the concept of collateral damage is probably near impossible, your Lordship."

"Exactly. Once again, your ability to cut directly to the point shows itself. My fellow Tschaaa feel that the killed young were purposefully targeted. An incident such as this is so alien, it is almost incomprehensible to them."

"That is because your species never really fought wars with itself. We have a long tradition of both accidental and purposeful genocide."

The Tschaaa Lord gave an equivalent of a sigh. "That is probably true. But whatever the reason, I had to explain it to them. It was the offspring of *my* loins, so it was *my* decision as to what should be done in response. I must do something."

"So, my Lord… what do you want to do?"

"First, my Director, be assured that your safety is not in question, at least not from me. I owe you my life, so it would not be honorable to blame you for the deaths of so many of my crèche. But I must take action against the Unoccupied States. I have also received notification that certain humans are organizing to refuse any further harvesting of dark meat from Cattle Country. So, I have two rebellions that must be dealt with."

One of the female attendants handed him a stalk of sugar cane, which the Lordship inserted into its hidden mouth. The chewing of it seemed to relax the large alien. "I will have to ask you for some more of your sugar cane, Director Lloyd. My supply is almost depleted."

"That can be arranged, your Lordship," Adam answered.

"Interruption of supplies of premium dark meat must not be allowed, so I will have to deal with that first. This despite my desire driven to strike back at the Ferals, the rebel humans who tried to kill me with the nuclear weapon. Now, my Director, how many armed humans could you muster in say, two weeks' time?"

Adam was afraid he would ask this. He was glad that he was not meeting with the Lordship personally, or he was certain that he would have quickly become fish food.

"Your Lordship, I have always been honest with you. I must confess to you that… obtaining human support to kill other humans will be extremely difficult, even people of color."

Lord Neptune interrupted. "Is that because of the wild, angry attacks the local members of my crèche made against your personnel?"

"Yes, Sir. They feel betrayed. They believe they sacrificed one part of humanity to survive but were attacked anyway, despite trying to defend against the attacking rebels."

The Tschaaa Lord paused, deep in thought. "Even if you either threatened them with harvesting, or offered great rewards for their help?"

"I am afraid, Lord Neptune, that neither would work to any great extent. I can probably find a few volunteers here in Key West who like to fight, and a few more mercenaries if I pay enough. Most of the Flying Squad personnel are gone, or have gotten fat and lazy, so I would be lucky if I managed to field a few hundred of them. The regular army I am in the process of building... Prior to this attack, I could field several thousand well-trained personnel. Now, that the word has gotten out about what happened—in large part due to radio reports from Deseret—I am afraid that many would defect to the other side if we tried an attack on the Unoccupied States. An attack on Cattle Country would probably result in large scale desertions after the first week when the forces were deep in country. And although I have a large Guard Force keeping the dark meat peoples in, they are not trained offensive soldiers."

His Lordship displayed some agitation. "I had an arrangement with the leader of Deseret a few years ago. I had decided that the fanaticism of the Deseret people's religion coupled with their excellent organization would result in further large scale destruction should I try to harvest their state. I asked them through a couple of Front Men to send out as many non-members of their religion as possible for harvesting, and I would let them live in peace. That is, as long as they stayed within the confines of their borders. I guess that arrangement is... turned off."

The Squid shifted his body again. "I have been ignoring them for the past few years, as Cattle Country has been set up. I have plenty of coastal areas under my control, and I figured they would soon realize that if neither side bothered the other, we could co-exist. I guess I was wrong."

Adam assumed that the Lord knew he had sent Captain Bender back by now, that Andrew had escorted him to Deseret. But neither he nor El Segundo had brought it up, so Adam decided to continue to play stupid.

"The media broadcasts from the Unoccupied States had that much effect?" the Tschaaa Lord asked.

"Yes, Your Lordship. It provided those outside your area of

control with human heroes. It showed that you are not in fact ten feet tall, but that you can be seriously attacked. The Rebels bet on the fact that no one wants another general exchange of WMDs, to include rocks. Which I guess they are correct in thinking, as I do not see any of your fellow Lords launching anything at the Unoccupied States."

Lord Neptune slumped a bit in his hot tub. "That is true. We all realize that true collateral damage in such an exchange of weapons would be devastating to the ocean ecosystem, as well as killing many young outright by errant warheads. The Ferals attempted a surgical strike against me, although large, that almost worked. Had it worked as they planned, the collateral damage would have been contained within the Marquesas Keys complex. As it was, thanks to the distances involved and the fact that our young were spread out, the casualties were light when you consider the millions of Tschaaa existing along the coastlines of North America. However, the psychic damage was horrendous. The unnecessary death of even one of our offspring is deemed unacceptable. The deaths of close to three thousand young and adolescents is considered a form of genocide."

His Lordship signed confusion with his social tentacles. "Which is why none my species understands the concept of abortion. How can a breeder who is sane kill its offspring in the bud? It is unfathomable."

Adam shrugged. "Some humans believe as you do. Others that the decision to give birth is the mothers to make. With the extreme reduction in our numbers, I have not heard of many selective abortions being done. Not to mention your mandates against them."

"Be that as it may, Director, where do I get soldiers and warriors from? I will have many Tschaaa volunteers, but my species are not suited for operations hundreds of miles from the oceans. They will be at a disadvantage for warfare in the interior lands. There are finite numbers of deltas, falcons, even with additional production. The same holds true with robocops, greys, modified harvester robots to fighter standards."

The Lord noticed Adam's raised eyebrows at the last part of his statement. "Yes, I have not been sitting, vegetating, while I have been recovering from my injuries. I have been reviewing many of your film records of your past wars, as well as fictional essays. You humans speak often of robot warriors, not just cyborgs. Therefore, I have already started the modification of some one thousand harvester robs to a fighter standard through the use of some of the millions of human weapons that have been seized. Small arms with ammunition can be attached instead of the specialized harvesting equipment, producing a mobile small gun platform. But they will have limited decision making or tactical planning capabilities."

"I will keep making limited numbers of my soldier class like my bodyguard here, and of course, numbers of greys and lizards."

The Tschaaa Lord seemed to perk up a bit as he discussed what he was doing. "I have also taken a page from your recent past. Your Hitler and your Stalin made use of slave labor to produce weapons. At the huge Baja Complex, I have taken more than a thousand Cattle from the former area of Mexico that had not been harvested or relocated to Cattle Country and given them the choice—work in factories making and modifying equipment, or else be chopped into steaks."

"I thought you had pretty much rounded up all the dark meat you could find?" Adam inquired.

"No, not in some of the more remote areas. I have let Feral humans exist in certain parts of North America, in small groups, keeping an eye in the sky on them. If disease suddenly swept through Cattle Country, I would still have access to a viable breeding population of humans in the wild, without having to tap those of you who are already in the controlled areas, providing services to me. I also maintain an 'us versus them' dichotomy. At least it worked up until last week, when the Tschaaa attacks on you Key West humans apparently derailed this model."

Adam was once more reminded of just how intelligent and adaptable His Lordship was compared to others of his species, not to mention humans. If he had been killed by the nuke strike, even El Segundo, his offspring, would have trouble replacing him. Without him, Adam doubted that the invasion over six years ago would have been successful, past blowing the hell out of everything.

"Well, Sir, I will do my best to obtain support for you. But I am not optimistic."

His Lordship positioned his tentacles in a way that could mean something between an inquiry and a statement was about to be communicated. "Adam, I have been in contact with James Kray, the Leader of the Church of Kraken."

Adam had always hoped the situation would never come which would necessitate the direct use of fanatical Church members. But it looked as if the Tschaaa Lord was about to broach the subject.

"Mr. Kray stated that he could have forty thousand armed personnel in thirty days."

Adam could not keep himself from snorting derisively. "Armed warm bodies they will be, your Lordship, not trained soldiers. I predict that half will run at the first sign of danger, the other half will wind up shooting more of their fellow Church members than the enemy."

"That may be, my Director. But, armed warm bodies will be of use to start an action against those humans who are resisting my control. It will also send a message to my fellow Lords that I am taking forceful action. That will be sufficient reason for many of them to slip back into their day-to-day inertia, content to stuff themselves on fresh dark meat." Once again, Lord Neptune had proven that had he been a human chess player, or the leader of a major human world power, he would be a force to reckon with, even on a bad day. "Kray claims he can have a like number of trained personnel within ninety days, if I help supply the human weapons and equipment."

Adam had heard through his intelligence sources that James Kray claimed a couple of million full-fledged Church of Kraken members. Thanks to his Lordship's directions, the Church had allegedly stopped its cannibalistic ways of eating other humans, which had been an attempt to be more like their role models, the Tschaaa. As many humans had done in the past, thousands were drawn to a religion based on a strong new belief or symbol in their search for something to replace the previous but now gone order in their lives. They identified with the apparent victor species—the Tschaaa—now the symbol of strength. The fact that some Tschaaa had started a form of spiritual belief or ancestor worship around the deep sea giant squid had just added to the attraction. Humans seemed to be drawn to large and strange beasties and monsters, most religions having at least some mention of such things in their histories. Witness the Old Testament behemoth.

"Well, your Lordship, as the saying goes, I would have to 'see it to believe it'. So, the… unfortunate aggression against humans at Key West does not affect his belief about working with your fellow Tschaaa?"

The Lord waved a tentacle at the screen. "He only cares about true believers. Since no Church Members were apparently injured by any Tschaaa, he has put forth the narrative that true believers are protected, as they are the true allies of my species."

The Tschaaa Lord blew a few bubbles from its gills, the same as a chuckle for a human. "I am still fascinated by ability of humans to adopt a whole belief system or mindset in a relatively short period of time. And with such fanaticism. Our culture and beliefs change very slowly. The adoption of the new beliefs revolving around your giant squids and a possible ancestral or supernatural connection with the Tschaaa is unique in the recent history of my people. Usually, it would take decades before more than a few individuals would adopt a new way of viewing the world around us."

The Tschaaa leader signed he was musing. "But here, on Earth, we already have substantial numbers of Tschaaa adopting a parallel belief to your Church of Kraken. Once again, I have to entertain the thought that this planet and its denizens are having profound effects on what it means to be a Tschaaa."

Adam considered for a moment telling the Lord that humans were having similar thoughts about what it meant to be human, humane, and the word humanity. However, he decided it would just muddy the waters.

Lord Neptune continued. "Be that as it may, my Director, I plan on using James Kray's followers, if for no other reason that they may make good cannon fodder. Crass and brutal, yes, but they in no way have demonstrated the abilities you and yours have in being a potential client species. I hope we can work through the unfortunate events of recent days. Much like your kind has worked to overcome racial and religious strife among groups in the past, I hope to make the casualties suffered on both sides of our temporary conflict a thing of the past. The humans you have brought into the rebuilding of your areas have been a source of pleasure to me. They have also demonstrated to me, and to the other Lords the potential of the Human Species."

The Tschaaa rounding up whole racial groups based on skin color had greatly simplified any conflicts between groups of humans. Now the "haves" and the "have-nots", were ultimately controlled by the decisions of the Tschaaa.

"Your Lordship, there is one large matter that must be dealt with, I believe head-on. That is the subject of genetic and body modifications secretly begun by you. The substances and nanites you introduced into our bodies and reproductive systems are rapidly becoming common knowledge, despite my efforts to keep the proverbial lid on it. I am specifically being accused of being behind it."

The Tschaaa Lord signed consternation with his tentacles. "I will record a message personally addressing this. I will assure your people that any unfortunate side effects will be dealt with and solved by my scientists. Physical harm to humans and their young was the last thing I wanted to happen. It was meant to have overall beneficial effects on your species, to make them a better client. I will explain this, and take what you humans would call 'the heat' off of you."

Adam knew that trying to explain the deep sense of violation his fellow humans felt, especially the women, would not be understood. First, the concept of rape or forced sex, seemed to be a completely foreign concept to the Tschaaa. And, of course, they were not Tschaaa, but still looked at as beasts of burden and food sources. The bizarre attempt by some ten limbed creature telling pregnant women that having their reproductive system secretly modified was 'no big deal' would go over like a fart in church. Such attempts at educating the Tschaaa about human sensibilities would be of little use. As much as his Lordship could speak like a human being, he would never really feel, think, or act like a human. There was just too many differences between the species.

"I appreciate the effort, your Lordship. I hope it will suffice."

"It must, my Director. Or else your people will be unnecessarily miserable." The large Tschaaa performed the equivalent of a stretch. "I grow weary, so I apologize that I must shorten our conversation. I must inform you that starting tomorrow, forces will begin to move into Cattle Country to stop any attempts to interfere with the meat supply. Which may mean some early harvesting. Some of James Kray's Church Members will be used, and based on your concerns, I will monitor their effectiveness. Then I will consider a direct response to the Unoccupied and Feral areas. I will also complete my recording at my soonest opportunity, hopefully broadcasting it tomorrow."

He seemed to lean in toward the screen and Adam. "You have been loyal to me. I will be loyal to you. I owe you that much for saving my life. I will insure that Andrew spends more time with you, for your safety. To lose you would be very painful to me."

"Thank you, Lord Neptune." The screen went black.

Adam sat still for several minutes. He knew the attempts to salvage the Lordship's relationship with the human population in the controlled areas, specifically Key West, may all be for naught. It had always been a balancing act of the most difficult kind, like juggling balls on a tightrope while someone shot large spitballs at you. He may have just fallen off.

In the outer office, Heidi and Andrew had waited. Heidi, being the curious and mischievous type, decided to try an experiment. She stood up in Andrews direct line of sight, and began to stretch. The short sleeved shirt she was wearing stretched taut over her ample chest. She then bent over so her tactical pants were stretched taut over her tight posterior.

"See anything you like, Andrew?"

A hint of a smile formed on the cyborg's mouth, his eyes obscured by his visor.

"Ms. Faust, you are the second person in about a week's time that seemed curious about my sexuality, or at least my ability to feel arousal and function. Yes, those 'parts' are still intact and operational. But we robocops, as you call us, have unique ways to experience sexual pleasure that seems as real as actual intercourse with another person. So yes, being a heterosexual male in my former life, I can still appreciate the finer points of the female form."

He continued. "So, do you want me to say that you have a nice body? Fine…" Andrew then switched to the exact monotone and stilted cadence of the movie character his kind was named for. "Petty-Officer-Faust. You-have-a-nice-body…"

Heidi burst out laughing and fell back into the padded chair in which she had been sitting. Andrew actually chuckled a bit.

Adam re-entered the outer office at that moment. "Well, I'm glad someone is having fun."

Andrew turned to look at him. "We completed a stress reliever exercise, Director. Ms. Faust may deign to show it to you later." With that comment, Heidi blushed a bit and stood up.

"Didn't mean to disturb you, boss."

Adam waved the comment away. "Hell, enjoy yourself when you can, Heidi. I've just been a bit preoccupied lately. Hopefully, based on the conversation I just had, things may be working themselves out."

"I am glad to hear that Director. Please let me know if I maybe of additional assistance, including keeping your new communicator operating."

"Will do, Andrew. Now, Heidi, I need to wrap up a couple of things, and then we need to meet the Admiral at the dock near his place—the Admiral's Cabin. He wants to show me something and refuses to tell me what it is."

Heidi frowned. "Do you want to take more security with you? There may be someone who doesn't like you around."

Adam grunted. "I'm not going to sneak around. If someone wants to whack me, they can have at it. I have no reason to mistrust the Admiral. He could have done me in years ago."

Andrew looked at Adam. "I will be nearby, Director, monitoring the situation. And before you protest, I have already been instructed to keep a closer eye on you."

"Oh, alright. But I don't want you eavesdropping. I would like to have a private conversation with the Admiral."

"Of course, Director."

A little over an hour later, Heidi and Adam walked down the dock near the Admiral's Cabin. Berthed at the end of the structure was a large, well-maintained Hatteras Sports Fisherman. Boats like this were few and far between, many having been sunk by the Squids in the early days of the invasion when they distrusted anything that floated and carried humans.

The Admiral was clambering around the sea craft, whistling some unrecognizable tune. He waved when he noticed Adam and Heidi. "Come aboard, Director. Susanne, Sharon, take the good Petty Officer Faust up to the seaside bar for a cool drink." The two women he ordered about were his "Amazons"—his comely nearly six foot tall bodyguards that accompanied him everywhere. The two women smiled warmly at Adam, coming up to kiss him on the cheek before leading away a pensive Heidi.

Heidi kept glancing back as they left. "Please, Heidi, relax," Susanne, the large brunette said. "Sharon and I would never let anything happen to the Director. He is our special friend. And I know that the Admiral feels the same." For a moment, Heidi sized up the two physically fit women, wondering if she could take them in a fight.

"You said 'special friend?" Heidi asked.

"Why, yes," the blond, Sharon answered. "The Director and the Chief rescued us from being used for 'entertainment' on a yacht in the bay. They killed a whole bunch of assholes, and freed us. Adam introduced us to the Admiral, and we became his daughters, then his Bodyguards. We have always been taller and bigger than most women, and both were well trained in Jeet Kun Do. So, we all go back some five plus years."

"No one hurts the Director or the Admiral when we are around," Susanne added. "They are like a father and an uncle to us. I sense, Heidi, that you feel the same about Adam Lloyd, the Director."

"Yes, I do. He and the Chief also saved my ass. So, I guess we ladies have a lot in common."

The two Amazons chuckled. "Very true. Come, we'll have some virgin daiquiris as we…"

"…are on duty, Susanne," Heidi finished her sentence. "Yes, we have a lot in common."

The Admiral had an ice cold beer in hand for Adam. He motioned for him to grab a seat on his large boat.

"I have always been fascinated by how well you keep this Hatteras, Admiral. Boats to me were always a hole in the water into which you dump money."

"They can be, Director. They can be." The Admiral intently watched the three security women as they walked to the seaside bar. After they were almost to their destination, within sight but not listening distance of the two leaders, the man known only as the Admiral suddenly had a change of tone. "Well, Adam Lloyd, are we both going to be alive this time next week?"

Adam's mouth dropped open. The his eyes, face, and whole stance seemed to change. "You are used to seeing the helpful clown, the Admiral, whose elevator sometimes stops short of the top story. A few cards short of a full deck." He chuckled at Adam's confused look.

"How in the holy frack did you…?" Adam began.

"How did I fool you and almost everybody else? Easy, because everyone wanted to be fooled. They wanted a helpful, non-threatening father figure with a great sense of humor. Someone who wasn't fully a grown up, to put people at east, and help them forget the fact that some alien a-holes are still trying to eat us. If only for an evening."

He took a swig of his beer. "I used to be a Naval Intelligence Officer, Major Craig Berndt. I was still in the Reserves when the rocks hit. Everything fell apart quickly, with Squids all over Florida by the end of the first thirty days. I was a manager of a resort hotel farther up the Keys. I hunkered down there, and hid, melting into the background. I tried to help as many people as I could to not get harvested, or killed by their fellow humans."

The Admiral sighed. "I soon saw that a happy-go-lucky older crazy man, was the most non-threatening. His Lordship soon had control of everything here, and began attempts to communicate with us. He liked my crazy sense of humor, so he used as labor. At least he stopped the harvesting."

Adam understood why Lord Neptune would be drawn to someone who seemed unusual. He too was unusual in comparison to his fellow Squids. His Lordship had soon begun to use the Admiral as a local organizer when he needed something from the local humans.

The Admiral continued. "Then, you and the Chief showed up. Something clicked between you and His Lordship. So next thing I knew, you his Director. Which was fine with me. It took the heat off of me, and with it the stress of dealing with his kind every day." He emptied his beer, went and grabbed another two, tossing one to Adam.

"You actually turned out to be someone with some morals. You *want* to help people, even if you have to pick and choose who is helped and who is sacrificed. Hell, you saved a whole shitload of young girls and women who are now my 'daughters'. You can adapt to that type of survival decision making—choosing who dies so that others may live. This 'Protocol of Selective Survival'."

The Admiral chuckled. "If I had to make decisions like that almost every day, I would really be nuts, not just acting eccentric."

Adam took a long drink from his first beer, and immediately started on his second. "Why drop your cover now? How do you know that I won't tell the Tschaaa that you have been faking everyone out for all this time?”

“Well, Adam, because you have morals about throwing one more human unnecessarily to the Squids. Which is why Captain Bender is home safe and sound. And, you seem to actually like me.”

Adam chuckled and shook his head. “I should have known that it wasn’t an accident that the Conch Republic had the world’s best intelligence service. You probably do know what we are doing before we do.”

“So, Adam, I ask again. We will be alive next week?”

Adam paused for a moment. Hell, he might as well fill him in on the whole situation. He probably already knew about half of it anyway, if he knew about Torbin Bender.

“First, Admiral, I need a rusty nail. And now, an explanation. It’s like this...”

Heidi and the Amazons were still sipping non-alcoholic drinks almost an hour later. Even in their shorts and tennis shoes, Susanne and Sharon were near six feet tall. Heidi could see the long, steely muscles in their arms and legs. They were the kind of women Heidi wanted on her side, not someone else’s.

“So, ladies, if I can ask a possibly rude question. Is the Admiral always a bit... off?”

They both laughed. “He can be a bit eccentric,” Sharon said. “At the same time, he misses nothing. He runs the restaurant complex, acts both as the Mayor of Key West and Governor of the Conch Republic. All everybody knows of him is as the Admiral. I think he acts a little bit over the top to help keep people in a lighter frame of mind.”

“But, do not screw with one of his people, especially all of us he calls his daughters,” Susanne interjected. “He is extremely protective, which is why he respects Director Lloyd so much. Your Director has whacked quite a few people who tried to hurt, rape, and even eat women over the past five years. That is why so many of us love him. He is a special friend. He must really trust you to have you as his bodyguard.”

Heidi shrugged. “This kind of happened by accident. However, he and the Chief did save me from probably a short life. So, I am loyal to him.” She looked up, and saw Adam and the Admiral slowly returning from the Hatteras. "Well, ladies, it looks like they are finally done." She stood up and began moving toward the two men, Susan and Sharon following.

"Ladies!" The Admiral greeted them loudly. "I see you have all gotten along just swimmingly. No hair pulling, no face scratching. Good."

Then, as if saying something in confidence, he lowered his voice. "Although I have to admit a good old-fashioned catfight floats my boat..." He winked at Heidi.

"Admiral. Stop that." Susanne scolded him. The Admiral suddenly took on a sheepish look. "Sorry, there goes my mouth overloading my ass again." The two Amazons rolled their eyes, then each took an arm in tow.

"It was nice to meet you, Heidi," Susan said. "Stop by here anytime. We are usually floating around somewhere, and will always be back."

"Likewise. Someday, when duty doesn't call, I'll buy you a beer."

"What about me, the Admiral? Doesn't the lovely lady want to buy me a beer too?"

Heidi snapped to, and saluted him. "Of course, Admiral. Anytime we are both free."

"Well, young lady, I am not 'free'. I'm pretty damn expensive, being an Admiral and all..."

Sharon poked him in the ribs. "Time to head back to your suite, Admiral. You need your lunch."

The wild-haired and bearded man flashed a broad grin at Heidi and Adam. "See how well they take care of me? Now, Director, Petty Officer, I will take leave of you both. Please stop by again soon."

"Of course, Admiral. Enjoy your day. Heidi, time to head back."

"Yes, Boss."

They walked back to the staff car Adam had obtained from the motor pool. He climbed into the driver's seat, Heidi in the passenger.

"Boss, is he always like that?"

"Most of the time. But, sometimes, he can get a bit serious."

Adam sighed. Too bad he could not tell her about what he had just found out about the Admiral. He would tell the Chief, but no one else. The Admiral's charade was quite productive. No need to screw it up. Adam knew, after telling him what the Tschaaa Lord had told him, that the Admiral was on the same page. He may need the Admiral's help if he and his staff needed to make a hasty retreat.

"Come, Heidi, I'll buy you lunch. There is a great little Mexican hole in the wall not too far from here…."

CHAPTER 5

WAR DOG: The official current name given to the lineage of Sergeant Fuzz, a huge Great Dane and German Shepherd mix breed tweaked with Tschaaa genetic modifications. War Dogs have won the reconstituted American Kennel Club competition as Best Breed some twelve times. The Breed is officially kept under strict breeding restrictions as War Dogs are seen as an integral part of the Allied Defense Forces. Attempts at fraudulent breeding of War Dogs is a Federal Felony.

-Excerpt from The Combined Works of Princess Akiko, *Free Japan Royal Family. "The Great Compromise," Appendix 30, definitions and vocabulary.*

MALMSTROM ARMED FORCES BASE

Abigail Young was humming to herself as she walked across the Base toward her home, carrying her cloth grocery bag. It had been a very busy month since she had first arrived, but she would not have changed it for the world.

She smiled and continued humming another song she had heard on a soft hits radio station. She had caught herself not only humming about two weeks ago, but realized she was also doing it with a smile on her face. This was not something she had done in Deseret. Maybe it was because she had a home.

The two bedroom duplex section was the first really personal "home" she had lived in the last six years, since fleeing the Hanford explosion. Her thoughts returned to the first twenty-four hours she was at Malmstrom. The key General Reed had provided to her worked just fine. Inside was a living room with a sofa and recliner, a small dining table in the dining area next to the fully equipped kitchen, two decent sized bedrooms—with a bed in one and a papasan chair in the other. She had the Lieutenant place her personal items in the bedroom with the bed. She then escorted him back out to the front door.

"Lieutenant Baker, I am in your debt for all your help, especially ensuring that my dear friend Captain Bender is returned to his wife in one piece." She stuck her hand out for a handshake.

It took a moment for Lt. Baker to take it. "Ma'am, I was just doing my job, but... I was wondering..." He began to stammer. Finally, he took a deep breath to collect himself. "Captain Young, if I came calling here, to see you... I hope it would not be too forward."

Abigail was suddenly in unfamiliar territory. She had been too busy and too focused in Deseret to entertain any type of personal relationship with a male, not to mention the possible stigma she carried because of radiation exposure from Hanford. Now, this very nice young man was trying to establish some type of possible "dating" relationship. She blushed.

"Lieutenant Baker --Todd, I... really appreciate all that you have done. You are a fine officer. But, I am in extremely new territory, and I need some time to get settled. And to be quite honest, I have been too busy to have what you may consider a normal personal life. Could I possibly ask that you... that *we* postpone any... 'calling' activity?" She gently removed her hand from his.

He paused for a minute, then gave a small smile. "I understand, Captain. I will check back with you in a month or so. Until then, if you need any help, please feel free to contact me. If I cannot help, I may be able to find someone who can."

He was so nice and so earnest. She almost felt guilty that she attracted him as much as she did. She tried to smile back, but actually felt quite bad about the situation.

"Thank you, Todd. Have a nice night."

Before she could say anything, he saluted her. She saluted back.

"You have a nice night also... Abigail." He turned and headed back to the Humvee.

Abigail shut the door, and released the breath she had been holding. She needed rest, but old habits die hard. She did a quick, cursory cleaning of her weapons on the dining area table, making sure they were functional and loaded. She checked the refrigerator and saw that it had already been stocked with some basic staples—milk, eggs, bacon, homemade sliced bread, butter, jam, cheese, a little fruit, and some small wrapped packets of meats. There was also a six pack of beer, a large pitcher of lemonade, bottle of orange juice, and a couple of small bottles of water. She took one of the bottles of water and retreated to the bedroom with the bed, now hers.

The bed looked new, as did the bed covers and sheets. She entered the bathroom and quickly washed up. She knew she badly needed a full shower, but was too tired to take one. She striped down to her skivvies, hung up her fatigues, then removed the clothes from her garment bag. Her dress blues, with both skirt and pants, and a summer dress the Prophet/President's wife had magically provided in her room before she left Deseret. She managed to put her spare underwear away in the dresser drawers, then collapsed on the bed, immediately falling asleep.

Abigail awoke just after 9:00am, temporarily confused until she remembered where she was. Immediately, panic set in as she feared she was late for something. She rarely, if ever, slept this late. Then, she remembered what the General had said about time off. She finally relaxed. She began to listen to the early morning sounds of the neighborhood and liked what she heard. There was an occasional vehicle, birds, a dog barking in the distance. No Jodie calls, no yelling, no marching. It was peaceful.

She stretched, then slowly rose from bed, making her way to the bathroom. She noticed her mouth tasted bad, so she found her toothbrush and quickly brushed her teeth. Padding barefoot out to the kitchen, Abigail regaled in the ability to walk around in just her underwear. Suddenly, she was famished. While her cooking skills were limited, her Uncle Buck had taught her how to make some mean wrecked eggs. She found a couple of skillets in the cupboard, some utensils, and quickly scrambled the eggs. She added chunks of bacon, some cheese, some small pieces of sausage. A little pepper, hot sauce she found, a dash of paprika, and... voila! A perfect breakfast.

Toasted bread and butter was a bonus, to which she added a glass of milk. She sat down, ready to christen her table. She bowed her head in prayer.

"Thank you, Lord, for this bounty I am about to receive. I am truly blessed. Please help me keep my friends and fellow soldiers safe from harm. May you bless the Church and the Prophet. Thank you. Amen." She had no rote memorized prayer she said each time. Everything she said was directly from the heart.

She almost inhaled her breakfast. Maybe the fact she had made it herself, in an honest-to-god kitchen, that added to her enjoyment. When she was finished, she actually let loose with an unladylike belch, and began to laugh. This was her home. She could do pretty much what she wanted, within reason, and without offending someone. It felt amazing.

Abigail cleaned up, washed the dishes and pans, and put everything away. Then she headed for a shower. The main bathroom had a combination tub and shower. And—wonder of wonders—brand new towels, soap, and shampoo. She began to realize the effort the General and his staff had put into this at such short notice. She felt a little choked up at the idea of the kindness of strangers.

Next, she decided to clean up herself. The hot shower was heavenly. She unbraided her hair and washed it, realizing how much it had grown. She stayed in, washing and soaping everything twice before she noticed the hot water was finally running out. She stepped out, and examined herself in the full length mirror on the back of the bathroom door.

There was no doubt about it. She was no longer a girl, but definitely a woman. Her whole body was firm, tight, with long steely muscles under her feminine curves. Now she suddenly realized what men were looking at. They saw this warrior with the body of a desirable princess—more of a warrior princess, to be exact. This combination was exotic to many men.

For the first time, she also noticed a gift wrapped package on a shelf above the commode. She picked it up, frowning a little. Then she saw the envelope with her name on it. Inside was a small hand written card.

"Welcome, young lady. In this package are a few things a woman often needs. I have heard you have beautiful long blonde hair. Please use the contents herein to keep it nice and healthy. I am looking forward to meeting you, Official Representative of Deseret. Please take your time and get settled in. I will be in touch."

It was signed Madam President, Sandra Paul, USA.

She opened the package. Aside from a small hair dryer, there was an ornate mirror, brush and comb set, with a couple of matching barrettes. All looked to be set in gold, antiques that had been handed down from previous generations. She read a set of gold inlay cursive initials, her eyes welling up with tears of recognition. The initials matched what she knew to be Madam President's maiden name. She began to cry. Strangers in this strange land were treating her like family, like they had known her for years. She couldn't help but feel a bit that she did not deserve this.

As she cried, she said a silent prayer. "My Lord Jesus Christ. Please make me worthy of this kind, Christian treatment from strangers."

She was finally able to regain control her of emotions. She blew her nose, wiped her eyes, washed her face again. Then she dried her hair, and used the brush and comb to work out any snarls. When she was done, her long blonde hair shone like it hadn't in quite some time. She smiled. She went to her bedroom dresser and found a special place for the set. Later, she would buy an everyday set of hair care items. These provided by Madam President were for special occasions.

She put on clean panties and a sports bra, the combination she always wore. The Prophet had said sanctified undergarments were no longer needed in the Mormon religion, instead asserting that it what was in your heart and soul, not what you wore, that was paramount. Next, she put on her well-worn sweatpants and top. She had no idea how many miles she had run in them, but was planning on many more.

As she exited her bedroom, there was a knock on the front door. Force of habit made her pick up the switchblade she had taken from the Kraken. She walked to the door, stopped.

"Who is it?"

"Aleks and friends, Abigail. What the Yankees here call a welcome wagon."

A bit surprised, she opened the door. She saw Aleks, bookended by two attractive women—a blonde and a redhead. They were the same size and body type as Aleks. Side by side, the three women looked like a Russian sports or Olympic team, with matching sweat suits and athletic bodies.

"Please let me introduce Afanasiy—called Fanny around here—and Inna. They are my fellow soldiers. We came here together as part of the original mission from Free Russia. The good General has *ordered* us to take the day off from our regular duties in order to help you get settled. May we come in?"

"*Oh*. Of course." Abigail blushed again. "I apologize. I am used to a barracks, with just enough room to swing a cat, as my uncle used to say. I'm still not used to having a...place of my own and visitors."

"No worry, little sister," Inna piped up in Russian. "You are family. Family cannot be rude to family."

"Little sister?" Abigail answered in Russian.

"Why yes, Abigail." Now it was Fanny's turn to elaborate. "Aleks told us about you. She said that you speak Russian like a native, so you must have Russian in you. You are also a good friend of Torbin, who we have previously adopted. So, we took a vote and adopted you. The one warning is that people around here call us the three sisters, a nice way of calling us the three bitches to our faces, as we take shit from no one. So, you may have to put up with some crap caused by us. Just call us if it gets too deep."

Abigail was a bit flustered at first, but she managed to collect her thoughts. "Ladies, I am honored. But I do not want to start under false pretenses. I'm not Russian. I am Romanian and Norwegian. I learned Russian and other languages because my mother was an interpreter first for Romania, then the United States. But, I am not Russian. Sorry for the confusion."

The three Russian officers looked at one another. Aleks shrugged. "Close enough. I am half Ukrainian, but Fanny and Inna accept me as a sister. So, welcome to the group." One at a time, all three women kissed her cheeks, then hugged her, smiling. They all giggled.

"As you can tell, we sometimes act like schoolgirls," Aleks explained. " It helps to keep us young, and to deal with all of the problems we face each day.”

Inna looked at the switchblade still in Abigail's right hand. She smirked a bit. “I think our little sister already knows how to handle problems. You will fit in just fine, Abigail.”

“*Oh. I'm sorry. I forgot it was even in my hand.*” Abigail started to put it down.

“May I?” Fanny held out her hand. Abigail handed the knife to her. Fanny hit the release and watched the blade spring open. She checked the steel edge. “Not bad. Decent steel. Spring opens well. Where did you get it?”

Abigail paused, before she responded. “I took it off a Kraken beast, a gang member. He tried to hurt Torbin and me.”

All three Russian women gave knowing nods, and Aleks spoke. “My husband has a tendency to attract trouble. Again, I thank you for pulling his proverbial chestnuts out of the fire.”

“He has helped me as well. I owe him Aleks. He has been an irreplaceable friend.”

“As he is to us, little sister,” Inna replied.

Aleks clapped her hands. “Now, to business. Show us your home, please. We will help you decorate as only three opinionated women can.”

Abigail was a little stiff as she awkwardly prepared to show her new home. This kind of socialization was completely new and foreign to her. She had never really spent spare time with other women, or men for that matter. It had always been eat, sleep, work, train, repeat—sometimes with the work involving violence.

They first went into her bedroom. “Well, at least the General provided you with a decent double bed.” Aleks sat and bounced on it, checking the springs. “This will not hurt your back. Or, a lover's back either.” The three Russians laughed.

Abigail blushed bright red. “I…” She could not get out a coherent thought.

“Look what you have done, Aleks.” Fanny scolded her. “You have embarrassed her. Please, disregard Aleks. She can be rude, crude, and socially unacceptable. She is even warping our friend Torbin…”

As they began to kvetch in Russian, Abigail began to shake. She plopped butt first on the floor, the carpet providing some cushion.

“Little sister, are you alright?” Abigail could only sit and shake.

"You goddamned fool. Do you not recognize combat stress when you see it?" Inna snapped at Aleks. Next thing, she was sitting next to Abigail, hugging her. Abigail began to bawl.

The three women huddled around her, letting her cry. Finally, five minutes later, she finally stopped. "I am so sorry. I'm acting like a big baby." Abigail tried to wipe her nose and eyes with the sleeves of her sweat top. Aleks kissed her cheek.

"You have not really had time to yourself, have you? Or time to *be* yourself, either alone or with friends, have you, little sister? Or to talk about the things you have seen, and done?"

Abigail swallowed. "I guess not. The last week or so, everything seems to be…bubbling up. I am losing control, and turning into a basket case. Worthless."

"Now look here, Abigail Young. No friend of my husband, Torbin, is *ever* worthless. My God! He told me how you saved him. None of us could have done what you did."

She took Abigail's face in her hands. "Abigail, when I told you that I owe you, I meant I can never *ever* pay you back. You saved my husband, the father of my unborn children. I, *we*, are here to help you—not because the General ordered us—but because we want to. You are not going through anything that the three of us have not experienced."

Abigail sniffed. "Really?"

"Yes, really."

Inna, still hugging her, explained, "All of us have had to… depressurize. We were trained as spies, and to be assassins too if necessary. Which has been necessary—many times. Since we met each other, we have helped to keep each other sane. I have no family left. The Squids took them. Aleks has a cousin or two. Fanny's mother is still alive. So, here and now, *we* are family.

Fanny then interjected. "There was a study in the first part of the twenty-first century, comparing how men and women could handle stress involving violence. They showed men and women pictures, films of acts of violence, and the results of violence. Women, especially when the pictures involved children, have a large amount of difficulty in dealing with, processing the violence then moving on. The psychologists and sociologists who did the study surmised they internalized it, and personalized it, because of their ability to reproduce. They held onto the pain and angst the representations of violence created. Men were able to de-personalize it easier. However, violence eventually gets to everyone, unless you are a sociopath. You are no sociopath. None of us are, contrary to what some people might think. Therefore, we have cases of combat stress, and post-traumatic stress syndrome."

Fanny continued. "Plus, with the threaten everyone faces of being eaten, the cases will increase unless we find a way to deal with it. We deal with it by being family, supporting each other, getting shitfaced, physically working out, and talking it out. You, Abigail, can do the same. And, if necessary, there are professional counselors available through the military hospital."

Abigail let out a deep sigh. She realized that having the three women around her gave her a feeling of security she had not felt for a long time.

Inna turned to Aleks. "She told you that you are to have twins?"

"Yes, she did."

Abigail shivered a bit. "I now must ask….did your husband tell you what…he found out about what the Evil Ones are trying to do…to women?"

"Yes, he did. I will get a check-up as soon as our local medical officials and scientists get a good handle on what to look for. If I have been… affected, it will be in the early stages. I come from very strong stock. No Squid is going to screw with my twins."

The women began to giggle. Then to laugh. Finally, they began to babble a bit in Russian, helping to de-stress. They had Abigail touch Aleks' stomach again, and again she sensed the lives developing. Suddenly, she was calm.

She kissed each woman on the cheek in turn.

"Thank you. I have made more new friends in the past week than I have since the Evil Ones came. I am close to the Twenty, but that is because we lived and trained together. So please pardon me if I become overwhelmed with… normal friendship."

"Well, little sister. We are about to do something that women friends used to do a lot before those slimy Squids showed up. We are about to go shopping."

"I have some money in my dresser…"

"No, no. I will pay." Aleks commanded.

Fanny stood up and opened Abigail's underwear drawer. She shook her head, and clucked her tongue disapprovingly. "Sports bras and Grandma panties are good for field maneuvers, not social maneuvers. Our friend Torbin picked some nice panties and such out at the BX a while ago. There are also other places we can go." Abigail stuttered a bit. "Torbin…p-p-picking out…women's underwear?"

"Why yes. My husband has many unusual skills. Of course, I made him retire that one."

"Much to our displeasure," Inna cracked.

Aleks huffed, "I will share many things with my sisters, but *not* my husband."

"Well, then," Inna shot back. "You are just going to help your sisters, including Abigail, to find men as good as Torbin."

This elicited a laugh from them all, even Abigail.

She turned toward Aleks.

"I must tell you that Torbin said you would help me with…lady things. To be honest, I guess you would say I am very inexperienced in being a woman among other people. A warrior, I know backwards and forwards; being a lady—I know very little."

Aleks took Abigail's hands and felt them, squeezed them, then her arms.

"My God, you are strong. Well, the first rule of being a lady, especially around men, is that you have to be a bit dainty. Contrary to what men say, we can hurt them all too easily. Then they cry and carry on like big babies."

Abigail laughed. In a blink, she was totally relaxed.

"Look at this beautiful uniform," Fanny exclaimed, still snooping. "It looks like Torbin's."

"Yes. My Prophet and President was a former Marine and modeled our uniforms after theirs."

"Well, little sister, we will flesh out your wardrobe. Then, you will be able to wrap men around you little finger without a uniform."

Inna looked at Abigail. "I think, sister Fanny, that Abigail has sufficient equipment already to wrap men up." Abigail laughed, but still blushed a bit.

They prepared to leave. Abigail made sure she had her house key and I.D.

"Here." Inna handed her back the switchblade. "It can come in handy if we run into a rude clerk."

They were still laughing as they left.

Four hours later, they were back, all carrying packages. Abigail felt almost punch drunk. She had never been "shopping" like this before. At all the stores they went to, all the sisters kept grabbing clothes items, holding them up in front of Abigail, passing judgment on the piece of clothing as it pertained to suitability for wear.

Aleks had held something very sheer and revealing in front of her. "Hm. This will be perfect."

Abigail then realized it was a set of very sheer dark negligée—bikini panties, top that reached down to thigh level, matching garter belt and nylons. The Avenging Angel's eyes nearly bugged out, and her mouth dropped open.

"No. Please. I cannot wear that. It is indecent."

Aleks stopped. She looked at Abigail for a moment, then spoke in a low tone.

"Little sister, I know you are a virgin. No, do not blush. You are lucky that you have had the time to be extremely selective as to who you wish to... give yourself to."

"This, is for that someone special." Aleks held up the ensemble. " Every woman needs something like this. Someday, you will meet that special man who will be that one. He will be the love of your life."

She sighed. "As the Amerikanskis say, I had to kiss a bunch of toads before I found my Prince Torbin. In my line of work, I had to sleep with some toads for my country. But when I found him, it was like all the rest—the past—did not exist. And that is why, Abigail, I owe you for saving him. I would die without him." A small tear began to form in her left eye, which she quickly wiped away.

Abigail looked at the negligée. It was... very pretty, but she still had to take a deep breath to center herself again. "I will bend to your opinions. I just have no experience in... sex, in creating sexual desire in men when I want to."

Aleks smiled. "My dear, down deep, *all* women know how to create desire in men. We just do not always admit to it. But, I will work with you as you wish, seeing as my husband promised that I would show you all the knowledge of feminine wiles he claims I have."

The sisters finally found what they wanted for Abigail. They then brought her to a hole in the wall diner that Abigail discovered was run by an expatriate Russian. Abigail was treated to a series of small dishes and foods which were a definite step above chow hall food, even the Doc's.

She turned down the vodka, though.

The four women arrived at Abigail's home, and made her sit while they unpacked the purchases and found places in her bedroom for them. Aleks hung a sign which read 'welcome' in Russian on the front door, and placed a bouquet of flowers on the main table.

"Come, little sister," Inna called. "See where we have placed all you clothes."

Abigail walked into her bedroom. Everything was expertly placed in the closet and in her chest of drawers. A nice business pants suit hung next to her Dress Blues. In the closet was also a basic black dress that every women needed in her repertoire. Several pairs of colored bikini panties shared the dresser with her basic granny panties. She even had a few pairs of panty hose and thigh high nylons. Of course, she had a few pairs of military xtyle socks, as well as sweat socks. They threw in a couple pairs of slacks, blue-jeans, some skirts, blouses, a formal dress, and another summer dress to keep the one the Prophet's wife had given her company, and now both the closet and dresser were full.

Inna and Fanny had looks of satisfaction on their faces.

"Later on, we will help you get some knickknacks and other items to gather dust. Every home needs them." Aleks told her.

Abigail went to woman one in turn, hugging them.

"I can never repay you all. This is like... Christmas and birthdays all rolled into one."

Inna snorted. "You are family. If you try to pay me back, I'll be very mad and hit you. And I hit hard."

They laughed. Moments later, the women began to leave, to give Abigail a chance to rest. "Remember, the General told you to take the next few days off," Aleks reminded her. "I will be back working tomorrow, but since I and Torbin live next door, just pound on the wall if you need something. I will send Torbin running to answer." Abigail hugged Aleks again, then they left. Abigail collapsed on her sofa.

That was about a month ago. Abigail, back in the present, kept walking, humming. The memory of those first days would always be a special for her, but her thoughts now turned to more serious memories.

Some nine days after the nuke strike against the Tschaaa Lord, the Squid had broadcast a message over the airwaves and internet to everyone who would listen. It had been the first time Abigail remembered seeing an enemy on television. After apologizing for his Tschaaa killing some of their quisling human allies, he admitted to having tried to "improve" the human species through genetic and organic modifications. Then, as if those announcements weren't enough, he also had one additional message.

"To the families of those who died or were injured during the attack on me and Director Lloyd—I will ensure that survivors will be well taken care of, using our superior Tschaaa medicine to repair their bodies. And to those females who were affected by my attempt to improve your species' health, fecundity and development—I will ensure that their health and the health of their offspring will be closely monitored."

The Tschaaa Lord then manipulated his social tentacles to communicate 'stern warning. "But be warned, we Tschaaa are in the superior position in the food chain. As the apex predator, we have the ultimate authority. You humans who work with us to improve your species' standing, work to be a productive client of the Tschaaa, you will be amply rewarded. We have already—with Director Lloyd's excellent help—brought your living standards back to close to what they were prior to our arrival.

"Those who resist and who attack us, like the Rebels and Ferals did, will be harshly dealt with. We are already beginning to harvest extra cattle who are beginning to resist us in Cattle Country. We will soon respond to the violence brought to our young with violence in kind to the Unoccupied States. Now is the last chance for the Madam President and her people to accept our control.

"There is a human saying from your twentieth century: 'You can be either part of the solution, or part of the problem.' Those who accept our direction and guidance will be part of the solution. Those who do not... will be dead and harvested. I will leave you with these thoughts. Have a pleasant day."

That had sped up developments in the Free Human sphere. Madam President had immediately broadcast a response, acknowledging all of the newscasts emanating from Deseret. For the first time she also gave the official story on the rumors of genetic and physical modifications of humans—primarily females—that the Tschaaa were attempting by secret insertions into the population. It was arranged that all women and girls would report to the nearest medical facility to determine if this "infection" had affected them. The President had also instituted an official draft for war service of all residents of the Unoccupied States, ages eighteen to fifty, and asked all of the local militias that had been formed to contact the War Department for coordination of resources. (War, not Defense. One should call it as it is.)

"I do not want to send our people off to war, but the Invasion and Infestation brought war to us. Our Congress will remain fully functional, as will our civilian rule of law. It may seem at times that the military has assumed martial law, but that is not the truth of the matter. To insure that is the case, again with the approval of the other elected representatives and our judiciary, I have reconstituted a Federal civilian law enforcement agency in the forms of a Marshalls Service and a Customs Service. The Marshalls will be the law enforcement agency responsible for the enforcement of laws and the investigation of crimes within the boundaries of the Unoccupied States of America. The Customs Service will set exit and entry controls, and enforce all laws and investigate all crimes involving the movement of people, goods, and services across the borders of the Unoccupied States. They will also coordinate law enforcement functions and investigations with foreign governments. Both of these entities date back to our original constitution of 1789."

She motioned to someone off screen. "I would like to introduce Paul Miller, the Commissioner of the Federal civilian law enforcement agency. Prior to the first rock strike, he had many years of experience in law enforcement and will be organizing this new endeavor. We are asking that anyone with law enforcement experience to please come forward, as well as any current sheriff, police, and vigilance committees to please contact him for coordination of resources. Law enforcement service will count the same as military service when it comes to the official draft."

Then, her "she bear" side emerged. "I will cut this short now, ending with this. We humans do *not* accept an inferior position to *anyone*. We are *not* cattle!" She slammed her fist on the podium from which she was speaking, sending her notes flying. "We and our other Free Friends will fight. We will fight to free all the People of Color being used as Cattle. No matter what the color of our skin, we are *all* humans!" She slammed the podium again. She glared at the television cameras. "To all of you Squids out there. As my Japanese friends like to say, 'Prepare to be sushi!'"

The last statement, and variations of it, soon created a cottage industry of placards, flags, banners, signs, stickers, patches, caps and t-shirts. A slang term for a military member became "sushi chef". Torbin's disabled vet friend Mike at the BX mall became moderately wealthy, having one of the few remaining t-shirt shops around.

Soon thereafter, General Reed told Abigail what he would like her to do. "Since you can speak more languages than I can shake a stick at, and have excellent training skills, I would like you to help in training new officers and soldiers, as well coordinating and interpreting for the influx of foreigners we are about to experience. Russians, a hand full of Romanians, a couple Germans, maybe some Finns. Of course Japanese, which I understand you are also picking up quite nicely. Sound good?"

"Yes Sir."

"Good. You start tomorrow."

All of the events she had just remembered ended one month ago. Abigail had been working ever since, with little else to do or think about.

So wrapped up she was in her review of recent memories as she walked, she almost did not notice the loud bark, cry of pain from a human throat, then the sound of loud cursing.

Abigail liked to walk this way because it was near the canine kennels, where the military working dogs were kept. She liked to see the dogs at exercise, to hear them bark. She planned on stopping in one day, to offer her services once she saw a way of not seeming too pushy. That thought was about to go by the wayside.

There was a loud crack as something broke thru a wooden gate near the edge of the canine runs. She turned toward the commotion and saw Him for the first time.

At first glance, he looked like a very large—nay, giant—german shepherd. Then Abigail noticed his muzzle was a tad bit shorter, and his ears flopped over at the tips, rather than stand up pointed like a shepherd. But he was huge.

The dog came bursting out into freedom, running and bounding almost like a large deer. Yards behind in pursuit were three people in uniform. One that looked like he had Senior NCO Stripes on his uniform yelled at her. "Lady, *freeze!*"

But the large dog had already seen her, and made a direct beeline for her.

"Harry, get the gun," the Senior NCO yelled.

Abigail then did what came naturally. She put her full grocery bag down, and sat down cross-legged.

The NCO thought he was about to see a murder by dog.

The huge animal went straight for her, mouth open as if to bite. Abigail gave a short whistle, then looked down at the ground. The canine slewed a bit to the side instead of hitting Abigail straight on. The dog saw long blonde hair in a ponytail, smelled a young female, and seemed to remember someone in his past. Then, he was circling Abigail, decelerating.

"Hey, fella. You're a big one. What's your name?" Abigail said in a normal tone of voice.

The giant beast kept circling her, first growling a bit, then slowing and snuffling in her direction. He reduced the size of the circles until he stopped still behind her.

Abigail let the dog sniff her hair, her head, and the side of her face.

"Hey, big fella, can I sniff you? Or how about a little scratch? Like on your chest and tummy?"

The dog came around directly in front of her. Keeping her eyes averted, she slowly reached her right hand up. She began to scratch his chest, very light at first. Then a little harder.

The dog began to grunt and groan in satisfaction. He put the paw of friendship on her arm as she scratched him.

"Well, I'll be goddamned." At the sound of the male voice, the canine whipped around, placing himself between Abigail and the Senior NCO. He snarled loud, showing a very impressive set of teeth.

"Sergeant, it's okay. I've got him," Abigail said quietly. She gently began to scratch the dog's ears. He stopped growling as Abigail spoke to him in soothing tones.

"Feels good, doesn't it, big fella. What's your name?"

A female voice responded, "Fuzz. His name is Fuzz."

Abigail chuckled. "Well Mister Fuzz, glad to meet you." At that, the big dog laid down and rolled over so Abigail could scratch his stomach.

A young woman in combat fatigues and E-5 Strips slowly walked up. Abigail noticed the name *Martinez* on her name tag. She was a short and stocky, fairly dark-skinned Hispanic, a lucky one who got away from the harvesters. She moved closer. Fuzz glanced at her, then ignored her, concentrating on the stomach scratch and rub he was receiving. He let out a small satisfied groan.

"You are Captain Young, from Deseret."

"Yes, Sergeant Martinez. Pleased to meet you. I'd shake your hand but as you can see, I'm a bit busy."

"Fuzz will at least tolerate women. He seems to hate men. I have been working with him since someone dumped him about a month ago, as he seemed to have received some prior training."

She then looked a little incredulous. "But what he is doing right now is….incredible."

Abigail grinned. "I had an Uncle who used to train dogs for hunting and protection. I spent some summers with him, so I picked up a little about dogs from him." She began to scratch Fuzz's chest again. "And, dogs just seem to… like me."

Abigail noticed the Chief Master Sergeant, former Air Force by the rank emblem on his uniform, was standing back with an incredulous look on his face. His name tag read Croft.

"I'm not trying to ignore you, Chief. It's just that if I keep scratching his chest and stomach, Fuzz here seems to stay calm."

"That's okay, Captain. I know he hates me, so I have Sergeant Thomas coming with a tranquilizer dart…"

Abigail looked at him. "Why? I have him calm now."

"Ma'am, he just bit one of my men for about the sixth time. We've been trying to get him settled and trying to start training him as a K-9 Patrol Dog. He seems to have had a lot of training already. Whoever dumped him by the back gate left a note telling us they were donating him and his training for the cause. He had been doped up when he was dumped, so we did not realize he had a problem with men. Like Sergeant Martinez said, he deigns to work with her when he feels like it, but goes ballistic when someone else tries to work him."

Abigail looked at Fuzz, whose eyes met hers. Maybe she was imagining it, but it was almost like he was seeing someone else, remembering someone important to him when he looked at her. Whatever ever the reason, Fuzz had quickly latched on to her.

"What's the game plan after you tranquilize him, Chief?"

Chief Croft looked at Fuzz. "We'll probably have to put him down. He is just too dangerous to let him loose."

Fuzz looked at the Chief, and a slow rumble began in his chest.

"Hey, relax Fuzz. Let me handle this." The Chief was a good six feet tall, but when Abigail rose slowly, with a steely look on her face, he actually took a step back. "No one dies today, Chief."

"Captain, all due respect, but you are not in my chain of command. I'm the kennel master and I decide what to do with my dogs when they become a danger to others."

Abigail did not waiver. "No one dies today. I'm taking him."

"You can't do that. I can't let you do that. If he hurt someone, it would be my ass."

Fuzz quickly stood.

"Down, big fella," Abigail ordered. Fuzz sat. She never took her eyes off Chief Croft.

Sgt. Martinez realized that Abigail Young was not going to back down. She saw a look in her eye that sent a shiver down her spine. Chief Croft was a good kennel master, but he did not have a killer's instinct. The young lady standing in front of her did, especially when defending someone or something she believed in. Today, Fuzz was that "someone".

"Chief. Captain Young is a Diplomat. Deseret's official representative." Sgt. Martinez was thinking as quickly on her feet as possible, trying to diffuse the situation before the Chief suffered the consequences, and a messy incident between governments occurred.

"So?" the Chief shot back. Fuzz was beginning to eye him like a hunk of beef.

"So, if she takes responsibility, I think she has some type of qualified immunity, or special dispensation, or... hell, I don't know! I just know that if she takes the dog I don't think General Reed or anyone else will hold you accountable. Besides, it gets the problem out of your hands. It also saves you having to bug the vet, doing a bunch of paperwork... You know, just another pain in the ass to deal with."

Maybe Chief Croft saw a way to save face and get rid of a big problem, or maybe he was really listening to Sgt. Martinez. Whatever the reason, he responded, and addressed Abigail. "You'll tell General Reed you took full responsibility for this dog? Since we didn't procure him under normal circumstances, we're not out any money except a few vet expenses and food. I know that I won't be faulted if he disappears. But he cannot be allowed to run loose."

"Don't worry, Chief. I'll make sure that any necessary notifications are made. And, no, Fuzz will not be running loose. When he goes with me, he's family. You have my word he will not be dumped again."

Chief Croft looked at Fuzz, who looked back with a gaze that said "What's next?"

"Okay, Captain. Contrary to what you may think, I do *not* like to put dogs down.   But I also cannot have the equivalent of a one hundred fifty pound 'land shark' running around, biting my people. I hope you know what you're getting yourself into."

Abigail relaxed a bit, then smiled. "Chief, after dealing with Eaters and Ferals, Fuzz will be easy."

Chief Croft grunted. "I hope so. I'll have Sgt. Martinez bring you his limited file, including his vet records. He has been kind of 'off the grid' because he was a drop off. He's such a big, healthy-looking dog, I believed we could use him. Apparently I was wrong."

Abigail looked at Fuzz, who actually wagged his tail. "I think he has potential. We'll get along just fine."

"Alright, Captain. You have a nice day." He turned and headed back toward the kennels. Sgt. Martinez started to follow him.

"Sergeant, one moment, please."

"Ma'am?"

Abigail stepped up to her and offered her hand. "You just did us—Fuzz and me—a big favor by helping defuse that situation. Sometimes I kind of get tunnel vision, especially if I think I may have to take some action."

Sgt. Martinez shook her hand. She knew that this young lady

would have not stood quietly and let the Chief euthanize Fuzz. Which probably meant the Chief would have been in the hospital and she would have been in confinement. But, she also seemed to have heart of gold when it came to canines. So, an expert in controlled violence Abigail might be, but a sociopath she was not.

"I didn't want to see Fuzz put down either, Ma'am. He has too big a heart to go like that. If you wait here, I'll bring his stuff to you."

Sgt. Martinez headed toward the kennels. Abigail looked at Fuzz. "Whaddya say, big fella? Do you want to go home with me?"

Fuzz thumped his tail once, then gave a small, low "woof".

"I'll take that as a yes. Are you hungry?"

Abigail began rummaging around the cloth grocery bag she was carrying. She quickly noticed that the quart of ice cream she had bought was beginning to get quite squishy. Although fall was setting in, it was still warm enough to melt ice cream, apparently. She pulled it out of the bag, noticing liquid drips of ice cream forming on the bottom of the carton. She looked at Fuzz.

"This isn't exactly dog food, but I hate to see it go to waste. Want to share?"

Fuzz's nose began to work as he realized the small container Abigail was holding just might have food. Abigail opened the quart of ice cream, scooped a small amount out with her fingers and stuffed it in her mouth.

"Mm. I have a weakness for peppermint. Want some?"

She held the carton down and Fuzz suddenly stuck his large tongue completely into the container. The cold did not seem to mind him as he proceeded to generally inhale the entire contents.

"So much for sharing. Just remember who's the boss, you big lug."

Fuzz dismantled the container and licked up every bit of ice cream. He was finishing licking everything for the second time when Sgt. Martinez returned. She broke into a large grin when she saw what Fuzz was eating.

"Begging your pardon Ma'am, but I thought I had you pegged right as a soft touch."

Abigail chuckled. "Guilty as charged, Sergeant." She noticed that in addition to a leash and a folder containing Fuzz's records, Sgt. Martinez had a large clear plastic storage bag full of dog food, a large food dish, and a blanket.

Abigail smiled at Sgt. Martinez. "Who's the soft touch now?" "I feel a bit guilty that I wasn't able to work with Fuzz, and get him into our system. I guess I just wasn't good enough of a handler. I'm glad you came along, Captain."

Abigail asked, "May I ask your first name, Sergeant?"

"Guadalupe, after the saint, Ma'am."

"I have been told by some new friends of mine that I am way too rough on myself. May I suggest, Guadalupe, that you and I are a lot alike. All we can do is our best. Sometimes our best is sufficient, sometimes it is not. That's where friends come in. They can make the difference. Please consider yourself a friend of Fuzz and I."

"Thank you, Ma'am. I appreciate that." Sgt. Martinez knelt down by Fuzz.

"Can I hug you one last time Fuzz?" The huge dog answered with an equally huge slurp to the face.

Both women burst out laughing. "Ew. Dog slime." Guadalupe protested, then gave Fuzz a big hug anyway. "If you ever need a dog sitter, Captain, please give me a call."

She stood, then glanced at the kennels. "Duty calls. It was a pleasure to meet you, Captain Young." She saluted, then turned around and headed for the kennels.

Abigail scratched Fuzz's ear. "You have a way with women, Fuzz. Just remember who you live with and check with me before a bunch of strange females start showing up in the backyard."

She did a load adjustment, tossing the demolished carton in the trash. She attached Fuzz's leash, threw the blanket over her shoulder and put the food and dish in her grocery bag. "As my father used to say, we're off to see the wizard."

She told Fuzz to heel, which he did at first. But his long, fast stride caused him to move forward as they walked. Abigail noticed Fuzz seemed to want to lead, search in front of her, as if looking for possible dangers. Finally, she decided to try something. First, she halted Fuzz. Then, she laid the leash across the great dog's shoulders, looping it under his collar. He looked at as if to say, "What's up, boss?"

Abigail gave the command, "Scout, Fuzz," in Romanian. He immediately began to walk ahead of her, zagging back and forth a bit, looking and smelling for possible threats while keeping track of

Abigail's location. Abigail's mouth dropped open a bit in surprise. Her Uncle used to train K-9s in Romanian as it was not a well known language outside of that country. He also prefer to train his dogs in the 'scout' function, off-leash. He used his dogs aggressively, teaching them a certain level of independent decision-making and action under certain circumstances. He had also instructed a few K-9 trainers in his techniques. Did one of them survive in this area of Montana, training this large dog in Uncle Buck's technique? Or had her Uncle somehow trained Fuzz over the last year or so?

She stopped, calling Fuzz back to her. Abigail looked in the folder Sgt. Martinez had given her. As far as they could tell, Fuzz was a shepherd and great dane mix, about two years old, and in excellent shape. He had been well taken care of before being dumped on the kennel's doorstep. Fuzz was around one hundred fifty pounds. His muzzle resembled a slightly shorter shepherd type, but his ears were a combination of the two breeds, the end flopping over a bit rather than having the wolf-like pointed appearance. All in all, Fuzz was a fine specimen. Chief Croft had found a large, wide collar for him, and there was base issued rabies tag attached.

Fuzz looked up at Abigail and tilted his head as if to say, "Well?" Abigail smiled. "You are a handsome dog, but I think you know that. Just don't let it go to your head." She shut the folder and stowed it in her grocery bag. "Scout," Abigail commanded once more in Romanian. Fuzz immediately went back to the slight zigzag pattern, glancing back once in a while to check Abigail's position. Her home was pretty much in a straight line from the kennels, so Fuzz kept in front of Abigail with ease

During the walk, a couple of dogs had barked from behind fences after getting a whiff of Fuzz. Fuzz had ignored them, other than a low frequency "woof" to let any animal in earshot that a large bad ass was passing through. About a half mile later, they arrived.

Abigail had Fuzz heel as she went up to the front door. She set down her load and used her key to open the door. Before she could do anything, Fuzz pushed past Abigail into her side of the duplex. "Hey, I didn't invite you in yet." Then she realized what he was doing, without any prompting. Tail and head up, his shoulder fur a bit up also, Fuzz went from room to room, checking for any potential threats that may try to harm Abigail, his new human. He returned to the entrance area, wagged his tail, and sat down, gazing with affection at Abigail.

"Thank you, Mr. Fuzz, for being concerned about my safety. Come on, let's go to the kitchen."

Woman and dog were in the kitchen together as Abigail put her groceries away. She placed Fuzz's dish on the floor, and put in some of the dry dog food from the provided plastic bag. She then filled a pot full of water and placed it next to the food. "Have some food, Fuzz." He was soon chowing down.

Abigail poured herself some lemonade and sat at her dining table facing the kitchen. She looked at the muscles under Fuzz's fur and could see the power in the very large dog. Over three feet at the shoulder, he was pretty lean, and would probably gain a few pounds from regular feeding. He should still be able to carry a slight increase in weight with no effect on his capabilities.

Abigail took his blanket and spread it by the sliding glass door that led to the fenced in backyard. The duplex had a large split back yard, the house sitting on a little under three quarters of an acre, most of it backyard. Fuzz finished eating, then found his blanket and laid down.

Abigail began making herself dinner. Slowly, thanks to Aleks and Torbin, she was becoming a pretty good cook. Torbin especially had a flair, probably would have been an amateur chef in another life. When he made something, it looked like it stepped right out of a pre-strike culinary magazine, with perfect presentation. Abigail did not care that much about looks, she went for taste.

She soon whipped up had a noodle dish, with some vegetables, fruit, and homemade bread. She placed it in on the dining table, Fuzz watching her. She smiled, then bent her head in prayer.

"Thank you, Lord, for the bounty I am about to receive. And thank you especially for sending me my new friend, Fuzz T. Dog. I think he will be an excellent Servant of God with me. In the name of Jesus Christ, Amen." She raised her eyes and looked at Fuzz. He thumped his tail, then laid his head down, and closed his eyes. He was soon lightly snoring.

Abigail ate her meal, reflecting on the events of the day in her mind. Fuzz was a well behaved dog, witnessed by the fact he did not beg for her food. He was a bit tired, as was she. The emotion of their meeting and his near death, had added some stress, which in itself can be tiring. Abigail enjoyed her meal, then took her dirty dishes to the sink and began washing them. She saw that Fuzz had woken, and was watching her at the sink. She smiled. "You like to watch women at domestic chores, don't you, fella?" He gave her a doggie open mouth smile.

She realized just how quickly they had bonded. You could tell when a dog picked you to be his human. They gave a certain look of devotion, of affection. And when you returned it, it blossomed into love and complete loyalty.

Abigail finished her kitchen chores, and turned back to Fuzz. She walked over and sat cross legged next to him. He put his large head on her right thigh, and she began to scratch his ears. They sat that way for several minutes, regaling in each other's company.

"Want to go outside, big guy?" Fuzz perked up, raising his head from her lap. The sun had gone down, the beginning of twilight. They both stood up and Abigail opened the sliding door. She watched as Fuzz leapt out in the backyard and walked around the fence line, marking his new territory.

Fuzz peeked into the fenced in yard of the other side of the duplex. The sliding door opened and she heard Aleks' voice call out loudly, "Torbin! There is a large beast in Abigail's backyard." Abigail quickly stepped out to disabuse Aleks of her concern. As she stepped out, Fuzz rose up, placing his forepaws on the four foot fence separating the two yards.

Torbin stepped out, exclaiming, "Shit! There is a beastie in her yard." Fuzz began to growl a warning and Abigail yelled at him.

"Fuzz—stop that! They are friends. Down." Fuzz glanced sheepishly at his mistress and removed his paws from the fence.

Abigail walked over to the fence line. "Sorry, Aleks and Torbin. I did not think you would see him yet."

Torbin asked, a bit worriedly, "Where in the holy hell did you get *him*? He looks like he could eat my head in one bite."

"I promise he won't. Fuzz, come here." The dog slowly walked to Abigail, never removing his gaze from Torbin. Abigail stood by the fence, scratching Fuzz's ears. "He has a problem with men, a habit of which I think I can break him. But he is a ladies' man, so Aleks, if you step over here, I will introduce him to you."

Aleks walked up to the fence and stood next to it. Fuzz saw her and began to work his nose to verify she was indeed a "she". Then he pushed his nose up to the holes in the chain link fence. Aleks slowly reached through and rubbed his muzzle. He rose up, putting his forepaws back on the fence so he could extend himself upwards.

"Oof. He is big!" Aleks exclaimed. She reached forward and began to scratch his chest. Fuzz opened his mouth in a doggy grin and let his tongue roll.

"Will he be my friend too?" Torbin asked. Abigail walked up and took ahold of Fuzz's collar.

"Alright, Fuzz. Meet Torbin, my friend." She pointed to Torbin, who cautiously moved forward, and began a light scratching of Fuzz's chest. Fuzz began wagging his tail in a slow beat, glancing at Abigail with a "see, I can play nice" look.

Torbin stopped scratching and pulled his hand back. "You definitely have a handful there. Think you can handle him?"

Abigail smiled. "After dealing with Eaters, Feral humans, and certain former Marines, he is going to be easy."

"Ouch. I am wounded. Aleks, defend me." Torbin feigned insult.

"Why, husband, when it is the truth? Come back here, big beastie." Fuzz went to the sound of her voice, then tried to sniff her stomach thru the fence. "Typical male. Goes for the genitals."

Abigail laughed. "Actually, he may sense you are pregnant."

Aleks was beginning to show. A complete examination and work up by the military hospital, assisted by Colonel Bardun and her expertise as an exobiologist, had determined that she had been exposed to some of the materials the Tschaaa had introduced to affect the reproductive system of human females. All done in order to modify the development and growth of human young. The amount of exposure appeared low, but the babies (male twins) were developing at a faster pace. Her due date was closer to seven or eight months rather than nine. Both of the twins seemed to be healthy in utero, but would assuredly be large babies. So Aleks, much to her chagrin, was already looking like she had swallowed a basketball. Because of this fast development—combined with the fact that hers was one of the first pregnancies affected—Aleks had been told to stop working the day before. She would only be allowed to go to work when General Reed called her in.

Fuzz sniffed Aleks' belly again. His tail wagged a couple of times, then she looked at Abigail. "Yes, big fella, she *is* going to have puppies—actually babies—but puppies to you."

Aleks laughed. "So, beastie, will you protect me like you will your new owner?" The oversized canine 'woofed', then licked Aleks. She laughed. "I will take that as a yes."

The three Humans talked for few minutes as Fuzz sat and watched them. Abigail was surprised how calm and patient he was, a complete switch from earlier in the day.

"Well, time for me to go in and make sure big fella here is settled in. I have tomorrow off, so I plan on buying a few dog things for Fuzz."

"Mind if I go along, Abigail?" Aleks asked. "I am already getting cabin fever from not being able to go to work."

"That, wife, is for you own good," Torbin interjected. "No one wants you suddenly fainting because our kids are developing so fast. I want you safe and comfortable."

Aleks sighed. "Yes, husband. But will your highness allow me to shop with Abigail? Or do you want to keep me barefoot and pregnant at home, doing nothing but stuffing my face?"

"Hmm, barefoot and pregnant—subservient—not a bad idea... ow."

Torbin kept underestimating the pain a Russian trained spy could inflict on an unsuspecting, albeit deserving, man.

A couple of hours later, after she listened to some soft hits radio and read the local newspaper, Abigail prepared for bed. She made sure Fuzz had water in a pan near his blanket. She planned on buying him a proper bed and water pan tomorrow. She had more money than she knew what to do with, General Reed having arranged a salary commensurate to her rank, and Deseret sending her "expense money" for use on incidentals involved with being the Official Representative to the U.S.A. Now, she had something, and someone, to spend her money on. It felt good.

Abigail brushed her teeth, put on some pajamas she had bought, and said a short prayer. She thanked God again for having Fuzz find her. This had been a good day.

She laid down, put her head on her pillow, and immediately began to doze off. She was awakened suddenly by a heavy body landing on her bed. She started to react in a defensive mode, then realized it was

Fuzz. He placed his large head on her thigh, his tail making a single 'thump' on the bed.

Abigail chuckled. "Well, Aleks keeps mentioning its okay to have a male in your bed if you love him. I wonder if she would count you as fulfilling that position." Abigail scratched his ears. Fuzz groaned in appreciation. She smiled and laid her head back on the pillow. In over six years, she had never felt so safe. Or loved. Both woman and dog were fast asleep in seconds.

CHAPTER 6

"Fundamentally, terrorist conflicts are about breaking the will of the enemy. To do this, one does not need to kill all of the enemy's personnel or destroy all of its resources. One simply has to destroy the idea that ultimate victory is possible. Victory or defeat then, boils down to a question of psychology."

— Andrew Silke, *Terrorism: All That Matters*

ATLANTA, CATTLE COUNTRY

While Fuzz had been finding Abigail, the populace of Atlanta was trying respond to violence, death, and terror.

Just two weeks from the nuke attack on the Key West area, and after the broadcast about the attack and the genetic/reproductive modifications, the Tschaaa Lord realized that Malcolm Carter had convinced most of Cattle Country to stop sending meat for slaughter. The Terror began the next day.

What appeared to be a standard robotic supply dirigible slowly made its way across the Atlanta Skyline. As per normal routine, it automatically slowed over the center of what was left of the city. The large supply container on its bottom opened its bay doors. This time, instead of disgorging food, booze, dope, some clothes, toilet paper and the like, large cylindrical glass containers fell from the airship. They shattered when they hit the ground or building roofs. Chlorine gas and fumes quickly filled the air.

Malcolm Carter, Mayor of Atlanta and leader of the Revolt, had managed to find or construct underground shelters for the majority of the inhabitants of Atlanta.

However, most were not gas proof. People soon found out the deadly effects of breathing chlorine gas. The ones caught above ground soon began to succumb, coughed, choked, their lungs seared from the chlorine gas. Then the gas began to seep into the shelters where panic and chaos ensued.

Malcolm, outfitted with a gas mask, observed the tableau from a ground floor office he had set up above his shelter. People ran, screamed, some fired shots in the air from the occasional firearm. "Goddamn idiots. Shooting and running does no one any good."

The center of the city was hardest hit, fumes wafting up and down streets, into basements, and into sewers. Those people hiding in underground locations were affected to various degrees, depending on the amount of gas that seeped in. The rate of serious injury and death was high.

Surprisingly, not a single casualty was harvested. No harvester robs showed, no Falcons swooped down to grab ahold of the dead or wounded. It was as if the Tschaaa said, "You humans in Atlanta are not even worth feeding to the lowest of the low. You are worth nothing."

Malcolm had tried to foresee this, tried to obtain as many gas masks, oxygen tanks as possible. But they had been very short in supply. He managed to obtain enough to outfit some response forces. Now, twenty-four hours after the gassing, with bodies beginning to swell and decay, Malcolm sent them his team to organize cleanup details to dispose of the corpses, and locate any injured that could be saved.

The teams were out some three hours, stacked the dead into a large pile for disposal. The plan was to burn them, telling the people that they bodies may be infected with a disease. This story might not be necessary, as there was no real area available for burial, the previous cemeteries having been destroyed or abandoned.

Some two thousand people of color had died outright, their lungs so damaged they had suffocated to death. Some had survived with damaged lungs and eyes. A number of these survivors would eventually die from diseases that attacked the injured areas. Initial counts showed some ten thousand residents were injured moderately or seriously.

Malcolm watched one group from his street level headquarters when the Falcons showed up. Everyone felt the signature generated electrical field, then the first ship arrived. Two others quickly followed. Before Malcolm could even shout a warning, the group of six men were seized by the metal tentacles emanating from the alien craft. Lifted up above the streets, they were eviscerated, torn asunder, their blood forming a red rain that wet the streets below.

Limbs and internal organs were scattered about, the robocops piloting the Falcons making no attempt to harvest anything. The dispatch of the six humans accomplished, they turned their attention to a building down the street from where Malcolm was concealed. Using their mechanical limbs and energy beams, they razed the building, floor by floor, in a matter of moments. After the craft reached street level, they tore into the subfloors with surgical precision.

Their efforts were rewarded as some dozen men, women and children were discovered hiding in the subfloors and basement. One by one they were grabbed by the searching mechanical tentacles, lifted high above the street, and slaughtered. At the last second, one child about six years old was saved, set back down on the street among the butchered remains of the other humans. The Falcons accelerated and were gone.

Malcolm swore, then dashed out on the street to where the young child was standing, in shock. He grabbed her up in his muscular arms, then sprinted back to his hiding place. He calmed the child down, eventually handing her over to Red, his female assistant. Malcolm had come to depend on her more and more. She had a knack at getting things done.

Joe, the large, former NFL lineman came back from his foray into the streets and saw the results of the Falcon's visit.

"This is *bad*, Boss. They usually do not waste meat like this."

"No shit." Malcolm snapped. Joe shut up, knowing the pressure Malcolm was under.

The Mayor took a deep breath. "Sorry I snapped at you, Joe. I knew the Squids were bloody minded and cold, but this. I have word that all the larger cities, Montgomery, Huntsville, Jackson, Birmingham, have all been hit with gas. The dead were just left to rot. Now, it looks like they are coming back with Falcons to make a point. What that point is I am still trying to figure out."

"I think they are trying to split us up, Boss. They're hoping someone will give in, one of the Mayors, or some other group, start sending people to them again."

Malcolm rubbed his jaw. "That could be it, Joe. But, we'll just have to try and hold on here, and hope the others do too. If we give up already, it will have been for fucking nothing."

Nothing else happened for a week. The people of Atlanta were terrified, but Malcolm somehow kept them from panicking and turning on each other. The biggest fear Malcolm had, short of the Squids flattening them with a huge space rock, was that the residents of Atlanta take out their fear and anger on their fellow citizens. They might even seize people and turn them over to the Squids themselves in an attempt to placate them, strike a separate deal.

Then disaster struck again. Falcons appeared over the city, the electrical field they generated the only warning. They dropped dozens of glass containers, which burst on the pavement in the center of the city. This time, it was mustard gas. Malcolm wondered if the Tschaaa Lord had been reading books on World War I and decided to adopt the relatively cheap terror tactics of gas warfare.

Mustard gas caused horrible burns externally as well as internally. It seeped into hiding spots, the wind blowing it down streets and alleys. People of all ages were soon screaming and dying. Once again, none of the Falcons attempted any harvesting, they only dumped their deadly cargo and then left. Malcolm had tried to use some ground to air weapons he had set up, but Falcons hadn't stayed around long enough for any response.

Within twenty-four hours, there were some three thousand additional dead, thousands more horribly burned. Things began to fall apart.

People of color from the various groups turned on each other, fighting over food, medical supplies and non-contaminated shelter. The remnants of the mustard gas stuck around in the low areas, being heavier than normal air. Someone would stumble into a small quantity, kick it up into the general environment, then would run screaming as the gas burned them.

There was not enough medical aid to handle all of the casualties, their moans and screams sounding like the damned souls of Dante's inferno. Malcolm finally organized a large number of his supporters, armed them, and passed through the streets trying to restore order. Many residents were beaten, stabbed, or shot as they resisted Malcolm's forces.

Joe contacted Malcolm on one of the forays about a mile from his headquarters office. "Boss, they did it."

"Did what, Joe?"

"A group grabbed some East Indians and Filipinos, tied and gagged them, threw them in some cars they got running. They headed out an hour ago, en route to Savannah. Someone said it was a peace offering to the Squids, taking fresh dark meat to the processing plants in Savannah."

Malcolm swore and cursed. "Goddamn those fucking idiots! That's what the Squids want, to split us apart."

He leaned up against an abandoned car. "I just didn't have enough time to get everyone organized, and ready. Who would have thought those fucking Krakens would strike back when they did. Another month I would have been ready for this." Malcolm picked up a nearby empty glass bottle and smashed against the nearby building. He stood still for a moment, thinking.

"All right, Joe, our public address systems are pretty well trashed. We need to organize some small groups to spread the word. We have to stick together, and get ready for the next attack. No more hiding in basements. It's fight or die, probably both. But at least if we die, we die free, not being cut up like a chicken for Sunday dinner."

"Joe, round up the trained men and women. We'll issue the heavy weapons we have, set them up for another visit by the Falcons and whatever comes with them. I thought the Tschaaa would hesitate a bit after they found out we weren't going to provide anymore fresh meat to them, that they would attempt to talk with us through some of their lackeys rather than massacre us right away, and waste all this prime rib. I thought wrong. His Lordship survived that nuke and already has planned a retaliation on anyone who resists them. It seems we are easier to hit than the Unoccupied States."

Joe smiled. "Well, Boss, at least things won't be boring."

Malcolm laughed. "No, Joe. It is definitely going to be a hot time in the old town tonight."

About a week later, the New Battle of Atlanta began in earnest.

CHAPTER 7

BATTLE OF ATLANTA, PHASE ONE

The first hint that a new phase in the Tschaaa response had begun was a sonic boom that shattered the surviving windows in the downtown area. Two Deltas broke the sound barrier at building level, actually causing a couple of weakened building walls to collapse. Luckily, no one was near enough to be injured. Unfortunately, that was the last of the 'luck' Malcolm and his people would have this day.

After the sonic booms, as people of color who dared to come out of the relative safety of their hiding places were scurrying for safety, a harvester ark landed on the remains of a flattened building. Within minutes, harvesting robots, now modified to be battlerobs, streamed out of the large cargo and processing craft. They soon demonstrated their new deadliness.

Malcolm had organized six-person armed response squads with the weapons they had on hand. Many were homemade weapons constructed on the advice provided by surviving engineers, teachers, scientists, and soldiers. Homemade could be very efficient under the right circumstances. A rocket launcher made from a salvaged piece of reinforced pipe was moved into position as the first battlerobs came traveling down Martin Luther International Blvd. on their six wheels. Looking like overgrown ATVs, the large eye-shaped globe extending from the central body of the vehicle began to shift and turn on the former human harvesting machine.

"Careful, wait until they're in range," the African-American leader of the team told his personnel as they set up the launcher. Slowly, one of the battlerobs trundled down the center of the avenue, its globe turning from side to side, searching for humans.

Fifty yards out, the gunner fired the rocket launcher. The rocket streaked toward the target, striking the side of the battlerob's globe. The warhead was a black powder shaped charge, so the explosion was rather low order, but had enough oomph to stove-in a portion of the side. The battlerob rolled to a stop as the globe began to throw off sparks and smoke. Finally, the ammunition of the human-built machine gun in the globe began to burn and cook off. The vehicle stopped and burned as plastic parts caught on fire. Within another minute, a second battlerob rolled up near the burning one.

"Hurry up and reload," The team leader instructed his people. They slowly slid the rocket into the tube, making sure no unburnt rocket propulsion material was left to set off the new rocket. Black powder could easily be set off if one was not careful with sources of heat and flame.

As they tried to complete the reload, the second battlerob began to fire the machine gun in its globe. Normally as a harvester rob, the globe would contain a large high intensity light to blind its prey to aid in capture. Now, the recognizable thump-thump-thump of a fifty caliber heavy machine gun was heard. The battlerob had somehow located the attackers at the corner of a former office building and was punching holes through the brick and cement. Two of the team members, including the team leader, fell dead. The four remaining humans ran, leaving the rocket launcher behind. Falling cement and masonry clobbered a fleeing woman in the head, knocking her to the ground. Her skull partially crushed, she died from internal bleeding of the brain within a half hour. No one was around to notice.

Similar scenes repeated themselves around the greater downtown area of Atlanta. The armed response squads fought as best they could with the weapons they had. By early afternoon, they had knocked out some twenty battlerobs, at the expense of some two hundred dead, and an equal number injured. Not a single body was harvested. The general populace huddled in their hiding places, petrified.

As a battlerob slowly wheeled down a wide street in the Downtown Atlanta area, the street sign long since gone, Malcolm crouched alongside Sahas Singh, a Sikh from a long heritage of soldiers. Singh had his traditional long hair wrapped up in his turban, his handlebar moustache long and waxed. He was sighting in the fifty caliber bolt action rifle on the approaching battlerob from the second floor window of the damaged office building.

"Got it, Sahas?"

"Yes, Mayor. Let us see what this rifle will do against that machine." He drew a breath, let it out, pulling the trigger at the end of his exhale. The rifle boomed, the fifty slug punching through the front of the wheeled robot's chassis. The battlerob jerked, stopped, and began to smoke and spark. The fifty caliber slug had done a good job of destroying its innards.

The Sikh started cursing as he tried to work the bolt for a follow-up shot. "The shell casing has split. The weapon is jammed."

"Time to move," Malcolm stated. The large Sikh scrambled to his feet and grabbed the large rifle. The two men ran down the stairs as fast as they could, into the basement. They had managed to dig a hole and make a passageway into the nearby sewer tunnels. As they exited, they heard machine gun rounds impacting the floors above. A following battlerob had determined from where the shot had originated and was trying to eliminate the threat.

With speed borne from practice, the two men made it to a ladder at a manhole on a parallel street. They climbed up, checked for the enemy, then out, replacing the manhole cover as quietly as possible. Then, dodging and hiding until they made it to Malcolm's basement level headquarters in a former hotel.

Big Joe was waiting for his boss in the office. Malcolm came in and plunked down on an old sofa. Sahas walked over to a workbench that had been set up along one wall and began working to clear the broken shell from the rifle.

"Well, Joe, one less robot. What're the updates on the situation?"

Joe paused for a moment. "Do you want the bad, the worse, or maybe some good news?"

Malcolm snorted. "Hell, might as well start with the bad news first. Lay it on me."

Joe sighed before continuing. "We got word by the ham radio. Montgomery just gave up. Jackson, Huntsville, Birmingham are basket cases, with no organized resistance; in fact, no organization apparently left at all. A few hundred people made a break north of Huntsville through a gate, and killed the trash guarding the barrier fence. Lost some bodies, not sure how many made it into Tennessee. Of course, Mobile, being a port, went down under about a thousand Squid the first week."

Malcolm swore. "Shit! People are folding like cheap suits. If I had about a month more time before those crazy bastards tried to nuke the head Squid, I would have had all the major population centers under some form of centralized control. As it is, the Mayors and other leaders went along with me because they did not want to be seen as supporting the Squids. Now, they can say they gave it the old college try, then start harvesting their bros again, probably starting with the injured and wounded."

Malcolm walked over to a battered desk and took a bottle of whiskey from the bottom drawer. He found a couple of glasses, poured a shot for himself and one for Joe. He knew Sahas did not drink alcohol.

"Well. What's the worse news?"

"Well, Boss, we knew the Church of Kraken has put soldiers in the field at some of the cities I just mentioned. That may have sped up their collapse. We just got word that there are groups of Krakens on all four sides of Atlanta. They have military style weapons, as well as support from battlerobs, those new soldier class beings, and some air support. Word is that in the other cities, they moved building to building, including the sewer drains, killing or rounding up all people of color. Now it's our turn."

Malcolm threw his shot back, then poured himself another. "Joe, my friend, we are about to be the current example of the Warsaw ghetto in World War II. But then, the Jews thought the Russians were coming to help, and the Allies air dropped some weapons into the ghetto. We have neither option from what I can see."

Joe frowned. "You don't think the Unoccupied States will help?"

Malcolm laughed. "We managed to get them word of what we

were doing, and have gotten exactly a four word reply—'Will try to help'. Since then, nothing." He took another swig of his drink. "I realize we caught them by surprise. They didn't think any of us are in any position to resist. But, they didn't exactly warn us about what they were going to do. I think they are glad the Squids are hitting us first, thanks to our refusal to supply any more dark meat. Now, they are circling the wagons."

Malcolm sighed. "So, what is the good news?"

"Red is waiting in the next room with someone who may be able to help us. I'll let him explain."

"Alright, Joe. Send them in."

A couple of minutes later Red, his East Indian assistant, came in with a slight, very dark East Indian man. He moved with an air of confidence, acting as if he were about to teach a college class instead of meeting a resistance leader in the midst of a war.

Red introduced him. "Mayor, this is Professor Bashir Gupta. As well as being a general engineer, he has an expertise in all things involving ancient warfare."

Professor Gupta stepped forward and offered his hand. "Mayor."

Malcolm shook his hand, noticing there was quite a bit of strength in his grip for being such a small-looking individual. "Well, Professor, I would say it is a pleasure to meet you, but right now I do not see much pleasure around here."

Gupta gave a slight smile. "I believe that is a grand understatement, Mayor. To cut to the chase, I have some Polaroid pictures from a still working camera I found amongst my things. It will give you an idea of what my friend Reginald Adams has been working on."

"Reggie Adams?"

"Yes, Mayor, an African-American like yourself. I believe the American term is that he is a 'backyard mechanic'. I would say he is a genius in making something out of close to nothing. I supply the designs, he makes them work with what we can salvage."

"So, show me what you have."

From out of a small folder, Professor Gupta pulled several photographs. "Here, Mayor, take a look at the first one. This is a multiple projectile version of a Roman ballista. As you can see, it fires five bolts at a time, with automobile leaf springs and cables used instead of wood forearms and catgut bow strings. You have to crank it to load it, but those five bolts can penetrate a battlerob at one hundred meters. We have made two of these weapons, and of course it does not require gunpowder to work." The Professor then pulled out the next photograph.

"This is a large, six-barrel homemade, hand-cranked gatling gun. The rounds are based on a .25 mm chain gun cannon round, but are loaded with black powder as it is easier to produce. Generally it will take two hands to crank it, so it is a two crewman weapon unless you have a very powerful individual. Your friend Joe here may be able to crank it one-handed."

Joe gave a slight grin at the mention of his name.

"You could motorize it, but the strain of too rapid a rate of fire would most likely cause the barrels to shatter, as they are reinforced piping. However, the size of the projectile and its mass, enables it to penetrate with a flat-on strike a battlerob at about a hundred meters. It would still be fatal to unprotected humans at a much further distance. We have one of these produced already, with another one in the works. We are trying to produce rounds for them, but have been slowed by the dearth of powder."

The scientist then produced the final photo. "This large, round device with the four protruding projectiles is a pneumatic weapon that uses extreme air pressure to launch the long spigot projectiles. The warheads on the tips are black powder, with a small partially filled canister of gasoline behind it, the fumes of which are very explosive. The long container behind this warhead can be filled with a flammable liquid, gas, or toxin— whatever you choose. But the more weight, the shorter the range. At a single degree of inclination with just the small basic warhead, they can reach almost two hundred meters."

Malcolm studied the photos. "Where have you been?"

"Well, hiding, of course."

Malcolm laughed. "Good answer. Coordinate with Joe here. Get us what you have, let me know what you need for more weapons."

"I also have some binary explosive warheads available, Mayor. As well as nitroglycerin. Get me some more chemicals, chemistry sets, I can make a substantial amounts of nitro and other explosives. I have a secondary degree in Chemistry."

Joe broke in. "We found a chemistry classroom at a junior college that hasn't been picked over. We should be able to find you some basic chemicals."

"Good. Make it happen, Joe."

Malcolm took the doctor's hand in his own. "Welcome to the Alamo, Professor. Joe there with his big knife must be in the role of Jim Bowie. I guess that makes me Davy Crockett."

The Professor smiled. "I know about the Alamo. But I plan to survive."

Malcolm laughed. "Who says we can't rewrite history? Now, gentlemen, let's get moving. Time to screw up the Squid's plans."

As Malcolm was finishing up his meeting with the Professor, Ray Sparks, Lieutenant to John Talbot in the Krakens biker gang, was organizing his fifty Church of Kraken force. He wanted them to enter downtown Atlanta from the west on what was left of one of the main thoroughfares. Sparks had gotten them this far aboard five pickup trucks and a Humvee with a Fifty Caliber on top. He looked at the horizon and saw the sun was steadily moving toward sunset. He fidgeted a bit. He wanted to start entering the city while there was still sunlight, its duration shortened by the autumn season. But trying to get fifty semi-trained personnel in an organized formation was like herding cats.

His second in command, a short, stocky man, a southerner originally from Georgia, walked up to him.

"Well, Boss, they have all their equipment, finally. But most seem to have forgotten the formations they were taught the last three weeks. The one good thing is they all remembered the weapons safety and handling the trainers beat into them, so no one has shot anybody…yet."

Sparks snorted. "Well, Jim, let's just get them on the road."

He pointed to the two Soldier Class beings standing in front of the transport vehicles. "As soon as they move, along with that battlerob, we are supposed to fall in behind. The theory is that they will draw the fire first, then we locate the meat shooting and maneuver around and dig them out. That is, if I can get these Churchers to maneuver."

All the Church of Kraken personnel had been issued an assault rifle gleaned from the millions seized worldwide during harvesting. They were given three thirty round magazines of ammunition, nothing else. A few had brought their own sidearms, showing that some had previous weapon handling experience. But, the fanaticism that made them want to fight against anyone resisting their Tschaaa Lords also led them to want to make suicidal banzai charges straight on. Sparks shook his head at the thought. ust wait after a line of them were shot down. Then let's see how suicidal the rest were.

James Kray, the head of the church, also called a Lord and Most Reverend of the Church, had made good on his promise. He provided the Squids with ten thousand volunteers for training the first month, with double that number being rounded up as this operation was beginning. Sparks had been told that there were two million official members, with an equal number hanging around the edges. Since you would be lucky to find a thousand flying squad members, the original Fifth Columnists of the Invasion, the Church of Kraken was the only viable source of humanity that could be used to invade Cattle Country, then strike back at the Unoccupied States.

The force of some ten thousand guards that helped keep the dark meat in Cattle Country were just that—guards. None of them would volunteer to go in after the revolting people of color. Keep them in, shoot them, maybe even chase a few down once in a while after they got past the fence, that the guards would do. Try to force them to do more and they would begin to desert.

Guarding the livestock was a job, not a career. The humans that did it, with some support from the robocops, came to the jobs as they were almost the only organized employment after the first year, and during the Long Winter, that provided room and board for the guards and their families. The food, shelter and trade goods the jobs provided meant that the people involved would not starve or die of exposure. The offspring of these people were some of the healthier humans that came out of the first five years, and were being groomed for further employment by the Tschaaa. But there were not enough of them to create an army.

The Krakens would be the human army to support Tschaaa warriors, which were a force along the shores of bodies of water but not efficient past a mile or two into the interior areas, away from water. And there not enough robocops or Lizards to create sufficient forces to attack and root out the Rebels. Greys were more support personnel, mechanics.

Now the Squids were faced with the fact that perhaps they should have destroyed all attempts to organize outside the Occupied Zones, rather than just ignoring them. But then again, the Tschaaa had never really fought a long term war. The few aliens who had resisted them in their first expansion into space were quickly overwhelmed, then were accepted into the Tschaaa sphere of influence. The Lizards were a full-fledged client species. No one had ever revolted and attacked the Tschaaa once defeated. Until now. Of course, none of the other alien species were seen as food either.

"Not as goddamned smart as you thought you are, you effing Squids, are you?" Sparks mumbled to himself. He may dislike minorities and dark-skinned people, but he had *no* desire to play footsies with the Squids beyond what he was doing now. If he could find a small community in some place he could hole up, he just might do that, especially if the perks he got—sex, drugs, and rock and roll—from the Tschaaa suddenly began to dry up.

"Boss, looks like the battlerob and company are getting ready to move." This comment from Jim interrupted his reverie about all things Squid. Sparks took a few strides toward the Church of Kraken fighters.

"Listen up!" Sparks bellowed. Although he had a slender, gangly frame, his voice was large and bold. "Get formed up, ready to march out! Remember the formations you learned. Do not bunch up. We will follow the battlerob out, until enemy contact is made. Grab your shit and get in place."

Sparks had a M-16 with a 40 mike-mike grenade launcher attached, the only one in the unit. Jim had a scoped sniper rifle, and a brace of Glock pistols across his chest. Sparks had a holstered six shot revolver. The purpose of the handguns, unbeknownst to the other Krakens, was to shoot deserters. James Kray had said there would be "no deserters". He did not intend to be made a liar.

Just as they were about to move out, following the Soldiers and battlerob, Sparks heard a smooth, rumbling roar suddenly come from the distance. He thought it sounded like an engine, but not one he with which was familiar. It seemed to be getting closer very quickly. Sparks looked up as he realized it was from an aircraft.

Sparks had made models of a F-51 Mustang in his youth, but had never seen one in flight. His mouth dropped open at the sight of the sleek looking propeller aircraft, marveling at the throaty power of the rebuilt Rolls Royce-Packard engine. Every being stood transfixed for a few moments.

Until the six 50 Calibers opened up.

Pappy Gunn, scrounger and armorer extraordinaire, had performed another miracle. An eighty plus year old fighter aircraft was back doing what it did best—taking the fight to the enemy where it was least expected.

In what was going to be repeated in another four locations around the outskirts of Atlanta, 50 Caliber rounds tore into the Soldier Class beings, the battlerob, and the transport vehicles. Nothing had been armored to withstand the pounding from the six 50s, not even the Soldiers. Especially not the Krakens.

The two Soldiers were down for the count, chests penetrated and bodies shattered. The battlerob's eye-shaped turret was sieved. Two of the pickup trucks burst into flame, gas tanks holed. Then the humans were chopped up.

Sparks and Jim managed to hit the dirt, rounds like huge angry bees whizzing by overhead. Many of the people from Church of Kraken were neither so quick nor so lucky. A 50 Caliber round tends to dismember the human body from pure kinetic energy, limbs and torso separated. One round can penetrate several bodies, each a fatality. The Krakens did not even have time to scream. Then the F-51 zoomed past. It was gone in seconds. A few moments later, the tableau was repeated on the next assault group, with similar results. The roar of Fifties could still be heard in the distance.

Sparks, his training and experience taking over, was up on his feet, weapon raised for the next threat. None appeared. He then began to check on the damage to people and machines. A quick inspection revealed a dozen dead, two dozen wounded. Some of the wounded would die in the next thirty minutes. A couple of Krakens began running in circles screaming, until shot dead by Jim. That helped to restore order.

"All right. See to the wounded. Get the good trucks moved so they don't catch fire too. You and you. Head up about a hundred yards, make sure no one is about to attack from the city. Move, goddamnit! You wanted to be in a war, now you've got it."

The other four units about to enter Atlanta suffered similarly, although the last one was relatively lightly hit as the Mustang ran out of rounds soon after it opened up, and they had some warning. One Soldier was knocked out, the battlerob damaged, and six Krakens killed, another six wounded. Only one pickup was hit. The Mustang took some bullet holes, but its tough design kept it in good stead.

When Malcolm got word of what happening, he had burst into gales of laughter. Red believed her Boss was now unhinged. Finally, Malcolm stopped, wiping the tears from his eyes. "Those crazy mofos. One week I'm getting fucked by them. The next, they're suddenly trying to save my black ass. I just wish they would let me in on the plan."

As sunset was on its last legs, the F-51—"My Ole Lady"—came in on final approach across the Georgia border, to a small hidden airfield south of Nashville, Tennessee. Because of its lower speed, and the Tschaaa's limited understanding of air defense, the eye in the sky ignored it. The F-51 made a clean escape. Ten minutes later, a Falcon began to orbit the greater Atlanta area.

Colonel "Flash" Gordon, USAF (Ret), greased the fighter down on the former stretch of highway on the first try. Quickly going into taxi mode, he made a beeline to a single plane hangar that was well camouflaged among a few trees and bushes alongside the road. Colonel Gordon braked, stopping the aircraft just short of the hangars rear wall. He went through shut down procedures, and cut the engine. A few more turns of the prop, and all was quiet.

The aircraft Crew Chief, Alfred Fritz, clambered up on the port wing and helped the seventy-something year old pilot unstrap and climb out of the cockpit. Soon they were both standing by the aircraft, looking for damage.

"I see a few holes, Colonel. I thought you said you would get my plane back in one piece." Every Maintenance Crew Chief referred to the aircraft they worked on as theirs. And they were always pissed when the pilot who "borrowed" it pranged it.

"Hell, Chief. I said I would get it back in one piece, not pristine. They were shooting real bullets. The last time I had that happen was flying SPADS in Vietnam." Gordon had flown Skyraiders, called SPADS after the biplane of World War I because both seemed out of date compared to all the fancy jets. Colonel Gordon would not admit to his real age, but everyone knew he was probably at least at the upper end of his seventies. Only through special dispensation from Madam President—in other words, he called in some markers—was he able to fly this mission. He had to agree to this being his one and only combat mission, and that he would train other pilots in the use of this aircraft.

Chief Fritz grunted. "Well, I count a dozen bullet holes, so I guess you didn't do too bad. How'd she fly?"

Gordon broke into a broad grin. "Like a dream, just like her namesake." My Ole Lady was a joking nickname he used for his love of his life, his wife Marie. She had not survived the first year after the rocks hit.

"Now, you get to hide it with the security team, until I can get someone else to get it out of here. If you sit quiet for a few days, it should be able to be moved elsewhere. You will probably have more problems with feral humans than the Squids. The Tschaaa really do not like to leave the coastal areas."

"Well, Colonel, a Cessna is in route to pick you up. So relax, and I'll start patching her up for the next pilot." Fritz turned and walked away. Gordon walked up and caressed the fuselage.

"You did well, Lady, like the fighter you always were. Marie, I know your spirit is here somewhere. You helped me do good like you always did." He blinked back tears. He caressed the plane again, feeling as if he was with his wife one more time.

"Thanks Babe. I'll make sure they treat you right." He knew Marie was watching from somewhere, would always watch over him until he went to join her. And now, he had helped put paid on the debt the Squids owed him.

He walked away, on the lookout for a cold drink.

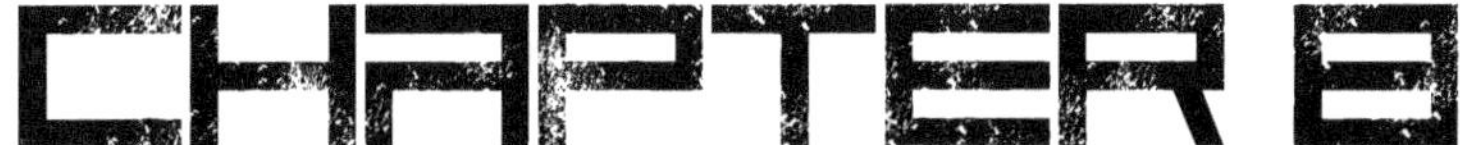

MALMSTROM, MONTANA

The morning after the F-51 strike, Abigail awoke to doggie kisses from Fuzz. It was an hour later than her normal wake-up time on a work day, which meant she actually had more sleep than usual as well. She appreciated the extra rest, and believed Fuzz had purposefully given her extra sleep time until he had to relieve himself. She scratched his muzzle, then moved to his chest.

"Good morning, big fella. I take it you slept well in your new home. Let me get up and I'll let you out." Fuzz backed away, and Abigail easily slid out of bed. She thought again how blessed she was to have come here. "Thanks, Lord," she said out loud. Then she moved to the kitchen.

She let Fuzz out into the crisp, clear air. Winter weather already approached in Montana; there had been snow flurries since the approach of the first day of fall. Fuzz seemed to take no heed. He went out and took care of his business, walking around marking the fence line to let everyone in the neighborhood know whose yard this was.

Abigail smiled as Fuzz used his rear legs to kick up some grass and spread his scent around. Then he pranced over to her with a "Well, where's breakfast?" look. She scratched his ears.

"Come on in, Fuzz. Typical male, wants attention, then a full stomach. Well, I still have some dog food for you. After that, I saw an ad in the newspaper last night. A vet downtown is having an open clinic—Doctor Emily Anders. So, you get to meet another lady, although she is a doctor. I just want a quick check-up by someone not trying to turn you into a working dog. How's that sound?" Fuzz gave his signature single deep bark in response. However, Abigail knew he was more interested in breakfast than meeting new people.

She fed and watered him. Then, poured herself a glass of milk. She watched Fuzz eat, and noticed the interplay of his muscles in his body. He definitely had been an active dog. Fuzz probably outweighed her a bit, Abigail now being about a muscular one hundred forty pounds on her now five foot eight and a half frame. But he gave no indications that he had any desire to challenge her Alpha status. Rather, he seemed to be devoted to her already.

As he finished up, Abigail told him, "Fuzz, I need to shower. I'll be in the bathroom, door open, so make yourself at home. Just don't chew up anything. We'll get you some chew toys or bones today."

Fuzz's ears perked up, so he must have recognized the words. Abigail smiled. She was going to spoil him and he knew it.

She shed her pajamas (she had several pairs now, glad that she no longer had to sleep in military issue skivvies) and looked at herself in the full length mirror. She liked the muscle definition she had developed, strong looking but definitely feminine. She had quickly learned just how attractive her body was by the way men looked at her. But she still was not ready to try what Torbin had referred to as the "dating scene". She still tried to control some of her own hormone induced feelings, knowing that even an Avenging Angel still had a biological clock aimed toward reproducing the species. Abigail still had the belief in finding her one True Love, the "Mister Right" Aleks had mentioned. The negligée Aleks had her purchase for just that person was in a special place in her closet, as it fit perfectly— almost too perfectly. When she tried it on and looked in the mirror, a very sexual being stared back. She had quickly put it away, knowing that it had a power all its own. She was not ready for that yet.

The warm shower was, as always, divine. When she wound up in the field again, which she knew she would, this would be missed. So she enjoyed it now.

She finished washing and rinsing her hair, let it drip dry for a few moments, then stepped out.

She felt eyes on her and glanced toward the bathroom door. There was Fuzz, sitting attentively, an open mouth doggie grin on his face. She laughed. "Typical male. Can't wait to catch a lady naked. Could you please turn around while I dry myself?" Fuzz, now knowing she was alright, turned and laid down in the hallway. Abigail could tell that she had obtained an ultimate protector. Fuzz would die for her and hers, which was an awesome responsibility she must never abuse. At the same time, in the back of her mind, she would risk death and kill for him, a canine, not a human. A bond developed over many millennia between dog and human kind was unique in the species of Earth. To think the Tschaaa thought that such a relationship could exist between them and humanity was an abomination.

She dried her body and her hair, then used the special brush set to brush her hair to a nice golden sheen. It was long, down past her shoulders now. She tied it back into a ponytail. When in uniform, she braided it into a tight style that did not interfere with her military cover. She had learned this braiding due to necessity during training in Deseret, if she wanted to keep her hair long. Now, she had it down to a science. But during her time off, she liked to let her hair down, literally. Looking at it in the mirror, she saw she should get it trimmed. Aleks would likely know of a place where she could go.

After a pair of bikini panties, socks, and a sports bra, Abigail put on a pair of almost new blue jeans, comfortable cowboy boots, and a light blue sweatshirt with a flowery design on the front. She liked blues, and would never be a pink person like some women were.

She went back to the kitchen and made herself some toast with jam. Fuzz did not beg, rather sitting at the opening of the kitchen and connected dining area. He definitely seemed to be "on duty" ever since he attached himself to Abigail. He was becoming more devoted with every passing moment. Abigail smiled as she finished her toast. She finished a glass milk as well, then washed her dishes in the kitchen sink. Fuzz stayed at the entrance way of the kitchen and dining area.

She walked out from her cleanup, knelt down and hugged Fuzz. The great dog gave a doggie open mouth grin, his tail thumping on the floor. "You big lovable beastie you. God must be smiling on me to bring a guy like you into my life. I think I might've fallen in love with you, Mister Fuzz T. Dog. I hope you don't mind." Fuzz turned his head enough to give her a large sloppy dog kiss, then followed it with another. Abigail snuffled her face into his fur, drawing in Fuzz's scent through her nose. She would never feel alone again as long as he was around. The bonding was complete.

Abigail stood up. "Stay here, please, Fuzz. I need to contact Aleks next door, and see if she wants to go to the vet with us." As she walked out the front door, she noticed Fuzz following her with his eyes. She left the front door slightly ajar so that Fuzz knew he could come running if he was needed. Abigail lightly knocked on the front door of their half of the duplex. It was just past eight o'clock in the morning.

"Coming," Aleks called out. Abigail heard her mutter as she made her way to the front door. "Is that you, Abigail?"

"Yes…" The Russian spy opened up the front door, holding her large stomach. "How are you, Aleks?" Abigail greeted her.

Aleks winced. "I would be just fine if these two males I am carrying in my stomach were not so intent in using my innards as a football field. They kick and punch so hard they wake Torbin up. I told him to go back and rest since it is a day off for him. But for a pregnant woman, especially one pregnant with two little Marines, there are no days off." Abigail knew that Aleks would much rather be working than pregnant. But, at the same time, she wanted Torbin's children. Since he could not carry them, she would be the one stuck with them until birth.

"I am going to take Fuzz to an open clinic at a veterinarian in Great Falls. I'd like for someone to give him a quick once over. Do you want to come, or just go shopping for doggie stuff with me when I return?"

Aleks winced as one of her children gave her a noticeable kick. "I think I shall wait here until my two little trolls calm down in my stomach. Get me when you come back. Hopefully they will be calmer by then. Maybe a shot of vodka… just kidding, little sister. It probably would not faze them anyway."

Abigail laughed. "I will see you a bit later, then. Then I will buy you lunch. A *big* lunch." The modifications and nanotech with which the Tschaaa had infected the human species, was causing a rapid fetal development in the two boys Aleks was carrying. Thus, she was literally hungry all the time. Her sons would be large, and already demanded much food. Aleks would eat for four at a sitting.

Aleks smiled. "I will take you up on that, my little sister. See you when you return."

Abigail said goodbye and went back to her place to retrieve Fuzz. She threw on a warm jacket. Late September in Montana could be nippy, especially since the Long Winter and subsequent changes in air currents and weather patterns. She locked up, and brought Fuzz to the attached garage. Abigail introduced Fuzz to the well-used but very serviceable Jeep SUV that General Reed had found for her. "An Official Representative has to have wheels to get around, especially four wheel drive in snowy weather." Unlike many women, Abigail had been given good automotive and vehicle field maintenance training in Deseret. Torbin told her she could set up shop as a "shade tree mechanic" if she ever needed extra funds, as she seemed quite adept at fixing cars and pickups.

"You'll make someone a fine husband someday, Abigail," quipped Torbin, for which he received a shot to the floating rib from his beloved wife.

"You be nice to my little sister, brute," Aleks scolded.

Abigail opened up the back of the Jeep, folded the rear seat down, and Fuzz leapt right in with no prodding. He apparently had been through this drill before. He managed to turn his large body around twice, then laid down with a satisfied grunt. Abigail shut the hatch, smiling. She jumped in the driver's seat, then turned her head back toward Fuzz. "Ready to go?" She heard a small 'woof', which she took as acknowledgement. She started the Jeep, carefully backed out, and then headed toward the main gate.

Just under a half hour later, she located the vet's office. With the simple name on the sign of "Great Falls Large and Small Animal Clinic" to announce what was in the long building, Abigail quickly located the parking area. It was still before 9:00am, so there were only a couple of cars in the visitor's lot. She parked with ease, grabbed the leash Sgt. Martinez had given her, and went to the back of the Jeep. She opened it, telling Fuzz to stand in Romanian so she could affix his leash. Fuzz understood both English and Romanian commands, but seemed to key on Romanian when the commands were about "working". She attached the leash and Fuzz easily jumped down from the Jeep. He automatically heeled as the entered the clinic, and Abigail approached the receptionist desk to check in.

"Hello, I'm Abigail Young with a new dog that adopted me. I was wondering if I can get a checkup for him."

The receptionist, a young lady probably around Abigail's age, smiled at Abigail's comment. "Yes, we have a lot of that around here. People think they adopt the dog, when actually it winds up the other way around. Are you from the Base?"

"Yes, Ma'am."

"And your friend's name?"

"Fuzz, Ma'am."

At the name, the receptionist eyes went wide and stared at Fuzz, who looked back, as if to say 'Yes?'

"Fuzz, from the Base? Ah, could you wait one moment please?" The young brunette slid off the chair and made a quick beeline into the back. Abigail looked around the reception area. There were two people with cat carriers, no one else. As she was about to sit down, a light brown haired woman with a doctor's coat came into the reception area. She saw Fuzz, and smiled.

"So this is the infamous Fuzz, land shark extraordinaire. You look awfully calm today, Mister Fuzz."

The woman approached Abigail, keeping an eye on the canine's reaction. He seemed to be watching her—alert, not aggressive. She extended her hand to Abigail. "Hi there. I'm Emily Anders, the senior vet here. Actually, to tell the truth, the only full time vet here. This nice specimen of dogkind is your buddy now?"

Abigail shook the doctor's hand. Emily was a slender, toned woman, probably in her late thirties, with longer than normal fingers that provided a firm, confident handshake. She was about Abigail's height, with a nice full face and feminine nose. She had a warm grin on her face as she shook Abigail's hand.

"Captain Abigail Young, Ma'am. Yes, Fuzz found me, moved right in. But I did not realize he had a…reputation off the Base. I hope it's not going to create a problem."

"No, of course not. There are not a lot of us veterinarians around, so we all talk when we get the chance. Dr. Shaw on Base was just talking to me the other day about the fact Fuzz kept working his way through the military working dog handlers by biting all of them, instead of putting up with being "busted". I guess he fights and will not give up, at least to men. But with you, he seems as quiet as a mouse. May I scratch his ears?"

"Fuzz, can the doc touch you?" Fuzz looked at his mistress, then moved forward enough to snuffle Doc Ander's hand. He gave it a quick lick, then allowed Emily to scratch his ears. He was soon grunting in pleasure.

"Yeah, I thought you'd like that. So, Abigail, what can I do for you today?"

"Can you examine him? I mean, I know the doctor on base did but, well, I just want to know if he has anything possibly wrong with him. He seems young, so if he has anything developing I'd like to treat it now."

"Sure, we can do that. I'll let my vet tech Wendy take you and him back to an examination room, get a weight and temperature. I have two cats I need to take care of first."

"Thank you, Doctor."

A stocky black woman came out from the back when the Doctor called her name. Abigail was a little surprised by Wendy's appearance, as there was not an abundance of African-Americans on Base. Even the military members having taken a high casualty rate. Fuzz snuffled her hand also, so the vet tech responded with an ear scratch.

"So, you are Fuzz. You have one heck of a reputation." She looked at Abigail. "Are you sure this is the same Fuzz…?"

"Yes, Ma'am. He just seems… calmer around me, that's all."

Fuzz extended his paw of friendship to Wendy, who took it, then began to scratch his chest.

Abigail laughed. "You just put Fuzz in hog heaven." Fuzz began to grunt a little in ecstasy. Both women were laughing now, the cat people in the waiting room looking at them like they were nuts.

"Come on, I'll take you back to the examination room." Fuzz let Wendy take his leash and walk him to the examination room, with Abigail in tail. In the Exam room, Wendy got a weight on Fuzz, the large canine standing perfectly still on the scale.

"This dog has been well trained," Wendy exclaimed.

"Yes, he has," Abigail answered. "But he still seems to really dislike men. Someone did something very nasty to him that he has not gotten over yet. But I am working on it."

Wendy wrote down the weight. "You have a solid one hundred fifty pound canine here. Looks like he is a Dane and Shepherd mix, his parents apparently on the large size. There are bigger Great Danes, but few Shepherds his size. He seems to have gotten the best genes from both."

As she took Fuzz's temperature, Wendy asked, "You're the Captain from Deseret, aren't you?"

"Yes, Ma'am. And you?"

"Call me Wendy, please. Wendy Johnson, from Georgia; at least the former state. I made it out just before the fuck... excuse me, the Squids closed it off as part of Cattle Country. I was in a veterinarian training program when the rocks hit. I made it out. I don't know what happened to my family. Somehow, got word that people were safe up here. So I started walking."

Wendy looked at the thermometer. "His temperature is in the normal range. Now, Fuzz, if you do not mind, I'm going to feel and squeeze you a bit. Okay?"

Abigail looked at Fuzz. "Fuzz. Sit." The last command was in Romanian. Fuzz sat. Then he let Wendy begin to gently squeeze and feel, manipulate joints. After a while, Wendy had Abigail order Fuzz to stand and she continued the exam.

"Hm. He seems like he is built like an athlete, all muscle. But... there are a few areas I want the doc to feel. Okay?"

"You're the expert. I'm just a soldier."

Wendy laughed. "That's not what I heard. Can I ask you a question?"

Abigail's ears turned a bit red, a bit self- conscious. "Go ahead, Wendy."

"Did you really... castrate a Kraken biker?"

Torbin and she had written a complete After Action Report of what they had to do to get to Montana. And of course, the "exciting bits" were soon leaked to everyone. Abigail sighed.

"Yes, I did. I don't want to brag about it. I did it because I had too." She hesitated. "I also slit a man's throat who tried to kill a dog I knew. That, I will brag about. People who go out of their way hurt dogs are evil."

Wendy looked at Abigail and saw something in her eyes that told her that one did not screw with this Lady's friends, upon penalty of great pain. She quickly changed the subject. "Were you born in Deseret?"

"No, in Washington State. My parents got me out when the Hanford Nuclear Storage Area blew up. I was sent to Deseret, my Uncle Buck got me there. My parents... didn't make it."

Wendy sighed. She had not found a single person who had *not* suffered a loss since the Tschaaa had appeared. The pall of death hung over everyone and everywhere.

"Your uncle is in Deseret?"

Abigail frowned. "No, he wanted to remain out in the Feral areas. I bumped into him on the way up here. He... prefers dogs to people, so he is headed up toward the least contaminated areas of Idaho."

At that moment, Emily knocked on the examination room door, then entered. "So, how are things going? Sorry about the wait."

"Well, Doctor, I've given a basic exam. Normal temperature, nothing serious that leaps out at me. But, could you check the bones and joints here and here?"

The Doctor knelt next to Fuzz. She prodded a couple of places. "Can you have him lie down?"

"Fuzz, down." The large dog dropped down and, without prodding, rolled over on to his back. Emily laughed. "Yes, I will scratch your tummy. I do not know what you did to him, Abigail, but he is one changed dog. Ever thought about being a vet? You sure have a way with canines."

Abigail shrugged. "I was trained to be a warrior. I'm good at it, so I figured this is what God Wants. At least until the Evil Ones and their minions are defeated, expelled. Then... who knows? I do love training dogs."

"Well, give it some thought. We vets are setting up a formal school so people like Wendy can get a formal veterinarian degree and license. Keep it in mind." Emily began to touch, gently squeeze, manipulate Fuzz's limbs, and check his body. She got Fuzz to roll over onto his stomach and she checked his spine some more.

"Abigail, do you think you can keep him relaxed enough that I can get an x-ray or two without having to sedate him?"

Abigail frowned. "Is there something wrong?"

"No, far from it. To put it bluntly, I have found some evidence of bone injuries, calcium deposits that would point to a much older dog, one that should be nearly crippled. Yet, he acts like a young dog, close to the two years of age Doc Shaw says he is. Some of the scar tissue, bone irregularities point to extensive injuries way out of the normal activities of any dog I have ever run across. So, do you think you can help me get some good x-rays?"

"Why, of course. I have some money with me to pay..." Abigail pulled a wad of large denomination bills out of her pocket, not being a "purse" person. Emily's eyes bugged out a bit.

"No. This is on me. Please, do not flash that much money around off base. Not everyone is as honest as you are here in Great Falls."

Abigail blushed a bit. "I'm sorry. I still act sometimes as if I am in Deseret. There, not only is it public shame to commit a crime such as theft, but if you three crimes then you are exiled. Unless you purposefully do serious bodily harm to another or an animal. Then you are publically shot." She said it so matter of factly that she did not really notice that the doctor and the tech's mouths had fallen open in shock.

Emily finally managed to say something. "They shoot people for... hurting animals?"

"Seriously injured, yes. When you purposefully abuse an animal, the Prophet felt the next step was that you would abuse a human. Thus, you stop it in the early stages. Butchers slaughter all animals as humanely as possible, many similar to the Kosher standards of the Jewish religion."

"Of course," Wendy interjected. "I imagine exile would probably be an early death for most people, unless they made it to a decent size town in the Unoccupied States and had a skill to sell."

Abigail nodded her head affirmatively. "In fact, we usually send them over the border with Arizona, toward California. The Prophet said you here should not have to deal with our... garbage."

Emily grunted. "That might not be such a bad idea for around here. But I digress. Please help me get an x-ray, and a little blood sampling as well."

"Yes, Emily. Whatever it takes. But I insist I pay for this extra work."

"Oh, make a donation then. We'll use it to help homeless and destitute animals. Now, let's get to work."

An hour later, Emily was looking at the blood sample under a microscope. Wendy was out printing the x-rays on a computer-connected photo printer. Enough cutting edge computer and electronics equipment had been salvaged after things fell apart in the rest of the United States, that when a power grid was re-established in the Unoccupied States, medical services were soon re-established close to pre-strike levels. The hacked and pirated power and info from the Tschaaa controlled areas also helped.

Abigail sat nearby with Fuzz, who was eating some dog biscuits Wendy had found for him. "You are definitely a ladies man, big fella," Abigail said as she scratched his ears. "And you are getting horribly spoiled."

She asked Emily as the vet stood up from the microscope, "Did you find what you are looking for?" Abigail asked.

Emily walked over to Fuzz and knelt down, looking in his face. "You are good friends with Major Bender, aren't you?"

"Yes, I am. I came with him from Deseret."

"Did he tell you about the modifications to the human genome and reproduction the Squids were trying on the trip here?"

"I take it that, in addition to the information Madam President gave during her recent radio and television address, all doctors received more in-depth information?"

"Yes, they did. Which brings us to Fuzz. Colonel Bardun, the astronaut, is an exobiologist. She has helped to, shall we say, 'map' what to look for in blood and cell samples that point to the introduction of the organic and nanotechnology materials the Tschaaa introduced to our species. Well, Fuzz here has indicators that he has been also exposed to these modification materials."

Abigail froze. Her voice caught a bit when she spoke. "Fuzz is, unclean… infected?"

Emily was taken aback for a moment, but then remembered where Abigail had been raised for the last six years or so.

"Hell, no! Just the opposite. He's as healthy as a horse. Whatever was given him is somewhat different in makeup from the stuff the Squids spread among us. It looks like it was modified specifically to interface with our dog friends. It makes him a superior canine specimen."

Emily began to scratch Fuzz's chest. "This big fella has the remnants and scar tissue of numerous injuries that should have left him crippled. But, whatever he received from the Squids or their minions, has given his body the ability to heal in a very efficient manner. Bone breaks left some calcium deposits, just enough to notice, but they seemed to heal quickly and in a manner that makes it hard to see any serious damage. His muscle seem to be of a denser cell structure. Pound for pound, he is stronger than any other dog his size. I think his bite strength is about one hundred twenty-nine percent of that of a typical grey wolf. So, he is closer to what we think a dire wolf would be in terms of strength and build. But, with the longer legs of today's canine He is part Shepherd, part Great Dane, and part… something else."

Abigail stared directly into Emily's eyes. "But he is… okay? Not sick, cancerous…"

Emily could tell that Abigail was suddenly worried sick. Just found someone who was devoted to her, and she to him, and now they may be taken away. She put her hand on Abigail's knee. "Captain, I do not lie to my patients, nor to my patient's family. Fuzz here is so damned healthy that he may outlive us all. His intellectual ability may have also been improved. The only question I have is, how did he get all those injuries? And as a side note, just how old is he really? The aging process in his body has been thrown off a bit."

Abigail had been holding her breath. She let it out, dropped to her knees from her chair and gave Fuzz a big hug. Fuzz gave a signature open mouth dog grin, with a little pant, a "heh" that passes as a laugh in the canine world.

"This is not funny, Fuzz," Abigail scolded him. "I was worried sick that there was something wrong with you. I don't share my bed with just anyone." Abigail realized what she had said a second after it popped from her mouth. She began to turn red.

Emily and Wendy began to belly laugh. Wendy was laughing so hard she had to lean against the wall to keep from falling over. The doctor rolled onto her back, laughing so hard she started to hiccup. Fuzz, thinking it was a new human game, pulled forward, taking Abigail with him and began to lick the vet all over her face. Which started the laughter all over again, this time including Abigail.

About five minutes later, Emily and Wendy had controlled themselves, wiping the tears from their eyes. Abigail was still chuckling a bit as she hugged Fuzz.

"Abigail, if you can give us a good laugh like that once a month, I be willing to have you come in for a free appointment. Boy, I haven't laughed so hard in I can't remember when."

Abigail smiled. "I sometimes say things that come out differently than what I meant. I guess I still have what you would call socialization needs, like dogs do. I was…sequestered to a certain extent in Deseret."

"Hell. You're young. I'm close to forty, with crow's feet that are starting to show. And I still say things that come out wrong."

A commotion began in the waiting area. A loud male voice, cursing and swearing, the receptionist not backing down. Emily dashed toward the sound of trouble, Wendy right behind her, with Abigail and Fuzz bringing up the rear. The hair on Fuzz's shoulders began to stand up, and a small whirring growl like a small engine revving up emanating from his chest.

"Fuzz…" He looked at Abigail, as if to say, "Hey, just getting ready."

A gangly, skinny, twitching and cursing man was standing in front of the receptionist, with a very beat up looking bull terrier mix sitting behind him, ears down as if afraid he would be struck.

"Look, you stupid bitch. She's a vet. My dog needs a vet. She has to see him."

The Doctor recognized the troublemaker instantly.

"Mr. Baker. I told you before, I will not see your dogs again. I will not patch them up so you can abuse them again."

The man called Baker swung around on Emily, glaring at her. "I have friends on the County Council. If you know what's good for you, you'll see my dog here and patch him up. Don't be such a stuck up bitch."

Emily began to seethe. "Get out. Take your meth-addled carcass out of here. This is *my* clinic. I decide who I treat."

Fuzz began to growl. Baker, noticing it, glared at Abigail. "You'd better heel your dog, Missy. Or it may get shot." His right hand moved a shirt flap so that a butt of a pistol was visible.

Abigail put the flat of hand in front of Fuzz's face, a "stop/stay" command and took smooth distance eating strides toward Baker. "Excuse me, Sir. But what did you say?"

"I said, 'Bitch, that you'd better heel...'"

His statement was cut off, as it is impossible to speak when ones adam's apple is being pulled out of your throat so that you can look at it. With her left hand, Abigail yanked the pistol from his belt. As she let Baker's adam's apple go, she slammed the butt of the pistol into his nose. Baker plopped down on his ass, and the bull terrier cringed.

"*Baker! Get out!*" Emily screamed. "And your dog stays here. I'll not have another victim of pit fighting and bull baiting on my conscience. Get out! Don't come back."

Baker, coughing, choking, rose to his feet. "She broke my nose. This isn't over, whore."

Abigail looked at him with cold eyes. "A friend of mine once told me that you should not write a check your behind can't cover. I think that is good advice... for you."

Emily heard the ice in Abigail's voice. She saw a side in the woman that reminded her of Fuzz. Now, he seemed like a big lovable dog. Then, a minute later, he is a being of destruction. Emily hoped she would not see a killing on her clinic floor.

Luckily, Baker managed to get to his feet, tried to stop the bleeding from his nose with his cupped hands. Emily threw him a large cotton bandage. "Here. You're bleeding on my floor." Baker caught the bandage and pressed it up to his nose. He turned and left, mumbling to himself.

The residue from the quick injection of a large amount of adrenaline into her body gave Abigail a slight case of the shakes. Fuzz moved up and nuzzled her hand. "I'm okay, big fella." She scratched his muzzle lightly.

Emily approached Abigail. "Are you sure?"

"Yes. Sometimes I get a few shakes, others I don't. When it's been a while since I have had to... act, it seems to affect me a bit more."

Emily wondered if she should ask some questions that bounced around inside her head. Then, the abandoned bull terrier began to whine. Before anyone else could act, Abigail signaled Fuzz to stay put, and then went over to kneel down next to the dog. The scared canine showed its teeth, as Abigail very slowly moved the back of her left hand toward the dog's muzzle, her eyes averted.

"It's okay, pup. No one will ever hurt you again. Can I pet you?" Her voice was low, calm. The dog's teeth disappeared. He sniffed her hand. Slow, steady, she moved her hands to the dog's head and began to lightly scratch its head. Then, she closed with the bull terrier and gently hugged it. It began to whimper and cry, then licked her face.

Tears begun to run down Emily's face. She quickly wiped them away. Dammit, she was tough, and had seen it all. She would not blubber like a baby.

"Emily, what's next for this dog?" Abigail quietly asked.

"Ah, a light sedative, examination, then I patch him up."

"He won't be... put down, will he?"

"Hell no. I only put down dogs and other animals if they are in extreme pain with no hope. I'll find a place for him, even if I have to build another kennel."

Abigail smiled, kissed the dog's muzzle, then slowly rose to standing. Years later, when Wendy would tell the story, she would claim she saw a halo like glow around Abigail. She turned back to Fuzz, began to scratch his ears. He gave a little grunt of enjoyment.

Emily made a slow approach to the bull terrier, gently patted its head. It licked her hand.

"Abigail, sure I can't convince you to desert, come work with me and Wendy? You have a heavenly touch with animals."

Abigail smiled. "Sorry, but God has a different task for me right now. Maybe later."

"The door is always open. Now, Wendy, can you help me get our new friend back to an examination table?"

Abigail looked at Wendy and saw she had a sawed off shotgun in her hands. Not just any shotgun, but a high end Beretta over and under with some engraved designs on it, the top end expensive barrels having been chopped off with a hacksaw. Since the first rock strike, functionality won out over looks and collectability every time.

"I see that I had another backup besides Fuzz."

Wendy smiled. "We girls have to stick together. Besides, Baker and his type have bothered us before. You would have thought that all the meth and crackheads would have died during the Long Winter. No such luck."

Emily interjected. "We had one dude try to jack us the first week we opened, wanted some drugs. Scared one of the dogs we were examining and had a hunk taken out his thigh. He took off. Wendy got the gun the next day."

"Did you say something about dog fighting?"

"Yes." Emily literally spit on the floor in disgusted. "You would think that with a bunch of BEMS infesting our planet, we humans would discover a bit more humanity and morality. No such luck. A bunch of us seem to want to be nasty, evil monkeys until the Squids eat all of us."

"They fight dogs… in pits?"

"That's the rumor. And the dogs they have brought here bear the scars of something other than hunting. Law enforcement has been too disorganized and weak to do much more than deal with the big crimes, like rape, murder, armed robbery. Everything else is basically ignored. I hope that new Federal Commissioner Miller can get things percolating, more cops on the street."

Abigail stood quiet for a moment. Then she spoke. "People caught fighting dogs in Deseret would probably be shot out of hand. May not be legal, but it would just happen." She glanced at her watch.

"I need to leave. Torbin Bender's wife, Aleks is waiting on me. We are going to go shopping for Fuzz here, since he had no money and can't speak human… yet."

"You're good friends with Major Bender?" Emily asked.

"Yes. You could say he and his wife, Aleks, have taken me under their wings. I live next to them."

"Well, he broke a lot of hearts in Great Falls when he up and married Aleks. His good looks and masculinity even started a couple of bar catfights, although the Tschaaa manufactured hormones and such may have had something to do with that also. Too early to tell."

Abigail laughed. "Yes. Although he's like more a big brother to me, I can see he might have that effect on women."

She tried to hand the pistol she had seized to Emily.

"No, you keep it. You may need it on the way home, in case Baker tries to screw with you, with the help of some of his friends. A little evenizer never hurt anyone."

Abigail examined it. At first, she had thought it was a replica cap and ball Colt Navy Colt. Then she noticed it had been converted to take .38 Special cased ammunition, and was loaded with five wadcutter rounds. Her Uncle Buck had taught her how to play poker, something she never told her parents. He mentioned it was good to have an ace in the hole, both in a game and in real life. Maybe this pistol could be an ace in the hole.

"Okay, Emily. That is probably not a bad idea. So, time to go, I guess." Abigail stuck her hand out and Emily shook it.

"Abigail, stop by any time with Fuzz here. I mean it. Consider it a social call, not an appointment."

"Okay, I will. See you later, Wendy. Thanks for all the help."

Wendy handed Abigail back the file she had brought with her. She patted Abigail's shoulder. "Watch yourself. And in the folder is a current rabies and registration tag. Keeps people from always asking questions."

The women said their goodbyes, patted Fuzz one more time, and Abigail took him to her vehicle. Wendy yelled after her. "See you at the Oktoberfest celebration next week."

"Yes. I'll be there with Aleks and Torbin Bender."

Wendy watched Abigail leave. "Man, she is *hot*."

"And, very straight. Besides, you have a very committed lady friend. Lesbians are not exactly overrepresented around here, thanks to the Squids and their lackeys."

The Tschaaa had pushed the fact that humans should reproduce, and provide more meat. Since homosexuals did not reproduce amongst themselves, requiring heterosexual activity to reproduce outside of artificial insemination, the Tschaaa and its minions, especially now the Church of Kraken, sent the "offenders" to the harvesters whenever possible. Just as all the homeless, infirm, many of the elderly, were quickly taken off the streets, anyone else not willing to try and reproduce were targeted. Thus, flight to the Unoccupied States when possible. Many humans did not make it.

"Well, Emily, I can still look at the menu."

"Spoken just like almost every guy-friend and lover I ever had. The problem is, they couldn't keep their hands off the menu items." They both laughed.

"Come on, Wendy. Let's clean up and see if we are going to have any more customers. I'll send Pam home. After Baker, she needs some time off. We can handle the receptionist job today."

The drive back to the Base was uneventful, no Baker or his comrades showing up to follow her. The gate guard waved her through, saluted the sticker on the front window that designated her not only as an officer but a government representative. Abigail chuckled for the umpteenth time that someone in the old days who would have just finished high school was now an adjunct ambassador. But disasters and wars created their own rules and needs sometimes. And the current situation qualified as both.

Fuzz was snoozing in the back of the SUV, not a care in the world. Sometimes dogs had it so easy.

She pulled up into the driveway next to her place and Fuzz was immediately awake.

Abigail exited the SUV and let Fuzz out of the back. He darted directly to the front door. Abigail let him in so he could fulfill his duties of checking for any beasties and bad guys who may have snuck in while they were gone. Abigail felt sorry for any being that Fuzz ever caught breaking in to their quarters. Just on his second day here, and he had already settled in, and found his function.

Abigail went inside and made sure Fuzz had some fresh water. Then, she went next door and knocked on Alek's and Torbin's door.

"Coming." Aleks called out. She came to the door and greeted Abigail.

"So, how did the vet's office visit go? Did Fuzz bite anybody?"

Abigail laughed. "Thank you for the vote of confidence. Actually, I almost 'bit' someone." She then told the story of the short, very short, dust up with the meth head.

"So, Emily Anders, the veterinarian, told me to keep an eye out as this Baker and his friends had a revenge complex."

"Come on, Abigail. I have something for you I was going to give you later, but you may need it now."

Abigail stepped in, standing by the front door after shutting it. Aleks was back in a flash with a good sized dark purse.

"Here, I have a duplicate. If you look closely, it has a hidden pocket for a pistol in the center of the bag, accessible from the side. Here, look? Now, reach inside."

Abigail reached in and felt a pistol grip. She slowly pulled it out. It was a five shot .38 Smith and Wesson Chiefs Special, nickel plated. There were five .38 Special Caliber hollow-points in the cylinder. The pistol was used but well maintained.

"I bought the purse, Torbin found the pistol. Now you have a purse and backup for a night out with the girls."

"But I don't usually carry a purse. I never had a habit of carrying a purse. I usually have a rucksack or small pack."

Aleks looked at her as a mother might look at a child who was having trouble understanding a concept.

"Young *ladies* carry purses. Packs are for field maneuvers and hikes."

Abigail was still learning the ways of a "normal" young adult so anything non-military still seemed a bit foreign.

"Don't purses just get in the way? Women always forget them, can't find things in them? "

Aleks sighed in exasperation. "Husband. Come here please."

Tobin came from the back of the duplex.

"Hi, Abigail. How are you and the beastie today?"

"Husband. Pay attention." Aleks held up the dark purse. "Would you want to see me carrying this, or a pack if I were wearing my tight dark dress and we went out for the evening?"

"Well, right now, I don't think the dark dress would be very comfortable, you being pregnant and all... ow. Don't kick me!"

"May I remind you that this pregnant belly is the result of your efforts? That it contains two large baby Marines already fighting and kicking? Now, answer the question!"

"Okay. Yes, the purse looks better." Torbin gave a sideways glance at Abigail. "Never marry a female Russian spy. They have no sense of humor."

Abigail tried not to laugh, but lost the battle. Soon, all three were laughing. Torbin gently put his hands on his wife's belly. "Fussing and feuding in there again, huh? Well, according to the docs, they will be out a bit earlier than normal, so that will help."

"Until then, I look more like a beached whale every day. But see, when you touch my belly, they calm down. They recognize their father."

"Yeah, and they know they'd better treat their mom right or I'll have something unpleasant waiting for them. They are extremely healthy."

"I think sometimes they are too healthy. Isn't there some joke about the baby slapping the doctor at birth instead of the other way around? I think with your sons, that is a distinct possibility." She turned back to Abigail. "Well? The purse?"

"I surrender. The purse is very nice. The pistol is very nice. You two are spoiling me."

Aleks reached forward and hugged her. "You deserve to be spoiled, little sister. Now, are we going to go shopping for that great brute of a dog of yours? You said you would buy me lunch and I am starving."

"You are always hungry, wife. Ow. That hurt!"

A little more than an hour later, Aleks was eating a large plate of broiled chicken as Abigail ate a bowl of spicy bean soup with black bread. Fuzz sat at her feet, being treated by the eating establishment as a service animal when they saw how well trained he was, how he watched everyone and everybody who came near Abigail and Aleks. Besides, Aleks was good friends with the owner, an expatriate Ukrainian who was visiting the U.S. when the first rock hit. His family had been with him, so somehow he made it into the Unoccupied States with no casualties. It one of the few total success stories from those days, the family surviving, and then thriving. He and his wife opened the European Café and American Eats just off Base, and it was a popular hangout for the troops, especially the increasing numbers of foreign personnel. Over a thousand Russians, several hundreds of Japanese, a couple of dozen Romanians, and some thirty Canadians now called Malmstrom home. Small numbers of non-U.S. personnel were scattered among the other military bases in the Unoccupied States.

Abigail was having trouble keeping a straight face watching Aleks eat. The woman who had been teaching her the finer points of being a young lady, of how to act as a normal person rather than as a warrior all the time, was now eating as if she had just killed something and was eating in her cave. Especially in the last two weeks, the sped up development of the twins in her womb (thanks to the Tschaaa and their genetic/hormonal meddling) had increased Aleks' and the twins' metabolisms, probably exponentially. Aleks was hungry almost all the time. When she ate, she often zoned out to all other activities, eating her food with a singular purpose.

Aleks looked up, and realized she was being watched. She stared at Abigail, who was trying to hide the beginnings of a smile. "What's so funny?" Aleks demanded, after chewing and swallowing another mouthful of food.

"Nothing. Nothing at all."

Aleks then realized she had chicken grease and sauce all over her hands and mouth. Her face turned red, and she began to curse quietly in Russian. Abigail handed her a spare napkin, then began to laugh.

"Fine. Laugh all you want. Just wait until *you* meet Mister Right, get pregnant and become a beached whale. I'm going to video it and email it all over the known universe. See how you like it. Being famished all the time, with two hungry trolls inside you." Tears were in her eyes, and Abigail now felt bad for having fun at her expense. Pregnancy under normal conditions was bad enough. This was not normal.

"Aleks, I'm sorry. The last thing I want is to upset you…"

Fuzz rose up in a quick and fluid motion, sticking his muzzle into Aleks' face and giving her a large slurping dog kiss.

"Ew. That is enough. I can clean my own face, thank you." But Fuzz would not stop until Aleks began to giggle. Then, he laid back down, his mission accomplished. The one with pups was no longer upset. "I think I will steal your dog, little sister. He is the one male, the one person who treats me with compassion."

Abigail took Aleks' hand. "I'm sorry. You have done so much for me and I'm laughing at you. Please don't be angry."

Aleks smiled at her. "I am not angry at you, just frustrated. I'm used to being an active Russian officer, not a babushka who is always hungry. But your hand looks inviting. Here, let me have a taste of it…."

Abigail snatched it back, both women laughing.

Aleks looked up at the entrance to the restaurant. "Speaking of a possible Mister Right, Ichiro just showed up. With a whole bunch of young Japanese officers about your age."

Abigail looked up and saw Ichiro Yamamoto as he walked in, some four fresh faced and very young looking Free Japan officers in tow, like ducklings following their mother. All of the Japanese officers, including Ichiro, had fresh pressed and immaculate combat fatigues on. Abigail felt butterflies in her stomach as she watched Ichiro.

Their eyes had then met for the first time, and an odd recognition had passed between them, as male and female warrior. And also, if Abigail was not mistaken, an attraction. Ichiro became as shy as she felt, having a stumbling conversation for a few minutes, each afraid of saying something completely stupid. Finally, Torbin had broken in. "Alright, you two. Sit down and relax. You are acting like you're afraid of farting in church or something. What? Don't glare at me, wife. They just need to relax. We're all friends and comrades here."

Aleks broke in. "Please ignore my rude and crude husband. He has the social graces of a slug. Please, have a seat."

They had parted that day a bit more relaxed. Abigail met Ichiro once more at the BX prior to him being whisked back to Japan. Again, they had been like two school kids, trying not to admit a mutual attraction. Why they had this effect on each other, Abigail had no clue. Ichiro was also older, more experienced, so Abigail assumed he would not be inexperienced with the opposite sex.

Ichiro had been gone for some time, though Torbin had said he would be back soon. And here he was.

"Ichiro. Over here," Aleks called to him. His face lit up when he saw her, then a wide smile appeared when he saw Abigail. Quickly he turned to his charges, snapping out orders of "Do *not* embarrass me in front of these friends and fellow soldiers." He approached their table with his little group, bowed in turn to Aleks and Abigail, who stood up, pregnant Aleks remaining seated. Fuzz, next to Abigail, rose to a sitting position so that these males, not to be trusted, would know they were being watched. At the sight of the huge dog, the young officers' eyes went a bit wide. But Ichiro only had eyes for Abigail.

"Ladies. So very glad to see you. And Captain Young, Abigail, I see you have made a new friend. Is he friendly?"

She shrugged, grinning. "Sometimes. We just met yesterday. Aleks and I bought him some canine comforts—food, chew toys, and a few other items a healthy dog needs. He is living with me now. Fuzz, this is Ichiro Yamamoto, a friend."

Fuzz's nose worked and twitched at the word "friend" as he took in Ichiro's scent. Now he would remember him. "May I pet him?" Ichiro asked.

"Try scratching his ears. Just move slowly. He has had some bad experiences in the near past. So far, he met Torbin and seemed to accept him. But he definitely prefers women."

"Ah, then Fuzz, we have something in common." Slowly, he began to scratch the large dog's left ear. Fuzz began to make small happy noises. Abigail smiled. Good, under the right circumstances, Fuzz would at least tolerate men.

Aleks looked at the Japanese officer's uniform. "You have different rank insignia. Is there something you are neglecting to tell your friends?"

Ichiro bowed his head a bit, slow in removing his hand from Fuzz's ear. "My country promoted me to Major. Because you and Torbin were promoted, and they wanted to keep us equal, have equal face."

Aleks knew that was so much bullshit. There was no reason that Free Japan would feel a need to "save face" about anything. Hell, they had provided eight jet interceptors for the U.S., something Madam President was chomping at the bit to get flying around the U. S. bases. The Unoccupied States was playing catch-up due to the heavy damage most military bases had endured.

"Tell me another tale, my friend. I see a conspicuous badge, decoration on your left chest. That is not due to your good looks."

One of the young officers began to talk quickly in Japanese. Ichiro turned and replied sharply to him, causing all four of the young men to snap to attention. Abigail broke in. "Please, Major. There is nothing wrong about them telling us you have received a... medal I think was the word he used. Aleks and Torbin have told me how hard you have worked. And Deseret knew about your part in Key West."

Ichiro turned toward her, a bit of surprise in his face. "You... speak Japanese now, Abigail-san?"

She smiled a bit shyly as she answered. "I already speak Russian and can act as a liaison with those forces. Since General Reed is using me as a coordinator and go-between with them, the Canadians, as well as Deseret, I also must be able to converse with the other major partner—Free Japan. I started using some education tapes, and found some Japanese speakers. But I am still just a beginner."

Aleks interjected. "It is rude to keep secret good fortune. And unlucky."

She looked at the officer Ichiro had berated. "I know you must speak English, or you would not have been sent here. Pardon me while I stand on my position as a pregnant lady and demand to have her curiosity assuaged. What medal is on his chest?"

The young officer looked toward Ichiro, his commander. The new Major sighed, gave him a small nod. The young man drew himself up to his full height, still about an inch shorter than Abigail. In very good English, he spoke, "Major Yamamoto is the first recipient of Order of the Golden Kite, reconstituted recently. It is an older award disallowed after the U.S. Occupation of Japan began. It was believed to have been too... militaristic following World War II. Our Constitution has been changed to allow such symbols of war again, as we *are* at war." The young officer puffed his chest out even more. "It is like... your Medal of Honor."

Ichiro blushed, bowed his head. "I am unworthy. I tried to talk them out of taking this action. It is too great of a responsibility..."

Aleks cursed in Russian and lurched to her feet, holding her large belly. "You saved my husband's life, nuked those bastard Squids and hacked a bunch of them up, and you say you are unworthy? Are you trivializing my husband's life? The life of the father of the two trolls in my stomach? Not to mention the others you helped bring back. Well, are you?"

Ichiro knew he had made a grave mistake. He had "pissed off" Aleks, something even Torbin avoided. Hell, it was rumored General Reed worked to stay on her good side.

In a quick move, he bowed low. "I am so sorry, Aleks-san. I in no way wished to disrespect you or your family. I just..."

"Just shut up and come here." She reached out and pulled him closer. She kissed him on both cheeks, congratulating him in Russian, then English. "If you must know, Torbin and the rest were put in for the New Medal of Honor. The process is at Madam President's desk. He also babbled about not being worthy, of not being a hero. Do you think I would marry just anyone? Carry this grand belly around for just anyone? Accept the fact that I am right. You deserve everything you are given."

The four young Japanese officers tried not to smile. That would have angered their Commander, who was like a God to them.

Abigail stepped closed and reached her hand out, bowing slightly. "Congratulations, Major. It is an honor to share this moment with you." Ichiro took her hand. Their eyes met and again something passed between them. They held each other's gaze long enough for Aleks to see that another spark had been lit. She smiled. Now she had something to tell Torbin that was new, and a bit unforeseen.

Ichiro released her hand. "I would be honored if I could help with your Japanese studies. You mentioned once before about studying my style of fighting. Please feel free to contact me and we will set up a time or two."

"Why thank you, Major. I will do just that."

"Please, we are not on the parade field. Please call me Ichiro."

"Okay... Ichiro. Will you be at the Oktoberfest celebration next week end?"

"Yes. General Reed has requested all non-U.S. units and delegations set up a booth or area with representations of their culture, traditions. He said we would be in for ... the long haul—I think that is the expression he used. He said we need to get to know each other as well as possible, as we would be shedding blood together. A very Samurai concept."

"Then I will see you there. I told Aleks I would help keep her and her soon-to-be-born offspring well fed."

Aleks snorted at this. "Like I said, just wait. You will not think it is funny when you are pregnant."

Abigail did not reply. She had not been in for one of the many exams she had completed in Deseret, motivated by the possible radiation contamination from the Hanford Explosion. The Elders and the Prophet in Deseret had strongly "suggested" she not consider child bearing so as to prevent any deformed children. But, no one had ever stated that she absolutely *had* been contaminated to such an extent to harm her ability to have children. Now, she was much freer, more independent here in the U.S. She would have to research the matter.

"Aleks, as uncomfortable as you are, it is still a God given miracle. I'll do whatever I can to help you and your babies when they are born."

Aleks smiled, squeezed Abigail's arm. "Thank you, little sister. You help keep me sane."

Ichiro bowed. "I must leave you now. I need to feed my charges and show them more of the Base. Till we meet again, ladies."

"See you later, Ichiro," Abigail replied.

Ichiro then spoke to the four young officers, and they fell in behind him as he led them to the ordering counter.

Aleks looked slyly at Abigail. "Handsome, aren't they?"

"They are all fine young men, Aleks. Now, shall we finish eating? I know you don't like to let food go to waste."

Aleks snorted. "Yes, make jokes now. Just you wait." Abigail laughed, and the two women sat down to finish their meal, Fuzz waiting patiently at their feet.

As they rose to leave, Ichiro reappeared. "Excuse me, Abigail-san. I thought you might enjoy this." He placed two small objects on the table in front of her. The Japanese warrior had found some colored paper to demonstrate his origami skill. A small figure that had to be Abigail stood next to a four legged one that had to be Fuzz, large even in this miniature state.

Abigail's eyes widened and her mouth opened. "Ichiro. They are fantastic. How did you do that?

He smiled. "My father and uncle taught me. It helped me to focus in my young years, when I was always in motion. I was not an easy child."

Abigail carefully picked them up, and placed them on her palm. She was beaming. She showed them to Fuzz, who sniffed the figures, discovered they were not edible, so ignored them. Abigail kissed Ichiro on his cheek. Then, she blushed, realizing what she had done. Ichiro grinned. "I am glad you like them. Now, I must leave. See you next weekend."

As he left, Aleks broke into a grin at Abigail's blush. "Not so calm, cool and collected, are you?"

This made Abigail blush more. "This is just so... nice. I am not used to getting such special presents."

"Well, little sister, get used to it. I think Ichiro likes you, as do many other men. Welcome to the eternal challenge of women— dealing with men who have the hots for us."

CHAPTER 9

My investigations, interviews of people involved, and studies of the recovered documents have shown me Director Adam Lloyd was not a one dimensional dictator as many have tried to portray him. Misguided he may have been, he was not eaten up with evil intent toward others, was not in the same class Hitler and Stalin.

-Excerpts from the Works of Princess Akiko, Free Japan Royal Family

KEY WEST, FLORIDA

Adam Lloyd sat at his office desk, reading an email. It was a short and sweet report about the aborted entry into Atlanta by the Kraken forces. He grunted as he thought about the chances of a reconditioned F-51 Fighter, older than just about every surviving human on Earth (the Invasion and Long Winter had been extremely rough on the very old and the very young), being used to successfully strike deep into Cattle Country. Once again, the lack of understanding on the part of the Tschaaa concerning general warfare, matters especially air defense, had been demonstrated. Their eye in the sky saw things, then ignored them because the Squids really did not understand threat evaluation. The concept of recognizing potential or possible threats was alien to them. On their world, threats had been categorized based on whether something attacked the Tschaaa, primarily the young. Once it did, then it was classified as an enemy, a threat. Just because a creature had lots of teeth and claws did not mean it was avoided; it had to try and eat a Tschaaa before it was designated as dangerous.

Adam thought their development in the oceans of their world must have been different than man's journey from trees to savannah. Man's brain had developed in such a fashion that everything different was treated as a threat until proven otherwise. The fact that in the early days, almost every predator was perfectly happy to try primate or monkey flesh was probably the primary reason for man's built in hyper vigilance. Those individuals that were wary of *everything* survived to pass on their genes. Possibly, in Adam's mind, modern society's dumbing down of this wariness and distrust of strangers as a means for all to "just get along" may have slowed the realization after the first rock strike that someone was attacking Earth.

The Tschaaa had set in place limited parameters for search and detection for the eye in the sky. Thus, an awful lot of aircraft and surface movement and activity were ignored. This attitude had now come to bite them in the ass in a big way, again.

Mary was in the outer office. Both she and Kat were beginning to show the early signs of pregnancy. Close examination and monitoring by Doctor Fredericks of some two dozen pregnant females that had definitely been 'infected' by the Tschaaa materials had so far not shown any dangerous effects. All the fetuses were developing at an accelerated rate, leading to their greatly increased metabolism, and the food intake by the mothers. At the time of birth would come the big test. Would they be delivered normally, especially as all the pregnancies were with twins, or would the sped up gestation cause complications? And what about the first year of growth, development? There were so many questions, all which made Adam pissed off because this whole development was accomplished in secret by the Tschaaa, driven by His Lordship.

At least the now two "sister wives" were getting along. They had bonded after their extremely nasty knockdown-drag out catfight.

Then, they had manipulated him into simultaneously impregnating them on the same night. This was before the revelations of the attempted Tschaaa developed modifications. But, knowing they would both be giving birth to twins gave them the sense of well-being and accomplishment many pregnant women feel. Having someone close to you experiencing pregnancy at the same time added to the positive attitudes, and feelings of security.

Adam sighed. He loved them both dearly. Having just one wife had never been in his plans, definitely not two. But now he knew he could not bear to live without them both. Jamey and Jeanie still shared his quarters, and occasionally his bed. Kat and Mary thought of them as sisters and were grateful they provided Adam with sexual outlets and activities that took the onus off of them. The two Wives knew they were not a threat to the family unit. In fact, Jeanie and Jamey looked forward to being "aunts" to the four newborns, just as they had enjoyed being bridesmaids at the small wedding Adam and his new wives had at the Base Chapel. Since the fallout, both physically and figuratively, from the U.S. nuke strike on His Lordship and the resultant time of rage by the Tschaaa against all humans, the positive feelings many Base personnel had for him were muted. Many no longer really trusted his "vision" of Squid/human relations. After all, what would stop the Tschaaa from having another moment of rage and attempting to harvest the Key West Base personnel, supposedly "friendlies".

So, a small wedding was best. Besides, none of the participants had surviving family members to attend.

The idea of man with two wives and two "aunts" who shared the marital bed would have been deemed weird and perverted in most circles ten years prior. Now, thanks to the Rocks and the Invasion/Infestation, almost every human institution had been at least modified, with some being destroyed. This especially applied to what constituted a "family". If five people said they were family, then they were. With entire bloodlines wiped out almost overnight, human society was rebuilding around new constructs.

Things finally began to settle down, with the majority of the residents of the Key West area getting back to what had been normal day-to-day living the last few years. The local Tschaaa and their minions were either bending over backwards to appear non-threatening or at least to not appear at all. After the initial rage, the counting of the dead by the Tschaaa (ten thousand and rising from the nuke and its aftermath—two-thirds of the victims young and adolescents), a new concept set in among the Tschaaa on Earth. They were vulnerable. They had last felt this when the Plague had hit their primary food source on their home world, leading to the great trek here to Earth for a replacement food source, dark meat. They had so quickly overwhelmed the human defenses, then survived the Long Winter with few problems, their sense of superiority and security felt as a species prior to the Plague had returned with a vengeance. Only to come crashing down again due to that same over confidence.

His Lordship Neptune and the other Lords had finally come to an agreement that, if they were to survive on a world still inhabited with dangerous feral humans, they had two choices. First, turn all of their resources and individuals—including robocops, lizards, and greys—to slaughtering or imprisoning every single human left on Earth, probably an impossible task in one lifetime. Or, second, work with the "friendlies" they were attempting to develop into a client species and contain the Feral humans, especially the ones organized into the Unoccupied States. Lord Neptune had pointed out that the humans residing in the U.S. seemed to be the main agitators. Deal with them, and the head of the snake may be cut off. It may grow back in Free Russia, Japan, or some other area, but that would take time. The former Americans seemed to be the driving force behind the organized resistance.

After a heated discussion, with His Lordship pointing out the human concept of scorched earth warfare, it was decided to use the virulent followers in the Church of Kraken, backed with Tschaaa weapons, Squid-manned Deltas, robocops in Falcons, the battlerobs, and small numbers of lizards and greys using smaller tactical weapons, would support large numbers of human Krakens armed with human weapons.

The Tschaaa had seized large numbers of weapons, leaving many in huge piles, some unprotected from the elements. His Lordship Neptune had also established a large manufacturing and reconditioning unit on the huge Gulf of Baja complex. Using some captured humans from Mexico that he had allowed to run loose as a backup source of dark meat genetic diversity, he had over a thousand humans working twenty-four hours a day in bringing small arms back to operational status. Already, some one hundred thousand rifle, pistols, and machine guns had been provided to the Church of Kraken "volunteers" being trained to assault the Ferals. But, as just proven by the quick and dirty single plane air attack, the Tschaaa controlled forces were far from being efficient.

Just then, the combination laptop-notepad communication device that Andrew had built for him buzzed. His Lordship was calling him on this secure device, in order to have a completely private conversation, with not even Andrew listening in (supposedly).

Adam connected, His Lordship appearing on the screen. No longer located at the damaged super complex at Marquesas Key, the Tschaaa Lord was floating at a very slow speed on one of three seagoing platforms the aquatic aliens had built on Earth. Three times the size of the USS Ronald Reagan nuclear carrier, its mass enabled it to ride out most storms or hurricanes. Though slow, its movement made it harder for anyone to attack it. The Lord was not going to be attacked again.

"Good morning, my Director. I see you are already working on the daily tasks and problems you incur as part of your position. By any chance have you received reports concerning Atlanta?"

"Good Morning, my Lordship. Yes, I was reviewing it just this minute. Unfortunately, some of my predictions were true."

The Tschaaa Lord signed frustration with his social tentacles. "Yes. Once again, your fellow humans accomplished something completely unforeseen. I thought my decades of study had given me some insight into what humans can be expected to do in most situations. Apparently, I have been horribly wrong. Why is that, Director Lloyd... Adam? You and I seem to understand each other. Why can I not understand other humans?"

Adam sighed. "You have, to put it bluntly, completely underestimated us. We humans are a nasty, warlike species who have waged global conflict for centuries. We have such a wealth of experience in long term killing of our own species, not to mention any other predator that threatened our survival. Thus, we have developed almost unlimited means and methods to attack and kill, as well as defend against such attacks. Your species has not. You developed a very homogeneous culture and population very early. Crèches allowed controlled breeding as well as controlled competition for power and breeding rights, preventing mass warfare. You have become used to dealing with species who were either so overwhelmed that they could never really provide real resistance, or species who accepted your dominance and tried to work with you. Of course, other than your original meat source, you did not try to eat the other species with established cultures, societies. Then you found us."

Adam considered his words carefully. "Your Lordship, you have been of two minds with us, almost schizophrenic in nature. You want to eat us, but you also want to communicate with us and use as a client species. One minute, you are scaring the crap out of us, the next minute you are trying to calm us, pet us like a faithful dog. You are doing all of this to a species that is very good at developing tools to slash, kill, and exterminate all who stand in our way. We have more books involving stories of war and conflict than all other topics. We have entire colleges whose sole purpose is to study war, to improve our tactics and strategy on how to kill people and break things. *You* decided to try and control *us*. We have forgotten more about waging war that you will ever know."

Adam stopped. He wondered if he had just gone too far, said too much. He knew this Lordship was the one who developed the majority of tactics and weapons to invade and occupy much of the Earth. He set up the current system of harvesting dark meat, of potential human clients. But the nuke strike had thrown that into disarray.

His Lordship stop moving for a moment, the Squid's flesh darkening to show negative emotions. Finally, Lord Neptune manipulated his two social tentacles into signs of resignation, then agreement. "Unfortunately, you are right, my Director. Your bluntness once again proves to me that my decision to use you in this leadership position among humans was correct. I guess we Tschaaa have a tendency, in your vernacular, of preferring to be fat, dumb, and happy. Now, I have barely been able to regain control of most of the major population centers in Cattle Country. But Atlanta still holds out. Out of the two hundred and fifty Church of Kraken members sent to probe the city, in one quick and simple attack, a hundred were fatalities, many others damaged. I also lost battlerobs and Soldiers. It has shaken faith in the ability of myself and my Crèche to deal with this problem and keep it from spreading. Already, there are reports of parts of Europe and the Near East where adult Tschaaa have been attacked, harvester ships and stations damaged, humans friendly to us killed. I am being blamed. I cannot afford any more… defeats."

As much as Adam wished he could just ignore this, to allow the Tschaaa Lord to sleep in the bed he had made, he could not. Any day, someone else could take over the Key West Base and the Reconstructed States, with all the inhabitants harvested just to be rid of them. The Tschaaa greatly preferred dark meat, but would kill and eat any human deemed to be a problem. So, Adam must not let Lord Neptune fail and fall. Not just yet.

"You have more Kraken humans going to Atlanta, true?"

"Yes. Over a thousand will arrive tomorrow. Luckily, I was able to use the survivors of the air attack to form a thin line around Atlanta. Many Cattle are still afraid, and are hiding rather than trying to break out. They may not realize how weak my forces are. I could flatten Atlanta, but that would be admitting defeat by burying much usable meat."

"Well sir, barricade, quarantine the entire area. Get more forces there. Have a tight ring around the city. Then, slowly lay siege to them. Light attacks here and there, just enough to keep them hunkered down. You will then starve them out over the winter. Move in during the spring, mop up the survivors. The cities under your control can provide additional units of meat, in addition to the ones killed trying to fight or flee. As long as you provide uninterrupted high quality fresh dark meat, your fellow Lords will soon lose interest in your problems. Show them success, they will adopt like tactics in their areas, and slow the spread of insurrection before it becomes organized."

His Lordship known as Neptune wiggled his tentacles in a sign of glee. "Yes! How stupid of me. This is mentioned in many of your books, films. Why did I not notice that?"

"Because, Your Lordship, you are not a warlike human."

After another half hour of dealings and discussion with His Lordship, Adam cut the connection and walked out to Mary's office. Sitting next to her was Kat. "What a pleasant surprise. My two wives together." He walked up and kissed each of them in turn. He mused about this odd turn of events—two sister wives who loved him and each other, both pregnant with twins. The fact they had been manipulated genetically and hormonally by the Squids definitely did not make them happy at first. However, they decided to accept the feelings their conditions generated, especially the love for each other and Adam. The children in their bellies were developing in a healthy but accelerated fashion. At night, the two women would put their bellies together so the half-siblings could "visit" while in the womb. They gently talked to the unborn, rubbing each other's stomachs.

He slept between them, sometimes being woken by them in the middle of the night, as they began to caress him, and each other. Soft, slow love making was the order of the day, and he did not complain.

He still had not had a real discussion with Jamey and Jeanie—his assistants and still occasional lovers— about this new dynamic of two pregnant wives, and what they wanted to do in the future. When he tried to talk to the "Barbie Twins" they smiled, told him not to worry, told him to worry about Kat and Mary, not them. They were happy helping with the children of Key West Base and would be happier with all the new twins that would be running around in the next few years. They had found a purpose in life, were adapted to existing under Tschaaa control. Which was another reason he tried to keep the situation with His Lordship from imploding or exploding. The thought of a bunch of Squid and harvester robots grabbing the residents of Key West made him ill. He would do anything to prevent it.

Both Kat and Mary stood up and gave him a group hug. "How're doing, Boss?" Married or not, Kat still called him Boss, and of course, she flashed her signature perky smile at him. The producer who said in another lifetime ago that her perky smile early in the morning, when things were going bad, was a definite plus didn't know the half of it. Lately, her smile and Mary's calm support were almost all that he looked forward to. Chief Hamilton, of course, was still a rock, but he always was. His smile, however, was not perky.

"It is going as well as can be expected. His Lordship is still trying to regain complete control in Cattle Country, while also figuring out what do about the Unoccupied States. Some of his fellow Lords wanted to start using Falcons and rocks to pound the Ferals into dust. They had to be reminded about the Long Winter, its effects on breeding areas, and the idea of scorched earth. We know the U.S.

forces have access to nuclear weapons, leftover ICBMs. That bomb on Marquesas Keys proves some of the warheads are still functional. I think Madam President would risk bombing everyone back to the Stone Age rather than cede complete control to the Tschaaa. Mutual assured destruction keeps us from an all-out nuclear and rock strikes war. At least as long as calmer heads prevail."

"Well, on a positive note," Mary said. "Doctor Fredericks says our babies are developing just fine, though faster. So we are hungry all the time."

Adam smiled. "Well, I'll get us all a nice big lunch. Any requests?"

"Lots of meat and cheese, Boss. I need all the protein I can get." Kat flashed a full grin.

Adam looked at his two ladies. "Did anyone tell you just how much I love you both? That without you, I'd be lost?"

At that comment, Mary began to tear up. "Dammit, don't be so serious. Of course we know, you big jerk. Now you've set off my waterworks." Kat handed her a tissue to dab her eyes, then hugged her.

"Come on. We've gotten through worse, haven't we? Especially when we were alone. We have each other now, and soon, four little ankle-biters running around. Adam, Boss, get us the food, okay? Low blood sugar and pregnancy are not a good mix."

"Sorry. This married with baby is all new to me. I'll call the All Ranks Club, have them make up a large plate or two of goodies for us. Okay?"

Both women smiled, nodded in agreement.

After making arrangements to have the food delivered, he had the two ladies join him in his office. The three sat on the oversized sofa, Adam in the middle, an arm around each wife. Mary and Kat each kissed him on opposite cheeks at the same time.

"Are you having any problem with the concept of two wives and four kids, all at once?" Mary asked.

"As long as I can find a way to keep us all safe, I'll work it out. You know I'm playing a balancing act. Since I have this room swept and secured of all electronic bugs, I'll give you some details on something I am working on." As the two beautiful ladies snuggled up on opposite sides, clasping hands on his lap, he began to tell them some plans.

A half hour later, he finished. "Well, what do you think? As a bug out plan, will it work?"

Kat went first. "How would hiding in Cuba be any safer? Aren't there still Squids there?"

"Other than some Tschaaa breeding along the reefs, after a severe harvesting the Lord in charge of the Cuban area and South America ignored it. The Chief found most of the surviving Cubans and has set them up providing us with high quality sugar cane, which seems to becoming almost as habit forming to the Squids as cigarettes with nicotine is to us. His Lordship Neptune convinced the younger Lord to cede the Cuban area to his control in exchange for additional high quality dark meat. Now, he has all the cane he wants, trades it with other Minor Lords for favors. So, he left some humans alone there, happy as long as he gets his sugar cane."

Adam began to gently caress the bare necks of his wives.

"No one will notice a few more humans, apparently there to harvest a cane crop. I doubt if anyone from the eye in the sky has looked at Cuba in months. The Chief constructed hurricane and bomb proof shelters in some caves in the mountains with power and water, using Tschaaa sun power technology along with human equipment. Short of the equivalent of complete worldwide nuclear war, we can live there for years, unnoticed."

"Even Andrew and his comrades wouldn't find us?" Kat interjected.

"That's assuming they would be looking for us. I think that if things get so bad that we bug out, that means that His Lordship is probably dead, which means we all just become general pieces of meat. No one will be looking for us specifically. If we keep our heads down, away from the water, we could go unnoticed for years. Unless, of course, the Lords in charge then so completely overharvest us that they start looking for individuals for slaughter. However, I think, thanks to His Lordship's examples, the Tschaaa Lords are learning resource conservation. Especially when it comes to dark meat. So, if we keep our heads down, we and our kids can have nice, long lives."

The three sat there quietly for a few minutes. Then, Kat kissed Adam. Followed by Mary. "How did I get so lucky? Most men have trouble finding one good woman. I have two."

Mary sighed. "Karma, I guess. You saved me and thousands of others from death and fates worse than death. Yes, others have died, probably for us. But you try to help. Which is more than most humans are doing today.”

"Not expecting anyone are you?” Kat asked.

“No, why?”

Kat gave an impish grin at Mary, who grinned back. Both women's hands moved toward Adam's lap.

"Now, ladies, this is a place of work. What if someone comes in?”

"Then I guess they'll get a free show,” Mary answered.

"Shut up and stop worrying, Boss. You deserve something special.”

CHAPTER 10

The decision by Madam President Paul to re-institute certain holidays as a means to insure bonding between all the disparate populations residing in or near the Unoccupied States was a correct one. How could she know that the acts of human bonding between former strangers would uncover an evil in their midst few could imagine?

-Excerpts from the <u>Works of Princess Akiko</u>, Free Japan Royal Family

OKTOBERFEST
MALMSTROM ARMED FORCES BASE
GREAT FALLS, MONTANA

The Oktoberfest celebration had the makings of a huge success. Madam President had mandated that all military installations sponsor a weekend Oktoberfest celebration, inviting the surrounding populace to attend. All of the foreign delegations and units were asked to put together cultural booths and displays, in an attempt to reconnect people from different cultures after some six years of isolation. Everyone must think themselves as humans first, whatever race and people as secondary. Humankind was in one big boat, and they would sink or swim together.

Veterans Day, Thanksgiving, and Christmas were to follow, as official holidays of the Unoccupied States of America. The New Senate and New House were finally organized at the former State House in Bismarck, North Dakota, a city that had suffered only very minor damage. Located far from any Squid installations, a circle of air and ground defense positions were emplaced to insure its protection from anything short of a major rock strike. It had a stately government rotunda and legislative center that was easily modified to handle the entire new crop of Senators and Representatives for a new Federal Government. Streamlined laws and regulations had been passed and implemented since the nuke strike on Key West. Still based on the original Constitution of the United States from 1789 (The original document was saved from Washington D.C. due to great sacrifice by a few—a story for another day.), people began to realize they had a civilian government in existence and control, once again.

The celebration had turned the parade and sports field into one large fairground. Every major military, cultural, and local group had been given an area to set up cultural displays, activities, food and souvenir stands, games and competition. Everyone had put their best foot forward.

When Aleks, Torbin, Abigail, and Fuzz had first arrived (early, to get a good table) Aleks had grabbed Abigail and went directly to the Japanese exposition. Ichiro had been placed in charge of the cultural display area, which had a good-sized tent and a large section of a sprinters track directly in front. The women soon learned why Ichiro had chosen this site.

Ichiro and Abigail were exceedingly glad to see each other, which was precisely why Aleks had chosen to go there first. She had seen the spark that had passed between them the week before, when Ichiro had created the origami figures for Abigail. They now resided in a small glass case Abigail had purchased, residing in a place of honor on Abigail's bedroom dresser. The Avenging Angel had a nice warm feeling every time she looked at the small, exquisite representations of Fuzz and herself. Having grown up the last six years with very little personal property, presents of such a personal nature meant the world to her.

As Abigail and Aleks approached the Japanese area, Fuzz following closely behind, they saw how Ichiro had selected and organized the site. Lined up at one end of the one hundred yard dash track were two Japanese rickshaws. By the tent was a roped off area where Japanese soldiers in Kendo gear were practicing their craft. Visitors would be welcomed to try their hand as well. There was another area where a demonstration of katana swordsmanship was being held by Japanese in traditional Samurai clothing and armor. This last area was where Ichiro was, in full splendor. Aleks led Abigail and Fuzz to where Ichiro was standing, sans his traditional warriors battlefield mask. Ichiro gave a large grin when he saw the ladies approach, keying primarily on Abigail.

"Abigail, you came. With Aleks and Sir Fuzz, I see." The canine, upon hearing his name, deigned to give Ichiro a tail wag. But when he saw several other Japanese in full traditional battle regalia --- fear producing masks and all—he began to growl, his fur standing up on his back.

"Fuzz. It's okay," Abigail reassured him, putting her hand on his collar. With the feel of his mistress' hand, and her command, the war dog relaxed a little. Just a little. He kept a watchful eye all those around him. The sight of the large dog aroused the interests of the Japanese personnel, including three women dressed in traditional Geisha-style dress. They were soldiers also, but had been politely asked by Ichiro to wear some traditional garb. He asked rather than ordered these young soldiers because he did not want them to lose face in front of their comrades. Japanese women soldiers fought and died alongside their male counterparts since just after the first Squid appeared.

Abigail saw the three young ladies and smiled broadly. "Why, their clothes are beautiful. They look so…feminine. Pretty. They are soldiers also, yes?"

"Yes, Abigail-San. All trained fighters. Sumie Sato here, the one in the middle, is one of our best jiu jitsu practitioners. I have seen her best men almost twice her size. Almost as dangerous as you are, according to Torbin-san."

At this comment, Abigail blushed. "Torbin exaggerates greatly. I am just a simple Warrior of God, doing what I must."

"You will start training with me, soon, Abigail-san? I would like to see your skill for myself. Of course, Sumie and others will be there to chaperone as well as assist, so that no one accuses me of anything... untoward."

"Ichiro, no one would ever accuse you of anything other than being a true gentleman. Is that not true, Aleks?"

Aleks had to try and keep a straight face, flashing back to a certain evening when the three Russian "sisters" had made an unannounced visit to Torbin's quarters just after they first met. What had started out as an attempt to use sex as an intelligence gathering tool had led to one of the great love stories that came out of this war—the love between Aleks and Torbin. But a certain young Japanese Officer had been well entertained also that night.

"He is an officer and a gentleman," Aleks quickly answered. "He will continue to be one if for no other reason that your big sisters will see to it, little sister." Now it was Ichiro's turn to blush.

"So, Abigail, next week. Contact me and we will begin. We can also practice your Japanese. Now, please come with me, and I will give you a tour of our cultural site."

With Fuzz providing a furry escort, causing many to step back upon his approach, Ichiro explained the various activities they were providing for all visitors. Ichiro explained the rickshaws. "I know how Americans love contests, games at their state fairs. So, each rickshaw will be pulled by two men, with a woman in the back to add a little bit of weight. They race to the end of the track, turn around, and race back. We have checked and rechecked the rickshaws to be certain they are safe and will hold up to the task. Of course, that means several soldiers have practiced and become quite good at this type of racing. So who ever beats them must be of superior ability."

Aleks sniffled. "Well, this is one activity I will not do. My two trolls add too much extra girth and weight. Any people pulling me would be at a disadvantage." She looked around. "And these same trolls are making me very hungry again. I see some rice cakes, sushi, and sashimi in that tent. I have some funds here..."

Ichiro looked taken aback. "You, pay? Never. You are my guest, the wife of my brother in blood. You will never pay for anything in my presence again." He looked so serious. Until Abigail began to laugh.

Ichiro gazed at her with a confused expression on his face.

"I am sorry, Ichiro. It is just, as much as my *big* sister has been eating, it may just break your food budget for this activity. Not to mention that you may run out of food."

Aleks bumped her hard with her very rounded hip. "You just wait. When I am back in my fighting trim, I will show you what big sisters *do* to smartass little sisters." Even Fuzz laughed.

After Ichiro had the sushi chef fix Aleks up with two stuffed bento boxes, including some tempura, Abigail had Fuzz escort her back to their picnic table, where Torbin had been patiently waiting, beer in hand. Abigail stayed, supposedly to get the full tour and demonstration of Japanese culture. However, Aleks saw the real reason. Abigail acted like a little school girl around Ichiro, and he seemed equally attracted to her as well. With a sly smile, Aleks allowed herself to be ushered off, realizing there was just so much chaperoning a big sister could do.

Abigail watched the kendo demonstration, then a full tea ceremony, both which fascinated her. Especially since a man in full Samurai garb performed it first, followed by one of the three 'geisha'. Ichiro explained in Japanese the significance of the ceremony. "The Japanese tea ceremony allows one to become centered, to block out all other pressures, problems. Thus, both men and women, especially warriors, are taught to perform it. It is said it can greatly reduce ones blood pressure if you are prone to that problem."

"You do this also, Ichiro?"

"Why yes, Abigail. I would be happy to walk you through it someday, explain the significance of each part of the ceremony, the serving of the tea. But if you want to learn how to do it, a woman should teach a woman. Women and men move differently, so it easier to follow another lady as she does it than some large handed man."

Abigail smiled. "Yes, Ichiro. I would enjoy both scenarios. Let me check my schedule, and see about a good time for both of us."

Ichiro smiled and bowed. Then he took her to where two geishas were showing first arrivals how to perform a traditional dance. Quickly, he forced Abigail to join in, despite protests that she was not dressed for it and was too clumsy. Within minutes, Abigail's natural flowing, graceful rhythm was brought to the fore. Soon, the two female-soldiers-as-geishas were concentrating on her, weaving more intricate moves and steps into the dance as others looked on.

Ichiro watched, a growing warm feeling in his stomach. How she, a hardened warrior, still had this youthful grace and exuberance. He shook himself from his reverie. He knew she "did something" to him when he was in her presence. He began acting like a young schoolboy around her, something he must control with all his responsibilities to all the new, young officers and enlisted men.

The music finally stopped, the two geishas bowing and applauding at Abigail. One giggled and said in Japanese, "We must ask the Major to bring her back. I would love to see her in traditional geisha garb."

Abigail bowed back, answered in Japanese, "I would like that, ladies."

"Oh, she speaks Japanese. Even better."

"I am just learning. Please bear with me."

"There is no problem. Come back anytime and we will help you with your studies."

Ichiro then approached. "I will have her return when her duties and yours permit, Lieutenants."

The two young women soldiers, instead of snapping to, suddenly produced fans, hiding their grinning faces behind them, acted demurely female and coquettish. Ichiro sighed. Let them take an inch with their feminine ways, they are soon into it for a mile. "There are some other guests approaching. A demonstration for them would also be nice." The two ladies were soon welcoming other local residents, and the demonstrations began again.

Abigail smiled at Ichiro. "I'm always shy, afraid to do new things at first. At least things not involving…soldiering. Hopefully, I did not make a fool of myself."

Ichiro smiled warmly at her. "You moved with a grace and a surety of someone who had done those dances for years. You are what Americans call a *natural.*" He gently took her hand. She gently squeezed in return as their eyes met.

There was a loud human bellow. Both Abigail and Ichiro looked up to see its source, the moment broken. The Sons of the North, formally Sons of Norway, had arrived, led by the ever loud and effervescent Rolf Knudsen.

"Come, little brothers! We have brought you mead, ale, and meat," Rolf bellowed. "We have come to sample your culture, and bring you ours. Today is a day for celebration!"

There was a dozen large Nordic men and half a dozen of striking, tall blonde females, most in traditional attire. Tobin said later that Rolf and company must have watched every Viking movie and tape of a television show to get an idea of what a Norseman really was. Then they picked out the most energetic parts, doubled them, and decided *that* was how a "Viking" acted. The Sons of the North had a pavilion set up toward the other end of the parade ground and sports field. There they had received permission to serve mead and home brewed ale along with traditional dishes and pastries. Now, apparently easily bored, they felt a need to bring a party to everyone.

Two of the large Sons of the North were quickly admiring a katana of one of the costumed Samurai. One of them proceeded to slice his hand open on the sharp blade, leading to gales of laughter from his fellows. A geisha/soldier quickly responded with a first aid kit, insisting with her batting sensual eyes that yes, he needed to be bandaged. Quickly, several of the Norskies were admiring her handy work, as well as the geisha. Two of the large blonde females responded and reminded their male counterparts that they were being watched by their women.

Others went to the food section of the erected tent, quickly stuffing their mouths with whatever they could find. Actual gold and silver coins appeared as the Sons of the North tried to buy all the food present. It was later ascertained by the Federal Authorities that the large population of Norwegian, Danish, Swedes, a few Dutch and Germans, who had resided previously in or moved to the Unoccupied States had been producing their own coinage, not trusting the use of left over and plentiful greenbacks. Going back to the old ways was being taken seriously.

Ichiro and Abigail responded to the food area, afraid nothing would be left for other visitors. Abigail quickly lapsed into Norwegian, to the joy of the Viking wannabees. Rolf had been too busy orchestrating his group's arrival to have noticed Abigail. When he heard her voice, he bellowed.

"Captain Abigail Young, shield maiden! You are here!" He swept toward her, Abigail sure he was about to crush her in a bear-hug, which she would not allow. But what he did instead surprised her.

Rolf stopped short, bowed to her, took her hand and held it to his forehead. He muttered some runic phrase. "I see you and obey you, milady Freyja. I pledge my loyalty to you." Abigail thought she had disbursed of his beliefs about her royalty, but now he was using a name from Norse mythology in referring to her. This had to stop.

"Rolf Knudsen." She began in Norwegian. "I appreciate your loyalty and your friendship, but I am not a royal lady, and I have no connection with the goddess Freyja. Please. I am a Christian. I cannot be associated with gods and goddesses."

Rolf grinned. "Whatever you desire, milady. But you do remind us of Freyja, especially your ability as a warrior. However, I will bow to your requests. Captain Young."

Rolf then bellowed. "Mead! This lady requires mead!" A large buckler of mead, still partially chilled, magically appeared in front of Abigail.

"I am not an alcohol drinker, Rolf. Though our Prophet now says small amounts are fine, I am not one to drink more than near beer."

"Just a small taste. To be connected with our people, who you are a part of. Please, just a sip."

Abigail smiled. His happy demeanor was infectious. "Oh, alright. Just a drink. I am curious how it tastes." She found it a nice, sweet drink from honey, but with an edge to it that Abigail recognized as alcohol. This nice tasting drink could easily get a young woman in trouble, so she quickly handed it back to Rolf.

"Thank you, sir. That is nice and quite refreshing. But, as Major Bender will tell you, I'm a 'lightweight' and would soon be intoxicated should I continue."

Rolf grinned broadly. "Maybe next time. I will eventually convince you of the heavenly qualities of mead."

Meanwhile, Ichiro had managed to convey to the Sons that they needed to leave some food for the rest of the visitors to come, but that there were other activities to experience. He pointed to the rickshaws and explaining about the fun race, which soon looked like it was a mistake. Bellowed Norwegian drew Rolf's attention, as well as Abigail's. She followed him to the one hundred yard race track, where the Norseman were milling around two male Japanese soldiers and Sumie, still in geisha attire.

Ichiro explained the rules in English for the contest.

"I have two experienced Japanese soldiers who, to be fair, have been practicing racing with the rickshaw. Sitting in the back will be the young lady in geisha attire, Lieutenant Sumie Sato. The purpose of this race is not only to win, but to insure the passenger in the back has a safe and pleasant ride. If you tip the rickshaw over, you must stop, reseat the lady, and then continue. So careful technique is required. I will give anyone so desired a small head start to handicap the more experienced Japanese personnel."

"So," Rolf asked "We pull this small wagon with one of our women in the back, up to the end of the one hundred yard track, turn around, and race back. That is the race?"

"Yes, my large friend. That is the race."

Sumie had been standing demurely by, coyly using her Japanese fan to cover her smiles, flirting with the large Nordic males to put them off their game. Then, one of them, apparently well into his cups, tried to grab her rice paper fan.

"Here, sweet thing. Let me try your fan out. It does not seem to be big enough…" The large bearded male was unable to finish his statement. One second he had a grip on Sumie's hand, the next second he was flat on his back. A foot sweep trip, twist and throw, too fast to follow to the unenlightened, and the large Son of the North was looking at the sky, with Sumie's dainty foot on his throat.

For a second, everything froze. Abigail thought an uncharacteristic *'Oh, shit!'*, certain violence was about to break out.

Then, uproarious laughter. The Sons of the North began to laugh and point at their fallen and embarrassed comrade. Sumie, for her part, quickly stepped back, bowing low to the fallen Viking. "Please, Sir. I am sorry. It is just this fan is a family heirloom. I am quite attached to it." She put out her feminine hand, manicured nails and all, coquettishly smiling, to help the large man up. He took it and jumped to his feet.

"You have hidden shield maidens, I see," Rolf bellowed. "Small, but deadly. Eric there will learn his lesson about being rough with strange women." Rolf and his comrades clustered around Eric. They slapped his back, pushing him, unmercifully ribbing him about being taken down by such a small lady.

"I am sorry they are so rough and crude, Ichiro. They're acting as if they never grew up." Abigail was worried that Ichiro would think less than kindly about some individuals who claimed her as being of 'their people' yet were acting like dolts.

Ichiro smiled. "Many of them are soldiers, to be facing death very soon. In fact, most of them grew up the last few years facing death on a daily basis. If not the Squids, then it was your Long Winter that threatened your survival. We in Japan faced little in comparison, other than food and energy rationing, now the occasional 'visit' by some young Tschaaa warriors looking for a duel. Which we handle quite well."

He shrugged. "So if they chose to 'let off steam' as you Americans would say, so be it. My personnel can take care of themselves, as you can see. The traditional Viking and Samurai warrior societies were probably not all that different in some respects. Though I have never heard of a Viking composing haiku poetry." Abigail and Ichiro both laughed, once again looking into each other's eyes. And once again, the moment was interrupted by Rolf suddenly yelling about the race.

In a few moments, the two Japanese soldiers were in place in front of their rickshaw. Rolf demanded that he assist Sumie in mounting the passenger area of the transport. The Japanese officer demurely smiled, once again using her fan and body language to transmit exactly what Rolf could expect and not expect. He seemed captivated by this small woman; this soft feminine creature one moment, a deadly snake the next. Abigail then realized what Sumie was doing. Much as Aleks and her spy sisters did, she was playing Rolf like a large fiddle, using her femininity to extract just the right behavior. But behind the silk glove was an iron fist. She was an intelligence agent, pure and simple. Someday, when she felt more comfortable, she would ask Ichiro, and maybe Sumie, about her true position. If Aleks were here watching, she could probably tell.

After helping Sumie into the rickshaw, Rolf addressed the other. He positioned himself in front of the rickshaw. Then he bellowed, "Brynhildr." One of the statuesque blondes appeared and proceeded to settle into the rickshaw. Ichiro noticed that only Rolf was standing in front of the rickshaw, checking the rail handles.

"Rolf-san, you need a partner to help pull. Otherwise, you will be at a disadvantage." The Japanese had lengthened the front rails so two persons could pull the rickshaw in tandem, turning it into more of a racing machine. They had also been braced a bit to prevent breakage during repeated races. This would be the first race of the day, so Ichiro wanted to make sure it went off well.

Rolf laughed. "Have you noticed how large I am? Your soldiers are the ones at a disadvantage."

Ichiro shrugged, then attended to his two rickshaw trained soldiers. Abigail, standing nearby, thought she heard Ichiro say something about not holding back. Maybe they had originally thought to throw a race or two in the beginning so as to generate interest, and not anger their guests. That concept apparently had just been shelved. The Japanese had apparently decided that the lithe runner's body structure the two soldiers had would blow Rolf Knudsen out of the race.

Ichiro approach the front of the two racing machines and stood between them on the center double stripe between the two racing lanes. "On the count of three, the race will begin. No contact is allowed between the two teams is allowed. This is not chariot race as in the movie *Ben Hur*." This produced some laughter. "You will race one hundred yards, turn, and race back to this point. Remember, you also have to provide a safe trip for your passenger. If she falls out, you must stop and pick her up before resuming the race."

Someone yelled from the crowd of onlookers, "I'll pick up that geisha and run off with her myself." More laughter as Sumie demurely and coyly smiled, covering her mouth partially with her fan. Anybody trying to run off with her would be sorely surprised.

"Any questions?"

"Yes," bellowed Rolf. "What is the prize for winning?"

Ichiro had not really considered a prize, thinking the race was strictly for fun.

"I had not considered a prize. What do you suggest, my large friend?"

"When I win, the two men must drink a full mug of mead. If by some chance the gods are angry with me and you win, I will… "

Sumie suddenly yelled out in perfect English and in a surprisingly loud voice, "Let me ride around on your shoulders for an hour. I would like the view from up there." Everyone laughed, Rolf the hardest.

"I may just have to lose on purpose." With that comment, Brynhildr growled something at him to the effect that if he lost on purpose, he would be walking stooped over, unable to give anyone piggyback rides. Rolf winked at her, chuckling. "It's a deal."

"So then, we are agreed," Ichiro stated. "Are the teams ready?

You are both ready. At the count of three, the contest begins. One, two... *three.*"

In professional sports, especially American football, there was the concept of "fast twitch", or explosive muscle types. This meant that even three hundred pound linemen could develop and be trained in the use of explosive power, shooting out from the line with great speed despite their size. They may not have the traditional sprinters more slender physique, but the linemen made up for it in fast twitch muscle mass. Rolf gave everyone present a demonstration of the concept.

The six foot six blonde giant shot out from the starting line, reaching the twenty-five yard line strides ahead of the two surprised Japanese. The lighter load of Sumie compared to Brynhildr did not matter. In fact, the Viking maiden was bellowing encouragement and instructions to Rolf, which seemed to make him run even faster. Rolf made it to the one hundred line three full lengths ahead. He swung hard around, Brynhildr leaning out on the side of the rickshaw as if she was in a motorcycle sidecar race, keeping the transportation device from tipping over. They began the return leg.

The Japanese team threw everything they had into the brace, turning at epic speed, yelling 'kiyis' as they strained to catch up.

Brynhildr yelled at Rolf, "Move, you fat cow! They are catching up." Rolf gave a loud Norwegian war yell and barreled toward the finish line. It was not even close. He won by almost four full lengths.

The Sons of the North exploded in jubilation, with their maidens joining in. Ichiro had a genuinely shocked look on his face. How this large, tall man could move so fast was a mystery to him.

He approached the winded Rolf, bowed in respect, then offered his hand. "Well done, my large friend. I was completely overconfident."

Rolf, between gasping breaths, replied, "Little brother, your people play well. Come to our great hall, any time." He stood up straight, and started to call for a drink of mead or ale. But his face was a bit pale, and he seemed to be woozy. Suddenly, Abigail was in front of him. "Rolf, please sit down."

"What?"

"I said, *sit down.* Before you fall down." Rolf sat, plunking down hard on the grass.

"Could someone find me some cool water, and a rag?" She looked into Rolf's face. "Why must men be so stubborn, so hard headed? You have been drinking alcoholic drinks all morning, which does not hydrate you well. Then, even in this cool weather, you begin to sweat because you cannot do anything at half speed. You are in need of some water, not mead, and to sit for a minute."

Rolf grinned sheepishly. "Yes, little mother."

"I am not your Mother! Does someone have that water?"

Sumie magically appeared with a pitcher of cool water, and handed Abigail a colorful silken scarf. Abigail soaked the scarf, put it on the back of Rolf's neck, then made him take sips of water from the pitcher, which looked like a beer mug in his huge hands. Sumie leaned over and whispered in his ear. "You would make a great sumo in my country, Rolf Knudsen. You have the heart of a samurai. It is pleasure to have met you."

Rolf's first impulse was to grab Sumie and lay a large kiss on her mouth. But, to everyone's surprise, her gently took her hand and kissed it. "You would make a perfect elfen princess of the old ways, milady. You are invited along with Major Yamamoto to our great hall. Anytime."

Sumie bowed, lightly kissed him on his brow, fluttered her fan a bit for effect, and was gone.

Just then, a commanding female voice called out in Norwegian. "Rolf Knudsen. Where is my grandson?"

"Here, grandmother." Rolf bellowed back, then tried to stand up, only to feel two surprisingly strong hands pushing him back down.

"Oh no you don't, private. You will sit for few minutes more." Abigail ordered him.

"Excuse me, Captain, but my brother and I are Corporals now."

"Well, congratulations, then. But stay seated. They can find you." Abigail stood up straight and glanced around her. She saw the oldest woman she had seen in a long time approaching her, flanked by two middle-aged women. The Invasion, and the Long Winter that followed, had been deadly on the old and the young especially. Many children had been harvested in the early days after the Tschaaa arrival, many others dying due to lack of food and adequate shelter. The old, needing medicine, food, shelter, died even when there was no harvesting in the area. So, the aged, the seniors, were not well represented in the general populace.

"There you are. What trouble are you in now? I see a young lady has taken you in tow, as usual."

"Grandmother, this is the woman I was telling you about. The shield maiden." Rolf knew he had screwed up the moment he used that term again. But Abigail did not seem to notice. She quickly stood in front of Grandmother Knudsen and performed a remembered curtsy, despite being in blue jeans rather than a dress.

"Elder mother, I greet you. It is an honor."

Grandmother Knudsen broke into broad smile, still showing healthy white teeth. Her face showed wrinkles, her hair was gray, but she still stood straight, almost as tall as Abigail. "Ah, you are one of us. I thought my big oaf of a grandson was exaggerating again. You speak Norwegian like a native born. How about Danish and Swedish?"

"Some, Ma'am. But I am only half Norwegian. The other half is Romanian."

"But you have a big chunk of Norwegian, the North, in your heart. I can feel it. May I take your hands, young lady?" Abigail held her hands out and Grandmother Knudsen took them.

"My God. You have strong hands. But they still look like a woman's. Your forearms are strong too. You have been raised as a warrior." The older women gazed into Abigail's eyes.

"You have other special gifts. You will be a unifier, not just a soldier. And I feel you are... sensitive to certain things, able to see into people, and tell who they are. Am I right?"

"Yes, Ma'am. I... see things sometimes. I especially can tell things about pregnancies. I can sense twins, and such. You have similar abilities, true?"

"Yes, young lady. We are a lot alike." Grandmother Knudsen then leaned forward and kissed Abigail on the cheek. "I would be honored if I could call you granddaughter. I have adopted many in the past six years. Only Rolf and his twin, Gunnar, are truly of my blood. We are the last ones of our specific family to survive. The rest were lost in Minnesota."

Abigail had a small lump in her throat. She had no elder relatives left, other than her uncle, wherever he was. The thought of having an actual grandmother created a yearning in her soul—a yearning for family. "I will be the one who feels honored, Grandmother Knudsen.

So yes, you may call me granddaughter."

Grandmother Knudsen beamed. "Please stop by the great hall of the Sons of the North. I am there most days. I can begin to teach you some traditional womanly pursuits—like sewing, knitting, and baking—in the old ways."

Abigail smiled back. "I would like that. Thank you." Abigail knew the older woman must sense her lack of knowledge in non-warrior pursuits, so there was no need for additional explanations.

"Now, my dear, please excuse me as I round up my wayward grandson and his friends. They need to help with the displays and demonstrations at our pavilion."

"Rolf. Come with me. Time to leave."

"Yes, grandmother." Rolf, now recovered from his weakness, called to round up the men and maidens. As the unofficial leader of the group, he seemed to have all their respect.

Rolf approached Ichiro. "I thank you for your hospitality and competition. Please come by our pavilion, sample out culture. And stop by our great hall off base any time. All warriors are welcome."

Ichiro bowed. "Thank you. Please give our best wishes to your honored grandmother. We Japanese know how precious the elders are."

Rolf clapped a large hand onto Ichiro's back, almost knocking him over. "I like you more every minute. Sons and daughters of the North, time to leave." The raucous group made their way back to their cultural display area. As they made their way, Rolf conversed with his grandmother.

"See, Grandmother, I told you Abigail was one of us. She would make someone a great wife."

"But not for you, grandson. I am sorry."

Rolf frowned. "Why not? Am I not good enough for her? Or she for me?"

The older woman sighed. "Grandson, trust me. Her path is in another direction. She has special tasks to accomplish. Besides, you have a host of young ladies already fighting for your attentions. Do not waste your time pining for something you cannot have."

Rolf kept frowning. Then he sighed. "You have never been wrong, Grandmother. I will heed your advice." He suddenly broke into a wide grin, and swept his grandmother into his arms.

"Put me down, you oaf! I can still walk," she protested.

"I am just demonstrating how I won the rickshaw race. Hold on." Rolf took off running toward the Sons of the North cultural display area, laughing like a fool.

Abigail approached Ichiro as he organized another rickshaw race. "I must return to Torbin and Aleks. They are probably wondering if I am lost. Fuzz will also likely come looking for me soon."

Ichiro smiled. "Yes. Your friends will think I kidnapped you." He bowed. "Thank you for coming, and helping me with the large ones. I am glad the Sons of the North are on our side."

"I will see you soon, Ichiro. I hope."

"Of course, Abigail. We must work on your Japanese, your unarmed combat skills, and your sword play."

She looked into his eyes. "I just like your company." She kissed him on the cheek, then turned and left. He was momentarily surprised, then broke into a broad grin. He began whistling some military march as he began to strut happily around the Japanese pavilion.

Abigail now made her way back to the picnic table she and her friends had staked out. Changing weather patterns had pushed really cold weather in this part of Montana back, Indian Summers being more of the standard. The sun was out, but it still being before noon the temperature was cool, not cold. She was happily humming, thinking about Ichiro and the activities she had just finished in the Japanese cultural area, carrying two large plates of barbecued meat from a "Tex-Mex" display, the one meant for Aleks brimming over. She had been sent on the mission to collect large amounts of protein by Aleks as soon as she had returned to Torbin and his very pregnant wife. He was sent out for drinks, near beer or soft drinks for Aleks and Abigail, beer or mead for him.

Abigail successfully reached the table without mishap, and was greeted with joy when she arrived. "Ah, *food*, to keep these two trolls in my gut satisfied. Place the big plate in front of me, I feel famished."

Abigail grinned. The extra speed of development of the twins Aleks was carrying, thanks to Tschaaa machinations, had turned her into an eating machine.

At that moment, she happened to glance up and froze. A face she had never really expected to see again was walking toward an area staked out by scavengers and other ne'er-do-wells. In addition to a party area for their people, the scavengers had also been allowed to set up a pawn shop operation, swapping items or paying out cash. Now, headed toward that area was the face of a man to which she had added a large scar in Evanston.

She had mentioned the incident to Torbin months ago while driving him back to Malmstrom. Five scavengers claiming they were from the Base on "official business" to check out Evanston had shown up after Torbin and his men left. They had tried to molest what they saw as two teenage girls—Abigail and Ruth—and "paid the piper" for it. Shot by Mathew, beat and gutted by the two young females, only this one, now Scarman, had managed to escape. But not before Abigail had opened his face with a knife he had tried to use on her.

She whispered in passing to Aleks. "Excuse me, there is something I need to take care of." Fuzz, sensing a change in his mistress, started to rise. "Stay" she commanded in Romanian, in addition to the hand signal and Fuzz froze. Now he was in a psychic quandary, caught between obedience and protection. Aleks saw a look on Abigail's face she had seen before, on other's faces. The killing look. Someone was about to possibly die here.

"Abigail. Wait." She tried to get up, her large stomach prevented her from doing it quickly. Abigail was gone. Aleks cursed, scanning for Torbin. He saw him a ways away, drinks in hand. She put her fingers to her mouth and let out a loud unladylike whistle.

Torbin had a drink carrier with two soft drinks, a near beer and a real beer in his hands, making his way through the increasing crowds. The recognized whistle made his eyes dart to where their table should be. He saw Aleks mouthing the name "Abigail" and pointing toward his right. He quickly scanned the crowds, saw Abigail walking in a gait he had seen before. She was in route to "take care of business/mess someone up". Something serious must be in the wind.

"Aw, fuck!" he exclaimed, looking for a place to set his drinks. He saw a table nearby with a young couple, Second Lieutenant John Brown and his wife. He was one of Torbin's new trainees, just recently graduating from officers training. Torbin strode over, setting the drink carrier down on the table of the surprised young people.

"Sorry to bother and intrude Lieutenant, Ma'am, but I need to leave these here for just a moment. Ma'am, I will come back so that we may be properly introduced." Then he was off, trying to catch Abigail.

"That is the Hero of Key West?' His wife Sue asked.

"Yes, honey it is. He's in a hurry, too. Wonder if he needs help…."

"John, you just wait here. If he needs help, we will know soon enough. Then, you can go."

Sue was a no nonsense farm girl from North Dakota, whose family had barely survived the Long Winter. She has met John as he was passing through. They met, fell in love, she followed him on his military career. He had no family, as he had lost them to the rocks. She was his family now.

He smiled at her. "Right, as usual. I think you are the common sense of this family."

"And you are the love of my life. Now, let's guard his drink carrier, and wait for what's next."

Abigail reached the edge of the scavenger display, tables, and pawn shop. She saw Scarman beginning to move to the back of a tent they had set up.

"Hey, Scarman. Remember me?" Her voice resounded strong and firm.

The tall, slender dark haired man turned toward the voice. He had already busted the face of some others who thought it was funny to call him that, the scar that ran from his hawk nose across his right cheek to his right ear flashing red when he was angry. Which was quite often since he had returned from Evanston. He spun around, looked and saw the source of the yell. And turned a bit pale.

"Girl," he spat out. "I don't know you, so I suggest you watch who you insult."

"You lie!" Abigail spat back. All conversation stopped around her. "You and four friends tried to molest two virgins from Deseret in Evanston. Only you survived. I gave you that scar. Now I call you out to answer for your crimes before God."

Another voice then broke in. "Hey, it's that bitch who sicced her dog on me at the vet's." The man known as Baker spoke up and moved forward.

"You lie also. Now, Scarman, or whatever your real name is, stand forth and deliver."

Most of the men and women around the scavenger area knew each other, worked together for the last few years. They had faced many dangers to provide needed supplies, for a price, to the survivors in and around Great Falls and Malmstrom after the Long Winter. That they had taken some of the supplies by force had been an ignored fact until a little over a year ago, when the developing government of the Unoccupied States had clamped down on independent scavenger operations. Now bitter that their source of riches had been slashed, scavengers were becoming a source of trouble as well as developing criminal enterprises, challenging the authority of the new State and Federal governments. They would be damned if one of their number would be called out by some pissant bitch from Deseret.

"Go fuck yourself," was the answer, as several men and women began to move toward Abigail.

One large, drunk individual with a prominent belly reached out to grab Abigail's shoulder. "Hey, good lookin'. How about given up some of that Deseret loving…"

His eyes bulged as Abigail grabbed and twisted the offending hand, crushing fingers together with very unladylike strength before spraining the wrist and putting him to the ground. He bellowed and grabbed his injured arm with his good hand.

"Who the fuck do you think you are?" A hard looking woman yelled, cocking her arm back as she approached.

"*Ladies and gentlemen!* Let us pause for a moment and reflect!" Torbin's "command voice" caused everyone to pause and concentrate on him for a moment. "Do we really want to mar these festivities with unwelcomed violence, or can we handle this matter in a civilized manner?"

There were some quizzical looks in his direction. "Who the hell are *you?*" Someone who apparently did not watch television yelled out.

"Do you mean that in an actual or a philosophical sense?"

"Stay out of this if you know what's good for you, soldier boy," someone joining the forward group chimed in.

"Now you've done it. Called a Marine a soldier. What an insult—I demand satisfaction!" Torbin counted heads. About a dozen men in and around with bad intent in their eyes and another half dozen women looking to fight. More might join in. He stood even with

Abigail, about two yards to her right.

"Why is it we attract violence, little sister?"

"The bad and evil must be challenged. They cannot be allowed to stand," Abigail spit out.

"I was afraid you would say that."

A friend of the man Abigail had put down cursed and rushed at her with a beer bottle. His testicles were quickly kicked up into his lower intestines with a front kick that was a blur. The fight began.

The woman who first approached Abigail tried to claw her face and received a smashed-in nose for her trouble. Two men rushed her to knock her down, pin her to the ground. One lost an eye, the other gasping for breath from a smashed adam's apple.

Torbin broke one man's jaw, dislocated an elbow, snapped a wrist almost in two. Sheer numbers took their toll, and both Abigail and Torbin were mobbed.

On the ground, Abigail bit the finger of a woman who was scratching at her face, broke the index and social fingers of the other hand that was up under her shirt, clawing her breasts. She grabbed the adam's apple of a man on top of her, pulled it out so he could look at it.

Then, through the hubbub, a loud, bellowing war cry was heard, followed with an instantaneous sound of thuds and something hard hitting bodies and breaking bones. A man on top of Abigail was sent flying off. Another man's face was smashed into a bloody mess as some type of club struck him off the Avenging Angel. Abigail heard a loud, recognizable voice cursing in Norwegian, yelling for Thor to come and watch what his Son was doing. It was big Rolf.

Rolf had ripped the leg off of a large picnic table, and was using it as a very effective war club. He took a moment to smash two men off of Torbin, then returned to Abigail. Rolf swung, smashed, and grabbed, almost in a berserker level of rage. Enraged scavengers came to their fellow's aid, only to receive broken arms and legs. A woman in the back drew a pistol, started to take aim on Rolf. A sheathed katana smashed her wrist, sending the handgun flying. Then it put her lights out with a blow to the base of her skull.

Just then, a loud police whistle blew. Followed by a bullhorn. "*Stand down!* Cease fighting. We will use deadly force if necessary!" There were not a lot of uninjured scavengers and friends left standing, so it appeared the fight was ending anyways. But if there had been one woman with a gun, there may be others, and Rolf was not bulletproof.

Rolf was panting, his mouth foaming a bit. Abigail saw his eyes were a bit glazed, so she did not know if he understood the instructions. She quickly stepped in front of him, and grabbed his face with her hands, speaking in Norwegian, *"Rolf.* Look at me. It's over. The enemy is defeated. Songs of victory will be sung."

Finally, his eyes focused. His face broke into a broad grin. "Abigail Young. I thought for a moment you were a valkyrie, come to raise me from the battlefield."

"No, my friend. You are very much alive." She kissed his cheek. "Thank you for helping us. I think I bit off more than I could safely chew."

Rolf suddenly kissed her back, then got a look of concern on his face. "Shield maiden, you are injured."

Then Abigail realized her bottom lip was bleeding, she had fingernail scratch marks on her chest. Her bra strap had been broken and her breasts were free, only partially covered by her torn shirt. She began to blush bright red. Rolf, seeing her discomfort, quickly shucked his outer shirt and covered her. Abigail winced as she put it on. "I think I have some damaged ribs also, Rolf."

"You and me both, Abigail." It was Torbin, bruised and battered, but a smile on his face.

There was a loud, growling bark, and the crowds around the scene of the fight parted. Fuzz, war dog, had arrived, dragging Aleks behind him. "You goddamn brute! Slow down! I almost fell!"

Rolf's mouth dropped. *"Fenris.* Devil wolf. You have come for battle."

"No Rolf. It's Fuzz, my dog," Abigail chided him.

"It is Fenris in the shape of a dog. See how he comes to fight by your side?"

Abigail grabbed Rolf by his ears, pulled his face down to look at her. "You. Are. Impossible. But you are a true friend. How can I ever repay you?"

Before he could answer, the bullhorn sounded again. "Now that we have your attention, a military police officer will to talk to you! Stay where you are!"

Half a dozen Military Police in battle rattle came through the crowd toward the combatants. Torbin recognized the officer in charge, the Shift Commander. Lieutenant Michael Hobbes, a Mustang officer like Torbin, was also a Marine. He had somehow made it from what was left of Washington State after two volcanic eruptions and the Hanford Explosion. A Fleet Marine, he hadn't seen the ocean since.

"Major Bender. I see you are having fun as only a Marine can have. May I ask as to what happened?"

"Well, my friend, Captain Young there was having a verbal disagreement with one man known as Scarman when someone decided to lay hands on her. So of course I came to the aid of a comrade in arms."

Lt. Hobbes looked at Abigail, now swimming in Rolf's huge shirt. He chuckled. "So that's what she looks like out of uniform. It looks like you two were definitely rolling around in the mud, blood, and beer. I know you're a Marine, but did you realize it was twelve to one odds?"

Torbin grunted. "Odds, smodds. No one beats on my adopted little sister and gets away with it. Besides, the scavengers and their friends are definitely in worse shape than we are."

"Primarily because you had an old style berserker by the name of Knudsen show up. Captain Young seems to be the only one who can calm him down once he gets going. But I guess beauty can tame the beast."

The injured Scavengers were all yelling and cursing at the MPs, demanding that Torbin and Abigail be arrested. Funny thing, Scarman and Baker were nowhere to be found.

"She broke my nose." A woman was crying, blood running between her fingers. Others were demonstrating broken bones, lacerations.

"That big fricking asshole there broke my arm with a club... I was just standing here, no weapons.... We were just minding our business when that Deseret bitch showed up!"

Lt. Hobbes was not happy. "I guess I'll have to take you all to the station, get statements from everyone. You were much too efficient with your mayhem. It would be different if they had weapons. That would justify your level of force, no questions asked. But I have to explain to the civilian authorities as well as the Base Commander why a giant with a club and an amazon with an attitude broke bones and maimed bodies."

"Excuse me, Lieutenant." A new voice was heard. Torbin and Hobbes turned to see Ichiro dragging an unconscious woman by her left foot across the grass toward them. He was carrying a pistol by suspending it with a literal chopstick down the barrel.

"Hey, tell that asshole to let Martha go," a shout came from the scavengers. "Goddamn slant-eyed freak," came another yell. Ichiro stopped, looked intently toward the crowd of angry men and women. He dropped the woman's foot, hand moving toward his katana. The crowd began to surge forward, swollen by some late arriving drunks, outnumbering the MPs.

"I suggest you all stay back!" Lt. Hobbes ordered. It looked like he was about to be ignored. Hobbes began to unsling his bayoneted assault rifle.

Then a large snarling, four-legged shape went snapping, biting, and dashing back and forth in front of the crowd. Fuzz proved how one dog with a vicious bite can cause a whole crowd of humans to reconsider moving in its direction.

"Shoot that fucking dog," someone yelled as a pistol appeared between two scavengers, pointed at Fuzz, the shooter hidden behind the bodies in front of him/her.The pistol was dropped without discharging as a shuriken star buried itself into the back of the exposed hand. Ichiro had moved without thought, his aim true.

"Lock and load! Pick your targets." In an instant, six laser dots from six rifles played back and forth over the crowd. At that moment, backup arrived, including a brace of patrol dogs, spoiling for a fight.

"Hands on heads!" came the command. Everyone sobered up immediately and complied.

"I was about to tell you, Lieutenant," Ichiro interjected. "I had proof these malcontents had many concealed firearms, which I believe they were supposed to check in prior to entering this fair site. This young... lady I have in tow owns this weapon. Only her prints and DNA are on it, I assure you." Then he smiled. "But I think that point was just demonstrated."

"Thank you, sir. Major Bender, if you and your friends could come down to the police station later, after you see to your wounds, I would appreciate it. Right now, I have a couple dozen people I need to search and then get to the civilian authorities. This sweet thing," Lt. Hobbes toed the unconscious form, "gets to stay in our gray bar hotel until she sees a Federal Magistrate, since I take it Major Yamamoto took the gun from her as she was about to use it."

"Very true Lieutenant, which is why she is unconscious."

"Now, if you will excuse me, I have a crowd of miscreants to deal with."

As Lt. Hobbes walked over to supervising the search and departure of the scavengers and their supporters, Torbin turned to Ichiro. "Had my back again I see, Ichiro."

The Japanese officer smirked. "Actually, I was watching Abigail's back. She is much more attractive to look at than you are."

"Hey, that's my little sister you're talking about. Say that around Aleks and you may be singing soprano."

Abigail came over with Fuzz in tow, Aleks behind them. The large dog was panting but looked very satisfied with himself. He might have gotten a piece of one member of the unruly crowd.

"Husband, there you are. How many new cuts and bruises this time?"

"No more than usual, Aleks. Abigail and I will go to the clinic to be checked out, if you can keep an eye on Fuzz."

"As long as he does not try and drag me all over the Base, I will. Your dog, Abigail, is a single-minded brute when he wants to be. Just like most men."

Abigail was patting Fuzz's head. "I'm sorry. It is my fault. I saw that man who attacked Ruth and I, and I saw red."

Torbin looked her in the eye. "Abigail, like me, you are used to just reacting in the field. We can't do that now. We need to let the authorities handle things around here. That is why Madam President is reconstituting many of the Government functions and services. She wants a more staid and normal existence rather than the old west."

Abigail sighed. "I know. I need to be 'civilized' more now too, I guess. I was trained to take care of things *now*. I guess I need to let others into the picture." She ruffled Fuzz's fur on his shoulders. "I can take him home, and fix myself up. I'm a trained EMT…"

"Captain, as the expression goes, a physician who treats herself has a fool for a patient, which applies to medics as well. You will come with me to be checked out. That's Major to Captain, not friend to friend."

Abigail looked down. "Yes Sir. Sorry to be trouble Sir."

"Oh, don't give me that self-deprecating crap. Just come with me to the clinic. You women are such a pain in the ass sometimes…ow. You kicked me, wife."

"That is Major to Major. Now, Abigail, for me and Fuzz, go get checked out. A broken rib that goes untreated can result in a punctured lung. I will ensure this beastie makes it home in one piece."

Abigail looked at Fuzz, who looked back. "Go and protect Aleks, my big fellow. That's a good dog."

With a "woof" and a single wag of his tail, Fuzz moved next to Aleks. Abigail gave Ichiro a warm smile, said she would talk to him later. Torbin noticed this interplay, and knew where it was heading. His wife would have to have a small talk with the sometimes naïve young woman.

Torbin and Abigail hitched a ride with an MP to the clinic at the Base hospital. He wanted to get this over with and go home. They both had a busy week scheduled, running a bunch of new butterbars through some tough combat and live fire training. With Universal Service, there were some one million available sixteen to forty-five year old humans to draw from. Madam President had told General Reed, now a Four Star and the equivalent of the old Chief of the Joint Chiefs of Staff (name changed to Commanding General of the Allied Armed Forces) to hit the ground running.

Torbin, with his status as Hero of the U.S.A. and extreme combat veteran, was pressed into the role of combat trainer extraordinaire. Torbin wanted back into the field, but he was told the Free States needed live heroes, not dead ones. So, a-training he would go. Abigail's excellent abilities and experience in the field made her a fine example for young female trainees to emulate. It also kept her from the sticky situation of fighting for a group of states with which Deseret had no formal treaty. Not to mention that as a Special Ambassador (the title the Prophet/President and the U.S.A. had created) if she was injured in combat with no formal treaty, it would be a very sticky situation. All of these positions and duties, plus her interpreter and foreign liaison duties, kept her very busy, a state on which she seemed to thrive.

While one group of personnel was going over Torbin's injuries, a female doctor was examining Abigail. A young enlisted troop had recognized her, saw Rolf's oversized shirt she was swimming in, and rushed to find her a replacement. A new silk screened T-shirt, from Torbin's veteran buddy's shop at the BX, with the phrase *"Caution: Sushi Chef in Training"* was given to Abigail to wear. She grinned. "Thank you. This is a great help. I owe you, and will replace it for you."

"Ma'am, begging your pardon, but you're an inspiration for many young girls. If you try to buy me another I'll be pissed. Just, please, keep being who you are. You give us all hope." With that, the young medical technician, probably Abigail's age, disappeared from the exam room.

Abigail realized that she did not even get her name. Just then, a doctor by the name of Major Rice, reappeared. An examination of her by technicians so far had revealed some bruised ribs, bruises on her arms, minor dents and scratches. When she found out that Abigail had not had any bloodwork done yet, something all women were having done since finding out about the Squid's modification program, the Major had a blood draw done. A technician specially trained to look for the early telltale signs of exposure to the Squid modification program had done a quick microscopic examination of the sample. What she had seen had puzzled her, so she gave the results to the doctor. Now she was puzzled.

Doctor Rica Rice was a Filipina who had been finishing her residency in the Great Lakes Area when the rock strikes began. She was newly pregnant with her first child, her husband also a resident doctor. They had at first tried to help the injured, then fled when harvester arks landed in the larger cities. The first ten days, every human that moved was harvested. Then, the darker skinned humans were weeded out. As they fled the area, her husband, a Caucasian American, was killed. Somehow, she escaped. In a daze, she had made her way west, trying to survive so that she could give birth to a healthy baby in a few months. People helped her when they found out she was a doctor, finding medical supplies for her to use. She and a group of many others from all races and walks of life, (later they named themselves "The Rainbows" for all the colors they represented) hooked up with the remains of some military units that were retreating to the interior. One day, she arrived at Malmstrom.

She volunteered for military duty, commissioned as an officer, gave birth to a healthy boy, now almost six years old. Now, she was giving back for all the help she and her son had received.

She flashed a genuine warm and sunny smile at Abigail. "Captain, it is a pleasure to finally meet you. Everyone in the hospital heard about you, especially from Aleks Smirnov, during her pregnancy check visits. But you have dodged a physical up until now."

Abigail presented a sheepish smile. "I've been busy getting settled in, Ma'am. I've just not taken the time to come here."

Doctor Rice looked at the medical history chart she had filled out. "Well, let's be a bit honest. You were kind of dodging us because of the radiation exposure scare the doctors in Deseret had put into you. True, Captain?"

"Yes, Ma'am," Abigail answered in a subdued voice. Rica sighed. "Let's take our rank and insignia off, shall we? Doctor to patient. You have no symptoms of any after effects from radiation exposure. I will complete a pap smear and a few fertility tests, which I am sure will show you are as fertile as the next young woman your age. Which means I will also see about getting you some birth control."

Abigail jerked with a start. "Uh, Ma'am. I am…a virgin. I am not experienced with sexual matters. I plan to stay a virgin until I am married, if that happens."

She finally smiled again. "If you tell me I am fertile, it will be a gift from God. There was fear in Deseret that I was…unclean."

Doctor Rice ears began to burn with anger. Anger that some doctor had allowed religious beliefs to cloud medical science. "*Unclean*? What type of diagnosis was that?

"Abigail, if you remain a virgin until your honeymoon, more power to you. I will do a very careful gynecological exam so as not to 'disturb' anything. But I am going to have Colonel Bardun, our resident specialist in exobiology, check your examination. Your body and blood have some…unique features that may show signs of exposure to Tschaaa material. No, nothing to be worried about. On the contrary, you seem to be as healthy as the proverbial horse."

She looked at the chart again. "The x-rays and the limited MRI show you have very strong, dense bones for a young lady. Your muscle tissue and structure is also very compact, dense, and efficient. Women's muscles are a bit more efficient than men's, though men have more muscle cells in numbers than we have, especially up top." She looked at another image. "Your cells seem almost... superior. Let me examine your arms and legs again.

A few minutes later, Rica whistled. "Not only does your body seem to have excellent healing powers, but your muscles feel like bands of steel. Remind me never to get you angry."

Abigail blushed. "That's how I got here, Major. I let my anger cloud my good sense. Two very good friends helped to save me from myself."

News traveled fast, especially since some of the more grievously wounded of the scavengers had been treated at the ER first, prior to being kicked off base. Rica Rice knew Abigail had done a lot of damage to her fellow humans. She had pieced together Abigail's history in Deseret. By all rights, since being a child warrior from age twelve, Abigail should have had some scar tissue, signs of healed trauma, or bad early development of bones and joints caused from too much physical stress too soon. The doctor could find very little.

"You will have a few bruises, aches and pains for a day or two. That's about it. Like I said, I'm going to forward the blood samples to Colonel Bardun for further comparison with some of the pregnant women who have been exposed to some type of Tschaaa modified DNA. But, they have not had any serious problems so far even while carrying babies. So please do not worry."

Abigail gave a slight smile. "I greatly appreciate your help, doctor. I have been told to be... concerned about my development, my maturing because I fled through the Hanford Explosion. I had resigned myself to the fact that there was too much chance of genetic damage to have children. If that is not the case... well, it is a very excellent present, one of many I have received since arriving here. I think God shines on Malmstrom more than you long term residents realize."

Doctor Rice chuckled. "Hey, I'm just a doctor. What plans the Universe holds for us is beyond my pay grade. Now, just out of curiosity, how often did you see a doctor in Deseret?"

"Almost monthly."

"What occurred during these visits?"

"Well, as with all of the Twenty, I received a physical, blood work, vitamin shots, an occasional short term prescription to take. As I matured, a couple of very nice female doctors explained the importance of breast examines for me, the signs of cancer I should look for. Of course, much of that was predicated on my exposure during the Hanford Explosion."

Doctor Rice paused for a moment. Just what was Abigail given each month? "Well, I will try and go through channels to see if I can somehow get your in depth medical charts from Deseret. From what I understand, I don't think you'll be going back anytime soon."

"No, Ma'am." Abigail had permission to make weekly telephone calls back to the Capital, as well as send letters, telegrams. They were trying to set up a secure direct computer connection to the President/ Prophet's office. So far, all the communication was that she was doing a good job, that they were in direct contact with Madam President, they knew what she was doing with the U.S. Military, and keep up the good work. Then they sent her some cash and a few personal items, like copies of the local newspapers. She still had more money than she knew how to spend.

However, she would let the doctor talk to the doctors in Deseret. She had learned a long time ago not to question things in areas outside her expertise. "Again, thank you very much, Doctor Rice. Am I finished?"

The Doctor smiled. "Yes. Colonel Bardun may contact you in few days. But feel free to come by anytime with questions."

As Abigail left, some young female enlisted personnel were nearby, speaking in low tones.

"Anything I can do for you ladies?" Doctor Rice asked.

A young Sergeant spoke for the group. "That was the Avenging Angel from Deseret. We just had heard so much about her that we wanted to see her up close. She's becoming a legend among the young girls and women in town."

"Well, she doesn't have horns or a tail." That comment elicited a few titters of laughter. "But, I suggest you all treat her with respect. I would not want to see her angry."

It was four days after the highly successful Oktoberfest. Abigail and Torbin were at work training a bunch of new officers in the fine art of killing. Aleks was stuck at home, looking to her own eyes more like a beached whale every day. She wished the twins could be magically transported from her abdomen to the bassinets they had for them.

Aleks was in the kitchen of her part of the Duplex, under the watchful eye of Fuzz. The large K-9 took his task of guarding the pregnant human quite seriously. When he was alone with Aleks, a knock at the door meant Fuzz was there before Aleks could be, getting between her and any potential threats.

Right now Aleks was cooking a turkey, supposedly practicing for Thanksgiving. Actually, it was an easy way to have a large amount of protein on hand to keep the trolls happy. They demanded a lot of extra calories. Fuzz was always spoiled by Aleks with scraps and snacks, out of Abigail's sight.

"What good is having a big beastie around if I cannot spoil it?" She asked Fuzz. He thumped his tail once. The weather was cooler, with chances of snow in the forecast. For a Russian, living in Siberia the last few years, it was nothing. Aleks laughed at how concerned even some native Montanans became at the first hint of snow.

"A fire or some heat source, some vodka, some potatoes and borscht, a warm body to curl up next to, that is all you need, Fuzz." The dog also gave her someone to talk to when home alone. She was not used to this imposed exile due to her condition. She was not at all the type of woman ready for mahjong games with the other pregnant women, eating coffee cakes. She was a trained spy, damnit. What did she have in common with the other dependent wives?

She had been initially angry about Abigail confronting that scavenger, and dragging Torbin into a nasty fight. But when she found out what had happened in Evanston, Aleks had told Abigail, "Next time, wait until I have given birth. I would love to cut that one's nuts off." As Scarman and the one named Baker had disappeared again, she might still get the chance.

Torbin had tried to get all big brother with Abigail, but Aleks came to her defense, explained the anger a woman feels when someone tries to manhandle their private parts. An argument ensued, leading to loud voices. Fuzz had walked up, letting out a low rumbling bark. The humans turned to look at him and he was staring at them, a bit agitated.

"I think Fuzz is trying to tell us that he does not like us arguing," Abigail commented. "I think he sees it as adversely affecting the unity of the pack."

Torbin snorted. "That's all we need. A four-legged combination referee and marriage counselor."

But they did stop arguing. The problem was that both Aleks and Torbin were hard-headed, stubborn, and opinionated. Aleks sighed. They loved the hell out of each other, so they always kissed and made up, sometimes ending up in bed. Aleks' pregnancy had limited their lovemaking, which also frustrated her. She had looked at her large stomach. "Trolls, you had better hurry up and come out. As much as I love you, I miss my alone time with my husband."

Fuzz choose that moment to walk to the double paned sliding French door to the backyard, and gave her that "I need to go out" look. "Okay, my beastie, let's get you outside. Let me know when you want back in." She walked to the door and had to maneuver her stomach out of the way to open it.

"You'd better appreciate this, my husband. I am getting tired of carrying two bowling balls in my stomach."

Fuzz went outside, and Aleks shut the door. She then went back to checking on her turkey and some stuffing she was experimenting with. A couple of minutes later, a sound of breaking glass came from the spare bedroom in the front of the house.

"What are you getting into, Fuzz?" She asked as she waddled to the hallway. As she rounded the corner to the hallway and started down it, she remembered Fuzz was still outside as she heard him bark. Then, as it came out the bedroom door, she saw the Eater.

Aleks screamed in fear and anger. How dare did this *thing* come into her home? Reflexes took over and she turned and made a grab for the hall closet door, where a semi-automatic Saiga shotgun resided. Her large stomach with twins threw her balance off and she started to fall, but steadied herself with the door knob. Then a clawed hand grabbed her left ankle.

She fell, turning sideways, still holding on to the doorknob. She landed more on her back than her pregnant stomach. She looked and saw a teeth filled maw not far from her captured foot. She howled "No!" and began kicking with her feet at the face of the creature.

Aleks did not hear the breaking double-paned door glass, nor the sound of Fuzz rounding the corner. One moment the Eater had ahold of her foot, pulling it toward its teeth, the next moment it was propelled into the drywall of the hallway, one hundred fifty pound plus of enraged canine slamming his whole body weight into the alien creature. The Eater was shoved completely into the wall, and left a body sized imprint. As the stunned creature started to slide out from the indentation, Fuzz latched his jaws on what passed as its throat. A twisting jerk of his shoulder and neck muscles and Fuzz ripped the throat area out, blue tinted blood splashing about. The Eater slumped to the hallway floor. Then the bud mate of the Eater appeared.

When Fuzz slammed into the Eater, time and space seemed to slow down. And Aleks heard a voice from her memories. "Smirnov. You fat cow. Are you just going to lay there and die? *Move!*"

During her spy training, she and the other trainees had suffered under the ministrations of a training instructor who went by the name Stalin. No one knew his real name. But every day he said, "You may hate me now, but what and how I am teaching you will save your sorry asses someday. Now move!" Cut and scarred, no one knew how many people he had killed. They just knew he was very good at it.

Propelled by the remembered voice, Aleks was on her feet. She threw open the closet door and grabbed the Saiga 12 gauge. Fuzz had met the second Eater head-on, not giving an inch. He reared up on his hind legs, his front paws clawing at the alien. His teeth severed three clawed fingers of the Eater's right hand as it tried to grab the war dog's muzzle. The creature let out a howling, screeching scream that Aleks would never forget. It grabbed Fuzz with its other clawed hand, trying to pull Fuzz's muzzle toward its open maw. Aleks had the Saiga now, and saw the open maw. She knew that the Eater could regurgitate highly corrosive stomach acid on near prey, blinding and maiming it.

Again, she saw in her mind's eye Stalin slamming them around during bayonet training."Think you will always be able to easily shoot your enemy? Think again, you sorry fuckers. Now *watch.* You will thank me one day."

Automatically, she went into a high throat thrust, up and over Fuzz and into the left eye of the Eater. She had no bayonet on the weapon but she had a heavy steel barrel. She stabbed it into the eye, ocher eye liquid squirting out. As the Eater began to scream again, she pulled the trigger.

What passed as the brain and the skull of the six-limbed monster was expelled out onto the hallway walls. The recoil almost jerked the shotgun from her grasp. But, pregnant or not, Aleks was still a strong woman. She hung on, bringing it back toward her for another thrust. It was not necessary. The Eater collapsed like a deflated balloon.

There was sudden silence, other than the harsh breathing of Fuzz and Aleks. No more creatures appeared. Aleks plunked down next to the dog, and threw her arms around his neck, blubbering in Russian, Ukrainian, and English. "You big, wonderful beast you. You saved me, and you saved my unborn children. You fantastic dog—I love you!"

Then she noticed the red blood that was not hers. She screamed and wailed as she realized her four legged savior was hurt. She did not hear the front glass door window shatter, nor the voice of a brave young woman who managed to climb through the opening she had created.

"Major Smirnov," the young officer's wife, Sue Brown, called as she rounded the hallway corner and saw the screaming, crying woman, the bleeding dog, and the dead Eaters.

"Call 911!" Aleks screamed, then fainted.

Abigail and Torbin were on the Live Fire Tactical Range Six, running a dozen butterbars through some tough drills. They were being forced to shoot, make decisions, maneuver, and give commands. Best to make mistakes here rather than on the battlefield. Two technicians were in the front, working on the P.A. system that was giving them fits. Thus they had no direct communications with the range house, their cellphones turned off.

They had just finished a course of Fire and Movement when Torbin's electronic hearing protectors registered a whistle. He turned around and looked. He saw the pudgy civilian Range Master, Mr. Arel, running as fast as he could toward them, blowing a whistle. He was in his sixties, had been involved in firearms training before Torbin was out of diapers. Too old for active military service, he still served the U. S. by training people for combat.

"Hold them up a minute, Abigail. Something's going on." Torbin started walking to meet the Range Master. Arel clambered to a stop, trying to talk between gasps for breath.

"Need you… back… at home. Wife… Eaters."

Torbin's blood went cold. He grabbed Arel's arm. "What the hell are you saying? My wife was attacked by Eaters?"

"Yes... Is okay..."

"Captain Young," he yelled before he realized Abigail was standing nearby, and had heard Mr. Arel.

"Go, Torbin. I'll clean up here."

Arel gulped. "His wife... was saved by your dog."

"Fuzz saved her? Is he okay?" Abigail's stomach flip flopped. Bad enough Aleks was almost hurt. Now, Fuzz.

"Don't know, Ma'am. Sorry."

Abigail made a quick decision. "Go, check on Fuzz for me. I'll stay here."

A surprisingly firm, loud voice cut in. Lt. Singh was a small East Indian female, just five feet tall. She had done alright in officers training, but was not known for speaking up. So the way her voice carried was a surprise.

"Ma'am, Sir. Begging your pardon. We can clean up here."

Torbin looked at her, surprised about what she just said. "Come again?"

Lt. Singh drew herself up to her full height. "We are Commissioned Officers, are we not? We may be in training, but we still are trained officers. Please trust me when I say we can handle putting this range in order. You and the Captain need to go now, to your friends and family. It's not like we are on a battlefield. Sir... Ma'am."

There were other affirmative comments from the other butterbars. One comment heard was, "We won't let you down. We wouldn't dare." Torbin surveyed what was to him were too many young faces. He felt a rush and a sense of pride. Young people stepped up for the first of many times since pinning their rank on. A small first step maybe, but a step nonetheless.

"Alright, you've got it. Lt Singh."

"Sir."

"This is your detail. Don't screw it up."

Unprompted, all twelve Lieutenants snapped to. "Sir, yes Sir!" They were telling Torbin they were a team, and they would insure Lt. Singh succeeded. They were coming together faster than he expected.

"Come on, Abigail, I'll drive."

They ran to their Humvee. Mr. Arel, finally having his breath back, turned at looked at the young officers.

"You just did yourselves proud. May seem minor, but you'll all remember this day." He turned and walked off. He just had a big dose of hope.

Legend had it that Torbin set a new land speed record in a Humvee. He used the siren and wig-wags to blow through one of the back gates. Then he was at the housing area. As he pulled up to their street he saw the mass of activity and vehicles around the duplex, including a large meat wagon/crash truck. His heart sank. An oversized cargo truck, the large square back was like a small mobile emergency room. It was usually on an active runway for aircraft crashes and fires. That was not a good sign. People entering his place in hazmat suits was also not good.

He found a place to squeeze in the Humvee and park. He and Abigail got out, and headed toward the duplex.

Then he heard a loud yell.

"Torbin. *Husband.*" He looked up and saw that it was coming from the back of the meat wagon. Aleks. Alive. And fighting with an EMT to keep the oxygen mask off her face, a good sign. He sprinted to the back, the two EMTs getting a look of relief on their faces. The female Sergeant started talking.

"Sir, we are trying to get her to the ER. But she refuses to go until she checks on the dog. She keeps trying to beat the shit out of us…"

"And I *will!*" Aleks yelled. "Fuzz saved me and our children. I will not leave until he is okay!" One of the twins chose that moment to kick her hard inside her stomach. She almost doubled over. Torbin laid his hands on her large belly and began to rub it, gently, speaking in low tones.

"Hey guys, lighten up. It's Dad. You need to calm down. Everything is okay." Aleks' agitation had transmitted to the twins, not a good thing. He caught his wife's gaze. "Babe, you need to calm down and let these nice people take you to the ER, to check on the kids. I'll make sure Fuzz is okay."

Aleks began to sob. "He took one out just as it was about to eat me! Then he fought the second one, giving me a chance to get the shotgun. Then there was dog blood all over. If he dies, I'll never forgive myself." Torbin hugged her, kept a hand on her belly as she bawled on his shoulder.

"Aleks, it's Abigail. I'll go check." Abigail dashed for Bender's side of the duplex. A man in a hazmat suit tried to stop her and she bowled past him. Then she saw vet Emily Anders with the base vet, a Major Shaw. Laying on the dining table was a very large dog. Fuzz.

Emily looked up and saw Abigail. "Aw, his human. Captain Young, if you please."

The man in the hazmat suit, now seeing the third person force their way into a contaminated area, threw up his hands in exasperation. If they wanted to risk dying over a dog, so be it. Abigail walked up, a cold, hard knot in her stomach. Fuzz, catching her scent, thumped his tail, tried to look at her. Abigail saw he was sedated.

"How bad is he?" she asked.

Emily answered. "It looks a lot worse than it was. He had a couple of cuts from smashing thru the sliding glass door. Then he had a bunch of those quills in his neck and muzzle from the Eater's arms. The good thing is they do not have those little hooks on the end like our porcupine does. So it is a matter of pulling them straight out with pliers, then slapping disinfectant on them."

She patted Fuzz's head gently. "We had to sedate him as he would not let any males near Major Smirnov. Sergeant Martinez had responded and helped me get him under control. Otherwise, they may have shot him to get to the pregnant Major."

Abigail looked at Emily. "How did you get here so fast?"

"Scanner traffic. I heard Eaters and came running. I want the chance of examining them every time I can. Then, I heard about a big beast of a dog kicking their asses, and knew it had to be Fuzz."

Abigail slowly reached out to Fuzz, scratched his ears. He sighed, now that he knew his mistress was here.

"Will he… be okay?"

Emily chuckled. "Okay? Hell, this hellhound is too nasty to let some monster put him down. He will be just fine after a night's rest. Like I said, there was blood, but nothing serious."

Abigail had a lump in her throat. "See what you did, you big brute. You went and got into a fight, and got hurt. What am I going to do with you?"

"Love the crap out of him," Emily answered. "And, when he is better, I would like to mate him with one of my bitches, a full blood

Dane. I cannot let a heart like his disappear. Hopefully the right genes will be passed on. Is it a deal?"

Abigail smiled. "Of course. Anything you want, Doctor. You just saved my big fella."

At her request, the two vets helped Abigail lift Fuzz and carry him to her quarters. There, she had him placed on her bed. "I'll sleep on the floor until he comes to."

Emily put her arm around Abigail. "Anybody ever tell you that you are one hell of a dog lover?"

Abigail teared up. The vet hugged her. "Trust me, he'll be just fine. Now, I need to get back to my clinic. Call me if you need anything."

Abigail wiped her eyes, patting Fuzz. "Relax, big fella. I'll be back shortly."

She ran outside to the back of the meat wagon where Torbin was trying to calm down his wife. The EMTs had managed to get an oxygen mask on Aleks to help her relax. When she saw Abigail, she ripped the mask off again.

"Fuzz. He is okay?"

"Yes, Aleks. The injuries were relatively minor, more blood than real damage. They gave him a sedative because he was so agitated protecting you, he wouldn't let anyone near. Sgt. Martinez from the kennel was on patrol, and she was a godsend, got him to let the medics see to you until the vets arrived."

Aleks cursed. "Such a worthless pig I am. I collapsed, fainted like a schoolgirl. Had there been another Eater, Fuzz would have been all alone." She began to cry. "I'm just a fat cow, worthless as a soldier."

Torbin knew it was hormones and pregnancy talking, affecting her.

"Babe, you are carrying twins that are kicking the crap out of you. Of course you fainted. Your circulation was probably all screwed up."

"That is no excuse. If not for that beautiful beast, I would be dead." Torbin hugged her, and let her cry out her frustrations. Finally, she stopped. One of the EMTs provided her some soft bandage material to use as a handkerchief. She wiped her eyes, blew her nose. Abigail then put her arm around her big sister.

"Aleks, Fuzz did what he wanted to do, which was protect you. He will be okay. Then, you can spoil him some more when you think I'm not looking."

Aleks kissed her. "Promise me you will let him watch over me, still? I promise I will try and not spoil him with snacks so much. I promise."

Abigail smiled. "I couldn't stop him if I tried. Those trolls you say you have in your stomach have been claimed by him as new pack members. So, he will not let anything happen to them, or you."

"Now, wife," Torbin interrupted. "You will go to the hospital for a quick checkup. I will be there soon. I need to secure our home and review the damage. Okay?"

His soldier and spy wife smiled. "Yes, husband. I hear and obey."

Torbin snorted. "Obey? That's a first."

As the EMTs began to secure Aleks in the meat wagon, Torbin noticed there was a familiar-looking young lady sitting in the back of another ambulance, having her leg bandaged.

He asked a Military Police Sergeant. "Excuse me. What happened to her?"

"Oh, you probably weren't told, Major. That's Lt. Brown's dependent wife. She heard the screams and kicked your front door window in, getting cut for her efforts. She'll be okay. She's the one that got there first, and called 911."

"Excuse me." Torbin walked quickly over to the ambulance.

Sue Brown was examining the EMT's handiwork, so at first she did not notice Torbin's approach. Then, she looked up, with instant recognition on her face as she saw him. She started to stand up.

"Whoa. What do you think you are doing? That looks like a bandage on your leg. I think you need to stay off of it for a while."

Sue smiled sheepishly. "I was a bit clumsy. Sorry I broke the door window, Sir."

Torbin examined this unassuming North Dakota farm girl, who was not a trained warrior. Yet, she had gone into harm's way when she heard screams for help. When Torbin saw people like her, outweighing the Krakens, the scavengers, the criminals still in human society, he had hope. Maybe they would be more than a bunch of nasty monkeys, intent on raping and killing each other, and actually band together to kick the Tschaaa off the Earth.

"Pardon me for a moment, Ma'am, while I get personal." He reached forward, gently holding her face and kissed her forehead. "Young lady, to say I appreciate what you did is one of the great understatements in the universe. I remember those who help me and mine. If you ever need help, feel free to ask. Off the record, just between you and me, no questions asked."

The Lieutenant's wife blushed. "I did what anyone else would have done, Major. Nothing more."

"Not true, Ma'am. Most people would have frozen. You went right in. Take it from one who knows. When it comes to fight or flight, most people without formal training choose flight."

He took her hand, gently squeezed it. "Tell your husband he had better treat you right. Anybody who helps save my wife and unborn children deserves the best."

Sue smiled, her eyes damp. "Thank you, Major. Coming from you… it means something."

"I'll get ahold of your husband. No, it's no problem. We had to cut training short because of this anyway. He needs to wait on you as that leg is going to hurt a bit." Torbin patted her shoulder. "Thanks again."

As he walked away Sue Brown thought about how someone who was such a hero could be such a real person. She also worried that her husband would be upset when he heard she was injured. Well, now he would know how she felt when she thought of him being hurt. Right now, she just wanted to give him a big hug.

Torbin had one of the MP units call the range, and then sent a patrol unit to pick up Lt. Brown. His wife needed him. Just then, he walked up and looked in the front door of his quarters. The hazmat personnel had finished cleaning up, tagging and bagging the alien remains. They still worried about possible infectious germs and materials form the Eaters, though other than the extreme stomach acids, none had been found yet. He looked at the french door, the broken front door window, and knew the hallway was trashed. Well, Aleks could bunk with Abigail until he repaired the damage.

"Excuse me, Sir." A voice came from behind him. He stepped back and quickly three workman in civilian clothes and carpenters belts walked by him, two of them carrying a large piece of sheetrock. They went right in to his home as he watched, surprised. He had not called any repair people.

He walked back to the MP Sergeant, a Staff Sergeant Sorenson. "Sergeant, where did these people come from? I didn't request any repairmen."

The Sergeant smiled. "Taken care of Sir. Compliments of my brother in law. He owns a good-sized hardware store, does construction on the side. I called him when I saw the damage. He wanted to help, knew it would take the Base civil engineers a while to get things organized."

Torbin became angry. "Goddamnit. I did not ask for any special treatment. I can take care of things myself."

"Sir, my brother-in-law just wants to help. You know, after what you did in Key West, everyone feels they owe you…"

"*Goddamnit!* Is this what's going to happen with anything I'm involved in? I'm just a grunt, just a Marine. I'm no hero. Show me a hero, I'll show you a bum."

Another voice broke in "Well, my mustang, I see you are pissed off again. Is my adopted daughter Aleks okay?" It was General Reed. When he had heard what had happened, he had responded as quickly as he could.

Torbin snapped to. "Sir. Sorry Sir. Aleks is okay, headed to the hospital for a full checkup. Just venting. This goddamn hero shit is getting old real quick. All I want is a field command, not be something placed on the shelf, dusted off for parades."

Then, an unfamiliar voice broke in. "Well, I guess the world *is* going to hell in a handbasket. I just heard a kick ass Marine *whine*."

Both General Reed and Torbin turned to the source of the comment. No one had seen Commissioner Paul Miller, head of Federal Law Enforcement arrive. He was standing back, arms folded, observing the tableau.

"Commissioner Miller. What brings you to our neck of the woods?"

"General, when Eaters, an alien life form, magically appear on a military installation, it is probably safe to assume they were smuggled from somewhere. Smuggling falls under my purview. So being in town, I came with a couple of investigators, some forensics folks. I don't want to step on any toes, but I need to find out how they got here, unnoticed. This may have been an old fashioned attempted murder, using a very unique weapon. Whatever happened, I need to find out."

"Well, investigate away, Commissioner. It frees my people up to insure no other Eaters are floating around."

Commissioner Miller turned to a still seething Torbin. "At the risk of losing my teeth, Major, let me tell you what, from a civilian perspective, this all means."

He pointed to Torbin. "You, whether you want to admit it or not, are a hero. By definition, a hero is one who has done heroic acts. Key West is an ultimate example of a heroic act."

"Now Commissioner…" Torbin tried to interject.

"Don't interrupt your elders. You know what heroes and heroic acts mean to the great unwashed civilian masses out there? After having survived some six years of being eaten, beaten, starved, and frozen in the Long Winter? It gives them hope. Hope with a capital 'H'."

He took a deep breath. "So pardon the hell out of me and the rest of the civilians if we want to be part of this 'hope' by helping a hero out when we can. It's a way to say 'Thank you'. You know about saying 'thank you', right Major? I think you just said it to that young Lieutenant's wife over there. And I bet you will say thank you to that big beast of a dog Captain Young has just taken for a well-deserved rest. So please, do not turn into a prima donna, complaining that the public won't let you alone. A 'hero' has additional responsibilities. Sorry, that is just the way life is. We need you to accept our 'thank you'. Got it?"

Commissioner Miller turned to the General. "If you want to chew me out for lecturing one of your officers, have at it. Sorry, but it needed to be said."

General Reed laughed. "Chew you out? Hell, I want you as a motivational speaker at the next Basic Training Graduation, especially for the officers. We forget what the civilians are living through, have lived through, and what they need from us. Feel free to remind us anytime."

Director Miller tuned to Torbin. "Well Marine, are you going to kick my ass, or shake my hand as I say 'thank you for your deeds'?" He held out his hand. Torbin took it, the anger gone. It was surprising how sometimes it took someone completely outside your experience to put things in perspective. He noticed some muscle in the beefy man, almost twice Torbin's age.

"You don't miss much, do you, Commissioner?"

"Years of being an investigator. It becomes second nature."

Torbin frowned. "Are you serious about that murder thing?"

"Well, you and your friends did a real number on some of Great Falls' not so finest during Oktoberfest. They may have deserved it, but that doesn't stop them from wanting revenge."

The Commissioner paused, looking around. "One reason while I'm in town is that there are a lot of rumors of things, animals, being moved around a lot, especially at night. You move things at night to hide them from prying eyes. Since this whole shebang of mine, Federal Law Enforcement, is still so new, I'm making sure we get a correct start on any investigations. I have a lot of new as well as rusty personnel. We have to get back in the swing of good old police work."

Torbin looked at his home. "If there is anything I can do to help..."

"Well, in the future, I may ask to borrow you from the General for some good old kick ass weapons and combative training. I understand you and Captain Young are the go to experts."

"We try, Commissioner. I'm willing, time permitting."

General Reed cut in. "I think we can adjust your schedule. I don't want someone being killed due to poor or no training."

At that moment, K-9 Handler Sergeant Martinez approached the group. The Commissioner saw her and turned to address her.

"Well, Sergeant, did your dog find anything?"

She snapped to and saluted General Reed and Torbin.

"So, my people are helping you out already."

"Yes General. I hope you don't mind."

"What's mine is yours, within reason. We're all in this leaky boat together. So, my good Sergeant, what did you find for the Commissioner?"

"Sirs, Ginger here picked up strong Eater scent from that bedroom window there, out to the curb there. Then nothing, except she seemed to catch a residue scent in the air when she raised her head, like maybe a vehicle had been parked there with something smelly in it. She showed interest a little ways down the street, then nothing."

The Commissioner looked at her intently. "Your dog is good?"

Her chest swelled a bit. "Sir, my dog's the best. She's a Shepherd/ Retriever mix, has a fantastic nose, with a strong hunting drive. And she *hates* Eaters. She'd drag me down the street if she had strong

Eater scent."

"Well, Sergeant, I think you verified what I thought. Someone figured a way to transport those BEMS without getting eaten themselves, then somehow sicced them on these quarters."

"Begging your pardon, Sir, but the forensic people told me there was Eater puke on the window sill."

Commissioner Miller smiled. "I love it when a story comes together. Put some Eater vomit, stomach acid as a trail of breadcrumbs that they cannot ignore, as Eaters queue in on other Eaters vomit. It tells them that something is being eaten. Then, they reach the cracked open window, smell prey on the hoof—dog and woman—and go into a feeding frenzy."

He looked toward Abigail's side of the duplex, saw her standing there, about to go in. "Think I can meet this beast of a dog, Fuzz, who spoiled their plans?" He asked the Sergeant.

"Sir, he's been sedated. If I may suggest another time?"

He looked at Sergeant Martinez. "You have a connection with him also, don't you?"

The Sergeant smiled a bit sheepishly. "I tried to train him first. He kept trying to eat the kennel master, and just about everyone else. If he hadn't found Captain Young, he would have been put down."

"Ah kismet. Karma. What a wonderful thing. Things often all fit in together for some bigger reason. Like pieces of evidence in an investigation." He looked at the three military members. "I know, I'm off on a tangent. But mark my words. This will all soon fit together."

"General, do you think you can get me the videos from the entrance gates so I can check for vehicles big enough to transport the two Eaters?"

"Your wish is my command. I'll get the Base Commander on it right away. He's at the command post right now."

"Thank you, Sir. Hopefully, I'll have some good targets for investigation in the next few hours."

Abigail went into her side of the duplex, glad to be away from all the hustle and bustle. She could hear the beginnings of the repairs to Aleks' and Torbin's quarters, happy that someone had gotten to it so fast. She would have been glad to have Aleks stay with her, but she knew that Aleks was more comfortable in her own place. She made her way back to her room and Fuzz. He was still crashed out on her bed, sleeping the sleep of the good and innocent. She smiled. He deserved all the tlc she could give him.

It was still late afternoon, working into evening, so it was early for Abigail to hit the rack. But, the stress of thinking Fuzz had been seriously hurt was draining. She got her field bed roll from her closet, spread in out next to the bed. She shucked her clothes, striping down to just her panties, slipping on an old t-shirt Torbin had given her. She stretched out next to the bed and Fuzz, was quickly asleep.

While Abigail slept, the civilian workman did quick work on Torbin's and Aleks' place. The hallway, bedroom window and french sliding door were soon as good as new. Torbin obtained the workers' names, said drinks were on him when they had a chance.

"Major, just kill a Squid for us the first chance you get," the senior man, Tom, replied. For the first time, Torbin Bender realized just how connected everyone was to the conflict. He had thought in terms of small actions by the military, forgot that each action he and others took invited swift retaliation on civilian areas. He had been living with a set of blinders, not thinking in terms of a long, strategic war and the effect this would have on everyone, not just the military. That ended now.

"I'll try to bring a tentacle back for you, Tom. Thanks again." He shook their hands and watched them leave. Then he went and found Sergeant Sorenson. He approached and stuck out his hand. "Sergeant, please accept my apology. I can be a real asshole sometimes. Your brother-in-law's people did an excellent job. I owe you and them."

Sgt. Sorenson smiled. "No problem, Major. They just like to feel useful. They have felt helpless for much too long."

"Well, tell your friends and relatives that I forgot who we really work for. The military exists for the protection of all the men, women, and children around the world. They do not exist for our own benefit. So, tell them thanks again, Sergeant Sorenson."

As Torbin was thanking the good Sergeant, Commissioner of Enforcement Miller was getting the first bits of information from the base entrance gates and his forensic personnel that tended to confirm his worst fears. But he was not ready to share them with others. Not yet.

Abigail slept on, as Aleks was brought home with a clean bill of health, her unborn children still not ready for a full birth yet. Torbin bundled her off to bed, his wife falling asleep in his arms. He said an infrequent prayer, thanking the ultimate boss for creating such a beast as Fuzz. Then he fell asleep, to dream of his unborn sons.

It was late and dark when Abigail was awoken with a slurping canine kiss.

She reached out to her furry friend. "How're you feeling, fella?" He nuzzled her, telling her he needed to go out. She got out of her bed, shivering in the cold. She used little artificial heat in her home, as she was used to using her own body heat as well as Fuzz's to warm the area they were in at any given moment. She let Fuzz out the sliding door, leaving it open despite the cold. She knew Fuzz would be wary of any closed doors between him and his "people" for a while. She concentrated and stopped her body from shivering, almost enjoying the cold. When Fuzz finished and re-entered the home, Abigail shut and locked the door.

They both returned immediately to the main bedroom, where Fuzz stopped at the bed and looked at Abigail. She smiled, crawled in first under the covers. Fuzz then followed, doing the traditional circling and nest making, then laying close to Abigail. This was the routine each night.

She put her left arm around Fuzz. "Big fella, you are better than any teddy bear. You are loved. Always remember that." Fuzz "woofed", and thumped his tail once. Abigail said a nightly prayer thanking the Lord again for having Fuzz find her, then set her internal clock. Tomorrow would be another busy day.

CHAPTER II

I have found during my research that most everyone, both the public and historians, forget about many of the characters who orbited the sphere of control near Director Lloyd. They existed and some would come to play extremely important roles in Tschaaa and human relations.

-Excerpts from the Works of Princess Akiko, *Free Japan Royal Family*

KEY WEST, FLORIDA

Adam Lloyd, Chief Hamilton, and Heidi walked down the dock to the Admiral's Hatteras yacht the morning of Fuzz verses the Eaters. The Admiral had asked the two men to come with him on a "men only" fishing outing, with his "Amazons" and Heidi to remain on shore. He said it was for "male bonding", but the three women knew it more likely a discussion of something the three officials wanted to keep as private as possible. The Amazons—Susanne and Sharon, respectively—had been with the Admiral some five years, being his now highly trained bodyguards and companions. They had become used to the Admiral's desire for secrecy, so long as it did not interfere with their protection of him.

"Permission to come aboard, Admiral," Adam called out.

"Permission granted. Stow your gear, grab a beer, and we'll be under way."

Adam turned to Heidi. "Here are the vehicle keys. I have no idea how long we will be out. Sometimes these fishing outings turn more into voyages of discovery. If you need to head back to Base, go ahead. The Admiral will make sure we get home safe and sound."

"If it's alright with you Boss, I'll just hang around with the two ladies here. I imagine we can find something to do."

Adam shrugged. "Suit yourself. I don't want you to feel stuck, waiting for me.

Susanne, the Amazon brunette, smiled. "Don't worry, Director. We'll keep her entertained and secure."

Adam smiled back. "I imagine you will." He faced the boat. "Shall I shove off, Admiral?"

"Yes. Undo the bow and stern lines. Daylights a-wasting."

The three female bodyguards watched as the Admiral made a skillful exit from the dock area, out to the passages and channels thru the reef areas. If someone did not know the Keys or the reefs, they could wind up with a trashed propeller and a broken prop shaft quite easily.

"He actually knows how to drive that thing, doesn't he?" Heidi asked.

"Yes, he does." Sharon, the blonde, answered.

"Now, let's head up to the main building. There is a nice hot tub there we can use." Fall in southern Florida was quite nice during the day, even if it was a bit cold at night. In fact, the daytime temperature was nicely warm, rather than hot and humid like the summer heat.

The three ladies made their way up to the hot tub and jacuzzi. Susan went to the nearby wet-bar and made margaritas for the three. They went to the jacuzzi, Sharon turning it on. "The filters were just cleaned, and the water flushed, so I guess you can say this is a 'virgin' pool."

Heidi laughed. "Virgin. Hell, I wish it could make me a virgin again."

The three laughed as they unselfconsciously shed their clothes, and climbed in nude. Heidi could not help but notice the tight and well-shaped bodies of the two Amazons. Nearly six feet tall each, their legs were long and shapely, hips smooth and rounded.

"I have to ask. Sharon. Susan. What did you do before you wound up here? You did not get those strong bodies overnight. Or, just since you hooked up with the Admiral."

"Well, Heidi, while you was joining the Coast Guard before the first rock strike, Susan and I were beach volleyball players. We were quite good, if I say so myself."

"Yes," Susanne chimed in. "We had gotten out of high school, and were headed to college or maybe an Olympic slot. A coach of the last team that had medaled saw us during a local competition put on by some major beer company, and really liked us. The fact we blew the competition away helped. We are both tall, fast, good spikers and servers. Not to mention having a kickass defense." The two friends laughed.

"We were on a small team bus the beer company had provided, heading to another put on competition as part of an advertising campaign. It was to be our last, the Olympic coach told us to call him just as soon as we were done. Man, you should have seen all the guys with their tongues hanging out.

All three women laughed. Then Sharon frowned. "The first rock hit while we were on the road up toward Georgia. Then another and another. The bus pulled over at a rest stop. Everyone was panicking around us. Things began to fall apart as Atlanta was hit. Then the harvesters started coming down." She shivered despite the warm water.

"One landed on the freeway, a couple of miles away, part of the first wave. Twelve hours in, the sun was down and we were huddled with several other women in the bus. About a half hour after the landing, the first harvester robs showed up in the rest area. The rest is a bloody blur."

Susanne slid over and put her arms around Sharon. "Every time we talk about this, it's like it happened just last week," said Susan. "We were friends from high school, first time away from our parents." A tear ran down Sharon's cheek. Susanne wiped it away and kissed her on the cheek. "We made it through, though. We had each other's backs, didn't we, Sharon?" Sharon smiled, and kissed her back.

"Somehow, we made it to Florida in a borrowed RV. Found this strange gentleman's club that had become an oasis in a desert of destruction and panic. That's where we met Hernando and John." Now it was Sharon's turn to continue the story. "After a short conversation with Hernando, the manager and now owner of the place by default, we put together a 'show' for the clientele. Hernando and John the bouncer became like big brothers to us after we made sure they understood we were nobody's bitches. They hired a couple of armed security guys, made sure we had plenty of guns and ammo, which they sometimes took as payment. Thanks to our prodding, we soon had a full time doctor for us and the other women, as Hernando located and hired some local talent to provide sexual services in a luxury tour bus they found. We talked them into building a workout room in the back, put some weight machines, treadmills and stuff, so we could keep in fighting trim."

Heidi looked at the two women. "I have to ask. What was the show you put together?"

"Why, some good old lesbian action." Susan answered. "Nothing keeps a guy's attention like two beautiful women fooling around with each other. And yes, we like men. But we also really like, love each other."

Sharon continued. "We added some catfight scenes, storylines, and gymnastics. We dressed in historical costumes. Soon, it became more like a theatrical production than a nudie bar. Broadcast television was pretty dead, except for some people who tried to keep a couple of local stations broadcasting in the clear. They only showed old movies, religious rants, pornography, or weird self-help shows depending on who was in charge that week. So, just like ancient men and women huddled around the campfire, telling stories to ward off the night and the demons, that was us in the club. There was no government, so the Toy Shop became a meeting place for locals to make deals, knowing it was a big neutral zone. No one wanted to screw-up a good thing—a place where you could relax, and drink alcohol that wouldn't make you blind.

Pablo, a Mexican hiding his family from the harvesters, showed up with this huge taco truck one day. Soon, we had a kitchen, and served food. The barter system set up meant people brought in fresh fish, meat, canned goods that were in good condition, and some fruit and vegetables. It became the community meeting place. We were not hit as hard by the Long Winter as most."

"So, what happened? Why aren't you still there?"

Both of the Admiral's bodyguards faces' turned into expressions of anger. "The fucking early Church of Kraken showed up," Sharon blurted out.

"Early one morning, at least a dozen armed men with those God awful Squid tattoos on their faces, necks, and chests showed up. They just came in shooting. A couple of them began hacking body parts off of the dead and dying. I swear to God I saw one start to eat pieces of raw human. This was before the word was put out that eating humans if you were a human did not make you a good Squid lover. The Tschaaa definitely do not understand cannibalism." "We were asleep when they hit. Susanne and I tried to run but were soon staring down gun barrels."

Sharon snickered. "I did crush one guy's nuts when he tried to grab Susanne. The rest of his fellow Krakens laughed and left him there."

"What happened next?"

"Well, they grabbed Susanne and I, surviving women and children. We never saw any of the guys again, so we assume they were killed, probably harvested. They loaded us into the back of a small moving van and headed south."

"Hours later, we were in Homestead, Florida. They had a shithole motel and someone's large yacht in the nearby Marina set up as confinement areas. We could tell some of us were destined to be playthings. Others were to be slaughtered. We saw some human torsos hanging from a meat hook."

"Then what? I know I'm being nosey, but I promise you'll hear my story also." People who survived harvesting and the Long Winter shared their stories as a way of bonding, as well as a way to say "See, I survived. I will survive."

The women smiled. Susanne answered. "Then the Director and the Chief showed up. And the ass-kicking began. The Krakens thought just two guys would be a pushover."

Sharon got a feral grin on her face. "Adam Lloyd walked up to the leader, and did not say a word. Just gutted him on the spot. His guts spilled out on the ground, and the Chief started shooting a 12 gauge, cutting people open with dime and buckshot loads. Then he pulled a huge Desert Eagle Pistol out from a bag and started blowing limbs off.

This was about two weeks after Adam and the Chief had made contact with His Lordship. He had made an arrangement to clean up Dodge City, and get things organized in exchange for no harvesting. And that is why Adam Lloyd is loved by many of us."

Susanne continued the story. "They found us chained in a back cabin, though we were able to watch the festivities through a porthole. At first I thought we may be exchanging one devil for another. Adam saw us, nude, chained. He found some clothes, had us cover up first. Then he cut us loose. We saved the chains as mementos of what we went through. We then knew the Director was... different. As well as the Chief."

Sharon spoke almost reverently. "Neither one tried to touch us. Ever."

Susanne sniffed. "He hooked us and the other survivors up with the Admiral. We've been with him ever since as two more of his 'daughters'. And *he* has never tried to molest us either. How two men in the same area keep such morals in a crazy world is a mystery."

"By the way, not a Kraken was allowed to live."

Heidi looked at the two women, trained protectors, hugging each other for support. And she thought she had it rough. No one had chained her up, tried to made her a human sex toy. It was funny how things looked bad until someone told you how rough they had it. Then, things did not seem so bad. Their story told, Sharon and Susan relaxed their grip on each other, laid back in the hot tub. Everyone was silent for a few moments. Then Sharon asked, "So, what's our story? How did you get here?"

Heidi smiled. "A bit simpler than your story. I was on a Coast Guard cutter a week and a half after the first rock strike. We were trying to sortie out from Miami Harbor without getting sunk by a marauding Delta or Falcon. Any vessel above about fifteen foot was treated as a threat by then. We were trying to get to open sea, try to lose ourselves in expanse of the Atlantic Ocean; maybe find some other surviving Naval units."

She snorted. "The cutter had just left the harbor, was about a hundred yards or so out from the inlet to Miami Bay when it blew up. I figured a Squid let loose a mine just as we were passing over a small reef area, timing it just right. Hit us right at mid-ship, split us in half. Suddenly, I was in the water in my floatation gear, all alone. I looked around for others, but soon discovered I couldn't find anyone else."

Heidi took a sip of her margarita. "The problem with thinking you are a true seafaring race because you have all these nice boats to run around in, is when you meet up with a *true* sea species, one that is born and dies in the ocean. You suddenly realize that you are just a rubber ducky in a bathtub by comparison." She set her drink down. "The Squids cleaned our clock within thirty days. I don't know how many capital ships were sunk. All I know is that the Tschaaa owned the oceans."

"Then what?" Susan asked.

Heidi gave a short laugh. "Somehow, I made it to shore. I started working my way down to city proper. As I was nearing some apartments and condos along the shore front, this young boy, about nine, ten years old suddenly stepped out from hiding. He saw the remains of my soaked uniform, that I was female, decided I could be trusted..."

It was like it was yesterday that she had seen him—a Cuban boy of medium complexion, slender build. He had approached her tentatively. Soaking wet, no cap, Heidi thought she must have looked like a wet rat.

As her mind filled with memories, Heidi's eyes filled with tears. Then she began to cry in earnest, trying to wipe the tears away. "Damn, I am such a big wimp. I can't even handle something that happened years ago." With that, she began to cry again. Then Sharon and Susanne were both hugging her, holding her as she sobbed. "He was like family," said Sharon.

Heidi managed to catch her breath. "He was like a little brother and a son, all rolled into one. And the fucking Krakens killed him." The three women sat silent, with just the sound of the jacuzzi in the background. Finally Heidi spoke. "I killed the Krakens who killed him and some of my other friends, part of a small family we were building. Then the Chief showed up. We all voted to go with him. Now I am here."

Heidi face stayed dark as she looked at the jacuzzi water. She stayed quiet for a couple of minutes.

Still really hurts, doesn't it?" Susanne asked.

Heidi took a deep breath. "Yeah. I'm missing some guts that were ripped out. Excuse me, ladies. I need to go to the bathroom."

Susanne and Sharon watched as Heidi went to the ladies room. They looked at each other. "We had each other, Susanne. That got us though."

"Yes it did, my dear. I think Heidi could do with a couple of close female friends right now."

"I think you're right. I have this desire to help her take the mind off her… pain."

Susanne sighed. "Yea, Sharon, I feel the same way. She's good people. I hate to see good people hurt like that. So, I suggest we just be good friends to her. I think she could use some women friends."

Sharon smiled. "Right as usual." She glanced over and saw Heidi approaching.

"Want a refill on your drink, Heidi?"

"Yes, please. Sorry I lost it…"

"Oh will you shut up. Damn, we all lose it from time to time. Here we are, worrying about getting eaten on a weekly basis, it would be a wonder if we didn't cry once in a while."

"By the way," Susanne interjected. "You are now officially a best female friend of ours. Sorry, no use arguing. *We* have already decided."

Heidi slid into the tub, went over and hugged the two Amazons. "Okay, I accept. But I doubt you two realize what you are getting yourself into."

"Trust us," Susanne answered. "We know *exactly* what we are getting into."

Heidi sighed, and continued her story from where she had left off. "The Chief showed up and gave me a chance to start over again. However, I had to accept the arrangement he and the Director had with the Squids." She shrugged. "By then, I had accepted the fact we had been defeated. Besides, I had a working relationship with the Squids in the area, they had gotten used to me, and I to them. I also realized that they eating us was what came naturally to them. Like us eating beef or pork. Being a predator does not make you evil."

Heidi's face took on a hard demeanor. "It was other Humans who had killed my little brother for meat. Like cannibals. That is evil. So, here I am. The Chief found me a job on the Base. Never had a chance to meet Adam Lloyd, he didn't start the in processing briefings and the evening socials until later. "

Heidi smiled. "Then I picked up the Director after his boat broke down. Now I'm his trainer and bodyguard. And thanks to that, I have two new girlfriends." She took a sip from the fresh cocktail Sharon had made for her. "Mmmm. That's good."

"No special guy friend?" Susanne asked.

Heidi shook her head. "I tried a couple of relationships. Enjoyed the sex with the men, but never really felt… close. And, gals are nice and soft, but don't do much for me. Sorry."

Sharon laughed. "I was kind of obvious looking at you, wasn't I?"

"Hey, I know I'm easy on the eyes, even to women. But sex with women, there is something… missing."

"I think it's called a prick," Susanne suggested.

That started up laughter again. They sat in the hot tub, sipping their drinks, enjoying the female friendship.

"Time for me to ask you both a question, ladies."

"Shoot, Heidi," Sharon answered.

"You two are a couple. What if Mr. Right came along? Or, could there be a Mr.

Right?"

The two Amazons looked at each other. They both nodded.

"Yes, Heidi," answered Susanne. "We still really like men, would like to start a family. We could even share a Mister Right—as long as I was the senior Wife."

"You? Senior? You'd have to fight me for that." Sharon shot back.

"Oh yeah?"

"Yeah." The two women suddenly closed in on each other, grabbing and playfully wrestling."

"Quit that."

"*You* quit that."

"Get your fingers away from there."

"You liked it before."

Heidi laughed. "Ladies. Come on. You're playing too rough. Someone's going to get hurt."

Sharon and Susanne hugged each other, laughing, kissed, and then separated. "We play like this all the time. We know how not to hurt one another. We feel bad when we spar, work out, and bruise the other. But we enjoy fussin' and fightin'. Like families do."

"Hmmmm. Want to work out some time? Spar or train together?"

"Hell, yeah." Sharon answered. Then, she closed in on Heidi in one quick move and began to wrestle with her in the hot tub.

"Hey! I didn't say now," Heidi laughed. Susanne joined in and the three women were soon laughing hard. A boat horn interrupted their play.

"Admiral's back. Guess we had better get dressed. I think his head may explode if he saw three pretty women, nude, in a hot tub." All three women laughed.

They went to the nearby locker room to dry off and get dressed. Sharon hugged Heidi while they were still nude. "If you ever get really lonely…"

Heidi unexpectedly kissed Sharon on the mouth. "You will be the first to know, sexy thing. But like I said, something is missing…"

"Yeah, still need a prick," Susanne joked. Which started them laughing again.

As they were finishing dressing, Susanne asked, "You're attracted to Adam, aren't you?"

Heidi paused for a minute while buttoning her top. "To be truthful, yes. If you say anything I will deny it. He's my boss, with two very nice and sexy sister wives. Both of whom are also pregnant. I would not do anything to screw that up."

"See, Susanne. I told you she was cool. But, two wives could become three…"

Heidi shook her head. "Too much drama. I don't know if I could share my man with another woman. I'd probably start a hair pulling contest."

The two Amazons smiled. "Well, we'll keep an eye out for you. Maybe we can find someone who can hold his own in the martial arts area also."

Heidi snorted. "Already found him. The problem he is on the Other Side. A certain Japanese Soldier who was with the group who tried to get Adam. The only person who ever cold cocked me. Believe me, I'd like to find out just how big his manhood was, after I pinned him and pantsed him." This started another round of laughter. They put their clothes on, and went to meet the Admiral's boat.

As Susanne and Sharon helped to tie the large Hatteras up to the dock, Heidi saw that fishing had been good. A large cooler that the Director had brought along was brimming over with sea life. Heidi stepped up and helped Adam and the Chief get the cooler onto the dock.

"Gee Boss, you did good."

Adam smiled. "The Squids seem to ignore a lot of the coastal species. They like the larger, predator marine species, like sharks, killer whales. The young warriors like the challenge of taking and eating something that can kill and eat them if given the chance."

Heidi snorted. "Too bad they didn't give us that chance. Dropping a bunch of huge rocks on us did not exactly give humans a sporting chance to fight them."

Adam shrugged. "They needed us as a replacement for their primary food source. They did not want to take a chance that we would deny them their dark meat supply."

The Admiral whistled a tune as he put the boat back in order. Finally, he joined the others. "Another successful fishing trip. Must be due to my superior nautical skills." At this comment, Sharon and Susanne rolled their eyes.

"Come on, Admiral," said Susanne. "Let's head inside and get you cleaned up. You said you wanted to check out your new chef at the restaurant tonight, to make sure he was working out."

The Admiral sighed, "Again, my poor memory betrayed me. I had forgotten that. This three hour trip went by much too fast." Heidi checked her watch. Damn. It had been three hours. Time went by fast when you were having fun. She smiled at the thought. This had been fun, and she had made two more good friends.

Adam noticed her subtle smile. She looked like she had some relaxed fun, private time.

The Admiral jumped to the dock. "I guess I smell like fish and sweat as usual, ladies. I guess I had better take a bath."

"Yes, Sir," Sharon answered.

"So, ladies, I will need my rubber ducky and someone to wash my back."

"Fine, Admiral. Susanne will find your ducky, and I'll wash you back."

"Can I get you to wash my front too?"

"Admiral!"

The Admiral smiled sheepishly. "Oh, I was just kidding. No one has a sense of humor anymore."

Unexpectantly, Sharon kissed the Admiral on his cheek. "You know we love you. But just remember we are your daughters, two of many. If you want something else, Susanne and I will get it for you. Deal?"

With that, the Admiral leered at Heidi. "How about you, Petty Officer? Will you help me with my ducky?" As Heidi's mouth fell open, the two Amazons grabbed their boss, one on each arm, and began to march him up the dock.

"Come on, Admiral. Time to keep you out of trouble," Sharon said, as she flashed her smile at the guests.

"I will call you later, Admiral." Adam called out. He was having trouble not to burst out laughing, knowing this persona of the Admiral was all for show.

Heidi gave her signature laugh. "I will have to admit, it is never a dull moment around him."

Adam chuckled. "You don't know the half of it Heidi."

Between Adam, the Chief, and Heidi, they got the fish and their equipment to their vehicle.

"Pardon me, Director, while I go and visit the little boy's room." Chief Hamilton said as he walked toward some public restrooms.

Adam looked at Heidi. "You had fun today, with Susanne and Sharon?"

Heidi grinned. "Yes Boss. I made myself two new friends, I think. Thanks for bringing me along."

Adam smiled. Then, his face took on a more serious visage. "Heidi. I need to ask you something important. But it has to remain completely secret."

"Boss, we've been working out, then doing this bodyguard thing for what, a few months now? I think you already know the answer."

"Yes, I guess I do." He took a deep breath. "If I bugged out with Chief, and my ladies, would you want to come?"

Heidi paused for a minute. "That bad, huh?"

"Yes Heidi, it's getting that bad. I don't know how long it will before Kray shows up with his Krakens and takes over."

"His Lordship knows I have been resisting attacking the Unoccupied States." Adam paused, his gaze drifting to the sea. "After the Tschaaa took out their anger on us, only a handful of people here in Key West can be depended upon to fight for the Tschaaa. I am surprised I have not had a bunch of desertions.”

He looked at Heidi, then took her left hand. “I really care about you. I would like for you to be safe. Plans have been made, with the Admiral’s help. Don’t look surprised. There is a side of him he keeps hidden. *That* is a secret too.”

Heidi swallowed and answered. “I’d like to survive. But I do not want to be a fifth wheel. If you bug out, I may go with you for a while, to make sure you are safe. Then, I’ll probably find my own way.” She looked into his eyes. “I really care about you, Boss. As a person, not as my boss. But. You have two nice, gorgeous wives, with kids on the way. A different time, a different place…” Heidi shrugged.

Adam felt the urge to kiss her. Heidi must have sensed that, as she put her finger on his lips.

“Don’t, Adam. We know where that will lead to. Way too many complications. Let’s just keep it the way it is, until something for sure happens. Okay, Boss?”

Adam gave a small smile. “I guess it will have to be. But I will hold you to the promise of at least seeing me and mine to safety. Deal?”

Heidi grinned. “Deal. Now, as soon as the Chief gets back, we can leave. I’m driving.”

“Oh, bossy now, are we?”

“You guys have been throwing back I don’t know how many drinks. I know how much I have had, being an ex-bartender. I drive.”

Adam threw her a salute. “Yes Ma’am.”

“That’s what I like, Boss. A man who listens to reason.”

CHAPTER 12

Just when humankind seemed to have demonstrated the lowest level of depravity and evil toward other Humans, Tschaaa biological, technological and genetic advancements enabled Krakens and others to sink to even lower depths of obscene and monstrous behavior.

-Excerpts from the <u>Writings of Princess Akiko</u>, Free Japan Royal Family

MALMSTROM ARMED FORCES BASE
GREAT FALLS, MONTANA

Four o'clock in the morning, and Torbin was awake again, sitting in their living room. It had been four days since Aleks had narrowly escaped death with the Eaters, thanks to Fuzz, the "Big Beastie" as she called him. Since then, every morning, Torbin woke up from the same dream. He was trying to reach Aleks as a shadowy Eater was coming at her, with his response at slow speed, the dream world having a molasses effect on his movements. Even more in the shadows were two human shapes, who laughed at his and Aleks' predicament. Then, he would jerk awake.

Torbin knew his dream was based on the comments of Commissioner Miller. Try as hard as he could, Torbin knew that he could not find any flaws to the argument that some humans had tried to murder his wife. The thought that they could slip away, not be punished, sent him into a seething rage. Which did not help his dreams, and thus his sleep.

He sensed his wife's presence before she spoke, then gently caressed his neck. "Cannot sleep, my husband? Bad dreams?"

He took her hand from his neck, kissed it. "Can't help it. I almost lost you. I was not here to help, would be a widower if not for Fuzz."

Aleks maneuvered her extremely pregnant stomach around so that she could sit on his lap. "*Oof*. Sorry I am such a huge pig. But I miss sitting on your lap, snuggling, as you Americans call it."

"Aleks, dearest, you are the lightest weight of all the burdens I carry. You can sit on me anytime you want. I love you."

Aleks kissed him, then whispered sweet nothings into his ear in Russian and Ukrainian. Torbin had come to understand them as statements about how much she loved him. No matter if he could understand everything she said. He could feel her love.

"Come, husband. Back to bed. Worrying about what could have been will just age you early. I want to keep you around for very long time. I don't give my heart to just anyone."

Torbin sighed. "I wish I had some of your Russian fatalism, acceptance. I just can't stand the thought that some assholes tried to kill you, and so far have gotten away with it."

Aleks kissed his cheek. "Patience, my husband. Remember, you were the spider, I was a fly. Good things eventually come to those who wait. I promise there will be a day of vengeance. We Russians are good at that. And my Ukrainian relatives were pretty good at it also."

A few hours later, he and Abigail were at the large sports complex on base with a new group of trainees. These were a fresh batch of basic NCO's, people with prior military experience that were now training to be First Line Supervisors, the backbone of any military organization. Many were older than Abigail, closer to Torbin's age. And she worked their asses into the dirt. Hill climbers, burpees, jumping jacks, push ups to be followed with some unarmed grappling. Later in the week, Ichiro would come and show them some of his techniques, some basic swordplay. The Armed forces were still working on an updated codified training system for all their personnel. Fighting aliens was not the same as fighting fellow humans, although they knew they would also have to fight those.

Torbin smiled to himself. He loved to watch Abigail work. First, she showed her enjoyment at the physicality of the training. At the same time, she made most of it look effortless. For her, it probably was. Yet, she knew when to stop, or not to push individual soldiers beyond their actual limits. Very rarely did she have to show any "D.I. anger" in the traditional sense. Usually, her presence seemed to make people feel a need to shine, not to disappoint her. On the rare occasion that someone took her demeanor as being weak, the person was quickly disbursed of that belief. One such individual wound up unconscious in the medical clinic. After that, smart people knew not to test her.

Torbin happened to glance around and saw a familiar figure approaching. Lt. Todd Baker, the one who had helped save Torbin's ass in Wyoming, came at a fast walk across the training field toward them. Torbin started to smile and call out some light greeting when he saw the serious look, almost a frown, on the young man's face. Now, what could be troubling the Lieutenant? Torbin had it on good authority that a local young lady who worked at the Base Exchange had taken a definite liking to him. And he had returned the feelings. This had helped disburse him of the crush he had on Abigail, something she could not return in kind. One very rough fact of the new order of things was that most people had lost large portions of their families. Some people, like Torbin, had lost them all. Thus, sometimes people latched on to each other just to have a sense of "family" of caring for and being cared for by another human being. Of course, this led to people mistaking pure loneliness for love, resulting in some unhealthy codependent relationships. Hopefully, this was not the case with to Todd Baker. Thanks in a large part to him, Torbin was still kicking, as opposed to having been turned into Eater excrement.

"Lieutenant Baker. How are you this fine day?"

Lieutenant Baker saluted Torbin, still with the serious look on his face.

"Sir, sorry to bother you. But could I have a moment of your time… alone?"

Torbin could tell that Todd Baker had a heavy weight on his shoulders.

"No bother," Torbin replied. "Hell, you've helped us train before. You know we can take breaks to handle important matters. I can tell by the look on your face that something is important, and it is the proverbial burr under your saddle."

The young Lieutenant blushed a bit. "That obvious, is it?"

"Come on, Todd, let's take a walk." Torbin turned and called out to Abigail.

"Captain Young, please excuse me for just a minute. I need to talk with the good Lieutenant here."

Abigail had looked up from her task of having the trainees complete their third set of sit-ups, having just finished another set of hill climbers.

"Of course, Sir. I have it under control." She flashed a quick smile at Todd, then returned to the task at hand. "All right, everyone up. On their feet. Time for another trip around the track."

When Abigail heard some grumbling, she was quick to respond. "I did not just hear some negative sounds, did I?"

"Ma'am. No Ma'am." The two dozen NCOs in training called out in unison. They had developed a respect tinged with fear of this young but very tough and experienced warrior. Everyone knew her as the Avenging Angel, her position in Deseret becoming her persona in the U.S.A. Behind her back, some people said she was an arch or even fallen angel, here to demand retribution of all who sought to harm her and her people. And Malmstrom personnel now included her people.

"Good. Because what do we say to negativity?"

The trainees responded in unison. "No negative waves. Never with the negative waves, Moriarty." A line from a classic sarcastic war movie, spoken in jest one day, had been taken in and modified by Abigail into a mantra. "Negative waves" were not allowed around Abigail Young's training area. And one had better *not* forget that.

Torbin chuckled as he and Todd Baker walked away, toward the far end of the sports arena.

"So shoot, Lieutenant. What's on your mind?"

"Major, I know who tried to use those Eaters to kill your wife. I know, because one of them is a family member."

Torbin felt both a chill and a feeling of rage, almost at the same moment. It seemed impossible, but Torbin felt both conflicting feelings almost simultaneously.

"Start Explaining. Lieutenant. And it had better be good."

The Lieutenant swallowed, then spoke. "Jack Baker, the one who gave Captain Young grief at the vet clinic, he is my older brother. He would never be called a 'good guy', by any means. But he is eight years my senior, and his nastiness helped keep my sister Pat and I, alive, after everyone else in our family were either killed or disappeared. We barely made it here from Arizona."

Torbin knew that Todd's parents had both worked at Luke Air Force Base outside of Phoenix. Both were active duty Air Force. The mother had been a fighter pilot, the father an engineering officer. Neither had made it out alive, thanks to roving Deltas and Falcons targeting all the active air bases.

The trip to Montana, like it was for most survivors, had not been easy. The Long Winter had also not helped.

Lieutenant Baker continued. "My brother fell in with the scavengers. His history of working both sides of the law since he was a teenager meant he fit right in. Scrounging, and maybe a little stealing is one thing. What he is doing now is something else."

Torbin stopped and faced the young man. "You need to spit it out. What exactly is he involved with?"

"Major, please believe me that at first I thought it was the drugs and booze talking. This last year, he has gotten into using any type of dope he can get his hands on. He has had plenty of money and gold to buy what he wants, because of what he is doing."

Torbin was getting impatient. "Look it, pardon me if I seem to be in a hurry, but since it was my wife they tried to kill, what did he do?"

Baker drew a deep breath before continuing. "He and a bunch of others set up a dog fighting ring. But, I have just found out it isn't only just dogs they are using. They use, breed... other things. To fight in their pits. Gamblers pay good money to bet, to watch. I know they have Eaters. Jack was so drunk and stoned the other night at the house, he said they had other things to fight. He laughed when I got mad, demanded he tell him. For the first time in my life, I beat the shit out of him." Baker stopped. "He pulled a gun, threatened to shoot Pat and me if I got in his way. Then he left."

Todd Baker was beginning to shake a bit. "He is my brother. He saved Pat and me. That got me the chance to join the military, pay back the fricking Squids. I owe him."

Torbin reached out and put his hand on his shoulder. "Todd, I know what it is like to have a brother. And to lose him. I hate to be mean about this but... I think your brother, the one who saved you, is gone. The being occupying his body is not the same brother."

Todd wiped a tear from his eye. "I know. Major. I am on my way to the Military Police, then the General's office. I'll tell my story, so they can stop him. Then, to the General, to...resign my commission."

"*What*? Like fucking hell you are! You saved my ass, now you want to quit on me? Over my dead body."

"Major, you don't understand. I purposefully ignored all the signs. I kept hoping something would happen, that he would go back to being the old Jack. He was not a saint, but he was not this... thing he has become. My inaction nearly got your wife killed. I'm not fit to command."

Torbin stood ramrod straight. "Lt. Baker. Near misses only count in horseshoes and hand grenades. And nukes. You will not beat yourself up over this. That's an order. Do you understand me?"

The young officer snapped to attention. "Yes Sir." He respected Torbin too much to disagree.

"Now, young man, we will go to the General together. I will not allow you to do something stupid like resign. We need all the fighters we can get. And, you have proven you are a fighter. On the way over, you can tell me where all these assholes your brother works with hang out."

Torbin asked Abigail to finish up for him as he and Lt. Baker had to go see the General ASAP. She did not ask any questions, as she knew that Torbin would not skip out on training unless it was very important. Abigail could tell that Todd Baker was upset, and she was worried, and sad. He was such a nice young man, who had at one time a major crush on her. But, as nice as he was, he did nothing for her in the subject of male/female attraction. Now Ichiro....

She snapped back to the task at hand. She had two dozen very sweaty, mostly winded NCOs in front of her. She decided that a change in the schedule was called for, given as it was now just her doing the training.

"All right, at… rest." They all went relaxed, trying to regain their breath.

"Let's all sit down on the ground. We are going to do what I call a little 'team building exercise'. Form a half circle, let's get to know each other a bit better."

She waited until everyone was in place. She looked out at a group of soldiers, half with prior combat experience to various degrees, the other half not, other than trying to survive to get here. They were E-4s to E-6s, training limitations preventing the Armed Forces from breaking the groups down more that. With the need to keep as many people on the line right now, trying to secure the orders with the help of local militias, training staff was at a minimum. That could easily bite them in the ass if they suddenly began taking large numbers of casualties.

The lack of a good training program for replacements would mean that the front line replacement troops would suddenly become cannon fodder due to poor training. Thus, Torbin and Abigail were trying to do everything possible to build a foundation for a Field Training system, where experienced NCOs and Junior Officers could provide newbies with some modicum of survival training as replacement troops hit the front line. A stop gap system, but until the Russians, Japanese, Canadian, and bits and pieces of personnel from other countries became completely integrated, it was the best they had.

"Now," Abigail began. "We are going to spend some time considering how we got here, what we expect each of us to do to defend the human race. Not just the U.S.A. The entire human race. Everyone has to be clear on that, what it means concerning what we, as soldiers, and supervisors, will have to do to survive. As well as keep our humanity, so we do not become Krakens." Abigail spit that last word out.

"Now, because I never ask anyone to do something I will not do, I'll start. Over six years ago I was in Eastern Washington when Hanford blew…"

Torbin had trouble sleeping that night. After taking Lt. Baker to see the General and the Military Police, Customs Enforcement and the Marshals service had also been notified. Torbin knew Commissioner

Miller would be chomping at the bit to track these assholes down and grab them. Trying to kill people's wives with BEMs, and the pit fighting, were not conducive to good order in U.S.A. society.

Torbin did not have a bad dream about Eaters and Aleks as with other nights. He just was so jacked up with the thought of revenge on his terms, his mind was racing with possible plans. Lt. Baker had told him where his brother and the others were apparently conducting the pit fights, and other possible illegal activities. A quick query via a hacking connection into the Occupied States and Tschaaa internet, bigger than their own, and he had found a past Google Earth image of the location, thanks to the former U.S.A. government.

Thanks to organized cyber hacking, not to mention a crap load of private hackers hooking up many a path into the poorly secured system, almost all the information recovered by Director Lloyd and his minions, plus input from the Squids, was available. The new internet and cloud was probably ninety-five percent of the pre-strike internet, including porn.

The alleged location was a former huge horse stable with a training/show ring, located some five miles outside of Great Falls. Lt. Baker had said that when in his cups, his brother bragged there was a large root cellar and a wine cellar on the property. Both had been expanded and modified to hold a lot of "somethings", the specifics of what was kept there his brother would never say. Todd Baker knew there were dogs. Beyond that, he couldn't help.

As surreptitiously as possible, Torbin had put his tactical gear together. He cleaned the .44 Magnum "Bear Gun" Madam President had given him. He loaded it with three rounds of the special armor piercing rounds that he had taken during the Key West raid for robocop suppression. The other three in the cylinder were now special hollow points he had gotten from his veteran friend Mike, of the t-shirt and variety shop at the BX.

Thanks to some smart marketing skills, and the fact he had one of the few silk screening operations left in all of the U.S.A, Mike was now basically rich. However, he kept working at his shop, now employing seamstresses and tailors to help make clothes and dress uniforms for everyone in the U.S.A., including the Allied Troops. Because of Torbin's fame, and the word that they were friends, Mike now had a booming mail order business. A privately run post office/private shipping company had been set up to connect all the Unoccupied States in a formal, organized manner. Madam President had told the owners of it that it would be allowed to run privately so long as it served the purposes of the U.S.A. And, they did not gouge its customers.

Mike was now on the Board of Directors.

Mike had handed Torbin a package a couple of days ago, after hearing the details of the Eater Attack. "Here, Marine. My own max load hollow points with liquid mercury in them for your Smith and Wesson. If the lead doesn't kill what you shoot, the expanding mercury will. If nothing else, it will poison whatever you hit."

Torbin had two speed loaders with Dutch Loads of AP and Mike's hollow points for the Smith. He also had a twelve round leather loop strip on his belt, with commercial heavy semi-wad cutters for hard hitting penetration. A dump pouch with another half dozen lead round nose that he had dum-dumed by cutting the bullets with his Ka-Bar rounded out his ammunition load. Torbin figured that once he got into the miscreants complex, he would find other weapons to use. Walking off with Alek's Saiga 12 gauge, or suddenly taking an assault rifle from the range would cause too many questions, especially from Aleks.

Winter was fast approaching so the days were much shorter. As Torbin was sipping the espresso Aleks had made for him that morning, he told her he would a little late getting home.

"I need to help Pappy Gunn and some Special Response Team guys try out some new night vision sights and equipment. So, I'll be home a little late tonight."

Aleks looked at him. He felt that she was looking into him, knew what he was planning.

"You just get home in one piece, my husband. Just remember that you have a loving wife with two, how you say, 'buns in the oven' waiting for you. Understand?"

He kissed her. "Aleks, did I tell you already today how much I love you?"

She smiled. "Yes. But you can tell me again, even though I can feel it."

"I love you, Aleks. You are what makes my life worth living.

Always remember that."

Aleks looked into his eyes. "Always know I will be here for you, Torbin. Always."

They kissed once more, and Torbin went to work, training troops again with Abigail.

He had told Abigail in basic terms what was going on after getting back from the meeting with General Reed. The General had even threatened to kick the young Lieutenant's ass if he ever mentioned "resigning" again. This was first time Torbin had seen him threatening personal violence in a serious way to someone. "So, Commissioner Miller will probably bring the Ferals to justice?" Abigail had asked

"Yep. It's off Base, so under the reconstituted civilian government jurisdiction. They will handle getting the people who tried to kill Aleks and Fuzz."

Again, he felt female eyes as they pierced his soul. He knew Abigail was examining him, trying to see what he may have planned.

"Torbin, my dear friend," Abigail began. "Just remember that if you need help in... doing something, I am always here."

Torbin glanced around, made sure nobody was watching as they were in uniform. Then he kissed her on the forehead. "Little sister, I know you are always there for me. What you can do is to keep an eye on Aleks, you and your big beastie, when I'm not around. Deal?"

Abigail broke into a broad grin. "Deal, of course. That is easy. Just make sure you always get home in one piece when I'm not around to watch your back."

"Will do, Abigail, Will do. Now, let's see what we can do to make today a memorable training experiences for our NCO Trainees."

It was dark as Torbin snuck up on the formal stable complex. He had a white sheet he had converted into a poncho as there was snow on the ground around the complex. If he saw some security, hopefully he could just drop to the ground and act like a small snow drift. He had forgotten how many times he had to sneak up past sentries at all hours of the day and night. Now, it was second nature.

So far, he had seen one guard at a large chain link entrance gate, who was kept busy with some comings and goings of various vehicles. Were they holding a fight tonight? He would soon find out. He had committed himself, there was no turning back. He made it to the chain link fence that the current owners and users had thrown up more as a warning than actual security. Large signs with pictures of slavering dogs were hung all along the fence line, proclaiming *"Beware of Dogs. They Bite." "Expect to Be Eaten."* was another warning sign. Torbin wondered if that was how they dealt with nosey neighbors—turned them into dog food.

The chain link fence was not even buried in the ground, so it was relatively easy for him to cut a chunk out of the bottom with his wire cutters, and then slither through. He had started to inch away from the fence, when he heard a "Pssst!" off to his left. He immediately slid to the ground, tried to look like a mound of snow covered dirt. He turned his head and looked to the left for source of the sound. Some thirty yards away, he saw some white cameoed figures just reaching the outside of the fence. They were in a spread out conga line, about a yard between each figure. Instead of his modified poncho camouflaged, the figures equipment looked like it was all official issue. Someone from the government was trying to get in just as he had done.

Torbin began the lowest and slowest crawl he could perform, moved away from the fence, in case they came down and found his hole. He observed a couple of the figures, wearing what seemed to be night vision goggles. Torbin liked to use his own natural night vision, which had always worked well for him once his eyes adjusted to the dark. The compound/stable had few lights showing. In fact, it looked as if the operators of this apparent facility had purposefully blacked out all the windows, to keep lights to a minimum. He bet they were trying to make it appear from the outside that few lights were on. Thus, it would appear to observers that there was little activity. Torbin would not be surprised if there was some heavy duty sound proofing modifications in the interior. All he could hear was some very muffled noise.

He moved slowly, keeping his eyes on the figures to his left. Two were now up to the fence, doing what he had done—cutting a hole as quietly as possible, then bending the cut material up to allow a person to low crawl through. Torbin had made it about twenty five yards from the fence when one of the two fence cutters motioned for the next figure back to come up and crawl through the fence. They seemed fairly efficient at this, so they must have trained and practiced in just this type of activity. Torbin stopped his crawl, lay still, and watched.

With practiced ease, all twelve figures were through and low crawling in toward the nearest building, a large stable. One small light shone out toward the rear of the structure, at right angles from Torbin and the strangers. Small slivers of light peeked through the edge of what appeared to be two windows. That was it. Everything else was blacked out. Torbin wondered what the heat signature of the stable was like.

Then, off to his right, he thought he heard a small door slide shut. The strangers did not seem to notice it, too concentrated on getting lined up as they crawled toward their target. Torbin looked toward origin of the sound. There was enough ambient light from a fairly clear sky and half-moon that he made out a figure moving toward the group. At first he thought it was a guard dog, but it seemed to be transitioning from two feet to four, then back to two. It motivated toward the dozen unknowns in this odd shambling, changing gait. But it was making good time. And the twelve did not see it. "Shit," Torbin whispered to himself. In one smooth motion, he rose up just enough to throw one of the two good sized stones he had brought with him. Want to sneak up behind a sentry? Throw a rock and make noise in the opposite direction, get the subject to look away from you. Then, move up on them in their blind spot. The improvised projectile struck the snow covered dirt just in front and to the left of the strange creature. It skittered to the left a bit at the rock's impact, and rose up. A chill went into Torbin as he realized that the odd figure looked like a large baboon.

Somebody from the group of twelve finally noticed the approaching figure. Four sounds of a silenced subsonic weapon and the figure sprawled out, then lay still. Whoever was in charge, saw this threat and made a tactical decision. A muffled order and all twelve figures rose into crouched "Groucho Marx" close quarter battle stances and moved in near perfect alignment toward the stable structure. Speed was now decided to be what was important. Torbin next noticed a thirteenth figure was on the ass of the armed individual farthest away, appearing to grip the belt of the person in front.

As he noticed that, he heard the muffled sound of the door as it swung shut once, then twice. Two more strange figures like the first were now moving at flank speed from where the last one had come, toward the assault line. Torbin sprang up and threw his last rock at the two threats, then drew his pistol. He must have hit one of them as there was a barking chattering, and one figure jumped up into the air, twisting about. Then all hell broke loose. Additional threats must have come from the other flank as someone began firing a silenced sub gun in three-shot bursts, toward where the light shown at the far end of the long structure. Larger, crouched figures emanated from an apparent exit point near the light. Large growls and odd barks began to fill the air, then loud howling. Within seconds, everybody was firing. Torbin thought he had heard the crackle of a portable radio just before this happened. The assault was on.

The two figures coming from Torbin' right had seen him now. They started to make a beeline when the firing from the assault line caused them to be taken aback. Too many targets, threats, and they were confused. They stood up and began giving alarm barks like baboons on the Serengeti do when seeing a threat. Torbin saw his chance, and dashed toward the assault group, hoped they did not shoot first, then ask questions. The "enemy of my enemy is my friend". Or so Torbin hoped.

He tried to keep an eye on the two baboon creatures to his right as he began to sprint toward the firing figures. Seeing one of the Assault Team member had his or her back toward them, they decided that was the prey to attack, were now distracted from Torbin. They began to run at full tilt on all fours.

Torbin's big .44 bucked in his hand as he shot at the running figures.

"*Friendly—don't shoot! Friendly—don't shoot!*" He yelled as loudly as he could, running toward the assault line. Someone noticed the baboon creatures now, and also began to shoot at them. Torbin was sure he had hit one, the other one went down in a hail of bullets.

"Who the fuck are you?" A voice yelled out.

"Major Torbin Bender, at your service."

He then heard a familiar voice. "Major, do you always head toward the shitty situations? Or do you just attract them?" It was Commissioner Miller.

"A little of both, Sir."

"Doctor Anders. Grab onto the good Major here." He turned toward Torbin. "Stay in back. We have a plan we know, you don't. Stay out of the way."

"Aye-aye, Sir," Torbin snapped back. The Commissioner grunted. "Goddamned gung ho Marines."

Emily Anders appeared and grabbed the back of his tactical vest, up under his makeshift poncho. She had a long, dark object in her hand, the length of an old fashioned knight stick.

"What's that?"

"Cattle prod. Don't touch the prongs unless you want a shock treatment," the veterinarian answered.

"Roger that." Torbin did not take the time to ask why she was here. Things were way too busy.

Another large, almost canine-looking beast burst out of the stable, under the lone light. It moved like a dog, but was the size of a black bear. Commissioner Miller fired a good dozen rounds from his 10mm ex-FBI MP5, as one of his men hit it with a shotgun slug. It finally went down a yard from reaching them.

"My God, what have they been doing here?" Emily blurted out.

"Come on," the Commissioner ordered. "We need to get through that door before someone locks it on us." They were some fifty yards from it as the Commissioner made a run for the opening. Torbin opened his revolver, ejected the empties, slapped a speed loader into his revolver and followed, Emily Anders still holding on. The Commissioner was so impatient he was moving before his troops even knew what had happened. Torbin, seeing no one on his six, quickly moved there. Miller kicked the partially open door, then slid through, button hooking to the left. Torbin hooked to the right, Emily still managed to hang on. For the first time, warning calls of "Police with a search warrant!" were given.

The interior was lit with some red "exit here" theater lights, nothing more. The Commissioner swung a bit wide toward the first horse stall on his left, Torbin went to the one on the right. They were in a good seven yards before anyone else followed. So far, no humans.

A beast burst from the stable on the left, screeching like the ape it used to be. The huge mutated chimp went for Miller as he raised his sub gun and fired. Three rounds and his gun stopped. The Commissioner stared into the face of death. He watched as its head exploded into a mass of red mist and brains. Torbin had double tapped it, an AP and a mercury loaded hollow point into the side of its skull. The .44 Magnum was deadly, especially in Torbin's hands. The former ape collapsed onto Miller's feet, almost knocking him over. He stumbled back, then regained his balance. He shot a look at Torbin. "I thought you were in the rear," Miller said.

"I was. Then the rear became the front. Are you okay?"

As the rest of the team started to enter, Miller nodded his head. "Remind me never to badmouth the Marines again. Alright, let's get moving. Check each stall. Shoot first, ask later. We have another team coming in from the other side, then another through the main gate, with six uniformed sheriff's officers." As he spoke, Torbin thought he heard some muffled shots from somewhere on the compound.

"Major, if I yelled for help, would the military show up?"

"They always have a couple of Special Response Teams on standby, with a chopper as well. Just say the word."

Miller paused. "This will *not* be Waco. I did not expect all of these... things to show up. A few Eaters, fighting dogs, but not this. We will keep going for a few, and see if things improve. But, well, this is not the charge of the light brigade. Alright, let's get moving."

They moved forward, checking stalls as they moved. They reached the end of that part of the complex without any more creatures showing up. They exited the first stable area, and passed into the next.

"There is a cellar of some sorts under this building, so look for stairs, trap doors, whatever. Stay frosty."

Ten seconds in, hell came back. A trap door flew open in the floor of a stable to their left and an Eater burst out. It bowled over one of the federal officers, latching onto his leg. A shot to its primitive brain pan stopped it, but not before it had crippled the officer. Emily jumped into action, quickly had his wound bandaged as they tried to secure the rest of the building, before entering the cellar. Another baboon creature showed up, barking and screeching before it was shot. Then another. And another.

"Someone is letting them loose piecemeal," Torbin stated as they shot down the last one.

"Yes, but from where?"

"Where was the main office, Commissioner? Every working stable had some type of business office."

The Commissioner smiled. "Remind me to offer you a job, Major." He got on his radio to the team coming in from the other side. Short conversation as they checked the rest of horse stalls. The found a trap door in another stall, covered it with weapons.

"Alright, the other team has the business office in sight. And there seems to be some armed humans in it. The main entrance team is in a firefight right now, with at least a half of dozen miscreants. We will continue and hit that group from behind. After, of course, we clear that cellar area here. The numbers of creatures running loose seems to have died down, for now."

With quick precision, Miller had a six man clearing team designated for the cellar.

"I'm going as well," Emily Anders cut in.

"Doctor," the Commissioner started to say.

"No, I am going. If what is going on that I think is going on, it's in the cellar."

"Look it, Doctor, this is not the old sci-fi movie *Them* and you are not the daughter of the myrmecologist who needs to see if the queen ants were all killed..."

"I. Am. Going." Emily had a stone cold look in her eye that made Torbin think of Abigail, just before she tore someone a new asshole.

"I'll be her bodyguard, Commissioner. Just let me borrow a 12 gauge."

Miller snorted. "Alright. It's your funeral. Agent Johnson. A loaded shotgun for the good Major, if you please."

Moments later, with the aid of some extremely bright flashlights, they were headed down the stairs, with Torbin and Emily bringing up the rear.

As soon as they hit the cellar floor, hell happened. Again.

Another "once an ape" came screaming at them, followed by baboon creatures. A mad minute, similar to Evanston, but on a smaller scale, began.

The Feds shot their shotguns, sub-guns, assault rifles. One man went down with a baboon at his throat. Torbin jammed his shotgun in its mouth and blew its brains all over the cellar ceiling.

Then a new breed of creature showed up.

"Weasels!" Emily yelled as long furry things, bigger than the largest house cat, exploded from den holes in the floor. The vet jammed her cattle prod into the face of one and cooked its brains. Then she jammed it into the side of one that was trying to bite Torbin in the groin. Torbin jumped from some of the electrical bleed off, but the weasel creature jerked off of his leg and lay twitching on the cellar floor. He proceeded to stomp its head in.

The attack stopped. Torbin turned to Emily, who was shaking and breathing hard. "My wife thanks you for saving my genitalia, Doctor."

Somehow, the vet produced a smile. "Did I ever tell you, Major, just how many women had a crush on you?"

"No, but please save that until we get out of here."

At that moment they heard the voice of a young girl. "Help us. Please!"

"Oh fuck, no," the lone female Federal Officer said as she dashed toward a locked room door. She looked through the barred window, screamed, and began to vomit. There was a chattering from an ape creature behind the door as it jammed its muzzle and teeth between the bars, snapping and biting. Torbin stepped forward, jammed his .44 in its mouth, pulled the trigger. The top of its skull disappeared. Torbin then laid his shoulder into the door, unbridled rage giving him the strength to break in the door.

Inside were three young females, the oldest no more than seventeen. One younger, about fourteen, was strapped to a table, naked, with bite marks on her body, claw marks on her sides and thighs. She was sobbing. The other two were secured to the cell wall.

Out came Torbin's Ka-Bar, and he cut the straps on all the captives. He then picked up the young lady from the table and she wrapped her arms around him, sobbed, shaking. Part of his brain said she reminded him of a young Abigail.

He was up the stairs to the main stable before he even knew it. Someone produced a space blanket, wrapped her in it, and got her some water. The team medic gave her a light sedative.

Commissioner Miller looked at the girl, then at Torbin. The female Federal Agent came up retching. Behind her, Emily was helping the two ambulatory young ones up the stairs.

"The word is given, Major," Miller spoke.

"Cell phone, please." Torbin took the phone and dialed a special number, unknown to most.

A voice answered. "Forest Fire Reporting. Where's the Fire?"

"Forest Fire, Torbin, 1775." Torbin then gave a classified code that changed each week, followed by the address of the stable complex. "Friendlies on site. Need Fire Response Soonest. Lots of trees involved."

"Response is dispatched. Turn radios to the following frequency..."

A few moments later and Torbin disconnected and handed the phone back to the Commissioner.

"About ten minutes, the calvary should be in the area."

Just then, one of the agents who had finished searching the cellar, called out to the Commissioner.

"Boss. The rooms at the end of the cellar are arms rooms, jammed pack with weapons. Must be at least a thousand rifles, machine guns, plus a bunch of pistols and shotguns. Ammo, too." The agent began passing out two five round boxes of 12 gauge slugs, and one of buckshot to the shotgun users.

"Wait here please," Torbin said to no one in particular, and went back down the steps. He ran down the hall to the armory and looked in. He whistled. There were rifles of every type you could imagine. His eyes went to a long one with a wooden stock. A 30-06 Garand, a late World War II shortened bayonet affixed to its barrel. Looped over it was a bandolier of loaded eight round en bloc clips. Torbin grabbed the weapon and the ammunition. He did a quick function check, saw the rifle had been lubricated, well cared for. It was probably from a private collection of some citizen who did not survive the first six years. He grabbed a clip and loaded it the correct way so as not to get an M-1 Thumb. Then he hurried back up the steps.

The Federal agents were checking their weapons, as Emily and the medic carried for the three girls. The female agent was shaking, pale as a ghost. Torbin met the Commissioner's eyes, nodding his head toward her. Miller said in a low tone, "She saw the chimp monster raping that girl. She'll stay here with the wounded." Miller motioned to the Garand. "I see you found a friend."

"Yes Sir. Had an old Gunny show me how to use this weapon. A rifleman's rifle." The Commissioner nodded in appreciation.

"Okay, time to move. Doctor, stay here with the ladies and the wounded agent."

Torbin handed Emily a revolver he had grabbed from an old west-style holster in the armory. "Here. This is a replica of an old Smith and Wesson .45 Top Break Revolver. Five rounds in it. You know how to use a pistol, right?"

"Yes, Torbin. My father taught me to shoot. I think I can handle this."

"It's more for humans, but it's better than nothing on the beast things."

"Time to go, Major," the Commissioner interjected.

"Okay. Watch yourself, Doctor."

Emily smiled. "Will do. You come back in one piece, Major. Understood?"

"Yes Ma'am."

The team stacked up quickly, Torbin at the rear. Then they move out the large swinging double doors of the stable, heading toward the next stable. Two smaller outdoor lights illuminated the area between the two stables, nothing more. As they were about to enter the next stable, large creatures came running around the corner of the building. These monsters had started out as something doglike, but now looked as if they had been crossed with an oversized hyena and something from a person's nightmare. Well over two hundred pounds, Torbin got a glimpse of some weird vestal arms or tentacles emanating from their front shoulders. The mouths had way too many teeth. He fired his Garand. There must have been a half dozen, two of them slamming into agents with open jaws even as they were sieved with bullets. An agent died with a crushed face and head before he knew what hit him. Torbin emptied his rifle, the en bloc clip pinging from the action after the last round. Torbin grabbed for another one as new threats appeared from out of the dark. Miller cursed as his MP5 ran empty, grabbing for his 10mm Glock 20 pistol.

"Eaters!" somebody yelled. Now Torbin knew someone had found a way to control these bastards, as they were ignoring all the fresh kill meat around and headed straight for the Assault Team. Only a few shots rang out as the rest scrambled to reload. An Eater was almost on top of Torbin, as he swung the rifle out to use the bayonet.

A segment of the darkness turned into a figure as a sword blade flashed, cutting the limbs off the left side of the Eater. It slid into the ground, letting go with the god awful mewling screech that a person never forgot. The clawed hands were cut off, then a blade penetrated its brain thru the left eye. It collapsed, dead.

"Ichiro. What the holy hell are you doing here?"

"Why saving you again, my blood brother. And I have some help."

From about fifty yards away, an animal horn blown by someone with strong lungs sent a call to arms sound reverberating out into the night. The Sons of the North had arrived.

"Shitfire. Don't I have any operational security and secrecy?" The Commissioner yelled as he emptied his pistol into an approaching Eater. Then, nothing else attacked.

A huge man dressed in traditional Viking warrior garb stepped out of the darkness. Of course it was Rolf Knudsen. Who else would suddenly show up, with a huge broadsword in his belt?

"Ah, we found you, brothers. But too late I guess. You have killed everything." He sounded almost sad. Upon hearing Rolf's pronouncement, the proverbial gods of combat stepped in with a vengeful, "Oh really? Watch this."

Out from the dark came more of the dog monsters, as large as black bears. People scrambled to bring their firearms to bear as Rolf let out a battle cry, producing a long spear and stepped in front of everyone.

"Get out of the field of fire, goddamnit!" Miller cursed as he reloaded his pistol.

Rolf braced the long boar spear with his right foot on the weapon's butt, catching one of the dog monsters full in the chest. The boar spear had two cross pieces a foot apart on the shaft, designed to keep boars that impaled themselves from pushing down the shaft of the spear and feeding on the human at the dull end, even while it died. It worked exactly the same way with this new threat. Snapping, jerking, and snarling, Rolf kept ahold of the spear as the monster died. Rolf bellowed praises to Thor, then drew his broadsword.

Torbin took out two more with his heavy 30.06, as a combined weight of fire dispatched the fourth one. Seven more American Vikings came out of the shadows, bedecked similar to Rolf. A baboon creature burst screeching from the shadows and was impaled by an arrow. Torbin glanced over to the projectile's source and saw that it was a female holding the bow. Tall, blonde, statuesque, the Daughter of the North had a look of satisfaction as the attacking creature flopped around, then lay still.

"Excellent shot, Brynhildr." Rolf bellowed. Torbin saw that even though she had traditional Norse garb and armor, the bow she was using was a modern compound bow, with attached spare arrow holder. She had two short handled single blade battle axes stuffed in her wide leather belt, a small quiver of arrows strapped across her back. Brynhildr looked as if she had just stepped out of an expensive Hollywood action film. This night, she was the real deal.

"Alright." Commissioner Miller began snapping orders. "You and you, stay with the Major and I. And with our new friends here. The rest of you, take the dead and wounded back to the doctor. We'll pick you up later." Miller picked up the assault rifle of the dead agent, then took a full magazine from the dead man's belt. With practiced ease he swapped out the full magazine with the partial, stuck the latter in a front cargo pocket. He had seen death many times before, and he would grieve for his lost agent later. Right now, he needed to take care of the living.

The six male Sons of the North lined up shield to shield in a practiced formation, Rolf and Brynhildr behind them. Miller grunted. "You want us to follow you? Anyone have a firearm?"

Rolf gave another large grin. "You may fire around us, and by us. We will not flinch. Let us be your shield wall. We will keep these beasts from hell away from you."

"Okay, it's your funeral."

Rolf laughed. "And a fitting one at that. To die in battle, taken to Valhalla by the valkyries. What could be better?" The Commissioner saw in Rolf's eyes that he was serious. He had learned never to question a man's religion, unless the man was trying to force it on him. He was not about to start doing something different now.

"Okay, lay on Macduff. Into the last stable through those barn doors. Then we can hit the assholes holding the main gate from the rear." He paused. "But first, raise your right hands." All the men raised their hands with broadswords in them, Brynhildr had an arrow in hers.

"Do you all solemnly swear to defend the Constitution and the people of the U.S.A. against all enemies, foreign and domestic?"

A chorus of "Yah, yes, of course." followed.

"By the power vested in me, you are all sworn in as Deputy U.S. Marshals for the next twenty-four hours. Don't make me regret this."

Rolf laughed. "My Commissioner, we will do what you tell us, as long as it involves killing the enemies you mentioned."

Rolf barked an order and his people moved in practiced unison toward the aforementioned doors. Torbin noticed Ichiro was walking by his side. "I don't suppose I could get you to stay back with the doctor?"

Ichiro smiled. "With respect, I am here because your wife and Abigail called me, afraid you were about to do something stupid. Impulsive. It appears that they were right. Now, I must get you back in one piece, or suffer their anger."

Torbin smiled. "Okay, but only because I don't dare make Aleks angry. Just do not get hurt on my account."

"I would never dream of it, Torbin-san."

With the shield wall they shoved open the barn door. No button hook, no criss cross entries, just straight in. Torbin was sure they had Kevlar under their Viking armor, so they would be almost bullet proof to small arms fire. Good combination of old and new weapons technologies.

They were in another dimly lit large stable. This one had just a few horse stalls along the sides, most of it open in the middle. Hay bales and horse tacking were spread out across the dirt floor. Maybe the last group of creatures were it, Torbin thought. Torbin and the others with firearms did a quick check of the few stables as they slowly walked past, making sure nothing would hit them from the sides or rear. A few huge dog tracks, nothing else was found. The group slowed as they reached the end of the building.

"Okay, when we exit through those doors, we will be in sight of where the miscreants are holed up," Miller stated. "We gunmen will get them in a crossfire with the Assault Team trying to enter through the front. We have a couple of flash bangs, which should help clear them out."

He turned toward Rolf. "If you and your people could watch our backs..."

Breaking glass interrupted his comment, as windows shattered in the south side of the stable they were preparing to exit. Screaming baboon creatures rushed at them.

With practiced ease, Rolf's people raised their large, circular shields, swung them up and over the others and reformed a shield wall in the new direction of the threat before the others could bring their firearms to bear. An arrow from Brynhildr's bow took one creature through its throat, and she drew another. A couple of shots were fired, then a dozen creatures were leaping at the Sons of the North.

Broadswords demonstrated their deadliness as the baboon creatures were clove in half, the swordsmen letting rip with battle cries. One actually made it past, to latch on to Rolf's left arm, which held a small buckler rather than a full shield. He laughed as the creature bit down, only to discover traditional chain link armor underneath. Rolf crushed its head with the pommel of his sword.

The other double doors of the stable, now to their backs, burst open. Whoever controlled these monstrosities had it down to a science, as the sacrifice of the baboon creatures allowed for an attack from a different direction, with no wall of shields for protection against them. Torbin yelled, "Behind!" as a pit-bull with a spiked collar leapt at his throat. Automatic reflexes took over, and he thrust the bayonet on the M-1 into its chest. The force of the contact almost bowled him over, but he managed to stand his ground. He pulled the rifle's trigger, the blast helping to free the bayonet blade from the now dead canine.

The pit-bull was the only "normal" animal among the attacking force. Once again, whatever means of control the criminal owners of this venture had, it enabled them to send various types of creatures at them, mixed up, all at the same time with no danger of distraction. They existed to reach and rend their target humans, nothing more.

Ichiro dispatched an Eater with his practiced technique, then used his katana to slice a super weasel almost in half. Shots were fired at the canine monsters, baboon creatures, once-an-ape animals. The other American Viking swordsmen were there, trying to get their shields between the creatures and the others. It turned into a complete melee of blood and guts.

A bear-sized canine monstrosity latched onto the shield of one of the Sons of Norway, crushing and shattering it as the creature knocked the man over onto his back. Even though reinforced with Kevlar, the shields could not stand up to the crushing might of the creature's jaws. The American Viking, unable to use his sword, pulled a dirk from his boot and began perforating the monster's chest and side. In a blur, a katana blade was sticking through the base of the modified canine's skull. It shuddered, then collapsed onto its original prey. The warrior, with Ichiro's help, heaved the dead body to the side.

"Thank you, my friend. That beast was being difficult."

Ichiro smiled, gave a short bow, and then went looking for another target.

Brynhildr had grounded her bow, and pulled her two battle axes from her belt. Letting out a war cry equal to any man's, she started swinging her weapons in an intricate pattern of death. She was selective where she struck, going for the soft throats, guts of the attacking creatures, so as not to bind her blades in bone. Soon she had her arms soaked with blood from gushing neck wounds and spilled gut sacks.

Then the threats were gone, or down. One of the two remaining agents was also down, his right leg badly bitten and bleeding. Brynhildr bent down, grabbed the emergency medic pack every one of the agents had on their belt and quickly had him bandaged up. He told her thanks and Brynhildr flashed him a smile. Then she was back up with her bow at the ready.

"Fuck!" exclaimed the Commissioner. "This was supposed to be a search and arrest warrant operation, not a damn monster hunt." He fumed, looking at his downed agent. "Screw this." Miller reached into a small ditty bag he had on his hip and withdrew a couple of round objects. He stepped over and handed one to Torbin, an M-26 shrapnel grenade. Torbin looked at Miller. "These are not usually law enforcement issue, are they?"

"No," answered the Commissioner. "But it is better to have them and not need them, than need them and not have them." He then turned to Rolf, who was checking his people out. One warrior had a cracked arm from a dog-monster bite, his mail armor stopping penetrating teeth but not the extreme crushing pressure of the bite. Later tests would show the creature's bite pressure was equal to a large crocodile. The rest had cuts and bruises, nothing serious.

"Rolf, can I borrow a couple of your warriors?"

Rolf grinned broadly. "Of course. They are not done fighting."

Miller then turned to his two agents. "Bowen, take your wounded comrade back to where the doctor is." Just then, his radio crackled to life. He answered it, listened to his earpiece.

"Well Major, your choppers are a minute out,.I think I can hear the rotors. The team is going to fast rope down on the business office roof, and take care of those inside. So, that leaves us to help take out those blocking the entrance. Ready?"

Ichiro stepped forward. "Sir, please allow me to accompany Torbin. That will free you to coordinate with the arriving military any last minute actions."

The Commissioner paused in thought for a few moments, then handed the other grenade to the Free Japan Officer. "You're right. You're thinking straighter than I am. I can see why General Reed values your opinion so much." Ichiro went to attention, then gave a short bow. He turned to his friend.

"Shall we, Major?"

"Absolutely, Major." Two Viking warriors formed up shield to shield, the two military men falling in behind their large frames. Both were almost as large as Rolf, thus allowing Torbin and Ichiro the ability to hide behind their bulk and shields. Torbin gave the order to move out and crossed the open area between the stall and the former tack/equipment storage shed, now the guard shack for the entrance of the compound. Torbin and Ichiro both had their grenades in hand, opposite hand social finger through the pin ring.

As they crossed the open area, a couple of shots rang out from the back of the destination building. The rounds impacted on the shield of one of the Sons of Norway. No follow up shots were taken, as an arrow streaked directly into the area of the muzzle flash. A scream of pain told them the arrow had struck true. Brynhildr had scored again. The two Majors pulled the pins on their grenades, then heaved them thru the back window of the structure. The warriors crouched down behind their shields, the Majors behind them.

The grenades blew a chunk out of the wall, eliciting screams from inside. Then, Torbin heard muffled cries of "We surrender!" as the front Assault Team finally made entry through the main gate. At that moment, the Military Special Response Team fast roped to the roof of the business office of the former commercial stables.

Torbin, Ichiro, and the two Sons of the North backed across the open area to the last stable building.

"Nice job, gentlemen," Commissioner Miller stated. "It took long enough, but things are beginning to come together..."

Rolf let out a bellow and started to run at some figures that were coming full tilt from the area of the business office. At the sight of the huge American Viking, they veered off at right angles toward the back of the compound. A large caliber shot rang out and Rolf went down.

Brynhildr let out a banshee scream of pain and rage, took off like a shot, bow in hand. Miller, Torbin and Ichiro followed closely behind. On the run, Brynhildr let fly an arrow and a figure went down, impaled through his thighs. Not pausing for a moment, yelling something in Norwegian, she let loose another arrow, which impacted a fleeing figure in the back. As that person sprawled face first into the dirt, the remaining two suddenly slid to a stop, yelling, "We give up! Don't shoot."

Brynhildr kept running at them at full tilt, slamming into them like a linebacker. There was a thrashing mound of hands and feet as the Daughter of the North tried to pound both of them at once with her fists, knees, and feet. Torbin would say later that only his arrival along with Miller and Ichiro prevented Brynhildr from beating or hacking the two men to death. It took a couple of minutes, but they finally untangled the woman warrior from the two miscreants, handcuffed them, and frog marched them back to where the others were. The one with the arrow in his back was in hell now, being deceased.

Brynhildr walked up and grabbed the one she had shot through the thighs with her bow and arrow, proceeded to drag him unceremoniously back to her fellow warriors by his wounded legs. He had been the one who had fired the shot into Rolf, so she had long term and very painful plans for him. She had the man's lever action .444 Marlin in the hand she was not using to drag the miscreant. When she reached Rolf, who was being seen to by the other warriors, she dropped her burden and strode over to the warrior. She knelt down in front of Rolf as he began to remove his clothes and mail armor. Brynhildr grabbed Rolf by his ears and began to scream at him, her face inches from his.

Torbin and the others arrived as she yelled at Rolf in Norwegian, a tear suddenly running down her cheek.

"Well, I don't understand the words, but the tone reminds me of Aleks. 'How dare you get yourself hurt! You did this on purpose just to piss me off! You uncaring brute you!' Or words to that effect."

Ichiro laughed. "And, she loves him like Aleks loves you."

At that remark, Torbin did a quick double take. He looked at the two Norwegians from North Dakota and saw that his Japanese friend was right. The look, the yelling, the concern was there. He wondered if Rolf realized it.

"That is the woman Rolf pulled in the rickshaw when he won the race at the Oktoberfest," Ichiro stated.

"I guess the race had a positive effect on their love life."

Brynhildr finally stopped her tirade, and let go of Rolf. The large warrior seemed like a scolded puppy, his eyes cast downward. Then in a blur, he grabbed Brynhildr by her braided hair and planted a firm kiss on her mouth. She kissed back, then pushed him away, slapping him. Rolf laughed, clapping his hands. Such were the mating rituals of the wild American Viking.

Rolf, now down to a bared, hairy chest, sat patiently as Brynhildr produced a long, very thin blade. She probed the area where the .444 caliber rifle round had hit him, digging shards of broken chain mail pieces out of his chest. The combination of Kevlar and chainmail had stopped the bullet, but the force had broken some links in the armor. Pieces of the broken lengths, small, sharp and thin, were shoved back into Rolf's chest. As Brynhildr expertly dug out the shards, stoic Rolf seemed to wince once. This resulted in Brynhildr poking him with the thin blade, admonishing him for being a baby. Rolf laughed again at her stern visage, said something to her in low tones. The female warrior tried not to laugh, to smile, but finally a giggle passed her lips, her eyes now twinkling.

"Ah, young love", mumbled Torbin. He got a warm feeling as a picture of Aleks flashed in his mind's eye.

Miller's radio crackled. He had a quick conversation with someone at the other end, then said, "Do *not* open those semi-truck trailers until I get there."

He turned toward Torbin and Ichiro. "Care to accompany me to examine a couple of locked and sealed truck trailers?"

"Yes, Sir. We are at your service."

One of Rolf's warriors with shield and sword joined up with them. "May I come too? I still have the desire for a good fight, if there are any beasts left."

"Of course. That is why I deputized you."

The four of them walked in the direction of the business office where the military team had fast roped in. About fifty yards from the office, in the shadows, were two semi-tractor trailers. Guarding their rear doors were two Federal Agents from the other Assault Team. "So Agent Cash, they are still sealed, yes?"

"Yes, Sir," the Agent answered. "And those look like our Customs Seals." The Commissioner walked up and used a flashlight to take a closer look. Wrapped through a bolt hole next to a small padlock was a metal seal. The Commissioner checked one, then the other.

"Yep, looks like some of ours. We'll have to figure where these came from, and see when they crossed into the U.S.A." Slowly, the Commissioner broke the seal on one of them, and stuck the seal in a pocket.

"Help us. Please, help us." The cry of a young girl came from inside. There had not been any motion, noise up till then from inside to indicate anything was alive in the trailer. The Commissioner yanked on the small padlock to see if it was loose. No such luck. In a blink, the large American Viking strode up.

"I will get in," he announced. Miller stepped back. The warrior struck the padlock downward with the pommel of his broadsword, breaking it open.

"What's your name?" Miller asked.

"Johann."

"Well Johann, get ready to open the door."

Miller looked at the four others. "Guns up, in case there is something other than a young girl in there."

Torbin took a bead on where the doors would open with his M-1. He had reloaded it with a fresh en bloc clip, so he had eight rounds of 30'06 at hand. He took a deep breath, then began to slowly let it out.

Miller nodded at Johann, who unbolted the doors, swung them open with ease. As he stepped back, a huge bull mastiff burst through without even a warning growl. Torbin snapped a shot off that sliced along the side of the huge dog's head. The stunning effect of the impact caused the canine to faceplant in the dirt, its front end now not working right. The Commissioner stepped up and fired a shot from his Glock 10mm between the eyes of the dog before it could recover. It collapsed, and laid still.

"Cover the doors. There may be more."

The Commissioner pulled his flashlight out of its belt holder and shone it into the truck trailer. The light illuminated three human bodies hanging upside down, large wash tubs below them. The tubs had streaks of blood on them, the bodies pale white where the light shone, other than some red streaks down the arms and faces of the dead.

"Help us!" The voices came from the back of the trailer. Before anyone could react, Johann put down his shield and sword and started to clamber up into the trailer.

Something that looked like it could be part human came screeching at Johann from the dark recesses of the trailer. Miller was a blur as he raised his pistol and double tapped two 10mm rounds into the figure's chest, the impact points could be covered by a quarter coin. The creature, propelled forward by its inertia, tumbled out of the back of the trailer, thudded on the dirt. It twitched, then lay still.

"Nice shot," Torbin opined.

"Just lots of practice," Miller answered.

Johann was up and in the trailer as if having human shaped beasts shot down around him was an everyday event. "Where are you, little ones?" Two young girls, around ten years of age, came bursting out of the darkness and grabbed Johanns left arm.

They were both nude, covered with scratches and blood. They began to sob.

"Come, Uncle Johann will get you home…."

Another screeching part human figure dropped down from the ceiling of the trailer, and started to claw at Johann. The Son of the North pulled an unnoticed Bowie knife from his sword belt in a blur of motion, burying the nearly twelve inch blade into its brain through the left eye.

"Have a fast trip to hell, devil spawn," Johann spat out. He yanked his blade out, let the creature collapse as he wiped his Bowie on his pants, and then sheathed it. Stepping to the doors of the truck trailer, he handed the two girls down to waiting hands. After he scrambled down, the two young girls grabbed onto him again. Torbin noticed that Johann was not just some young pup, he had grey in his beard.

"You have children, don't you?" Torbin asked.

"*Ja,* though they are now older than these two. They need covering, clothes..." In a flash, Torbin had removed his white sheet camouflage poncho and handed it over, and Ichiro peeled off his dark ninja top. They soon had both girls bundled up, still latched onto Johann.

"Come, little ones. We must figure out a way for me to carry my sword, my shield..."

"I will carry them, Johann. It would be an honor." Ichiro stood straight, then bowed low to the huge man.

Johann nodded, "Thank you, young sir. Now, little ones, we go to where it is warm, and there are nice people. You must tell me your names as I carry you, okay?" He strode back toward the stables, a young girl in each arm, laying up on his shoulders. Ichiro followed in step, shield and sword in his grasp.

Torbin looked at the two human like figures. "Commissioner, ever take any anthropology classes?"

"Yes, Major. Why?"

Torbin shined a flashlight beam at the two figures. "Homo erectus or their first cousins, though these may be the idiot cousins. They have no weapons, hand axes. Must have been bred and raised to be naked guard creatures, nothing else." He looked directly at Miller. "What screwed up human could do such things? Slaughter, drain the blood out of young kids? Have mutant chimps rape them?"

The Commissioner hesitated before he replied. "The assholes we just caught are some of them. I am getting my forensics team to go over this place with a fine tooth comb. It'll be good experience for them. They have already recovered some laptops and records. We will find out who else is involved, trust me. Though the attack on your wife came from here, I'll bet on it."

He glanced at the other still unopened trailer. "I think I'll scope that with a endoscope we can shove through a wall. Let's see what's in it before we disturb it. I've had my fill of surprises for one day."

Torbin grunted. "I think I saw Scarman, the one who Abigail dealt with before. Brynhildr stuck an arrow through his legs, drug him back over there. I think I'll go over and check on him..."

"Just make sure all you do is 'check' on him. I need him in one piece."

"I promise. I think karma just hit him with a ton of bricks when he tried to shoot Rolf."

"Well, stop her from messing him up also. I need to interrogate all of them."

"Your wish is my command, Sir."

As Torbin started to walk off, Miller called after him. "Just what where you going to do, here, by yourself? Kind of outnumbered, don't you think?"

Torbin stopped shrugged. "I'm a Marine. We don't look at odds. We just do what we have to."

He turned and left, and the Commissioner chuckled. "Crazy ass Marines."

As Torbin walked back to the stable where the Emily was at, the now rally point for everyone, he heard an uproar in Norwegian. He picked up the pace.

Just inside the closest set of doors they had passed through before continuing to the next stable, and the guard/tacking shack, he saw all the Sons of the North talking loudly in Norwegian. They were gesturing at the twelve prisoners which sat in a line in the stable, handcuffed.

Sgt. Wall, the NCO in charge of the fast rope team that had taken the office, saw Torbin and motioned toward him. Torbin walked over to him.

"Major, these Vikings are angry as hell over the treatment of youngsters. I think they want blood." Sure enough, just after he said that, there was a group yell and the Northmen walked toward the prisoners, swords in hand. Torbin started to step in front of them when Brynhildr beat him to it. Yelling, hitting them on their chests, despite the armor, she soon had them stopped. The Daughter of the North lectured them, often slapping her own profound chest.

The typical male in Torbin mentally remarked about her physique before he stepped toward the warriors. Now, her point made, Brynhildr spun around and went straight to Scarman. She grabbed his hair, yanked an ax from her belt.

"Brynhildr, wait!" Torbin called out.

"No worry, Major. I will not kill him... yet."

Then she had her face in the scavenger's face. "By all rights, I should scalp you like people did during the Indian wars in the Dakotas. But I won't. The good Major and the Commissioner need you well enough to answer questions. The arrow thru your legs hurt, didn't it?" She pushed the ax head into his wounded legs, resulting in a cry of pain.

"One of my sisters already marked you, and gave you your new name. I should give you a matching scar on the other side." She tapped his other cheek with her ax blade. "But I won't. Maybe later. After the government is through with you. Mark my words, the things you did to those children will be paid back tenfold."

Now, she lightly patted his cheek with her open hand. "Remember that while you are in your cell. No matter what happens, ten times will be your punishment from me and mine. See you later." Brynhildr gave him a feral smile, then stood up and walked back to her brothers in arms. They were soon slapping her back, her arms, and she slapped them back. Viking affection. It reminded Torbin of the fictional Klingons in Star Trek.

He nodded to Sgt. Wall, who nodded back, and went back to helping a couple of agents watch the dozen prisoners. Five of the "Fighting Pit Crew" as they were now being called, were dead. One by Brynhildr's arrow, one by the shrapnel grenades he and Ichiro had thrown into the entry guard building, three by gunshots. One of the gunshot deaths had been the result of the fast rope attack, where one of the "Pit Crew" was slow to give up. Three of the surviving prisoners had bullet wounds and Scarman had the arrow shaft through his legs. Two others including Baker, the Lieutenant's brother, had cuts and bruises from a beating administered by Brynhildr. The rest had minor shrapnel and flash bang injuries from the entries in the various buildings. One agent was dead, killed by a dog-monster. Two had mangled legs, waiting for MEDEVAC. Two others had bullet wounds, while several others had bruises, cuts and scratches. None of the military fast rope team had been injured.

Torbin made his way to Emily, who had five young girls, the oldest about seventeen, sitting around her on some stools and a bench someone had found. The two agents with leg wounds were laying nearby, beginning to nod off from the morphine Emily had administered. Sitting a few feet away was the female agent, last name Fromm. She was staring off into space, white as a ghost. Emily saw Torbin approach and glance at the female Agent.

"I gave her some morphine too. She's having trouble processing what she saw." Emily shivered as she said that.

Torbin put a hand on her arm. "Are you okay?"

She flashed him a brave smile. "Yes. Though I had to use the pistol you gave me on that super weasel over there." She motioned with her chin, and Torbin for the first time saw the dead creature about ten yards away in the stable dirt and straw.

"First time I had to shoot an animal since I became a vet. Usually I just put them to sleep."

Torbin nodded, then added "Hopefully, it will be the last."

Right then, large Johann, with the aid of Brynhildr, came carrying cups of hot steaming something.

"Someone ordered hot chocolate, yes?" his voice boomed. Then the five young girls had something to take their mind off of the hell that had been. The former business office had a stash of goodies apparently, as cookies were produced, plus donuts and rolls. The five youngsters went after the bounty as if they were starved. Which they were.

Torbin felt his rising anger in him, which he tried to control. He knew what these five young ladies had been through. Two others of their number, as well as the only boy found, were hanging, bled in preparation to butchering in the truck trailer. For the first time in a long time, a red mist began to form in front of his eyes. Before he realized it, Brynhildr was kneeling in front of him.

"No, Major. That way leads to madness." She had seen a look that she had seen before, something that could turn into berserker rage, and then some. She laid her hand on Torbin's arm.

"You have a wife and soon two young ones, we all know. Concentrate on them."

Torbin slowed his breathing. The rage passed. He smiled at Brynhildr. "You remind me of someone I know."

"Abigail Young. Yes, she is one of us, an adopted daughter of Grandmother Knudsen. And your good friend." Brynhildr stood up. "Now, excuse me, but I must keep Rolf and his friends out of mischief."

As she walked away, Torbin turned toward Emily. "You know

Doctor, some rise to the occasion, like you and Brynhildr. In fact, a lot more recently than I ever imagined. Makes me feel good to be a human.”

Emily smiled. “I know, Major.”

“It's Torbin. We just faced old man death together. I think we are on first name basis now.”

“Uncle” Johann began to talk to the female children. “Not too fast or too much, little ones. Chew slowly, eat slowly, so as not to hurt your stomach, and get sick. Like this.” He then proceeded to stick a donut in his bearded mouth and make slow, exaggerated chewing motions with his mouth. The girls began to laugh and giggle. Then, one of the two he had rescued, named Jewel, dropped her cup and food, began to bawl. In a flash, Johann had her is his arms. “Here, little one, it is okay. You are safe now.”

“They are all dead. My mommy, my daddy, all dead. I have no home!” She wailed with the pain of knowing her old life was gone, forever. Big Johann gently stroked her hair, murmured encouragement in her ear.

“There, there. Uncle Johann is here. You can come live with me, my wife. I have children too. I would love to have more.”

Emily felt obliged to interject a little reality. “Uh, Johann, child protective services... ”

“She stays with me.” His voice was suddenly cold as ice. “All who try to take the little ones without family will suffer such pain as they never imagined. We Norsemen take care of children. Those who harm them are scum.”

Torbin knew what he said was true. The current Government may try to exert some authority, but they would be riding a whirlwind. Torbin began to see that the Sons of the North may be loyal to God and country, but it had its limits.

“I think we just met Father Christmas incarnate. That's who you remind me of, Johann.”

Johann's demeanor softened. “Yes, Major. My wife, Freda, tells me so. I have played Father Christmas at school plays when my children were quite young. I guess at heart that is who I am. How about you Jewel? Want to live with Father Christmas?” The young girl wrapped her arms tighter around Johann. Then, she fell asleep.

“Uffda, I will have to figure out a way to carry my shield and sword, and not wake Jewel.”

“I will carry it again, Johann-san.” It was Ichiro. He had found an old army blanket and made himself a poncho to replace the dark Ninja top he had given one of the captive girls. It was below freezing, so decent clothing was definitely needed.

Johann looked at him. “Thank you, little brother. Your help is appreciated.”

Torbin took this as an opening to ask a question that had been nagging at him a bit. “Ichiro, just how did you and your large Nordic friends get here and find this place?”

Ichiro, smiling slyly, answered. “Your wife is not the only highly efficient intelligence agent, or spy if you wish to use that term. I have several in my employ. One of them, Sumie Sato, quickly ascertained this location. Knowing you, I readied myself and started my journey here.

“But not before I had called friend Rolf from the rickshaw race. I knew I would need… backup as you say.”

“None of your own troops, Ichiro?”

“This is personal, my brother. I cannot use my position, and the soldiers under my command, to deal with a personal issue, putting them at risk. So I called on Rolf, knowing he would obtain some qualified civilian help.”

At this he shook his head. “I thought they would bring firearms. Instead, they come as sword carrying warriors, as myself. But, it worked out in the end. Their shields, size, swords worked quite efficiently.

“Pardon, Torbin. I must now help Johann take his charge to a vehicle they have hidden.”

Torbin turned and saw the other four young girls queuing up to follow Johann. Government protocol be damned, they knew who they wanted to be with. Johann saw the look of consternation on Torbin’s face.

“My full name is Johann Munsen. I am in the phone book. Or, go to the Sons of the North Hall, and they will find me. The children will be safe with me and my family. We have a good female doctor in our community, who will check the little ones over. Then you and the Commissioner can question them all you want.”

Jewel stirred in Johann’s grasp. He kissed her forehead. “My wife,

Freda, always wanted a girl. We have three boys, two of draft age. Now, she will have a house full of little girls. She will be very happy. And thus, I will be happy."

Emily stood up and approached Johann. She had to go up on her toes to kiss his cheek. "Johann, you are a saint. When all these girls are well enough, bring them to my vet's office. I have lots of dogs to play with."

He grinned. "I will do that, my lady. Now we must go, get these ones in baths, then beds." He turned to go, Ichiro following him. The other Sons of the North, including Rolf, were picking up the remaining girls, lifting them up on their shoulders to give them all pony rides. That way, they could still carry their swords and shields. Brynhildr brought up the rear.

Commissioner Miller appeared, started to say something. Then he stopped. "I can talk to them later," he said, thinking out loud. "We have enough evidence to hang all these Krakens."

"Krakens?" Torbin asked.

"Yes. Over Half the prisoners have those god awful Giant Kraken tattoos on their chests. Church of Kraken through and through. Now I get to find out how long these assholes have been operating in my backyard."

He turned to Torbin. "I will have to send a forensic doctor I have on staff to try to get some rape kits tonight, if possible. If not, so be it."

As he watched Brynhildr bringing up the rear of the procession, he said "Excuse me," to Torbin and quickly went to catch up.

"Excuse me young lady, Brynhildr is your name?"

"Yes Sir. Brynhildr Jorgensen."

"Do you have a draft notice yet?

"No, although I am twenty one years old. I expect to be called up for service any day now."

"Do you want to be in the military?"

With that, she stopped. "Why so many questions?" Brynhildr asked bluntly.

"Well, Ms. Jorgensen, I am about to offer you a job that counts as government service. One that will give you a little more…autonomy than starting out as a boot soldier."

"It is Miss, Commissioner. We so called Norskies have no trouble with young women being maids, unmarried women. We do not need a special title to express our individuality."

Paul Miller chuckled. "Well, you definitely are not afraid to speak your mind. But I need an answer to my question."

The tall and buxom blonde thought for a moment. "I do not suffer fools easily, no matter what their rank. I train with Rolf and the others because I know they are not fools. And they will listen to me as a warrior, not just a woman. So, yes, I do like some autonomy as you call it."

"You do know how to follow orders though, right?"

Brynhildr laughed. "Let us cut through the bullshit, Commissioner. Could I listen to you? Yes. See, I was watching you also. So I know you are no fool. Thus yes, tell me to do something, I will do it. But if for some reason I think you are being a fool, I'll tell you." She smiled. "And I hope, like Rolf and the others, that you will listen to reason."

Miller laughed. "It is nice to have someone around who is the antithesis of a Yes Man." He reached into a pocket and removed a business card. "Give me a call at this number in a couple of days. I will be tied up on this crime scene for a while. But, I think with a little of my training, I definitely could use you in law enforcement. It might be in something… special. By the way, what subjects do you like in school?"

"I do well in Biology, Chemistry—all of the sciences. Why?"

"Just trying to get a feel for your expertise in other things other than shooting arrows, throwing things, and beating the crap out of people."

Brynhildr laughed. "I assure you, I'm good at other activities. I'll call you in a couple of days, to see if you have changed your mind."

"I don't think so, Miss Jorgensen. I know what I want and need." He stuck his hand out. She took it in a very firm grip, shook it.

"Pardon me Sir, but I must catch up to my fellows. I will call you." With that, Brynhildr turned and walked quickly to catch up with the other "Norskies".

Miller watched her leave. "Yes, I think this may be a very fruitful relationship," he said to himself. He then turned back to the task at hand, a huge crime scene.

The Commissioner walked over to where Emily and Torbin were sitting, conversing as they kept an eye on the two wounded agents.

Emily seemed to be showing something to Torbin.

"So, what do we have here, Doctor?"

The vet looked up at him. "Good, I was about ready to come looking for you."

"This," she began as she held up an object about the size and shape of a D cell battery. "Is what seems to be used to control all of these genetic monstrosities. I took this one from the brain of that crazy weasel creature I shot. Luckily, I missed this little gem. A bit of twisting and prying and viola, here it is." Emily pointed to the end that had been inserted into the super weasel.

"See how there looks to be multiple tiny contact points, as if you were plugging in a cell phone to a charger? Inside the creature are some miniature circuits and wires that infest the motor and decision portions of the brain. Not a lot, just enough so this, when activated, provides stimulus to the amygdala, prefrontal cortex and related areas. I'll have to do a complete autopsies on examples of all these beasts to figure out the exact wiring, stimulus points. But I think it is safe to say that the areas of aggression and movement are connected. They probably received a little bit of conditioning so they knew to attack strange humans and specified targets, not the other beasts and creatures."

The Commissioner shook his head. "Well, I guess I will have to find some refrigeration units to preserve all these monsters for further examination. Torbin, does the military have access also to some people that can help with the autopsies? I can't see the good doctor doing it all herself. And my forensic people are definitely not experts in animal physiology."

"If you call General Reed directly, and explain what you have, I think he'll help you find some of the right people somewhere in the U. S.A. All of these… things are potential weapons on a large scale. The thought of even one other location like this place scares the hell out of me."

"Commissioner," Emily asked. "What is in the other trailer?"

He sighed. "It looks like some type of mobile lab. We put a spy camera through the wall to make sure there was nothing alive, moving in there. We didn't find anything, so we popped it open. They are going over it with a fine tooth comb. The first thing we found appears to be a Tschaaa organic growth vat, like the ones in which they grow their grays. It might also be similar to the ones Colonel Bardun saw on Platform One."

Emily involuntarily shivered. Everyone had been told the story of what the Tschaaa and some sick humans were trying to grow in space. "Did you find...?"

"No, Doctor, no fetuses or babies growing in there. But it looked like some type of canine body was in a very early state. I hope you and some geneticists can help us figure out things like this."

"Now, if you will excuse me, I need to do some more coordination. I'll give the General a call, see if I can keep the response team here for a while to help with security."

"Did you find the fighting pits?" Torbin asked.

Miller grunted. "Yes. Those...assholes—pardon my French, Doctor—have a good sized arena built directly under the former stable business office. It is all wired for sound and video, with a few "box seats" for special VIPs to watch the festivities live."

He paused for a minute, seemed hesitant to continue. Torbin had seen the look he had on his face before.

"Something worse than what we have seen so far?"

Miller directed his gaze to Emily.

"Go ahead, Commissioner. I've been around the block a few times. Just because I'm female doesn't mean I can't handle bad news."

"Well," Miller began. "A quick cursory examination of some of the tapes and DVD show that in addition to dog fights, creature fights, they also used...people. Especially young girls. Some were used in catfights, others were pitted against animals, the monsters." He looked away and spit.

"I'm going to have to eventually bring in some cadaver dogs in to search this whole compound, as I think there are some human bodies, or at least bones, buried here. I think some missing persons cases will be cleared up. No matter if we only recover one set of remains, based on what we know now, all twelve of the prisoners are facing a firing squad."

Shooting was now the official method for the death penalty. Quick, easy, no gallows to be constructed, no gas chambers, electric chairs, or lethal chemicals needed.

"So you'll have to interview the five little girls about what they...

saw," Emily said.

"Yep. As much as I do not want to make them live through it, I'll have to."

Paul Miller paused. "Sometimes, being in charge really sucks." He excused himself and went to make more arrangements.

Torbin addressed Emily. "So, when are you going to tell me how you came to be here?"

The vet smiled. "The same as you, Torbin Bender, warrior extraordinaire. I was snooping around, trying to collect some info as I thought the powers that be were moving too slowly. I was wrong. Ran smack dab into the Commissioner. I told him he would have to waste a couple of his men to sit on me, or he could let me go in with him. After all, a trained veterinarian would be a help with any fighting dogs they found. But instead we found a bunch of creatures that only a mother could love."

Torbin laughed. "And I thought I was nuts for wanting some payback. You risked your life to help some fighting dogs."

Emily shrugged. "That is what I do. I help animals—especially dogs, cats, and horses. Someone has to do the heavy lifting."

She motioned toward the prisoners. "My friend Baker is over there. I knew he was up to no good for a while. But I never thought he would be involved with young girls…"

"Well, Abigail knew him from the little incident she had in your office. Plus, the brawl we had with his buddies at Oktoberfest, from which he ran. But the worst of it was his brother is Lieutenant Baker, who saved my ass in Wyoming." Torbin explained to Emily how he had come to this place, about the older Baker's involvement with the attempt on Aleks' life with the Eater, and about how much he knew what was going on inside the compound. "He knew about all the beasts, so he must have known about the youngsters. I think we have a community of really sick puppies here."

At that time the ambulances arrived for the wounded and injured, including the Krakens. The medics and EMTs went straight to the injured agents, eliciting cries of complaints from the Krakens and their partners in crime. In one quick motion, Emily walked toward the prisoners. Torbin saw her move and started following, wondering what she was thinking.

Emily had the cattle prod she had brought with her in her right hand as she approached Baker. "Hey, Baker. Got yourself in over your head, didn't you," the vet stated.

The skinny man, looking much the worse for wear, glared at her. "Go fuck yourself, bitch. Always thinking you're better than everyone else. But you're just a stuck up…" The rest of the insult was quickly cut off by volts of electricity coursing through his crotch area. Emily had jammed her cattle prod onto his inner thigh and hit the on button. Baker started to shake and twitch as some eight thousand volts coursed thru his lower body.

"Emily. Stop that!" Torbin's loud admonition made her jerk it back. The Marine grabbed the doctor and walked her back into the stable, away from the prisoners. The twelve miscreants suddenly became very quiet. The realization that they were at complete mercy of someone else, a mercy that could be removed, made them shut up. Now they were someone's little bitch, rather than the other way around.

Emily began to shake in Torbin's grasp. Then, she was hugging him, holding tight. "What they did to those little girls…and to not even feel guilty. I am so goddamned *mad*." She began to cry. Torbin held her in the hug, gently rubbing her back. He knew she needed the release of a good cry. So, he did what any good man did when a woman began to sob. He became a silent source of strength, letting her know he was not going anywhere, that it was okay to cry.

After a few minutes she stopped, still hanging on. Then, she untangled herself from him. She wiped her eyes with her hands until Torbin magically produced a handkerchief form some hidden pocket. She used it to finish wiping her face, blowing her nose. She smiled sheepishly at him. "So much for the tough old veterinarian, used to seeing death in all of its forms. Sometimes even dealing it to put some poor animal down. I'm mad about what they did to the animals here. But what they did to young girls, using animals in sick perverse ways….I want to castrate them all with a dull scalpel and no anesthesia."

"I'd hold them down for you, Emily, if I could. But, well, we have to let the law take its course. I almost screwed this up for the Commissioner. If I had come a day earlier, they may have been tipped off, and started destroying evidence. And witnesses."

"You mean there is a limit to what a Marine can do?"

He sighed heavily. "Yes. I would have been dead meat after ten minutes and those monster-dogs got wind of me. One man, even a Marine—God forbid anyone of the old corps hear me say this—would be dog food."

Emily kissed him on the cheek. "Yeah, I almost did the same thing. Blinded by the thirst for revenge. I guess someone upstairs had the angels working overtime saving us."

She started to give the handkerchief back to Torbin. "Keep it. I have lots of spares. I have a very pregnant wife at home with trolls in her stomach. She has mood swings that are like the onslaught of hurricane season."

Emily looked at Torbin, her face a serious mask. "You really love her, don't you?"

"She's my life. Her and the two boys in her belly. That's why I came here. To make sure no one tried that shit with the Eaters ever again."

Emily found herself once again a bit jealous of Aleks. Why couldn't there be more eligible men like Torbin around? The universe was inherently unfair.

Commissioner Miller returned at that moment. "Major, time for you to he. The General contacted me, said he wanted to see you, Ichiro, and Rolf Knudsen in uniform at 0900. Something about military members going off on half-baked operations without a certain General knowing about it."

Torbin shrugged his shoulders. "Well, I guess he could throw me in the brig. Might be a vacation for me, no wife to threaten to kick my ass."

Miller laughed. "Be glad you have a wife, Major, and soon kids. It starts to get lonely at the top, without companionship."

Emily then put her two cents in. "That goes for us older women also, Commissioner. I love dogs, being a vet is what I always wanted to do, but never having started a family…."

Miller looked at her. A very attractive forty-something, if he didn't miss his guess. "So, if I may be so bold, Doctor, you had no husband or kids…"

"No, Sir. Too damned busy with my career, my business. My parents and younger sister survived, after the Squids came. I'm one of the lucky ones—my immediate family survived."

Miller grunted. "Yes, most of us have few family left. I had an ex-wife, a boy and a girl in El Paso. I have no idea if they made it or not."

"Well, in your position now, can't you get someone to help look for them?"

"Now that wouldn't be very fair to everyone else missing family, Doctor, would it?" With that remark, Miller expressed just how dedicated he was to doing things the right, the fair way. It meant that he would not abuse his immense law enforcement power. It was hard enough keeping the military in line, without civilian officials going off on a tangent.

"I guess not, Commissioner."

"And with that," Torbin interjected. "I bid you adieu. Don't mind if I take the M-1 with me, do you?"

"Keep it, Major. You earned it. Besides, if you see something that got away from here, do me a favor and take care of it. We need new species of predators like we need holes in our heads."

"Will do, Sir. Emily, stop by my home first chance you get. My wife will want to thank you for saving the family jewels" That prompted a laugh from Emily.

"Doctor, I'll have some of my agents get you home, just as soon as we can."

"No hurry. And call me Emily, please. I think we are to first name basis after tonight."

Miller smiled. "Okay, call me Paul then, please." He turned and stuck his hand out to Torbin.

"Thank you, Major, for helping me stay in one piece. It's been real."

The two men shook hands. "Stop by sometime, Commissioner. My wife will want to pick your brains about tonight."

"I will definitely do that. Be careful getting to your vehicle."

"Yes, Sir." Torbin turned and began to retrace his steps to his original entry point at the hole in the fence. Emily watched him leave.

"Definitely a hero for the times, don't you agree… Paul?"

"In spades, Emily. Now, if I can pick your brains about animal physiology one last time before I get you home…"

Torbin made good time to his hidden vehicle, then back to the Base. He knew he would catch some hell from Aleks because once again, he had put himself in danger. Since she had become pregnant, she had worried about being a widow, and having to raise two sons by herself. Torbin knew some of that was the hormonal effect of being pregnant, as she was a trained spy and soldier, and knew the chances of death in this war. They had discussed it when they had first committed to each other. Carrying two children in your body changed your attitudes about almost everything.

But there were times when a man just had to do what he had to do, something women had a hard time understanding.

He parked his SUV and grabbed the M-1 from the back. Locking the vehicle, he headed to the door. It was near the witching hour, but of course the house lights were still on. He heard Fuzz's warning "woof", which told him that Abigail was keeping Aleks company. He reached for the doorknob, but it opened from inside before he could unlock it. Aleks stood in the doorway, with the "What in the hell do *you* think you are doing?" look he had come to know so well.

"Aleks…" he started to say, but never got past her name.

"Well. I see you have a new man toy. And is that blood on your shirt? And of course you expect me to wash it out." Then she broke into a litany of Russian and Ukrainian that Torbin knew by experience was cursing and chewing out his ass, while at the same time questioning his family heritage.

In a flash it hit him what he had seen, done tonight. Stuff that normal people never had to experience or see. Nor should they. With that, he exploded. "No, goddamnit, *not* tonight! I just had to do things, see things no one should have to see or do. I did it for you and our kids—so no one would ever try and screw with them again!" Abigail stood behind Aleks with Fuzz, a look of concern on her face. Torbin was good about holding his personal emotions in check, so this explosion was out of character.

Aleks' eyes widened and she began to stutter, stammer.

"No. No more, Aleks. I am now going to grab the bottle of scotch and go out back for a series of well-deserved drinks. I will come back in when I am good and ready. Abigail. Nice to see you, thanks for keeping Aleks company." With that he brushed by the two women, went to the kitchen, grabbed the bottle of scotch and headed out the back sliding door. The same door Fuzz had trashed saving Aleks. Torbin was so incensed, he did not even notice that Fuzz slid outside with him.

Aleks stood, frozen. Then she began to shake, then sob. "What have I done, little sister? I have never seen him so angry. So... hurt. What have I done? He will hate me..."

Abigail hugged her. "It will be okay, Aleks. He loves you more than you can imagine. I'll go out and talk to him. Just let him cool down a bit. Something... very bad happened tonight. I will find out what it is. Okay?"

Aleks stopped crying long enough to nod, croak out "Yes, thank you." She then sat down on the sofa, tried to gain control of her emotions.

Torbin stood out in the fenced in backyard, taking a big swig of scotch when he heard a "woof" and felt a dog muzzle pushing his non bottle holding left hand. He looked down at Fuzz. "Well, are you going to chew my ass, literally now, for pissing off the pregnant lady? I know you are very protective of her. By the way..."

Torbin knelt down in front of the war dog.

"Mr. Fuzz, I have not really officially thanked you for saving the love of my life and my unborn children. Yeah, I bought you a couple of steaks, but we have not had a man to man talk... or at least male to male talk." He gently began to scratch Fuzz's ears, kissed him on his nose.

"Without you, my wife would be dead. My two unborn sons would be dead. Thus, I would be dead, at least inside." Tears began to run down his face. Fuzz licked them away, and Torbin buried his face into the big dog's fur, gently sobbing.

Abigail had quietly slipped outside, was standing in the shadows. To see Torbin, a best friend, like an older brother, in this much emotional pain cut her inside like a knife. But she knew that to barge in now would just embarrass him. So, she stood back, watching her dog do what dogs do best... provide unconditional love to humans who were hurting.

Torbin finally stopped crying, wiping his eyes as Fuzz kept nuzzling him. "I thought you didn't like, trust men. I guess I'm an exception. I'll take that as a compliment." He sat cross legged on the ground in front of Fuzz, ignoring the snow and the cold.

"I wish you could have been with me tonight, Fuzz. We could have used you. Some young girls we rescued could have used you also.

Nothing like a big, furry, warm dog to make a person feel safe, loved. As it was, I had to kill some…things that were probably were once your cousins. But some asshole humans fucked them up, made them monsters. Therefore, we had to shoot them. I am very sorry. I've come to understand that dogs are better than most people I know at being 'human'—moral, nice, loving. So, accept my thanks for everything you have done for us nasty monkeys and my apologies for anything I may have done to you and your kind."

Fuzz, war dog, barked and extended the paw of friendship. Torbin sat his bottle down, and shook it. Fuzz gave him a large doggy grin, with the huffing laughter unique to dogs but often not noticed. Just then, Torbin noticed Abigail in the shadows.

"Hello. Have you been their long?"

"No, not long."

Torbin slowly rose. "Just having some male talk with your best bud here. I can see why you like him so much."

Abigail walked up to Torbin, and embraced him. "You are a 'best bud' to me, Torbin Bender. A big brother. You've always been there for me." She gently stepped back from the embrace. "Always know that I'm always there for you, and your family."

"Aw, hell, I know that."

"Well, know that Aleks loves and needs you more than anybody. Which is why she gets so upset sometimes. She is so very scared she will lose you to something stupid. Especially since she cannot go and soldier along with you right now. So, she's very frustrated."

Torbin let out a big sigh. "I'm just getting used to this… everlasting love thing. I've never felt it before either, never thought I would start a family. So, I know I screw things up all the time. But I do so love that crazy Russian-Ukrainian inside there. So, everything that looks like a threat I take very personally, and want to take it head on. Which is what I did tonight."

"It was bad…."

"Abigail, it was the worst. The story will no doubt hit the news, as Krakens were also involved. But, well, some young girls were used, abused…" Torbin began to shake.

Abigail hugged him again. "You did good, big brother. Like you always do. Just go inside and let Aleks know how much you love her, tell her what happened. She will understand."

She stepped back from Torbin, his shaking stopped. He pushed the scotch bottle at her.

"Here, hate to drink alone."

"Torbin, you know I have no experience with drinking strong spirits."

"Here, just a sip. Puts hair on your chest."

At that, Abigail giggled, a sound that always made Torbin feel nice, that all was right with the world.

"I don't think I need hair on my chest, Torbin Bender. But I will take a drink for you. Okay?"

With that she took the scotch bottle, taking a drink. And she began to sputter. "Oh! How do you get used to this? Or enjoy this? It tastes… bitter, hard."

"It just takes years of practice. We Marines have become quite good at it." He retrieved the bottle and took another pull from it. "Well, time to face the music. Once again, thanks for being you, Abigail. You really help Aleks. You and Fuzz here, the hairy human."

Abigail smiled. "It's my pleasure. You are family to me." With that she kissed Torbin's cheek.

Torbin opened the sliding glass door, went in. Aleks was sitting at the dining table, a look of pain on her face. As Torbin entered, she started to stand. "Hey, pregnant lady. Just relax. Rest. Everything is okay." He kissed his wife where she sat, and she clung to him.

"Torbin, my husband, I do so love you. That is why I get so… upset when you're in danger. Please, do not be angry with me. I cannot stand your disapproval…" She began to sob, cry.

Torbin knelt next to her, holding her tight. "Aleks, I love you more than life itself. Anger is temporary. My love for you is forever. Remember that."

Abigail and Fuzz quietly snuck out as Torbin and Aleks loved each other. Love like they had was rare in the crazy world. Best not to distract them.

As Abigail walked out and shut the front door, an unfamiliar Jeep pulled up in front. Fuzz immediately began to growl his nose working. Then, he stopped, his tail wagged once. It was someone he knew.

Ichiro exited the vehicle, saw Abigail and smiled. She immediately walked up to him, smiling.

"Hello. Ichiro. And thank you for helping get Torbin back in one piece." With that she walked up and hugged him. He smiled, hugged back. Abigail looked into his eyes.

They had started to train together just this week, Ichiro teaching her the finer parts of the use of the katana, as well as traditional Japanese bowmanship. She had taken to it like a fish to water. After the first lesson, Ichiro had introduced naked bladed swords.

"You must have been a Samurai in a previous life, Abigail. You act as if you have done the techniques before, many times." Ichiro had soon found out her speed and skill was second only to his. And he thought that may be temporary.

Everything clicked, with the hour soon turning to two or more, Fuzz had sat patiently, watched. He seemed to sense his human mistress really enjoyed this. If she was happy, he was happy.

Now, this night, they looked into each other's eyes, and something really clicked. They began to kiss, deeply. After a few moments, Abigail gently pushed away.

"Ichiro, this is new to me. I ask you for your patience. Aleks would say I am a bit stunted when it comes to relations with…men." Then she looked deep into his eyes. "I must be certain of what I am feeling. I am a babe in the woods with this. Fighting, violence I know. Love…" She stopped, suddenly realized the word she had just used. She blushed, completely unsure of herself.

"Abigail, know this. You tell me what you want. There is no reason to be embarrassed. You are who you are. Which to me, is someone very special, desirable, lovable…" Now he stopped. Lust he understood. Now, he felt this unfamiliar warm feeling in his stomach, his heart. Two confident warriors in all senses of the word, now stymied and unsure because they were entering the field of true love.

For a few moments there was silence, neither person spoke. Then Ichiro began anew. "Abigail Young, you may have as much time as you want to consider what your heart says. I will do likewise. But please do not feel a need to distance yourself. I still want you to train with me."

Abigail paused, then answered. "I'll still train. I enjoy it too much to quit. I…enjoy your company. I just ask we go slowly with anything more personal…or serious." She smiled at Ichiro, wanting to do more, but terrified that she was not thinking, would be hurt, and would hurt Ichiro. These unfamiliar feelings were too confusing right now.

Ichiro took her hand and kissed it. "I must go now, Abby. General Reed wants me in his office in the morning, probably for what you Americans call an ass chewing. No matter. I did what I had to."

"Thank you again, Ichi. Blame me if you must. Tell the General that I asked you officially as the formal representative of Deseret."

"No. Abby, it was my decision, made because Torbin is my blood brother. A Samurai does not make excuses for doing the right thing, no matter if it is against orders. I will weather the storm. It will be alright. The General is a fair man." He kissed her hand one more time, smiling. "I will call you tomorrow."

"I'll be waiting for it, Ichi." With that, Ichiro went to his vehicle and left. Abigail released the breath she had been holding.

She turned around and almost stepped on Fuzz. He had been sitting quietly, patiently, invisible to the two humans. He gave an open mouth canine grin. Abigail smiled, scratched his ears. "Eavesdropping, are we? But tonight, my beautiful beastie, you may think what you want. I think you like Torbin and Ichiro, and are learning to trust males. Good. Because they are not going anywhere." She patted him. "Come, bedtime and nice dreams. All's right with the world. The men in my life are safe, including you." She and her friend went to her home, for a blissful sleep.

CHAPTER 13

BISMARCK, NORTH DAKOTA

Madam President Sandra Paul opened the large bay windows of the now Office of the President, U.S.A. It was well below freezing outside, normal for North Dakota this time of year. But she craved—no, needed—the fresh, cold and crisp air in her face right this moment. She needed to feel the wintery air to help wash away the effects of the images of horror she had just viewed in her email. She stood there, feeling the icy cold on her face. There were times like these that she felt very, very, old.

"Madam President, you risk frostbite. Please close the windows." It was George Williams, her Special Assistant and man of many hats— Chief of Staff, chief cook and bottle washer. And most importantly, her dear friend.

She took a deep breath of cold air, then started to close the windows. As she did, she heard the former State House clock tower begin to chime twelve noon. She turned and saw George standing respectfully in front of her large desk, the Presidential seal affixed to its front.

Bismarck, the capital of North Dakota, had been lightly damaged during the rock strikes/Invasion. A nearby U.S. Air Force radar targeting site used by bomber crews on practice bomb uns had been attacked, and a single Delta had fired a couple of cannon shells in the tallest business building in the downtown. That was it. No harvester arks, no flying squads, no robocops snooping around. Just the even more horrible than normal Long Winter. The birth of the oil industry in North Dakota years prior had provided the populace of both North Dakota and the surrounding states a sustainable source of fuel and power to survive the extreme conditions. The fact that people were used to extreme cold and snow kept a large portion of the population alive. The tradition of tough farmers, a lot of them of Norse heritage, rounded out the survival characteristics of the now Unoccupied States of America citizens. They also provided help to almost all who fled from coastal states and overrun military installations during the retreat.

When it came time to pick a New Capital, the location of Bismarck on major highways and rail lines, its distance from both coasts and the Gulf, along with its undamaged legislative buildings made it the ideal choice. It also had an operational and decent-sized airport, now the home of a small air force and transport service. Over the last couple of months, both former military and civilian assets were being repaired and moved into the Bismarck area. In addition, ground to air anti-aircraft weapons and a small unit of Free Japan F-15 Silent Eagle interceptors were now in place. The Japanese kept their small number at F-35s at home. The President could not blame them. The Japanese had been working overtime to help rebuild the USA air assets, which until now had been primarily helicopters and a contingent of former private aircraft. Some former USAF Aircraft were coming online (a few Interceptors and some A-10s found stashed in various locations, along with some transports) to supplement the craft the Japanese had salvaged from American Naval assets in and around the Japanese islands. The small contingent of Canadians had brought down a serviceable F-18 along with some ceremonial but still operational twenty-five pounder artillery pieces. They also stated they knew where some more F-18 assets were stored, as well as some weapons and ammo, including some Canadian Leopard tanks. They would just need help recovering them.

Other than a couple of I-Hawk missile batteries provided by the Japanese, as well some salvaged ex-Naval Phalanx anti-aircraft gun systems, it had been the Russians who had been a godsend for providing heavy anti-aircraft missiles and gun systems. The U.S.A. forces had salvaged a small number of man portable Stinger missiles, a couple of ancient Redeyes, and an old Chaparral tracked system from some National Guard storage area. Then the Russians had shown up.

Over a thousand SA-7s shoulder launched systems from all the various types, a few Sa-8s and SA-4s, then a bunch of anti-aircraft cannon had appeared in Alaska. Slow fishing vessels, coastal freighters, some Russian Cushion air assault craft had provided a lifeline, transporting people and equipment across the Bering Straits to Alaska. SU-23 twin mount anti-aircraft cannon, a couple of Quad Mount ZSU-23 tracked systems, some hundred 14.5 anti-aircraft guns removed from stored obsolete tanks had been sent over, with a quantity of ammunition. Madam President had reports on her desk of other treasures in the pipeline. The fact the Russians never seemed to throw anything away was enabling her to throw up a ring of protection around the major surviving cities and bases.

Add twenty-five hundred crazy Russians, many of whom were Spetsnaz, with AKs and RPGs, and a hard fighting force was taking shape. An additional small force of trainers were also en route. Some one thousand Japanese had also shown up, many barely out of basic training. The Americans had been told additional training was on them, which was why Torbin, Ichiro and Abigail were so vital.

Now, however, there was a threat already in her own backyard, one that had been hidden apparently for a while. A threat exacerbated by the fact that humans seemed to be right in the center of it.

George Williams saw the troubled look in her eyes. He had almost forgotten how many years he had known her, well before he had become her Special Assistant, now basically her Chief of Staff. He was very protective of her, almost exceedingly so. Madam President, Sal to a few close friends, had been friends of his wife, son and daughter for years. With only a surviving daughter, Madam President had grown closer to the tight inner circle of friends, becoming a family-like unit. This was the new normal among the survivors.

"Just had to look at those emailed pictures from Commissioner Miller, didn't you? I asked you to let me handle it."

"What kind of President would I be if I only dealt with pleasant things? I can't go through life looking at pictures of pink bunnies, and nothing else."

George sighed. There was not a single day that he did not wish she was not so damned stubborn, so willing to take the full weight of everything on her shoulders. It was beginning to really age her. She had become President of the surviving states by default, there being no one else who could or would step up to the plate. George often told God how screwed up this was. Why just her? "So, now that you scarred your eyeballs for life, what is the next step?"

George then saw the "spine of steel" appear. Once Madam President made a decision, was about to go after someone with a dull fish knife, it was like she became a thing of steel, no longer human. Since Ichiro Yamamoto had appeared with his unique sword skills, George thought of the Samurai's katana as the epitome of what she was. This extremely sharp, strong blade, but with the ability to bend and bounce back. Metal with great strength that was not brittle.

But everything, everybody had its limits. Just not today.

"We hunt them down, the Krakens, their sympathizers, those sick individuals that find what was done to those young children entertaining. We prosecute them if we must, as I have to prove we are a Nation State based on laws. But if we have to kill them outright, so be it."

The Iron Lady of England had nothing over Madam President. She continued.

"We broadcast the images of what these pieces of shit did to innocent children and animals. Those dog monsters may have started as offspring of someone's pet, companion. And the evidence of bestiality, the DVD images uncovered so far..." She began to shake with anger. The leader of the Free Allies gripped the back of her chair so hard George thought she would break it.

"Sal...," he said in a soft, low voice. Slowly she released her chair, then reached into a right hand drawer to remove one of her signature handkerchiefs. The steel blade began to dab her eyes in an attempt to save her makeup.

"George, I am going to have to do something else unpleasant today."

"What is that, Ma'am?"

"Young Alesha Taylor. Our dark skinned answer to the Director's Kathy Monroe. Instead of a nice, calm intro to the wonderful world of broadcasting, she gets to handle this story, warts, sick images and all."

George drew in a short intake of breath. She could have been his daughter. A young person of color, just turned twenty one years of age, the President's man felt very protective of her. She had barely survived fleeing here with her mother some six years ago, the rest of her family all butchered by the Squids. She had just started a teenage modeling career when the rocks fell, had undergone a special hell of seeing family members captured and killed, while she and her mother fled. Somehow, her mother, Glenda, had kept her alive, fed, clothed during the Long Winter. She landed a job near Great Falls, Montana. Then Glenda was struck down last year with MS—Multiple Sclerosis. She had volunteered for some experimental treatments using Tschaaa medical science, nanites, and was just in the first stages. Now, it was the daughter's turn to take care, support the mother.

"Madam President, do you think it is a good idea to show…"

"Hell yes, it is!" She snapped back. "The Director, his wives, his supporters, the Squids and all their minions, everyone in the world with access to a screen is going to *see* what humans are doing in the name of serving the Tschaaa. See how they like the thought of their daughters being raped by mutated apes, forced to fight each other and hell creatures, for the benefit of some sick pleasure. My mother told me years ago that you are judged by the company you keep. Let's see how normal people react when they see the company the Squids keep, what miscreants they consider as friends. Yes, Miss Taylor will have to help me get the message out."

She paused. Then spoke. "She is supposed to be here for a meeting in a few minutes, correct?"

"Yes Ma'am."

"Well, I guess we'll see then what will be her reaction, after seeing these pictures, videos."

George knew that it was useless to argue with her. She had made up her mind. He just hoped it would turn out alright.

A few minutes later, a statuesque dark-skinned female entered the Presidential Office. Alesha Taylor still carried herself with the calm confidence of a professional model, along with the runway figure. Tall, close to 5'10", with the four inch heels she was wearing she was now an even more imposing figure. She smiled and walked directly up to the President, hand extended to shake hers.

"Madam President. Finally I get to meet you in person. It is an honor."

The President felt a firm handshake. As a professional politician, she had learned the importance of a firm handshake in the "world of men" that she had entered. Since the Invasion by the Tschaaa, traditional roles, and worlds of influence had all but disappeared. Only the need of women to give birth and rear children kept a semblance of the traditional roles in place.

"Oh pshaw. Just remember I am the First Citizen, not royalty. I am here to serve. As are you, I hope."

"Of course, Ma'am. I jumped at the chance to do something… constructive. The human race needs a professional model right now like it needs a collective hole in the head. But if I can be part of a way to spread the word of the evil we face, to counteract the propaganda of the blonde bimbo, then I'm your woman."

She saw the President examining her intently. Alesha knew that something else had just entered the process of her becoming the face of the U.S.A. on public media. "Well, as George has no doubt told you, I am often very blunt, and I cut through to the chase. Please step over to my computer desk, and have a seat." Alesha complied, sitting before a blank screen.

"What you are about to see has only been seen by a handful of people, outside of those who conducted the raid. We lost two good agents at the compound you are about to view. One died there. The other…" Madam President paused, "She committed suicide hours after seeing, experiencing what you are about to see. So, after this, there is no stepping back, you will be presenting this on your first broadcast tonight. If you can."

Alesha took a moment to prepare herself. She looked at the President, with a look of steel similar to what George saw in the President's eyes.

"I am ready if you are. Like they used to say, I didn't come here to whistle Dixie."

With that, the President touched the keyboard to the images on the screen, and then stepped back. Fifteen minutes later of viewing the videos and the still pictures, Alesha stood up, and stepped back herself. She was shaking, which the President saw was from rage. A rage that she had seen in hard people, when faced with an unjust, evil situation. The former model turned toward the President of the U.S.A.

"Ma'am, let's go get those pieces of shit. I didn't flee literal hounds, dog packs to have to put up with … this. If you can't use me as a broadcaster, give me gun. I'll replace the agent who killed herself.…"

Madam President took her right hand in both of hers. "We have enough gun carriers right now. What I need is you, a face and a voice for good. Welcome aboard. But I warn you. It will not get easier."

CHAPTER 14

In the early hours of the next day, Adam Lloyd was reviewing the recording of the broadcast from the Unoccupied States in his office. This was the third time he had slowly gone through it, stopping and looking at individual frames. Reviewing the U.S.A.'s version of Kathy Monroe, he knew they had a voice and a face for their message of Resistance.

Alesha Taylor had started her first broadcast simply enough. "Good evening, my fellow humans and citizens. My name is Alesha Taylor. Starting tonight, I will be seen on this broadcast station, as well as on internet feed, presenting news and information. This broadcast feed is originating from facilities near the New Capital, Bismarck, North Dakota. Yes, a lot of the news and information will be provided by U.S.A. government sources. However, I have been given the right to both verify the information I am given as well the right to refuse to broadcast something I feel is false, biased, or untruthful. I will not simply be a mouthpiece for those in power, like a certain pretty blonde that broadcasts from the Occupied States, who everyone has come to know. I will work my hardest to provide factual information that improves your lives, and serves as a reminder of the freedom which we enjoy. This same freedom is not enjoyed in the concentration camps of the Cattle Country, nor in the Tschaaa-controlled areas of this world which we call Earth, our home. *Our Home, not the home of the Squids.*"

The camera switched and she turned slightly to the new primary feed camera. "Tonight was originally planned to be a hello, how are you, get acquainted broadcast. I was going to give you details on an upcoming awards ceremony for a K-9 warrior and a civilian that demonstrated exceptional courage and valor." She paused, then continued.

"But then Federal and local law enforcement agents conducted a raid and served a search warrant on a compound and former commercial horse stables on the outskirts of Great Falls, Montana. The original reason was to break up a dog fighting and illegal drug operation. The agents quickly discovered a level of evil and horror not normally associated with the U.S.A. We think that the Tschaaa—the Squids—have a monopoly in their controlled areas on such activities. Now, it has been found in our own backyard."

Alesha paused, swallowed, and began again. "I suggest that young children be removed from the room, and not be allowed to view the recorded images we are about to show you. The images you are about to see are are *not* for the squeamish. They were obtained from helmet cams and other cameras used by the agents during the raid, to record the details of the action, as well as for evidentiary use in court. The next fifteen minutes are an accurate sampling of the entire raid. And yes, I can say this because I used some of my own sources to verify that there was no photoshopping, no Hollywood-style production activities going on. This raid happened. Again, watch this at your own risk."

The next fifteen minutes were of scenes starting with the first approach to the stables, the first beast attacks on through an overview of the results after the compound was secured. Some were close-ups of snarling dog-monsters, baboon creatures, mutated chimps, and the giant weasels as they attacked and were shot or hacked down. Vikings were seen with large swords and shields in a couple of scenes, a surprise to most viewers. Adam thought, Where did they get these soldiers, these warriors?

The most horrific and disturbing scenes were the ones involving the children. Parts of their nude bodies and faces were obscured for privacy, but one could still see the sorry state they were in as they were rescued. Probably the most effective part, from a purely propaganda aspect, was the scene where a large bearded man was seen opening the doors of a semi-truck trailer, and the humanlike creatures that attacked as the agents tried to rescue a couple of little girls. The sight of the huge man using a Bowie knife to slay an attacking hominid creature, with the comment of sending it to hell, could not have been more effective if it had been part of a Hollywood epic. And this was real.

Then, the pictures of the three child-sized bodies hanging, after having been bled out.

The recording next went to a line of dead monsters and creatures, mutated and modified so that their own mothers would not have recognized them. Examples of all the major types were lined up side by side, the camera panning down for a good look of each.

Next, the line of prisoners. Close-ups were taken of two with huge Kraken tattoos on their chests, their shirts having been removed for the full effect. Several had smaller tattoos. All the tattoos were of high quality, colorful, done by someone or some ones who knew what they were doing, had some artistic flair. If not for the subject matter, people would have found them attractive.

Finally, Alesha was back on the screen. "I was told that in many instances of evil, some good can be found. These following pictures are just that—examples of good, of humans helping humans."

There was a view of five young girls sitting in a semi-circle, eating and drinking hot chocolate, now at least partially clothed. Someone had cleaned their faces, and tied back their messy hair. Adam caught the glimpse of Torbin Bender's profile, and chuckled once again. How that Marine always got himself in the middle of things was surprising. Adam guessed it was because he always charged to the sound of gunfire, into harm's way, like many an ancient warrior. He knew he would be criticized once again for letting him go, but the Director did not care. Sometimes you had to do what was right, humane, and honorable, damn the consequences.

The final section of film was the huge Viking from the trailer, as he carried a sleeping little girl, snuggled securely in his large arms. A Japanese man was following him, carrying what was probably the

Viking's sword and shield. Then the camera panned to the four other girls being given piggyback rides by four other equally large warriors, with a statuesque blonde female bringing up the rear, a compound bow in hand. Adam shook his head. How could the Tschaaa and Krakens hope to match soldiers such as these?

Alesha continued. "Special Deputy Marshals took custody of the five young girls, insuring they had nice, clean beds to sleep in that night, in safe and loving homes. Before we go to a break, after which Commissioner Miller will talk more about the raid, and investigation, I have something personal to say."

Alesha then looked directly into the camera, which zoomed to a close-up.

"My mother and I had to flee hounds to get to the Unoccupied States. I lost the rest of my family, who were either killed or imprisoned because they are humans with dark skin. But I also know that, in a pinch, we are all capable of being menu items for the Squids.

"So this is for all you humans out there, all over planet Earth. Which side would you rather be on? Would you rather be working with fellow humans, trying to keep the rest of humankind from being eaten? Or would you rather be on the side of these Krakens, these Squids, who mutate, modify native creatures into monsters, including our canine friends? Who use and abuse young girls in every way imaginable, and then gut and slaughter them?"

There was steel in her eyes and in her voice. "So for those who are enjoying Tschaaa technology, medicine, plenty of food, the restored internet—are you willing to pay the price? This price? Sacrificing our young for the pleasures of an alien infestation and its minions? Just because it's someone else's children and relatives being abused, eaten?"

A tear ran down her face, endangering her makeup. "I know my answer. It's old, maybe archaic to some. Liberty or death. Whatever it takes, defeat the Squids, the Krakens, the Director. No more. I repeat, no more dead little girls and boys.

"Now, to break please, so I can fix my makeup."

At that moment, Adam Lloyd knew his Mission was lost. The message Alesha had just given, using the film footage, would resonate around the world, would shame others into action. Out of sight, out of mind. That could not work any longer, with these images personalizing the death that had been hidden, primarily in Cattle Country. Things would explode. The Earth may be made uninhabitable, a scorched Earth policy like the Russians used against the Nazis, but that would mean for the Tschaaa also. Salvaging just one part of humankind was no longer an option. It was all or none.

There was a light rapping on the door. "Adam, it's Mary. Kat and I need to talk with you." They had trouble sleeping just like he had after watching the broadcast. They had all slept together as usual, but the two sister wives kept jerking from bad dreams all night, Adam waking them and holding his two loves until they fell asleep again. He dozed a bit, that was it.

"Sure, come on in."

The very pregnant blonde and brunette came in. Kat was noticeably upset, Mary had her arm around her. He stood up, went to them and got into a group hug. He kissed them both, then Kat spoke. "Boss, I can't do my job anymore. I cannot put a spin on things like this anymore. I guess I have been fooling myself about the type of people, the creatures we are actually dealing with. The Krakens are being supported by the Squids, His Lordship. Those goddamned photos… the little girls… " She began to cry.

Adam knew this would happen as soon as he saw the broadcast from the U.S.A. He wondered if he could keep doing his job. The Tschaaa may claim ignorance of what was going on in Montana, but they were ultimately responsible. And he was partially culpable also, since he helped His Lordship in all his dealings with humans, including the Church of Kraken. Ignoring this was not an option.

"Consider yourself on extended maternity leave. I'll find someone else to be the face of the Occupied States. I have to meet with James Kray this afternoon. Maybe he can provide someone. Let him and his people explain all this… shit we just saw."

He sighed. "I expect a call from His Lordship anytime now, either expressing concern or asking questions about the broadcast, maybe both. Then again, maybe neither. Maybe he knew about that compound all along. Maybe there are a bunch of others."

Kat wiped her eyes, and blew her nose. "Think that is a possibility?"

"Hell, they tried to modify all women secretly and quietly. They said it was for our own good. It was bad enough when our own previous government used to say that. Having a bunch of tentacle aliens claim they know what is good for us…that raises the insanity to a whole new level."

"What's next?" Mary asked.

"We just hunker down. There is still a remote chance something may break for the good. If not, then we try and do what we discussed." Kat and Mary both nodded, knowing Adam was talking about his bugout plan. "I imagine I have a bunch of messages from people wanting to see me today, Mary."

"You've got that right. Professors Joseph and Sarah Fassbinder want to see you later this morning. Major Grant is on her way here right now, she couldn't sleep either. I expect more will follow."

Adam sat silently in thought for a few moments. How do you spin the unspinable? You don't. There were no valid reasons for what happened in Great Falls, Montana. Those types of experimentation and manipulation were pure abuse of human beings. Hitler and Joseph Stalin had nothing on the Krakens and others behind this despicable level of evil.

"Well, some will try and say the broadcast was fake, propaganda, a Hollywood production. But, Kat, you can tell. Any signs of image manipulation?"

Kat shivered. "Hollywood—hell, the porn industry—could do wonders with special effects and computer graphics. But those pictures of those…creatures looked too real. You can't fake the scenes of those five young girls. I don't think anybody under Madam President would allow little girls to be run around nude, and abused for the sake of propaganda. If *she* got wind of something like that, someone would be personally castrated by her. Then shot."

Adam snorted. "Yes, I will give her that. She has a strong sense of what is right, is not afraid to fight for it, take action on her own. I often wondered if the roles were reversed, if somehow I was up there, and she had met His Lordship, Neptune. What would she have done?"

Everyone was silent for a while. Then Mary spoke. "She would have tried to gut our many tentacled overlord, and been killed for her efforts. We would all be dead, except for a few put in with the Cattle, or the Ferals. Any semblance of organized human society would probably be gone, as without your attempts at working with the

Tschaaa to save some humans, there would be no reason for the Tschaaa Lords to listen to our Lord Neptune. You showed what cooperating humans can do for the Tschaaa in the future. Besides being meat on the hoof." Mary paused, then continued.

"Adam, things happen for a reason. Without you, here, the Krakens might be in charge. Other than items which helped them in their screwed up religion, everything else would be gone. You saved people. You just could not save everyone."

No one spoke for a period of time. Adam shrugged. "We'll just have to take it as it comes. I imagine I'll find out more very soon from His Lordship, and during the meeting with Reverend James Kray this afternoon. I already know that he has been put in charge of offensive actions against Atlanta, and the U.S.A. He is going to use his cannon fodder followers of the Church of Kraken. We'll see what his reaction to the broadcast is."

He hugged his wives. "We'll make it through this. We've all been through worse. Now Kat, go ahead and go home. I know Jane Grant will want to talk to me, so I'll tell her your change in status. Mary, please try to handle the requests to talk to me, keep it in some semblance of order. I'll see who I can. Hopefully those who see me will spread the word about what I think, to cut down on people coming in. If you get too run down, take off. I'll handle my own phone calls."

As the three went back into the front office, Adam saw Heidi sitting in her normal place in the corner, with a good view of the entrance way. He glanced at his watch.

"I know I didn't call you in this early."

Heidi gave a wan smile. "Didn't have to. I knew you wouldn't be able to sleep, and would be here."

Adam chuckled. "You know me too well, like an ex-wife. Well. It is going to get busy today with visitors. Hopefully they will all be friendly."

"If not, I'll handle them, Boss, After all, that's what you pay me to do."

He looked in her eyes. "Thanks, Heidi. Just remember, you can quit this gig anytime you want. You weren't drafted."

Heidi responded with her throaty, cheerful laugh that Adam had always enjoyed.

"What, quit and have to go back bouncing around on a boat all day? I think not. Besides, who would you find to replace me, with all my charms?"

Adam laughed. She always could get a good laugh out of him. Yes, she was rather irreplaceable.

"Okay, I gave you your chance. Don't start whining later."

"A Coastie whine? It'll never happen."

With that, Adam went back into his office to wait for the first visitor.

Professor Fassbinder and his very pregnant wife Sarah came in a few minutes later. The sun was barely rising above the horizon. Adam knew this was going to be a long day for everyone. Probably everyone with access to an over the air television or computer new internet hookup had seen "The Broadcast". (In later history, that became the name for it. No special identifier, just The Broadcast. Everyone alive knew what it meant.)

Joseph's face was long, and Sarah had puffy eyes from crying. Adam welcomed them into his office, and shut the door. "Can I get you both anything to eat or drink?"

"If I weren't so pregnant, I'd say a double shot of scotch was in order," Sarah answered.

Joseph shook his head "No".

Adam sat down in a chair opposite the married couple, the coffee table between them. The two professors were sitting on the large sofa everyone who visited found so comfortable and inviting.

"I'm not going to try and make any attempt at grand explanations about what everyone has seen on the broadcast last night. Yes, it appears real. It has no characteristics of a photoshopped or computer-created product. The creatures, the people were real. And because of that, I have to accept responsibility for what happened."

With this, Joseph seemed to wake up from his funk. "How so? You weren't there in Montana. Those weren't your people."

Adam let out a sigh. "They may not be 'my people', but I have supported the system that allows their existence. Therefore, I'm afraid that I'm at least partially to blame."

"What about his Lordship?" Sarah snapped. "Has he contacted you yet, expressing some condolences? Tried an explanation of what happened? Those poor, frightened children, filmed as they were rescued... What type of fucking explanation does he have for *them*?" Sarah's cheeks were now flushed with rage.

"None, yet, Professor. I don't know if that is because he is still processing what happened, he knew it was happening, or he just does not really care." Adam paused, looking off as if at something in the distance no one else had seen. "I have a meeting with Reverend Kray of the Church of Kraken, head of the Krakens, his followers. I am definitely waiting to see if he will be a mouthpiece for His Lordship. I know he has been in greater contact with the Tschaaa since he was given the task of pacifying Atlanta. I know also that he is been told to plan an Invasion of the Unoccupied States, using his half-trained fanatics. The details I'm supposed to find out today, this afternoon."

There was a pause in conversation, all three deep in their own, private thoughts. Then Joseph Fassbinder spoke. "This has to stop. We cannot allow such activities, no matter where, to continue." The Professor voiced an opinion that could easily be a death warrant if the Tschaaa Lord found out, if he were behind the activities in Great Falls. But Andrew, cyborg robocop, had been sweeping the Director's Office for any bugs. Although people would think he was nuts, Adam trusted Andrew when he said the office was entirely bug free, that none had been placed by anyone, including Lord Neptune. Otherwise, many conversations would never have occurred.

"I agree, Joseph. But we are limited as to what we can do, other than insuring nothing of this nature is allowed in the Keys."

Sarah broke in. "We are buying guns. If Andrew and his ilk decide to take action against us, they may be of little or no value. But I'll be damned if I am going quietly, into the dark night, my unborn children becoming Squid food without a fight. The Holocaust, never again."

Adam allowed himself a small smile. "You are not the only local resident with that frame of mind, Sarah. I think our... existence under the Tschaaa has reached a turning point. The attack by the Squids immediately following the nuke strike was bad enough. They have attempted to act conciliatory after that. But, as of today, over fifteen thousand Tschaaa are counted as casualties as a result of the attack, directly or indirectly. Eighty percent of those were young or adolescents. That is something the Squids will never forget... nor forgive."

"So," asked Joseph, "What's next?"

"We protect ourselves as best we can. If I were you, I'd prepare for some kind of bug out. I'll try to warn people if I think we are about to be made 'meat products,' but I cannot guarantee much time to flee. Or any real help."

Joseph grunted. "Well. I don't plan on returning to Platform One anytime soon. If someone tries to force me, I am definitely gone."

"Speaking of, how are the Olson twins doing with their saucer research?"

Joseph furrowed his brow. "The research is producing some exciting scientific results, but they are being run ragged by the asshole Minor Lord running the Platform. He is still angry over the embarrassment of losing the space plane, two humans, and some Delta fighters trying to intercept it. So, he threatens all the humans on the space station with 'produce or die'. I'll send you an email, Adam, with the most recent video of their tests. Bottom line, when activated the saucer takes them somewhere, elsewhere. It only works with the Olsons, no one else. It's like it is a living being that likes them, ignores everyone else."

"Where do you think 'somewhere' is?"

"That's the weird part. It appears to go into what can only be described as a completely different, unknown universe. The Tschaaa and their related starcraft can access a form of hyperspace, a small dimensional shift or warping of this universe that allows the craft to exceed the speed of light. They warp space in front of the craft, changing the properties and physics of the area. Then, the craft enters the area at a speed that, in relation to "normal space", breaks the speed of light. Some scientists say they bend or fold a section of space, allowing them to travel a shortcut between two points, timewise. However you explain it without the math, it works. But it requires a crap load of energy, provided by tapping into a highly efficient use of matter, anti-matter. Dark energy and dark matter. So, only smaller ships, and scouts are used in this manner.

"The saucer disappears, reappears in a different section of the galaxy, universe, we don't know. We try using the Tschaaa extensive and our limited star maps to try to extrapolate where the craft is. Usually, you should be able to find some recognizable star or sun looking in a 360 degree search around the saucer. But, so far, no joy. Not even close."

"So, Joseph, the theory is that it is one of the eleven multi-verses of string theory. Correct?"

"Spot on, Director. The problem is, we cannot discover its relationship with *our* universe, galaxies. Where and how the two bubbles we picture the universes as being connect, position in reference to each other, they have not figured out yet. They take their little trips, two dozen so far, take some photos, sensor readings, and then return. But that still cannot triangulate or use some other means of reference to figure where the saucer travels to in reference to Earth. Though they have found out something else. Is this room secure?"

"Yes. Andrew sweeps it for bugs, takes out any he finds as he says he has no orders about allowing surveillance devices in this area. He says that His Lordship has not authorized any bugs to be placed. If the Tschaaa Lord had, Andrew would have done it."

"You trust him?" Sarah asked.

"Yes. Andrew is brutally honest. He may be of originally human stock, but he has received some programing which requires him to follow directions to the proverbial letter of the law. Conversely, the ability he and his brothers have for independent thought and action is greater than any other Client or creation of the Tschaaa."

"Hm," interjected Joseph. "That seems to be programming conflict looking for a place to happen. Independent thought verses stone clad directions. Sooner or later, there is going to be an internal argument."

Adam shrugged. "If it happens, it happens. I haven't seen any inkling of that yet."

There was a short lull in the conversation, as Joseph mulled how over how to present his information. "Well. I might as well be blunt. Thanks to the Star Map info the Squids had given, the Olson twins have figured out where the Squids came from. They found the area where the Squids' homeworld is."

Adam froze. "Who knows this?"

"Just them and us, you included as of today. They mixed it in with a report on the saucer results. In with some math formulas they slipped the coordinates of where the Tschaaa homeworld was apparently located. I can find a way to slip them to you, if you have a way to camouflage them, secure them from prying eyes."

"No problem, Professor. The Tschaaa are kind of blind when it comes to electronic surveillance of the internet. They understand bugs in an office. Hacking a computer? Not really."

Joseph looked at Adam. "So you never really pushed their vulnerabilities to them?"

"I told his Lordship after the last fiasco around Atlanta that humans understand real total war, using everything to win. He acknowledged it. But for all his studying of the 'human condition', he still doesn't really understand us, our capabilities. Were it not for the surprise of large rocks hitting us, then the saboteurs disrupting our responses, and finally the airstrikes by the Deltas and Falcons, the Invasion would have failed. In a standup fight, even with the Falcons' kickass capabilities, they would have been brought to a standstill. This would have required them to completely decimate us from space, probably making it difficult to colonize this world. The Long Winter would still be going on, the seas becoming too cold for the Squids reproduction crèches to function, at least on the scales they are now. And even more of us would have died."

He paused. "The Tschaaa would have probably grabbed a large breeding stock of us, and then left. And we would be living in caves and city sewers, trying to survive until things warmed up."

Sarah looked at him. "Sometimes, I think that might have been better in the long run. No Squids and Krakens rounding us up, eating us, at least some of us, on a monthly basis. We would have to start over. But maybe we would be more humane to our brothers and sisters."

They were all quiet for a while, deep again in their own thoughts. Finally, Adam broke the silence. "Well, like they say. If wishes were horses, beggars would ride. So, to end this conversation, I am doing what I can to deal with the... savagery we saw on that broadcast. can't make any promises. I believe we have reached a tipping point in our relations with the Tschaaa and its virulent supporters. What happens next..." He let the statement hang.

Sarah managed to stand up with her very noticeable belly. She suddenly grabbed ahold of Adam and kissed him on his cheek. "We have had some disagreements, but I know your heart has always been in the right place. Unfortunately, I don't think you will be able to achieve your dream."

Adam snorted. "After the Squids attacked us indiscriminately after the nuke attack, basically saying we all look alike, I knew my chances of completing my original Mission, the Protocol of Selective Survival, were poor. Us being an indispensable Client Species, is probably not going to happen. At least in my lifetime."

He sighed. "But I'm very stubborn. So I keep hoping."

"Well, Director," said Joseph. "Just remember you have a lot of personal support. If you yell for help, we will come."

Adam took his hand and shook it. "Thanks, Professor. I appreciate it more than you know. Now, if you will excuse me, I have a line of people waiting to talk to me. By the way, babies okay, Sarah?"

"Yes. They are developing, healthy but at a faster rate. Which means I'm hungry all the time."

"Well, I'll have to make sure we set up a spread for Thanksgiving this year. At least we can have fun eating ourselves silly if nothing else."

Jane Grant showed up a few minutes later. She had a hangdog expression on her face that Adam had never seen before. Jane was one of the most positive, can-do people Adam had ever met. As his Operations Officer, she coordinated what happened on Key West Base.

"Major, you do not look happy. But I can understand that, given the circumstances."

Jane managed a half smile. "No, I have to admit. I don't see much to be happy about right now."

Adam looked at her. She had been one of his most loyal people. And now she was suffering for it.

"Jane, I know this is not easy. Everyone I have talked with realizes the trick-bag we are in right now. My plans no longer seem viable…"

"Stop right there, Commissioner. The Krakens may have screwed things up, but your original idea is sound, given the situation we were in. You've help save a bunch of people from the slaughterhouse."

He snorted. "Yeah, at the cost of many others. I just have to face the fact that I was fooling myself. When you try and dance with the devil, you may not like the music or the results."

They sat facing each other, Adam's office quiet except for the ticking of an old grandfather clock he has salvaged a while ago. Once the most powerful person in the northern hemisphere, second only to the Tschaaa Lord, he now realized the recent occurrences showed just how powerless he had become. It was if a huge shift in the timeline had happened, unbeknownst to all until the ripples it produced began to make themselves felt. Now, he felt like he had just been run over by a tidal wave.

Jane stood up, and stepped closer to him. "Boss, Adam, could you stand up for minute?" Adam stood up. Jane hugged him tightly. "I know this blows military decorum all to hell, but... I love you. I always have. You and the Chief saved me from death or being some local warlord's plaything. If things had been different... maybe I would be have also been one of your wives." She tilted her head back and looked up at him. "But I chose to serve you as a military officer. I was always told that an officer and a lady does not sleep with the boss. It destroys the professional relationship." She took a deep breath, let it out, her eyes a bit wet now.

"But I can still love and serve you as long as I can. So, here I stay." She kissed him. He kissed back. Before they knew it, they were on the large overstuffed couch, kissing, squeezing, and fondling each other. Within minutes, Jane Grant's Air Force blue slacks were pulled off, as were the panties beneath. They kissed each other deeply, and the immediate joining of their bodies was a perfect fit. It took just a few moments and then both the participants were experiencing very human orgasms.

They lay in each other's arms, Adam gently caressing Jane. "That was not supposed to happen..." began Adam.

"Yes it was," answered Jane. "Or it wouldn't have happened." She took his face in her hands and looked at him. "This is probably the only time this will happen, given you having two lovely wives who I happen to like and respect also. But... it needed to happen. I needed to tell you how I feel, and to know how you feel about me." She kissed him.

"This will always be one of those fond memories I will have until the day I die. Which is the way it should be. Now, to spoil the mood, we both need to get back to work and try to salvage this mess we just inherited from those asshole Krakens."

Adam smiled, kissed her lips. "Always the professional. I think I need to promote you, and not because we just had sex. But because you have been working way above your pay grade." Then he turned serious. "But promise me something."

"What, Adam?"

"If you see that it is time to leave, then leave. Do not stick around out of loyalty to me. I want you to be safe, and survive. Head for the U.S.A. I think they will take a defector with your knowledge. Promise me that."

Jane looked into his eyes, knowing again why she loved him. Some would say it was at least partly due to the Tschaaa screwing around with everyone's hormones and DNA. Jane knew better. He did care about those around him, more than himself.

"I promise."

"Good. Now, Kat is officially on maternity leave. We need to find another face for our broadcasts. Reverend Kray is to meet with me later. He may provide me with someone who may be a bit over the top. But, to be truthful, I don't care."

Jane sighed. "Well, I can fill in, and we already have a couple of news readers. But of course, nobody with Kat's presence." Jane paused for a moment. Then, she spoke again.

"You probably heard we had a Russian defector last week. A good-looking redhead, Inna Popov, if I remember her name correctly. She skipped when the powers that be wanted her to fight in North America. As soon as she got a chance after arriving here, she deserted."

"Why?" asked Adam.

"She said that she was not in the mood to fight for some Yankee capitalists. Apparently her family was big in the Politburo before the breakup of the Soviet Union. Their belief system rubbed off on Inna, who appears to be an unapologetic old style Marxist. The thought of fighting for the capitalist warmongers is repulsive to her."

"How can we use her?"

"She has a background in mass media and propaganda. But she does not want to be on camera, as she still has some relatives who survived in Russia. So, she is willing to help us, and thus the Tschaaa, not because she is pro-Squid, but rather that she is Anti-Capitalist U.S. A. She may be a bit nuts, but she has the voice for radio."

"Well, use her then. If she turns out to be a fake, maybe a plant, she sure can't hurt us as much as the goddamned Krakens did in Montana. As long as she helps us survive here in Key West, and keep things under control, fine. The U.S.A. is going to get a big boost from the film they showed, and from the new young black lady they are using as their version of Kat. I expect people to defect, as well as the number of people coming to us from the Feral areas to drop off, maybe even disappear. We need to keep us from having riots in the street, or all out combat with the Squids until we have a means to save as many people as possible. I honestly do not think things will ever be the same."

Dressed again in her uniform, hair and face in place, Jane smiled. "Well Director, no rest for the wicked. Let me know if our Reverend Kray comes up with anyone we can use. Hopefully, no one with a big squid tattoo across their face. That would be a definite turn off on tv."

Adam sighed. "I will, Jane. And thanks for being… you."

Jane gave him a quick peck on the cheek. "I can't be anyone else."

Adam visited with other residents of the Base, listening to their concerns. He tried to allay their fears, give them hope. But he also told them to have a backup plan in case everything fell apart. He could do no less, or no more.

Then it was time to meet with the one person he was loathe to see, James Kray. From the first time Adam had met the Reverend James Kray, titular head of the Church of Kraken, now called in short hand the Krakens, Adam had not liked him. Tall, slender bridging on skinny, he reminded Adam of a cross between a praying mantis and a vulture. When he looked at someone, the look in his eyes and face seemed to reflect a predatory sizing up of the subject in his gaze as a potential meal. Adam swore Kray sometimes held his hands as if he were an actual a praying mantis about to grab its prey.

Kray showed up with two huge bodyguards who were probably televised professional wrestlers in life before the Squids. Now, they had the large, stylized Kraken tattoos on their faces, the dark blue ink obscuring their ethnic heritage. Kray strode through the outer office as if he owned the place, ignoring Mary. But she had already seen him arrive in front of the building on the hidden surveillance camera, alerting Adam.

So Adam met him at the door to his office, spoiling the Reverend's grand entrance. "Reverend Kray. How are you today?"

The Reverend stopped, giving Adam a smarmy smile. "Good, Director. And ready to get on with the duties His Lordship has given me." Neither man extended his hand in friendship, for a handshake. They were forced to work together. That did not mean they had to like it, or each other.

The two hunks started to follow Kray into the Director's office when Adam spoke up. "Sorry Guys. Private meeting."

The Reverend frowned. "They go everywhere I go. Security, you know."

"Oh come now, Reverend. Are you saying you are afraid of talking to me alone? Do you think there is a threat here somehow? Only one group has ever tried to whack me here, and they didn't succeed. And they had a nuke".

"Well, Director, I notice you have a bodyguard over there," he motioned to Heidi standing near Mary's desk. "As limited as it is."

Heidi snorted. "I'll show you limited." The two huge men, apparently not liking her tone, started to step toward her. "Come, on guys, if you want a dance, my card is empty."

Adam knew that despite the size difference, Heidi would have them both gutted with her knives in about five seconds. Sometimes it was the size of the fight in the dog, not the size of the dog in the fight.

"Now lady and gentlemen," Adam interjected. "Let's not get into a pissing contest. We are here for friendly meeting. Right, Reverend?"

Kray nodded. "Yes, we are. You two wait out here, don't let anyone disturb us. Shall we, Director?" He motioned toward the office. Adam saw that Kray just had to seem like he was in control, was in charge. The thought of having to listen to other people's input was completely alien to him. Listen to the Tschaaa Lord, follow his directions, he may. Anyone else, especially other humans, forget it.

The two guards posted themselves at the entrance to Adams office, like two large pillars. Adam entered, went to his desk and hit the automatic closing mechanism. He sat behind his desk, having moved a padded chair directly in front. Adam was making sure that the Reverend understood that they were on *his* turf, not someone else's. Sad that he had to play these games, but some people only understood when you made them face reality. And the reality of the situation was that, at least in Key West, Adam was still in charge.

"Can I offer you something to drink, Reverend?"

"No, I'm fine. The subjects at hand are pretty basic, so this should not take long."

Adam leaned back in his chair. Under his desk, in a fast draw holster, was a slab side Colt .45, locked and cocked. Just in case things went South. But, Adam doubted it. Reverend Kray was used to dealing with victims, not people who fought back. If someone fought back, well, one of his Kraken minions took care of it.

"Well, as they say, shoot, Reverend."

Kray gave him an almost feral smile. He was going to enjoy what he was about to say. Which meant pain and strife for some unfortunate soul. "I am putting together an assault force to attack the Unoccupied States. We need to get some revenge for what they did to our Lords. Killing all the young with that nuclear weapon...it cannot be allowed to pass without a response in kind."

Adam had already been told by Lord Neptune that Kray had been given the authority to strike back, as well as to decimate and reduce Atlanta. So far, the Atlanta Operation had been turned into a case of wild expectations with little results. Casualties on the Kraken side had been high, despite support by battle robs, a Falcon or two, and a few Deltas. The Tschaaa were trying to recapture control of Atlanta, not only to get the Cattle there back for harvesting, but also to send a message that resistance was futile. The rest of Cattle Country had fallen back in line within a few weeks. All but Atlanta. Humans would have just reduced it to rubble in one massive air attack. But the Tschaaa did not think like humans. They hated to waste 'good meat'. The plague that had made their original primate food source deadly and unusable, plus the long trip to Earth to obtain a replacement source had been spiritually debilitating for many of the Squids.

To say the Tschaaa Lords had "food issues" was an understatement.

That, plus the fact the oceans on the planet were teeming with life and vitality, revitalizing the Tschaaa breeding Crèches to levels not seen for thousands of years, made the Tschaaa loathe to destroy anything more. Enough destruction, leading to the Long Winter, had been done during the Invasion. Now, they wanted to keep any more destruction of the Earth's environment to a minimum.

"So, how does that affect me and mine, Reverend? Don't you

have a couple of million followers of the Church to call on? You already have a few thousand investing the Atlanta area. Surely you can spare a few more to attack Madam President and her people."

Kray's smile turned to a look of frustration. "I have many faithful. What I lack is equipment and training. Especially heavier weapons. That is why I was sent to you by His Lordship."

Adam sighed. He knew this was coming. He just kept hoping it would come later than sooner. "To be honest, Reverend, thanks to that fiasco in Great Falls, with Krakens abusing and killing children, getting any volunteers to help you and yours is going to be tough."

The Reverend's frustration was turning to anger. "We *all* serve the Tschaaa. I need your help to complete my mission, my orders. I was told you would give me that help. Case closed."

Adam chuckled, which he knew would anger the Reverend more. "Reality is, my dear Reverend, I could order a bunch of people to give you in depth training. I could order them to train all you people, as well as provide thousands of trained personnel, but that would last for about a week."

"What do you mean, last about a week?"

"What I am saying, Reverend, is that, thanks to the images your people provided to the media people of the Unoccupied States through their obscene actions, the name 'Kraken' is becoming synonymous with psychotic sacks of shit."

You could hear a pin drop. Kray glared at him. Adam ignored the glare. It was about time this idiot was given a dose of reality.

Finally, the head of the Church of Kraken spoke. "So, you are saying your people would refuse to follow orders?"

"I am saying they would say 'Yes Sir,' show up, then drag their feet until they could desert to the Feral areas."

"They would be shot." Kray blurted out.

"Yeah, right. Start a gunfight with a bunch of STRAC troops who are well-armed and are furious with your people over what Krakens did to those children. They will gut your forces, then scatter when the Falcons and robocops show up. Even if Lord Neptune ordered a total annihilation, it would start such a shit storm that you would have a whole other Atlanta on your hands. Maybe several. Maybe they would help the Cattle break out. Just imagine that scenario."

Adam got up and went to fix a drink. Kray was seething. But the

Kraken leader knew Adam was right. Finally, he spoke again. "So if I told everyone that the… actions in Montana were the work of some renegades, unsupervised, doing what they willed…"

"Oh, come on, Kray. Do I have a big red 'S' on my face for stupid? We both know they had support to get all those crazy beasts made, bred, manufactured, whatever the hell. The Tschaaa had to be helping with the modifications to Earth fauna made in such short order. We had some good scientists, but most are probably dead. The survivors are either under Tschaaa control, in the U.S.A, or hiding in the uncontrolled, feral areas. The equipment used had to be of Tschaaa design. The growth tank on the broadcast was definitely from Tschaaa stores.

Adam walked back to his desk, sat down and took a slug from his double. "Most of our labs and scientific areas were either destroyed in the Invasions or abandoned during the Long Winter. And those that may have remained occupied, functional, were concerned with surviving, not playing the Isle of Doctor Moreau."

He continued. "Look, I know we are at His Lordship's beck and call. But I also know that he has become painfully aware of his lack of control over us pet humans. We may be on the verge of becoming a client species, but the nuke strike and now this… obscene disaster that was broadcast all over the world. It brought back memories of the Holocaust, Soviet gulags, the Killing Fields…" He took another drink.

"Bottom line, I can probably get a few volunteers to train your people. I can turn over some of the M-1 Tanks, the Bradley Fighting Vehicles. I know that His Lordship is assembling a lot of small arms, and probably a few larger weapons, using slave labor at the huge complex that covers Baja California. But, beyond what I just said, it's going to be in your hands. Your people and their buddies in Great Falls just made us take a big bite of a shit sandwich. Tastes good, doesn't it?"

They heard a familiar voice in the outer office. Andrew, assigned cyborg robocop, was announcing his presence. Then they heard an unfortunate exchange.

"Hey, the Reverend says no one goes in… ack!"

One of the two huge bodyguards had apparently tried to dissuade Andrew from his task at hand, which was to enter Adam's office. The automatic fortified door Adam had installed after the failed attack on him activated and Andrew stepped through as if it were a day in the park. Suspended a foot off the ground, one in each of his powerful hands, were the bodyguards. In Andrew's grip, they looked like rag dolls.

Kray jumped to his feet and Andrew stopped directly in front of him. "Reverend. We have had this discussion before. I do not take orders. Humans do not get in my way. I give orders. You and your people move out of my way. Director Lloyd learned that fact years ago. Why can't you and your people?"

Kray began to stammer. Adam jumped in. "Andrew, please. They are turning blue. Can you release them? Please?"

"Since you asked so respectfully, Director, yes." He let the two large men drop and crumple to the floor. Kray glared at Andrew, but knew he was helpless to respond. Slowly, the two bodyguards began to come around. Heidi had been watching this and was trying not to burst out laughing.

Andrew glared at Kray. "I have noticed that some of you humans are much too wrapped up in your own importance. I suggest you start developing a bit less hubris to keep you from causing many problems for yourself and those around you."

Kray stood for a moment, clearly angry to have been called out. "Yes Sir. I will ensure my personnel understand their…relationship to you." Kray then turned to Adam.

"So you will supply me some support?"

"Have your people start heading toward the former Eglin Air Force Base in the panhandle area of Florida. The large range area that was used for weapons testing and development we use now as a training center, especially with our limited heavy equipment, armor, and so forth. I'll have some tanks and such you can use, once you have trained personnel. I'll see how many trainers I can get. No promises, for the reasons I have already stated."

Kray gave him a wry smile. "I guess I will just have to make do with that." He looked at his two bodyguards, who were finally on the feet, but wobbly. Kray gave a bit of a Prussian bow to Adam, then Andrew, clicking his heels a bit.

"Till we meet again. Gentlemen." He then walked directly out of Adam's office, through the outer office, then down toward the main entrance. The two subdued bodyguards trailed behind.

Adam looked at large Andrew standing stoically in the office. When Andrew saw that Kray and company had left, gave Adam his typical small smile. "Sometimes one must play a certain role to get a point across."

"So, Andrew, we're okay? I haven't... overstepped any boundaries?"

"Of course not. Otherwise I would have let you know." Andrew's mouth shaped a more wry smile. With his eyes covered by the protective visor, his face was sometimes hard to read.

"You don't see me suspending you and Heidi as I did with those two less than efficient examples of humanity, do you?"

"Hey, big guy," Heidi jumped in. "That would not be cool. You would not be on my Christmas list anymore if you did that."

"Why, Heidi, I did not know I was on your list. Thank you for telling me. Now I have time to come up with a present for you."

Heidi grinned. "Well, now you know. Do you need my clothes sizes, any other personal info?"

"You forget, Heidi. I have many additional sensors, capabilities wired into me. I know your measurements within a millimeter. I know when you gain a pound, and where."

"TMI Andrew. TMI. Please, don't start blabbing things."

Adam began to laugh, then Heidi and Mary, who was still sitting at her desk, observing the activities.

Mary glanced at the surveillance system screen. "He's leaving, Director. And he looks none too happy. I don't think he likes being reminded he is working for others, that he is not in charge of his own future."

Adam snorted. "Welcome to the world of the Tschaaa. I thought he worshipped the Squids as ancient Krakens originally, as God-like creatures. Now, the more contact I have with him, the more I realize he is worshiping some esoteric Kraken God above the Tschaaa, with whom he is becoming more frustrated with every day. He wants Tschaaa weapons, more direct support in dealing with Atlanta. He wants the city leveled. But His Lordship has said no. Now, he wants to attack the Unoccupied States."

"He has been told he has the chance to prove his abilities," opined Andrew. "But he and his fellow believers are being used as warm bodies, disposable fighters. Kray wants to be more important, but Lord Neptune realizes Kray's severe limitations, which is a main reason why His Lordship still keeps coming to you for many things, Adam."

Adam studied Andrew. "Does His Lordship realize how dangerous this … frustration on the part of Kray can be?"

Andrew paused for a moment. Then he answered. "His opinion is that if push comes to shove, some of my brothers and I will visit the Reverend and his people. And we will deal with the problem with extreme prejudice. It would be messy and destructive. But, once Kray no longer has use, or becomes too much of a problem, he is gone."

Adam did not say anything for a moment. He knew that the same answer applied to him as Director. As a favored "pet" he would be given more leeway. But, push comes to shove, the results would be the same.

"Well, Andrew, I guess all we can do is take it day by day. And, due to our Kraken friend's actions in Montana, the next few days are not going to be pleasant."

CHAPTER 15

Some historians say the Chinese had the first really grand government bureaucracy. Since that time, every group of humans has deemed to necessary to form a bureaucracy in support of their daily operations. The Unoccupied States were no different.

-Excerpts from the Works of Princess Akiko, *Free Japan Royal Family*

BISMARCK, NORTH DAKOTA

Hours after Adam had his meetings on the fallout from the U.S.A. broadcast, Madam President was just finishing up her work day. It had been over twenty-four hours from the time that everyone within eyeshot of a television or computer screen had seen the images of the hell-spawn, a new name becoming popular for the mutated Earth fauna, as well as the five surviving girls. Much like Pearl Harbor, the Kennedy assassination, 9/11, and when the first rock struck, everyone would remember where they were when they saw the horrific images. People would have thought that, after having friends and relatives butchered already by the Tschaaa, that there was nothing more that could shock their sensibilities. They were wrong.

The North Dakota state capitol complex had been turned into the new Unoccupied States of America Federal Capital. Buildings had been added onto, areas expanded to house the Congress (Sixteen Senators and thirty-two Representatives, divided evenly for the time being between the eight member states). Elections every two years, with six year terms for the Senators, two for the Representatives, like the old days. No political parties as of yet. There wouldn't be, if she had any say in the matter. Each elected official worked for their state, and the citizens of that state. Bismarck was in driving distance of all the Congressmen, except for Alaska, so there was limited overhead expenditure in housing and transportation. In fact, several apartment buildings in the Bismarck area had been purchased and refurbished (though in a pretty spartan way) for use by the officials and their limited staff. No more frills, free haircuts, subsidized meals, etcetera. Everyone lived on their basic salary, with the Federal government providing a few support items—office space, computers, telephones, and of course, paper. What government could run without paperwork?

The official salaries, budgets, and support systems had been in existence just over a year. Before that, Madam President had been a benign dictator in fact, as there was little governmental structure to call on, or to advise her. She had the military, which had been the extent of government assets. Accepted as the President because she was one of the few surviving elected officials, and the only one willing to take the job, she had been running the operation of this new country by the seat of her pants since the end of the Long Winter. And her pants had become threadbare. Thank God, enough people had stepped forward to add some civilian control once again. Militias, vigilance committees, county and town councils had helped create a framework, a working organizational structure for a representative Republic once again.

The first day of Congressional activities of the new term had been a week before the nuke strike. During a combined meeting of both Houses, after a very meaningful prayer for guidance, sufficient basic legislation had been passed to create a functioning new federal government. Then, two days later, after creating a secure meeting area, she had laid out the basics of the attack on Key West. Just the bare bones that, yes, there was a plan to bomb the Tschaaa Lord and company. Can we do it?

There had been a very short subsequent discussion of what steps had been taken to protect the U.S.A. from any counter-strike, and to determine if there a likelihood of a counter-strike based on what they knew of the Tschaaa and the Director. Then, to the President's surprise, all of the newly elected Representatives and Senators had stood up unheeded. A retired U.S. Senator, Joseph Biggs, the elder statesman who had now re-entered politics, spoke. At seventy-five years of age, he was one of the oldest survivors, and a dear friend of Madam President before the Invasion.

"Madam President," his voice rang out despite his age. "Do what you must. My colleagues and I vote for the first act of war against the invading Tschaaa. May God speed the young men and women of our military. And God bless the human race." There was a round of applause and of cheers, which filled the new House of Congress. At that moment, Madam President knew she was the leader of a group of Americans. And then, there was no turning back. She had just stuck a large thumb in the eye of the dragon.

Senator Biggs was elected in Congress to fill in as Vice President until a formal election could be held. If she was killed, there would be continuity in the Office of the President.

Vice President Biggs was now at the former U.S. Air Force Academy in Colorado Springs, Colorado, a functioning full scale military installation. Maybe someday, there would be another military academy there. Right now, four years of officer training was a luxury that no one could afford. She and Joe tried to stay a bit separated, as they kept expecting an attempt to whack them any day now. Atlanta was surrounded as the last bastion of resistance in Cattle Country, so there were less distractions for the Squids. They should be planning revenge. At least, that is what a human would be doing.

She was putting papers in her satchel to take them back to the Presidential residence, a rather large house that had been owned by a well-to-do businessman, now deceased. He had gotten into the oil industry boom in North Dakota on the ground floor, and had made some millions. Then the Tschaaa had shown up. His surviving family members had sold the residence to the New Federal Gov't, then had headed for the hills of Montana. They did not want to be around when the Squids came calling on this upstart government.

There was a knock on her office door. It was late at night, so she had already sent her limited staff home. She heard a familiar West Texas drawl. "Ma'am, the State Troopers outside tell me there are some people here asking to see you."

The owner of the West Texas drawl was her driver, former Texas Ranger Andrew "Andy" Jackson. He had been one of the most senior, and oldest, Rangers when the Squids had hit. In the continuation of a long history of service, the Rangers had aided the local military and state forces in resisting the Tschaaa's taking of Houston, Galveston and Corpus Christi, as they took control of the warmer waters of the Gulf of Mexico.

Andy had told her it had been a short and nasty fight.

"Rocks hit the city centers, along with the military bases. Then the Deltas and Falcons came in and shot at anything moving. Harvester arks showed up, spittin' out those goddamned—pardon my language, Ma'am—harvester robs. Then robocops, a few grays, lizards, and those traitorous flying squads of humans.

"We fought them for forty-eight hours, almost straight through. The robocops finally formed a line and started blowing us to hell and gone. I think I'm one of three Rangers that survived."

His family had been living in Alpine, Texas. He had managed to make it back, and with the rest of West Texas, hunkered down. The several thousand inhabitants of Alpine, Texas were a hardy lot. They banded together and weathered the Long Winter together, fighting off bands of Ferals. Sol Ross College located there helped provide some scientific and technical help. They may not have flourished, but they survived. Even most of the elderly lived, not a normal occurrence post-Invasion. Far from the Gulf, as well as the Pacific Ocean, they were left alone by the Tschaaa.

Then one day, Andy said he had heard that the Unoccupied States of America was up and running, trying to preserve what the original states had stood for. He had been experiencing a feeling of frustration, helplessness. Texas Rangers had not been in the habit of admitting defeat. The Alamo meant something to them. One Riot, one Ranger had been a mantra for years. Andy lived it, breathed it, felt it to his core. There may only be one of him but, dammit, he was Texas Ranger. Maybe one of the last.

With the help of his very tech savvy daughter, he put out feelers through the new internet that had sprung up from the Tschaaa controlled areas and the Unoccupied States. Sure enough, Madam President was looking for a few good men, and age was not a concern.

So he talked it over with his family—wife, two sons, and daughter. Alpine would be stagnant, trapped in time for years, maybe forever. The family packed everything up into a pick-up, trailer, and a SUV and headed north. His eldest son had gotten into some trouble, had done some prison time before the rocks set him free. The thought of a complete "do over" for him was a Godsend. They headed to Malmstrom Military Base, sending out job feelers. Madam President got wind that a Texas Ranger was looking for a job. Sandra Paul took one look at him, hired him on the spot as her driver/bodyguard. The rest was history. After some two years of bouncing around while his family found a new home in Great Falls, Andy Jackson was now a part of Madam President's office, just as George Williams was a part. A couple of times Ranger Jackson had to handle unruly constituents that were getting violent. The word got around that the tall, lanky man in the Stetson was the real deal, not some drugstore cowboy wannabe claiming to be a Ranger. And his Texas Ranger Commemorative Smith and Wesson .357 Highway Patrolman was fully functional.

So when Andy came and told her there was a crowd of people wanting to see her at 10:00pm at night, she knew that he had already surveyed the situation and knew that the people would not be dissuaded by him saying the President was unavailable. It also meant that he thought it was something important.

She smiled at the Ranger. "So, are they carrying pitchforks and torches?"

He chuckled. "No. Ma'am. The have a whole bunch of candles. Some look like luminarias, like Mexicans and Texans put out this time a year in the Southwest."

"Hmmm. That's a switch. How many are there?"

"Close to a thousand, I think. With a few kids mixed in."

Madam President's jaw dropped a bit. A thousand people on a cold, sub-freezing night in North Dakota, coming out in mass? What was happening?

She walked over to her coat rack and threw her parka on, grabbed a heavy scarf her sainted husband had given her years ago.

"Time to go meet them, Andy. If they braved this weather to see me, I owe it to them to make it worth their while. Let's go." She turned and strode purposefully out toward the stairs leading to the building entrance. She did not see the small smile on the Ranger's face. Once again, her aggressive, take charge attitude gave him a positive jolt in his soul. With her in charge, he knew the Squid's days were numbered. As he had often wondered before, why couldn't there have been more like her six years ago? People may not have given up so quickly, going to hide in holes.

The President soon found herself at the top of the wide front steps, looking down onto a small sea of lights. She should have known that Andy would not have exaggerated. Now, the question was, why were they here? Well, the only way she would find out is if she went and asked.

She walked down the steps, taking her parka hood down as she neared the crowd. They were respectively standing back from just two State Troopers who had blocked their way up to the front doors. Demonstrations of civil disobedience, attempts at harassing the Man, authority were things of the past. Everyone knew who the real enemy was. She smiled and called out as she walked down the steps.

"Hello. What brings all of you out on this cold, snowy night? What can I do for you?"

A familiar sounding voice called back. "The question is, what can we do for you, Madam President?"

She looked at the source of the remark and saw a slender black man standing in the front of the crowd. Her mind quickly scrolled down her list of possible names and faces, and hit on one. Jerome Washington, father of Sergeant George Washington, Medal of Honor winner from the nuke raid on Key West. Posthumously.

She stepped down a couple of steps closer, holding her hand out. "Mr. Washington. How are you this brisk, cold night in Bismarck?" Mr. Washington worked his way up the steps and shook her hand. Madam President had presented the Medal of Honor and flag from his son's coffin personally to the man and his wife. Director Lloyd had made good on his promise to Torbin Bender. All the remains of the deceased soldiers had been quietly passed back into the U.S.A. It had helped grant closure to the families, surviving relatives.

Jerome Washington had been one of the few people of color who had brought his whole family successfully up from what was now Cattle Country. A pharmacist by trade, he and others had set up a Pharmaceutical Training Academy, as pharmacists were in short supply in the Unoccupied States.

A slender, almost skinny man, Jerome Washington had the strong voice of a man of stature, strength. "I think I can speak for almost everyone here. Madam President, please know that we are here for you. If you need something, just ask." He paused for a moment, then continued, "We know that, after seeing the… horrific pictures, images from the broadcast last night that we have been fooling ourselves. We thought he Squids would not touch us, would ignore us. Out of sight, out of mind." There were murmurs of assent from the crowd.

"Many of us were angry when you launched that strike against Key West. We thought you were asking for trouble, poking a stick into an ant hill. After all, they had left us alone for some six years. Who cared about those being butchered in Cattle Country? Out of sight, out of mind."

His voice quavered a bit, but Jerome continued, "Even though I had lost relatives directly to harvesting, I chose not to speak out, to agitate for action to help others. I chose not to speak out because… I was afraid." There were more voicing of agreement from the crowd.

"I was selfish. I had saved my immediate family. Time to live a new life." A tear ran down his cheek which he quickly wiped away to keep it from freezing.

"I was angry and hurt when my son, George, was killed doing what he thought was right. I started to blame you, Madam President. Now I must ask your forgiveness for that blame."

"Now, Jerome, there is no need to apologize for…." She began. But the slender dark man held up a hand to stop her.

"Please, let me finish. I have to say this. You were right. I was wrong. The evil the Squids have visited on us what we cannot ignore. It is now permeating even up here in the so called safe areas. Seeing what those beasts, those Krakens did in the name of the Tschaaa Lord can't be allowed to exist. To see those young bodies hanging, like pieces of meat…" There were now sobs from the crowd. Jerome swallowed, somehow continued.

"So, Madam President, let it be known from this day forward. We are here to take America back. Maybe the world back, God willing. Or, we die trying. Like my son George."

She struggled to hold back her tears. Somehow she did. She grabbed Jerome Washington's hand with both of hers. She turned to face the crowd.

"Thank you. Thank you all. I promise I will do everything to right as many wrongs as I can, to drive this…Infestation from our country. And your support, you coming here…is more than I ever hoped for. Thank you. Everything I do is for you. Please remember that." She was shaking a bit, and not from the cold. One person began a solitary, slow clap. Then another person matched it. Then another. All in time.

People put down their candles, or handed them to others. Soon, almost half of the crowd was involved with the timed, simultaneous applause. It reverberated around the surrounding governmental area. Each time they people clapped, Madam President felt an infusion of strength, energy. She now knew they had reached a turning point. There would be no going back to the days of fear produced apathy. Five abused young survivors, three slaughtered ones had seen to that.

Finally, the clapping began to slow down. Then, almost as I it had been planned, one person was left clapping in that slow rhythmic style. Then, as the final clap sounded, a voice was heard.

"Never again."

Then a chorus. "Never again."

Then silence, except for some sobbing.

She continued down the steps to the crowd, began moving amongst them. She hugged, kissed, and shook hands, as everyone gave her words, looks, gestures of encouragement. Finally, she separated, went part way up the steps. She turned around, faced the crowd.

"Thank you all. I will work to make sure I never betray the trust, the confidence, the support you have shown me tonight. I am your very humble employee. I thank you again."

She let out a large sigh. "Now. I suggest we all go home, get some rest. Have a hot toddy. I know I need one." People began to laugh, gave a few more shouts of encouragement. Then the crowd began to disperse. But as they moved on, the people left behind all their candles and luminaries. A large soothing glow continued to bathe the front of the Capitol building as everyone went home. The President stood there, waiting until the last person had left. Soon it was just the two state troopers, Andy and her. She smiled, turned, and walked back up the steps.

"Come on, Ranger Jackson. I'm going to grab my briefcase, then go home, get some sleep. You need to do the same. And apologize to your wife. I didn't mean to keep you so late."

Andy looked at her. "Ma'am. Has anyone told you lately that you are one hell of a human being?"

She stopped. Then, she hugged him. "Coming from you, that means a lot. Thank you." She let go of her bodyguard. "Come on. Tomorrow is going to be one hell of a busy day.

The President of the United States did not even know the half of it. At first light, people began to line up at anything that even remotely looked like a recruiting or government office. Former hidden veterans came out of the shadows, confident now that there was a chance to begin the fight anew.

Draft boards? Not even needed now. Everyone volunteered to help, somehow, somewhere. The dam had broken. A flood had been released, a huge wave created.

On the receiving end would be the Tschaaa and their minions.

CHAPTER 16

Commissioner Paul Miller maneuvered the SUV up the semi-improved road toward the Munsen homestead and smithy. The Munsens were located some five miles outside of Great Falls, off an older county road. He glanced over at the person in the front passenger seat.

Brynhildr Jorgensen, new Federal Law Enforcement Special Agent, was sitting confidently next to him. She did everything confidently. Nothing seemed to phase her. Throw a problem at her, and you had better watch out, she might just hit a line drive right back at you. Paul Miller thanked the gods of law enforcement that he had stumbled upon her and convinced her to come work for him.

About two days after the Raid (everyone now knew the first one as The Raid, although the Director had hit a couple of similar sites already), Brynhildr had shown up at his office, an older, rather scruffy gentleman in tow.

Paul had maybe five hours of sleep under his belt, as he and others sifted through all the information—files, samples, and papers—they had collected at the compound. His burning need to find any other sites of such depravity was at him like an ulcer. He worried even that he was developing one, based on his continual sour stomach.

Brynhildr had shown up in what appeared to be a tailored business pants suit that fit her perfectly in all the right places. Just an inch under six feet, broad shoulders, walking with an air of confidence, people stepped aside as she neared the Commissioner's office. The fact that she was built like the proverbial brick outhouse did much to impress the men in the office. Paul had told his people that someone of Brynhildr's description might be by, to just send her in when she showed up. And here she was. With what was soon be identified as a present in tow.

She knocked on his door, and stood, waiting for him to tell her to enter. "It has been two days, as you said, Commissioner. I've brought someone who may have information you might find interesting."

Paul came from around his desk, thrust his hand out for a shake. "You definitely don't beat around the bush, Miss Jorgensen." He shook her hand, then stuck it out to the older man. "Commissioner Paul Miller, at your service. Mister…"

"Peters, sir. John Peters. Brynhildr came by, thought I would know something."

"Well, what about, Mr. Peters?" At this the older man hesitated, looked away. Then Brynhildr cleared her throat rather loudly, causing him to jerk and glance nervou at her. Paul could tell her look was one of "Don't you dare back out now."

"I live…several miles outside of Great Falls. I have a small farm. The road that runs by my place continues on up to another farm. That one was vacant until….about a month ago." He began to shake, then burst out. "I don't want any trouble. I'm just trying to support a family. Daughters with dead husbands, kids—they need a place to live, food to eat."

Paul went to his desk, pulled out a bottle of Scotch and three glasses. He quickly poured a drink into one, which he handed to Mr. Peters. "Here. Try this. And I can tell you that any information you give me will be worth some funds, money for your trouble. That is, if it is what I think it is."

Peters slugged the drink down. Paul refilled it, leaned back on his desk, and motioned the man to sit down.

He looked at the farmer. "Scared, aren't you? Someone

threatened you."

Mr. Peters looked down. "If it were just me, I'd tell them to go fuck themselves. Excuse my language Ma'am. But I have young ones staying with me. Like the ones on the tv." He drank some more scotch.

"Please give me your hand, Mr. Peters." The farmer complied. "I hereby give you my solemn word that you will be protected, even if I have to get General Reed to loan me a platoon of those Russians that we have bouncing around. But, I need to know. It's a bunch of Krakens, with another compound. Right?"

Peters nodded his head yes. "There's been a bunch of large trucks the last week or so. And this note in my mailbox." The man handed an envelope to the Commissioner. In it was a note that simple said "We are watching you." A Kraken symbol was in the area a signature would be.

Paul looked at Brynhildr. "They're still there, aren't they?"

"Yes, Commissioner. Checked it myself."

"The same?"

She sighed. "Yes. Unfortunately, the same."

Paul went back to his desk, unlocked a drawer with a combination lock, and pulled out a form and an envelope.

"Here. Ten thousand bucks are in that envelope. Get you family out of there. Brynhildr, can a few of your people…"

"Already taken care of. People will think his friends and family are visiting. Just a bunch of square heads. No threat." At that remark, Paul smiled. Yeah, right. No threat. Just some crazy Vikings.

"Please sign this. Payment for information. The first of others, if this pans out. Now, please wait here. I'll need someone to take a formal statement…" Brynhildr magically pulled some papers from a small briefcase that Paul noticed for the first time.

"Already taken care of, Commissioner. And here is a draft for a Search Warrant."

Paul scanned the statement. He chuckled. "Well. Special Agent Brynhildr Jorgensen, I guess you work for me know."

She smiled at him. "Yes sir, I guess I do."

Paul went to his telephone, and called his information center.

"Initiate a recall. All tactical teams. We have another pit."

The rest had been pretty quick. Paul Miller obtained an Emergency Presidential Warrant, something they had come up with for the duration of the next year with a strong sunset date. Until everything was set up and working like it used to in the old U.S.A, the Court System was too small to handle a lot of Emergency Search Warrants. So, for one year, starting about four months prior, a Special Executive Branch Warrant was created to handle situations like this, where the Tschaaa and Krakens were involved. The Commissioner had a Night Time Exigent Circumstances Warrant that he could serve this night. At the sunset date, it disappeared, with the law written to prevent another such law for a period of one year. No more expanding Patriot Acts or such, with no one really knowing the details.

With the help of a General Reed provided A-10 and an attack chopper (courtesy of the Russians) as well as a Cadillac Gage Commando Armored Car with three men and a 50 Caliber, the Commissioner had more than enough fire support for his fifty armed personnel to serve the search warrant. Brynhildr went in after he had come up with some credentials and I.D. for her, including a brand new badge. He wanted someone with experienced eyes who knew what to look for when it came to the creatures and equipment. Paul stayed back, overseeing everything. Let the young people get the thrills. He had seen enough on the last Raid to last him for a lifetime.

It went a lot faster and smoother. A large semi truck smashed through the main gate this time, followed by a bunch of gun carriers. It resulted in six dead tattooed Krakens, several captured hangers-on. Only one monster was released, a huge boar like creature that took about thirty rounds before it went down. Another dozen were found still locked up, including a huge cat-like creature that looked like it started out as a Bengal tiger. It took a while, but sufficient tranquilizers were found to sedate all the creatures. A section of the Bismarck Zoo, long empty, was used to secure the surviving creatures for study. Oddly, only a couple of the monsters had been "wired up", which probably was the reason the agents hadn't faced an onslaught similar to the original Raid. Now, there were enough specimens to keep a team of zoologists and biologists busy for months if not years.

After that, it had been a crazy couple of weeks.

Now, they were headed to the Munsen spread to check on the young Raid survivors as well as for the Commissioner to pay some penance. It was coming up on ten o'clock in the morning. This same evening, a formal memorial service was finally going to be held for the two agents and three young ones who had died. Following that, an awards ceremony, stretching all the way back to the original Eater attack on the Bender-Smirnov household.

As they neared the residence, Paul asked Brynhildr a question."You never did tell me where you obtained that hidden law enforcement training you sprung on me that first day you came in."

Brynhildr gave a small smile. "During the Long Winter, I read a lot. There wasn't much else to do other than try to stay warm, and not eat much. My uncle had been a Federal Agent years back. He kept all his manuals, books. I read them, watched some discs when we had power available. I have a good memory."

Paul chuckled. "I was sandbagged. That hasn't happened very often."

"Well, Commissioner, you're the one that offered me a job, few questions asked."

Paul turned his head just enough to be heard easily by the person in the back seat of the SUV.

"Emily, are the chicks and turkeys doing okay?"

Doctor Anders, local vet extraordinaire, answered back, "Just fine, Paul. Bruno and I are keeping a good eye on them."

Emily had been working overtime, helping the Commissioner with the examinations of the mutant creatures developed from Earth species. She had been especially helpful in getting the old zoo back up and running, in order to have a place in which to store the creatures. Emily had said the large Bengal Tiger creature may have originally come from the zoo, as many zoo animals were cut loose by well-meaning handlers when the Squids began tearing things apart. One species released from captivity that had fared well in the Long Winter were the buffalos.American Bison were allowed to roam free on the Central Plains one again. Two large herds now moved back and forth from the Canadian border all the way down to Texas, and the Gulf of Mexico. Without man slaughtering them, they were making a huge comeback.

Due to circumstance, Paul and Emily had been spending a lot of time together. Which was fine by Paul. She definitely brightened things up. So when Paul had mentioned he wanted to visit the five young survivors, as they were being called, Emily had asked if she could come along. Paul readily agreed. With Bruno, the pit bull fighter rescue, tagging along as requested by Emily. He had trouble leaving the vet's side, ever since Abigail and Emily had taken him from Baker, the former scavenger, and now prisoner in maximum segregation.

Brynhildr was the go-between, the Munsens being part of her Nordic community. Paul quickly discovered that, among all the others things the young woman had been doing, she had also been visiting, keeping track of how the five young girls/ladies were faring. So, here they all were, at the entrance gate to the Munsen Farm and smithy.

The gate was open, so Paul slowly drove through. Some one hundred yards up, he stopped the SUV in the turnaround in front of the house. About fifty yards off to his left was the blacksmith shop and forge, where Johann Munsen—Uncle Johann—worked his metal magic. The Commissioner had done some checking after Johann had taken the five youngsters, just to be on the safe side. Years of law enforcement had made him a bit cautious about people who seemed too good to be true. But Johann and his wife Freda were definitely proverbial pillars of the community. And Johann, besides shoeing horses, could do wonders with a piece of steel or iron. Need a plow fixed? He was your man. A blade of some kind? Ditto. In fact, Johann had made some replacement barrels for some local's hunting rifles that the owners claimed were better than the originals.

He parked the SUV, and everyone exited the vehicle, Bruno the pit bull mix staying close to Emily. Immediately a strong looking but rather short woman came to the front porch. The visitors had kept their parka hoods back so that their faces could be seen, the outside temperature hovering below freezing necessitating warm clothes. Paul recognized the woman from some photos he had obtained as Freda, the matriarch of the Munsen clan.

She broke into a wide smile when she saw Brynhildr, calling out a greeting in apparent Norwegian which Brynhildr answered with the same pleasure at meeting. Paul knew he would have to learn some Nordic language, as the push for the old ways meant that Norwegian, Swedish, Danish, German—you name it—were being used more and more on a daily basis with the increase of immigration from former

Minnesota, Wisconsin, and parts of Canada. He had good information that small groups had made it all the way from Europe in the past couple of years. A Free America, even if abbreviated, had a strong pull.

Freda was dressed in a long dress, belted, with long sleeves and warm leggings underneath. Good fur lined boots protected her feet from the snow, as she crouched down off the porch to hug Brynhildr. After her greeting of the fellow community member, she turned to greet the others with an equally big smile.

"I recognize you, Commissioner Miller, from the news. And Brynhildr has told me all about you, Doctor Anders. Welcome. Come in. Can I offer you warm cider, some mead, orale?"

Paul approached Freda and went to shake her hand, which turned into a hug and a kiss on his cheek. She did the same to Emily.

"I hope whatever Brynhildr told you was nice. I can be a real pain sometimes," Emily said.

"Come now, doctor. You helped save my new little ones. What could possibly be bad about that?"

Just then, four young girls, ages ten to fourteen, all came out on the porch to see the visitors. Paul had trouble believing they were the same girls that had been rescued some two weeks ago. Long dresses, leggings and boots like Freda, hair braided in long pigtails, washed and alert, they beamed good health. They came out giggling, in a rush, and were stopped in their tracks by Freda.

"Young ladies, let's not forget what I have taught you. How do we greet visitors?"

Suddenly, all four lined up, then curtsied as one, saying in Norwegian a greeting that translated as, "Welcome, gentleman and ladies. May we offer you a warm fire, a warm drink, friendly conversation?"

Paul stood quietly for a moment, a little stunned. They acted as if they had grown up here, that the horrible experiences of the past months had never happened. Well fed, well groomed, well cared for, they were bouncing back with a vigor which Paul had not thought possible. Not after seeing their dirty, bruised, scratched and naked bodies at the Compound that night.

"Mrs. Munsen, please accept my wholehearted thanks and praise for the way you have taken care of these four young ladies. This is a hundred and eighty degree change from two weeks ago."

Freda stepped up, and grabbed his arm. "Come, Commissioner, I have not done anything special. Anyone here would have done the same. Come in and we will fix you all some warm drinks. Mead, heated ale, hot cider I can easily offer all of you. I may be able to find some tea and coffee. I am sure these young ladies can find some of the cookies and pastries we have been making for the memorial service." With the last statement, the four girls began quietly talking to each other, then, one after another, went quickly into the homestead.

"Ma'am. Whatever you have that is non-alcoholic. I am still on-duty."

"I am also," Brynhildr interjected.

"I'll take whatever is easiest for you, Ma'am," Emily added.

"Well, come on in then. And call me Freda, please."

"Only if you call me Paul."

Freda giggled a bit, letting them know she was still young at heart. "Alright, it's a deal. Now, inside where it is warm. Please feel free to bring in your dog, doctor. I can tell he's rather attached to you."

Paul paused for a moment, looking around. "I counted four youngsters. There is a fifth, the oldest, Hannah Weitz. Is she here?"

"Oh, my poor manners. Of course she is. She is out helping my Johann in the forge. Here, I will call for her." Freda stuck two fingers in her mouth and let out a loud, shrill, unladylike whistle.

A moment later, her husband Johann stepped out from the blacksmith shop. "Yes, Mother," His voice boomed.

"Visitors for Hannah. Please get her."

He waved affirmatively, turned to talk to someone in the shadows. A few moments later, a raven haired young lady stepped out. With a long dress, leggings and boots like the other females, she was also clad in a heavy leather protective apron like Johann. Her long raven hair was tied up into a bun with a scarf over it. She was removing some thick gloves as she approached, began to smile as she recognized the visitors. She called a greeting in Norwegian, to which Brynhildr responded. Again Paul felt a little bit like a clod. Five youngsters were learning a second language in a matter of days, and he still had trouble remembering his Border Patrol Spanish, all four months of it.

Hannah walked with a confidence and strength the Commissioner would have not thought possible after what she had been through. Hannah was seventeen, the oldest of the captives, and had survived some two years of life in the pits. Of all of the survivors, she was able to give within a day of their rescue very detailed statements of what she and the others had suffered at the hands of the Kraken. Paul still felt a pang of guilt having to send agents and medical staff out with in twenty-four hours to take rape kits, examinations of the five young victims. But sometimes, command decisions were not pleasant. The guilt he felt was a big reason for him to be here.

Brynhildr and Hannah met a few yards from the porch, hugging each other. Brynhildr, an inch shy of six feet, was large, some five inches taller than Hannah. But even up against her, Paul could see Hannah was definitely filling out. Her shoulders were broader than he remembered. Her arms, even covered, looked strong as she hugged her dear friend.

There was an unexpected loud whining and Bruno, brown-colored pit bull mix, made a beeline toward Hannah. His ears were back, he was wriggling and twisting his body as if he was in the throes of some strong emotional event. Which he was.

 Hannah, seeing the dog, kneeled down. "I know you," she called out as she was quickly on the receiving end of some very passionate doggy kisses, Bruno pushing and rubbing up against her as if he were trying to become one with her. Hannah hugged him back, rubbing his body, scratching his ears as tears began to run down her face.

Emily had started forward when she noticed Bruno reacting. She knew by his body language the dog was no threat to Hannah as he approached her. But she was very puzzled by his reaction after apparently recognizing Hannah's scent. Then it dawned on her.

 The vet walked slowly up to the re-acquaintance activity and quietly spoke. "You and Bruno met in… the pits."

Hannah looked up with wet eyes, but with a big smile on her face."Yes, Ma'am. We are both survivors. We even slept together a few times. Then he disappeared. I thought he was dead."

Emily knelt as the other adults looked on. "I think he wants to be with you. I think you are his human." She looked at Johann who had walked up, pulling his thick gloves off. Before she could speak, Johann did.

"I can tell this large hound will not be happy about leaving you. And I can tell, Hannah, that it is the same with you leaving him." The big man paused for a moment.

"Think he can be taught to guard livestock? Those damned coyotes and raccoons are killing off my chickens and geese. I could use another dog since ours died."

"Yes, Uncle Johann. I can get him to do that."

"Good. It is settled." He looked at Emily. "I take it you are in agreement with this?"

Emily stood up. "Shake." She stuck her hand out. Johann took it, a slight quizzical look suddenly on his face.

"Congratulations. You just adopted, and Hannah was just adopted by, Bruno, pit bull mix. I warn you, I will check back to make sure he is being treated right. I take my veterinarian duties very seriously. As a former patient of mine, I'll always be looking out for him."

Johann gave a wry smile. "I knew when I met you on the Raid that you were a force to be reckoned with. Any woman who tries to rescue and help creatures like the ones we killed that night... you are one with much honor. I give you my word I will insure this dog is well taken care of."

Hannah stood up and gave Emily a huge hug. "Oof. Easy on the ribs, dear. What have you been doing, Hannah, weightlifting?"

"Next best thing, doctor, Working with metal," Johann answered for her.

Emily looked at the young lady, still a girl in many ways. "You like that, Hannah? Kind of hot, sweaty and dirty."

Hannah showed a small smile. "I have been hot, sweaty, and dirty many times over the past couple of years. Working with the forge, shaping iron, steel... it may look dirty but steel is clean. It has a clean strength, formed from clean heat, fire. Steel is honest, does not betray you if you work it right. And steel gives you strength with which to resist your enemies, those who wish to harm you." Hannah paused, her demeanor now serious. "I will never be without steel again."

Paul Miller saw, once again, the results of the sins that the Tschaaa had visited on humanity. It was bad enough when humankind just tried to deal with its own members. Now, these aliens seemed to accentuate everything that was bad with the human species, gave it additional tools and reasons to abuse fellow men and women even more. As if they needed that.

For the umpteenth time, a person just leaving childhood behind had to deal with violence, horror, death on a daily basis. The universe was definitely not fair.

"She works as hard as any two grown men," Johann interjected. "She is the best assistant I have had in years. That includes my own sons."

"Now, Uncle Johann," Hannah protested. "You are exaggerating."

"What, I, Johann, exaggerate? When have I ever done that?"

"Poppa, you must be joking," Freda broke in.

"Now, Momma..."

"Husband, you are well known for what you call your storytelling over a mug of mead or ale."

Johann displayed his best sheepish look. Freda strode up and hugged him, and he bent over and kissed her. "Without my wife, I would be a lost puppy. She keeps me grounded, and out of trouble. Well, usually."

With that, the young girl called Jewel, one of the two ten-year-olds that Johann had personally rescued from the semi-trailer, came back to the porch.

"Please, Aunt Freda, Uncle Johann, our welcomed guests. The drinks and snacks are ready." When Paul looked at young Jewel, it was hard to remember the naked, dirty, bruised and scratched little girl they had found cowering in the trailer. Bright, healthy, and cheerful, Aunt Freda and Uncle Johann had worked a miracle. Five, to be exact.

"Before we go in, could I have some help for a moment? I brought you two free range live turkeys, six Bantam chicks, and some rice and flour. With Thanksgiving coming, I thought you could use help feeding these additions to your family."

Suddenly, Johann looked stern. "Commissioner, with respect, we need no government hand out, and expect none. We took these five fine young ladies into our home because it is the right thing to do. We don't ask for assistance."

"Poppa. Don't be so pig-headed." With that they began to argue in Norwegian. Now it was Paul's turn to interrupt.

"Excuse me." He spoke rather loudly and with authority. The couple stopped arguing, turned and looked at him. "The items and fowl I have brought are bought with my funds, the government has nothing to do with it. I ask you to accept it in behalf of our five survivors. It is offered as atonement, penance on my part."

"Why?" Hannah blurted out. "You helped save us."

"Because, my beautiful young lady, I should have known what was going on in my own backyard. All of the signs of Kraken shenanigans, criminal acts were floating around for quite some time and I did not put the facts together. Because of that, I have at least three dead children on my conscience. I don't like that. So, I owe you survivors. At least take the items in the name of the three who did not make it."

Everyone was silent. Hannah broke the spell by walking up to the Commissioner and putting a hug on him like she had done to Emily.

"Oof. You are strong." And Hannah began to quietly cry.

"Come on now. I don't do well with girls, women crying. Especially when I cause it." Hannah held on tight, refusing to let go. Paul began to stroke her hair as he used to do with his own children when they were upset. Brynhildr quietly walked up, spoke something softly into Hannah's ear in Norwegian. With that, Hannah looked into Paul's face.

"Commissioner, please. Never, ever claim fault for what happened. The fault, guilt lies with the Krakens, the Squids, and all those evil ones. You and the others who showed up that night. You were our saviors. You'll always be in our prayers." She turned her head then toward Johann. "Uncle…"

"Ach, say no more child," Johann replied. "Once again, my wife and the other women folk are right. I'm much too hard-headed and stubborn, for my own good. I think it must be from being kicked in the head by all those horses I was shoeing."

Freda huffed once. "My love, you were hard-headed and stubborn from the first day I met you. Twenty-five years later, little has changed."

"Well, my loving wife, had I not been so stubborn, you would have run me off, married the Olson boy."

"I would not have. You exaggerate once again…" and they began again to kvetch at each other.

Brynhildr broke in. "Please. I have my mouth ready for some hot cider and cookies. Can you continue this discussion some other time?"

With that, the married couple laughed, then hugged and kissed. Johann let go of his wife and strode over to Paul, his hand outstretched. Hannah moved aside, and Paul took the very large hand into his. "Accept my apology, please Commissioner. I am not used to having government officials actually try to help me. They have been absent for almost six years. I'm used to doing things on my own."

"No apology necessary. And please call me Paul. As Major Bender says, once you have faced death together, you're on first name basis with each other."

"Then you must call me Johann. Good. That is settled. Mother, can you help me find a place for the new livestock?" And with that, they began to move the turkeys to a nearby pen, took the chicks into the house so that the four younger girls could see them, hold them. Nothing like soft little baby chicks to make kids happy.

An hour later, Paul, Emily and Brynhildr were finishing up hot cider, cookies and pastries. The five young ladies were sitting next to them at the table. The four younger ones, ages nine to fourteen, liked to sit close to the three visiting adults, holding onto their arms, liked the secure human contact with people they associated with rescue. Hannah, some seventeen years old by her count, was a bit more reserved. But she still had a beaming smile that often flashed during the hour long conversation.

Hannah then looked at the clock. "I am sorry, but I must excuse myself. I have just a little bit more work to do on a project I am doing for the memorial service tonight."

Johann, frowned a bit, but then motioned for her to go.

Freda spoke as she got up to leave. "Please leave yourself enough time to clean yourself up for this evening. I want no blacksmith soot on the dress and jacket we have made for you to wear."

"Yes, Ma'am." Hannah then went to each of the visitors, curtsied, and then gave them all a quick hug. When she swiftly departed for the forge, Bruno automatically followed her, having been snuck some goodies by Paul and Emily when no one was paying attention. Freda looked at her husband after the young lady had departed.

"Poppa, please do not work her so much. She needs to learn more kindly pursuits."

"Me work her? She is the one that is always pushing to do more.

Hannah has caught on so fast, is constantly finding new things to work on, that I am always trying to keep up with her. When I said she did the work of two normal men, I was not exaggerating."

Paul looked at the large man. "Sir, I know she's about the age of majority, can vote when she hits eighteen, but I wish she had more time to be a regular teenager."

"Is there such a thing anymore, Commissioner?" Brynhildr interjected. "The Tschaaa have changed everyone's life."

"I know, Paul. My wife and I try to give all these fine young girl-children a resemblance of how we were raised. And as you can see, they are turning out just fine. I'm as proud of them as if they were my blood."

"We are survivors, Uncle," Jewel broke in. "We have not forgotten what has happened. But you and Auntie are giving us so much love..." Her eyes began to tear up. Emily, sitting beside her, reached over and hugged her. Jewel returned the hug, now smiling. Emily kissed her forehead, then spoke.

"Johann, Freda, you both deserve medals. Hopefully no one from the State Child Protective Services will give you any grief for taking all five under your wings."

"They won't," stated Paul.

Johann and Freda both looked at the Commissioner, the unspoken question of how he knew that hung in the air. Paul Miller smiled a bit. "Sometimes being at the beck and call of the President has its benefits. Especially when communication is a two-way street. Madam President sent CPS an email, then a letter with a Presidential Seal stating that she considers these five young survivors as Special Wards of the U.S. Government. Yes, once all the courts are up and running, someone could try an end run. But right now, especially after the response to the broadcast, no one is going to buck her. Everyone knows now she was right all along about us not being forgotten by the Squids and their followers. What happened here in Great Falls was years in the making."

The four girls could understand what he was saying, and knew now that their future with Uncle Johann and Aunt Freda were secure. In a quick motion, they were all clustered around Paul, all tried to hug him at the same time. The Commissioner protested. "Hey, it was the President that set this up, not me. Thank her tonight when you see her. She wants to talk with all of you."

Freda's eyes widened a bit, then she clapped her hands. "Children. Come, quick, we must clean up. Then, we have to make sure all of you are washed and dressed correctly for meeting with the President. She must see her decision was the correct one. So, let us get to work."

Paul and Emily tried to help clean up, but they were just in the way of the whirlwind of activity. Already, Freda Munsen had everyone organized, efficiently doing what need to be done. Emily and Paul retreated to the porch, putting their parkas back on. As they stood on the porch, Emily grabbed Paul's arm, looping hers around his.

"Commissioner Paul Miller, did anyone ever tell you how nice a man you are?"

"Quit it. I'll get a swelled head."

"Would you go on a date with me?" Emily asked. Paul sputtered a bit, all of a sudden out of his element.

"If you say no, of my canine friends and I will be very displeased. They may pee on your feet the next time you come to my clinic."

"Emily, I am not exactly a spring chicken…"

"And neither am I. Now, speaking of chickens, are you going to chicken out? I asked you for a date. You should be used to women taking non-traditional approaches."

He looked into Emily's eyes. He then realized just how much he enjoyed her company. "Yes, Emily, I'll go on a date with you. Though I am horribly out of practice. And we will have to work it around our work schedules."

"Of course. Good." Emily squeezed his arm. "Now, let me say goodbye to Bruno. I'm going to miss having him following me around everywhere. But he and Hannah belong together."

He watched the vet walk toward the forge and smithy building. Not for the first time did he notice how attractive she was. And smiled. Everyone needs a bit of fun and affection in their lives. Maybe this was his chance.

The memorial ceremony for three dead children was to begin at 6:00pm in the large auditorium on Malmstrom Base. The two agents killed had already been buried by friends and family, so tonight would be a remembrance. But for the three dead youngsters, it would be a funeral. They had held off on a burial for two weeks, tried against hope to find some friend or family who knew who they were. Paul Miller had their first names from the survivors—June, David and Cheryl. That was it. Ages were only approximate based on the autopsies and examinations. They all appeared to be caucasian. No identifiable marks, other than scars from the abuse they had suffered.

Three coffins were donated by the local funeral parlors, as were cremation services. It was decided that, not knowing if the Squids and Krakens had tried to inject them with any foreign bugs, it was better to err on the side of caution and cremate them, destroying any chance of the spread of some weird disease.

After the memorial/funeral, there would be an awards ceremony and then an interview by a certain broadcaster. Which was the reason Alesha Taylor was there an hour early. She had to prepare the two special recipients.

The dependent wife, Mrs. Brown, had been easy. After telling her the exact questions she would be asked and letting her know how great she looked in the new dress she had gotten, Sue Brown had finally calmed down a bit. "I'm sorry Ma'am," the young wife said. "I've never been on television before. I don't want to make a fool of myself, and embarrass my husband."

"This from a woman who tried to take on Eaters barehanded? Come on."

She blushed. "I just did what anybody would do, I tried to help. Fuzz did all the hard work, fighting those Eaters."

With the mention of the dog, Alesha felt a quick stab of fear that she quickly suppressed. She needed to get through this night, get by this fear. Then she planned on getting a bit smashed.

"You'll do just fine." She flashed her best smile at the woman, then sent her to back to her waiting husband. Alesha took a deep breath. Now, she had to meet the war dog.

She walked to the back of the stage and waited. Almost immediately, she heard the sound of human footsteps, and the sound of a dog snuffling a bit as it checked out all the new smells. Captain Abigail Young, resplendent in her dress blues, came with a very large dog at her side. Sergeant Fuzz, K-9 War Dog. He was now rapidly becoming a national symbol, a hero. Lassie, Rin Tin Tin, every Hollywood dog hero rolled into one, in the flesh. Alesha tried to take a step forward and froze. Waves of fear she had not known still existed froze her like a statute as Captain Young, seeing her, came forward with a smile and her hand extended. Then she saw the look of abject fear in Alesha's eyes as the broadcaster fixed her gaze entirely on Fuzz.

"Fuzz, halt. Sit." She gave the commands in English, so that Alesha could understand. Fuzz responded as if it were Romanian, being bilingual. Abigail slowly stepped up to Alesha.

"You are deathly afraid of dogs, aren't you?"

Somehow, Alesha croaked out, "Yes."

Abigail smiled a bit. "Well, Fuzz is not a dog. He is just a big teddy bear in disguise. See, I'll show you." With a couple of quick commands, Fuzz stood up, took a step forward. He then laid down, rolled over on to his back, legs up and sprayed out, his tongue lolling out the side of his mouth. He did not move.

"That's his 'dead bug' impression. Major Bender helped develop it." She took Alesha's hand, slowly lead her forward. The black woman began to shake.

"It's okay, Ma'am. I've got complete control. Now just kneel down, and I'll let you see how soft Fuzz's teddy bear fur is."

Somehow, Alesha let Abigail guide her hand toward Fuzz's chest. "Scratch, here, and here. That's it."

Alesha scratched the soft chest and stomach fur of the canine. And of course, thanks to thousands of years of relations with mankind, Fuzz's right rear leg began to jerk and kick a bit as he let out little grunts and sighs of doggy pleasure.

"See, he likes that."

Alesha kept scratching, as a tear ran down her cheek.

"Were you bitten once?" Abigail asked.

"Chased and tracked. I heard my relatives get dragged down," Alesha answered, her voice quavering.

"Well, dogs are shaped by the people around them. So there are good ones and bad ones. Just like us."

Alesha was shaking a bit, so Abigail decided to try something else. "So, Ma'am, go ahead and stop scratching. Now, go ahead and sit back a bit while I reposition Fuzz."

Alesha was wearing a nice pants suit so she sat back cross legged. Slowly, Abigail had Fuzz rise up, and move to the broadcaster's right side. She then gently took Alesha's right arm and placed it around the canine's neck.

"Go ahead. Hug him like he is a person. He is, you know. He just has four legs instead of two."

Alesha slowly, cautiously followed Abigail's directions. Later she would think about how trusting she was of this stranger. After all, she knew Abigail Young only by reputation. As she began to hug Fuzz with one arm, Abigail took her left arm and had it join her right, slightly turning her body. Before she knew it, Alesha was feeling Fuzz's soft, warm fur on her cheek. Fuzz began to laugh in the slight huffing manner dogs do that often goes unnoticed by humans. At that, Fuzz's tongue lolling with pleasure from his mouth, Alesha began to gently sob. Fuzz, realizing this nice lady was sad, did what dogs did with sad humans. He gave her a doggy kiss, a lick, then another as he tried to lick her tears away.

"Sorry about your makeup Ma'am. Fuzz loves to give women doggy kisses. He is quite the ladies man."

Alesha began to hug Fuzz a bit tighter. She had not realized how much she had missed the feel of a teddy bear like large creature. She had blocked out all her childhood experiences with dogs after the near fatal escape of her mother and her. Now, these memories all came rushing back. The memories of warm fur, happy barks, rolling around on grass as a family dog licked and nuzzled her. She buried her face into the furry shoulder of Fuzz, feeling the muscles underneath.

Finally, Alesha let go, leaning back a bit. Abigail had Fuzz sit in front of Alesha, so they could easily see each other. The pretty black lady wiped her face with her hands, then smiled. "My makeup is trashed. Some of it's on Fuzz. Sorry."

Abigail smiled. "No need to apologize. Like I said, Fuzz is a ladies man. He's used to getting makeup on him."

Fuzz extended the Paw of Friendship. Alesha took it, and shook it. Then, she leaned forward and kissed him on the nose. He caught her with a quick slurp before she could back out. Alesha giggled.

"I feel like a little girl again, on a summer afternoon. I grew up with dogs. I have just blocked almost all my memories out since my mother and I escaped." She paused. "My mother had to kill one with a knife she had as we fled from the main group. It was going after me when she jumped in front, let it bite her." She shivered. "As we ran, we could hear the screams of the others as the dogs and assholes got them. Some were my cousins. We haven't seen a family member since."

She looked at Abigail. "Thank you and Fuzz for helping me recover some pleasant memories, the summers I had with dogs before the Squids showed up. I have forgotten how nice it is to hug a furry dog, get licked in the face. Unconditional love from a dog is something I've completely missed due to my fear. Now, I can think about having a dog in my life, and my mom's life."

Abigail looked at Fuzz. Then, she spoke to him in Romanian, touching Alesha to draw his attention to the woman even more. Whatever Abigail said, he seemed to understand it. "What did you tell him? And is that Romanian? I had heard that you talked to him in Romanian."

"Yes, it is Romanian. Someone, possibly connected to my uncle the dog trainer at one time, trained him in Romanian. Sometimes it helps when other people can't tell what you are saying. When I speak Romanian to him, he knows it is serious."

"So, if I can be nosey, what did you say?"

"I told him that he needed to guard you. To protect. You are now one of a handful of people he has filed away as being worthy of protection. Which means he will kill for you. Not to be taken lightly."

Alesha shivered. "Is that what he was doing when the Eaters tried to get to Major Smirnov?"

Abigail gave a wry smile. "Yes. Though some of that is because she was pregnant. He thinks of it as with pups, so he is protecting future members of "his" pack. See, we belong to him. He only listens to me because he loves me. And I love him."

Alesha snorted. "That's like a lot of men. Other than the one woman they love, the rest of us are just so much window dressing. And sometimes that one woman is treated like window dressing."

The two women chuckled a bit. Then. Alesha stood up. "I need to get cleaned up. This whole shebang is going to be televised. Afterwards, I interview Mrs. Brown, then you and Fuzz. I don't think you'll need any preparation. You seem able to handle almost anything."

"Well, I'd not go that far. Warrior related things I'm good at. With other subjects and activities not warrior-related I have gaps and blind spots. Including social activities with men. How men and women are supposed to act around each other away from military operations or fighting still confuses me."

Alesha laughed. "Lady, it confuses everyone. Especially when we have Squids trying to screw with our hormones and DNA, at the same time as we are in danger of being eaten by them."

Alesha stuck her hand out. "You'll do just fine. Just wait after the memorial and award services by the stage entrance. My producer will let you know when to come up for the Interview. We'll wait until people are leaving, then do the interviews with the backdrop of the ceremonial area. Seeing that big U.S. flag behind us as we talk will focus the audience on what the story we are trying to tell."

Abigail looked a bit puzzled as she shook the proffered hand, "What story is that, Ma'am?"

"It's Alesha. Ma'am is my mom. The story is that no matter what the Squids and their minions throw at us, we'll bounce back. Because of people like Mrs. Brown and yourself. And people like Fuzz there. The bastards cannot keep us down."

Alesha introduced Abigail to her Producer, Patty Lindstrom, a middle-aged stocky brunette with soon to be permanent facial worry lines. As Patty walked Abigail and Fuzz back toward the seating area, Abigail noticed in passing some workmen bringing equipment into the auditorium. She started to answer some background question that the Producer had just asked when Fuzz topped and stood stock still. Abigail stopped and looked to where Fuzz was looking, his nose working furiously. A low growl began in his chest, the sound that his action engine was revving up. Abigail quickly stepped up and touched his collar.

"What is it, Fuzz?" Now noticing his human was with him, he began to walked purposefully toward where the workmen was unloading large boxes and pieces of equipment.

"Excuse me, Ma'am," Abigail threw over her shoulder to the Producer as she went with Fuzz.

Two of the men had just finished manhandling a very large box from the back of an electric moving cart. Though made of thick cardboard, the bottom had been reinforced with wooden slats. Fuzz was agitated and went straight to the box, growling.

"Hey lady, watch your dog." A greasy-looking skinny man called at her.

"What's in the box, gentlemen," Abigail asked with a smile.

"None of your fricking business." This came from a stockier, taller man.

"No need to be rude. It's just that my dog senses something… wrong." Fuzz, heard the aggressive tones of the two men and tried to keep an eye on them and the box.

"Well, it's just equipment for this ceremony. Don't ask me exactly, I'm just paid to de…."

Something in the box moved, shaking the box. Fuzz went nuts, growling, barking and circling.

"Equipment doesn't move…" Abigail did not have the chance to add 'on its own' as the taller man slashed at her with a box cutter. He didn't stand a chance. Before he realized it, he was down on the floor with a broken wrist and dislocated elbow, screaming. The skinny man tried to run and draw a pistol at the same time. He made about two strides when Fuzz slammed into him. The K-9 probably weighed as much the skinny man and had more muscle. The result was the man was slammed into the wall next to the double loading area door, the pistol he was pulling knocked from his grasp. He screamed as Fuzz sunk his teeth into the man's groin, the canine jerking and twisting his head. The war dog released and the man slumped to the floor, still screaming.

Then there were many Military Police with assault rifles around everywhere. They recognized Abigail, as they had all trained with her and Torbin. "Captain Young. What is going on here?" The NCO in command asked as his men covered and then began to restrain the two injured men.

"There is something alive in that box they don't want anyone to see. They tried to pull a box cutter and a pistol on Fuzz and I."

Sergeant Renfro, a tall redhead, laughed. "Didn't know you, did they?"

"I guess not, but the box is still moving." Whatever was in the box was now becoming agitated also. Then Abigail heard a cry and almost scream that she had heard many times before.

"Eater. It's an Eater!"

"Shotgun!" Sgt. Renfro commanded. An E-3 stepped up with a buckshot loaded 12 gauge pump. He pointed at the box just as a claw began ripping the side of the box open. Two point blank rounds stopped the escape attempt of the Eater. By now, everyone in the world was showing up. The President was to arrive at any time. She couldn't if things were not secure. Not to mention all the people who would be in attendance.

The Military Police checked every single box after locking down the area. A Hazmat team showed up, wrapped up the Eater containing box with heavy duty plastic and then removed it. Alesha and her Producer Patty were shuffled off to the side as all this was being done, and watched. Fuzz, not trusting the humans' noses, checked every single box with his nose, then walked over to stand with Abigail.

"Good dog, big fella. Everyone missed that. But not you." She scratched his ears, and Fuzz grunted in appreciation. Then she turned her head and noticed Alesha and Patty standing, a large MP in full battle rattle next to them. She turned and walked toward the two women, Fuzz automatically in tow.

The MP snapped to attention, and saluted. "Good afternoon, Captain Young."

"Good Afternoon, Corporal. I'll stay with them if you can be used elsewhere."

"Yes Ma'am. Thank you. Just wanted to make sure they were safe and out of the way." Abigail knew it was probably more of the latter than the former reason. The Corporal turned and saluted them, then Abigail. "Ladies," he said, then turned to regain his unit.

Alesha looked at Abigail. "I just happened to turn around and saw all that. Are you and Fuzz always this quick and... deadly?"

"When need to be, Ma'am, I mean Alesha." The broadcaster looked at the Avenging Angel. She had been told stories about this young lady, younger than herself. She had to admit she had hesitations, questions when she had heard that Abigail was from Deseret, thanks to the stories about how they had treated people of color. Now, after the time with her and Fuzz, then seeing her in action, Alesha could not imagine Abigail doing anything wrong, hurtful, to the innocent. To the enemy, to evil doers, she was a wraith.

"That thing woke up too early, was going to be released during the ceremonies, services, that was the plan, wasn't it"

"Probably, yes, Alesha. Many people would have been injured in the panic. The Eater might have hurt, even killed people before being brought down."

"One of them could have been me, Patty here, or the President."

"That was probably the plan. Even with no fatalities, the terror they generated would have been a strong message that they are a lot stronger, these Krakens and Squids, than we realize. That we exist at their pleasure, nothing more."

Alesha shivered a bit. She looked at Fuzz, who seemed nonchalant about the whole affair, now that the Military Police had taken control. "He sensed something wrong, didn't he?"

Abigail smiled. "He has a good nose, is always on duty, and like all dogs, *hates* Eaters. I have heard they have a similar reactions to Squids, lizards, and grays. Dogs can tell that they did not originate here on Earth, and do not belong here."

"Can I pet him?" Patty asked.

"Yes. Fuzz, come closer." Fuzz stepped up and Patty began to pet, then scratched his ears. He groaned and grunted in appreciation. The middle-aged woman smiled.

"We owe him. And you. You two make quite the team. I think that will show through during the interview."

"If I don't get too nervous," answered Abigail. "I'm not used to being on television."

"You'll do just fine," said Patty. "I've been in this business for almost twenty years, survived the Long Winter. I can see naturals when I see them. You two are naturals for television."

Before Abigail could answer, someone called out, "Ten hut! General in area."

Abigail automatically came to attention, and saw General Reed approaching. Fuzz automatically stood to also, sitting tightly next to his mistress. General Reed saw her, and veered off toward her.

"Captain Young. I understand you and Fuzz have been busy again. I thought you were here for a ceremony, not to work."

Abigail snapped her signature parade ground salute and the General returned it. "We couldn't help it, Sir. Fuzz got a whiff of the Eater, everything else just followed."

The General looked at the K-9. "Sergeant, I wish you could talk human. I would sure like to know what goes on in that brain of yours. Well, I'll guess I'll just have to be satisfied with the results."

Fuzz looked at him as if to say, "What did you expect?" Fuzz did what came naturally to him. Protecting his humans was his natural function. And he did it quite well.

The General then looked at the broadcaster and her producer. "Ladies, I can tell you got a good look see at the workings of this big beastie and his mistress here. I hope you can get what they do across to everyone watching tonight. This will let people know the type of personnel, soldiers we have in this war."

"Yes, General, that is what we hope to do," Alesha said. She stuck her hand out for the General to shake. "I hope I can interview you sometime, about your job."

The General shook her hand, then snorted. "I am old, boring, and not sexy enough for television. I'd put everyone to sleep. Keep the televised interviews with the youngsters on the front lines, like the good Captain here. She and Fuzz are a lot more photogenic than I am."

"Now, if you will excuse me, I need to make sure everything is secure for Madam President." He turned to Abigail. "Carry on, Captain, Sergeant Fuzz." He gave her a quick wink with his off eye so the two media people did not see it. Abigail snapped a salute back, trying not to smile. Sometimes, he felt like a father to her. It was a nice feeling.

After he walked away, Abigail turned to Alesha and Patty. "I'm going to head down, to get a good seat. Most of the pall bearers of the three coffins are my friends. I like them to see me, know I'm there for support. Dealing with children's deaths is difficult."

"We'll see you at the end, Abigail." Alesha responded.

Abigail found a seat on the aisle, toward the back so that she could get up and leave with Fuzz if necessary. After her big fella found that completely unexpected Eater, she was paranoid. Fuzz also seemed to be on high alert now, watching and sniffing everyone who came by. She sure hoped nothing else happened.

General Reed would have staff members looking at everyone and everything, trying to discover how they got in with an Eater. Abigail knew the solution to it happening again. Put a dog at every door and gate. Almost any dog would do, as they all went nuts when they smelled Eaters.

Abigail sat and watched as the five survivors came in and sat in the front row, under the watchful eye of Freda Munsen. Fuzz started to show unusual interest in the girls/young ladies, his nose working overtime.

"What is it, fella? You've smelled young girls before. What's different now?"

Fuzz, whined, looked at Abigail, and then looked at the survivors. Abigail sighed. No use putting it off. She would have to take him up to the group, see what interested him. They walked up to the front row, and she approached Freda Munsen.

"Excuse me, Ma'am," She said in Norwegian. "Sorry to bother you…"

Freda Munsen broke into a large smile. "Captain Abigail Young. Brynhildr and Grandma Knudsen have both spoke highly of you. It is a pleasure to finally meet you. And the famous Fuzz."

Abigail smiled back. Once again, her reputation preceded her. At least in this case, it seemed to be a positive one.

Before she could speak again, Fuzz went to the oldest looking, dark-haired young lady, and sitting in the middle. She and the dog's eyes met, and Fuzz began to wag his tail, something he did not do on first meetings. The young lady broke into a wide grin. "I know you. We've met before." And she reached out and began to pet the canine and then scratch Fuzz's ears.

A puzzled Abigail looked first at the war dog, then the young lady. She saw Abigail's puzzled look, and stood up. She gently moved Fuzz, then curtsied. "Captain Young. Hannah Weitz, Ma'am. Sorry your dog is showing so much interest, but, well, we've met before."

"When?"

Hannah took a deep breath, to calm herself. "The pits. He was there also, quite a while ago. We spent some time together, were moved together. Then he disappeared. I thought he was dead."

It was like a light went off in Abigail's head. "Did you see him with anyone else? Did you see him with a large, muscular man, well built?"

Hannah paused for a moment. "No. Ma'am. But I did hear two men arguing about him. I was in a cell. I couldn't see out so I never saw the men who were arguing, just heard them. One said that he was too good of a dog, that someone named…Buck, would be very angry to see such a dog being used for…the pits."

Abigail reached out and took Hannah's hand, smiling. "You have no idea the gap you just filled in about Fuzz. Buck would be my Uncle, who I described. But since you didn't see him, said that he'd be angry about what they were doing... now I know he was never there. I knew that in my heart, but I needed confirmation."

"I can't imagine anyone related to you, Captain, would be involved in such things."

Abigail frowned a bit. "Sometimes the ones you love get involved with things that you wouldn't like, that are bad, even evil. You can't always pick your relatives, family."

One of the younger girls piped up. "Aunt Freda picked us as family. And it's great."

Freda stood up. "My manners are horrible today. I apologize. Ladies, let's all stand up and introduce ourselves to the good Captain."

All of the young ladies, mostly still girls, were dressed alike. All had dark velveteen dresses, almost black, with matching jackets. Abigail knew these would have taken some work to make, and looked at Freda with appreciation. Two were ten year olds, one was twelve, the last fourteen. Of course Hannah, at seventeen, was the oldest. One by one, they curtsied and introduced themselves.

"My name is Jewel, Ma'am." She was the first ten year old. Pretty light brown hair.

"My name is Susan, Ma'am." Susan, the second ten year old with Jewel when she was rescued by Johann from the truck trailer, had dark auburn hair.

Next, the twelve year old, a darker brunette, introduced herself. "I am Sharon, Ma'am."

Finally, the fourteen year old, Anne, the blonde. Abigail did not know until later that she was the one Torbin had rescued from the rape by the mutated chimpanzee. "My name is Anne, Ma'am."

Abigail grinned. "It is so very nice to meet such fine young ladies, Mrs. Munsen. And I don't know how you managed to produce such beautiful dresses. You must sew like a dream."

Freda smiled. "Oh, don't carry on so. All of these young ladies had to help. Even Hannah, when she wasn't working in the forge. I was a professional seamstress before the Krakens, both alien and human, came to our home. So it was not all that hard to teach these young ones. Especially since they are such quick learners."

The younger ones seemed a bit embarrassed by the praise. Jewel then began to study Abigail more intently, as if she was searching for something.

"Jewel, you look like you may want to ask me something. Please go ahead."

"Is it true you killed and castrated some Krakens?"

"Jewel. Don't be rude," Freda jumped in, afraid such a blunt question from such a young girl would offend.

Jewel turned her gaze downward, embarrassed at the rebuke. "I'm sorry. We have just heard so many stories about you."

Abigail quickly knelt down, looked the young girl in the face. "It's alright, Jewell I'll answer that. Yes, I did do that to some Krakens who tried to hurt and kill some dear friends of mine. Including some four-legged friends, like Fuzz here. It was necessary, so there is no guilt."

"Are you an Avenging Angel, as we have heard?" Anne asked.

"That is my title, and my position in Deseret, my home. Here, I represent my state, and help Major Bender and others to train soldiers."

"He's the Hero of Key West, the one who killed a Squid with a knife," Anne added. "And helped to rescue us."

"Yes, and he is one of my dearest friends. We met fighting Eaters."

Freda looked at Abigail, reached out and took her hand. "We would be honored if you came over someday to our home, and visited. I know these young ladies would enjoy feeding you some of their cookies and other baked goods. They are getting quite handy in the kitchen. And Hannah is quite handy in the forge, with my husband, Johann." Abigail looked at Hannah, noticed her strong looking frame.

"You work with steel, Hannah?"

"Yes, Ma'am. Uncle Johann is teaching me. In fact, I made some special items for tonight, for the three... who did not make it." Hannah and the others became much more serious, all smiles now gone.

Abigail looked at Freda. "I would be honored to visit, Mrs. Munsen. As long as I can ask a favor."

Freda smiled again. "Please, call me Freda. And what would that favor be?"

"Could you teach me some... sewing skills? I have very few. I have learned how to sew socks, buttons, and wounds as an EMT. But that is it. I would like to learn more…ladylike skills, traditional skills. I will not be a soldier forever, I hope."

Freda broke into a grin. "Of course I will. You have supple, strong fingers. It will be easy." She suddenly hugged Abigail. "You are an inspiration to all young women and girls. This large dog of yours is a legend already." Freda released Abigail, and scratched Fuzz's ears. He let out his typical dog sounds of appreciation, letting everyone know he was in dog heaven.

Abigail knew it was time to leave before Fuzz made a nuisance of himself "Please excuse me. I must go back to my seat before it is taken. Hannah, it is so good to have met you, and to have found out about Fuzz's background. And all of you young ladies are so pretty and nice. You make me feel like a clod."

"Never, Captain Young," Hannah jumped in. "You are someone… special to us. You and Major Bender. And of course Uncle Johann and Aunt Freda. We five are so very lucky."

With that, Abigail hugged all the young ladies, and said her goodbyes. Fuzz mooched additional pets and ear scratches, stole a couple doggy kisses, which led to giggling. Abigail smiled. Such a ladies man.

"I will call you, Freda."

"You'd better, or I will have Brynhildr track you down for me."

Abigail laughed. "Now I know I will be there."

She and Fuzz made their way back to their seats. As she sat down, she marveled at how healthy the five survivors now looked. Freda and Johann had done such an excellent job of clothing, feeding, housing—and yes, loving them—that they had blossomed in just some two weeks' time. Abigail thought they should get some type of medal for their voluntary efforts. With no government help, they were adopting and raising five strangers, turning them into excellent citizens and human beings. How many people could claim such successes?

The large auditorium began to fill. There were not just military types, there were also many civilians from off-base. The broadcast by Alesha had generated such an outpouring of both support for the five young ladies as well as anger and sorrow over the three who had not survived that everyone wanted to be involved somehow. Attending the memorial service was at least one way they could express their feelings, show support for the survivors. Soon, there was not an open seat in the entire building. Television cameras had been set up to record and broadcast the memorial service, as well as the awards ceremony, so many a bar and restaurant were set up to handle the overflow of people who could not find a way to fit into the auditorium. It would've been fascinating to have known how many people outside the U.S.A. watched the broadcast.

Soon the venue was packed. A few more people were squeezed in with folding chairs, with the Fire Marshall looking the other way for a few moments. This was important to people, so the rules were bent a little. Fuzz sat calmly by Abigail, but did not miss a thing. If a threat showed itself, Fuzz would have reacted immediately. Abigail looked at her four-legged companion and smiled. He was such a fine dog, such a fine "person", she knew how lucky she was. And now, thanks to Hannah, she had another piece to the puzzle of his history before Malmstrom.

After the auditorium had been as packed as anyone dared, a voice spoke over the P.A. system. "Ladies and gentlemen, please stand for the Presentation of the Colors, and the national anthem."

An Armed Forces Color Guard marched down to the front, turned toward the audience. A high quality recording of the Star Spangled Banner began, and everyone sang along. Only eight states may be Free, but dammit, they were still the United States. And old glory and the anthem harkened back to times and conditions they hoped to recapture. The colors were then retired.

"Please remain standing as the departed are brought forward."

Abigail watched as the three caskets were brought forward. Among the casket bearers were Torbin, Emily Anders, Rolf, Uncle Johann, Brynhildr and Commissioner Miller. Those who were part of the Raid, who had rescued the five survivors, felt a responsibility to help place those they were too late to rescue in their final resting place. The rest of the positions were filled by Sons of the North and Special Agents. The slow procession was done in silence, until the three caskets were placed on the stage in front of the auditorium so all could see. The casket bearers then retired back to their seats in the auditorium. A military chaplain, Major White—formerly U.S. Air Force assigned to Malmstrom Air Base and trained in interdenominational services—then came on the stage. A video screen suspended at the back of the stage was turned on, displaying a scene of a beautiful sunny big sky Montana day.

"Friends and neighbors, those who helped to rescue the survivors that fateful day, I welcome you to on this bittersweet day. Bitter because we are having to lay to rest three young people struck down before their time. Sweet because they are in a better place, with passed loved ones, and because we are all gathered here to pay tribute to these dearly departed."

The chaplain paused for a minute, glancing at some notes. Then, he placed them aside. "I had some prepared comments, a bit of a sermon. But I could not do them justice. I didn't know these three young children. Commissioner Paul Miller has done his best the last two weeks to locate friends, relatives of the departed, but to no avail. However, we have here one person who at least knew them a little. Who knew of their tribulations before they left this earthly coil. And she has asked to speak on their behalf."

The chaplain paused, looked into the audience. "Hannah Weitz, could you please come forward?"

Hannah stood up and walked to the stage. She carried herself with a grace and confidence of someone of many more years of age and experience. In her shiny dark hair Freda had woven some bright garlands, almost forming a halo. The hall was so quiet one could hear a pin drop.

She made her way to the dais on the stage, the chaplain meeting her, taking her hand. They embraced, and the chaplain, smiling, stepped to the side and rear of the stage. Abigail noticed Hannah had no notes, no prepared written comments. But she could tell the young lady knew what she was going to say. And she started in a firm, projecting voice for such a young person.

"Thank you, Chaplain White. I know the three departed appreciate you being here. As they appreciate all you in the auditorium being here, witnessing them on their journey of being laid to rest." A couple low sobs were heard. Hannah continued.

"My name is Hannah Weitz. I am one of the survivors. I am the one who survived the longest in captivity, some two years. During this... hell—yes I will use that word—I met June, David, and Cheryl. I never knew their last names. I met them in passing, as we were all condemned to the pits by some evil, sick monsters that walked on two legs. I will not call them humans, as they acted like no human being I have ever met. But they harkened back to another set of monsters my family has had to deal with." She paused for a moment, as if to let her remarks sink in to those in attendance.

"You see, I am Jewish. I come from a long line of Jewish people. Among those were two great aunts and a great uncle. They were part of another hell. The horror of the Final Solution, the Holocaust. They survived the concentration camps of Hitler and the Nazis. And today, the descendants of the Nazis are the Krakens. And like the Nazis, they need to be wiped from the Earth." There were a few murmurs of agreement, then they died down. Hannah continued once more.

"I do not know how long the three departed, the dead were kept as prisoners. As I said, we only met in passing. I was used many times for entertainments in the pits. I fought and was forced to… perform other acts upon threat of slow death if I refused. I survived. I survived because my great aunts and uncle survived and told the rest of the family how they did. What did they say? I will sum it up in two statements."

"Never give up, never surrender. And you must survive to be a witness, a speaker of the dead. That is what I am today. A speaker of the dead. Not just these three here. But also the two agents who died freeing me. And all the other victims, many unnamed, buried in various locations. Or fed to the Tschaaa. Or their beasts."

A person was heard retching, and a couple of people were escorted out the back of the auditorium. Hannah took a drink of water from a bottle the chaplain had left her. Then once again, she spoke. "I am a speaker of the dead. Thus I must witness to the wrongs, the evil done. Which I have been doing, and will continuing doing in upcoming legal hearings and trials to come. Plus, there is one other action I must insure is done." Hannah paused once more.

"I must insure that, what became the mantra of my people after the Nazis, becomes the mantra of the human race. That is, never again. Never again will we allow even the least of us to suffer as the dead have suffered. Never again will we allow people, just because they are different, maybe have a darker skin, be used as fodder for the evil ones, the Tschaaa, Squids as we call them. We must never give up, never surrender. We must be willing to die rather than surrender. For if not, if we are willing to sacrifice others so that we may comfortably survive, then we are scum. We are as evil as the Krakens. We are as alien as the Squids. We will have become the personification of Ba'al, of Satan, the evil one." She fixed the assembly with an iron gaze.

"Today, in this place, we must swear our allegiance to this task. This mission of stopping the evil that are the Tschaaa, the Krakens, the Eaters, the monsters created from our earthly creatures. We must fight, resist, unto death." As Hannah paused for a moment, some people started to applause, to loudly express support. With an authority of one mature beyond her years, she held up her hands in motion for them to stop.

"Please. This is not about me. This is about the dead. I don't want applause, expressions of support. I request that we all absorb what I have said, and decide what this means for all of our dead, all human dead, both in the past and in the future. I do have one small item to add, then I will be done."

Hannah pulled what looked like an oversized silver dollar out of a pocket. "Thanks to the efforts of those men and women who came to save me, the other survivors, as well as help from God and bit of luck, I am here to speak of and for the dead. Thanks to the love of Johann and Freda Munsen, I have a new family with my fellow survivors. And thanks to Uncle Johann's forge, I have been able to create some symbols for what I present to you today, as I speak for the dead."

She held up the oversized shiny silver coin. "On this coin I have tried to recreate symbols of every known, organized religion. I do not know what the dead here today believed in. Nor what other dead believed in. But I believe that they have gone on to a better place, an afterlife. This coin is a symbol of that belief, that hope." She turned the coin over, broadcast cameras trying to focus in close on the coin in her hand.

"On the back are listed the three names of the three to be laid to rest today. And, the numbers the Nazis tattooed onto the arms of my aunts and uncle. For all of the decedents, family members were required to memorize these numbers so as to never forget. I did it as the first step to start a chain of remembrance of all those who have died, will die as we fight this good fight. I am placing one in each casket of the three here today. It is something I needed to do. I think the three here today will understand."

She looked at the assembled people. "I'm now done. I've now

finished speaking of the dead today. Hopefully others among us will assume the mantle as a speaker of the dead when needed. I thank you for your patience, and your support. I close with this mantra, this request. Never give up. Never surrender. Never forget. Never again." Hannah walked to each of the caskets and laid a coin on each. Then, with a gravitas and regal bearing no one would ever forget, she walked off the stage. Uncle Johann was there to meet her and escort her back to her seat.

Abigail watched her and realized Hannah had gone up to the stage as a teenage girl. She came down as a woman. Abigail knew that people would speak of this moment for years to come.

Everyone sat still, quiet. Then, the pipes began to play Amazing Grace. Three bagpipes played the mournful yet uplifting song. And people began to sing. Many were crying, but they still sang. As the last verse was sang, the pipes finally fell silent. The chaplain came back to the stage. "It is time for the departed to take their journey to their final resting place."

The same Honor Guard that had brought the caskets in, went to retrieve them. During this, the chaplain opened each casket and placed the coin Hannah had forged gently on the head pillow. In each casket was an urn containing the ashes of the person, it having been decided that for safety from some unknown mutated disease they might have been infected with, cremation was the safest method of burial preparation. The general public did not need to know this. Waiting outside were three hearses to take them to a newly created gravesite on a small hill overlooking Great Falls. Finally, the three were in the confines of the hearses. A special police escort was provided, with the chaplain to officiate at a short graveside interment service. Representatives from all the local churches, synagogues, tabernacles, mosques, and kingdom halls were there to pay the final respects as the caskets were laid to rest and buried. The dead would not be alone.

A huge tent had been set up outside, with old military field stoves to provide heat as well as warm drink in the winter weather. A short break was provided between the Memorial Service and Awards Ceremony so that people could shift their emotional and intellectual gears. Those who wished to could leave. Very few did. Abigail put her parka back on and took Fuzz outside for a short break. She walked with the great dog, seeing people watch them with a mix of curiosity and respect. After Fuzz had taken care of business away from the auditorium, Abigail took him over to the huge tent to obtain some hot cider. Various organizations had also prepared hot rolls, donuts and cookies. Abigail obtained a couple of donuts, and went out to sit on some side steps. She shared the repast with Fuzz, thinking about what she had just found out from Hannah about Fuzz and the Pits. She scratched his ears. "Well, big fella, now I know for sure why you have a dislike for most men. You and Hannah alike were made to fight, risk death for the amusement of some sick bastards. Now I also know God was smiling on me when he allowed you to survive and find me. You are one of the best things that has ever happened to me."

Fuzz moved his head and looked into her eyes. Right then, Abigail could swear he was thinking "You are one of the best things that happened to me too." She hugged him tightly, reveling in his soft fur. He gave her a quick slurp on the cheek and Abigail chuckled.

"Well, time to go back in, Sergeant Fuzz. It'll be your turn soon enough to be on stage." She and her best friend made their way back to their seats.

Soon after Abigail had found their seats once again, people began filing in. Again, the auditorium was packed. Many were staying in the refreshment tent to watch the ceremony on live feed. Finally, as people spoke in low tones, the first bars of "Hail to the Chief" were heard, signaling that Madam President was in route.

"Ladies and gentlemen, the President of the United States."

Everyone stood out of respect as the President came down the center aisle. She stopped here and there along the way, shaking hands, saying hello. She did a quick detour to the survivors' seats. She grasped Hannah's hand, hugging her. Then Madam President spoke. "Young Lady, that was one of the most moving, most beautiful orations I have ever heard. You are truly a speaker of the dead. It is an honor to meet you."

Hannah blushed a bit. "I did what had to be done. Ma'am. And thank you for saving us."

"Oh, pshaw. I did nothing. Commissioner Miller and Uncle Johann here, they went in and saved you."

Hannah looked into her eyes. "But you set it in motion. Without you, this would never have happened."

Madam President felt tears welling up, fought them back. Time to be strong, to forget the images in her brain of that awful day, the pits. This was a time of honoring the living. She thanked Freda and Johann for "adopting" the five survivors, stayed long enough for the four younger girls to curtsy and introduced themselves. It made the President think back to more innocent times, before the coming of the Squids.

Then she made her way to the front stage as some poor technician played filler music. All during this time, Ranger Jackson hovered nearby, backed up by some plainclothes agents and an outer ring of MPs. The Eater Fuzz had found set everyone on edge. The Presidential Seal was on the podium/dais as she stepped up and gave a big smile to the public and the cameras. The Vice President was watching from Bismarck, tucked away so that not all the leadership could be wiped out all at once.

"Good evening, my fellow citizens. Tonight, we have some positive activities here at Malmstrom Armed Forces Base. We are going to pay homage to and award some citizens who stepped forward to help others, putting their lives at risk in the process. Without further pomp and circumstance, could I have General Reed and Commissioner Miller front and center please."

Paul and John were both a bit taken aback as this was not according to plans discussed prior. They quickly made their way to the stage, knowing that cameras were filming everything. They stopped in front of Madam President, with General Reed saluting. "Present as ordered, Madam President."

She gave a broad smile. "I know this is not according to plans, but, being a woman, I reserve the right to change my mind." This led to some light laughter from the audience.

"Commissioner, General, in these rather voluminous envelopes I have Presidential Citations for the units and personnel involved in the Raid on the Pit Compound. Thanks to your combined efforts, we shut down a cesspool of evil and depravity, saving five young ladies at the same time. I know, Paul, some of your agents wished to remain anonymous due to ongoing investigations, so I decided to do the presentation of these citations this way. I know you gentlemen will insure that every deserving individual will receive the just rewards. So, in the name of the Office of the President, I now present these citations, along with the thanks of all the citizens of this fine land."

As she handed the packets to the General and the Commissioner, loud applause and cheers broke out in the auditorium. After the very somber memorial, the assembled people needed some positive outlet. As General Reed and Commissioner Miller made their way back to their seats, Madam President addressed the assembly again.

"This whole operation began when a certain Major and his wife, Majors Bender and Smirnov, were on the receiving end of an assassination attempt using Eaters. This was the tip of the iceberg, of the festering evil we discovered in the Pit Compound. During that assassination attempt, a certain military dependent wife, unarmed but unafraid, without any concern for her own safety, rushed to help. She could have easily been torn asunder by the alien life forms. But that did not dissuade her. Would Mrs. Sue Brown please come to the stage, please."

A very nervous Sue, in a brand new dark blue dress, made her way to the center of the stage. She had practiced in her new high heels so as not to fall down and embarrass herself and her husband. Sue was not used to being the center of attention, being just a strong, no-nonsense North Dakota farm girl. Her long brown hair had been expertly coiffed, paid for by Aleksandra. Aleks had insisted, getting Sue down to a hair salon run by a Korean lady in Great Falls who was rapidly becoming the go to person for special jobs. Now up, with ringlets down the sides, she looked like she was going to a school prom.

Sue approached Madam President, and stuck her hand out to shake. The President took it and, with a big grin, then pulled the young woman in for a hug. "You are gorgeous, my dear. Not like you looked when you went to help Major Smirnov, I bet." The stage sound system picked up any conversation within fifteen yards of the dais.

Sue nervously smiled. "No Ma'am. I was out jogging. But please, I did nothing special. Fuzz did all the heavy lifting. I showed up after the fact."

The President gently turned Sue toward the big video screen that was suspended on the wall above the stage. "Let's let a couple of pictures tell the tale."

The first picture must have been taken immediately after Military Police Forces had arrived. It showed the inside of the Majors' quarters, with a large dog standing near where Aleks was laying, a look of "don't you get any closer" on his face. Kneeling next to Aleks, with her back to the camera, was Sue in her jogging suit. Laying in the hallway were the remains of two Eaters. Also noticeable was the very large Eater-sized hole and indentation in the hallway wall.

"The Military Police said that Sergeant Fuzz let you get near the Major, but none of the men. He seemed to trust you."

Sue shrugged. "I've always liked dogs. I guess he sensed that."

"You kept Aleks still, her airway clear, away from any detritus of the Eaters until EMTs could get by Sergeant Fuzz."

Sue blushed, shrugged her shoulders. "I guess. Ma'am. I just did what I thought was right."

Then the next picture came up. A Hazmat-suited soldier was lifting the head of an Eater up, the one with its throat ripped out. Ichor was dripping from its mouth and throat, some of it acidic as it was noticeably singeing the floor. There were murmurs from the audience.

"Ladies and Gentlemen, as you can see, even a dead Eater can be dangerous."

Madam President turned toward the Lieutenant's young wife. "As I said, you went in, having to break a glass window, cutting yourself in the process, with no concern for your own safety. I think that is something special. Something that should be recognized." She stepped over to the dais, and removed a large flat case from it. She stepped back and opened it.

"Sue Brown, here is a Presidential Medal for Valorous Service. It is designed to be presented to those civilians who have gone the extra mile in the service of their country, of their fellow citizens. If anyone deserves it, it would be you."

Sue began to stutter, protest. "Please, Madam President. I did nothing special…."

The President smiled. "One nice perk of this job is I can say I'll be the judge of that. I'm the President." People began to laugh.

"Lt. Brown. Front and center."

Sue's husband, in dress uniform, marched up to the President, and saluted. "Lt. Brown reporting as ordered, Ma'am."

"Lieutenant, please be at ease and do the honors of placing this medal around your pretty wife's neck so all can see."

"Yes Ma'am." John Brown removed the shiny gold medallion from the case, spread the necklace length ribbon attached, and careful so as not to muss her hair, put it over her head, around her neck. He said in a low voice. "I love you so. I am so very proud of you."

Sue began to tear up. From a sleeve of her woman's business suit, the President pulled one of her signature colorful handkerchiefs. "Here, my dear. Keep it. I have many more."

Suddenly, people were applauding. Then standing and applauding. Then cheering. Sue dabbed her eyes, her husband beamed. Finally, Madam President held up her hands. "If you would please take your seats again. We still have one person to honor." She turned to the young Lieutenant.

"John Brown, I suggest you take very good care of this young lady. She is very special."

He smiled, a lump in his throat. "I know, Ma'am. I know." He went to attention, saluted. The President saluted back. He then turned, and escorted his tearful wife from the stage.

As everyone began to take their seats, a low roar finally beginning to die down, Madam President's voice rang out. "Captain Young, Sergeant Fuzz, Front and center."

From off stage came Abigail and Fuzz, marching in time, off leash. They stopped in front of the President, Abigail resplendent in her dress Blues, Fuzz with a special vest around his chest and front shoulders displaying his rank. The Captain saluted, and Fuzz sat, raising his right paw as if in a salute.

"Captain Young, Sergeant Fuzz reporting as ordered, Ma'am." Madam President saluted back, then looked slightly down at Fuzz, who had now lowered his paw. She smiled, adding, "At rest, both of you please. Relax a bit, you both deserve it as I have heard you two were already busy tonight."

"Yes Ma'am. Sergeant Fuzz found an Eater hidden in a large box being delivered."

The President chuckled. "And I heard you two took down the two miscreants trying to deliver it."

"Yes. Ma'am. Then the MPs showed up, took care of the Eater with a 12 gauge."

Madam President turned and addressed the assembled citizenry. "The two men arrested were trying to insert an Eater in such a way that it would wake up from its tranquilized state, break out of the box, attack and panic whomever it could. So, I know I owe my life and well-being to these two warriors. And possibly some of you." She turned back to Abigail and Fuzz. She had a large case in her left arm that she brought up and opened. As she did, the picture of the Hazmat person lifting the Eater with the torn out throat was flashed again on the large display screen.

"Sergeant Fuzz, on the day in question, two alien Eaters were inserted into the residence of Majors Bender and Smirnov. They proceeded to attack the unarmed and pregnant Major Smirnov. Without hesitation, no thought of your own safety, you broke through a glass sliding door and met the two attackers head on. The picture displayed on the screen is the Eater you killed by ripping its throat out. You then engaged the second Eater, placing yourself between it and Major Smirnov. This enabled her to retrieve a shotgun and finish it off. You were injured in this attack, but Major Smirnov was not, thanks to your actions."

The President removed a medal from the case. "As President, I am proud to award you the Silver Star for your bravery. You demonstrated the virtues we all want to see in our Armed Forces Personnel. A grateful country thanks you for your valor. Captain, would you do the honors of pinning on the Silver Star."

"Ma'am, begging your pardon, I think he might like it if you would."

The President smiled as she looked at the K-9. "I think you are right, Captain. If you could hold the case, please." She knelt down next to Fuzz, looking into his eyes. His mouth was open in what looked like a doggy grin. The most powerful woman in the U.S. then carefully pinned the Silver Star onto Fuzz's K-9 vest. She hugged and kissed the war dog on its muzzle. Fuzz stole a doggy kiss, licking her. Madam President began laughing. "Typical male. Steals a kiss every chance he gets."

The audience began to laugh along with the President. She then stood up. "Captain, I also have a Purple Heart here for the wounds he received. Would you do the honors?"

"Yes, Ma'am. I would be honored." Abigail took the decoration, knelt, and pinned it on Fuzz's vest. She then stood up, and saluted him.

"Madam President, I have never worked with a more deserving soldier."

"I agree, Captain. I wholeheartedly agree."

The President then turned to the assembled citizens."I have arranged for a demonstration of Sergeant Fuzz's capabilities, if the good Captain thinks he is up to it. And I will assure you, Captain, he is under no threat of injury."

"Yes Ma'am. So, we are ready when you are." Abigail bent over and whispered something to Fuzz. Immediately, he was up on all fours, alert. The hair on his back began to stand up, and he moved so that he was a little in front of Abigail.

Two Military Policemen pushed out a large table on rollers, there being a definite weight to what was under the large tarp on top of the table. They centered it on stage, locked the rollers and stepped back. As they had approached, Fuzz had shifted his position, always ensuring he was between the MPs and Abigail. Now, she could hear the slight growling in his chest, the sound that his "fight engine" (what Abigail called it) was revving up. With a nod from Madam President, the MPs reached forward and ripped the tarp off the object on the table.

Gasps were audible from the audience as they saw a life sized replica of a Tschaaa, a Squid. Made out of fake, rubberized flesh, it was one of many being produced with the help of 3D printers so that military trainees had something real to fight, shoot, and study.

One word from Abigail, and Fuzz exploded toward the training aid. He hit it with so much force, open muzzle and teeth going for the large right eye, the fake Squid was knocked half off of the table. Then Fuzz began to flex his shoulder and neck muscles, ripping and tearing from side to side. Pieces of fake skin began to be ripped and flung about as a few people screamed from the audience. Fuzz twisted and pulled, soon yanking the Squid off the table and onto the floor. The war dog ripped the grasping "hand" off one of the social tentacles, twisting and flinging it off the stage and toward the front row of attendees. A couple of people jumped up from their seats.

Fuzz then scrambled around toward the "rear" of the fake creature, began to tear into the arms. He seemed to be in an almost frenzy of destruction. At this time. Madam President called out. "Captain Young, *time*."

Abigail yelled the command "Out!" in Romanian. It took a

moment for the command to sink in, then the K-9 stepped back from the trashed training aid, still growling. Abigail slapped her thigh and Fuzz was there. Abigail knelt down and began to pat and praise her four-legged companion

Then the applause. Followed by yells and shouts, turning into a chant of "Fuzz, Fuzz, Fuzz." The people had a new hero. Under the din the President walked over to Abigail and Fuzz. She bent over and began to scratch the ears of the war dog.

"Glad to have finally made your acquaintance, Sergeant Fuzz." The canine "woofed", turned and licked her hand. The President then stepped forward and held up her hands, motioning to stop the display of appreciation. Finally, the audience calmed down, but with most people grinning, chuckling, murmuring toward their neighbors. They were, in the vernacular, jacked.

Madam President stepped forward, not needing much help from the sound system to project her voice. "I asked for this demonstration for a specific reason. There is a propaganda circulating among the Tschaaa controlled areas that they want us to be a Client Species. To enjoy all the perks and benefits of Squid technology just as long as we allow a minority of humans to be served up as meat, as fodder. They apparently try to state that our relationship with our dogs, with Fuzz and his brethren, is a model for a future relationship between us and this alien, ten-armed invasive species." She paused, looking out across the small sea of faces.

"After seeing Sergeant Fuzz here, willing to fight and possibly die for us and we for him—as I know Captain Young would do in a heartbeat—is there even the remotest chance we could be a loyal companion to a slimy, nasty Squid, as our canines are to us?"

"*No!*" It exploded from every single throat.

"Could we be a helpful companion to some weird species that would just as soon *eat* us as look at us?"

"*No!*" Again the answer shook the building.

"Could we acquiesce to serving some culture as a helper species when they look at serving us up as a menu item?"

"*Hell no!*"

The President knew this was being broadcast well beyond the borders of the Unoccupied States. She knew that a response could be swift and nasty if the Tschaaa wanted it. But she also knew that they did not think like humans. Even if they did, it was time to take that chance if people ever wanted to be out from under the yoke of alien oppression.

She smiled. "I knew you would say that." Laughter exploded. She turned to Abigail and Fuzz.

"Thank you for your service. We couldn't accomplish what we want to do without people like you and Fuzz here. And yes, Fuzz is definitely more of a person than a Squid will ever be."

She then turned back to the assembled citizenry. "This ceremony is now complete. I thank you for your support. In closing, I would like us to sing a rousing version of *America the Beautiful*. How about it?"

Music emanated from the speakers and everyone began to sing. Those who did not remember the words did a good job faking it. Madam President noticed that Abigail had a very nice voice. Although Fuzz's attempts at a few howls were none too successful. The song finished, the singing stopped.

"Go with God, my fellow citizens. The future begins today." Applause broke out, then began to die down as the people got up to leave. Madam President made sure her mic was turned off as she went to Abigail and Fuzz one more time.

"The Country owes you both, Captain Young. Remember that. If there is ever anything you need…"

Abigail blushed a bit. "No Ma'am. You have done so much for us already. I would like to thank you for something, now that we are no longer on microphone."

"Please, my dear, go ahead."

"Ma'am, the brush set you left me the first day I was here. I know it was from your family. It's too special for me to accept and keep."

The President looked into the eyes of the Avenging Angel. She was becoming a daughter of the U.S. And a daughter to her. She smiled and took Abigail's hand. "My dear, I knew you were special when I first learned about you. Special people need special things. So the brushes and combs are yours to keep. Consider yourself family. Now, it is time to leave."

Abigail stepped back and saluted. "As Major Bender says, via con Dios, Madam President."

The President saluted back. "Go with God also, Captain Young and Sergeant Fuzz." She then turned and went toward Ranger Jackson.

"Time to leave, Andrew, before I turn into a pumpkin."

The Ranger laughed. "Ma'am, you would never be mistaken for a pumpkin. Pumpkins don't have steel in their spines." She smiled in response, then took his left arm to be escorted off the stage.

CHAPTER 17

The world is a dangerous place to live, not because of the people who are evil, but because of the people who don't do anything about it.

-Albert Einstein

Yeah. Just needed someone who cares about him. Dogs are simple. You love them, they love you back. You fight for them, they'll die for you. Simple.

-Dogman

BANKS OF THE COLUMBIA RIVER
OREGON STATE

Now called The River Bar, the former bar and grill had seen better days. It was still a step above the level of a "dive", so the kitchen still worked and the beer wasn't watered down. Located near the banks of the Columbia River, at what used to be The Dalles, the bar was now the center of a small community made up of bits and pieces of abandoned buildings, houses, vehicles, and some tents. Most of the beer was provided by a revitalized brewery in Portland, Oregon. Although a distance away, the road system was still sufficient for a trailer load of beer to be delivered about once a month. Bottle, barrel and kegs were available. Some wiseass had called the new brew Octopus Beer, slang name Wussy Beer. It actually was quite good

The alcohol menu was rounded out by locally produced wines, home brewed backyard beers, ales, and a still out behind The River Bar that produced what was called Bust-Head. The saying was, "If your head feels like it's been busted, you've been drinking Bust-Head. Guaranteed *not* to make you blind." A little bit of tweaking, different types of mash, fruit, and anything else that would ferment produced a variety of booze under the Bust-Head label. Aging was measured in hours, days, weeks or months. A bottle with a "12" on the label could mean any of those passages of time. People who cared actually asked what they were getting.

Of course, behind the bar were some pre-Squid bottles of the "good stuff" were kept for special occasions. Scavengers who came in with decent bottles of pre-Squid alcohol could get a premium price for it. But woe to those who tried to pass their home brew off as the good stuff. They wound up floating in the still irradiated Columbia River. Even though personnel under the control of Director Lloyd nearer the tri cities area were using Tschaaa technology to clean up the Columbia, and filter out the radioactive crap left over from the huge Hanford explosion, smart people did not make it a habit to eat the fish or drink the water. Water was provided by rain barrels, a few surviving water towers, streams and creeks. But even that was filtered using Tschaaa organic organism-based filters.

Near Portland, Oregon there was a small Squid presence, with a robocop overseeing a county council that organized the some fifty thousand surviving humans in the Occupied area. Since the Tschaaa did not travel up the contaminated Columbia River past the other huge filter and decontamination complex they ran some two miles east of Portland, The Dalles was considered Feral territory. People were allowed to go to Portland, to trade, buy things. But get out of line and you were whacked, then fed to the Squids.

The bar had a couple of operational televisions, hooked up to huge satellite dish and a fifty foot tall conventional antenna constructed from pieces of electrical power towers. The televisions could pick up anything broadcast for thousands of miles. Sometimes, they even picked up signals from Asia.

Tony the bartender was the owner of The River Bar. No one knew his real last name. He had been called Tony the Bartender since taking over the place some five years prior. He smiled and laughed, but was not afraid to bust a head, or dump a body into the Columbia. Tony even allowed sex workers to ply their trade in his establishment for a small fee, as long as no one was rolled. He found a doctor who would stick around and examine the women to keep them free of associated diseases. If they did give someone a serious disease, they'd wind up in the Columbia. You had to have some standards.

Both televisions were on the same feed, broadcasting live a ceremony from the U.S.A., which was almost over. Tony liked to keep abreast of world affairs, so when something was being broadcast live, the pornos and old films were turned off. Things were winding down, as Tony watched the cameras pan across a small sea of people leaving an auditorium in Great Falls, Montana.

The picture changed and some good-looking black woman was interviewing a young, pretty white girl that had a huge dog next to her. Tony quickly turned up the sound. "….and so, Captain Young, you consider it excellent fortune that you and Sergeant Fuzz here found each other," the attractive broadcaster was asking the sharp-looking female soldier.

"Yes, Ma'am. I call it providence."

At the sound of the voice, a large, muscular man sitting at the end of the bar looked up from his beer. His eyes focused on the image on the screen. "Turn it up. Please, Tony."

"Sure, Dogman." The volume of the television increased, drawing the attention of three other rough looking individuals further down the bar. They struggled to focus on the picture through their blurry beer goggles, tried to discern the figures and what they were saying.

"That was some little show the President arranged for Sergeant Fuzz, wasn't it?" Alesha Taylor asked.

Abigail Young chuckled. "Yes, Ma'am, but Fuzz here adapts well to strange situations. He has an excellent native intelligence, better than most people I have met."

"I noticed that you only had to say one word in Romanian, and he knew just what to do.”

“Yes, Ma’am. He recognized the outline of a Tschaaa, artificial life-sized model or not. But I think they may have had some old Squid scent on the model also, judging by how Fuzz’s nose was working just before he reacted.That’s also how he took out the Eaters. He just slammed into them, all teeth.” The camera focused on Abigail, all smiles. “Someone said once I had to make sure Sergeant Fuzz was kept under control, to keep him from being a free running land shark.” She scratched behind his ears. “But sometimes a land shark has its uses.”

Alesha began to laugh on camera as one of the three drunks spoke up. “Hey, that’s the Deseret bitch. You know, the one we heard about. Took out some guys on the way to Malmstrom.”

His companion, a larger, hairy individual barked out with laughter. “That’s right. Look at that nice piece of ass.” He had a leer plastered on his face. “I wouldn’t mind teaching her a few new tricks. That would be a night to remember.” All three began to laugh, slapping each other’s backs, taking gulps form their beers. “Tony. More beer,” The large one called out. Then he noticed the figure at the end of the bar was staring at him. He was not used to strangers daring to even look in his direction.

“What the hell are you looking at?” He blurted.

“Nothing. Absolutely nothing,” Dogman answered.

The large man’s beer soaked brain told him that he had just been insulted. He was over six feet tall, large and hairy, with some muscle under his beer fat. He was used to beating the crap out of people who pissed him off, especially after he had some ‘beer courage’ in him, like now. “Oh, a smartass. How’d you like your smart mouth closed for you?”

Tony tried to break in. “Hey, no problems in here. Take it outside, Mitch. I don’t want my place busted up.”

The one called Mitch sneered. “The only thing that is going to get busted is his smart mouth.” Mitch had barely uttered his threatt, when a very large shape detached itself from the shadows, a low growl emanating from its mouth. The huge Mastiff pup, just under two hundred pounds and only a year old, moved toward Dogman.

The three men at the bar froze, speechless for a moment. It appeared that the unexpected addition of a huge dog with equally huge teeth had made them have second thoughts about any trouble. But then, Mitch's beer courage got the better of him, his two drunk friends following along like the lap dogs they were. Mitch reached for something concealed under his loose shirt tails. "I'll just use my gun on that son of bitch. Then I'll..."

He never finished his statement. The large caliber pistol he was pulling out was stopped at his belt level by a short handled double bladed throwing ax Dogman had concealed under the bar's top edge. It buried itself between Mitch's eyes with a thwacking sound. His body stood upright for a moment. Then it toppled backwards like a fallen tree.

Everyone froze for a few seconds. The skinnier of the two remaining men screamed like a little girl, clawing at his waist as if going for a concealed weapon. The Mastiff, after a single word from Dogman, stopped that action by lunging up quickly and latching its jaws about the face and head of Skinny. His screams were broken off with an audible crunching sound.

The final drunk turned to run out the door. A slim throwing knife buried itself at the base of his skull, and the dying man fell forward onto his face. He lay twitching, then went still. It took a few seconds, then Tony came back to life. "Goddammit, Dogman. How am I going to explain this to the law? They'll close me down."

"What law?" The large muscular cut man answered. Tony stood with an open mouth for a moment. Then he began to laugh. "You're right. Force of habit. Once in a while I think it's seven years ago, when I owned my old place."

Tony quick walked around to the main door, looked out. No other customers nearby. He grabbed and put up a sign which read, 'Back in Fifteen', then shut and locked the door. "Come on. Help me clean up the bodies." The two strong men soon had moved the three bodies out the back door of the establishment. Tony had a large cart on a set of tracks he had built. The cart could be lowered down by a thick hemp rope to the Columbia River's edge, an easy way to get rid of non-recyclable trash. There was no more EPA to worry about. Besides, how could a little bit of trash make the radioactive water any worse?

The three bodies were soon splashing into the water. Tony and Dogman had relieved them of their cash, their weapons and anything else that looked valuable. Some large shapes moved toward them in the water. Numbers of very mutated and huge catfish were now a major predator in the area, smart enough to hang around the river's edge near the bar. They had learned that at various periods, Tony provided some edible and tasty trash. The fish were soon chomping on the three bodies.

"When's the marshall due back?" Dogman asked as they walked back inside. There was a man nearby who had established himself as the marshall by default, as he had once been a sheriff's Deputy. One day, he showed up with a badge, gun, Pr-24, Bowie knife, taser, and pepper spray. He said he was the law. But his main job was running a small diner a few miles up off the Columbia.

Tony snorted. "He comes by here about once a month to collect his 'mordida'. For his 'protection', he gets a keg of beer and a bottle of Bust-Head which he sells to his diner customers who pass through. Most of the regulars in the area come here when they want a drink. The only other times he comes here is when I call him."

Marshall Masters, his true last name, had responded a couple of times to large fights at The River Bar. He had quickly established his technique as hit first, ask questions later. After a couple of folks were shot for causing him trouble, the locals soon learned to leave him alone. Although, if you called him for assistance and hadn't done something piss him off, he would show up to help.

"Luckily the regulars don't show up tonight until later. Those three drunks were just passing through. No one will miss them for long while, I wager." He eyeballed Dogman. "Now, are you going to tell me what brought this on?"

"The young lady on the television is my niece. No one insults my niece."

Tony looked at the muscular man. "So being a badass runs in the family?"

Dogman shrugged. "I did teach her about dogs, and how to train them. I also might have shown her a thing or two about how to take care of herself."

Tony chuckled. "From what I know from the people passing through, she has more of a reputation than just being able to take care of things."

"Whatever. But you don't mess with my family."

Tony looked at the pile of property and weapons the two men had removed from the dead men. "Want any of these pistols, Dogman? One's a big .45 Colt."

"No thanks. I have enough guns. I'll split the scratch, gold and silver with you."

"Okay." Tony soon had everything divided into two piles on the bar.

"Two hundred each in greenbacks, six gold coins and ten silver. Here, take this ring, it looks like gold. And here's about five bucks in old U.S. Mint coin."

Dogman pulled a cloth bag out from under his shirt, scooped everything into it. His Mastiff sat patiently watching. "Do you have anything I can feed Matt here?"

Tony reached under the bar and pulled out a small bag. "Here. Buffalo Jerky." He tossed it to Dogman. The black haired man reached into the bag, and pulled out several pieces of jerky. He handed a piece at a time to the huge dog, who took it gently from his fingers.

"Man, that dog is *big*. Where'd you get him?"

"Some guy had him staked out near his house with little food and water. I'd tried to buy him, the asshole told me to get fucked. Now he's fucked." Dogman said it matter of fact, with no emotion. Tony did not ask what he meant in this case. He could imagine.

"He looks healthy now."

"Yeah. Just needed someone who cares about him. Dogs are simple. You love them, they love you back. You fight for them, they'll die for you. Simple." Matt nuzzled Dogman's hand with his huge nose. Dogman began to gently scratch his muzzle and ears. The Mastiff groaned a bit. He was in dog heaven.

"I would have liked to see that whole interview of my niece."

Tony smiled. "Wait right here." He went to a back room, and came back out with a disc. "Here. I record a lot of these specials, live news. Sometimes a whole bunch shows up, then I can't watch the old boob tube. So I record it. You have a disc player, yes?"

Dogman took the disc. "Yeah, I have one. I'll bring this back ASAP." Tony waved off the comment.

"No hurry. I know you'll be back. What little family we have left is important."

Dogman stuck his out his huge right hand. "Thanks. I owe you."

Tony grinned. "I don't really feel a big need to talk about what just happened. I'll call it even."

Dogman looked at him, deadpanning. "Something happened?"

Tony began to laugh. Dogman was 'good people'. He had known him for a couple of years. Tony considered him a friend, and he believed Dogman felt the same. Friends were hard to come by if the Feral areas. They shared a beer, as Tony waited for his grill man to show up with some supplies Tony had sent him to get. It worked out just fine, as there had been one less set of eyes to worry about. The grill man showed up with the first of the regular group for tonight. Tony switched one of the televisions over to a porn channel.

"See you later, Dogman."

"I'll be back tomorrow." With that, the Adonis with the huge dog walked outside. A couple of women who came in tried to chat Tony up about the handsome stranger. Tony shook his head. "You'll have to talk to him. Dogman doesn't like people to talk for him."

Dogman drove his massive RV down to a campsite a couple of miles away. He parked, got out, and unfurled the side awning. Then he rolled out a bunch of plastic fencing to show his dogs the limits of their territory. He walked the Mastiff and his three Dark Mask Curs out, let them do their business, then brought them back inside the fence. Four large food dishes were set down, and each dog sat in front of one of them. He fed each in order, the Alpha female, Pepper, getting hers first.

He was down to these four dogs, having found decent homes for several others as he had rescued them. Their former "owners" were dead dogfighters pushing up daisies, as Dogman thought they were the lowest scum possible. Taking innocent animals and having them hurt each other for entertainment was the height of perversion and evil. Dogman had seen some of the images from the Pit Raid in Great Falls, talked to some people who had been through the area. Those involved and still breathing were lucky Dogman had not been on site.

He grabbed himself a beer and put the recorded disc in his player. He quickly found the segment of the interview with Abigail. He sat down and watched his niece recount recent her history with Sergeant Fuzz. He listened intently when she talked about how the War Dog had been trained by someone. Judging by the description, it was probably someone Dogman had trained prior to the first rock striking the Earth. Dogman had quickly lost track of the previous instructors he had trained, especially when he had evacuated Abigail to Deseret. If he found any had been involved in dogfighting operations he would castrate them himself.

When he Abigail stated she had just found out that Fuzz was a survivor of the Pits, Dogman felt a mixture of rage, then pride that his niece had been able to rescue this fine example of the canine species. Abigail had been his best student. She had a way with dogs that was second only to him. A rare smiled formed on his face. He was so glad she had turned into such a fine young lady. He still felt guilty about leaving her in Deseret, but it was the safest place at the time for a young girl, just shy of her twelfth birthday. He knew that he and her parents had provided her with survival tools that had would serve her well. Dogman knew that if he personally had stayed, someone would have been injured or killer. He did not suffer easily those who tried to judge him, or force their beliefs on him.

Watching Abigail as she and the female person of color finished the interview with comments about a rapidly approaching Happy Thanksgiving, Dogman realized something. Torbin Bender had promised him that he would insure that Abigail was taken care of, and was safe and healthy. The Marine had fulfilled his promise. Dogman owed him now. Someday, he would have to pay back Bender for ensuring his niece's well-being. With that thought, the large and muscular man decided it was time to fix his meal. He carefully stopped the disc, and removed it from the player. He would have to find a way to buy this from Tony. It was too special to just let it disappear.

Now, he knew he still had some buffalo steaks in the refrigerator. Of course, some of the meat would wind up in his dogs' stomach. He let a very rare chuckle pass his lips. He knew he was sometimes actually a very soft touch. But that was a secret he kept between him and his dogs.

CHAPTER 18

THANKSGIVING
MALMSTROM UNITED ARMED FORCES BASE
GREAT FALLS, MONTANA
UNOCCUPIED STATES OF AMERICA

Abigail was checking on her pies for the umpteenth time that hour. The plan was to eat at twelve noon at the huge dining table Torbin had found and placed in his and Aleks' and side of the duplex. It was getting close and Abigail was afraid her pies would not be done, too done, bad crust, bitter filling—the list of her worries was almost endless. Finally, Shannon Bell, the oldest daughter of the Bell Clan from Wyoming and pilot-in-training, stepped in.

"Ma'am… Captain, please. You're wearing yourself to a frazzle. Everything will be just fine. If something does go wrong, well, it's not like we are in danger of being shot."

Abigail shut the oven door, again. "Please, call me Abigail. You're a guest in my home, not to mention your mother said she was adopting me. I'm not thinking as a Captain right now. I'm thinking as a worried… homemaker. I guess that would be the right term."

The slender, brown haired Shannon smiled. "Okay, Cap… I mean Abigail. But please. The pies look great. Your bread looks great. The rolls look great. You have a natural flair for baking. You're an extremely fast learner. Everybody will enjoy stuffing themselves with your baked goods. Trust me, okay?"

Abigail smiled nervously. "Guns, weapons, tactics, fighting—that all comes second nature to me. But *this...*" She waved her arm across the kitchen. "I like my own cooking, probably because I am used to it. And it is better than chow hall food. But to serve someone else... This is nerve wracking."

Shannon stepped up and put her hand on arm of the Avenging Angel. "You're worried that a certain young man of Japanese descent might not like this, aren't you?"

Abigail stopped and looked at her. "Is it that obvious? Damn. Oops, sorry. Cursing solves nothing." She was not used to having an audience judging something she did. In the field, you just acted, reacted, and could tell immediately by the results if your actions were correct. Usually, if you were screwing up, the amount of bullets whizzing by or advancing enemy screaming at you increased. Here, the judging of the results seem so vague, almost esoteric. Tastes could often vary a lot, especially between cultures. Now, with six years of absence, formal Thanksgiving was being reintroduced to humanity in the Americas. So what would everyone's expectations be, especially Ichiro, a Japanese visitor? Abigail felt like she was carrying the weight of great expectations on her shoulders. She did not want to disappoint. She was not used to failing.

Finally, she spoke. "Shannon, I know you're right, that I should be confident. But my gut still says something can go wrong, and that I will embarrass myself in front of all my new friends and family."

Shannon gently squeezed her arm. "Your family and friends will support you and love you no matter what happens, or what mistakes you make. If for no other reason than they know what a good, honest, and faithful person you are. So please, don't worry so. Besides, we have an ace in the hole if something goes really wrong."

Abigail glanced at another one of her adopted sisters a bit quizzically. "What do you mean?"

Shannon had an impish smile on her face. "Well, we can feed any mistakes to the dogs. Fuzz and his new mate won't complain that maybe the pie crust is a bit dry. They'll wag their tails and ask for more. Not to mention the good Major and Commissioner Miller."

Abigail began to laugh. "I guess you are right. Aleks keeps saying that men are dogs. I guess we can verify that if need be today."

Shannon then added one last thought. "Abigail, I hope this is not too personal, but, well, Major Yamamoto has eyes only for you. Short of poisoning him, nothing you do today will be wrong. Trust me. He has the 'look'."

Abigail brightened, then frowned a bit. "Do you think my pies could poison him?"

Shannon put her face in her hands. "Stop it! You're giving me a headache. Shut off the oven and open the door a bit. As it cools down, it will still keep the pies we leave here warm. Pick two, I'll grab the rolls and bread."

"Pick two? Which two? Which are the best…" Shannon let out a small cry of frustration, then began to laugh. Finally, realizing what she was still doing, Abigail began to laugh also. She hugged Shannon. "This is to pay back your mother and sister, since they are not here. Please pass this hug on to them."

Shannon smiled. She knew the full story of what had happened at Abigail's first meeting with the Bell family, just how much combat and violence related stress she had exhibited. Her mother had adopted Abigail on the spot. From what Shannon had heard, many people have adopted Abigail Young as an extended family member. Her inherent goodness had that effect on people. Everyone wanted to make sure she was happy and secure. At the same time, everyone knew that the Avenging Angel would not allow any harm to come to her friends and family. These feelings created strong, unbreakable bonds between all the people involved.

This was the first that Shannon had seen Abigail in anything other than a calm and confident state since she arrived at Malmstrom. In a relatively short time, she and Fuzz had become popular symbols of what was right with humanity. All of the stories about her, from the trip from Deseret, the "Oktoberfest Beat-down" to her handling of Fuzz and his subsequent defense of Aleks Smirnov had turned her into a modern living legend. Every young girl and woman Shannon had met looked at Abigail as a role model to emulate. People were purchasing t-shirts with pictures of her and Fuzz on the front and back. Fuzz had his own "land shark" drawing that started out as some posters, now had gravitated to his own line of t-shirts and other products. One day, Abigail had remarkably received a very large check in the mail, apparently from some people making money off her "brand". A short note included stated that the authors of the check felt guilty they were making a bunch of money off of the actions and reputation of Abigail and Fuzz, and so they felt morally obligated to share the wealth.

After conferring with Torbin and Aleks, Abigail had started a retirement fund for Fuzz and all other War Dogs in the form of a charity. A small amount was funneled off to help current veterinarian offices in the U.S. provide services. Since then, other checks had arrived. It looked like it would be an ongoing activity. These were the effects that the Avenging Angel and the War Dog had on people. They brought the best out in them, not just hero worship.

"Come on, Abigail. It's time to take your bake goods to the Thanksgiving table."

Abigail sighed. "I wish things were more normal, that I could spend more time in these traditional activities, providing food for friends and family."

Shannon chuckled. "The 'normal' traditions were put on permanent hold when the Squids showed up. I think women have had to adapt to changing conditions through the ages, and during wartime have had to trade combat for domestic duties. After we rid ourselves of the Squids, maybe we can start thinking about having children and families again. Like in old television sitcoms."

Abigail nodded. "That's true. I just long for the days of holiday diners before the Squids showed up. The last six years of being trained to become a fighter seem like a blur at times. I wish there was a way in which we could get a 'do over', start over without the possibility of being eaten hanging over our heads. Someday, I would like to start a family, if I can." She had a slight faraway look when she said this. For the first time, Shannon saw a different side to Abigail. Usually all business about killing Tschaaa or Krakens, now she was talking about creating life rather than trying to end it.

Shannon patted her arm. "Come on. Let's enjoy the day, Give thanks." The two young women loaded up with pies, bread, and rolls, walked out the front door of Abigail's side of the duplex and in through the front door of Tobin's and Alek's side.

Fuzz watched them enter from a vantage point by the large sofa in the living room. Lying next to him was his mate, Princess. The large female Merle Great Dane who lived with vet Emily Anders had been introduced to Fuzz a few days after Oktoberfest while she was in heat.

It started out like a fairytale meeting. Princess and Fuzz sniffed noses, and immediately both their tails began to wag. Then, she had laid on her back, her her belly exposed as if to say "I surrender. I'm yours." Emily's mouth had dropped open.

"My God. I have never seen *that* before. Do you want to stay, and make certain that it will turn out okay?" Emily asked.

"No. I will not want someone watching me when I finally find... the one for me. I will give Fuzz the same privacy."

She walked out the door, as Emily stated, "As a vet, I need to make sure this goes alright, no injuries. Hope that doesn't piss you off."

"No. Do your duties as a doctor. I understand."

Emily had laughed to herself. Abigail had such a moral and innocent outlook toward things. Not like her, the old jaded vet.

And from all appearances, the two dogs looked made for each other.

Dogs ancestors were primarily monogamous, the alpha male and females of a pack doing the bulk of the mating. Fuzz and Princess had apparently decided they were the alphas, even if the other pack members were humans. Whenever they were near, they gravitated toward one another, acting like married humans.

Emily knew that was anthropomorphizing the canines, but it still seemed like that was the case. In the long run, it did not matter. Princess would have some very nice puppies.

Emily was sitting on the couch, holding hands with Commissioner Paul Miller. He had made good on the date promise to Emily soon after the request. One thing had led to others, so they were now an "item."

When Aleks had demanded that Emily came over for Thanksgiving, so that she could personally thank her for saving her husband's testicles from the weasel creature, Emily said she had to bring Paul as her date. Aleks not only agreed, but insisted.

Emily started to get up to help the ladies entering.

"No, Emily, you're a guest," said Abigail. "You stay seated, while

Shannon and I help Aleks. Besides, there is only so much room in the kitchen."

"You bent my arm, Abigail," Emily said with a smile. "I'll stay here and keep Paul and the other dogs company."

Paul looked at her with a raised eyebrow. "One of the dogs now, am I?"

Emily gave him a peck on the cheek. "Yes. The most handsome one at that. Just remember how much of a complement that is from someone who thinks dogs are better than most humans."

Paul grinned, and put his arm around her. She made him incredibly happy. In fact, his employees, had all said he was almost acting like a normal human being. Almost. Sometimes out of the most horrible situations, like the Pit Raid, came something good.

Aleks checked the large turkey in the oven. In the backyard, Torbin watched a second bird in a large roaster. Wrapped in his parka, braving the cold, he sipped a beer. The one thing he was a bit short on was suds. He had been too busy to buy any more. Oh well. The Commissioner had brought a couple of bottles of wine, Aleks had a couple more stashed away. They had vodka and scotch, plus Ichiro's sake. They also had un-spiked hot cider for the teetotalers, like Abigail. He wasn't certain whether or not Shannon Bell drank alcohol.

Ichiro was putting the finishing touches on an origami centerpiece for the table. Next to each guest's place Ichiro had made another origami creation, representing the person sitting there. He had also neatly folded the cloth napkins into perfect little peaks, prompting Torbin to say he would make someone a helluva wife someday. Ichiro had retorted that at least he would be good at something, as opposed to Torbin, who was only really good at passing gas.

The two turkeys were large, but Aleks was eating for four, with her two unborn sons each possessing an unusually fast metabolism. Of course, they also had extra stuffing, mashed potatoes, bread, rolls, and pies. Emily had brought her family's recipe for cranberry sauce, and a bunch of freshly made potato chips. There were a couple of food stands that specialized in making fresh potato chips, kettle corn, and flavored popcorn. The reconstituted junk food industry was still in its infancy, so unless someone wanted old and possibly stale chips from a pre-strike bag, the fresh chips were the way to go. Torbin for one hoped large amounts of bagged chips never again caught on. The fresh ones were so much better.

Aleks opened the french door, and poked her head out. "How is it coming, my husband?"

"Almost there, love. Just a few more minutes and I can remove this bird from the heat." She nodded. Both of the turkeys had been live, free range.

Just the previous day, Aleks had taken them from Torbin, chopped off their heads, gutted and plucked them with practiced ease. He had been pleasantly surprised.

"You never told me you knew how to gut and prepare a live bird."

"You never asked, my love."

"Where did you learn this skill?"

"Well, Torbin, truth be told, I was raised on a farm. I joined the Russian army because I was bored and wanted adventure. I did not want to be, as you say, barefoot and pregnant. Now look at me."

"Well, Aleks, you're not barefoot." He received a piece of turkey innards in his face for that smart remark. Damn, she was fast.

"As I was explaining, I learned how to prepare a bird, kill and gut a hog, slaughter a side of beef if need be. I also dressed a deer once." Aleks washed and wiped her hands, then started gutting the second plucked bird. "Bluntly, gutting a pig is not all that different than gutting a man. I've done both."

Torbin had looked at her for a few moments before commenting. "I hope you do not plan on practicing that technique on me any time soon."

Aleks stepped over, grabbed him and kissed him, hard, leaving some turkey grease on him. "Don't even joke about that, Torbin. I love you and want you in one piece. Especially when these two trolls pop out of my stomach." With that, he had held her, hugging her for a few minutes.

"I guess life with you, my dear, will always be full of surprises."

"Any other way would bore you, husband, admit it."

He laughed. "Yes, you have me pegged. Now, I'll get out of your way and let you do your magic."

And now, he was admiring his very pregnant wife, standing in the open sliding door. A warm feeling coursed through his body. He stepped back from the roaster, stepped up and kissed her.

"Do you know how much I love you, Aleks?"

"I think I do. But what brought on this sudden expression of affection?"

He looked into her eyes. "This is the first Thanksgiving we have had since the day the Squids showed up. Since then, I have a loving wife, two strapping sons on the way, a bunch of new friends, and some fool is going to give me a medal of honor for doing something I would do for free... kill Squids. No matter how bad things are, we seem to be going up rather than down. And again, I have a beautiful loving wife, something that I never imagined would happen in my wildest dreams."

Aleks began to tear up a bit. "You just have to make me cry, in front of guests, don't you?" She stepped out into the cold and maneuvered her pregnant stomach so she could hug her husband and her love.

"Out of the whole mess of the past six years, you, my crazy Yankee imperialist, have made my life worthwhile. We will get through this together, raise two fantastic sons, maybe more, and grow old gracefully. With that, I'll be happy and satisfied. I love you." They hugged again for a few moments, then Aleks gently pushed away.

"I must get back to the turkey so that we will have something to serve our guests, and the trolls in my stomach." She smiled, then went back inside and closed the door. Torbin returned to his turkey.

"Damn, I'm lucky," he said to himself. "Or maybe like Abigail says, 'Someone up there likes me.'"

As the women in the house finished the table preparation, Fuzz suddenly stood up, his hair bristling as he went to the front door. Seeing this, Abigail grabbed a carving knife she had been sharpening and approached the door as well. Ichiro went for his katana, and Aleks, seeing Fuzz and Abigail move, stepped out near the dining table with her hand on her now ever-present Makarov pistol. No more a pregnant woman depending on a canine to defend her. Any Eater would get a face full of lead. Princess stood up, placing herself between the door and Emily. Paul Miller had his hand on a five shot revolver in a pocket holster. Anybody trying to cause trouble at *this* house had made a very bad decision.

But no sooner had Fuzz reached the door, then his hair returned to normal and he suddenly wagged his tail. He had caught the scent of someone he knew and liked. The next minute, someone knocked on the door. Abigail being the closest, answered it.

On the threshold were Brynhildr and the five survivors, all dressed in nice long hooded coats, long dresses, leggings and boots. The young ones were carrying covered plates with some type of food. Brynhildr had two large tankards in her hands.

"I see you, Abigail. Happy Thanksgiving." Brynhildr spoke in Norwegian flashing a big smile.

"I see you, Brynhildr," Abigail answered. "Please, come in out of the cold."

"Yes, come in, make yourself at home," Aleks directed. "We have plenty of food for everyone if you would care to stay."

Brynhildr and the five young ladies came in, Hannah smiling and petting Fuzz as he licked her hand. She would always be someone special to him.

Abigail had to admit she always felt a bit insecure, almost jealous around Brynhildr. Rolf called Abigail 'Shield Maiden', but to her, Brynhildr was the epitome of a shield maiden female warrior. Tall, sure of herself, able to kid around with all the other males, and able to give just as good as she got. She was quick and easy around men, yet let them know what her boundaries were as she was having fun. Abigail still felt clumsy, unsure when put in strictly social settings. During training and combat, she was suddenly sure, confident with men and women. Outside of that, she always felt uncertain what to say or how to talk.

With both Ichiro and Torbin she could be more herself. However, she always had this little gnawing insecurity in the back of her mind that she would say something stupid to Ichiro, and he would leave her. What she did not know was this was impossible. But when Brynhildr was around, as when Ichiro trained her in some bow work, Japanese style, Abigail felt a pang of jealousy, which she suppressed. But, it was still there.

The younger girls brought their plates to the coffee table near Paul and Emily. They curtsied, then hugged the two familiar faces. They turned to Aleks, Abigail and Shannon. As the oldest, Hannah spoke for the rest after they had performed the now programmed curtsy and stood in a line.

"We have brought you some cookies, a pie, some traditional Nordic pastries. We hope you enjoy them as much as we enjoyed making them for you. Brynhildr also has a tankard of ale and a tankard of mead."

Aleks stepped up to them, smiling. "My, you are all so pretty and polite. Please place the food and drink on the large coffee table. What brings you to my home, my dears?"

"Brynhildr said Major Bender, Major Yamamoto, the Commissioner, and Doctor Anders would be here today. We have some things to show our Thanksgiving for helping us find our new life." The four younger survivors quickly produced an intricate crocheted shawl and doilies for Emily.

"My God. I haven't seen things like this in years. How did you do this beautiful work?"

"Aunt Freda taught us. It was fun," Jewel answered. Emily stood up after carefully handing the new treasures to Paul and hugged and kissed each young lady.

"Thank you all so very much."

"It's little compared to what you have done for us," Hannah answered. "Now, if the two Majors and the Commissioner could come here. I have something for you each."

The three men, who had helped save the five survivors, came forward somewhat self-consciously, Torbin having come in from the broiler when he heard they had new company.

From under her long hooded coat, Hannah produced three felt wrapped bundles. She carefully sorted and handed one each to the three men. In the two bundles given to Torbin and Paul were slender six and a half inch blade combat knives, a full edge on the main, a half edge on the back. Both were razor sharp. The handle was leather wrapped.

"These are based on a M-3 combat knife from World War II, used during the years of the Holocaust," Hannah explained. "If you look just in front of the handle, you will see a Jewish star engraved there, with the words 'Never Again'. I think, given the current situation, it fits."

Paul looked at his. "This is impressive. You made this yourself?"

"Yes Sir. Uncle Johann showed me some pictures from a book he had, I figured out how to do the rest. My apologies that I have no sheaths."

Ichiro carefully unwrapped his. He suddenly sucked his breath in past his teeth with a slight hissing sound.

"I used a Tanto design for yours, Major Yamamoto. I tried to match the repeated folding techniques of steal shown in a book on Japanese katanas. Hopefully, I did an adequate job."

Ichiro examined the pronounced temper pattern that marks a high quality blade. He stood ramrod straight, held the Tanto out with both hands, and began to bow his head until it almost touched the blade. He began to rattle off in rapid fast Japanese as he repeated the bowing.

"I don't speak Japanese…" Hannah began, then Abigail broke in.

"He is saying he does not deserve this, that you must be the reincarnation of a Japanese swordsmith to have made this. Ichiro, English. Please."

Ichiro stopped. Then stood up straight again. "Hannah Weitz, I am honored to accept this. I feel I am not really worthy of such a gift. I was there to help my brother Torbin that night, nothing more."

Hannah smiled. "The reason you were there does not matter. The fact you were there does."

Torbin turned around and walked out through the back door without saying a word. Aleks knew something was wrong.

"Excuse me, I will be right back." She moved fairly quickly despite her bulk.

Brynhildr looked at Abigail. "Your friend is upset about something."

"Yes, he is. Aleks soon will find out what it is. Now, can I offer you anything?"

Brynhildr and Hannah exchanged a look. The dark-haired beauty said, "We need to get back. There is a full meal waiting for us. We just wanted to bring these items to you."

Abigail glanced toward the backyard. "Well, I'll walk you out. Maybe Torbin will come out before you leave."

The young ladies all said goodbye to Emily and Paul with hugs and kisses, then caused Ichiro to blush by doing the same to him. Abigail had to smile. Ichiro was such a staid, upright samurai. It was fun to watch him deal with an unfamiliar situation, like being hugged and kissed by four young girls. They then said goodbye to Fuzz and Princess with ear scratches and pats. The Dane looked as if this was expected because of her royal personage.

As they exited the home, Brynhildr said to Abigail in Norwegian, "Your family name is Jorgensen, correct?"

"Why yes, that was my father's family."

With that, Brynhildr stopped and extended her hand. "We are cousins. That is my family name. Cousins maybe many times removed, but cousins nonetheless." Abigail took her hand, surprised. She had never given it a thought that she could somehow be related to a New or American Viking as they were called in the Unoccupied States.

As Brynhildr grasped her hand, she said, "Since we are family, please realize that I'll always be there if you need help. Hopefully you will return the favor. And, more importantly, you have nothing to worry about me interfering with your relationship with Ichiro."

Abigail suddenly blushed. "How could you tell? Were my concerns that obvious?"

Brynhildr smiled. "I'm a hopeless flirt. It is a skill I use to disarm men, and to make them do things they think are their idea. I see the effect that has on other women when their men are involved. So yes, I noticed. But blood is thicker than lust. Remember that. I'll never do anything to hurt you, cousin."

Abigail smiled, then hugged Brynhildr.

"Uff da. You are strong like they say, Abigail. Coiled steel you are."

Abigail laughed, let go. "The epitome of a Shield Maiden says I squeeze too hard? Come now, you are pulling my leg, as they say."

Brynhildr stepped back, then felt Abigail's arms, shoulders. "Remind me never to do anything that might make you angry at me. I've never felt such compact, coiled strength in a woman. How did this happen?"

Abigail shrugged. "I have been trained as a warrior for some six years. Maybe that and my father's genes. Or my mother's. My Uncle Buck—my mother's brother—is built like a modern Hercules. Women have been known to actually swoon over him. It was funny to watch, even as a young girl."

Brynhildr cocked an eyebrow. "Hm. If Rolf angers me too much, maybe you will help me look up your Uncle?"

"So Rolf is your…boyfriend?"

Brynhildr laughed. "Yes, I guess you can say that. We are like two bears. We fuss, slap each other around, playfully of course, and then he proposes his undying love for me."

"And you, to him?"

Brynhildr sighed. "Yes, I suppose it is written on my face when I talk about him. I was not looking for a soulmate, but I guess I found one by accident. I have other plans. I do not wish to be tied down with children right now. But later...." She shrugged.

Abigail smiled. "Now, it is my turn to say that Rolf, despite his constant declaration of loyalty to me, is nothing other than a good friend. So now, cousin, I guess we are even." Both women began to laugh, and intertwined their arms as they walked to the SUV. In these apocalyptic days, it was nice to find more family.

As the visitors were in the process of saying their goodbyes, Aleks threw on her parka and joined Torbin outside. He was standing next to the broiler and staring at its contents.

"My love, what is the problem? Hannah was just trying to…"

He thrust the wrapped present at her. "Here, a present. I have my Ka-Bar."

Aleks unwrapped the knife, noticing the intricate workmanship. "Husband, my love, why does this upset you so? I don't want to see you this way. I need to understand."

Torbin threw his meat fork across the backyard, making Aleks jump.

"Because, goddamnit, a young seventeen year old girl should not be making killing instruments. She should be making jewelry, rings, crocheting doilies. Not making knives to kill enemies." He began to shake with rage.

"I carried Anne, the little blonde out from the downstairs dungeon. She looks like Abigail must have at that age. Some sick fucks were using her a *plaything* for some mutated ape. And the worse thing about it, was that it was all humans, people there. No Squids. We did it to our *own*." A tear of rage ran down his face, and he quickly wiped it away. Marines don't cry, at least not in front of people.

Aleks wrapped her arms around Torbin, squeezing him tight. They stood like that for a few moments, the only sounds were the murmur of a suburban neighborhood, and their breathing. Finally, Torbin patted Aleks' arm.

"Okay, I've got control now. Sorry I'm such a pain in the ass. I love you so much, I don't want to be a millstone on your neck."

Aleks kissed him. Then grabbed his ears, to make him look her in the face. "Do not beat yourself up. It makes me question my taste in husbands. I love you. We will get through this together. Da?"

Torbin smiled. "Da. See, you're a learnin' me Russki."

Aleks slapped his chest. "Now, come with me. You have to thank Hannah. I will gladly use the knife if you do not want it. It has a nice gut cutting blade, good balance."

"Ouch. I keep forgetting what you do for a living. Yes, let's go so I can apologize for being a jerk."

Aleks looped her arm through Torbin's. "You may be a jerk, but you are *my* jerk. Don't forget it."

Brynhildr was about to get into the driver's seat when she saw Torbin and Aleks exit the house, and come toward them. Hannah also noticed them and quickly got out. Then, all of the others were out, standing around the SUV. Torbin approached Hannah, and stuck out his hand. "I apologize for being such a jerk. Sometimes, things just hit me funny. That is an excellent blade. You need to be proud of your workmanship."

Hannah brushed by his hand, throwing her arms around him in a big hug. Suddenly, all four girls were wrapped around him, hugging, kissing him, giggling. Aleks began to laugh, then cry a little, then laugh. Abigail walked over and hugged her.

Hannah managed to step back. "Thank you, Major Bender. You save us. That is all that matters. No apologies are necessary."

Anne stood in front. "Thank you for carrying me up the stairs that day." The other three chimed in. "Thank you, Major Bender."

Torbin, for once in his life, was speechless. He just stood silently and received their gratitude.

Jewel broke off and walked over to Aleks. "You are going to have twins?"

"Yes, two little trolls. Would you like to feel?"

"Can I?"

"Of course." Aleks pulled up her clothes enough so Jewel could feel her belly.

"Oh! A baby moved."

Soon all five of the young women were gathered around, touching Aleks' stomach. They began to giggle as they felt the life within her move about.

"Someday, I want children," Anne piped in.

Her assertion made Aleks chuckle. "Just make sure you have a husband that will give you children, not trolls like I am carrying."

Abigail and Brynhildr both began to laugh. Torbin put on his best hurt face. "I am hurt. I am cut to the bone. Once again, I, Torbin Bender, Marine extraordinaire, am insulted beyond belief." He dramatically placed the back of his hand on his forehead as if to swoon. The old Torbin was back.

"Come here, husband. It is time to go in and finish up the Thanksgiving meal."

"I will see you later, cousin." Brynhildr called to Abigail.

"And I you, cousin."

With that, the survivors and Brynhildr loaded into the car.

"He's a nice man," auburn-haired Susan declared.

"He's more than just nice," Brynhildr interjected. "He has honor and bravery. He is a protector of the weak, the young. He is what a warrior and a husband should be. Use him as a model when you begin to be interested in boys. Men like him will not disappoint you, young ladies."

Hannah gazed at Brynhildr. "Is Rolf like him?"

Brynhildr laughed. "Yes, in a rougher way. But he has a good heart. That often is enough." She started the SUV and headed back for the Munsen home.

Abigail, Aleks and Torbin went back into the house. Torbin shot a quizzical glance at Abigail. "You and Brynhildr are cousins?"

"Yes," Abigail answered. "We are both named Jorgensen. So, somewhere, there were sisters and brothers, eventually cousins."

"You never mentioned your birth name before."

"You never asked, Torbin."

"Come, help me with the finishing touches for the meal," directed Aleks.

Within half an hour, hot, steaming turkey was on the table, along with mashed potatoes, gravy, sweet potatoes, cranberry sauce, green bean casserole, bread, rolls, butter and honey. On a small side table were Abigail's pies, along with the pie and sweets the survivors had brought. Everyone found a seat, with Torbin, the man of the house, at its head. He looked at Abigail.

"Being as I am a bit rusty at saying grace, how about if you do it, Abigail?"

"I would be happy to." She grabbed Ichiro's hand with her left, and Shannon's with her right. Everyone around the table linked hands, and bowed their heads. "Lord, please bless this gathering of people and food here on the first day of Thanksgiving in years. We humbly ask you for your aid and your love as we embark on another year of reclaiming our country, our heritage, and our humanity. In Jesus' name. Amen."

As they began to pass and serve food, Ichiro smiled at Abigail. "You are quite good at the blessings, Abby-san. It must come from your heart."

She smiled a bit sheepishly back. "It does. I feel blessed for having you, my friends, Fuzz, and my health. I know that is not all by chance." Ichiro took her hand and squeezed it as they looked into each other's eyes.

"Hey, you're holding up the food. Make with the goo-goo eyes later."

"Husband."

"Oops. Sorry. Please pass the cranberry sauce."

An hour later, they were cleaning up after the repast, everyone stuffed more than they had been in years. Torbin plopped down into an easy chair Aleks had found for him. Everyone had shared the tankard of ale, which had been a good replacement for the lack of beer. Everyone had sipped the mead, even Abigail.

"You know, Paul, there is one thing I miss."

"What's that, my good Major?"

"Football, American style. Football and Thanksgiving seem to go together. Now, unless I want to watch a tape of a game, there are none I can watch."

"Have to agree with you, Torbin. Just another reason to kick the Squids' asses as far away as we can."

At that time, Shannon Bell and Abigail began to distribute wine glasses to everyone. Then they came around with bottles of wine. After everyone had a glass of wine, Aleks came forward, water in her glass instead of alcohol.

"A toast. To good friends, to good food, and to a good birthing of the two trolls in my stomach.

"Here, here," Torbin exclaimed. Abigail sipped her wine, as did Ichiro. All the rest quickly finished theirs off. Then everyone sat and let their food digest. Torbin and Aleks cuddled up in the love seat. To everyone's surprise, Abigail sat on Ichiro's lap, and put her arm around him. Shannon smiled. After what her mother and sister had told her about their first, stressful meeting with the Avenging Angel, it was nice to see her acting like a normal young woman with a boyfriend. Shannon felt a little left out as she had no male friend, but having a family style dinner like this was great. A boyfriend could come later.

Torbin then proceeded to belch, which resulted in a slap and admonishment from Aleks. "Hey, it's not my fault. Blame those great pies of Abigail's. Fruit pies always make me belch."

Abigail smiled. "I'll second what Torbin just said," Paul Miller interjected. "Your crust was divine, young lady. Like my mom used to make." Abigail beamed. Ichiro saw her reaction, feeling a warm glow begin to grow as he noticed how happy she was. No guts, no blood, no violence to talk about. Just good times with a special person. At that moment the Japanese Samurai realized that he was hopelessly in love. He would not push Abigail into anything, as she had said she needed time. But he realized that no matter what happened, she would always have his heart.

"Hey Shannon," Torbin began. "How's the pilot training coming?"

"Well, Sir, just finished an abbreviated ground school last week. Since I had some thousand hours flying with my father, Retired Colonel Bell, they are sending me straight to OJT after Thanksgiving. I start as a co-pilot of a rescue chopper. Later, I don't know what my assignment will be. Right now, we have a lot more helicopters than any other aircraft. So, pilots go there first."

"What would you like to do?"

Shannon shrugged. "I'm easy. Whatever is needed to fight Squids and Krakens, I'll do. I'm still pissed off those Krakens tried to hurt my family to get to you and I wasn't there to help. I joined to be an officer and pilot to make a difference. So, wherever they need me, I'll go."

Torbin remembered a young Marine who had the same opinions. Him. It was déjà vu to hear the new young officer express the opinions he had held years ago, before the Squids came. Now, he just wanted to be near the action, to have a chance to close with the enemy, kill as many as possible and drive them from his country. "Well, Shannon, Abigail and I trained you in close quarter combat. Someone else a lot smarter than me will have to train you in the finer arts of combat flying."

Shannon grinned. "Yes, and you ran my ass into the dirt. I don't know how you two do it, day in and day out. How many troops, soldiers have you trained so far?"

Torbin though for a minute. "Since Abigail showed up? I've lost count. Abigail, do you know?"

Abigail, who had been enjoying sitting, snuggling a bit with Ichiro, had been keeping track of the conversation just in passing. Now, she was being forced to respond. Her brow furrowed.

"Since the Pit Raid, and everyone lined up to volunteer, I've lost count how many people we have come in contact with. Now that we are training all ranks, not just supervisors, officers, it seems like we see a hundred faces a week. Ichiro here is doing a lot of unarmed combat training, as well as blade and improvised weapons training. But I just heard the Russians are sending us a dozen trainers, arriving this weekend, supposedly the toughest they could find. Torbin and I have been told we will have to integrate them with our training, I guess supervise them. The plan is to use them in a lot of the initial basic training. Most of our people are on the front lines, in combat units. We trained some NCOs in the train the trainer concept, who will train people on the job. But that was a stop gap. We have to go back to full mobilization style training, make sure people will have a good chance to survive once they hit a combat unit."

Aleks suddenly laughed.

"What's so funny, Love?" Torbin asked.

"I just thought of someone who trained me. It would be fitting that he would be sent here. If you can survive his training, you can survive anything the Squids can throw at you."

Then she shook her head. "But I don't even know if he is still alive. He had a tendency of angering everyone in authority, especially political types. They may have sent him on some suicide mission just to get rid of him. He was too tough for the Squids to eat."

Torbin stretched. "The conversation is getting too serious. Since we don't have football to watch, how about a game of Monopoly? Then I can teach my Russian wife here the finer points of Yankee Capitalism while we snack on leftovers."

Aleks snorted. "Russia is no longer Marxist, my ignorant husband. Any game requiring intelligence and mental quickness will put you at a disadvantage. Just remember that."

"See what I put up with? Get them pregnant, they still won't stay quiet on the farm... *Ow!* Why must you always jab me in the same rib? I'm going to have a large bunch of scar tissue there when I get older."

"Keep doing what you are doing, you may not get any older, husband."

"And with that loving exchange," Paul Miller interjected. "Bring out the board. I'll warn you. I'm cutthroat when it comes to Monopoly."

CHAPTER 19

"A well-regulated militia, composed of the body of the people, trained in arms, is the best most natural defense of a free country."

-James Madison

"So that this nation may long endure, I urge you to follow in the hallowed footsteps of the great disobedience of history that freed exiles, founded religions, defeated tyrants, and yes, in the hands of an aroused rabble in arms and a few great men."

-Charlton Heston

JOINT BASE ELMENDORF-RICHARDSON/ J-BER
ANCHORAGE, ALASKA

Customs and Immigration Officer Richard Head was not happy. He had been called out from his turkey dinner to handle a Russian aircraft that was not supposed to be in until tomorrow. And it had declared an Inflight Emergency, which resulted in every emergency vehicle on J-BER (pronounced Jay-Bear) being called out to meet it also. Even though Russia was an ally, Commissioner Miller had mandated that "everyone" entering the United States be "customized". Way too much contraband was being smuggled in, not to mention that some of the so called refugees were actually followers of the Church of Kraken trying to gain entry covertly. So, he and a few MPs were working instead of being home with their family and friends. After all, this was the first official Thanksgiving celebration since the first rock hit. So, it was a big deal, and now it had been interrupted because some "Ivan" decided to come in a day early. Not cool.

The Li-2, a Russian licensed copy of the old DC-3/C-47, was apparently the last of its kind flying. It had already made several trips to and from Siberia, its low and slow method of travel meant it was totally ignored by the Tschaaa eye in the sky. Anything traveling at less than about three hundred knots was completely ignored, even after that B-25 WWII bomber had been used to insert Major Bender and company into Key West. The Squids seemed to have trouble adapting in how their surveillance functioned when new threats arose. They had a tendency of just maintaining the same systems and methods.

Be that as it may, the Russian Gooney Bird was struggling to make the airfield. The officer thought it sounded as if the engines had been pushed just a little too far, and were now quitting on the job. But the pilot, a grizzled old veteran who had flown in Afghanistan during the Russian Invasion, would do his damnedest to ensure that the Li-2 would not *dare* to crash on him.

The aircraft came straight in, both engines quitting at the same time. The Russian pilot demonstrated his skill by greasing the plane in on a dead stick landing. He let it roll to the end of the runway, applying only minimum braking. Finally it stopped, with some two dozen fire and rescue personnel standing by, ready to inundate it with foam and water. But nothing happened. The passenger door on the right side, opposite of a standard DC-3, opened. A ladder was deployed.

The flight suited senior pilot was off first, surveying the assembled rescue personnel. "Typical Americans. Always react with wasteful numbers to a minor problem," he grumbled as another figure came down the ladder after him. This person was dressed in Spetsnaz fatigues, with no name tags or rank. Scarred, weather-beaten face, head shaved, and smoking a cigarette with a holder, the second arrival was built like a cross between a bear and a fire hydrant. He looked like a solid piece of iron, barely topping five foot nine.

"Hey, buddy. Put out that cigarette," an Assistant Fire Chief yelled at him. At the sound of the voice, the solid man surveyed the personnel spread out around him and located the source. He marched toward the Assistant Chief, who repeated his warning, eyes wide. "Goddamnit—put that cigarette out! There may be fuel vapors around. Put it out, or I'll have you sprayed down."

In a calm but penetrating voice, Mister Solid replied, "Do that, Comrade fireman, and you will have to remove a hose nozzle from your rectum." He kept walking, then continued. "There are no fumes because Comrade pilot dumped what little fuel he had left over the bay. The plane may look old, but it has many modern conveniences."

The Russian's demeanor let everyone know that he was not to be trifled with. And he was right. The rescue crew tried to restrain their laughter at the idea of a hose projecting from their chief's ass, as he had the reputation of having either his head or a stick up there already. The fireman sputtered. Before he could say anything else, the Russian asked the assembled personnel, "Where is the Customs House? I have orders to check in with my personnel."

One of the junior supervisors called out and pointed across the tarmac. "All the way down at the other end of the tarmac, Comrade. If you wait, we can arrange a ride."

"Thank you, but my people and I need the exercise. The plane will need to be towed, and unloaded."

"No problem," the junior supervisor replied, then got on his radio. With that, the Russian turned on his heel and marched back to his aircraft, the Assistant Fire Chief still sputtering.

When he reached the plane, the solid Russian pulled a beret from his pants pocket and put it on. He yelled some commands in Russian into the open doorway. As if by magic, eleven other identically uniformed Russian soldiers came scrambling out of the aircraft, each fielding a small pack. They formed up in column formation, one man handing an identical pack to the now identified commander of this small unit. The Russian barked a command and they all were at regard attention. Another command, they did a right face. The man then proceeded to march them a few feet before he commanded them into double time, packs and all. And off they went to the the Operations building.

"Asshole," the Assistant Chief finally blurted out.

"Dare you to say that to his face, Chief," someone called out from behind one of the fire trucks. The rest of the crew laughed, while the Assistant Chief stormed back to his command vehicle.

Customs Officer Richard Head heard the sound of combat boots in unison approaching. He stood up from behind his desk so that the personnel would notice him upon their arrival. A dozen uniformed Russian Soldiers entered through the doors in front, slowing down to quicktime. They came to a halt at the command of the apparent leader. Given a left face, eleven Russians soon stood at parade rest. A solid bear of a man approached Head, snapped a quick salute, and presented a stack of passports to him.

"Senior Training Instructor Stalin reporting for Customs and Immigration Inspection with eleven personnel."

Head took the passports. "You're a day early."

"Vagaries of war, Comrade."

"Here. Each person must fill out one of these declaration forms. And I have a manifest that says you have some cargo in your custody."

"Yes, Comrade. One hundred and ten SKS rifles, a like number of M-66 bolt action rifles, all with attached bayonets."

Head examined the manifest. "Why so many bayoneted rifles?"

A hint of a smile finally showed on the Russian's mouth. "Why, for bayonet training, of course."

Richard Head was beginning to get irritated. "A thousand rounds of ammunition for each type of weapon. A handful of Sa-7s RPGs and related rounds. And side arms for all your men. Anything else?"

"Just three presents I have for some Russian officers at Malmstrom."

"You'll need to open them. And your passport only has the name Stalin on it. No first, middle names. Is this an attempt at a joke?"

"No joke, Comrade. That is my name. I know who I am. I need no extra names."

Head regarded him with a dubious look. "I didn't think Stalin was a name anyone still used."

Instructor Stalin shrugged. "Why not? It is a good Russian name."

The Customs Official kept staring at the Russian, who appeared as if he no worries in the world.

"Open the presents. I need to make sure they are not drugs or other illegal merchandise."

"Run them thru your x-ray machines. It will show you what they are without ruining the wrapping."

"Look it, Stalin, or whatever you go by. I'm in charge, not you. Show me the packages and open them. That's an order. Damnit."

Stalin stood still, calmly staring at the Customs Officer.

"That's it." Head started to reach for the Russian's personal pack. It would be the last thing he would know for a half hour. He would wake up with a headache and would try to locate the Russians, but would fail.

Stalin stepped around the inspection table and over the prostrate body of Head. He rumbled through the desk and found a stamp he was looking for.

"Comrades. Front and center."

Within minutes, Stalin had stamped each passport with the correct visa stamp and forged the initials of the unconscious Head. The Senior Lieutenant of the group looked at a Stalin with a worried, concerned look the instructor had seen many times before.

"Comrade Senior Instructor Stalin, is this necessary? Must you once again use force rather than just go through the process like everyone else?"

Stalin grunted. "I do not suffer fools easy, Comrade Lieutenant. Time and this war wait for no man. We have a chance to hit back at the Squids with the Yankees and the Japanese. Some minor bureaucrat will not be allowed to derail our efforts. Besides, I am impatient to visit some prior students of mine already working with the Allies." Stalin pulled a black passport out of his bag, and he quickly added a stamp and initials on the correct page.

"Comrade Stalin, that is a diplomatic passport for a Diplomat, embassy personnel. How did you get that?"

The Senior Instructor smiled. "Do not worry. You are all innocent of any connections with my actions. They will only deal with me. Now, young Lieutenant, form up your men. We leave now."

Within moments, they were marching in tight column formation out of the operations building. They proceeded down the boulevard, toward the way off base. Stalin would find a hotel for his people to stay in while he located the land transportation they needed for the long trip from Alaska to Montana. He noticed a red fire and rescue truck leading a deuce and a half down the same street. The fire truck hit its siren for a second. Stalin peeled off from the formation and met the approaching vehicle. In it was the young supervisory fireman.

"Hey, Comrade. I have your equipment in the truck. Where do you want it?"

"I will jump on board and direct it. That you very much, Comrade fireman. I owe you a drink. Perhaps some vodka?"

"Maybe later. I'm still on duty. You have a safe trip, Comrade…."

"Stalin, young man. Senior Training Instructor Stalin. I will not be hard to find. Just ask around."

The Fire Supervisor grinned. Yes, with a name and the demeanor like his, Stalin would not be hard to find.

Stalin saluted the fireman, then quickly scrambled onto the deuce and a half. He was pleasantly surprised when he saw the driver and co-driver were both young women, two very attractive brunettes. The driver was a Sergeant, the co-driver a Private First Class. He grinned.

"Comrades. Thank you for bringing me my equipment. Tell me, do you have time while I find lodging, and a place to store my equipment? Or do I need to drive the truck myself?"

The Sergeant smiled. This Russian looked like he could take a bear down. Yet there was something about his demeanor, despite his scars, that was oddly attractive. He had no rank, so he must be a civilian.

"Well, Sir, today is Thanksgiving, and we are on a skeleton crew. We were called out because they thought your plane would be spread out all over the tarmac, and we would be picking up pieces of the cargo for the next twenty-four hours."

"Hm. So you were called out on your holiday. I understand this was the first one of this type to be celebrated since the Squids appeared, da?"

"Yes," the Private answered. "We have a turkey dinner supposedly waiting for us at the chow hall. But I don't know how long they'll hold some for us."

Stalin smiled a bit. "Take me to a hotel that has rooms for my men and I, and a place to park this truck under guard. I will then treat you to any meal you wish. I am very good at obtaining meals for my men. It is what you Americans call scrounging."

The Sergeant grinned. Why not, she thought. "Okay, Sir. As long as you call our dispatch, and tell them that you need our assistance for the next twenty-four hours. I know they don't want to interfere with anyone else's Thanksgiving."

"Then it is a deal. Shake, in your parlance. I will also need to know your names in order to inform your dispatch."

"Sergeant Stephanie Seymour, and this is Private First Class Kristen Smith, at your service, Sir."

"Please. No sirs. I am not an officer. Senior Instructor, or just plain Stalin is fine."

PFC Smith looked at him quizzically. "Stalin?"

"Yes. That is my name. I have no others, even though the Customs Officer did not believe me. I know who I am."

Sgt. Seymour smiled. "Well, crawl into the cab, Stalin. It's cold out. I think I know of a hotel that will fit your needs."

Early the next morning, Stalin woke up on the comfortable hotel bed. Both women were next to him, one on each side. Sgt. Seymour had kept her promise and found a hotel with a large enough parking garage to accommodate the truck. Stalin had arranged for shifts of two men each to secure the weapons and other equipment during the night. A call to a prearranged telephone number and Stalin had set up a time to meet in forty eight hours with other trucks that were being convoyed down the Alaskan (ALKAN) Highway, across Canada, and down to Montana. The deuce and a half was theirs to use now, and the two women soldiers would get a ride back to the Base. But before that, Stalin kept his promise.

Some palms greased with actual gold and silver, and the hotel management came up with turkey dinners with all the fixings. Stalin then made his way into the kitchen, and somehow managed to concoct borscht as well as some potato dishes. And, of course, a large quantity of vodka was located. Sergeant 'call me Stephanie' Seymour sat next to Stalin with a very satisfied look on her face after having stuffed herself with his culinary offerings.

"I know this is better than anything we could have at the chow hall. Neither I nor Kristen have any family left, so this was definitely a good way to restart Thanksgiving for us. How can we repay you?"

Stalin poured the Sergeant another glass of vodka. "Oh, I will think of something…"

Stalin knew he had a certain animal attractiveness that had a strong effect on women, despite all of his scars. In fact, with some women, it was because of the scars. Women, especially in this day and age, wanted a strong man that could help protect them and give them strong, healthy babies. The arrival of the Squids put a premium on fighting qualities to keep babies from being harvested.

Kristen, the PFC, stirred on his left side. This would be a night to remember. Stalin smoothly extracted himself from in between the two women, and headed to the shower. Nothing like American plumbing and hot water. He then dressed and repacked the few things he had taken out. The two women were just beginning to wake now, and saw him getting ready to leave.

"Alas, my sweets, I must see to my men. Please stay in this room as long as you like. I have paid for another night, but will be busy all day. Early tomorrow morning, we start the long drive to Malmstrom Allied Base."

Stephanie stood up, nude, and walked over to kiss him. "Any time you pass through, please look us up. I can't thank you enough for a great Thanksgiving."

Stalin gave a small smile. "I will remember that, Comrade Stephanie. This was my first exposure to your American Thanksgiving. I will look forward to experiencing other Yankee holidays if they are all like this one." Kristen then approached and kissed him goodbye as well. He hugged them both one last time, and then left.

Stephanie looked at Kristen. She smiled, and hugged her friend and fellow soldier. They had covered each other's backsides for the past two years. In a way they were the only family they had left. Like siblings, they were willing to share most things for the sake of their small bonded unit.

"Well duty calls. Come on, Private First Class Smith. Time to get showered, dressed, and have some leftover turkey for breakfast. Then back to the J-BER. We still need to earn our pay."

CHAPTER 20

"There are no Holidays in hell."
-Anonymous

ATLANTA, GEORGIA
CATTLE COUNTRY

Malcolm Carver watched as the top of the downtown office building burned. A half hour prior, as the Unoccupied States celebrated Thanksgiving, a twin engine aircraft later identified as the B-25 left behind by Torbin Bender and company in Florida had dropped two twenty gallon drums on the center of Atlanta. One hit the top of the tall structure and exploded, throwing its cargo of homemade napalm all over the roof. The second drum fell to the street below, where it broke apart but did not explode. The liquid contents ran down into the sewers and nearby basements and parking garages, spreading fumes and flammable liquid. Fortunately, nothing had been set on fire. As they evacuated the residents from the underground warrens, they lost one man who had been overcome from the fumes in the confined spaces. But they had been lucky. If both bombs had exploded at ground level, the flaming substances would have resulted in a high number of casualties among those hiding underground.

At last count, there were just over fifty thousand surviving people of color hiding in Atlanta. Now, minus one more.

He glanced sideway at his "new best friend", as he jokingly referred to him. Dawoud Amin had dropped from the sky, literally, a week before. Coming in a sailplane glider that had been launched covertly just outside of Cattle Country, Dawoud had used a catapult assist as well as two small rocket motors to propel the glider up to some five thousand feet. Dawoud had expertly ridden the air currents to make a silent landing in downtown Atlanta. A trained Islamic terrorist, member of a sleeper cell in the U.S., he was the only surviving member of his group. Now he used his skills against the aliens who were killing his darker skinned brothers around the world. For some six years he had hidden his dark skin from the harvesters, until one day arriving at Malmstrom Armed Forces Base, where he offered his skills to his former enemy.

"How did you give up your mission to serve Allah and kill the infidel?" Malcolm had asked.

The tall, slender Dawoud had given a cynical laugh. "Allah has apparently given up on us. He allowed these beasts to show up and begin eating us. It must be a form of punishment. He has turned his back on us until we prove our worthiness again by killing this new enemy in His name. The eating of human flesh by intelligent beings is an abomination. If we stop this, Allah may return to us."

"You said 'may'."

Dawoud shrugged. "If it is the will of Allah. No man may know all of Allah's desires. We try to follow his word—the Qur'an. But we apparently failed and now must redeem ourselves. Only Allah may make that decision."

Dawoud had brought a few goodies with him. "Pappy" Gun had sent some early production examples of an 'ace in the hole' he was developing—3D Printer produced weapons. Two single shot, bolt action .223 caliber rifles made from spun plastic/ceramic medium had proven quite accurate, and were now referred to as poor man's sniper rifles. Though only good for about a dozen shots until they began to show pressure cracks, they were still very accurate for the first few rounds. Dawoud had already taken out two sentries on the outskirts of the ring of armed personnel the Tschaaa and their lapdog Krakens had thrown up. Dawoud had brought a small spark radio set that he used to tap the out old morse code to a relay listening post hidden in Tennessee. He used this to communicate the success of the weapons so that more could be provided.

In addition, Dawoud had brought two small .32 caliber pistols with matched silencers, also 3D Printer weapons. Six rounds in an integral magazine, the pistols might last for twelve shots on a good day before breaking. In a shoulder holster, Dawoud had a 3D printer copy of a Czech Skorpion machine pistol in .32 caliber. It would last for at least the twenty round magazine it came with, maybe a second mag if you were lucky. But all of these weapons were fairly light, cheap, quickly made, and disposable. Perfect for behind the lines operations, and Atlanta was definitely behind the lines.

Dawoud had also brought a small quantity of plastic explosives, plus an encyclopedic knowledge of improvised weapons, explosives, and booby traps. The fact that the Unoccupied States had sent him to Malcolm out of the clear blue sky, after the F-51 air attack, was a good harbinger of things to come. Then, Dawoud had met with Professor Bashir Gupta and it was a match made in heaven. Or hell, depending how you looked at it.

Gupta had looked at Dawoud in respectful surprise when he began outlining all the improvised explosives he could manufacture with the chemicals and materials at hand. "Are you certain that you do not have a Doctorate in Chemistry or Chemical Engineering?"

Dawoud snorted. "The only Doctorate I have is from the school of hard knocks and street warfare. I was taught by the best on how to make weapons out of almost anything."

"You used them against Hindus as well as Christians, yes?"

Dawoud hesitated before he answered. "Yes. I was a warrior for Allah in every sense of the word. I will not apologize for who I was. It was the result of the times I lived in. Now, times have changed."

Gupta smiled. "Yes, times have changed. I think God, Allah, Shiva—whomever you pray to—has decided to teach us a valuable lesson."

"What is that?" It was Dawoud's turn to inquire.

"There are worse things in the universe than the fact someone worships a God in a different way than you do. One of those worse things is that there are beings in the universe that find us quite tasty." Dawoud had laughed long and hard at Gupta's response.

Now, Malcolm and Dawoud were watching as two battle robs led a patrol of Kraken human soldiers into what was downtown Atlanta. The burning office building provided a little extra warmth on this cold morning. The enemy forces made their way slowly down the thoroughfare, weapons ready. They scanned the buildings for snipers and other threats, having been on the receiving end of both the past weeks. Now, it appeared as if the Krakens were beginning to put more pressure on the holdouts in Atlanta, no longer content to just starve them out. However, they still seemed hesitant to just raze Atlanta to the ground for some reason. Malcolm suspected he would never entirely understand alien psychology.

Dawoud watched the approaching Krakens with an almost feral glee. As the battle robs reached the center of the street, he told Malcolm, "Watch this." He pushed a button on the command detonator he had made from a cell phone. Just as a wheeled battle rob drove by an abandoned car, a shaped charge detonated, shooting a jet of molten metal into the side of the bulb-shaped turret. The Tschaaa built machine began to smoke and spark, then jerked to a halt. The humans scattered to what cover they could find, a few shots fired at the origin of the blast. Dawoud and Malcolm, some one hundred yards away and well concealed, both smiled as they watched the action. The Krakens yelled back and forth for about ten minutes, the remaining battle rob searching for a target. Made from a harvester bob, it keyed on motion. If one stood still, it would often miss human shapes.

Finally, the patrol reformed, Malcolm hearing yells of "booby-trap" being thrown about. They slowly moved about twenty yards closer until a battle rob fell into the large tiger trap in the street. The street surface had been replaced with a tarp, stained and painted to make it appear as if it were the original street pavement. Stretched super taunt, it held up until the machine was almost completely suspended. Then it gave way, the battle rob falling into the sewer drain below. The Krakens yelled as it fell, scrambled to the edge of the pit trap and looked down in. The Squad Commander yelled commands to find some rope, cable, anything to be used to lift and pull the battle rob out. Dawoud looked at Malcolm and nodded. Malcolm clicked a small hand held radio he had three times.

From a concealed catapult a block over, a large gasoline filled tripled garbage bag was launched. The large bag arced high in the air over a parking lot connecting the two streets. None of the Krakens saw it until it was too late. The bag hit, burst. A small detonator Dawoud had made sparked, and flaming liquid was all over. Two Krakens were inundated, turning into running fiery torches. One, a female, fell into the pit with the battle rob, screaming. The other flaming Kraken tried to fall and roll like children were taught in grade school. He ended up rolling into the pit too, screaming as he fell. Suddenly, everyone broke and ran, firing wildly. One Kraken ran down along the remaining storefronts close to the buildings. In his mad dash, he tripped a deadfall trap. A trash can full of watered down but still potent battery acid cascaded over him. Screaming in pain, he dropped his assault rifle, and began to run blindly about. His fellow Krakens tried to yell directions to the blinded soldier but he was screaming in pain, clawing at his eyes. Running and stumbling in ever widening circles, he soon joined his two fiery comrades in the trap pit. There was a thud as he hit the surface below, and his screaming stopped.

"Quickly, Malcolm. Have the men get into the pit to recover the weapons. They may send more battle robs." A short broadcast, and pre-placed forces were in the pit with fire extinguishers. Two others ran to the battle rob up on the street. With practiced ease, they broke open the maintenance hatch in the back of the turret, and removed the machine gun and ammunition. Luckily, the shaped charge blast had entered underneath the weapon box in which the machine gun had been built. The controls had been fried, the electronic-organic hybrid brain knocked out, but the weapon was still serviceable.

Twenty minutes later, the area around the ambush scene was deserted. Malcolm and Dawoud made it back to the hidden underground command post Malcolm had established in a large storage room connected to sub-floor of a parking garage. Three stories down, he felt safe from bombing attacks. They soon had the results of the ambush. Three usable assault rifles, although one would need a replacement stock. Surprisingly, both of battle rob machine guns were workable, as were two rifle grenades that had been recovered from the one shot launchers placed in the front of the ex-harvesters. It was a good haul.

Malcolm grinned at Dawoud. "You bring us luck, my friend. Guns and dead Krakens. The only thing that could make it better would be a Thanksgiving turkey."

Dawoud chuckled. "No one mentioned anything about me bringing a turkey when I flew the glider here."

From a desk chair in the command post, Red spoke. "I could come up with some roasted rat right now. There are also rumors that a cat was caught and skinned a block over." The gorgeous young woman looked at Dawoud with what Malcolm could only describe as a smoldering gaze. Dawoud seemed to attract her as no other man, not even Malcolm, could. He smiled to himself. Love and lust found themselves in the oddest places.

"Whatever you could provide, my good lady, would be most welcome," Dawoud said, giving a short bow. This elicited a grin from Red, who then hurried to find them something to eat. Malcolm chuckled.

"You know she has the hots for you, Dawoud."

"Yes, my friend. She is very attractive."

"So..."

Dawoud looked at Malcolm. "I am still enough of a good Muslim that I would have to take her as a wife before I would have sexual congress with her. She would be my third wife."

Malcolm looked surprised. "You have two more in the Unoccupied States?"

"Yes. They helped me get to Malmstrom, to offer my services. We have four children."

Malcolm laughed. "You are a man full of surprises."

Dawoud smiled. "But first I would have to explain to Red that she would be the most junior wife. She would have to convert to Islam, if Allah and I can reach a reconciliation." He paused.

"She would have to hold her own against two other wives. I have already had to break up some catfights they had."

Malcolm laughed loudly. "Before she gets back, let me tell you about how I first saw Red...."

CHAPTER 21

3:00am Christmas morning and Aleks could not sleep. She sat at the kitchen table of the duplex, sipping some tea she had made. The trolls, her twin sons, were active in her womb. They were moving, shifting around restlessly, as if preparing for something to happen. Aleks knew it was a proverbial crap shoot concerning the due date, the Tschaaa attempts at human fecundity modifications having sped up the gestation period.

As she was the first human female in the area that had been identified as carrying children affected by the Tschaaa organisms and modified DNA strands, hers was the test case. Doctors Bardun and Rice had been fussing over her for months, watching the quickened development of the babies. They had provided Aleks with some high protein drinks to help provide the necessary nutrients for the rapidly growing twins. Aleks was always hungry, eating prodigious amounts of food to keep her babies happy and satiated. Between the drinks and the food, the trolls were developing into *big* babies. They had talked about a Caesarean, but Aleks had insisted that her pelvic region would be of sufficient size to handle the birth, "as long as they don't both try to come out at once."

As she sat sipping her tea, allowing Torbin to sleep, she thought of the events over the last month since Thanksgiving. First, a blast from the past, in the form of a certain former instructor of hers, had appeared. Comrade Stalin, Senior Training Instructor extraordinaire. Torbin had recounted the story about the day the scarred, solid Stalin marched into General Reed's office.

"Senior Training Instructor Stalin reporting as ordered, Sir." Ramrod straight, in almost accent-less English, he stood in front of the General. For one of the few times in his life, Stalin's eyes had widened a hair in surprise when the General had answered in flawless Russian.

"Comrade Stalin, I believe you wished to be called," General Reed replied as he stood and extended his hand. He had been told that Stalin was some odd form of "civilian" in the Russian system, not military but also some special category all his own. Stalin had created the title Senior Training Instructor years ago, and no one had ever disagreed with him about it. Possibly, it was rumored, out of fear. He was a legend in the tight Spetsnaz and Intelligence communities.

"You speak Russian like a native, General. But you are not Russian, da?"

"I was married to a Russian. We had two sons."

"You used past tense," Stalin commented.

"Yes, Comrade. They were in Moscow, visiting relatives when the Tschaaa struck. I have not heard anything since. I assume they are no longer with us."

Stalin did not speak. He could have told the General that the Moscow area had been a disorganized mess after the rock strikes. That there was always the chance that she survived in one of the many little enclaves that had sprung up as the surviving Russian military fled east to Siberia. But he knew that the General had probably thought of this before.

General Reed then produced a bottle of scotch. "I prefer scotch to vodka, Comrade. But would you have a drink with me?"

Stalin had smiled. "We Russians may drink a lot of vodka, but that does not mean some of us have not developed a taste for other types of alcohol. I could certainly use a drink after the long drive from Alaska."

General Reed produced some ice cubes, and poured a couple of substantial drinks. He raised his glass toward the Russian. "A toast to future cooperation and operations against the Squids between our countries."

"I will drink twice to that, General."

They then sat down, and began to talk turkey. Stalin laid out his expertise in training, especially with regards to building an efficient fighting force using the people they had on hand in the shortest period possible.

"I know, General Reed, that we do not have the luxury of time. The longer we wait to take action, the more entrenched the Enemy becomes. The majority of Tschaaa ships are beginning the preparatory actions for their trip home, leaving certain groups behind. If we make it appear too costly for the Tschaaa to keep a permanent presence on Earth before the starships leave our solar system, they may just pack up and *all* go home. If not, then it becomes a War of Genocide. I do not see us existing next to species that will try and eat us any chance it gets, not as co-equals."

General Reed saw in Stalin a warrior that had probably seen more action than a dozen soldiers combined. He also saw a man with a spine of steel connected to a very fast acting intellect. Why he was not a General of the armies in Russia would be a mystery if General Reed really looked into the matter. The fact he was sent here pointed to the idea that someone wanted him out of the way. Stalin probably was one of few survivors who knew where most of the skeletons from the USSR and pre-strike Russia were buried. That would make some people—political animals mostly—very nervous, Squids or no Squids. Well, their loss was the General's gain.

"When can you and your people start, Comrade?"

"Tomorrow morning, General. When the first cock crows."

General Reed smiled. "0700 will be fine, though that is close to sunrise this time of year. You will be under the direction of Major Torbin Bender, as well as working with some personnel from other countries, including our Japanese allies."

Now it was Stalin's turn to smile. "Ah, Comrade Bender. The Marine who killed a Squid with a knife. It will be a pleasure to compare notes with him."

"Good. Here is a map outlining where the main training areas are located. Meet the good Major at this temporary building next to the gymnasium and field area. That is what they use as their offices. They don't spend much time there, which is why it is so spartan. We keep paperwork to a minimum. A form almost never helps someone learn how to fight and survive."

General Reed stuck his hand out. "Time to shake on it, Comrade, as us Yankees put it. But I must warn you. Shake my hand and I will work your ass off. I don't have time for people looking for a vacation in a foreign country."

Stalin glanced at his muscular posterior. "Well, General, others have tried to work my ass off. It still appears to be attached."

General Reed laughed as the two shook hands. Stalin had obtained a file on General Reed before meeting him, as any good spy would do. Though his flawless Russian had surprised him a bit, he knew General Reed's background. Stalin looked into the General's eyes as he felt the metal of the man in his grip. Stalin was an excellent judge of character. It had helped him survive all these years in a system that often made the weak disappear. He liked what he saw. Stalin stepped back and gave a short bow.

"Thank you, my General. Thank you for giving me another opportunity to serve in this all important fight."

"Hell, Comrade. I thank you for coming. I need some Russian steel here. My wife taught me the value of it years ago."

As Stalin left, General Reed did not realize the hidden meaning in the phrase 'my General' that the Russian had used. Stalin had decided that the General was *his* General. That meant he would follow him to hell if need be, and protect him from all enemies. Stalin would kill or be killed for General Reed, that was the extent of his loyalty. The fact that the General spoke Russian like a native and had married a Russian probably helped. But the bottom line was that Stalin had decided General Reed was his General. Woe to those who interfered.

Aleks had also been told by Torbin about the first meeting he, Abigail, and Ichiro had with Stalin the morning after the Russian had checked in with General Reed. Torbin had received a short telephone call that the Senior Training Instructor and his people would be reporting to the training area the next morning. The General had been sparse with the information on Stalin, as he wanted Torbin to make an independent evaluation of the Russians.

At 0650, Torbin and company were in their offices when Stalin knocked loudly on the outer door. Torbin met the Russian instructor at the entrance.

"Comrade Bender. Senior Training Instructor Stalin reporting as ordered by my General Reed." He stood ramrod straight, Torbin seeing a person he would later describe as hewn from a block of granite, scars and all. Torbin stuck his hand out. "Welcome aboard, Comrade Stalin." He glanced past him and saw eleven men standing ramrod straight at Parade Rest in a two line formation. All were dressed in identical Spetsnaz urban camo fatigues with pistols and fighting knives. Torbin noticed that Stalin had no such accouterments, just a set of fatigues with no rank. A cloth name tag with STI printed on it was over his right pocket, that was it.

"So, Comrade Bender, where do we start?" Stalin asked as he finished shaking his hand.

"Well, since I was told you are ready and raring to go, we have one hundred alleged retreads who will be here at the training facility at 0730 hours. I say alleged as there are limited ways to check out their stories of previous training and service. They have been checked out this last week as best we can, but as they say here, the proof is in the pudding. They all seem to know basic military customs and courtesies. The questions that remain are twofold. Just how much service do they really have, and are they here to serve or to spy."

Stalin cocked an eyebrow. "So some may be here under false pretenses, and may even be Krakens?"

"That's right. After finding those Pits right under our noses, anything seems possible."

Stalin paused for a moment. "I will have complete control over their training?"

"Yes, for thirty days, a couple days break at Christmas. Just no actual killing or maiming them. I know you will be tough, but I can't have a bunch of corpses showing up. We need soldiers and some do have family members around."

Stalin smiled. "Comrade, the training will be excruciatingly tough. More so, I dare say, than your Marine Corps training. But I promise there will be no unnecessary injuries. Fatalities, well... if they kill themselves, I have difficulty stopping that. And, if I guessed correctly, this will be a chance for you and my General to decide if our methods will be compatible with the type of soldier you want. True?"

Now Torbin smiled. "You hit that right on the head, STI Stalin. We have to get a codified training program in place that can be completed at all the Allied Armed Forces Bases in the U.S. By the end of January, with your assistance, each base or training location should be set up to turn out at least a thousand trained personal a year. Then, we will need to increase that exponentially over time."

"Now, let me introduce you to Captain Young and Major Yamamoto."

Ichiro, after his little "problem" with a certain deceased Russian officer, was always a bit reserved when meeting Russian personnel. He bowed respectfully, shook Stalin's hand, welcoming him to Malmstrom. If Stalin noticed any coldness in his demeanor, he did not let on.

When Abigail shook Stalin's hand, he cocked his head a bit, studying her.

"Excuse me, Comrade Captain, but your reputation precedes you. So my men may be a bit… curious to see if reality equals reputation."

Abigail was fast on the uptake before Torbin or Ichiro could say anything. She had heard this all before, the idea that the Avenging Angel from Deseret was all just hype. In flawless Russian, she answered, "So, Comrade, what would you have me do? Eat rocks, spit nails?"

Stalin fell silent for a moment, surprised at her excellent Russian. He had information that she was good with languages, but not like a native Russian. A hint of a smile formed on his lips.

"How about a little bayonet training with me? My men know how much I like cold steel, and how nasty I can be with a rifle. This will show them your mettle."

This conversation was all in Russian, so Torbin understood maybe two words of it. Ichiro understood a bit more, getting the gist that Stalin would like to demonstrate a bit of Russian military training, using Abigail as a subject.

"Of course, Comrade," Abigail answered. "You have sufficient equipment with you?"

"Yes, Captain Young. We have a vehicle full of everything we will need. Shall we?" He bowed a bit, motioning Abigail to proceed first toward his men. Torbin figured Abigail understood what was going on and, trusted her judgment. He just followed her lead. As they walked down the small ramp to the cement former parking area that served as a military training formation area, the Russians snapped to attention in formation. Stalin ordered in rapid fire Russian for two men to bring several of the bayoneted training rifles from the truck. There was snow on the ground around the cement area, trainees having shoveled the snow from the formation area and walkways. This was still definitely winter weather in Montana, so the temperature was just beginning to climb to freezing level. The Russians, other than Stalin, were wearing winter camos with long sleeved undergarments and gloves for warmth and the stereotypical Russian fur hat. Stalin wore no gloves or extra undergarments, acted as if it were an early spring day in the park.

As the two selected soldiers ran to get the rifles, Stalin put the rest of the formation at Parade Rest, then at ease. He then explained to them in Russian what was about to happen.

"Captain Young has 'requested' a demonstration of some of the training skills we will be using to bring trainees with prior experience up to standards as combat soldiers. This will include the infusing of an aggressive, combat spirit into anyone who wishes to fight alongside us Russians. What better way than with a bit of bayonet training, da?"

Suddenly, the Russians all smiled to themselves. They has seen this before. Someone was about to be taught a hard lesson by Comrade Stalin, as well as some humility.

"Captain Young, would you care to address the trainers?"

Abigail stepped up, and in flawless Russian spoke. "It is an honor to have you experienced soldiers here to help us prepare for war. I look forward to working with you."

The Russian personnel felt to shocked silence at the Yankee's command of their language. It did not hurt that she was also very pleasant to look at. A few appreciative murmurs were heard until Stalin stopped them with an icy glare. Just then the two detailed soldiers appeared with several rifles each. A tarp was spread out on the cement and the rifles laid carefully on it.

"Captain, an SKS or a Myosin Nagant 44 bolt action? Your choice. Both have folding bayonets attached. It helps bone-headed soldiers from losing them."

Abigail smiled at the comment. "SKS, if you please. I've handled one before."

"Lieutenant Ivanovich."

"Yes, Comrade Stalin." The young officer snapped to attention.

"Please select two SKS rifles for us to use. Ensure they are cleared and safe. It would be embarrassing if the good Captain was accidently shot."

"Yes, Comrade Stalin."

Torbin watched all this with a watchful eye. The Russians seemed to be both in awe as well as scared of Stalin. Torbin was getting the impression that Stalin was a bit of a legend amongst the Russian military establishment. It would be interesting to see if he lived up to that reputation.

Upon seeing the rifles, Torbin quickly figured out the drill. A little bit of bayonet training. Stalin probably wanted to see if Abigail knew about cold steel. He smiled to himself. A Russian was about to get a big surprise.

Lt. Ivanovich stepped in front of Abigail, and holding a cleared SKS in his left hand, saluted with his right. "Lt. Ivanovich, Ma'am. Here is your requested weapon."

Abigail saluted back, took the offered weapon, did a quick check of the chamber to insure there was nothing there, then held it at high port and pulled the trigger. Stalin noticed this with an appreciative eye. The young woman was comfortable around weapons, and also seemed to have the strength to easily manipulate them. Good. His estimation of American Forces went up a tick. Stalin took his SKS, checked to insure it was cleared as well. He then unfolded the foot length bayonet with a nine inch blade. Torbin noticed the bayonet blade had been sharpened to what looked like a razor sharpness. He cleared his throat, stepped forward.

"Excuse me, Comrade. Do you have any training sheaths for the blades?"

Stalin gave him a quizzical look, then spoke in English. "Why? What good is training if it is not realistic enough, if there is no danger of getting hurt? One can be injured in combat, yes?"

"It's okay, Major," Abigail interjected. "I believe Comrade Stalin has sufficient experience that neither one of us will be allowed to be seriously injured."

Stalin grinned at her comment.

"You are also a politician, I see Captain," he commented in Russian. "Praising me will not make me feel merciful toward you if you are found wanting."

"Neither will it make me any less aggressive toward you, Comrade, despite your elder age," Abigail responded with a smile.

Several Russians gasped. Who would dare to risk insulting Stalin like this? She must be mad.

The Senior Training Instructor only gave a hearty chuckle. "Ah, Spirit. I like that in a soldier, a warrior. Alright, my young Captain. On guard position."

Abigail brought up her weapon, bayonet pointed at Stalin, with the butt of her weapon near her right hip. She was perfectly balanced on both her forward left and rear right feet. With a practiced eye, Stalin could see Abigail was relaxed and confident. She had done this before. Good. Stalin always looked for a good workout.

"And now, the dance begins," the Senior Instructor said.

Stalin made a feint with his point toward Abigail's face, to see if she would overreact. Abigail simply moved her body just enough, positioned her weapon just right that had Stalin continued through with his thrust, the bayonet would have slid past its target, being sufficiently blocked to prevent any possible contact. Stalin recovered and smiled. Finally, someone not so awed, afraid of him, or so inexperienced as to prevent a decent response.

"I do not like this, Torbin-san." As Torbin glanced at his friend he saw, for the first time he could remember, a distinctive worried look on the Japanese soldier's face. Torbin realized it was the look of a man who saw the love of his life in danger, and wanting to jump into action. Damn. He had not realized just how close the two had gotten. But this was duty. This is what they did. Torbin could not step in and still say he trusted Abigail's abilities. She had made her bed, she must sleep in it.

"What's the matter, Major? Don't think the good Captain can take care of herself?'

With that, Ichiro's face became stoic. "No, Major Bender. I know she can. But if she is injured, Stalin will have to face me."

Torbin did not reply. He knew that, career and mission be damned, Ichiro would fulfill the duty he thought honor dictated. He would try to kill Stalin if Abigail sustained a serious injury.

Stalin began a standard repertoire of attacks he used in his training course. He tried low and high attacks with the point, slashes with the blade edge, and follow through with butt strikes. Abigail seemed to flow, move, and parry every attempt. Stalin began a more aggressive series of attacks, and Abigail started to give ground, slowly. Stalin watched as the young woman was pushed back to the edge of the cleared concrete, to within a foot of the snow covered ground. The Russian made slash at Abigail's legs, then swung the rifle butt around to knock her rifle away, to be followed by an unobstructed butt smash toward her face.

She was not there. Somehow, seemingly a blur, the Avenging Angel spun to her left, out of the way of the butt smash, the Russian's right side. Stalin was so surprised that he almost continued forward onto the snow covered ground. But years of experience took over and he managed to regain his balance and spun around himself to face Abigail in an on guard position.

"My turn," Abigail said in English, and unleashed her attack.

Smacks of wood hitting wood, the ring of steel on steel reverberated as Abigail was an almost blur of motion. Torbin knew she was fast, but not *this* fast. Only Stalin's years of experience, his automatic reflexes seemed to save him. A look of solid determination on his face, he once again tried to press an attack. He went in low, a long full thrust to Abigail's middle that not even he could have pulled at the last moment to prevent a substantial injury. But once again her body was not there. She was behind him, having leapt and twisted like some gymnast. He managed to spin around, and rushed her with his rifle at high port. Rifle smashed into rifle as he tried to use superior mass and strength to push her back, over power her. And hit a brick wall.

For the first time in recent memory, Stalin's eyes widened large in actual surprise. How could this woman, whom he assumed he outweighed by at least twenty kilos or so, be able to stop this attack?

Then Abigail moved. Stalin found himself sliding by the young lady, a bit off balance from pushing so hard, having tried to overpower his supposedly smaller foe. Somehow he took a blow behind his right knee. His leg buckled, and Stalin tried to roll in the direction of his fall, so that he could go with the blow, get out of the vicinity of Abigail and get back to his feet. Then he saw stars.

A few moments later and he was on his back, sans rifle, a bayonet blade at his throat.

"Yield, Senior Training Instructor Stalin?" A firm female voice asked.

His eyes focused. He heard his men begin to protest, possibly thinking some trick had been pulled. He yelled out in Russian. "Stop. Or else." Everyone froze. Then, Stalin, on his back, began to chuckle. Then guffaw loudly. Finally, a belly laugh. Abigail tried to stop herself but actually let out a girlish giggle.

"May I be allowed to rise, young lady?"

Abigail withdrew her bayonet blade from his throat and stepped back. Stalin quickly scrambled to his feet, still laughing. He grabbed Abigail, hugged and kissed her on each cheek before she could protest. He spun and faced his men.

"Today, history has been made. An Avenging Angel has taken down this old devil. I think she deserves some recognition."

Lt. Ivanovich commenced slow applause, which all of the Russians soon joined in rhythm. Then Torbin and Ichiro.

"You must be part Russian, da?" Stalin asked above the din.

"No Sir. Romanian and Norwegian."

Stalin laughed again. "Hell, close enough." He met Abigail's gaze directly. "You can protect my backside anytime you wish," he said in Russian.

"It would be an honor, Comrade Stalin."

"Now, after work, I must buy you a drink. Many drinks. "

"I drink almost no alcohol. I am Mormon."

Stalin shrugged. "Then I will drink your portion. And buy drinks for the two Majors here."

The clapping having stopped, Ichiro stepped up to Stalin and Abigail and bowed. "A contest befitting samurai. I am glad no one was seriously hurt."

Stalin saw Ichiro's demeanor, and the way he and Abigail suddenly locked eyes. He had seen this look before. "You would have gutted me with your sword had I seriously hurt the good Captain here, would you not?"

It was a day for firsts, as Ichiro suddenly began to stammer, stutter in apparent protest. The scarred Russian held up his hand. "Please, no denials. There is nothing wrong to protect, even seek revenge for a loved one. I would do the same."

Both Ichiro and Abigail turned shades of crimson, and Torbin burst out laughing. He glanced across the training area, saw some trainees approaching from the opposite end of the large, snow covered field. "Comrade Stalin, prepare to meet your mission."

Stalin glimpsed the approaching personnel. He barked out, "Alright, Comrades. New meat approaches. Time to make ready."

He turned and looked at Torbin. "Today will be a long, hard one for them."

Torbin smiled. "I wouldn't have it any other way."

That night, Torbin and Abigail had told Aleks about the Russians. When he mentioned Stalin's name, Aleks' eyes widened. "Did you say Stalin? Just Stalin?"

"Yes, my dear. He said he only needed one name. And by the way, Abigail here kicked his butt in bayonet training."

Aleks mouth fell open. "You defeated him with a rifle and bayonet?" she demanded of Abigail.

"Well, he was quite good, so I think it was more by luck than any... why are you staring at me like that?"

Aleks grabbed her husband's arm. "He is solid, scarred up, looks like he was cut from a block of rock?"

"Why yes, Aleks. You know him personally?"

Aleks went pale. "I must sit down," she said as she plunked down on the sofa.

"Dearest wife, what's wrong? Are the trolls kicking too much?"

Aleks took a moment to catch her breath. "Remember what I told you about when Fuzz saved me from the Eaters? What I did, what he did?"

"Why, of course. What..."

Aleks held her hand up to stop him. "There was another person involved."

"Why of course. A certain dependent wife showed up."

"No." Aleks took another deep breath. "Senior Training Instructor Stalin was there. At least his voice was."

Both Torbin and Abigail stared at her as if she was having a brain fart of some type. "Fuzz hit the first Eater, who had ahold of me, and freed me. I froze for a moment." She looked at Abigail. "Your big beautiful beastie saved me from that one. Then the second attacked. And I just sat there. Until I heard a voice in my head calling me a fat cow, telling me to get up or die. So I got up, grabbed the shotgun. Then the voice reminded me of my bayonet training. I used a high thrust to get by Fuzz, and shoot the Eater in the head.

"It was *his* voice; it was *his* training that helped save me, and helped Fuzz from being permanently injured. I got up, trolls and all, and helped. I owe Stalin. He told all of us that, despite us hating him for his cruel toughness, his constant beating on us, that we, his trainees, would someday appreciate what he had taught us. How he had taught us. And he was right. He helped save my life and the lives of our unborn sons. I owe him. As do you."

Torbin went to his wife and kissed her. "I guess I really owe him then. I'll tell him in the morning…"

"No, my husband. I must go and thank him in person."

"Well, not tomorrow. Stalin is just finishing getting the trainees sorted into new platoons. He needs tomorrow to finish this process."

"The day after tomorrow then. I will ride in early with you, and find a ride home."

"No, I will get you there and home. My position has a few perks. Being able to help my pregnant wife is one of them."

Aleks smiled at her husband in agreement. Then she turned to address Abigail. "Little sister, you beat a Russian legend today, with one of his weapons of choice. There are stories, probably true, that he challenged Cossacks, Syrians, others from foreign lands to duels when they offended him while they were training in Mother Russia. He does not suffer insults to his honor, nor insults to those under his command. To include trainees. He may scream, curse, and insult you all he wants. But have an outsider try…."

Abigail looked a bit sheepishly. "Had I known that, I would have let him win."

"No. He'd see that, and would lose all respect for you." Aleks cocked her head as she looked at Abigail, then grinned.

"This is grand. My little sister, an Avenging Angel, defeated one of the nastiest men alive. This will be a story I tell my trolls when they have grown."

"Please," protested Abigail. "Don't make it any bigger than it already is. Now it sounds as if people will be challenging *me*."

Aleks laughed. "As my husband says, 'No good deed goes unpunished'."

Aleks' amusement was temporarily cut short by her two sons moving restlessly in her womb. They had been especially agitated the past twenty-four hours. "Calm yourselves, my children," she said in a low voice as she rubbed her very large belly. "Let your mother have a few more quiet moments, then we can go back to bed."

She thought of the day she had gone in to see Stalin at the training area and he had seen her pregnant stomach...

Torbin and Aleks arrived at the training area so early, it was still night out. Yet, Stalin was already there. He had been creating a "problem platoon". It was on the third day of its creation. Twenty-five of the trainees, most of them having exhibited some characteristic that pissed Stalin off, were now in a platoon receiving his "special" attention. And now, despite Torbin laying down the law to these "experienced" troops, some were on the verge of revolt.

It was below freezing, so Aleks was bundled up in a thick parka to protect her unborn twins. She exited the SUV on her own before Torbin could get out and help. No way did she want to seem dependent on anyone, especially not in front of her former instructor. She marched through the snow to Torbin, then they started up toward where Stalin was haranguing the troublemakers. Stalin was in his regular fatigues with the ubiquitous fur hat that was always shown in the movies. He had a set of gloves stuffed in his belt, which he only used when handling metal weapons. He seemed immune from any frostbite until the temperature dropped well below zero. Torbin had told his wife that he thought Stalin had alcohol or antifreeze in his body rather than normal blood. Aleks had laughed and agreed. He had all the trainees lined up, with rifles extended on stretched arms above their heads. They had gloves on, earflaps of their fur hats down over their ears. They looked as if they had been in that position for several minutes before Torbin and Aleks had arrived, and they were none too happy about it.

"Alright you assholes. We were going to start with some bayonet training, but since two of you are unable to hang on to your weapons because you say your fingers are too cold, well, I'll just have to warm things up a bit. Anyone's arms getting tired?" Stalin heard someone grumble under their breath.

"What was that? Someone say something?" He cupped his right

ear with his hand.

"Oh, so now you have nothing to say. Training Platoon Leader Smith."

A slight female in the front row, beginning to shake, answered, "Yes Senior Training Instructor."

"Take them twice around the track, in formation, weapons above their heads. That ought to solve this bitching problem."

"Yes, Senior Training Instructor. Platoon, by my command. Left, face. Forward, harch."

A Left Guide began calling cadence. "Left, left, left, right, left..." "*Goddamnit! Double time!*" Stalin boomed at the trainees. He did not yell, or scream. He boomed. They took off as if shot from a cannon. "Keep in step. This is a formation, not a gaggle of geese."

Suddenly, one older troop slipped on a patch of ice and fell. The platoon kept running. "Man down! *Man down*, you stupid worthless fuckers! You leave a man behind, I'll shoot you in the leg, and leave you all behind!" Suddenly, two trainees in the rear doubled back, helped the man up, and helped the older man sprint back to the formation.

"That's better." With that he turned toward Aleks and Torbin.

"Major, you are here early. You have someone with you who looks familiar."

"This is my wife, Major Aleksandra Smirnov."

Stalin stopped, stood still for a moment. Then, a small smile formed on his face. He snapped to attention and bowed. "Major, I had heard some of my former trainees were here. When I last saw you, you were barely out of Basic Training. Someone thought you would make a good spy, an intelligence operative. That was about a year before the Squids showed up."

"Yes, Senior Training Instructor Stalin. After... surviving your training, they decided I was officer material. I pulled some field operations, had my bars pinned on me the day before the first rock strike."

Stalin looked at her belly, switched to Russian. "Pregnancy becomes you, Comrade Major Smirnov. You look very healthy, fit even with twins inside of you."

"How can you tell? Did someone tell you?" Aleks demanded in Russian.

"No, Comrade Major. I have been around enough to tell by the way a woman looks when pregnant that she is definitely going to have more than one child. And, the way you are carrying you children, I predict they are also boys. Da?"

Aleks snorted. "You always were too smart."

"It helped keep me alive, Comrade Major. Now, I know there must be a reason you are out here this time of morning. What would that be?"

Aleks continued in English. "I came here to thank you. Your training so many years ago helped me survive a recent attack. It also helped my two trolls in my belly survive."

Stalin's brow furrowed a bit. "Now, I'm puzzled. I had not heard of any attacks here."

With that, Aleks broke into a quick and dirty explanation of what had happened that fateful day, when the Eaters came calling. "As Fuzz, Captain Young's War Dog, came to my defense, I heard a voice calling me a fat cow, telling me to get up or die," Aleks explained. "That voice was you. You had yelled at me so many times I guess I had internalized it. Either that, or you somehow reached across time and space to help me." She stared him in his eyes. "Well, what was it—a memory, or are you psychic?"

Stalin glanced from Aleks to Torbin. "Majors, I have been accused of being psycho, but never psychic."

Aleks continued. "Your bayonet training kicked in, and I was able to get a shot into the second Eater, and keep Fuzz from being seriously hurt. So, I am here today to thank you. On behalf of my unborn sons and myself. Thank you, Comrade Senior Training Instructor Stalin."

Torbin interjected, "I thank you on behalf of her husband, me."

Stalin did not respond immediately. Then, with an uncharacteristic twinkle in his eye, he spoke. "So, Comrade Major, calling you a fat cow, among other insults that I will not repeat in front of your husband, did you some good. Da?"

"Yes. Just don't get any ideas to start again, or give my husband here any training in Russian insults. Your training, plus hours of scrapes, cuts and bruises learning cold steel from you, saved me. Without that, the insults would have been much less effective."

Stalin gazed at Aleks' prominent belly. "May I be so bold as to feel the young ones kick?"

"Since you helped save them, I do not see why not. Husband? Any problem?"

"No. I don't think our Senior Training Instructor is trying to cop a feel. If you have no problems, I don't."

Aleks opened her parka, pulled up a thick sweater and shirt. Stalin gently placed his large scarred hands on her belly. A few moments later, he gave a rare smile. "They move with strength. They take after their parents, I can tell." He nodded at Torbin. "You did well to marry a strong Russian woman."

"Only half Russian," Aleks interjected.

Stalin shrugged. "Half is enough. That and a Marine who kills Squids with a knife, how can the children be anything but strong and tough."

Torbin stuck his hand out, and Stalin took it. "Thanks for training my wife. It served her well." An unusual bond was thus formed between the two men, based on a pregnant woman. But lasting bonds had been based on stranger things.

Stalin turned around and saw that his "F Troop" was well into its second lap.

"No jodies or marching songs?" Aleks asked.

"They have not yet earned the right. I put all my bad eggs into one basket, with a few good ones unlucky enough to be stuck with them. It did not take my men and I very long to weed out the troublemakers, the ones with what you would call 'attitude'—a lack of knowing when to keep your mouth shut and listen."

"You are dealing with them personally?" asked Torbin.

Stalin showed a slight smile. "It is better to focus their hate onto one person. And it is better that I can take care of problems in my own way, without making others nervous."

Torbin grinned. "I can understand that. Just like General Reed and I have said, try not to kill them or maim them. Tough training does no good if your product is deceased."

"You are correct, Major. Now, I see Captain Young and Major Yamamoto approaching. Which means the other three platoons will be falling in soon with my men." Stalin saw his platoon rounding the final bend of the second lap, rifles still extended above their heads. He knew some of these people thought they would get a free ride based on their supposed prior experience. Stalin was quickly finding out that a lot of this claimed experience was either exaggerated or outright false.

As they neared him, he shouted another command in his booming voice. "Training Platoon Leader Smith! Form them back up where they started. After that is done correctly, I may let them lower their weapons." No one dared grumble, even if they could. Some of the older troops looked a bit pale in the face. They soon were lined up, somehow still keeping the rifles suspended above their heads with their fatigued arms and hands. Satisfied, Stalin boomed out again. "Training Platoon Leader, put them at rest."

"Yes, Senior Training Instructor." Smith put them at ease, then rest. This allowed them to lower their weapons at last.

Abigail and Ichiro walked toward Stalin, who called a greeting in their direction. "Good morning, my Lady of Cold Steel, and her friend the Samurai. It is a fine crisp morning, is it not?"

Torbin turned and looked at the approaching Abigail. "My Lady of Cold Steel? What's that, like your third title someone has come up with?"

Abigail looked a bit uncomfortable. "Please. My Title as Avenging Angel was an official position, rank in Deseret. All of the other names you people keep trying to give me are becoming ridiculous. I am not a shield maiden, valkyrie, a Lady of Steel. I'm just Captain Abigail Young, here to help in the fight against the Squids. Nothing more."

Stalin smiled. "I will have to protest the last part of your statement. 'Nothing more' is a serious underestimation of your skills and abilities." He continued, "If the title Lady of Cold Steel sounds too ostentatious, then I withdraw it."

"I like it," Aleks interjected. "You are a lady, little sister. But you handle blades and cold steel quite well from all reports. I think it is a fitting show of respect for a superior warrior, as well as a person."

Abigail sighed. "Fine. I won't protest all the nicknames I have received since coming here. I can see most are out of respect or affection, sometimes both. I just don't feel special enough to warrant all this attention."

"But you are special," Ichiro uncharacteristically blurted out.

"Ah, the President of her fan club speaks," Torbin teased. Ichiro blushed a bit and gave his blood brother a nasty look.

"What? What did I do to deserve that look? I just spoke the truth."

Further conversation was interrupted by a loud verbal exchange coming from the 'F Troop' formation. "I'll call her a fat bitch if I want to. I don't care if she is pregnant or not. Why is she so frigging special?"

The source of the overly loud comment was a large black woman. Six feet tall, and well over two hundred pounds, she was larger than some of the male trainees. And she knew it. Stalin glared at the formation. "Excuse me," he said softly as he turned from the conversation with the others and quietly made his way toward the formation. Platoon Leader Smith was trying to get the trainee to be quiet before she drew negative attention, and did not notice her attempts had failed until Stalin was on top of her.

She saw the Senior Training Instructor, her eyes went wide, and she tried to call the formation to attention. "At ease, Smith," Stalin said as he walked by, heading toward the tall trainee in the rear rank. "I see Trainee Jefferson has voiced another loud opinion. Please, pray tell me, what has warranted another outburst?" Stalin spoke in a normal tone of voice as he stood in front of the woman, inches taller than he.

Jefferson was used to telling everyone her opinion, using her size to intimidate many into not disagreeing with her. In simpler terms, she was used to being a bully.

"What kind of bullshit is this? You drag our asses out here, freeze them off, then make us stand here while you socialize with some fat white bitch. We're all Veterans of the U.S. Armed Forces, and I got away from Georgia when everyone else was being eaten for being black. I came here to join up and fight, not play fucking games."

Stalin responded quietly. "So you say."

"What?"

"I said, Trainee Jefferson, so you say."

Her face turned a bit purple. "Are *you* calling *me* a liar?" Jefferson yelled out.

"What if I were?"

"You white Commie piece of shit..." She took a step to grab him. Stalin bent and twisted a bit, then swung a lightning fast jab into the front of her groin below the belt buckle. Her eyes bugged out and her mouth dropped open, then she fell to her knees, holding her crotch.

She tried to curse but instead made unintelligible sounds as she dealt with her excruciating pain and shock to her private area.

"A bit of a lesson to be learned from this demonstration," Stalin said loudly. A well-placed punch to the groin can be effective on either male or female if done correctly... though it does seem to do more damage to men than women."

Every bully has his or her toadies. One of them tried to come to her defense. A tall and lanky white male in his twenties stepped out of rank toward the Training Instructor. In the blink of an eye he was on the ground, a combat boot on his neck, his arm twisted up in an unnatural position.

"*Who's next?*" Stalin boomed.

No one moved a muscle.

"Major Bender, a word please."

Torbin marched over to where Stalin had the trainee wrapped up.

"I must apologize, Major. I have lost control of this group of questionable humanity and they have demonstrated a definite lack of military decorum and discipline. This has embarrassed you and your fellow officers due to my inadequacies and the inadequacies of these supposed 'retreads' as you Yankees call them. I must ask for your forgiveness for myself as their Senior Training Instructor and for them as members of the Armed Forces."

Torbin tried to keep his reserve, look stern, and not laugh. He knew what Stalin was doing. He was deflecting the effect of the violence at the same time telling the platoon that they were in this together. He may be a mean son of a bitch, but he was *their* son of a bitch.

"No need to apologize, Comrade Stalin. I know that the members of this platoon will wish to make amends for the disreputable actions of a few." Torbin looked around and projected his voice a bit. "Am I right in that assessment, Trainees?"

Those with actual valid military experience and attitude led the rest of the people in a loud, "Yes Sir, Major Bender."

"Louder! Show the Major you mean it." The Russian boomed.

"*Yes Sir, Major Bender!*"

Torbin called over to Abigail. "Captain Young. Other than the two trainees on the ground, please march the rest of the platoon over to the gym, and let them warm up a bit prior to the other platoons showing up.”

“Yes Sir. Trainees, form on me over here. Hop to it. Now!”

They knew of Abigail’s reputation, history, as they did Torbin’s and Ichiro. They knew better than to question people they knew had fought and killed people, Squids, Eaters. At least most did. As they formed up on Abigail, she let them know something in no uncertain terms. “The woman the trainee referred to as a ‘fat bitch’ is a Major in Russian Intelligence. She is also my ‘big sister’, and Major Torbin’s wife. She went through training with Senior Training Instructor Stalin years ago, under much worse conditions. I suggest you treat her with respect or you may have to deal with her after she gives birth to her twin boys. Someone who kills people, Eaters, is not someone to trifle with. Platoon Leader Smith.”

“Yes Ma’am.”

“March them out, to the gym. I’ll follow.”

“Yes Ma’am.” Within moments the training platoon was marching across the exercise field to the gym.

As this was occurring, Torbin and Stalin were dealing with the two trainees still on the ground, with Ichiro appreciatively looking on. Torbin bent over to the slowly recovering Jefferson. “Have you seen the error of your ways, trainee?”

“Fuck you,” she hissed between clenched teeth.

Torbin shook his head, and turned to the young man Stalin still had pinned to the ground.

“This is trainee Kant, Major. He is in dire need of some unarmed combatants training.”

Torbin bent over and Stalin reduced the pressure of his boot on the man’s neck.

“You understand there is a war on, right Kant?”

“Yes Sir,” Kant managed to say.

“Would you like to be shot for mutiny, for attacking an instructor in the performance of his duties?”

Kant’s eyes widened a bit. “No Sir.”

Torbin stood up, looked at Stalin. “Well, STI Stalin?”

The Russian shrugged, then released the man, stepping back. Kant managed to get to his feet, holding his injured right arm with his left.

“Go to the gym, trainee, let Captain Young take a look at it. She’s a trained EMT."

"Yes Sir." Kant stumbled off.

The large, strong woman, still cursing and threatening, took this moment to try and stand up. Stalin kicked her hard, knocking her to the ground. On her back, Jefferson spat out, "I'll fuck you both up, you racists."

Torbin frowned and glared at her. "I guess she thinks she is the only one who lost people to the Squids, that only people of color were eaten. Guess what, dumbass. You may look tastier, but the Squids eat everyone in a pinch. They just think dark-skinned people make better Cattle. By the way, I've lost a lot of good troops who were of a darker persuasion than me. Pissed me off just as much if I had lost a red-headed viking." He pulled out his cell phone, hit the speed dial for Security Control.

"Yes, this is Major Bender. Could you send a couple of units for a transport to the brig? We're at the training facility and field... Thanks, we'll be waiting." Torbin sighed. Why did people have to make it so hard on themselves? He looked at Jefferson. "Some MPs are coming to take you in. Try and fight them and I won't be responsible for your injuries. You'll get your day in a hearing or court to spout all the crap you want. I suggest you take the path of least resistance." With a look of abject hatred on her face, she tried to spit at Torbin, who deftly dodged it. He shook his head and turned to Stalin. "Want to bet she fights the MPs, Comrade?"

"That is a given, Major. Let us instead bet as to how long it takes for them to subdue her."

"Done. I say they clock her in twenty seconds."

"Hmmmm. I say thirty seconds. There are some muscles under that flab, and she is quite angry."

They were both wrong. It took a full minute and tasers to get her cuffed. Then she was dragged to the paddy wagon.

After Jefferson had placed in the transport vehicle, Stalin walked over to Aleks, who had been calmly watching all the activity. It brought back some not so fond memories. Stalin stood at attention, clicked his heels, and gave a short bow. "My utmost apologies, Major Smirnov. I do not think you came here to be insulted today."

Aleks grunted, replying in Russian. "I seem to remember I tried to kick your balls up into your throat after you had called me worthless one too many times."

Stalin gave a small smile. "And you nearly succeeded. You were—I can tell you now—one of my best trainees. I knew you would succeed. I just did not think I would see you again. Especially not here, with twins in your belly, and a Marine for a husband."

"Which brings us back to why I came here." Aleks maneuvered around her large pregnant stomach, reached up, and kissed Stalin on both of his cheeks. "I thank you for helping me survive to this point. I will expect you to visit us at our home someday, after I give birth. My sons will need to meet another one of their many unofficial godfathers."

This brought one of Stalin's rare full grins to existence, which looked as much as a grimaced snarl as a smile on his craggy face."I would be honored. I will bring the vodka, to see if Marines can hold their liquor as well as they claim."

"They can, Comrade, trust me. They can."

Another internal kick brought Aleks back to the present. This was the most active her twins had been since the Christmas pageant at a large hall downtown.

It had been a night of friendship, music, food and drink. Brynhildr, Abigail's cousin, in full Valkyrie garb, had first belted out a Wagnerian ballad. Then, she had followed with *Silent Night* in the original German. By the time she had finished there was hardly a dry eye in the hall.

Her boss, Commissioner Miller, had said to her later, "You never told me you had the makings of a professional singer."

"You never asked. Besides, what has that to do with being a Special Agent?"

Paul Miller had grinned. "Not a damn thing. But it makes an old man feel good."

Brynhildr harrumphed. "If you are old, I am but a child."

"Now you understand."

The young children clustered around Abigail and Fuzz. She had told the organizers that Fuzz would come inside to check things out, as he had done at the awards and memorial service weeks earlier, where he had discovered the concealed Eater. Of course, no one complained. They were glad they had such coverage for free. Having a four legged hero also added something special to the pageant, especially to the children. Rin Tin Tin, Lassie, Benji, every former canine media celebrity rolled into one, which was what Fuzz had become.

Her reverie was suddenly broken as Aleks felt an odd sensation. Then, her water broke.

She looked at the pool on the kitchen floor. "You trolls just could not wait until your father and I had opened up Christmas morning presents, could you?" Something told her things would be happening fast.

"Husband!" she yelled, then put two fingers in her mouth and let loose with a very unladylike whistle. She heard Torbin bound out of bed, then saw him with his Ka-Bar in his hand.

"Torbin, my water broke. The trolls want a Christmas birthday. Grab my suitcase, I will get a towel and head to the car…"

"Like hell you will," interrupted Torbin. He grabbed the wall home phone, and dialed Central Security Control. "Hello, this is Major Torbin. The download has begun. Please call General Reed. We'll wait for the crash truck. Yes, thank you."

"What are you doing?" Aleks questioned her husband.

"Orders, love. General Reed said in no uncertain terms that you would not be taken in a POV. We are to wait for the heavy duty ambulance they are sending. You are the first woman to give birth after the Squids screwed with our genes and hormones. You are to be treated with kid gloves."

Aleks flushed with anger. "No one asked *me* about this. I am not some weakling. I am a Russian officer…" The rest of the conversation was cut short as a contraction hit. She plunked back down into her chair. Torbin quickly stepped to her side, and grabbed her hand.

"Remember your breathing, dearest…"

"Oh shut up. Women have been doing this without the help of you oafs for thousands of years." Another contraction. Seven months would be on the edge of a premature birth. Tests had shown that with the effects of Tschaaa tinkering, it would be the new norm. It looked like the actual birth sequence might also have been greatly accelerated.

The large crash truck, used as a small emergency room on the flight line for serious aircraft crashes, arrived in record time. The fact they had been personally primed by General Reed had led them to practice for this event, including the response time. They had it down to a science.

Torbin helped his wife to her feet, just as someone knocked on the door. It was Abigail, using her spare key to open it. "The babies are coming? Your whistle woke up Fuzz and I." The aforementioned K-9 was directly behind her, and tried to force his way around. "Hey. Who's in charge?" Abigail said to him, and he started to whine. He smelled Aleks, and seemed to know what was about to happen. Two legged puppies were on their way.

Seeing Fuzz and hearing his whine, tears of joy flooded Aleks' eyes. "See what saving me did, you big beastie? You are going to have two young humans to take care of now. "

Just then, the crash truck arrived outside, the emergency lights flashing through the windows. Abigail stepped out the front door, and waved at them to hurry. Then she dashed to the closet and grabbed Aleks' large parka. She wrapped it around her adopted big sister as the EMTs came in. For once, Fuzz did not complain about a bunch of strange humans being around. He sensed what was happening.

As they hustled Aleks into the oversized ambulance, her contractions sped up. The female EMT Sergeant yelled at the driver. "Tell the Emergency Room the babies are coming now! We'll just have a delivery en route."

Torbin looked at the Sergeant. "You can do this?"

She flashed a quick smile. "Did I ask you if you can gut a Squid with a knife? You know your job, Sir. I know mine. Hop in, we're leaving."

Abigail had to hold a whining Fuzz back. He wanted to escort the pregnant human and her children personally. After all, he had protected them up until now. As the crash truck accelerated away, all of the neighbors came out of their houses to watch, and one yelled out. "The Major's having her babies?"

"Yes," Abigail answered. "And quickly. Impatient Marines, you know."

Suddenly, people began to cheer and applaud. Torbin and Aleks were their people. Abigail gazed down at Fuzz. "Come on. We'll clean up inside and then go in my SUV. I know you can't wait any more than

I can. I'll see if I can sneak you into the hospital, okay?"

Fuzz seemed to give her a knowing look, then barked.

Two blocks from the house, the head of the first twin appeared. Before they knew it, he almost literally popped out. Aleks luckily had a broad enough pelvis, almost as if she had been made to give birth to accelerated babies. Then, the second twin followed mere seconds later. Both were over nine pounds, explaining Alek's enormous belly. Both were born with dark hair, and opened their eyes a bit on their own, each giving a small hiccup instead of a loud cry. The female Sergeant, a big grin on her face, did a quick toe and finger count as each came out. She set them up on Aleks chest as she prepared to tie off and cut the umbilical cords. Torbin pulled out his Ka-Bar. "Please, sterilize and use this. It means something to me."

The Sergeant did not question the request. An alcohol wash on the blade, quick cuts with the razor sharp blade, quick tie offs, and it was done. Two beautiful baby boys were sitting on Aleks' chest, taking nourishment from their mother. Gage, the first one out, was on Aleks right breast, and Tristan, his younger brother by a few moments, was on her left, both concentrating on suckling.

Aleks beamed at Torbin through teary eyes. "Your sons are gorgeous, my husband."

Tears of joy began to run down Torbin's face. For once, he did not hide his tears. He had two good reasons for being so happy.

"That, Major, has got to be one of the easiest and quickest deliveries of twins on record," the EMT Sergeant opined. Torbin suddenly hugged her, and kissed her cheek.

"I owe you, Sergeant… what in the hell is your name?"

"Sergeant Robins, Sir. Just doing my job." She untangled herself from his grasp as the other EMT checked mother and children over again.

"All healthy, Major. Doctor Rice is waiting to admit Major Smirnov, though. Just as a precaution. She'll meet us at the ER door."

Moments later, the crash truck was at the ER. One of the male EMTs had the doors open in a flash, and standing at the ER entrance were Major Rice and Colonel Bardun. Having been notified by Central Security Control, both women had made it to the hospital in record time. Major Rice had even brought her six year old son along.

Christmas morning or not, this was an important birth.

Both of the officers broke into wide grins when they saw Aleks on the gurney with her two sons.

"Those are two gorgeous looking babies, Aleks. And it looks like they came out just fine," declared Major Rice.

"Hey, they're boys. That means they're handsome, not gorgeous," Torbin protested.

"Bottom line, they look healthy as hell, Major," Bettie Bardun interjected. Torbin helped get the gurney down and the two doctors quickly clustered around the mother and children.

"Eight, nine, ten. All fingers and toes accounted for." Rica Rice was checking everything twice. After working out with Col. Bardun the possible ramifications of Aleks having been "affected" by the Tschaaa, they had checked and rechecked everything during Aleks' pregnancy. Bettie Bardun had helped work up special protein drinks for Aleks during pregnancy and had others standing by now that she given birth. Rica Rice had monitored every stage of the babies heightened development, fretting over every ultrasound, x-ray, blood test, and examination. Of course, she never let on to anyone how concerned she was about this birth. Aleks was literally the first known pregnancy directly related to Squid tinkering with female hormones, DNA, pregnancy and fetal development. What happened this day would be a template for the unknown numbers of other affected pregnant women to follow.

"Come on, let's get her into the examination room."

Torbin followed his wife's gurney in as two orderlies and the two doctors made certain everything was as it should be. In the examination room, Aleks finally allowed the Doctors to remove her sons from her breasts. They checked heartbeats, respiration, etc.

"Col. Bardun is going to hang on to the placenta and afterbirth, and run some diagnostics on them. It will help prevent us from poking and prodding these two anymore than we have to. We will just need workups on their blood and cellular development."

"They are fine, Doctor Rice. A mother knows. They are my big, beautiful sons, two of the best things that have ever happened to me." Suddenly, she sensed where Torbin was standing nearby, and grabbed his hand. "Come closer, husband."

Torbin moved in and Aleks pulled him in and hugged him.

"You have given me two beautiful sons, my love. I never imagined this would happen. I love you. I always will."

She began to tear up as Torbin kissed her neck, then whispered into her ear, "You are the best thing that has ever happened to me. You will be in my heart. Always."

Rica and Bettie tried to remain detached, professional, but couldn't. They wiped tears from their eyes, gazing at each other with stupid grins under their surgical masks. This was a great day.

"Okay, Aleks, which one is this one?" Bettie asked.

"Gage, the oldest. The other, Tristan, is just maybe thirty seconds younger."

Rica handed Tristan to Aleks. "I have never seen two more identical babies. How you will be able to tell them apart is beyond me."

"I just know. My husband will just have to learn."

"Come on, let's get Aleks and her babies to her room," directed Rica Rice. "We're going to hold you for observation for twenty-four hours, Aleks. Doctors' and General Reed's orders."

"If you must, but I feel fine. Without all that extra weight, I feel light as a balloon."

Aleks was soon placed in a private room. After an exam, it was decided there was no reason to hook her up to any monitoring machines. She seemed in excellent shape, especially considering she had just given birth to two large boys.

"I'll put a cot in here for you, Major Torbin," Rica said.

"Just get me a bedroll, Ma'am. I'll sleep on the floor."

"Oh, Torbin. Don't be stubborn. I have this nice soft bed. Don't be such a hard-ass Marine," Aleks scolded.

"Hey, that's one of the endearing qualities that made you want to marry me. Admit it."

Aleks looked at Torbin, a slight smile on her face. "Here, take your sons. I must visit the ladies room."

"Here. I'll help…" Bettie Bardun began to say.

"No need, Colonel. If I could manage to pee with two large trolls in my belly, I can do it now that I am a lot less burdened." She slid to the floor with ease.

Rica produced a hospital gown, the hated type with the opening in back that a patient could never quite keep closed. "Please put this on while you're up. Hospital rules."

"You people just like to make us as uncomfortable as possible with those damn gowns, Doc," Torbin grumbled. "Makes us want to go home, and open up the bed for other patients."

"Hey, I didn't design them. They've been around for as long as I can remember."

"Quit changing the subject, husband, and take your sons. They will want to be fed again soon, and I really have to pee."

Torbin took his two sons and sat in the well-stuffed reclining chair provided in the room. It suddenly dawned on him that this was the first time he ever held his sons. As a shit-eating grin started to form on his face, he heard a small click. He looked up to see Colonel Bardun with a small digital camera.

"Thought we should memorialize this moment. I know I would want to if it were my children."

Torbin smiled at the tall woman. "You are good people, Bettie Bardun. As are you, Rica Rice. I owe you big time for all the time and effort you two spent making sure Aleks delivered our sons safely. I'll always remember those who helped me and mine. Ever need anything, just holler."

"Just doing our jobs," Rica answered. "In this case, it was my distinct pleasure. My son asks me all the time about you, the 'Hero of Key West', and Aleks, the Russian spy. He thinks you two are cool."

"Tell him his mother is the cool one. You make sure kids come out with all their fingers and toes. How cool is that?"

Rica flashed him a smile. "I'll let you tell him that. He's with me today, down by the nurses' station. I didn't want to leave him at home alone this early, and I didn't want to dump him onto someone on Christmas morning. This is family time."

"Well, as soon as my wife comes out of the bathroom, I'll pass Gage and Tristan back to her, and visit your son."

"I am here, my husband," Aleks announced as she stepped from the bathroom. "Go and entertain Rica's boy. You'll have plenty of time to watch me feed our sons. A young boy is probably fit to be tied being stuck in a hospital on Christmas morning."

Rica smiled. "Thank you both. He'll be thrilled to meet a person who's been on television, and in the newspapers. The more strong male figures he sees and meets, the better it is. He misses never having known his father, other than through pictures, and my stories."

Torbin noticed a haunted look in Rica's eyes. It had been years, but she still really hurt. She must have really loved him. Probably as much as he and Aleks loved each other.

"Consider me gone. If you don't mind, Doctor, I'll take your son to the cafeteria. I need a cup of coffee, so I'll get him something to eat. Young boys need food in the morning to feed their growing bodies."

Rica paused for a moment, looking, examining Torbin. Finally, she spoke. "You know, for someone with a reputation as a hard-ass, you sure have an empathetic side."

"Hey, don't let that get around. People will think I'm soft."

The three female officers all laughed at this statement. The thought of anyone thinking the Hero of Key West as "soft" was one of the more humorous concepts they had heard lately.

"I don't think there is any danger of that, Major," Bettie Bardun remarked.

"Anybody else want something? No? Then, off I go." He bent over and kissed his wife. "You look beautiful."

She snorted. "You say that to all the women who just gave birth."

"No, you're the first. See you in a bit."

"We'll stay a while, to observe your wife and your sons," explained Rica. "We just want to err on the side of caution."

Torbin nodded, then left the room. Bettie Bardun turned and smiled at Aleks. "You are one lucky woman, Aleks. Now, mind if I hold your sons for a moment? I promise I won't drop them."

Torbin made his way to the nurses' station and saw a slender young dark-haired boy sitting, with a stack of comic books piled on the chair next to him.

"Hi there. You're Major Rice's son, right?"

The boy seemed startled a bit by being addressed by an adult. He stood up quickly, dropping a comic on the floor. 'Yes, Sir. Richard, Sir." He was a bit bleary eyed, tired, and now nervous.

"Well Richard, I'm Major Torbin Bender." He stuck out his hand to shake the boy's. Richard had a firm handshake for one so young. Suddenly, Torbin's name sunk in and his eyes went wide.

"You're Major Bender? The Squid killer, like in the comic book?"

"What comic book is that, Richard?" Torbin asked, with a quizzical look on his face.

"H-h-here, Sir. I dropped it." He bent over, and picked it up nervously. Torbin took it and looked at the cover.

A very muscular depiction of Torbin Bender was on the cover, a gun in one hand, a huge bowie knife in the other. He was slaying smaller versions of real Tschaaa warriors, with bluish blood flowing everywhere. Protecting his back was a larger than life Ichiro, wielding a katana a good foot longer than his real one. Severed tentacles were flying everywhere.

"Who did this? Do you know?"

"The kids at school say they're making them in Minot, North Dakota. They sell them in a bookstore downtown. This is the first issue. I have two others, here with the other comics."

He started to show Torbin. "That's okay, Richard. I can only read one at a time. Say, I need some coffee. Let's go to the cafeteria. I'll get you some breakfast while I'll tell you what really happened."

Richard's mouth fell open at Torbin's suggestion. "You will? You'll tell me?"

"Sure. You're the son of a friend of mine—your mother—who just helped my wife deliver two handsome, healthy sons. The least I can do is tell her son the real deal."

Richard broke into a big grin. "Man, wait until I go back to school. They won't believe I talked to you... Sir."

"Tell you what. I'll even sign and write a note on the comic. That ought to convince them," Torbin suggested. "What do you want for breakfast?"

"Can I have pancakes? My mom is really busy these days, and doesn't make them much anymore."

"My good man, you can have anything you want. You're with Major Torbin Bender, Squid killer extraordinaire. I think I'll join you in those pancakes. They sound great."

A half hour later, and Richard was finishing up a huge stack of pancakes, with Torbin not too far behind. He hadn't had pancakes in a while either. They tasted surprisingly good this morning.

"So, that's what happened. I managed to kill that one Squid, I think the 'man upstairs' was smiling on me that day. Then, Petty Officer Faust tried to cut me and Ichiro—Major Yamamoto—knocked her out. She was good. Too bad she's not on our side."

Richard swallowed his last bite of pancakes, and guzzled some milk. "Then you fought your way out?" He finally asked.

"Yes, but not with a bowie knife. I had a captured automatic rifle, and Ichiro had his sword. Although the comic got one thing right. There were Squids *everywhere*. Somehow, we made our way up to the causeway."

"Then you fought a robocop?"

Torbin laughed. "I shot at it to give Ichiro a chance to get away. The robocop threw a rock at me, and hit my helmet so hard it put a dent in and knocked me on my butt. Then he captured me."

"He? It was a *man?*"

Torbin paused, and regarded Richard more closely. "His name is Andrew. He is part man, part machine. A cyborg. He captured me, then saved me from being torn apart by a bunch of crazed Squids. He took me and turned me over to Deseret. Captain Abigail Young helped get me home."

"Captain Young? The Avenging Angel?"

"Why yes. Is she in that comic also?"

Richard looked through the stack of comics, pulled one out. "Here, Issue Two."

Torbin opened it and found the comic book version of Abigail. The illustrated version was a very voluptuous female, with everything about two sizes bigger than it was in real life, and a hint of a halo around her head. The comic book author took the "angel" literally in some respects, but made her look like a shield maiden in others. She kicked the ass of any Eaters or Krakens that came around.

"The third issue tells about... the Pits."

Torbin slowly opened it up, looked at the pages. This one showed the beasts, the creatures surprisingly realistic. Too realistic. There was the part about Torbin finding the young girls in the cell. The way the comic artist drew the look of horror on Torbin's face suddenly made him shiver with the memory. He dropped the comic to the table.

"Everything okay, Major?" Richard asked with a nervous quiver.

"Yeah. Just brought back some bad memories. But things turned out just fine. We rescued the five survivors. They have a good home now."

"People... soldiers died." Richard said.

"Yes, young man, they did. For a good cause."

"My dad was killed by the Squids before I was born." Richard tried to say this in a matter of fact manner. But Torbin could see in his eyes longing… and sadness.

"My dad was killed also, Richard. By the Squids. As was my mother, and my Brother."

They sat silent for a moment.

"You miss your dad, don't you Richard?"

Richard's lip quivered a bit, then he stopped it. "Yeah. I never got to see him for real. But my mom has told me about him. She says I look like him. She has a couple of pictures of him, and I guess I do."

"You want to know a secret? I miss my dad too, Richard. So, we have something in common."

"Yeah."

They sat quietly again for a moment. Then Torbin broke the silence.

"I'd like it if we were friends, Rich. Can I call you Rich?"

The young boy gazed intently at Torbin. "You want to be my friend?"

"Yeah. We both lost our dads to the Squids. Friends help friends get through bad times together. Losing your dad is a bad time. So, I'd like you to be my friend. Then we can help each other. Okay?"

Suddenly, Richard smiled. "Yeah, I'd like that."

"Great. Shake." The young boy shook Torbin's hand.

"Now you are an official friend of the infamous… Squid killer." The last part Torbin did in a deep falsetto. Richard began to laugh. The laughter was music to Torbin's ears.

A few minutes later, Rica Rice appeared to recover her son. As she saw Richard now smiling while drinking some hot chocolate, her stomach did a little flip flop. He usually looked rather serious, and smiled infrequently. He no longer seemed sad or depressed. He just seemed… somewhat unhappy. As she stood back and watched him for a moment, he began to laugh. A lump formed in her throat as she he heard his boyish laugh. She held back the tears, smiled, and walked over to the table.

"Time to go, Richie." She addressed Torbin. "Hopefully he wasn't too much trouble."

"Trouble? Nah. That's me. My middle name is Trouble—just ask my wife." Her son began to laugh gain, and she saw a twinkle in his eyes which was a very rare event these days.

"Major Bender was just telling me what really happened in Key West. He said a robocop knocked him on his butt with a rock. Nothing like what the comics say."

Rica gave him a quizzical look. "Rich was just showing his comic collection. I didn't know I had my own comic. Guess I'll have to see about getting royalties."

Richie interrupted. "See, Mom, he signed this one." He opened the aforementioned comic and showed it to his mother. Rica picked it up and read the inscription.

"Let it be known that this comic book belongs to one Rich Rica, friend to Major Torbin Bender, *aka* the Squid Killer. Woe to any person, Squid, Eater or Kraken who harrasses or bothers said Rich Rica and his comics. For the Squid Killer knows and sees all."

Below was written a P.S. "This warning also applies to creatures, beasties and nasties of the night. Be warned." This was followed by Torbin's official scrawl that passed as a signature. Penmanship had never been his strong suit.

Rica tried to hold back her tears. "Honey, could you go get mom a soft drink, my regular? I'll wait here with Major Bender."

"Sure, Mom." He grinned as he went to the soda dispenser.

Rica took a deep breath, as a tear ran down her face. Torbin grabbed a napkin and handed to her.

"Hey I didn't mean to upset you. If I did, said something wrong…"

"Torbin Bender, you Sir, are a Saint. I have not seen my son laugh like that in…aw shit." She began to cry. Torbin stood up and put his hand on her arm.

"Hey. It's okay. He's a kid. They're very resilient. Especially when they have a Mom who loves him to death. Come on, dry your tears. It's Christmas morning. He's got presents to open."

Rica took a deep breath, dabbed her eyes. "Major, you just gave my son and I Christmas presents that I will never forget. You made him laugh."

"Well, I always was a class clown. Got me in a lot of trouble in Basic Training."

"You meant that about being his buddy, his friend?"

"Hell, yes! Good kids like him are our future. Thanks to the Squids and our own screw-ups, they have a tough future facing them. So, if I can make it a little better for or a kid like Rich, of course I will. Just remember, I don't just throw my friendship around. You are also my friend Rica Rice, who took care of my wife and sons like I couldn't."

Rice smiled, then squeezed his hand. "I am really honored. Especially that my son has a friend like you."

Richie came back then with the drink. He smiled at his mom and she smiled back. Then he hugged her. "Merry Christmas, Mom. Can we go home and open presents now?"

"Yes, we can. First, you can walk with me up to Major Bender's wife's room for a last quick check. And you get to see some twins. Someday they'll grow up, and you can play with them."

"Okay. Major Bender, is your wife a spy?"

Rica started to say something but Torbin jumped in. "Yes, she is. So don't you try and get one over on me. She is really good at catching people trying to tell stories that aren't the truth, watching people when they least expect it. Maybe she'll put a spy camera in your classroom, at school, make sure you're behaving yourself."

Rica couldn't help herself. She began to laugh. "Hey, look. Your mom's laughing. How fun is that."

The now smiling trio made their way back toward Aleks' room. "Your mother here really helped my wife and our sons, young man. So, if I say she is cool, she is cool. Alright?"

"I know she's cool." Rich said very unexpectedly. "She's a doctor. She helps fix people, soldiers up. Like you."

Rica suddenly hugged her son as they walked. "I think you bring the best out of my son, Torbin."

"Nah. Just good genetic stock. You and your husband. And a loving mother."

Just there, there was an explosion of sound, yelling from Aleks' room, the sound of an unfamiliar voice. Then a metal bed pan came flying from the room. Torbin took off like a shot. Rich ran after him. "Richie, stop!" He did not hear his mother.

Torbin turned into the room's entrance and ran into a young lady in heels, woman's suit, with a microphone that she jabbed at his face. "Major Bender. Sally Reid from K…." Her statement was broken off as Torbin broke her wrist and dislocated her elbow with a quick defensive arm twist. She began to howl in pain.

Her cameraman was a big beefy man, over six foot tall. He made the mistake of swinging the camera at Torbin. He blocked the arm, trapped it, and then dislocated the elbow by raising the arm up against the normal joint motion. As the cameraman tried to swing at Torbin with his free arm, the "Squid Killer" proceeded to smash him in his face with his right fist. He punched again and again, a red haze over his eyes, turning the man's face into a bloody mess.

"Husband. Torbin. It's over. Let him go!" Aleks' voice finally cut through his rage. He let the now unconscious man drop to the floor.

Suddenly another new female voice was heard. "Sally. What happened? I told you to stay with me..." Torbin rounded on a young butterbar with glasses. "*You!* You brought them here?"

"Ah, I just had them here for some interviews of personnel working on Christmas..." She started to back up as Tobin still had murder in his eye.

"Hey, buddy..." A man with Sergeant stripes on his arm reached out to grab Torbin's arm, apparently an assistant to the Second Lieutenant.

"Let him alone!" A small boy flew into the Sergeant, planting a perfect blow straight to the family jewels. Rich Rice had come to the defense of his new friend with a vengeance. The Sergeant grabbed his testicles and collapsed into a heap on the floor.

"Richard, no!" It was his mother, Rica. The Major grabbed her son, pulled him back. "Stand here." Responding with her physician training, she quickly entered Aleks' room.

"My sons and I are okay, Rica. I cannot say the same about the young lady and man."

Rica took one look at the two downed people, and began calling for help. "I need a backboard and a gurney in here. Now! I have a concussion with possible neck injuries. A broken wrist, maybe arm." She glared at the young female Lieutenant. "What in the hell are you all doing at Major Smirnov's room?"

"I, I, didn't know they were here. They snuck off when my Sergeant and I turned our backs. I told them not to wander away from us." The young Lieutenant with the name tag of Carson was panicked, in over her head. Rica now addressed the young civilian reporter on the floor.

"What were you thinking? This area is off limits to people just wandering around."

Between painful sobs, as orderlies and nurses showed up with a gurney and backboard, local television news reporter Sally Reid blurted out a story. "We came here for an exclusive photo. These are the first kids born from a mother infected with..."

"*Infected?*" Rica Rice screamed. "How *dare* you make such a judgment. They are my patients. How dare you interfere."

Lieutenant Carson tried to come to her guest's defense. "Ma'am, they didn't realize..."

"Shut up, butterbar. I ought to..." Torbin started to advance on her, his anger boiling again.

"What in all that is holy is going on?" It was a familiar voice. General Reed was suddenly on scene.

"Major. Stand down." His Command Voice cut through the din, and everyone listened.

Torbin snapped to attention. "Sir. Protecting my wife and sons, Sir."

General Reed stepped up, saw the crying female reporter on the floor, the bloody cameraman, the Sergeant with the smacked testicles trying to get up off the floor. He spun toward Lt. Carson.

"You. Get your Sergeant here, call your Commander, and be in my office in an hour."

"General, I...."

"Did I ask for an explanation? Did I? Move. Now." The Lieutenant saluted, bent over and helped her NCO up off the floor.

Sally Reid, seeing the General as she was helped into a wheelchair, decided at that moment to try and spout off. "I'll sue. Freedom of the Press, the public's right to know. This beast had no right to break my arm, beat my cameraman..."

"Shut up!" Torbin had rarely seen the General this angry. Everyone froze.

"Do you realize there is a war on? Do you realize you are on a military installation, in a controlled area you have no right to be in? Do you?"

The reporter started to protest and the General was suddenly an inch from her face. "I should have you dragged out by the MP's, and dumped in the snow out the main gate. You are screwing with a man's family here."

"General, please." Rica broke in. "They're injured and in our hospital. I can't allow them to just be dumped in the cold."

General Reed turned at looked at Major Rice, saw her son standing a few feet back. He suddenly stepped into Aleks' room. "Major Smirnov. Are you and my godsons okay?"

"Yes General. See, like good Marines, they sit here quietly, ignoring the violence around them, waiting for your orders. Sir."

General Reed chuckled. "You, Aleks, have the unique ability to defuse a situation."

He turned to Rica Rice. "You're right, Major. I'm letting my feelings get in the way of being a Commander. I defer to your medical judgment."

He looked at her son. "Richard, is it?"

"Yes Sir."

"So, what is your part in this?"

The boy paused, then blurted out. "I hit the man in his balls. He was trying to hurt Major Bender, my friend." The six year old boy stood, a bit defiant, defensive of his mother and friend.

General Reed looked at Torbin, still at Attention.

"Major Bender, at ease. You seem to have a big fan here. One who at a young age will smack a man in the groin for you." He then turned back to the doctor, who was trying to keep an eye on the efforts to get the injured to the ER.

"Major, you have quite the young soldier there. I can tell he's protective of his mother, also."

With that, General Reed stepped up to the young boy, stuck out his hand. "General John Reed, Richard. Please to make your acquaintance."

Richie took his hand, shook it like his mother had taught him. "Major Bender calls me Rich, my Mom Richie. Not Richard."

General Reed laughed. "Well, can I call you Rich, like Torbin here? Good. Now, if you will all excuse me, I have two newborns to fuss over." He looked at Torbin's right hand. "You need to take care of that hand. Don't want blood all over your sons."

"Yes Sir."

Rica handed him a bandage and some gauze. "Here. I'll check it later."

"I'll help," her son interjected. Rica looked at her young son, suddenly more alive than he had been in weeks.

"No more fighting, alright?"

"Yes, Mom."

She looked at Torbin. "And you, no more fighting, alright?"

"Yes, Mom."

Rica tried to keep a straight face, and failed. She actually giggled a bit. "Please, you are impossible. I don't know how your wife puts up with you."

"Neither does she." Torbin looked at Rich. "Want to help me clean up my hand?"

"Yes, Major."

They went down the hospital hallway and found a spare men's room. Torbin went to the sink and began to wash the blood off his hand.

"Does blood bother you, Rich?"

"No, Major. My mom sometimes has blood on her. She explained that this happens sometime when you're a doctor. I'm used to seeing it."

Torbin noticed that most of the blood was the cameraman's, but it looked like part of a tooth was in one of his knuckles. He picked it out and then used some bacterial soap to wash it well.

"Rich, need to tell you something. I lost my temper there, and did more damage than I needed to. I should have just thrown them out. I didn't, so I was wrong."

"But you thought they were hurting your wife, your babies."

"Yeah, when I saw that flying bedpan, I thought something was very wrong. But I soon saw it wasn't. I really hurt those people." He looked at the young boy.

"What I am trying to say is, when you have the ability to hurt people, you have to control it. You fight to defend yourself, others. You fight just enough to do those things. Then you stop. Hurting people from anger is wrong. Understand?"

Rich looked at him for a moment. Then he spoke. "My dad fought to save my mom. He died. But he saved mom. So I'm here."

"And he was right. He would be proud of you, Rich. But he would not want a son who fights at school all the time. Understand?"

"Yes, Major."

"Come on. Let's get you back to your mom, buddy."

"I am your buddy, really?"

He looked at the young boy, having to grow up too fast in a world where some aliens were trying to eat him, given the chance.

"Hey, you just jumped in and smacked a guy in his ding-a-ling to help me. Of course you're my buddy."

Rich smiled, then gave Torbin a quick hug. "Let's go find mom."

General Reed was in with Aleks, alternating holding his two Godsons. It felt good to hold, feel this new life.

"They definitely are healthy," he opined through the surgical mask he had donned. He felt the less exposure these newborns had to strange germs, the better. "Take after their parents. Came out tough."

Aleks smiled. 'You do not now the half of it. These two enjoyed using their mothers' innards as punching bags. I am surprised I have no internal injuries."

The General handed Tristen back to Aleks, who quickly put him to nursing again.

Contrary to what American traditions had been, Aleks and her upbringing in Russia saw no problem with men seeing her substantial chest as she fed her sons. If some guy got a thrill from seeing her with a baby attached, so be it.

"So, you'll have them christened, baptized soon?"

"Yes. I am Russian Orthodox. I would like to have them baptized like I was."

"No worries, Aleks. The Chaplains on base can perform just about every religious ceremony there is, denomination be damned." He grunted. "The Base Commander was telling me the other day that they are studying traditional Nordic ceremonies, to keep the Sons and Daughters of the North happy." He shook his head. "I never thought I'd see the day that Thor would be almost as important as Jesus in the Norse communities. Instead of dying out, I guess beliefs in Thor's hammer, the old ways, were just waiting in the wings, ready to fill the void left by non-belief in current religions. The Squids showed the weakness or lack of caring by a traditional God toward us wayward children. So, people look for a warrior god."

Aleks snorted. "There is but one creator. You can call him any name you want. He can be all of them. After all, he is all powerful God."

"Well, I won't knock believing in Thor and Valhalla. Seems to make for some very nasty warriors, which I can always use."

General Reed looked at his watch. "Time to go. I have to meet those idiots who brought those local reporters into the hospital, plus call the Base Commander. And I left Captain Young and Mister Stalin outside, as I did not want too many people visiting you at once. Stalin was getting to know Sergeant Fuzz, who is itching to see you also. His nose says you are here, with your sons."

He shook his head. "That war dog has definitely claimed you as someone to protect. As well as your sons."

"Of course. He saved me, them, from those Eaters. We are all members of the same pack. Or so Abigail explained to me."

"Well, Aleks, she seems to be spot on." The General then leaned over and kissed Aleks' forehead.

"You keep yourself safe and warm. Take your time coming back to work. These two trolls as you've called them are what's important. They're the future for the U.S."

Aleks flashed a bright smile. "I will, General, soon to be godfather when we christen them."

"But I will be getting back into fighting shape. I have been a fat cow long enough." With that, they both laughed and the General left.

Torbin came back with Doctor Rice and her son, Rich. "One last check, Major, and I'm gone. My son here has presents to open. That is, if Santa has shown up."

"Mom, Santa is a nice story," a mature sounding Rich stated. "But I know it is all about giving. I have some things for you."

"Wait just a darn minute." Torbin suddenly acted all agitated. "You mean there isn't a Santa Claus? I've been acting nice instead of naughty all these years for no good reason? Aleks, at least you could have told me there was no Santa."

Aleks gave him an exasperated look. "You, my love, are a clown. A lovable one, but a clown nonetheless. Now, introduce me to the Major's son. I have not formally met him yet."

Torbin made a grand sweeping gesture toward Rich. "This young man is Richard Rice, known as Rich to his friends, like me. His tribal name is Crotch Crusher. Watch out for his mean left hook. It's a nasty one."

Rich blushed a bit, and his mother looked at Torbin as if she thought he was a few cans short of a six pack.

"Young man, come over and meet my sons, please. And I apologize for my husband. He is the American poster child for Crazy Clown Syndrome."

Torbin feigned being hurt as Rich went up to Aleks' bed. She held Gage up to Rich. "Say hello to Gage, the eldest one by a few seconds."

"Hello, Gage," Rich quietly said as he reached his right hand out to touch the baby. Gage managed to grasp his index finger as he was being touched.

"See, my son says hello. You will be friends someday, when he is older. Tristen, say hello also."

Rich gently touched the hands of the other twin, who also grasped a finger for a few moments.

"Your mother here made sure there were healthy and born without any difficulties. For that, I will always be in her debt."

"My mom is a good doctor. Everyone knows that."

Rica thought again how lucky she was to have a son like this. "Now, Richie, we have to go. The Major is in good hands. I'll be back tomorrow to discharge you, Major, if everything is okay. I know that Major Bender here will insure you are not bothered."

"Yes," Aleks answered. "He is good at that. I guess I'll have to keep him, especially as he helped provide me with two beautiful sons."

"Handsome. Boys are handsome. Girls are beautiful. I'll learn you yet, wife."

Rica laughed and Rich smiled. Torbin went over to him. "Give me five, buddy."

Rich figured out what he wanted, having seen some older movies. "Now, up high. Now down low... Oops, too slow!" Rich laughed, then gave Torbin a quick hug.

He went to his mother's side, who was beaming. She put her arm around him. "Goodbye for now. See you later." They turned and walked down the hall.

"We'll stop by the ER on the way out, make sure the ER doctor has those two injured civilians taken care of," Rica told her son while walking.

"Yeah, Mom. Major Bender told me he was sorry he lost his

temper. That I shouldn't do that."

Rica Rice thought once again that that Torbin must have had children in his prior life. He seemed to know what to say, and what to do.

"The Major is a very smart man. It's good he is your friend."

"Yeah Mom, I know." Rich grabbed and hugged his mother. "I love you, Mom. Merry Christmas."

"Merry Christmas right back. Quick check, then its present opening time."

Torbin went to his wife's bedside, and kissed her. "Doin' okay?"

"Yes. Of course. I have a loving husband and two healthy sons. Once I'm at home, I can start working on getting back to my fighting weight. I do not want to be a fat cow."

A new voice entered the conversation. "You are not a fat cow, Major. You would not be here if you were." Stalin entered with Abigail behind him, Sergeant Fuzz at her side. Stalin had a wrapped present in his hands which he presented to Aleks.

"Merry Christmas, though your husband might want to keep this under wraps after you open it. Hospitals sometimes have different opinions about what is appropriate."

Aleks smiled. "Thank you, Comrade Stalin. First, however, my sons and I have an appointment with the big beastie there. Come here, Fuzz. Say hello to the new pack members."

Abigail had the General "grease it" with the Hospital Commander that a canine would be allowed into a room with two newborns. After the Commander realized which canine was involved, he grinned. "Hell, General, he's a Sergeant. And a Hero. If he can't come in, who can?"

Fuzz had an open mouthed dog grin as he approached Alek's hospital bed, then his nose began to work a mile a minute as he smelled Gage and Tristan. Torbin took Gage, Aleks held Tristan, and maneuvered the babies so the war dog could greet the two humans he helped to save.

Fuzz gave a very small lick to the cheek of each newborn, then began to whine a little bit, acted like he was trying to say something.

"Yes, big fella," said Abigail. "They are handsome and healthy. And once they are older, you can play with them."

Aleks looked at the dog, then handed Tristan to Abigail. "Come here, Fuzz." The canine went over to Aleks who bent over and hugged him. "Thank you for being you. Thank you for being there to save me and my sons."

A tear ran down her face and Fuzz licked it off. He gave the huffing dog laugh that many people cannot recognize as such. But those that do could tell he was happy, contented. He was with human members of his pack who he loved and who loved him. And now there were two puppies (two legged, but pups none the less) to take care of, to protect. That was fine with him.

Abigail was holding Tristan, beaming. "What a beautiful, I mean handsome, young man you are. You'll grow up strong like your father." She glanced over at Aleks. "If you ever need a babysitter, check with me, please. I know Fuzz would just love it."

"Don't worry, little sister. I won't forget you. After they're settled in at home, I plan on getting out some. I need to work off this baby fat I have put on."

"Well, Major, feel free to come by my training classes if you want a good workout," Stalin interjected. "But it's one size fits all, so you'll have to keep up."

Aleks snorted. "I may just take you up on that, Comrade Stalin. As long as you do not start calling me a fat cow among you other choice names."

The Training Instructor laughed. "I only use words of endearment and encouragement on those who need it for motivation. I think you are well past that stage. But please, open up your present. I think you might see its usefulness."

Aleks cocked an eye, then picked up the wrapped package. It felt a bit heavy, so she knew it was not some bit of jewelry, or knick knack. She tore open the wrapping paper, and found what appeared to be a large pistol case. With practiced hands, she opened it.

"That, my good Major, is the latest version of the MP443 Grach pistol, with fifty rounds of ammunition. Nine millimeter 7N31 high velocity armor piercing to be exact. I heard three of my former students in spy-craft were assigned here. So I brought some presents they could use, not pretty baubles."

An appreciative Aleks picked it up, held it in her hands. "This feels good, balanced. Definitely better than my old but serviceable Makarov. Seventeen round magazine I see."

She smiled at Stalin. "I didn't know you cared about your former students."

Stalin shrugged. "We are all in this together. And I know any of my trainees who survived the last six years must be a cut above the norm. So, for the good of Mother Russia, and now our new American friends, I figured it would be a good idea to provide what newer equipment I could obtain."

Torbin looked at the pistol with a practiced eye. "We'd call that a right good shootin' iron around here. I appreciate you wanting to keep my wife well protected and alive."

"Major, one does not want to see excellence go to waste due to poor equipment. And, she is Russian. So I feel a bit protective."

"Half-Russian," commented Aleks.

"Close enough. But the excellence statement stands. I remember you and your two fellow women now that I've come here. Comrades Kuzlov and Popov I eventually remembered as being superior intelligence officers and field operatives. As are you. Rough I may seem, but I give credit where credit is due."

Aleks looked at her former instructor. As much as she and others had hated him at the time of the training he had put them through, it had served its purpose. All three of them were alive today. And now Aleks was a mother with two beautiful bouncing boys.

"Here, Comrade Stalin. Take Gage from my husband. Let us get you acquainted with two children who are here in part due to your efforts."

The Russian took the newborn from his father, holding him with ease. He let Gage try to grasp his gnarled fingers as he flashed his smile that looked more like a grimace.

"Already he has a strong, Russian grip. Comrades Putin and Josef Stalin would be proud of these two. In an earlier time, Major, you would have received an award for producing such fine future citizens of the Motherland."

"Well, we are in America now. And my husband is a Yankee. So their health is good enough for me."

"By the way, what happened to our friend Putin?" Torbin asked.

Stalin shrugged. "Dead most likely. Moscow was hard hit, as were all our governmental, command, and control centers. The Squids had things pinpointed. So, if you were up in the higher levels of government and were at work the first week, you were most likely targeted.”

He frowned. “It is sad that some people like a certain worthless Colonel who had his demise here survived. I believe there is a saying in English that the ‘good die young’. In Russia, that seems to apply to the competent.”

He looked at Torbin, still gently holding Gage. “You did us a favor by getting rid of that one.”

“Who said I had anything to do with that?” Torbin replied back.

“Well, not maybe personally. But you helped with, shall we say, creating the necessary environment.”

“Let’s change the subject to more pleasant matters,” Aleks said. “You will have to come to my sons’ christening and baptism. General Reed said he would insure a Russian Orthodox Ceremony was available. I know you are still Russian Orthodox, Comrade.”

“Yes. I still have the cross with my ID tags. I would be honored to attend. And I knew my General would be able to arrange such things. It is nice to see that competence survived here in the U.S.A.” Stalin gently gave Gage back to Torbin.

“Your son is getting hungry, I can tell.”

 “You’ve had experience with babies, have you?”

Stalin gave a slight smile. “Let us just say I have handled offspring in the past.”

Aleks snorted. “What Comrade is trying to say is that he was quite the cocksman in the past. You never did get married to anyone, did you?”

“Aleks, let’s be nice to our guest,” interjected Torbin.

Stalin gave a short laugh. “Always the blunt Major Smirnov. Can I help it if women want my babies but not me? A husband who is never home, whose claim to fame is violence is not seen as, how you say, a ‘good catch’ in the greater scheme of things. But I help the mothers of my children when they want or need it.”

Abigail gave Stalin a disapproving look. “But don’t you want to be in your children’s life?”

“Well, like you, my Lady of Cold Steel, I have a special mission, a calling right now. Maybe in the future, when the Squids are gone or dead, I can try being what you Americans call a ‘house husband’.”

Aleks laughed at the thought of that. “I hope that happens. I would love to see you in an apron, sweeping the kitchen floor."

Stalin smiled, then glanced as his watch. "Well, there is someone else I must visit this fine Christmas morning. So I will take my leave of you. Again, congratulations to you two Majors. And please let me know when the christening is scheduled."

"Will do, Comrade Stalin." Torbin answered.

Stalin departe as Abigail kept kept fussing over the two newborns. Aleks could tell she was beginning to have the urges of motherhood.

"So, little sister, think you would like one of these trolls of your own?"

Abigail smiled, then blushed bit. "Someday, when I am no longer needed to fight. And, if I can."

"You can, Abigail. You said you could sense that I was carrying twins. Well, I can sense you are fertile. Ignore all that bullshit they fed you in Utah. You had no more exposure to radiation than the rest of us have, thanks to the Squids."

"Thanks for your confidence, Aleks. I hope you're right."

"Trust me. I just gave birth to two healthy sons despite the interference of the Squids, and someone trying to kill me with Eaters. Like you Americans say, I am on a roll."

The Malmstrom Confinement Center had been expanded so it could double as a Federal jail for persons awaiting trial, including civilians. Since it was on base, it was also more secure than one in the public venue.

Stalin entered the military side of the facility, and showed his ID and passport. The soldier at the entry control point examined them, looked at Stalin.

"Who was it you wished to see, Senior Training Instructor Stalin?"

"A trainee by the name of Jefferson. I helped put her in here. I would like to see how she is doing."

"Wait here, please. I need to get the Duty NCO."

The young Corporal was confused as Stalin seemed to be a civilian but had some sort of connection with the military chain of command. He could not understand why anyone would want to visit someone on a holiday when they were the one who helped put her there.

He returned with an E-5 NCO, O'Neil, a big and tall red-headed

Irishman with a New York accent. Sgt. O'Neil looked at Stalin with a smirk on his face. "You sure you really want to see her? Her attitude has definitely not improved since you sent her here."

Stalin shrugged. "It is Christmas morning, the time when we celebrate the birth of Christ. What better time to show a bit of compassion?"

"Okay, it's your funeral. Come through this door and empty your pockets. Nothing goes in, nothing comes out. Understand?"

Stalin showed a hint of a smile. "Of Course, Sergeant. Whatever you say."

Stalin had already pegged the Sergeant as being a bit of a bully, the NCO believing he was wasting his time playing nursemaid to prisoners on Christmas morning.

Five minutes later, he was in front of the cell holding Jefferson.

"Porsche Jefferson. Stand up, face the door, show us your hands. You have a visitor."

The large black woman stood up as directed. Sgt. O'Neil unlocked the cell door, motioned Stalin in.

"You have ten minutes."

"Thank you, Sergeant." Stalin entered, heard the cell door close and lock behind him. He then saw why Jefferson had not moved closer. Her right leg was manacled to a solid ring cemented to the floor by her bed. Stalin frowned. Then he noticed her face.

The bruises were more recent than the ones she had received from the MPs. Her right eye was almost swollen shut, and she had a proverbial fat lip. She glared at him with her one good eye.

"What the fuck do you want? Come here to gloat?"

"No. As you are still assigned as a trainee, I am still responsible for you. At least until and if you receive a court-martial and sentence. So, have you been fighting?"

Jefferson have a short hard laugh. "No, I've been getting beaten. Seems the Crackers here don't like it when you call them Crackers. They can call me whatever they want all day, but if I smart off... well, you see what I gets."

Stalin frowned again. "So, you say you are getting beaten due to your race?"

"Either that, or because I'm a woman."

"That makes no sense. Half the new recruits here are female. So many males were lost during the Invasion and harvesting the first year that in the U.S. there is a sixty/forty split between females and males. In Russia, it is seventy/thirty. So, more women will show up for military service. Trying to get rid of them means we have less personnel. That is counterproductive."

Jefferson snorted. "I'll let you figure it out. But I'm getting my ass kicked at least once a day."

"What have you been fed?"

"Gray loaf."

"What is that?"

Jefferson sneered. "Never been in jail, huh? Well, they take your meal, run it through a blender, then pour it a pan and bake it. Comes out gray, usually funny tasting."

"Why is that done?"

"Supposedly if you throw your food, or refuse to eat it. Which I haven't done. I'm big. I need my food."

Stalin stood quietly for a moment. Then he spoke. "I'll be back."

He called out and after a couple of minutes, the Corporal showed up. They walked back to where Sgt. O'Neil was sitting with his feet on the desk.

"So, done with your visit?"

"Why do you feel it is necessary to beat a person who cannot escape, and who is not trying to escape?"

O'Neil did not like to be questioned. Especially by some foreigner. He jumped to his feet. "Look here. This is *my* facility. I'm in charge. So, Ivan, if you don't like it, tough shitsky. Go complain to someone who cares."

Stalin kept a composed demeanor as he kept looking at the big man. This just irritated the Sergeant more.

"Are you trying to piss me off, Ivan?"

"Did I say my name was Ivan?"

"Oh, a smart ass. Get the fuck out of my facility."

"I will leave when I have answers."

"Look it, you fucking Commie bastard… " the large man started to come from around the desk, reached out to grab the Russian. And stopped when steel fingers grabbed his adam's apple and squeezed. The Corporal stepped forward to aid his Sergeant as the big man's eyes bulged from the pain and having his breathing interrupted.

"Another step and I crush his throat," Stalin said calmly. The Corporal froze.

"I do not like big bullies. Especially those who get pleasure from beating up women, no matter how large the woman is." O'Neil had several inches in height and a definite weight advantage, but he seemed to be a baby in the hands of the Russian. O'Neil had reflexively grabbed Stalin's arm when the Training Instructor had grabbed his adam's apple in an attempt to relieve the pressure and pain. It was like grabbing a bar of steel.

"Now, I am going to first arrange for a decent Christmas meal for Jefferson, with which no one will interfere. Then, later today, a medic will examine her. All of her injuries will be documented."

Stalin pulled O'Neil ever so slightly toward him, causing strangling noises to emanate from the NCO's open mouth. "Woe betides anyone who causes additional injuries to the young woman. I will make it my personal mission to make the life of such a person a living hell."

"And before you start thinking about taking some action against me," Stalin continued. "Let me explain the reality. I have a diplomatic passport from Russia. The worst you can do to me is to force me back to Russia. My government will not allow the U.S. to punish me, only to send me home, maybe to a gulag. But I have survived a gulag before, and I can do it again."

Stalin shoved O'Neil backwards, the large man stumbling over the chair behind the desk. He fell heavily to the floor, lay gagging and choking. Stalin fixed the Corporal with a dead stare.

"Hey, buddy, I just follow orders." The Corporal blurted out.

"Then these are your new orders. Jefferson gets treated like everyone else in confinement. No worse, no better. I will ensure she behaves, and does not require any further physical restraint. If she refuses to abide by your instructions, call me. I will ensure it is the last time she causes you problems. Understand?"

"Yes Sir."

"I am not a Sir, not an Officer. I am Senior Training Instructor Stalin. Repeat that please."

"S-S-Senior Training Instructor Stalin," repeated the Corporal.

"Good. Now, help your Sergeant. He may need medical attention. I will now make arrangements for the actions I want done."

Stalin telephoned Lt. Ivanovich. Christmas or no, the Lt. quickly located a full holiday meal and had it over to the Confinement Center in record time. As soon as Jefferson had scarfed down the first decent meal she had in days, despite the damage to her face, a female medic appeared. Stalin arranged for an examination in the small infirmary the confinement facility boasted. The young NCO was not happy with what she saw as she completed the examination, made notes, took some photos. She stepped outside to talk to Stalin, the Military Confinement Specialists leaving him alone with the prisoner. Maybe they hoped she would try and escape from just him. No such luck.

"She is in training status, under you?" She asked Stalin.

"Yes, Sergeant. But she has resided in this fine establishment since the beginning of the month. I will be contacting General Reed about expediting her return to my training."

The Sergeant's eyes widened a bit. "You can contact General Reed directly?"

"Yes. He is the one who brought me here, to this base."

The Sergeant paused for a moment, mulling something over in her mind.

"Could you get my findings directly to him, without me getting screwed for jumping the chain of command?"

"Of course, Sergeant... White your name tag says. If that is what is necessary. But I need some explanation as to why this is necessary."

"Well. Senior Training Instructor Stalin. Let's us just say that some reports concerning the well-being of some females on this base, especially people in confinement, have been sidetracked, lost. When I heard you needed a medic here, I volunteered to come. Most of the hospital staff do not want the headaches associated with 'problem' areas."

She swept her hand to include the whole confinement facility. "This has a reputation of being one big problem area. An awful lot of injuries are generated post arrest here. But, there is a war on. Or so I've been told."

Stalin scrutinized the young NCO for a moment. A nondescript twenty-something with light brown hair and glasses. She was about five foot five, medium-build and average-sized, she had a bit of steel in her brown eyes. Stalin decided he liked her.

"What is your first name," asked Stalin.

"Candy, short for Candice. And yours?" That steel again. She was not one to be bullied, intimidated.

"Stalin. I have just the one name. I know who I am, others soon learn. So, I took a name that fits my demeanor. It also permits me to do things knowing no one can ever locate any of my surviving family, as my records were lost years ago."

Sgt. White gave a small smile. "I wouldn't be surprised if you had something to do with that loss."

He shrugged. "Could be. But that is ancient history. Provide me with a copy of your reports, I will get them to my General, authorship kept quiet."

Sgt.White stuck her hand out. "Deal. Shake, please."

Stalin shook her hand, receiving a firm, strong hand shake.

"You are not Russian, are you?"

"No, Mister Stalin. Heinz Fifty-Seven." When Stalin seemed not to register what she was saying, White explained. "My ancestors seemed to like to marry outside the tribe, clan, whatever you want to call it. I am primarily caucasian, which is all I know for sure."

"Well, my good Sergeant. I do believe that Darwinian selection was kind to you and your family. And please, my friends call me Stalin."

Candy smiled a bit more. "So, we are friends now? You hardly know me."

"I am an excellent judge of character, Sergeant. It is time for me to let you leave. Get me your finished report. I am easy to find. Now, please go and enjoy the rest of your Christmas."

"Thank you. Merry Christmas… Stalin."

"Merry Christmas, Candy White."

He watched her leave, then stepped back into the small infirmary room of the Confinement Facility. Jefferson had finished buttoning up her shirt. She looked at Stalin. "That Sergeant likes you."

He grunted. "Could be. Contrary to my reputation, I am quite likable."

Jefferson gave a hard laugh. Then spoke."Why'd you do this? Why'd you get this meal, get me fixed up with a medic?"

"Why not? No, that is not a fair answer."

He locked eyes with the large black woman.

"I hate to see potential go to waste. You are big, strong, with fire in your belly. I just have to get you to direct that fire, that anger against the Squids and their scum allies, not your fellow soldiers. If I can do that... Well, I think you would be an excellent Squid and Kraken killer. If not... "

He let the sentence hang. Jefferson sat in silence for a moment, then spoke. "You are really going to get me out of here, and reassigned to you?"

"If I can, yes. But, you will have to start over with me. And this will be your last chance. Come at me again, I will break you."

A chill went up Jefferson's spine. He said it so matter of factly. That he would put her six feet under without breaking a sweat.

She stood up slowly, suffering from the beatings she had received. She tried to stand at attention.

"Senior Training Instructor Stalin. Trainee Jefferson asks for another chance."

A small smile formed on Stalin's mouth. "You have it with me. Now I just have to convince the Powers that Be. Come. Time to go back to your cell. Think you can march there?"

"Yes, Senior Training Instructor."

"Good. Let's go."

Stalin marched her back to her cell, past the Corporal, Sergeant and three MPs, one an officer. He placed her in her cell, and shut the door. The Corporal ran up, and glanced in the cell."Uh... "

"No, Corporal, she will not be chained again. She will behave herself if you behave yourself. Understand?"

"Yes, Senior Training Instructor."

Stalin looked through the small cell window.

"You will behave yourself, *da*?"

"Yes, I promise," Jefferson answered.

With that Stalin turned and walked toward where the Sergeant was trying to have a conversation with two enlisted MP's and a Lieutenant Shift Commander.

"Good morning, Lieutenant."

Lieutenant Michael Hobbes turned toward the Russian. "Comrade Stalin, Your reputation precedes you. Have a little disagreement with the good Sergeant here?"

Stalin feigned surprise. "No disagreement, Lieutenant. Just an explanation of the errors in his management of this facility."

Hobbes laughed. Torbin, a fellow Marine, had already told him about Stalin, explained that he was a drill instructor's drill instructor, and made some of their Marine DIs look weak. He was also very protective of the people under his control.

Hobbes looked at Sergeant O'Neil, still rubbing his throat. "I'll pass your complaints up the chain of command. But don't expect them to do much. I told you a long time ago about what would happen if you kept up with your attitude adjustments for people you don't like. War does not give you an excuse to abuse and bully people."

Sgt. O'Neil started to protest, then noticed Stalin looking at him with ice cold eyes.

"Yes Sir," he croaked out instead.

"Well, like they say, 'Merry Christmas to all and to all a good night.' Comrade Stalin."

"Lieutenant." The Russian made a small bow toward Hobbes.

As the Lieutenant left with the two MPs, one asked. "Sir, what'll you think will happen now?"

Hobbes laughed. "I think General Reed will have a short talk with Stalin, then it ends. Unless O'Neil really tries to push it, slaps some more people around. Then he'll be assigned to some forward observation post along the border. That crazy Russian has a hell of a lot more pull than you or I have. I think he just took a bully problem by the horns and solved it. At least temporarily. Now, gentlemen. Let's go get some Christmas chow before someone else calls us."

CHAPTER 22

ATLANTA, GEORGIA
CATTLE COUNTRY

Malcolm Carter was sitting, looking at a scrawny and battered artificial Christmas tree. He was wondering what gastronomic miracle Red would find for them today. Somehow, she always found something for Big Joe, Dawoud and himself to eat that wasn't just gruel. She also helped out Bashir Gupta and Reggie Adams in an attempt to keep them well fed as they helped produce weapons from almost nothing.

Since Thanksgiving, there had been no further attacks. Some

snow and cold had hit Atlanta. Now, the Krakens seemed to be satisfied to just wait them out. Malcolm would not be surprised if it was because someone thought all this inactivity as well as problems finding food would cause the humans in Atlanta to start fighting among themselves.

Up until last week, Dawoud had managed to get small supply balloons, gliders and a couple of small drones to drop food and medical supplies as well as the occasional weapon into Atlanta, courtesy of the U.S.A.

Then, a Falcon was seen heading to the border with South Carolina. Dawoud had received a morse code message soon thereafter. The Falcon had turned the area up to ten miles from the border into scorched earth. Since then, nothing. Malcolm had done what he could to create sources of food, including attempts at greenhouses, and small breeding pens for animals. Someone had come up with rabbits, pigeons, and guinea pigs to breed for food. Rat catching had become an art. Stray cats and dogs had long since disappeared.

Now, people were crawling through the vacant buildings, as well as any abandoned vehicles, looking for something the previous owners had left behind that been missed before. Big Joe had stumbled upon a cache of wine and liquor that enabled Malcolm to have the scotch on the rocks he was having right now. This was one of the few times when Malcolm had used his position to selfishly covet something for his own use. He figured if it helped keep him sane and functional, other people should not complain.

He had also managed to scavenge some items to be used as presents, especially for Red. Every little bit helped to keep hope alive. He, Joe and Dawoud were sitting around the dining table they had found and moved into their basement office. Dawoud, being a lapsed Muslim, still found the idea of Christmas rather amusing.

"You celebrate the birth of your Prophet on a day that you are fairly certain he was not born, but rather on a day that coincides with the pagan Winter Solstice? With fir trees from a part of the world where Jesus never visited? And you think Islam is bizarre."

"Hey, it's the spirit of the thing that is important," Joe interjected.

"Well, at least Islam teaches everyday charity to other people, especially the poor. Islam needs no special day to give gifts to relatives or to help others in need."

Malcolm glared at Dawoud. "No, you just went around sending relatives and friends in as suicide bombers during other people's celebrations."

The lapsed Muslim shrugged. "I will admit we let our extreme ideals get out of hand. Now I think Allah is punishing us for our transgressions by turning his back on us, and letting the demons eat us."

Red brought an Indian rice dish with bits of meat and peppers in it to the table.

"Let us give thanks for what we have, rather than argue about the past, what should be. We can enjoy the spirit of Christian Christmas without believing in all of its teachings."

Not for the first time did Malcolm notice what a gem he had in Red. Her intelligence and organizational skills had been a godsend. She also had an ability to diffuse conflicts, no matter how sensitive the subject. Dawoud smiled at her. "Ever the peacemaker. You are a woman of many talents as well as being beautiful." Red smiled back with smoldering eyes. He and Red had developed a "thing" since the former terrorist had arrived in Atlanta. Malcolm knew they strived to keep it discreet, but passions often won out. Dawoud, despite still claiming to be a faithful husband with two wives at home, could not ignore Red's exotic charms.

The men each served themselves a portion of the dish, while Red brought another plate of a mixture of vegetables and noodles, as well as some fresh bread. She then sat down and prepared herself a plate, sat down.

"I'd like to say grace, Boss," stated Joe. Malcolm glanced at him. "Sure, go ahead. I hadn't thought of it."

Joe reached out his large hands. "We need to join hands." Soon, all were holding hands with heads bowed.

"Lord, whatever name you want to go by, please bless this meal that Red has prepared. We give thanks for your bounty and your blessings. Thank you also for the friends, now our family, that you have allowed us to find, have, and enjoy. Thank you for the life and times we are sharing with these special people. And all God's people say, *Amen*."

Malcolm looked a bit surprised. "That is one of the longest

speeches you have made in a long time, Joe. I didn't know you had a flair for prayer."

Joe suddenly seemed a bit self-conscious. "I usually don't have a need to say much, Boss. Today I did."

"Well, my very large friend," Dawoud said. "I think if Allah is still listening to our prayers, he must have heard this one. It was quite good."

Red reached over and grabbed Joe's large hand again. She lifted it and kissed it.

"You are a man full of surprises. I honor our friendship."

"Thank you, Red. Hey Boss, gift giving after eating?"

"Sounds good to me, Joe."

"Wait," Dawoud protested. "I have no gifts to give. Not being Christian, I did not even think of it."

Malcolm waved the comment away. "Like Joe said, it's the spirit that counts. The spirit of giving to your friends and family. Gifts do not have to be physical in nature. An action to help someone can be a gift."

"That is true," Red chimed in. "Your presence here has been a gift."

Dawoud smiled. "Since you say it, Red, I will accept it."

Red smiled back, a twinkle in her eye. "And with that, shall we begin our meal? I am hungry even if you are not."

At that comment Big Joe laughed. "Not hungry? I was born hungry. That's why I'm so big."

"And glad I am for that fact, my large friend," Malcolm said. "Now, this looks delicious as usual, Red."

"I also have a potato dish still warming. I know how much you Americans love potatoes."

"Well, as they're native to South America, that makes sense. Can I interest anyone else in a drink?"

CHAPTER 23

NEW PRESIDENTIAL QUARTERS
BISMARCK, NORTH DAKOTA

Madam President was entertaining George Williams and his family, as well as Ranger Andrew Jackson and his family. For the first time in a while, the President's daughter Sarah was also present, with her six year old daughter, Beverly.

George's fraternal twins, a boy and a girl, were sixteen. Their names were George the Fifth and Ellen, respectively. Both were tall and slender, taking after their mother Meagan rather than George's massive fullback build. They had also inherited their mother's movie star looks. In an earlier age, they would have been childhood models.

Ranger Jackson's children were full grown, the eldest, David, being twenty-eight. David was as tall and lanky as his father, with many of the same facial features. His stay in prison prior to the Tschaaa invasion had made him reserved, a bit uncomfortable around people he did not know. Now, thanks to his father's move to North Dakota, he was being given a second chance. However, it seemed he still had no real idea what to do with it.

His brother Samuel was bit shorter and stockier, taking after his mother's side of the family. Felicity Jackson had come from a long line of Texas Cattle Ranchers, and was a strong woman, able to hold her own. She was close to five foot ten in height, as was her daughter, Barbara. Andy often kidded that if he needed back up in a fight, all he had to do was call his wife and daughter and sic them on the opposition. That usually resulted in a reproof from Felicity about being too crass. But had she not been tough, she would not have survived the last six plus years. Samuel was twenty-six, and Barbara was two years younger at twenty-four. Samuel had been in line for a pro baseball slot out of college, but the Tschaaa had put a kibosh on that. Barbara had been preparing for pre-law. Now, both had joined up with the U.S. Armed Services. Both had been schooled in firearms and self-defense by their father, a fact had helped them accelerate through their training.

Samuel was a First Lieutenant in Mechanized Infantry, with Barbara being trained for the Judge Advocates Corp, one of the few lawyers in the military. They had been a luxury up until now, but the increasing numbers of Soldiers, Airmen, and Marines had forced General Reed to revitalize the military legal system. Nothing could help destroy the morale and fighting effectiveness of an American-based military than service members thinking they were slaves with no rights. If that was the case, why fight an enemy that promised more freedom, at least for the lighter skinned?

George's twins would soon have to make a choice, as Universal Service was expected for citizens ages eighteen to age fifty. You could sign up at sixteen under some circumstances. George Five, as his parents called him, was quite good with all things computerized and electronic. His father thought his skills might be of use in cyber warfare when the time came. Ellen had a knack with animals. After meeting Emily Anders, George had put her in contact with his daughter. Hopefully the good doctor could get her a slot in the veterinarian college she and others had set up. There was a shortage of all types of medical personnel for both animals and humans. The increasing importance of war dogs meant that there was almost as much need for medical support for K-9s as human soldiers. Fuzz had easily demonstrated how dogs could take care of infiltrators and sense alien life forms. The need for K-9 talents would only increase.

Right now, David was odd man out, still trying to find a way to support the war effort beyond repairing roads and digging drainage ditches. George knew of the man's predicament. Andy could not afford to carry him, nor use his position with the President to get him special position when here were thousands of other young people in the same situation. George also knew that Ranger Jackson did not need to be distracted from his job as the President's driver and personal bodyguard by worry about his son.

While Madam President and her daughter were playing hostesses this Christmas morning, preparing a breakfast for all those assembled at her insistence, George addressed Andrew Jackson.

"Ranger, could I have a private moment with you and David?" The Ranger replied with an inquisitive expression.

"Well, Sir, if that's how you would prefer to spend your Christmas. I don't want anything to interfere with time with your family."

"It will just take a few minutes. A quick trip to the entrance way." The Ranger nodded, heading over to where his son was listening to the others talk about what young people usually do. David rarely had much to say. His prison stay had limited the subjects he could talk about even if he had wanted to discuss something. A quick word, and both Jacksons were following George out to the large entrance way of the small mansion that was now the Presidential residence. Both wives and mothers noticed but held their questions. They would get the information from their husbands soon enough.

"I don't wish to beat around the bush. Here is Commissioner Miller's private phone line number. You are to call him first thing tomorrow. He is expecting the call."

David broke his usual quiet demeanor and asked, "Why? Am I in trouble?"

"Far from it. Paul Miller thinks he can use you."

"He knows of David's record." It was as much a statement as a question from the Ranger.

"Yes. He knows everything. In fact, he probably knows some things about you and I that we would just as soon keep quiet. Paul has a way of getting people to tell him things."

"Yet he still wants to talk to me. Why?" David had a cold look in his eye. Prison had taught him not to allow himself to be pushed around, unless you wanted to be someone's bitch. It was an experience he had avoided, and didn't want to start now.

"Commissioner Miller told me that some of the best cops he had worked with had a previous life that was not exactly sterling. To put it bluntly, he said sometimes it takes a thief to catch one."

"I wasn't a thief," David jumped in. "I killed someone. Unless he wants me to be an assassin, I don't know what he could use me for."

"Son..." the Ranger began.

"No, Dad. This is mine. I appreciate everything you did for me to get me up here. But it's my life, pure and simple."

Andrew Jackson saw his own stubbornness and hardness reflected right back at him. David had always been a bit of a hard case even before winding up in prison. He definitely had not been softened by his experience of some two years before a Tschaaa strike had freed him. The Ranger had been surprised he had even come back home, instead of taking off with some of his cell mates when the walls were knocked down. He could have easily become a Kraken.

"I think that iron you have in your gut and backbone may have something to do with it," George answered. "Like I said, Paul Miller has already checked you out. But he is not the type to beg someone to take a job. Just the opposite. He wants people with fire in their bellies who want to do something. Your choice."

The three men stood silently for a moment. Then David spoke. "No charity. Dad, y'all didn't have anything to do with this, did you?"

"Dammit, son, don't be so hard."

"Why not? You are!"

"And it nearly killed me." Andrew Jackson, possibly one of the last Texas Rangers took a second to compose himself. "I never told your Mother how close I was to going kamikaze on the Squids around Houston. I'm not used to defeat or failure. So, yeah, I quickly learned a little humility. That's why I'm here. To give my family and myself a second chance at life, and at fucking up some Squids. In that order."

George had never known a Texas Ranger before. Now he could see where the expression "One Ranger, One Riot" came from. No one spoke. The David broke the silence.

"Okay, I'll talk with the Commissioner, and see what he has to offer. But I'm nobody's bitch. So if he has some hidden agenda, or he's doing this to make himself feel better..."

George broke in. "David, there are those people in the world that are straight-up, with no hidden agenda. Paul Miller is one of them. Will he get something out of this bargain? He thinks so. I'll let him tell you what it is. But no, this is not charity. Like a lot of people who suddenly came out of the woodwork after the Pit and the Five, it's a second chance to matter. Madam President has given many a person a full pardon. The past, pre-Squid, is the past, period. You can be part of history, or you can watch it go by. Your choice."

David stared George directly in the eye, holding the gaze for few moments. Then he extended his hand. "Thank you, Sir. I can tell you're what they used to call in the old west a straight shooter. I always liked that history. Guess today we have another frontier like the west was then."

"You won't regret it, Son," his father said. "The Commissioner has a bit of the old breed in him, like we used to call them in the Rangers. What you see is what you get."

"Okay, I guess it's in the Commissioner's ball park then. Let's find out if he likes what he sees."

Just then, the private secure line of the President rang. George started to intercept it but Madam President beat him to it with an "I'll get it." She answered it with her typical cheery, "Good Morning", then stopped to listen. Suddenly, a wide grin broke across her face. "Thank you, General. That news just made my day. You have a Merry Christmas as well, Sir." She put down the phone, began to pump her fist and cry, "Yes!" Then she danced around the house—twisting, twirling, and laughing.

"Mother? Are you having a fit? What's going on?" Her daughter asked as she came in from the kitchen.

"What was the call about, Ma'am?" George asked.

She suddenly danced over, and grabbed George. "Excuse me, Meagan, while I borrow your husband for a dance partner." George's wife began to laugh as she saw the woman everyone else knew as the President, cuttin' the proverbial rug with her husband.

"Alekssandra Smirnov just gave birth. Two outstandingly healthy baby boys, as Abigail Young predicted. Mother and sons are doing great." Then she laughed again. "Though our prodigal Major just messed up two local news reporters who snuck in to get some unauthorized photos. That boy. Always in the mix with somebody." She stopped dancing.

"Beverly, there are a couple of bottles of Cold Duck in the pantry. This calls for a toast."

"George, you'll have to give Alesha Taylor a call. She'll have you smooth over things with the local news media. They just got started last month in the larger cities, trying to regain some of what we have lost. Can't have them thinking we're going to beat up on them just because they piss us off."

"Yes. Madam President. I'll get right on it…"

"You'll do no such thing. You will first drink a toast to the birth of two sons of our future."

Quickly, glasses were produced, the bottles opened, the Cold Duck poured. Everyone had one, the President leaving it up to the parents about the minors drinking. But even her Granddaughter would get a sip to mark the occasion.

Possibly the most powerful woman on Earth raised her glass.

"Ladies and gentlemen. A toast to our newborns, to two young boys, who will grow into men. They will be the type of men our world will need in the future if we are to survive. How fitting that their births are on the same day we celebrate another's birth that gave us hope, and shaped our futures. I think the result of that birth still watches over us, and is smiling at the two baby boys, Gage and Tristen. To the newborns and their parents. Good fortune and a Merry Christmas."

The toasts rang out. For a moment, hope was suspended in time. Hope and joy would not disappear in the coming year, but both would sorely tested.

CHAPTER 24

Aleks had finally gotten their sons to both drift off to sleep. Torbin was snoring in the easy chair next to her. She smiled. It was getting late in the evening. This first day of life outside the womb had been primarily one of eating, sleeping, and repetition of both. But the majority of the time had been nursing. Somehow, Aleks' milk supply had held up. The special protein shakes that Bettie Bardun had developed were a godsend.

They knew that the Russian's body had been modified to work at a higher metabolic rate during pregnancy, as had her sons' development. Without the support of a strong scientific community, the higher need for sustenance in the womb and by the newborn might lead to a high degree of infant mortality through miscarriage, as well as late illness due to immune systems weakened by insufficient food. The Tschaaa had really been pushing the envelope, walking a tightrope between life and death of the young. But since it was human young, what was the cost to them? A lesser number of veal steaks? Every time Aleks thought of this, she became very angry. She could not of losing her two sons. They had all been put in increased danger by the Tschaaa meddling with human genetics. Future mothers may not have her toughness, or the level of care that the military hospital could provide. Even one unnecessary death due to the Squids' selfishness was one death too many.

Her twin sons were sleeping in twin bassinets near their bed. She would stay awake until Torbin woke up. No way would she allow the two newborns to go unattended during this first twenty-four hours.

She sensed someone was watching and looked up. There was a young enlisted woman, medium height with a runner's slender body, looking in the room. She was an E-4 by the stripes on her sleeve and wore the field uniform of an EMT. She was not one of the normal support staff assigned to the floor Aleks was on. However, she had been checking up on Aleks between the normal rounds of the floor nurses.

"Pssst. Young lady. Please come here." Aleks tried to say as quietly as possible so as not to wake her sons or Torbin. The young woman paused, as if unsure whether she should come in or just leave. Then, decision made, she came in.

"Ma'am? Is everything okay? Do I need to get the assigned nurse..." She spoke in very quiet tones, as had Aleks.

"No, young lady. Everything is just fine. The men in my life all have full stomachs and are sleeping."

She noticed the EMT had a necklace with what appeared to be some kind of silver cross on it that she was handling like someone would a traditional worry stone, rubbing it between her thumb and forefinger.

"That looks pretty. May I?" Aleks gestured with her hand.

The E-4 suddenly realized what she had been doing, and turned pink.

"Sorry Ma'am. I should keep this out of sight due to uniform regulations."

Aleks smiled. "I won't say anything if you don't." With that, the young enlisted soldier stepped close so that Aleks could hold the necklace piece.

Aleks looked at the small piece of jewelry and quickly saw it was not a cross.

"Is this supposed to be a small sword, a blade of some type?"

"Yes, Ma'am." Then her demeanor became very guarded.

Aleks looked into the eyes of the young woman.

"Corporal, is it? I noticed you checking in on me and mine, and I know you are not assigned to this floor. May I ask why? But first, you know my name, what is yours?" She looked closely at the uniform name tag in the reduced light.

"Anderson."

"Your first name?"

"Ashley, ma'am."

"So why the interest? Does it have something to do with your necklace?"

With great hesitation, the young woman answered. "I... just wanted to make sure you were okay. I'm sorry if I seem weird, if I offended you...."

Aleks grunted. "Why would I be upset that someone cares about me and my children? Now please, I'm not used to what you Americans would call a fan club."

Ashley then explained, reluctantly, "The piece of jewelry is a blade. It stands for cold steel."

Then, Aleks knew. Even when on maternity leave, being in intelligence, Aleks kept her ear to the ground. She had heard that some of the younger women seemed to be closely following Abigail's "adventures" and using her as a role model. This role model business went so far as to have led to some kind of small, private group. Of course, word of Abigail's little demonstration with Stalin had spread through the rumor mill like wildfire. Abigail had even remarked that every young woman she saw, whether military or not, seemed to be treating her with the utmost deference.

"This has to do with Captain Young, yes?"

"And you, Major. Cold steel is a symbol, a symbol of what we women must do to insure our children survive in a better world. It means we must be like blades of steel—strong, but flexible. Sharp and deadly, but controlled.

"We are the Sisters of Steel. It has been a secret, up until now. We didn't want people to think we are some weird fringe secret society, not to be trusted."

"Instead, like the Three Sisters, the unofficial group my Russian compatriots and I formed," Aleks suggested.

"Yes Ma'am."

Aleks sat in her bed for a few moments, processing this information. She beckoned Corporal Anderson to come closer. "Would you like to hold one of my sons... sister?"

Ashley nodded her head with a smile. "Yes, Ma'am. It would be an honor."

She and Ashley carefully picked up Gage and Tristen, trying not to wake them. Their stomachs being very full with mother's milk, they slept the sleep of the innocent. Torbin kept sawing logs in the recliner.

"They are so handsome, healthy, Major. I hope I can have such a family someday."

"If you want to, you will. By the way, do you mind if mention this... special group to Captain Young? I'll make sure she does not think it is weird."

"Yes, Ma'am. She would hear eventually anyways. I don't want it to be a source of trouble or embarrassment."

"Of course not. Here, help me put my sons back to bed."

Soon, Gage and Tristan were once again dreaming the dreams of babes—warmth, mother, milk, and love.

"I must go back to the ER, Major, in case we get a call out. Thank you again for letting me hold your sons."

"Thank you for being a guardian angel, Corporal. My sons appreciate it."

Ashley reached into her top pocket, and pulled out a small folder envelope. She opened it, and took two silver items out.

"I just remembered. I picked up another order of these that Hannah just finished."

"Hannah Weitz?"

"Yes, Ma'am. She makes these symbols for us. Here. One for Captain Young. One for you. Befitting the persons who are the basis for these symbols of hope."

Aleks teared up a bit, and motioned Ashley closer once again. She hugged the Corporal, kissed her on both cheeks. "You do us honor. Remember that."

"Yes Ma'am. You show us what honor is all about." With that, Corporal Anderson stepped back, gave a quick salute, and was gone.

Sisters of Steel. How befitting the times, Aleks thought. She looked at her sleeping sons. You two are going to have such a large number of unofficial aunts watching over you."

Just then, Torbin began to wake up.

"What? Sorry, babe. I didn't mean to sleep so long. Here, I'll watch the kids so you can get some rest. Anything going on?"

Aleks smiled. "Nothing to worry about. We women have it under control. I love you, husband."

"I love you too, babe. Now, get some rest, please."

CHAPTER 25

A little over a week after the birth of Gage and Tristen, it was Adam Lloyd's turn to be in a hospital for both of his wives to give birth. Doctor Fredericks was to oversee the births, looking for any abnormalities caused by the secret modifications and alterations by the Tschaaa that she had initially discovered. "I am surprised I have not been disappeared after spilling the beans," she confessed to Adam as the two women went into labor.

"I think that Lord Neptune realizes that the same abilities you possess that allowed you to discover this hidden process of change to the female genome and functions are the same abilities that will allow you to make sure they work the way the Squids wish them to work."

She shrugged. "No matter. I have found your wives pelvic areas have the ability to handle the births of such large babies with such ease. Although not entirely outside the size norm for human babies, they are definitely big. Especially considering they are twins."

She shook her head. "I will probably spend the rest of my life trying to understand the Squids' ability to modify the basic functions of life of a whole slew of species. They are definitely ahead of us on the intricacies of reproduction and controlled growth."

"Do the basic sequences of DNA here on Earth make it easier to make such modifications?" Adam asked.

"It could. That is something I have begun to look into, along with all of my other duties."

"Doctor, if you need help, just yell. I owe you. Humankind owes you. The first successful births of babies affected with Tschaaa modifications has just happened in the Unoccupied States. This is thanks in part to the information you developed, and passed on to their authorities."

Doctor Fredericks smiled. "You are glad you let a certain Captain, now Major, go are you not? Despite the complaints that you did?"

"I'd do it all again. He's a soldier and a man of honor. That's a disappearing breed. And now, he's a father as well."

"Ach, my assistant says the babies are crowning. Already. Excuse me." The good doctor put on her surgical mask and reentered the birthing room.

It was all over in fifteen minutes. As in the case of Aleksandra Smirnov's twins, Kat and Mary each gave birth to healthy twins in short order. Kat gave birth to twin boys, Mary to twin girls.

Everything was sped up once again, with both women having sufficient pelvic characteristics as to not require a cesarean. The children were all born with full heads of hair. The boys, William and Adam, were blondes; the girls, Kathleen and Marian, were brunettes. All four easily came into the world, appearing very alert for newborns.

"One, two, three..." Doctor Fredericks counted each and every digit; looked, examined and, with a gentle touch, prodded the four children. She broke into a wide grin. "Wunderbar. I wish all births were so successful. I will keep the afterbirths for tests and examination. Now, it looks as if all four are already looking for breakfast."

Kat's and Mary's breasts had swelled noticeably with milk the last few weeks, as if their bodies were working overtime in preparation for the births. They had already pumped and stored a substantial amount of milk in order to reduce the uncomfortable swelling and weight. Now, each breast had a child happily attached.

Adam, surgical mask in place, came into the delivery room. "My God. Almost a basketball team in just fifteen minutes. They are beautiful, like their mothers."

Kat began to cry.

"Hey, why the tears?" Adam asked.

"I'm so fucking happy. A washed-up adult movie star, giving birth to two fantastic sons. No way could I have guessed this would happen."

"Hey, sister, I do *not* want to hear you beat yourself up." Mary ordered her from the next bed. "We're in this together. Don't you forget it."

Adam had a large lump in his throat. He never could have guessed he would be a father of four children. Especially all at once. "I love you both so much," he finally murmured. He hugged and kissed each wife in turn.

The doctor cleared her throat. "Now my good Director, go get yourself a drink while we let these ladies rest and feed your babies. We will keep them overnight to ensure there are no surprises. The Chief has already posted himself at the door to guarantee they are not bothered."

The doctor then hugged him. "You did good, Adam Lloyd. They will grow up healthy and wise."

Adam left the room, and located Chief Hamilton sitting in a nearby chair with a sawed-off pump 12 gauge. "Expecting company, Chief?"

"Better to have it and not need it, than to need it and not have it. Besides, I'm their godfather."

Adam laughed. "That's godfather as in helping raise the kids morally and spiritually, not godfather as in making people offers they can't refuse, right?"

Chief Hamilton smiled. "Affirmative. But as weird as things are right now, I'm not taking any chances."

Adam checked his watch. "I need to run to the office, and see if there are any fires to put out. I'll be back."

"Take your time, my friend. This is easy duty." The Chief stood up and handed Adam a box he had concealed under his chair. "You'll need these, if you believe in tradition."

It was a box of Cuban cigars. "I got those from our friends with the last cargo of sugar cane."

Adam stuck out his hand. The Chief stood up and grasped it. "Thanks for being my friend all these years, Chief."

"Hell, that was the easy part. Now, go and have that drink and kick back for a few. You'll be busy enough when the ladies come home with the little ones tomorrow. I know I was."

Adam had spaced on the fact that Chief Hamilton was once a father himself.

"Willie, I hope someday you find someone new you can share your life with."

The Chief shrugged. "If I do, great. If not... well, I had a good life until the Squids showed up. I'll always remember that."

Off all of the things Adam had difficulty connecting with the Tschaaa showing up, the loss of the Chief's family was probably the worst. Possibly because it was personal.

"Now, Boss. Take off. I'll keep an eye on them."

Adam arrived at the office to find Heidi Faust setting at Mary's desk, answering the telephone.

"Yes, Sir. I'll pass that on to the Director. Yes Sir, he is still at the hospital. I'll pass your good wishes on to him. Have a nice day."

"What are you doing here this early, Heidi? I didn't call you."

"Well, Boss, you should have. What good is security if you don't use it."

Adam shook his head in slight disbelief. "I guess news travels fast, even early in the morning."

Heidi flashed her smile, which started with her sparkling eyes. "Congratulations on becoming an instant father, four times over."

Adam walked over to the desk and Heidi stood up to hug him. "Thanks, Heidi. You've been as much of a friend as you have been a bodyguard. I'm blessed."

He stepped back and produced a Cuban cigar. "Do you like cigars, Heidi?"

She laughed. "I have on occasion smoked them. I will definitely not turn down a Cuban, that's for sure." She took the cigar, then smelled it. "Nothing like the smell of good tobacco. Brings back fond memories of my father. Oh, speaking of father figures—that last phone call twas from the Admiral. He'd like your permission to go visit the moms and newborns."

"Of course he has permission. Hell, he's like an older uncle to my wives. If not for him, half this place would not even exist."

"Well, give him a call when you get a chance. I think he wants to talk."

Adam nodded. "I'll do that. First, I need to contact His Lordship." With that, Adam went into his private office and shut the large double doors. He pulled the laptop communicator Andrew had set up for him from his locked desk side drawer. A few quick adjustments and commands, and he had a secure video feed with Lord Neptune. Every time Adam thought about the alien Lord choosing that name—his original Tschaaa name was almost unpronounceable by humans—Adam chuckled to himself. His Lordship had definitely watched way too many Earth movies.

But then again, it seemed most Tschaaa Lords preferred to be referred to as a name or title from some Earthly reference rather than trying to anthropomorphize and translate their name into some Earth language. His Lordship had once told Adam that trying to "translate" his name into something recognizable would have resulted in a sentence length name talking about the positive characteristic his sire had seen in him. Sires of the young did the naming. His Lordship said his name in English would have referred not only to his intelligence, but also the weird way he looked at things. Adam guessed a Native American name like Sitting Bull or Crazy Horse—names that referred to some attribute of the individual—would have been the closest to the idea behind Tschaaa names. When Adam had mentioned the name Crazy Horse as an example, Lord Neptune had laughed in his Tschaaa manner.

"That name would have been a close fit in some Tschaaa's opinion. At least the 'crazy' part."

Adam pinged the Tschaaa Lord's communication device and waited for an answer. It came quickly in the form of a video feed of His Lordship lounging on a bed of fresh seaweed. The Tschaaa apparently liked the feel and smell of Earth seaweed.

"Ah, my good and faithful Director. You are calling me about the birth of your young. This is indeed an auspicious occasion." The Tschaaa universal translator was quite efficient.

"Once again, Your Lordship, you have the advantage of prior knowledge."

Lord Neptune moved his tentacles and arms in signs of amusement, laughter. "Andrew contacted me with the good news as soon as he had it. Congratulations on the birth of four healthy children. I take it that our improvements to your species seem to be working."

Adam grit his teeth a bit at that last statement. Every woman who had signs of "modifications" in their genome, hormones, reproductive cycle had visions of giving births to monsters thanks to Tschaaa meddling. So far, other than complications due to the rapid growth of the fetuses, which resulted in women giving birth to twins in seven months, all reports were favorable. The wife of Major Bender, Aleks Smirnov, had by some quirk of fate beat all other known "modified births" by at least twenty four hours. Adam had received notifications of nearly one hundred births so far, not all of them apparently involving those "modified". The worst complication reported was the increase of caesarean births due to the very large size of the twins versus a mother's pelvis." Of course, the real test would be seeing how the children developed in the next months. Would the accelerated birthing and growth have dire results? Only time would tell.

The Tschaaa Lord continued, "I am used to multiple births, triplets and larger numbers at one time, but we recognize that carrying more than two new young to term at one time could have been deadly for some human females."

New young. Yes, the current batch of humans were "new", and hopefully improved. If this accelerated growth resulted in mental abnormalities, high incidents of cancer, or an early death, then the long term gain would be naught. But then again, the Tschaaa would have larger quantities of "veal" around for consumption. He had not told Adam how this specifically affected the occupants of Cattle Country. Adam did not even want to know the level of "infection" in the walled and fenced off three state area. He had enough to worry about.

"Well, Sir, so far, so good. I have four apparently healthy bouncing babies—two boys and two girls, as well as two tired but very happy wives."

"Excellent. I will prepare a personal message for your breeders. Please let them know that anything they require for the healthy growth of their young will be provided. I suppose I am experiencing emotions similar to what a human godfather must feel. I may not be related, but I feel a bond, a responsibility to them." Adam did not tell him how weird, almost sick that sounded. He had once been told of the Future Farmers of America. The children and teenagers raised animals they felt close to, only to see them slaughtered for meat. But then again, pigs and such were not considered sentient beings.

"I will pass that on, your Lordship. Thank you."

"Thank you, Director, for your continued support. Now I must contact James Kray. He needs to brief me on his operations and preparations."

Adam knew that Kray and his Krakens had taken over primary responsibilities for dealing with the Resistances in Atlanta, as well as preparing a counterstrike against the Unoccupied States. Adam had no desire to know the details. His attitude toward such things had changed since seeing the Tschaaa's reactions to the nuke strike and the televised images of the Pit Raid. Now, he was more focused on keeping as many humans outside Cattle Country alive as possible. He would never let on, but his trust of Lord Neptune was extremely low.

"I will talk to you later, your Lordship." The connection was broken.

Adam knew he and the other parents of these "new" children were so far very lucky. No monsters, no deaths at birth. Thalidomide-like effects, deformed bodies and minds, so far were absent. So far. If they ever appeared, there would be more hell to pay.

He put away the secure communicator, then began to check his voice messages and emails. Ninety percent were related to the newborns and their mothers, mostly congratulations and well-wishes. He then heard a familiar voice in the outer office.

"Hello, Heidi, is the Director available?" It was Andrew's voice. It was still a mystery how a person that large could move around so quietly. Had he not spoken, Adam would not even have known he was there.

Adam rose from his chair and walked to the double doors. "I'm always available for you, Andrew. You know that."

"One should not be rude if it isn't necessary, Director. Everyone needs their privacy." Andrew held two large flower arrangements in his arms.

"I take it those are for Kat and Mary?"

"Yes, Adam. I also have a large amount of diapers and other such necessary items in my Falcon parked at the Sportplatz. Let me know when I can transport them to your residence."

"Anytime, friend. By the way, do you smoke cigars?"

Andrew paused, as if accessing a computer program.

"I never was a smoker before my conversion to a robocop. That poses an interesting question—what would the experience of me smoking a cigar be like now?"

"Does that mean the answer is yes, you'd like one?"

"Don't mind if I do, Adam." Andrew set down the two sets of flowers, and took the offered Cuban cigar.

"Supplied by the Chief, if my guess is correct."

"As usual, Andrew, you are spot-on." Adam produced a Zippo lighter and lit the cigar.

"Those flowers are beautiful, Andrew," Heidi commented.

"Yes, they are nice," Andrew replied between initial puffs. He then proceeded to blow exact smoke rings. "This is rather nice. I guess I was missing something six years ago. It is an interesting interface with my sensors." He puffed some more on the cigar.

"To your point, Heidi, I obtained or rather, picked those flowers myself. And arranged them. My first attempt at it."

"Andrew, you never said you had an artistic side to you." Heidi smiled. "I know you are a man of many talents, but not flower arranging."

"I appreciate your comments, Heidi. I find myself exploring new interests these days, pushing my envelope so to speak. Recently, the interface with my more mechanical side has made me appreciate my human parts even more. Intellect without humanity, feelings, seems to... lack something."

Adam interjected. "You are the becoming the epitome of a Renaissance Man, Andrew—trying to explore, experience, and understand the world around you."

A small smile formed on Andrew's lips. "Now you are the one spot on, Director. I think that is exactly what I have been doing. Odd that with all my access to data, I didn't make this observation myself."

"It's a matter of perspective. Sometimes someone looking from the outside in notices things about the inside."

Andrew blew more perfect smoke rings, and smiled again.

"I will have to visit new fathers more often, so I can score more free cigars."

"Well, my cyborg friend, if things keep going the way they are, you may have many more chances to score cigars."

Andrew paused for a moment, once again apparently scanning databases via his many interfaces with both Tschaaa and human information networks. "In addition to the two born first to our favorite Major and his wife in the U.S., and now your four healthy newborns, I have reliable information on one hundred more mothers with evidence of manipulation to their reproductive systems giving birth to healthy twins. There is also definite evidence of some thirty other women with signs of manipulation and modifications by Tschaaa medical science in Key West. I am trying to obtain specific data in the other Tschaaa controlled areas, but it has been more difficult. I think some people are afraid to come forward, because they fear that they will lose their children.

"So far, the Unoccupied States have been rather closed-mouthed other than Major Bender's offspring. Probably because Aleks Smirnov, his wife, seems to be the first test case."

Adam decided that, in spite of his instincts, he had to ask the question. "What about in Cattle Country? Or the Feral areas?"

Andrew looked directly at Adam, no longer puffing on his cigar, "Due to the recent attempt at revolt and resistance in walled off Cattle Country, exact numbers are unknown. I believe it is substantially more. Information is even less reliable for the Feral areas. Unless they seek medical aid, some mothers may not realize what is going on until they suddenly go into labor very early. Or else they experience severe problems during birth due to the size of the babies. This does not even address miscarriages. Without close medical observation, the miscarriage rate may be very high."

Adam's expression must have taken a dark turn, as Andrew quickly added," I am sorry if what I say is too raw. I no longer see a need to lie, or try and sugar coat the facts. Unpleasant truth is still the truth. It is something we must face."

"How do *you* feel and think about this, Andrew?" Heidi suddenly broke in.

"I feel bad about any child, unborn or born, hurt by attempts to make them 'better', or to make their gestation period shorter. I believe that if I were in charge, I would not have found it necessary to try and modify the human genome in such a rapid and drastic way." He paused and flicked the ash off his cigar into an ashtray Adam had purchased years ago at a yard sale. "But then again, I was not in charge."

Adam scrutinized Andrew. He once again realized there was more to the Robocop that meets the eye, and that the Tschaaa had no clue what they had helped create. "Well, my friend, I guess we just have to take things as they come."

Andrew responded with a small smile. "Yes, Director. We are friends. And we do have to make the best of bad situations." He stubbed out the cigar in the ashtray, then placed the remaining stogie in a small hidden body compartment.

"I will finish this fine cigar later. Now I must depart." He paused. "Jeanie and Jamey are approaching. Probably to talk to you."

Adam suspected that, like the others, they would like to say congratulations and ask if they could visit soon.

"Thanks, Andrew. Heidi, send them in when they get here, please."

"Will do, Boss."

"I will speak with you later, Director. Again, Congratulations."

"Thank you, Andrew. Come by later for another cigar."

"I will do that, Director."

Adam sat and waited. He had not had a lot of time to spend with the "Barbie twins", who were not related but looked like they should have been. They still stayed in adjoining rooms to his suite, but with his sister wives both pregnant, they had slept with him exactly once. And that sex had been at the prompting of Mary as pure stress relief. They both still worked at a daycare, helping with all the young children as teacher's aides to Professor Sarah Fassbinder, also very pregnant. She should be giving birth any day now.

He heard the bright happy voices of the two women as they greeted Heidi in the front office. Adam stood up and made his way to his office double doors.

"Ladies, come on in. Andrew said you were coming."

"Can't surprise you with him around," Jamey said with a smile.

"We came to congratulate you and your wives on the safe and healthy births," said Jeanie. "Like the ancient Greeks, we come bearing gifts. But don't worry, they don't hide anything."

"You two are way too honest to conceal anything. I know that."

Out of a large basket they were carrying between them, they produced four matching baby blankets, two blue, two pink. Embroidered on the blankets were the names of the newborn, chosen well before birth. Out of the basket also came four matching little teddy bears.

"All handmade by yours truly. Hope you, Kat, Mary, and the little ones like them."

Adam, for one of the few times in his life, was speechless. He had so underestimated these two women, probably because he had viewed them primarily as sex objects for so long. Perhaps because he was now a father, Adam suddenly realized the complete "wrongness" in the way he had treated them all these years. He now saw that he had "two diamonds in the rough" all this time right under his nose. We walked over and hugged them both, again a large lump in his throat.

"If there is *ever* anything you two want or need, just say the word. I've taken you for granted for years, and I used you."

"Well, truth be told, we used you also, Boss." Jamey met his eyes when she said this, a previously unnoticed firmness in her gaze. "We love you, but let's face it—we love each other more."

"Yes," Jeanie added. "We saw a good thing, a way to be safe and relatively comfortable when all those around us were starving and dying. Or being eaten. You saved us from that fate and worse, so we latched on to you."

Jamey continued, "You are not the bad person some people think you are. We came to love you, and to want to help you try to rebuild humanity, even if on a very limited scale. Hopefully, we did actually help."

Adam realized this was the probably longest conversation he had with them since he could not remember when. It made him embarrassed to have to come to grips with his own crassness. "You both helped keep me sane on many occasions. You helped so many of new arrivals with children, the children who had suffered the horrors of wondering when their next meal would be, and if they would be the next meal for a Squid. I just never told you this because I was a boneheaded asshole wrapped up in my own self-importance. Please, I beg your forgiveness."

Jamey suddenly started to cry. Jeanie put an arm around her. "Damn, you just made this even more difficult. But you couldn't know."

"Know what? Did I do something wrong?"

Jamey pulled some tissues from a pocket, dabbed her eyes. "We think it's time we leave, Director. We need to get out on our own. It's time to proudly admit we are a couple, and no longer hide that fact. If the Squids or Krakens want to eat us because we're not breeders, so be it."

Jeanie turned from watching Jamey, back to the Director. "I know there are many groups who believe the sexes only exist to promote the species through reproduction, but I don't care. What I do care about is loving my life partner. Which is Jamey here." She kissed her love and smiled.

"You know that can still stay here, if you wish. You have an important job to do. I can set you up in separate quarters…"

"No, Adam," said Jamey with her newly found firmness. "It's finally time to go it on our own. We will move off base. We already have a place to move to. The Admiral even offered us jobs if you wanted to replace us."

"Why the hell would I want to do that?"

"Because, sometimes, when people feel rejected they get nasty. Sorry if we did not have one hundred percent faith in your reaction. But, well, we aren't perfect. If we misjudged you, we apologize."

Adam regarded the two women he had known for years with great respect and love. He knew that they had reached a turning point in their lives, just as he had. The feeling of potential loss he had was bad, but he also knew he was paying the price for taking them for granted.

"Please. You can at least stay working on Base as long as you like. I'll get you an all access pass, twenty-four hours a day. The thought of you two not being around, to help the newcomers, to see my children grow… Shit, it hurts." The last part he had blurted out. "You're family. The thought of not seeing you again is tearing a big hole in me."

Jamey and Jeanie held each other close, tears in their eyes. Suddenly, they were both hugging him as well. "Goddamnit Boss, you are *our* family too," Jeanie exclaimed. She kissed Adam on his cheek.

"We're not dying, not yet. If you really need us that badly to keep working here, we'll keep doing it."

"Yes," added Jamey. "I guess we acted as if we were leaving the state or something. We just need our space, and you and the ladies need space also. Especially with four newborns."

"You'll help them at the nursery when they're old enough?"

"Of course we will! Hell, we can be the two married aunties every family should have." Adam hugged them both tightly, not wanting to let them go. He felt very vulnerable right now, for the first time in years. He was so used to being in charge of everything. He could try and force them to stay with all the power he had here. But that would make the idea of family a lie. No, it was time.

He kissed them both again. "Okay, let me know if you need help moving. I can always round people up."

"Thanks, Adam. Jolene has already arranged some help for us. She's the one who helped us find the house we are moving into. Susan and Sharon both said they would help too."

"Just make sure the Admiral realizes that you're not part of some arrangement he's thinking of creating. He has too many "daughters" as it is."

"I know all these years we've been rather passive, Boss," stated Jeanie. "But with all this crap going on with the Squids screwing with us women, screwing with what makes us tick, we need to take charge of our future. The relationship we had with you was unique. That's it. We won't be sharing another man's bed."

"No, we won't," Jamey agreed. "We love you. That's why we stayed. We knew we were safe ages ago, even if we left the Base. But you are our family. What we had will be special…forever."

They all stood quietly for a few moments. People on the outside would never understand the bond they had. To many, he was the Director, with three mistresses, then two wives and two mistresses that were at his beck and call. But they were all wrong. They all lost their blood relatives, and so they had created a new family. It would last as long as there were members still alive.

"I suppose this is it for now. Later on, please stop by and see Kat and Mary. They are going to feel a bit lost also with you two not kicking around here every night. Even if you don't see me very often, you have to visit them and the kids."

"Of course. We're family!"

Jeanie and Jamey said goodbye to Heidi and left to check in with the school and daycare. Adam stood by Mary's desk lost in thought, Heidi sitting in the chair. Finally, Heidi rose.

"Come on, Boss. They're not dead. They love you as family, and always will. Just like when the kids move away. They are still family—you just aren't in each other's hair every day."

Adam's focus turned to Heidi. "You're not planning to leave, are you?"

"Hell, no. And have to work for a living? You're stuck with me, Director Lloyd. For the duration."

Heidi put her hand on his arm. "Everyone's family in this office, Boss. You know, I think of Andrew as the weird cousin that stops in, makes us think differently, and shakes things up. But he's family too."

"You really think he considers us as adopted cousins or some such?"

"Trust me, Boss. Women usually are a bit more perceptive about things like this. He'll be a dotting uncle to your four children. Woe to anyone who screws with them. He'll hit them like a freight train."

Adam frowned. "Even if the Tschaaa Lords think otherwise?"

Heidi automatically looked around, checking to see if anyone was watching or listening. "Boss, I think he is attached to us, especially to the children. I've heard him talk with you. I don't think there is going to be anymore harvesting of veal around here for the Squids. The human part of him won't let it happen."

Adam sighed. "Come on. I need a drink, and I'm ordering you to have one with me. Whether or not you're on duty."

"Yes Sir. You twisted my arm."

New life in the form of newly birthed babies gives humans hope, and love. As a mother, I too have felt the joy of holding the children you just gave birth to in your arms, letting them suckle life giving mother's milk from your breasts. This is something men will never understand. The Tschaaa Invasion and Infestation tested all the mothers of the world. Little did the Tschaaa Lords realize that mothers, both human and alien, would rise to the occasion, thus leading to actions no one— not even a certain cyborg named Andrew—fully foresaw.

-Excerpts from the <u>Collected Works of Princess Akiko</u>, Free Japan Royal Family

Blessed are Women
Whose Hearts and Souls
Are Joined Together by Laughter and Tears
Who Fight for Life, Against All Fears
Who Face Evil, With Blades of Steel
Because They Shall Be Known as
SISTERS OF STEEL